WESTERN

NEW

SPEEDY

Also by Max Brand
in Thorndike Large Print

The False Rider
Dead or Alive
Fightin' Fool
The Seventh Man
The Dude
Border Guns
Lucky Larribee
The Long Chase
Destry Rides Again
Torture Trail

MAX BRAND

BRAND

SPEEDY

Thorndike Press • Thorndike, Maine

Library of Congress Cataloging in Publication Data:

Brand, Max, 1892-1944.
   Speedy / Max Brand. -- Large print ed.
      p. cm.
   ISBN 1-56054-001-X (alk. paper : lg. print)
   1. Large type books. I. Title.
[PS3511.A87S6   1990]   90-34621
813'.52--dc20   CIP

Thorndike Press Large Print edition published in 1990 by
arrangement with G. P. Putnam's Sons.

Cover design by James B. Murray.

The tree indicum is a trademark of Thorndike Press.

This book is printed on acid-free, high opacity paper.

1

When John Pierson had a dog and a gun, he
felt as though he owned the entire range of
the Rocky Mountains from head to heel. And
he had the gun and the dog with him, and
there were still two days of clear vacationing
before the moment when he had to turn back
towards his home. He loved his home and he
had made it worth living. He loved his work,
and he had made it worth loving. But still his
heart was half the time running out the window of his office and plunging off among the
blue peaks that he could see.

It was not often that he got there in person.
A week end here, and a fortnight in the slack
season of the year were about all that he could
afford. But he took what he could in the way of
mountain days.

He was on foot. He had been raised on a
horse, but when his time was so short, he
generally felt that one got closer to the heart of
things by walking. And so he walked now, with
a good, free, powerful stride, in spite of his

closeness to fifty years of age. He went uphill with a strong drive; he went downhill on springs. He was a big fellow, built like a rock, bull-necked, brown-faced. The tan on the back of his neck had been built up layer by layer since the days when he was a tow-headed boy riding range on a Texas ranch.

He was given a slightly professional touch, perhaps, by the short cropped mustache that he wore; it was still jet black, and glistening, though his hair was very gray. And in the keen, straight-looking blue eyes was the soul of the acquisitive man. Even the glance with which he surveyed the mountains he loved was almost that of one estimating their acreage, regretting that sheep were not browsing on the difficult patches of upland grass, or that cattle were not dotting the lower valleys.

In one of those lower valleys he paused so long that the dog lay down in the grass and began to roll and play with itself, as though confident that the day's work and sport were over. For the master was lost in delight.

It was not much of a valley. It was a little broken ravine with a twisting, singing line of silver water thrown along the length of it. But it had groves along the banks, or single big trees thrusting out at a slant, holding green sunshades, as it were, over picnic grounds. And there were thickets of blooming shrubbery, and here a patch of rocks thrust up through the soil, glistening, the bony knees of Mother Earth breaking through a threadbare place. But mostly the water was enchanting. For sometimes it roared over a little cataract and multiplied itself with shadows, and in all ways tried to imitate a real river. And again it shot down a steep flume with a hissing sound of speed; but finally, it paused entirely in a large pool.

The very soul of John Pierson had paused there, also, and while the dog rolled in the grass, he was probing the mirrored mountains, the sky, the white blowing clouds that were quickly lost in the shrubbery along the banks, like sheep; and then the quick shadow of a soaring hawk skimmed across the water.

Down there below, where the water broke down from the pool and began to wrinkle as it gathered speed — there ought to be fish in that spot, among the rocks — good brook trout, basking there, loving their shadows and scornful of man! He saw exactly where he could stand, first here and then there, doing his casting. It was not long before lunch. He had shot nothing. And he determined that he would eat fish this day! It was one of his boasts that when he adventured into the mountains, he never took with him more than his rifle and his fishing rod and salt. Nature had to provide for all his needs — nature and his ability to harvest her gifts.

He screwed the pieces of the rod together and then tried the balance and whip of it with an expert hand. He was proud of that hand; the wrist was steel-strong, even now, when he was deep in middle age. And his touch was delicate, and his eye was sure. He would be able to fish that stream as no one had fished it before, as no one might fish it again. The trout that escaped from him would die of old age, he assured himself, as he selected his fly.

He whipped out a sufficient length of line, smiling with delight as he listened to the sharp, small whistling of the thread cutting the air. In the cañon above, he could hear in the distance the talking of the little river, a musical, excited conversation. Farther down the stream, there was the harsh crashing of the water as it tripped over a ledge of rock and smashed itself into foam and spray on a base fifty or sixty feet below.

But though this sound was both steady and ominous, it was not loud. It needs only a little distance of the thin air of the mountains to muffle noise. Indeed, to the ear of the lawyer, there was just enough sound to make him conscious of the voice of the mountains; there was enough sound to make him dream in the upland quiet into which he would be plunging, before long. He would lift above the valleys before the midafternoon. He would be shouldering among the peaks, where only the wind talks, and the insects sing and whisper in small hushing waves of sound.

He was content. He was mightily content, and now he made his first cast — the line flew far, and flicked the water as straight as though its length had been ruled.

He admired that cast, the accuracy of it. Like the true fisherman, the fish were only in a corner of his mind, and his way of catching them was all that mattered.

He had dropped the fly just on the verge of the shadow that sloped down beside a big rock, and he had half finished reeling in his line, when the strumming of a guitar, nearby, smote his ear like the roar of trains, the disputing of voices, the whole angry noise of civilized, hurrying, foolish man.

And then a voice, pleasant enough, a man's baritone voice, rang through the glade, singing:

"Julia, you are peculiar,
Julia, you are queer;
Truly, you are unruly,
As a wild, western steer.
Sweetheart, when we marry,
Dear one, you and I,
Julia,

11

You little mule you,
I'm gunna rule you,
Or die!"

The lawyer finished reeling in his line and then put the rod, for a moment, over his shoulder. He looked for the singer with an air of personal insult. He had been snatched back too suddenly into the follies and vanities and idiocies of the youth of the world.

And now he found the musician, just finishing, his mouth wide on the last note. He was lying on a grassy ledge not twenty feet from the fisherman; the guitar was in his lap, his coat was rolled to support his head comfortably against the bank at his back.

The wrath of the older man overflowed. For he could see worthlessness in the tattered clothes of this boy, and in his too-handsome face. Good looks, when they pass a certain point, always appear a trifle effeminate, a weakening of the true male character. And this lad was made with the scrupulous care that should better have been bestowed on the making of a reigning beauty. He was slim, delicate, dainty. He had big, brown, sleepy, indifferent eyes. His rather swarthy skin bloomed with color. And he was set off, with the vanity of one who knew his good point, by a necktie of flaring yellow and blue.

The lip of John Pierson curled with wrath and scorn.

"Young man," he said, hotly, "d'you know that these mountains are not the place for young ragtime fools?"

He wanted to thrash the boy. He wanted to make him jump and howl. There was in him a great possibility of the family tyrant, though as a matter of fact his only child was a daughter who ruled him with an easy and impertinent adroitness. He knew that she was the monarch of the house, and yet he loved her all the more. But his sense of failure with her, made him a little more absolute in his dealings with others in the world.

The musician, pushing himself languidly up on one elbow, first plucked a blade of grass and began to bite at it absently, studying the stranger.

"Is this a reservation for tired lawyers, sir?" said he.

And as though to point the insolence of his remark, he raised his hat and bowed a very little to John Pierson.

The wrath of the latter flamed higher.

He could hardly say what irritated him most in this speech — the air with which it was delivered, the goodness of the English and the enunciation, or the happy guess which it contained as to his profession. Everything combined with the place and what had gone before to madden Pierson.

He said, "Your kind of nonsense ought to be kept for Mexican cafés. Are you a Mexican, young man?"

"No such luck," said the boy.

He resettled the coat under his head, so that he could regard Pierson more comfortably, without quite sitting up.

"No such luck," snapped Pierson. "You rather be one, eh?"

"Oh, you know how it is," said the other, yawning a little, and covering his mouth with a graceful, slender hand. "You know how it is, Mr. Lawyer; one grows a little tired of hearing the eagle scream, because it's usually yipping about work. 'Work, work, young man. In work is salvation. The kingdom of God is in the muscles!' And that sort of thing."

It was the most offensive statement that Pierson had ever heard. He guessed that a philosophy of indolence lay behind it, and vice is never so damnable as when the vicious justify their actions.

"You, I take it," said he, "are a fellow who doesn't care what the eagle screams?"

"Not a bit," said the other, "except when it turns me out of bed. I came up here to rest a little, but I see that the eagle has spotted me. He's screaming in my ear, again."

At this not too subtle reference to himself, the heat of Pierson increased.

"If we were a little nearer my home town," said he, "I'd find a more secure place for you to rest, my friend. Where you wouldn't spoil a landscape. They'd find something for you to work at, for about thirty days."

"No, no," said the youngster.

He showed his hands, smiling.

"For here," said he, "you see hands which have never yet been stained by work or fee!"

2

Never in his life had John Pierson met with a human being who so thoroughly irritated him in every way as did this lad.

"How old are you?" he asked.

"Twenty-two, sir," said the boy, with a false humility.

"College, eh?"

"Part way, sir."

"Stop calling me 'sir!' "

"Very well, sir."

Now, in his own town, throughout his community, and in many ways it was a large one, Pierson was a man of great influence and power. His word was respected, his advice followed. Throughout this same mountain district, there were few people, no matter what their position, who would not gladly have bowed to him. Here was the exception, and a most unpleasant one it proved. He was even angry with himself because a worthless waif moved him so much.

"My boy," said he, "I will make a bargain

with you. This place happens to suit me. There must be a thousand others where you can lie on grass just as soft as that. I'll give you a dollar if you'll stir along."

The boy nodded, not as one assenting, but one considering.

"That's a matter," he declared at last, "that needs a lot of considering. In the first place, there's the question of the way this bank fits my back. Nature isn't such a handy cabinet maker, you know."

"Humph!" said the lawyer.

"Then there's the fish to consider," said the boy.

"The fish?"

"I've been seeing the glint of 'em down there in the water for some time. I'd hate to disturb 'em as long as the sun is shining like this."

"But after it stops shining?" suggested the lawyer.

"Oh, then I'd eat a dozen of 'em with a lot of pleasure, thank you."

"A very good speech for the perfect opportunist," said the man of the law.

"Finally, and the thing that seems to close the question," went on the handsome tramp, "there's the matter of my profession."

"Ah-ha," said the lawyer. "And what might your profession be?"

"Acting," said this brazen-faced lad.

"You're an actor, are you? What parts do you play?" demanded Pierson.

"Sometimes," said the boy, "I'm a son who's been disinherited by a cruel father. Sometimes, I've been robbed by greedy lawyers."

"Stuff!" said Pierson. "You mean that these are the tales you tell to credulous fools?"

"Sometimes," went on the boy, "I'm about to go to work to earn enough money to finish my school course. Sometimes I'm recovering from an attack of the great white plague."

"Consumption, my foot," said Pierson. "You're as healthy a specimen as I ever saw."

"When one plays many roles, one needs makeup," said the boy.

He seemed pleased as he related his roguery; whatever annoyed the older man seemed delectable to him.

"Then again," said the boy, "I've been the son of a rich American owner of mines in Mexico. He and the whole family murdered, myself knifed and shot almost to pieces by Mexican brigands, I have fled north out of the country, and so I find myself destitute, but determined, one day, to return to the land where I have been wronged, and revenge my dead father and brothers and sisters upon the murderers!"

The lawyer nodded.

"In fact," said he, "You're a professional beggar."

"If you heard one of my yarns," said the boy, yawning, "you'd give it a more complimentary name. I ought, in fact, to be a writer; but even writing, in short, is a form of labor."

"I suppose it is," said the lawyer. "Tell me, my young friend, do the dolts to whom you tell the Mexican story ever ask to see your scars?"

"I have even stripped to the waist," said the boy. "It's something that I don't like to do, but if I find, say a Texan who doesn't like greasers, I've stripped to the waist to show where the bullets struck and the knives cut. That is generally worth several hundred dollars."

"You're a thorough rascal," said the lawyer.

"It's my profession," answered the boy. "You can't blame a man for what he does inside his profession."

"Profession? Stuff! You make up the scars that the idiots think they see on your body?"

"You know how it is," said the youngster. "When one is shouldering his way around the world, one bumps into various obstacles that are capable of making wounds."

"Such as the toss of hobnailed boots," suggested the lawyer.

"Yes," answered the boy, without appearing to take offense, "or it may be the iron-framed lantern of a shack."

"You work the railways a good deal, I suppose?" said Pierson.

19

"Horses are usually too slow for me," said the boy.

"Yes," nodded Pierson. "I dare say that when you leave a place you usually have to leave fast."

"And go far," remarked the lad.

"Now and then," said the lawyer, "you will meet up with a dupe of a former day, too?"

"Now and then," agreed the boy, cheerfully. "But on the whole, this is an amazingly large world."

"You're young," said the lawyer. "As you get older, you may find more thorns on the bush."

"As I grow older, I grow more expert," said the lad.

"Tell me," said the lawyer, "what you call yourself?"

"An entertainer," said the boy.

In spite of himself, Pierson was forced to chuckle.

"And what name do you work under?"

"I've been called a good many names," answered the tramp, "some of them long, and some of them short. I've been called more one-syllable names than almost anyone in the world, I suppose. But the one I prefer is Speedy."

"Speedy?"

"You will see how it is," answered the tramp. "I sometimes give people a fast ride, and they generally have quite a bill to pay at the end of it."

"If you come into my community," said Pierson, "you won't take many for more than a short ride."

"No?"

"No," said Pierson.

"What's your town, if you please?"

"Durfee."

"I've heard of that place. How many people?"

"About ten thousand."

"Ten thousand? That's plenty. Ten thousand is a whole world of opportunity, to me. When do you go home?"

"In about three days."

"Very well," said Speedy, "I'll guarantee to be there. I'll guarantee to call on you at once, and let you know where I am, and whom I'm working on. And in spite of you, I'll promise that I'll come away with a good slice of coin."

"Impossible, you impertinent young rat," said Pierson, swelling more and more with his anger.

"Well," said Speedy, "I'll make you a bet."

"Very well. I'll take the bet."

"You give me odds, of course?"

"I give you odds? Why should I give you odds?"

"Because I hope that you're a fair sport. Here I am putting my cards on the table. I'm the

21

mouse entering the lion's den. I'm going to go to your home town, where the celebrated legal power and brain, Mr. John W. Smith, is like the very blood brother of God Almighty, and there —"

"My name is John Pierson," said the lawyer, coldly. "I'll bet you three hundred dollars to one hundred that you don't make enough in Durfee to pay your end of the bet."

"Good," said the boy. "That's only an evening's work for me. The day I tell you on whom I'm intending to work, I'll guarantee that I get the money in hard cash. I'll collect from you the next morning."

"The next morning you'll be in jail for vagabondage," said the lawyer.

"I'll accept another bet at evens, on that account," said the boy.

"Perhaps you've never even been in jail, my lad?" suggested Pierson.

"I've been there," said the boy. "Once I even rested for a week, but that was because an unlucky Mexican had put a knife through my leg."

"Through the leg?" asked the lawyer, doubtfully. "Mexicans don't stab people in the leg!"

"This one started his knife for my heart," admitted the boy, nonchalantly, "but I kicked him in the face, and that rather spoiled his aim."

"I suppose," said the lawyer, frowning, "that

you're an expert gunman, yourself?"

He maintained his scowl for a time. After all, there was a light in the boy's eyes that might not be altogether effeminacy.

"I never carried a weapon in my life," said Speedy. "It's not my way. Guns? Horrible things. They shoot men into prison. No, no, I never carry weapons."

"You carry the weight of a good many beatings, then," said the other.

"Now and then I've had a stick broken over my shoulders," admitted Speedy. "Now and then a bullet grazes me. Now and then a knife is stuck in me. But you know how it is — this is a world of sweets and sours, and —"

"You worthless, hypocritical —" began the lawyer.

And then he checked himself.

"I apologize," he said, ironically. "I forget that you simply are one who works inside his profession."

"Exactly so," said the boy, "and also —"

He also stopped.

For this time an interruption came from the little brown and black mongrel, whose wits and nose served Pierson.

It had started up a rabbit among the rocks. The rabbit had jumped the stream, and the brave little puppy had unwisely attempted the same feat. The result was that it fell plump into the middle of the stream, and was now whirling round and round, barking a call for help, as the water swept it rapidly down towards the brink of the waterfall.

3

The lawyer loved all animals, but above all he loved this little brown and black mongrel. He had used thoroughbred pointers before, and he had been amazed by the ability of the cur to do as much as any of the others. It was, perhaps, a little overeager. That was its only fault, and it is the best of all demerits in a young dog. For the rest, it was picking up the right education to a surprising degree; and it loved hunting as much as its master did.

Now, when he saw it spinning on the brink of destruction, he uttered a great cry, that choked short off in the middle, so furiously was he running to the rescue. But he knew, before he had taken ten strides, that he would be too late. It was a bitter moment for John Pierson, and the more so when he saw, or thought he saw, the appealing glance of the dog fixed specially upon him as it was carried down to destruction.

Then a slim form went by him, the tramp, the lazy and worthless sponger, Speedy. He ran like a deer, with a sprinter's high action, with a sprinter's long and powerfully reaching stride. It seemed that his toes barely tipped the earth as he fled towards the danger point.

The lawyer shouted hoarse and short in appreciation and amazement. For how had the boy managed to get down from his higher perch so suddenly and appear in this fashion in front of the race?

Even the tramp would be too late, however. That appeared clear. But, reaching the bank of the little stream, he threw himself headlong in, with a long, beautiful, flat dive.

He struck the water below the dog, well beneath it down the course. The power of the current jerked at him, and yet he found his feet with a wonderful dexterity, and instantly scooped the puppy out of the current and flung it well to the shore.

In that effort, he overbalanced. The smooth, powerful sheet of the current was striking him above the knees, and curling to his waist. Now, as he staggered, it seemed to rise in a wave and strike him with a renewed power. Over he went, fighting with his arms to regain his poise, but fighting in vain. Over he went, and though he turned in the water like a snake in the effort to regain his feet, the force of the water had him at too great a disadvantage, and he shot over the brink of the cliff.

The lawyer stood stock still. The moment, the dreadful picture, was burning into his brain, never to be eradicated. And he remembered one thing that would never leave his mind. It was the fact that the boy had not cried out. Silently, like a hero, he had left this life, and left behind him, his wretched trickeries, the thousand deceits of his profession. But his heart was great. John Pierson swore that, from that moment, his heart would be enlarged to look upon rogues with a tenderer understanding.

Then he saw the mongrel standing on the verge of the bank, below the rim of the fall, and barking furiously.

"He has seen the body!" thought Pierson, grimly, and strode forward to see.

What he saw made him cry out like a madman with joy.

For there was Speedy hanging by his hands from a projection of rock just under the lip of the waterfall. He kicked his feet above fifty feet of empty space which lay between him and the cruel teeth of stone on which the stream was shattering.

But even now, the boy swung his body like a pendulum and shifted his grip to another jutting bit of the stone.

What a handhold to swing by over the lip of destruction! The spray from the falls had covered the stone with moss and with green slime. And one slip of the fingers would be the last slip on this earth for Speedy!

Yet, as he swung there, he deliberately turned his head and smiled and nodded at the lawyer.

It swelled the heart of John Pierson to the bursting point.

How could he help? He got out farther towards the ledge, lay flat, and stretched out his hand. But there was still a good distance between him and the place where the boy was working slowly, from point to point.

Now one hand gave way. The boy hung by the grip of the other, only, and at that moment, inspired by the devil, a contrary gust of wind cuffed a sheet of the falling water aslant and struck it heavily against the body of the boy.

"The end!" said Pierson.

But it was not the end. With a desperate effort, his body convulsed by it, Speedy managed to reach out to a fresh hold with his left hand, and now behold him, under the very hand of the lawyer.

"Here!" shouted Pierson.

His arm was strong, his wrist was steel, his body was anchored by a very solid and substantial weight. In a moment he had both of the boy's wet hands in his. And what a grip they gave him! He was amazed at the strength in

Speedy, the idler.

Then, heaving up with all his might, he swayed the boy high as the armpits up to the edge of the rock.

Speedy was in a moment lying on his back on the grass. He lay with his arms thrown out to the side. He lay like a cross upon the green. There was no working of the face, no exaggeration. Only the flare of the nostrils, the stern straightness of the upper lip, the heaving of the breast in long breaths, told Pierson of the strain through which Speedy had been passing.

For his own part, he was shaking from head to foot. He sat down by the boy and pulled out his feet and watched a thing that oddly pleased him, but that oddly touched him in a raw spot.

It was the little mongrel, Brownie, making his demonstration of joy and of gladness of living, and of gratitude, not to his master, but rightly enough, to his deliverer from danger. And now, sopping wet as he was, he lay curled on the not less soaking breast of Speedy's coat and licked his face, and beat his tail frantically, whining.

Yes, it was very right that he should make a fuss over the boy. He certainly had earned Brownie's devotion. And yet the heart of John Pierson was a little sore. He was ashamed of this secondary emotion. It made him feel smaller than ever.

At last the boy sat up, held himself there on the stiff of both arms for a moment, and then rose to his feet. The lawyer watched him, but said not a word, for there was not a word to say.

And, calmly, deliberately, Speedy peeled off his soaked clothes, wrung them out, and laid them on shrubs to dry. Pierson noted, with interest, that if the outer clothes were shabby, the underclothes were scrupulously clean. Moreover, the body underneath them was clean, and brown as if from long seasons on beaches — the rather scrawny body of a young boy, but outfitted with stringy muscles that explained at a glance how the athletic feats under the brink of the waterfall had been accomplished.

Well, many an idler might be an athlete as well, trained by swimming, by tennis, by dancing and riding until he was as tautly stringed with power and muscle as any football player or day laborer.

These things occurred to the somber eye of Pierson, as he considered the boy.

He had filled his pipe, and now he was smoking and thinking of many things — and, for the first time in a good many years, not of himself.

Said Speedy:

"That's the coldest water that I've seen in a long time."

He turned his back to the sun, that it might

dry that part of him more quickly.

"That's snow water," said Pierson.

He thought it odd that these should be the first words interchanged between them, after the boy's heroism. But, the more the event receded in time, the more impossible it was to speak of the thing. What made it perfect was that the cause for the courage was so small. If it had been a child say – well, it would not have been half so admirable.

He looked back at the spot of the bank where the toes of Speedy had gouged deeply into the ground as he took his header into the stream.

It seemed to be at the very edge of the falls. And he, Pierson, would never have been able to attempt such a feat. Furthermore, if he had, by this time he would be a pulpy, smashed and broken corpse, pounding to pieces among the rocks where the water shattered itself in volley after volley.

"Speedy," he said, "I want to say something to you."

"I'll tell you something first," said Speedy. "Don't you say it. Let it be, please. You're going to give me some good advice and wind up with calling me a lot of pleasant names; you're going to apologize for telling me a few home truths, just before this, and you'll probably offer me a place in your sun. But don't you do it."

31

Even now the lawyer could be a little vexed by the cool insight of the boy.

But he said: "I wish you'd listen to me, Speedy."

"I won't though," said the boy. "It's happened a couple of times before that people have got a wrong idea about me. Hell, I know that I'm not all bad. But I know that I'm a damned long ways from all good, too. I don't get away from that, Mr. Pierson. And it makes me sick to cash in on a foolish impression, unless I've worked to make it, professionally. And just now," he added, with a smile, "I wasn't being professional."

"No," burst out the lawyer, "you were being —"

He checked himself before the extravagant word. It had been well enough earned, but something told him that it was not wanted. He could see the relief spread on the face of the youngster as he made the pause.

"What do you call making a fool professionally?" he asked, at last.

"I'll tell you," said the boy. "We're all men, we all have a share of brains, we all want money, we all want an easy time. Well, your dollars are your treasure; your wits are the soldiers that guard it. If I can put your soldiers to sleep, I take your money. That's my game, and it's a good game. It beats chess all hollow."

"You hate to make a false impression," grinned Pierson, "unless you've intended exactly that thing. Is that it?"

"That's it," said the boy. "That's part of it. Now, you and I understand each other a good deal better. Brownie and I are friends. And I warn you − if I take that three hundred − no, it's four hundred dollars − off you in Durfee, I'll dance on your front porch and laugh in your face, Mr. John Pierson!"

4

The house of John Pierson in Durfee was not pretentious. His wife and daughter were often at him to build a much finer place because, as they pointed out, his income and his fortune both warranted such an outlay. But he continually refused.

"If I build a big house," said he, "people will be afraid to come to me. They'll know that the fees they pay are what support me. They'll begin to figure out my income. As it is, they can't tell. I take a good many charity cases. They never know just what I rake in. Believe me, my dears, there is nothing that makes a man unpopular in a small Western town so quickly as a large income which they know he bleeds out of the town without producing anything."

"Producing!" said his wife, on this evening of his return from the mountains. "Producing indeed! I should like to know what man in Durfee produces more hard work than you do!"

"That's very well," said Pierson, who was at

heart a very fair man, "but you must understand that after all, what I produce is only words. I don't raise grain or cattle, or dig minerals out of the ground, or turn trees into lumber, or make cloth, or do anything else that has a concrete value in the eyes of the world."

"Stuff!" said his wife. "You keep the affairs of people straight!"

"There is nothing," said Pierson, "that men hate so much as paying for advice."

"There's no use talking any more, Mother," said Charlotte Pierson, the daughter of the family. "Father is beginning to philosophize, and you know that when that happens neither of us can argue with him."

"I know," said Mrs. Pierson, "and it's tiresome. I'm going into the house and let you sit out here with your philosophy and your thoughts about that tramp in the mountains. I should like to see that boy, though."

"You probably will," said Pierson, "when he comes to try to win his bet."

"I never heard of such nonsense as that bet," said Charlotte. "Of course he can't do that. Because you'll even have a chance to warn the proposed victim."

At this point, a slender man walked down the street, paused, and then turned in up the path towards the Pierson veranda. He walked with a leisurely step, and when he came to the foot of the steps, he said: "Is this the house of Mr. John Pierson?"

"It's Speedy!" said Pierson, springing up in excitement. "Charlotte, call Brownie, will you? Come up here, Speedy. I'm glad to see you. Mary, this is Speedy, about whom I was talking to you."

The boy paused again, a step from the top, and bowed to Mrs. Pierson. Charlotte could be heard calling Brownie from the back porch of the house; and presently there was a scampering of the dog's feet as it tore through the house, barking with excitement.

"He'll know you, Speedy," said Pierson, half kindly, half jealously. "The little rascal —"

Here Brownie knocked the screen door wide open with a blow of his forefeet, and sprang up straight at the stranger and then began to leap and whine and bark as though his real master had just come back.

"There you are," said Pierson. "I told you so. Brownie, let him alone, now. Down, sir, down!"

There was some impatience in his voice. He could not be altogether pleased when he saw his favorite hunting dog making such a demonstration over another man.

Then Charlotte Pierson came out on the porch. The lamplight caught in her blonde hair and set it shining about her face. She was twenty, straight as a string, brown as leather and pert as an unbroken mustang, running wild.

"Charlotte," said the lawyer, "this is Speedy. I told you that he'd turn up!"

Charlotte did not hesitate. She went forward and thanked the stranger.

She even let her hand linger in his, while she looked more closely into his face; for he was so dark that, in this light, it was hard to see him with any accuracy.

Her father was somewhat angered. He did not see why his girl should be so familiar with a tramp, no matter what good qualities that tramp might have.

So he broke in: "How did you get here so soon, Speedy?"

"Why not?" asked the boy. "I came on the same train that brought you."

"The deuce you did," said Pierson. "You couldn't have done that, Speedy!"

"That's the train I came on," persisted the tramp.

"I had an idea that you might try that trick," said Pierson, "and so I warned the conductor, and he warned the brakeman. I know that both of them watched for you every minute."

"It wasn't an altogether easy trip for me," admitted the boy. "I started on the coal tender, and then I had to shift to blind baggage. They chased me off that, and it was the rods for a while, and then the top of the last coach, and, finally, I got pretty tired, so I came down and sat in a seat, and finished the ride on the cushions."

"What!" exclaimed Pierson. "Didn't they see you?"

"Sure they saw me — with my coat off, and a smudge of soot across one eye and the bridge of my nose — that's as good as a complete mask, you know. And I had my sleeves rolled up, and a plumbing wrench in my hand. The conductor just thought that I was going back to Durfee from a railroad repair job down the line."

Pierson lay back in his chair and laughed heartily. So did Charlotte. But Mrs. Pierson said that she could not understand what it was all about.

"It means that he beat me," said Pierson, frankly. "And now, my lad, what's your next step in Durfee?"

"My next step is to win the bet," said the boy.

"To win the bet? You mean that you're really going to try?" asked Charlotte.

"Why," said he, "the bet's made, and so I'll have to do my best."

"Oh, but Dad would let you off," said she.

"Oh, but I wouldn't," said the lawyer, hastily.

"Dad!" cried Charlotte, in reproach.

"Certainly not," answered Pierson. "If he

can't win the bet, he'll have to go to work to make the hundred dollars that he'll owe me. Because if I win, I want an honest hundred, young man! Two hundred, in fact, is the whole bet, if I put you in jail for this job! And I think that thirty days in jail would give you a good chance to think your life over!"

"John, you're letting yourself go. You're brutal!" said his wife, angrily. "After a poor boy has —"

"It's all right," said Speedy. "I just wanted Mr. Pierson to name the man he wants me to try for the hundred dollars."

"Great Scott," said Pierson, "you mean to say that you'll try anyone I name for you?"

"Certainly," said the boy. "A man's not a real musician unless he can play a good tune on a bad instrument."

Pierson began to laugh.

"Of all the brazen-faced —" he began.

His own laughter stopped his words.

"All right," he said. "And I'll tell you what I'll do. I'll pick out the hardest man in town. Wait a minute. Mary, who's the tightest man in town?"

"Old Tom Jenkins," she answered, without hesitation.

"He never gave a penny away in his life," agreed the lawyer. "But there's someone tighter than he is. Charlotte, what's your choice?"

"Mrs. Hilton," said the girl. "She's given away so much that she —"

"I beg your pardon," said the boy. "I can't try a woman, because I never make them professional clients of mine."

"Hello!" said Pierson. "You limit yourself with a lot of self-made rules, it seems to me. But I'll tell you what, my boy, I'll name a harder subject than either of the ones the ladies have suggested. I'm going to send you to a man who works on every charity committee and never spends an infernal cent. He never gives to beggars because he says that no man needs to go hungry in a country as full of honest work as ours. I don't think that he ever spent a cent in his life, except on himself. He's never married, because he never could bear the thought of buying a wedding ring! That's the kind of fellow he is. I'm not exaggerating."

"You mean Mr. Chalmers," said Charlotte, breaking in. "But, Dad, that's not fair. He's the district attorney."

"What of that?" answered her father. "He's the district attorney, and he's as keen as a hawk. The moment he begins to suspect the nature of your profession, as you call it, he'll have you in jail so fast that your head will swim. But that's my choice. Mind, I can't hold you to it. But you asked me to name the hardest man in Durfee, and you see that I've done it. Now do as you please."

"I'll try Mr. Chalmers," said the boy, nodding. "He sounds like a promising fellow, to me."

"You'll find him a hard nut. I haven't exaggerated about him!"

"Well, I believe that, too," answered the lad. "But you know that the hardest nut is packed with the sweetest meat. Will you direct me to Mr. Chalmers' house?"

"It's three blocks straight down that way, and a block to your left. You won't miss it. It's a big white house, with a lot of trees in front of it. The reason he's living in such a big place is because his father gave it to him. I'm always wondering that he doesn't take in roomers to fill up the spare corners of the house."

He did not like Mr. Chalmers. As a matter of fact, he had run against him at the last election.

"Very well," said the boy. "I'll go to Mr. Chalmers' house."

"You'd better not go straight off," warned Charlotte. "Mr. Chalmers will be at dinner, now, and if you disturb him —"

"No fair, Charlotte," said the lawyer.

"That's all right," said the boy. "People give better from the table than they do from the street, I suppose. Goodbye!"

He started down the steps.

"Hold on!" said the lawyer. "How long a start

41

am I to give you before I come over and warn him?"

"Well," said the boy, "whatever you'd call a sporting start. I don't care. You can come over with me, if you want."

"Tut, tut!" smiled Pierson. "I'm not that sort of a fellow. But I take it that you're a fast worker, and I'll give you only fifteen minutes."

"Oh, shame, Dad!" cried Charlotte.

But the tramp was already halfway to the gate.

5

Samuel P. Chalmers was giving a dinner.

He rarely gave a dinner to more than one man at a time; this evening he was saying to his guest: "Two people can talk, discuss, sir. Three makes the development of a subject impossible. I wanted to have you alone with me, tonight, Mr. Chase. Because you are the man in Durfee whose opinion counts most with me. I wanted to consult you quietly, and personally, about certain matters of policy."

Mr. Chalmers affected a grand style, not only in his speech but in his clothes. He wore tails and parti-colored waistcoats, with a double loop of bright golden chain draped across it. His neckties were the joy of the matrons and the despair of the men of Durfee. Anyone other than Chalmers would have looked foolishly overdressed in such cravats; but they seemed to go well with the broad sweep of his blond mustaches, which he kept well and cleanly away from his bright pink lips.

Mr. Chase was a large rancher; and his

support had, practically unassisted, elected Chalmers over Mr. Pierson. That, added to the fact that people felt that Pierson already had held the office long enough. They had nothing against the latter.

And Mr. Chase was flattered.

He said: "Yeah, when you come to think of it, there ain't any way so good of settlin' things as to go and have a good talk with a man. Seems like trouble gets all ironed out pretty slick, before long."

"It does," said Samuel P. Chalmers, "and therefore I thought that I would have you alone, Mr. Chase. Your experience in the world, and the brilliance of your achievements as a business man —"

"Askin' your pardon, Mr. Chalmers!" said a timid voice.

The district attorney had a piece of meat on the end of his fork. He turned rather wildly and saw a timid face, a great, frightened pair of eyes at the window. He turned farther, with a growl.

"What the devil is this?" he said.

"I tried the front door," said the timid voice, "and they said that you was busy. And then I tried the back door, and they up and said there that you was still busy. And they said that they'd take and throw me over the fence if I didn't get away, but I kind of had to see you, sir. So I just looked in through this window and —"

"Who are you?" snapped the district attorney.

"I'm Mort Waley's boy, sir."

"Mort Waley? I don't know any Mort Waley. Where do you come from?"

"I come from over in Grant County, sir."

"I have nothing to do with Grant County," said the district attorney. "Run along, my lad. What's brought you here, anyway?"

"It was Pa that sent me, sir," said the boy. "He's kind of laid up, or he'd of come himself. He said there was one place to find justice in the world, and that was from Mr. Chalmers, down here in Durfee. So I just walked down, sir."

Said Mr. Chase, his fat face reddening a little: "You gotta reputation, Chalmers. Doggone me if it don't warm me up a good deal, to see how folks come to you for a square deal."

Mr. Chalmers expanded. It was true that he knew few people in Grant County, and that he never had heard of a man named Mort Waley. But a compliment is never paid uselessly to a vain man. His own heart warmed. He cleared his throat.

"Come in, my lad," said he. "Come in, come in. I'll have the front door opened. Not exactly my business hour, Mr. Chase," he added, with a deprecatory laugh, "but the law demands all

45

the time of its servants!"

Said Chase, the rancher: "You go right on. I'd rather be hungry than see folks stay in trouble when they might be helped out."

"Don't you bother about the front door, sir," said the boy. "I could climb right in here."

And straightaway, he put his knee on the window sill, and climbed through.

He made a sad picture. He had no coat. His trousers were badly tattered. The shirt was missing, and had apparently been wound around the bare feet of the boy. The rags of the shirt were bloodstained! Blood spotted the floor with darkness where the youngster stepped.

Mr. Chalmers was a man of strong expression.

"By the Eternal God!" he exclaimed. "What outrage is behind this?"

The boy shrank as from a blow. He raised a hand to protect his face. He shrank shuddering back against the wall.

"I ain't meaning no harm, sir," said he. "I'll clean up the blood on your floor."

"*You'll* clean it up?" said the district attorney. "*You'll* clean it up? My poor lad, who has done this to you?"

He advanced and laid a fatherly arm about the shoulders of the lad. Humped shoulders they were, with the bones thrusting out a little.

Then he turned towards Chase, whose broad,

rather heavy face was pinched with pain and with pity.

"Shaking like a leaf, poor child," said Chalmers. "Sit down here, my boy. Who did this to you?"

"Nobody, sir. I dunno what you mean?"

"You don't know what I mean?" cried the attorney, his voice rich and ringing with indignant sympathy. "I say, who reduced you to wander barefoot through—"

He was about to say "wilderness" and suddenly realized that the term was a shade Biblical for the stomach of Mr. Chase.

So he paused on "through."

"Dad was laid up," said the boy. "And this here was the last day. He told me to come runnin' to you."

"Not another word," said the district attorney, "until you've had food and drink. Sit down here, if you please! Sit right down here — yes, at the table, by God! I beg your pardon, Mr. Chase. I should have asked your permission, first, but —"

The rancher stood up.

"Don't be a damn fool, Chalmers," he said, bluntly. "The kid's sick. He's wobbly. Bring him over here and shove some food into him."

"You have a good heart, Mr. Chase," said Chalmers, gratefully.

"Hell, man," said Chase. "It's your house. I'm

doggone glad to find out that they lie that called you a proud man, Chalmers. All I gotta say is that you're gunna have my vote every time, and the votes of all my friends."

The effect of this speech was to make Chalmers bless the day that brought this youthful vagabond to his door.

By this time, he had brought the lad to the table, and now he forced him to sit down. But the boy looked in terror at the long, bright board, and at the heaped plate which the Chinaman now brought in and set before him with a pleased grin. For every cook loves to set forth his best before the truly hungry.

"Go on," said Chalmers, bursting with Good Samaritanism, his eyes stung with tears brought by the sense of his own virtue, "eat, my lad, and afterwards I'll hear you."

"If you please, sir," said the lad, shrinking in his chair, "I wouldn't feel none too good eatin', when Pa ain't had a bite for two days, since he was laid up."

"Two days, eh?" said the district attorney, darkly. "And what laid the man up, my lad?"

"It was three days back," said the boy. "He didn't count the shots, right, and when he went into the shaft the next morning, to clean out the broken ground, the last shot went off. It kind of tore off his left leg at the knee."

"My God!" said Chase. "The poor devil! I

remember seeing — go on, boy! How did you take care of him?"

"I come when he hollered," said the boy, "and he was layin' on the ground, with a good holt on his leg above the knee, with both hands, and there wasn't no leg to be seen nowheres below the knee —"

He paused and shook his head, his eyes blank with wonder, still, as he recalled this strange moment.

The two men interchanged glances. The lad was a good lad, it appeared, but a little lacking in the wits.

"Pa told me to go and start up the fire and heat a stove lit till it was red hot, which I done it, and then brung it to him with a pair of tongs and —"

His eyes withered shut. He clenched a fist and raised it before his eyes.

Sweat was streaming down the face of Mr. Chase.

"We know the rest, son," said he. "We know the rest. It's all right. You don't have to tell me. I remember seein' — but that don't matter. Go on and tell me how your old man is resting now?"

"Why, he's restin' pretty good," said the boy, his stopped voice coming back with a gasp. "He's restin' pretty good, I guess. I partly drug and he partly hitched himself along until we got him to the cabin and into a bunk. He says that one day he'll walk better than ever on one wooden leg. He says that a wooden leg, it sure saved a pile of wear on shoes. I reckon he's right."

Chase laughed, shortly.

But the district attorney shook his head.

"A picture of a brave heart, told in a few simple words," said Chalmers.

"He's a fellow with guts," said Chase, through his teeth. "Then two days without food, eh?"

"He was gunna go down to town, that same day, and try to borrow some flour, because he'd run out of money. And then he hoped he'd make a good strike in the mine, and in the two days that would be left, he'd get out enough gold to pay back Mr. Pierson and —"

"Mr. Who?" exclaimed the two men together.

"Mr. John Pierson, of Durfee. Pa was pretty broke about six months back, when Mr. Pierson come along on a huntin' trip and seen the mine, and looked it over, and liked the color that was showin'. Pa said there was a big vein about to open up, and Mr. Pierson, he said somethin' I didn't mostly understand about development, and capital, and words like that; and he would lend Pa a hundred dollars for six months, and if Pa didn't pay back the money by the end of that time, he was to give the mine to Mr. Pierson, and —"

"By the Lord!" cried Chase, "I never knew why I didn't like Pierson, before. I know now."

The Chinaman came into the room.

He announced that Mr. John Pierson was calling.

6

"Bring him in!" said the district attorney, scowling as if with hatred, at the boy. And the lad shrank from the grim eyes.

"And you walked down here in bare feet?" he asked.

"Mostly I run, sir," said the boy. "Till I kind of give out in the feet."

"You tore off your shirt and wrapped it around your feet, and you kept on running!" said the district attorney, through his teeth.

"I reckon you seen me!" said the boy, his great eyes opening in the simplest wonder.

Chalmers smiled bitterly at Chase.

"A poor, simple, honest lad!" he said to Chase. "I'll see justice done to him even if he doesn't live in my county. I'll see justice done to him if it's the last act of my life!"

Just then, the cheerful voice of Pierson said at the door: "Is this right, Chalmers? Shall I come in here? Sorry to disturb your dinner, but —"

Both Chase and Chalmers were upon their

feet. They turned on the intruder with thundering brows.

Chalmers, in place of answering, pointed a long, heavy arm at the boy.

"Pierson," he said, in a terrible voice, "this is your work!"

It was a little difficult for Pierson to recognize Speedy in the tousled hair, the shrunken, bowed body, the haunted eyes of this youngster.

But now he chuckled, easily.

"By the Lord, Speedy," said he, "you're making a mighty good play for your money!"

And he laughed, more loudly.

"It's a hundred dollars he wants, isn't it?" he asked.

Chalmers was taken somewhat aback; but Chase exclaimed: "Yeah, a hundred dollars — of blood money! Blood that you're takin', Pierson."

To the surprise of the district attorney and his first guest, the lawyer laughed cheerfully again.

"This is a great dodge," said he. "The little rascal says that I'm extracting blood money from him, does he? Is that the dodge?"

"Yes," said Chalmers, fiercely. "I'm not to be laughed down, Pierson. I tell you, this thing is going to be sifted to the bottom!"

"Oh, rot," answered Pierson, with a sweeping gesture. "This youngster is making a fool of you — two fools. He's a professional swindler and loafer. I bet him three hundred to one hundred that he couldn't wheedle a hundred dollars out of you. Another hundred at evens that I'd have him in jail before morning."

The first doubt struck Chalmers a hammer blow.

He turned on the boy.

"What's this about?" he demanded.

The boy merely gaped. His eyes were greater than ever.

"You've scared the youngster to death," said Chase. "Leave him to me. Son," he added, gently, "you understand what Mr. Pierson says?"

"No, sir, I dunno that I quite do," stammered Speedy.

Then he started up and clutched the arm of Chase.

"Oh, my God," he said, "doncha go and let him put me in jail, or Pa'll starve. He'll lie waitin' for me, and starve to death! If you're gunna jail me, go and send some flour and bacon to Pa. *You're* a kind man; you got a kind face. Doncha —"

"Oh, what rot," said Pierson. "Are you two going to be taken in with this play acting? I tell you —"

"Wait a minute," said Chase. "How long before this money is due to be paid?"

"Pa said it was due by midnight," answered the boy.

"There you are," said Chase. "And Pierson, I'll wager, would stand here and argue till the time was up. But by heaven, I'm convinced right on the spot. Look here. So, here's a hundred dollars and —"

He put the money before Speedy. The latter drew back from it. Bewilderment spread on all faces.

Only Pierson cried out: "You see? I told you that the agreement was that he should get the money out of *you*, Chalmers!"

"Pa didn't say nothin' about askin' help from anybody but Mr. Chalmers," said the boy. "I couldn't be takin' money from nobody else."

Suddenly he rose and stood stiff and proudly before them. But his voice was quiet as he added: "The Waleys ain't beggars, I reckon. I didn't come here to ask for no money. Pa, he sent me down to ask Mr. Chalmers for justice. I ain't gunna take no money from nobody! The Waleys, they ain't beggars. They never *been* beggars!"

The speech had its effect.

Mr. Chase gathered up his sheaf of money and sat down, heavily.

"Now, then," he said, "I wanta see you two smart fellers, you two lawyers, figger out this thing together!"

And he waited, scowling up at them, alternately, under his brows. The boy began to tremble violently.

"I'll be goin' on," said he, and turned towards the door.

Chalmers caught him and forced him back into the chair.

"Justice is what you're going to have, my poor boy," said he. He lifted his voice until it had the electioneering ring in it. "I thank God that Samuel P. Chalmers can work for naked justice rather than for golden fees!"

He was proud of that speech.

But Mr. Chase said, rather shortly: "Well, let's do something about it, then!"

"Wait a moment," said Pierson, who was gradually turning a bright red.

"I've waited long enough," thundered Chalmers. "Your disgraceful piracy and —"

"Oh, shut up, man," said Pierson. "You explain to me, if the boy's cock and bull story is the truth, how I could know that he was here at this minute, bulldozing you, Chalmers?"

Chalmers gasped. He turned again to the boy.

"You heard that question?" he asked.

"I dunno how he would know it," said the boy. "I dunno how he would know that I was comin' here. When I seen him tonight, I just begged him to let Pa have a mite more time, account of his leg being blowed off, and I said that the only other hope I had was to try to get Mr. Chalmers to help us —"

"There you are, Pierson," said Chalmers. "Now tell us what rat hole you'll next try to dodge into to mask your infernal greed, your brutal, grasping knavery. There is a law somewhere that can be called down on your trickery. At least, there is honest public opinion that shall be called on. The people shall know of this, Mr. John Pierson!"

Pierson was a violent crimson. Sweat streamed down his face. He stared at the boy as though he wanted to throttle him. And then he broke into a choked, wild laughter.

At last, turning sharply around, he exclaimed: "Look here, you two madmen!"

"He calls us madmen, now," said Chase, sourly, bitterly.

"Look here," said the other. "If the boy's story is true, his feet are worn almost to the bone — to judge by the rags on them. But I'll tell you. If you look close, you'll see that the red is red paint, or red ink, and his feet are as sound and whole as the feet of any of us."

"Very well," said Chase, with the sneer of one who submits to a last test, but whose mind is already made up. "We'll look at the poor youngster's feet. Boy, take off those rags!"

"Yes, sir," said Speedy, with amazing willingness.

And he slowly unwound the rags, making a little face as he got the first one off his foot, with a tug at the end as though it were stuck to the raw flesh.

And they saw — and Pierson with the rest, his face agape with bewilderment — a foot covered with clotted blood. The toes were choked with mingled blood and mud. Yes, fresh blood, freshly oozing, for it newly stained the hand of the boy.

The snort of Chase was like the challenge of a wild stallion. Yet his voice was carefully controlled.

"I reckon that's about enough proof," he said.

"This damns you forever, Pierson," said Chalmers. "This will drive you straight out of this town!"

"It will," said Pierson, savagely, "unless I can prove that there never was a man named Waley, that he never had such a mine, and that this boy is what I called him before — a professional humbug."

"Pierson," said the district attorney, dramatically pulling out his wallet, like a revolver, from his breast pocket, "from this time forward, I hope that your form will never darken my doors again! I must say that I've always suspected you of sharp practices, but now I know what you are!"

He counted out a hundred dollars and placed it in the hand of the unwilling lad, who drew back from it, protesting.

"No, my boy, no, my young friend," said Chalmers, "this is not charity, neither have you been a beggar. This is only justice — the beginning of a wave of justice which, I hope and pray, will wash you onto a happy shore of —"

He was about to pause, for he hardly knew what word should follow "of," but here Pierson cried: "Well, you've let yourselves in, you two. Now I'll tell you what's going to happen — I'm going to have you laughed out of the town, Chalmers. I took you for a man of sense. And now you've been cheated out of your eyeteeth by a clever young rascal. By the Lord, I still can't believe it — though I see the money in his hand. I can't believe it! You pass for men of sense. And yet there he stands with the money in his hand. All right, my lad, you've won. You've got the bet won. But now, Mr. Wiseman, Mr. District Attorney, I call on you to arrest this boy for swindling."

Mr. Chalmers stood spellbound. He was partly white and partly purple, for of all things in this world, he most dreaded ridicule. And there was a certain ring of savage triumph in the voice of his political rival.

But now the boy said: "All right, Mr. Pierson. You admit that I've won the bet. I won't have to jump through the window. I have the hundred. Now I return it to you, Mr. Chalmers. I thank you. I apologize for taking up so much of your time. But I hope that the entertainment has been worth while."

And he bowed, and smiled, and glided towards the door.

7

By the time John Pierson reached the front door of the Chalmers house, he was beginning to think that perhaps this little adventure might be worth all of four hundred dollars and even more. He was reasonably sure of it, when the district attorney followed him, and from the front porch shouted: "This is a damnable trick on your part, Pierson. This is a trick, a low, deceiving trick, to appeal to my foolish and soft-hearted humanity. But I see through you, Pierson. I've always seen through you. You won't be able to make me a laughing stock through this, as now I demand your assistance to lay hands upon the worthless puppy who was your tool, in this matter."

Pierson stood still, near the front gate of the yard. He was counting from his wallet, four hundred dollars into the hand of the boy. And, as he finished, he turned with a chuckle:

"You're a laughing stock already, Chalmers," he said. "This business will roar you out of town. People will learn from this just what a windy joke you are, and always have been!"

This was language brought home with a smash, but Pierson's heart was still sore because of his political defeat. And he relished mightily this opportunity to get a little of his own back.

So he went on laughing, while Chalmers began to roar again and again from the front porch. At last, Chase came out, and taking his friend by the arm, told him bluntly not to make a further fool of himself, and so got him back into the house. Already neighbors were opening doors and murmurs of interest came drifting through the air.

The lawyer at the front gate was saying to the boy: "Come along with me, Speedy. I've several things to say to you."

"I can't go along," said Speedy. "I have to stay here to do one thing more."

"Then answer me one question."

"Certainly."

"How did you make your feet seem to be bleeding?"

"They didn't seem to be. They were."

"Tut, tut," said the lawyer. "Don't tell me that!"

"It's true, though," insisted Speedy. "After all, a tablespoonful of blood makes a pretty big stain."

"But where did you get the blood?"

"Out of my feet, man! I simply made a small cut behind the ball of each foot, where the skin's tender and the blood's near the surface. The movement of walking kept the drops of blood leaking out. It isn't painful, but, as you saw, it makes a good lot of blood. And a bit of sticking plaster on each cut will make it as sound as ever. You should have asked me to wash my feet. Then they could have seen through the sham. But people get excited and careless, at times like that. They're apt to believe their eyes, and eyes are almost never right, you know."

John Pierson paused in thought. There was much in the last remark of this odd youth. Finally he said: "I want to see you again, Speedy. Shall I?"

"I'll be in the town long enough to get a new suit of clothes," said the tramp. "And then I'll go on again. I need an outfit. I was trimmed down almost to my guitar, when I luckily met you, and since then I've been thanking my stars."

"Will you come to my office tomorrow?" asked Pierson. "It's been growing in my mind almost ever since I met you."

"Thanks," said the boy. "You don't mean that you're going to try to reform me?"

"No. Not that. You have a pretty thick skin, I take it?"

"I don't pride myself on it," said Speedy. "But I suppose that I have a pretty thick skin, all right."

"Now, then, listen to me. I have some work in mind that will need the thickest skin in the world. It's not dishonest, but it's a gamble and a chance, and a good chance. I want to put it up to you. What do you say?"

"I always liked chances," said Speedy. "And I always liked long ones. I'll come in tomorrow at the end of the morning."

"No, come early in the afternoon, because our talk will take a long time," said Pierson.

So it was agreed. They shook hands, and Pierson went up the street, while the boy waited behind until the door of the Chalmers house opened, and Mr. Chase came down the front steps hastily, making rumbling sounds in his throat. It seemed certain that among other things, Mr. Chalmers had not cemented his friendship with Chase any more firmly on this night of nights!

At the gate, the boy stepped out from the shadow of a tree.

He said: "May I speak to you for a minute, Mr. Chase?"

"It's the young whippersnapper, again," said the rancher, stopping short. "I want nothin' to do with you, friend. And you want nothing to do with me, if you know what's good for you. Goodnight!"

"I want to talk to you for half a minute," replied the tramp, quickly. "I went there to make a joke of Chalmers. Not of you. I'm sorry you were there, because you're real, and he's only a sham. I couldn't make a joke of him; he's a joke already."

Chase sputtered for a moment, and then he exclaimed: "By the jumping lord jackrabbit, if you ain't right. You got a brain in your head, young man. It's all right, the way you pulled the wool over my eyes. I ain't one that pretends to sharp sight with men, anyway. I can see a hoss, a cow, or a sheep. But that lets me out."

"Goodnight, then, Mr. Chase. And no hard feelings, sir," said the boy.

"Why, boy," said the rancher, "doggone me if you ain't pretty clean speakin', too. I take a sort of a likin' to you."

"You ought not to go on trusting your impressions of me," warned Speedy. "You've already found out that it doesn't pay."

At this, the other chuckled.

And he said: "It's been worth more than me bein' made a fool of tonight — worth a lot more, because I've had a chance to see through one special kind of varmint. I'm gunna make a change in lawyers right pronto!"

He waved goodnight, and went with a firm, heavy stride up the street, a rather weaving step, such as one often sees in men who have spent most of their lives in the saddle.

The boy watched him for a moment; then he went to the smallest hotel in Durfee, down by the railroad track, and got a little room, and turned in. He was very tired. He simply wrapped himself in a blanket, and without taking off a stitch, he fell asleep as soon as he had closed his eyes.

He slept smiling, as one whose conscience is absolutely whole; and when he wakened in the morning, he was singing in five minutes. Ragged and unkempt he went down to buy his breakfast. But when he had finished a busy morning, a very neat young man sat down to lunch, dressed in a natty brown suit, with a broad-brimmed hat of tan color, and a tie to match. There was nothing showy about him, but he looked as though much money had flowed through his hands, and as though he expected the future to deal kindly with him, also.

After lunch, he went to his room for a siesta. And then, fresh and wide awake, he found the office of the lawyer. It was in a small wooden shack; and the "shingle" of John Pierson was not in large letters. But the building was itself a relic of the old, early days of Durfee, and the people looked upon it with affection, and with respect on a man who was willing to content himself with such quarters. It made Pierson seem more an intimate part of the town's life, and in the West, townsfolk like to see men who identify themselves with the life of the community.

Chase walked out from Pierson's door, as the boy came to it.

He himself reopened the door.

"Here's another client for you, Pierson," he called. "And I reckon that he'll keep you busier than I do!"

But he shook hands with the youngster, and then closed the door after him as Speedy went inside.

There was triumph in the eyes of Pierson, as he took the boy into his inner room.

Said Speedy: "I imagine that it was worth four hundred dollars, after all, Mr. Pierson?"

The lawyer laughed.

"Worth ten times that much," he said, brushing back his short black mustache with a nervous gesture of thumb and forefinger. "And still more than that. It pried Chase loose from Chalmers — that wind-bag! And it put him in my hands. You've made your peace with Chase, it seems! How did you manage that?"

"I stayed behind to apologize to him," answered the boy. "You know, Mr. Pierson, I don't live off honest men — unless they make bets with me!"

The two of them smiled at one another, with understanding. It was a bright day for Pierson, and he could endure remarks far more stinging than this one. Then he sat down, waved the boy into a chair, and leaning his elbows on his desk, he plunged into his idea.

He said: "Speedy, there's a big ranch on the Rio Grande. Thousands and thousands of acres. You don't measure a place like that in acres. You measure it in miles and leagues. You don't walk over it. You ride. And you ride hard, and change horses in the middle of the day, if you want to get around the land and back to the main ranch house by nightfall."

"I've seen a couple of places like that," said the boy. "Spanish landgrant somewhere at the bottom of 'em, usually."

"That's what's at the bottom of this one, too," said the lawyer.

He paused, and cleared his throat.

"Now, then," he said, "in the house on that ranch lives a man eighty years old. He lives alone. His wife is dead. His one son died a good many years ago. He thinks that he has no heir. But he's wrong. He has a granddaughter, and I can prove her claim to the place — the whole estate — all of those millions! Unfortunately, other people also know her claim. And they're trying to get her married to one of themselves. She doesn't know that she's an heiress. But what she does know, apparently, is that she doesn't want to marry. They've wooed and sued her, but they've all failed. Now, then, it seems to me that you're the sort of a fellow who succeeds best when the work is the hardest. Half the brains you invested in winning four hundred dollars from me, would be enough to bring that girl into camp. You'd find yourself a rich man. And then I come in. Not for a split. I simply want the regular legal fees for handling that property when the old man dies, and the land goes into your hands. That's my case as simply and shortly as possible.

"Now tell me whether you want to remain a hobo, or marry a fortune?"

Said the boy, without hesitation: "Thanks a lot. But the fortune can go hang!"

8

The lawyer rose a little, as though somebody had lifted him in his chair by the collar. In fact, his coat bunched loosely and wrinkled between the shoulder blades.

Then he settled down again.

"You're playing for time. You don't mean what you say," he replied, bluntly.

Said the boy: "Maybe I didn't tell you before, but in my games, I leave the women out."

"Why?" asked the lawyer.

"Because I don't like to fool with them," said the boy, and he frowned.

"Because you think that they're too easy?" insisted John Pierson.

Speedy shrugged his shoulders.

"I'm not ready to marry, even if I could," said he. "I prefer a free life."

"Every man has to settle down some day," argued Pierson.

"That's what the anchored ones say," replied the boy. "It's put the white on your head. Why d'you want me to turn gray, also?"

70

At this, Pierson laughed a little.

"You have a way with you, lad," he admitted. "But here you're wrong."

Speedy waited, but with the manner of one who is polite, though he considers that the subject is closed for further discussion. The lawyer, silently, got out a box of cigars from a drawer of his desk, offered them vainly to Speedy, and then cut off the end of one and lighted it.

Through the smoke he squinted towards the boy, seeing him only in part, concentrating on his serious problem.

At last he nodded.

"I think you're right, after all," he said. "I jumped at a thought that came into my mind, but I begin to see, now, that you're right."

Speedy agreed, silently, with a gesture. He made himself a cigarette with adroit speed, and not a grain of Bull Durham fell to the floor. He lighted the cigarette, flicked out the match and placed it without a sound on the ashtray. The lawyer noted the singular graceful dexterity of every act.

"No," went on John Pierson, "I was thinking of your cleverness, and the way you accomplish the things that you want to do. However, this is something that you couldn't manage."

The boy raised his head a little: "No," he said, "I'm not a ladies' man."

71

Pierson looked down, scowling to cover a smile. Very little except the handsome tramp had been dinned into his ears by his daughter since the night before.

But he looked up as solemnly as ever.

Then, shaking his head, he went on: "Whether you're a success in the eyes of the ladies or no is not the question just now in my mind. No, not at all. Your cleverness could jump that hurdle, I think. No, it's a matter of the men that fence her in. No, it would never do. They'd kill you out of hand, my lad!"

In the brown deeps of the eyes of the boy appeared a glimmering light. For that light the lawyer had waited.

"Oh, they'd kill me out of hand, would they?" said Speedy, gently.

"We'll talk no more about it," said Pierson. "The fact is that I thought of you because, Speedy, in spite of your profession, I like you. Because of Brownie I have a reason. Because of yourself I have a reason. Most of all, I think I admired the impudence with which you made a fool of me, last night. And I have an idea that once you gave your word, you could be trusted to the end of the world!"

The boy waved these compliments aside, with a saintly, rather pained smile.

"But about the man-eaters —" he began.

"No, no, no!" said Pierson, shaking his head. "Now that I think the thing over, I'm horrified because I ever dreamed of dragging you into the business. No, I was entirely wrong. Utterly and entirely wrong, of course. I wouldn't dream of it. Here you are, a fellow who never carries weapons, even — no, the thing would be murder."

"But —" began Speedy.

"I'd have your death on my conscience all the days of my life!" said Pierson, resolutely. "Let's talk of something else, Speedy!"

The tramp sat forward in his chair.

"It may seem odd to you," he said, "but you know that even bare hands and bare brains have handled gunmen before now!"

Pierson raised the flat of his hand and pushed the subject away from consideration.

"I understand," said he. "The idea of a difficulty to be overcome — that rather attracts you, doesn't it? But I wouldn't draw you in. You think that I'm talking of a few reckless border ruffians, but you're quite wrong. No, no! Devils! That's what they are, my lad. I've been down there and looked them over, myself. I've seen fellows who could fan their guns so accurately that they could blow the lettering off a sign a hundred yards away. I'm not simply talking. It's a thing that I saw with my own eyes!"

"Sign posts are not men, after all," suggested Speedy.

"I know what you mean," agreed the lawyer, sympathetically. "But the fact is that they're a chosen lot of devils, down there in the place I refer to. A chosen lot, by heaven! They'd as soon kill a man as a rabbit. And they do. Constant shooting scrapes, d'you see? And a man who tries to make eyes at that girl is marked down in a moment!"

"Then they must be killing one another off at a rate that will make the place safe for strangers, very soon," said the boy.

"You'd think so, but you don't understand the angles of the game," replied Pierson. "No, no, my boy! All of those ruffians have long ago found out that she won't look twice at any of them. They're sure that she won't elope with one of the old hands. It's strangers that they watch."

"Is the girl a half wit?" suggested young Speedy. "If the whole countryside knows that she's an heiress, do you mean to say that she has no inkling?"

"The whole countryside doesn't know," said Pierson. "Only two men down there have the facts in hand. They're both ambitious, but they're both likely, one of these days, to tell her the truth, because each one of 'em will be afraid that somebody else will pick the plum.

You see, I've sketched the thing in very crudely. Only, believe me that I don't exaggerate. The finest shot in the world be taking his life in his hands if he went down there with the purpose I suggested. As for you — it would be plain suicide. You'll wonder that I didn't think of all of this before. But you know how a dream jumps into a man's head, and he tries to realize it when he wakes up. Well, the mist has blown out of my brain, now. Let's talk of something else, Speedy."

The tramp stood up, restlessly, and turned towards the door. Then, hastily, he came back again, and dropped his hand on the edge of the lawyer's desk.

"Down there on the Rio Grande — down where the girl is — that's a real dropping off place, is it?" he asked.

"You bet it is!" answered Pierson, heartily. "The men in the spot I'm talking about are born with a knife in their teeth, and they learn to shoot the eyes out of running jackrabbits before they can walk."

The boy drew a great breath.

"I never thought much of the Rio Grande," he said, "but that's because I never took a good look at the country around it, Mr. Pierson. But from your description of the scenery — why, I see that's it the very next place where I'm to go."

"Come, come," said the lawyer. "You don't

mean what you say! Forget all this, Speedy. I beg you to forget it."

"Ask a man to forget the lungs he breathes with!" said Speedy.

"You mean that you seriously have the thing in mind? No, but then there's the question of the girl. She's not the sort you would like."

"No?" said Speedy, mildly.

"No," answered the lawyer. "She's a pretty thing, but she's a shrew. A man wants a gentle woman around him. Something to work for. But she's a wild caught mustang, if ever there was one!"

"Mr. Pierson," said the tramp, "may I ask you a favor?"

"Certainly," said the lawyer, putting much heartiness in his voice. "I'll do anything for you that I can!"

"Then give me the name and address of this man-tamer!"

Pierson jumped up.

"Don't ask me to do that," said he. "I've promised — but don't hold me to my word, Speedy!"

"I do hold you," said the boy.

"Confound it!" exclaimed Pierson. "You mean that you'd go down there and try to marry her?"

"In spite of the guns, I'd like to try it. And as for the girl, well, wild horses have been gentled, too!" said the tramp.

Pierson strode to the window. He turned his back on the boy and spoke loudly, angrily, without turning his head.

"You've cornered me, Speedy," he said. "But if I have to tell you, I have to! Her name's Mary Steyn, and she lives near Villa Real."

"Mary Steyn — Villa Real," murmured the boy, thoughtfully. "I'll look her up as soon as a train can get me down there!"

Suddenly he crossed the room and stood at the shoulder of Pierson. The latter, little by little, turned. A grin was on his face, triumph in his eyes. For a moment they stared at one another fixedly.

Then Speedy nodded.

"You took me in, that time, Mr. Pierson," he said. "It was all a little game to bait me, eh? A red flag for a bull. Was that it?"

The lawyer broke into ringing laughter. He dropped a hand upon the shoulder of the tramp.

"Speedy," he said, "you know that turn and turn about is fair play, eh?"

"Yes, I know that," said the boy, soberly, "but this was a good, full turn, after all. Well, I've told you that I'll do it. And I will. But you tell me what strings you have on me!"

Pierson shook his head.

"Not one!" he said. "Suppose that you should

win — and honestly I think that your wits may give you one chance in three — you may care to remember John Pierson, and remember that he's a lawyer capable of dealing with estates. But there's not a string or a hold that I have over you. But, by the way, I'll be glad to finance you for any expenses that —"

The boy grew suddenly crimson to the roots of the hair. He said not a word.

But Pierson took a quick little step back from him.

"I beg your pardon!" said the lawyer.

9

The house of Art Steyn was not a beautiful one. It was just a sprawling shack of a ranch house, with three rooms in it. In one room, the punchers ate with the family, which consisted of Mary, the adopted daughter, and Steyn himself. Mrs. Steyn, who had taken the waif in, those years ago, had long since died.

Neither was the situation of the house charming. It was simply backed against a bald, brown hill. There were no trees near it. Even the water had to be carried a hundred feet from the corral troughs. And the sunburned grasses that covered the rolling country for leagues around wore into well-defined trails near the place — though there was no real road — until finally the ground was beaten bare by many hoofs all about the immediate vicinity of the shack.

And yet, every Sunday morning, cow punchers from distant parts of the range were sure to come trooping. What attracted them? Perhaps it was the music which Mary pounded out on a rattling piano that stood in a corner of the long dining room. Perhaps it was Mary's lively tongue. Perhaps it was Mary's brown, pretty face. At any rate, they came like bees to honey. And Art Steyn used to sit behind the veil of his seventy years and smile dimly at "the boys."

Those Sunday meetings served more purposes than merely to see and hear Mary, or to eat the liberal cold lunch which, with beer, was regularly served to all guests, and no questions asked. In addition, the place was a sort of no-man's land, where weapons were never drawn since the day when poor Jay Minter was shot to death by the outlaw, Sam Willys. Mary Steyn was only fifteen, then, but she was already a cause for war among men, and after the death of Minter, an unwritten law declared that no man should either wear or use artificial weapons at the Steyn house. When a rider arrived, he hung up his belt and guns on a peg on the dining room wall. That was his first act; afterwards, he spoke to those present.

And, because of this good custom, it came about that sometimes deadly enemies met under that roof and regarded one another coldly, but without either violent words or violent actions following.

That was not all. Hatred is generally based on ignorance of the other man. And many a hatred softened and mellowed into actual friendship in the good-natured atmosphere of the Steyn house.

On this Sunday, for instance, Rudy Stern, when he came through the doorway, stopped with a shock, for he saw the face of a puncher who had recently come off a more northerly range. It was Alf Barton, big, powerful, solemn of speech, a fighting man. He was not sure death, like Rudy Stern, but he had been man enough to stand up to Rudy in a memorable battle, long ago. And Rudy had been looking for him ever since the two of them were discharged, on different days, from the same hospital.

The story was well known, and when the pair eyed one another, a silence swept in a wave across the room. The girl who was rattling the piano, noticed it, and spun about on the stool.

She saw the cause at once, and did something about it.

She went to Rudy Stern and took him by the elbow.

"You come along with me, Rudy," said she. "Hey, Alf!"

Barton turned, lumberingly, and glared at the girl's companion. However, slowly, step by step, he went to meet them. The two men eyed one another as though they were hunting for places to strike.

Said the girl, as she halted Rudy close to the larger man: "What's the matter with you two fellows? You shot each other up once. Isn't that enough? Now, you quit it! You're throwing a chill into the whole party. Rudy, Alf Barton's a man, and a real man, and you ought to know it. Alf, you know that Rudy has an edge on you in a gunplay. You may be brave enough to die, but why die today? Rudy, you're a bully by nature, but you're not going to start your tricks in this house! Look here, the pair of you. A pair of better punchers never forked a horse. Now, you either get out of here, or else shake hands, now!"

Alf Barton stood rigid and formidable, even then. For it was true that Rudy was the better gunman of the two, and Barton for that very reason would not give way. But Rudy, perhaps a little conscious that his great reputation made it possible for him to bend from his high position, suddenly thrust out his hand, with a smile.

He said: "Alf, old boy, you certainly socked me in Miller's place. But Mary's right. This is no place for us to wrangle. Besides, for my part, I'm glad to forget all about that. I've got nothing against you except that day; and the only thing that I've got against you on that day is that you shot too damn straight. Let's shake and call it quits!"

Barton colored a little. But he took the hand of Rudy in a great, honest grasp.

"I'm a mighty happy man to forget everything, Rudy," he said. Then he admitted, in his straightforward way: "I'm gunna stop payin' life insurance, now!"

The whole room laughed at this sally, and the laughter swept away the last iota of bad feeling between the two. They marched up to the piano, arm in arm, and bellowed loudly in discord in the next chorus that Mary played. The whole room was singing.

Under cover of that song, a grizzly veteran of the range entered, hung up his guns, and went to a corner, where he sat down and smoked a pipe. And presently another of the same type came in, and followed suit. He even drifted into the same corner where the first one had gone.

And it was he who said, half an hour later, lighting a second pipe: "Listen, Jack. I wanta talk to you."

Said Jack, "Damn your ornery hide, that's the only reason that I'm here — is to listen!"

"If you talk like that, Jack, I'm gunna take you outside and slam you!"

"Shut yer fool face, or the girl'll hear you."

"Ay, I forgot about her."

"I wanted to talk to you about that steer. It's a lie that I picked it off your range. That runnin' iron brand must of been the work of —"

"Hold on. I ain't here to argue. I ain't been close enough to you, since that day, to ask you face to face. It ain't been safe to get within rifle shot of you. But now here I set and I ask you, man to man, is it the truth that you're telling me?"

The other stared at him out of keen eyes.

Slowly, bitterly, he said: "No, it ain't the truth. I've lied to you, partner."

"Lie or no lie," said the other, with a sudden heartiness. "It shows the man you are to admit it. Son, we'll fix that matter up peaceable. And the load off my shoulders will be worth the price of twenty steers."

Said the other: "It wasn't the price of the damn steer. It was just that I wasn't gunna be outsmarted by you. Partner, you'll see I'm square. I'll settle it right here and now!"

This small conversation meant much, but it passed almost unnoticed. There was hardly a Sunday when two or three old enemies did not meet in this extra legal court and settle difficulties. And if a very moot point arose, old, faintly smiling Arthur Steyn would be called in to act as the judge. Quietly, in five minutes of talk, he was generally able to straighten out everything.

Now, it was when the merriment was in full swing, and at least twenty men or more were in the room that from outside the house came the sound of a guitar, and a ringing, clear baritone voice which accompanied the piano and the singers inside, a voice that cut through the others by the purity of its rounded tone in spite of the distance of the singer.

"Hello!" cried Mary, as the piece ended. "There's a real musician floating around here! Wait till I get him. This is going to be a party!"

She ran to the door.

And there she saw the player of the guitar standing.

She stopped with a frown.

"Only a tramp — a lowdown hobo!" she exclaimed with a cruel loudness.

For the boy before her was dressed in rags; his toes thrust out at the ends of his shoes; his necktie was askew; a tattered hat was on his head. The sling which supported the guitar from around his neck proved, as it were, that he was a professional mendicant, singing for his living. Now, in an equally professional manner, he lifted his almost brimless hat and bowed to her, and then straightened with a smile on his brown, handsome face.

"Miss Steyn," said he, "I've come a long way to see you. I hope there's something to eat in your kitchen!"

"Look here," said the girl, sternly. "We don't like hoboes, around here. One of your kind burned down the barn, a couple of years back. We want no more of you. Get off the place! Or if you really are just down on your luck, you'll find a woodpile around there behind the house. Go on and tackle it, and we'll feed you when you've earned your meal."

He kept his hat in his hand. The wind waved his tousled hair. His smile did not grow dim.

"Nothing that I'd like to do," said he, "better than to chop some of that wood and get the good hard exercise. But I've a vow that keeps me from it."

"You have a vow?" she asked, disdainfully. "What sort of a vow have you made?"

"Never to raise a callus, ma'am. You know that when a musician wants to keep his touch —"

"Musician? You low hobo, I'll give you five minutes to get off the place!"

And she turned abruptly back to the piano and played the next piece which was being clamored for.

She had scarcely ended when the mellow voice of the tramp broke in upon her, singing:

> "Julia, you are peculiar,
> Julia,
> You are queer.
> Truly,
> You are unruly
> As a wild western steer.
> Sweetheart, when we marry,

Dear one, you and I,
Julia,
You little mule you,
I'm gunna rule you,
Or die!"

There was laughter from the crowd, laughter from the girl, also, but she said: "He sings pretty well, but he's a hobo. I gave him five minutes to get off the place. Say, Fat, you go and throw him off, will you?"

10

Fat Ginnis was a hardy fellow who hardly deserved his nickname. His face was fat; the rest of him was as hard as wrestling with mustangs and beef could make a man.

He merely said: "Say, Mary — where d'you want me to throw him, and how far?"

"Don't hurt him," she called over her shoulder. "Just start him on his way. That's all."

"I'll start him, all right," said Fat, with the tone of one who would finish him, also.

And he disappeared through the doorway with long, determined strides.

The merriment grew, inside the house. Beer was served in the following manner. Two kegs were carried in and hoisted onto the long central table, and over each was appointed an overseer and bartender, who filled the glasses in turn and tried to keep the liquid from dripping on the floor.

However, as Mary said: "We can get another floor, but we can't get another crowd together as good as this one!"

A series of toasts began, and the first, as usual, was to Mary. It had hardly been downed, and she was laughing, and the first roaring of cheers had died a little, when the voice of the singer floated clearly though faintly in from outside the house:

".. . You are peculiar,
Julia,
You are queer,
Truly,
You are unruly,
As a wild western steer . . ."

The words seemed to have a peculiar aptness, at the moment, and the face of the girl flushed with anger.

"Will one of you fellows go and see what Fat Ginnis is doing out there, to let that hobo hang around and spoil the party for us?" she demanded. "Will you go, Doc?"

Doc waved his hand. He rose, shifted his quid — he had been taking his beer without removing the quid from his mouth — and tightened his belt. From a peg on the wall, he took down his hat, carefully adjusted it on his head, and then stepped out into the glare of the sunlight.

Someone laughed, looking after him.

"He'll kill that hobo!" suggested someone.

The girl was singing out after him: "Don't break the kid up for life, Doc. Just slide him along on his way."

But Doc gave no sign that he heard, and his wide shoulders, muscled as only a lumberman's shoulder may be, had a resolved swing to them, and he was leaning forward in his stride.

Other men in the place envied him. There was not a fellow there who did not ache to win a smile from Mary Steyn.

However, Doc would handle the business very well, no doubt. If he did not let himself in for a manslaughter charge, or some such thing, it would be well. There was an ugly story, somewhere current, about a certain Canuck who had died in the grasp of Doc.

Now the fun began again, under Mary's supervision. She loved these Sunday parties, and all week she looked forward to them, but her chief care was that the pleasure should be distributed, and that no one should be slighted. She had her favorites, of course, but the vast base of her popularity was composed of two elements — one, that no man could have her, and two, that she was equally nice to everyone.

When a girl makes a choice and shows a preference, the rest of the world of men promptly turns its face from her and cares not a whit if it never sees her again. Mary Steyn never had made that mistake. And if a too importunate wooer appeared, she simply winked at any of a hundred bold-handed ruffians, who promptly showed him that the air was better in other parts of the country.

Now Mary was busy for a time in moving through the corners and the distant angles of the big room, finding the oldsters, sitting beside them for a moment, making their grim eyes light up and smile back at her. And it was in the midst of just such a moment that she was suddenly aware that the entire rest of the room had fallen silent, while through the open doorway streamed the words of the infernal song:

> "Sweetheart, when we're married,
> Dear one, you and I;
> Julia,
> You little mule you,
> I'm gunna rule you,
> Or die!"

It was the hobo singer again, and his voice was raised and more powerfully ringing than before.

Amazement had stilled all sounds in the room. Amazement stilled the very heart of the girl. And into her mind's eye, once again, stepped the powerful form of Doc, as he had gone out to battle, a man in a hundred, a man in a thousand, even, when it came to physical combat.

Had she made a mistake about the boy?

No, she remembered the almost loathesome beauty of his face, his brown skin and ruddy color in the cheeks, the deep, soft brown eyes, the femininely flashing smile —

No, she could not have made a mistake about him as a man. But whatever little mystery it was that detained both Fat and big Doc should be looked into at once.

Said one of the men in the room: "Ma'am, what kind of an hombre did you say this hobo looked to be?"

"He's a worthless, shiftless tramp whose pride is that he never had a callus on his hands. A guitar-playing loafer and hobo. That's what he is. He looks like a girl in disguise! But I wish that something could be done about him!"

Ready faces surrounded her. But they were graver faces, now, she noted. Whatever the mystery was that lay in the disappearance of both Fat Ginnis and Doc, it was plain that a real man was required to handle the hobo now.

Her eyes picked up the men, one by one, and discarded them. Gentleman Joe Wynne was not there. She was beginning to miss him more and more, when he absented himself from one of the parties, or came dashing up very late in the evening, when most of the others had gone. He was the Achilles who could do all things — beat a Mexican throwing a rope or a knife, and shoot the eyelids off the hardiest gunman that ever pulled a Colt and fanned it.

There was Rudy Stern, as good as Gentleman Joe, when it came to gunwork, but not such an able man of his hands. A terrible and efficient warrior was Rudy, but if he undertook this battle he would probably invent a weapon offhand and kill the young tramp.

She wanted no more killings around the Steyn house!

Then she saw Alfred Barton. Alf was the biggest and the strongest man in the room. They said that he knocked a mustang down one day with his bare fist, and that the mustang stayed down for half an hour. A glance at him made the story appear easily credible.

So she said: "Alf, I hate to bother you. You've hardly more than come in. But I wish that you'd go out and see if Fat and Doc are shooting craps, or watching a hawk fly, or what. D'you mind?"

Alf Barton laughed.

He could pull a gun and he could shoot it, but he never was thoroughly at home with weapons. His hands were his medium. Whether it were catch-as-catch-can, or fists, or a roughhouse combination of the two, he was at ease and at home. He spread his elbows at the board and smashed bones!

And to do this little favor for Mary Steyn?

So he laughed, for an answer, and started for the door.

"Don't be rash, Alf," called the girl. "The hobo has some trick, maybe!"

He waved his hand over his shoulder without so much as turning his head towards her, and continued until the sunlight flashed upon his blond head. Then the edge of the door cut him off from view.

Every man in that room yearned to follow; but no one would break up the party, except at a sign from Mary.

She said: "If we followed along, it would make that tramp feel too important, even while he's taking his licking."

Straightaway, the buzz of talk began again, but this time there was only one theme; what had happened to the first two; what would big Alf Barton do to the stranger?

And the buzz grew denser, but softer, as the minutes slid by. Mary Steyn, to be sure, noted the passage of the time, and her amazement and her anger grew.

What was behind the whole thing?

All three were men; the last two were carefully picked men, worthy to fight a battle with ten. But — none of them came back!

And now, in the midst of her bewilderment,

the thing she dreaded, which had become a pulse of sound at her ear, sounded just outside the door:

"Julia,
    You are peculiar,
Julia,
    You are queer . . ."

And there stood the hobo in the doorway! He had not altered.

If he had had three encounters with three formidable men, no one could have guessed it. His rags were the same. The same remnant of brim adhered to his hat. His face was unmarred, and, for all that she could see, his breathing was not interfered with by any recent violent exercise.

Women hate mysteries and problems. And Mary Steyn was preeminently a woman.

She stamped on the floor.

"If one man can't handle him —" she cried out.

And then she paused, for a quiet voice called from the farther end of the room:

"Come in, lad!"

That voice took the case out of her hands. It rarely interfered, but when it spoke, it was absolute. For it was the voice of old Arthur Steyn himself.

"Come in, lad," he said, "and sing us another song. I like your style!"

The hobo took off his hat and bowed. It was a deep and graceful bow.

"What will you have, sir?" he asked.

"Something old," said Steyn. "Some old darky song would please me best. Mary, play something at the piano and —"

But Mary had suddenly disappeared from the room.

11

She had slipped out through the door, and
turning the corner of the house, the first thing
that she saw was the form of Doc loosely sitting
in the saddle, slouched over to one side, with
his head hanging on his chest, and the air of a
man who has been shot through the body. He
held onto the pommel of the saddle to support
himself. His hat was off. It remained somewhere unheeded behind him, even the sombrero sacred to a cowpuncher.

His head flopped up and down, as the horse
began to trot.

"Doc – has been beaten – within an inch of
his life!" she gasped to herself. "And he's going
home, shamed!"

Well, Fat Ginnis might have done the same
thing. But where was the great Alf Barton?

He was not in the woodshed nor was he
behind it. He was not behind the great corded
pile of wood which was waiting to be cut.

Had he disappeared from the face of the
earth?

No, running on, breathless, beside the barn she found him lying face up in the glare of the sun. His face was running crimson. One eye was open, but it looked up at the terrible sky without sense. The other eye was closed; it would remain closed for some days to come, she could guess!

His very clothes showed the signs of struggle. His coat was ripped almost from his back. His shirt was torn open across his breast.

What monster, part grizzly bear and part mountain lion, had dropped upon poor Alf Barton?

Not that slender, worthless hobo, with his singing voice and his guitar, surely! Such a thing was impossible!

She kneeled beside Alf, putting her body between him and the cruel sun. She took his head on her lap and with her handkerchief, she dabbed at the blood upon his split and swollen lips.

Then a flicker of life came back into the fishy, open eye — It winked. Alf Barton pushed himself slowly to a sitting posture, where he supported himself upon trembling arms.

His head hung down, not in shame but in sickening weakness and in pain.

She, still on her knees, laid a hand upon his shoulder; she could feel the big muscles dissolved to pulp, and shuddering under her touch.

"Alf," she said, "it's Mary speaking. Tell me what on earth happened. I'll take care of you. Not a soul shall know. What did the scoundrel do? Did he strike you from behind with a club?"

He looked vaguely at her. His breath rattled in his throat, but he seemed to be recovering little by little.

Then he raised a hand to his head, and fumbled at the crown of it.

"No," he said, "I reckon I half remember that part of it. That was where he slammed me up agin the barn, and my head socked the edge of a plank. That was kind of towards the end."

His thick mumbling voice horrified her. But she was fascinated more than she was shocked.

"D'you mean," she said, "that the hobo did it — all by himself?"

At this, he raised his head higher, inspired by a rising heat of indignation.

"All by himself?" he echoed. "He ain't all by himself. He's got a whole bag of tricks for company. He ain't never alone. He's got more legs than a spider, and three pairs of hands."

"He — did — these things — to you — with his hands?" she cried.

"I didn't say that," answered Alf Barton,

shaking his bleeding head. "It was my hands that he used."

"Alf, you're crazy," she said. "How could he use your hands?"

"Ask him!" he replied, angrily. "Don't you go and ask me. How do I know? When I reached for him, I just seemed to hit myself. That's all that I know about it. When I rushed him, I just tripped on the place where he'd been standing, and sailed right on and lit on my face. When I stood off and sparred at him, he picked a straight left out of the air like an apple off of a bough and turned around, and bore down, and just about dislocated my arm at the shoulder. After that I didn't have nothing but a right, left to me. But a right was enough — if only I could of pasted him once."

"He's a professional prizefighter?" exclaimed the girl.

"He ain't," said Alf Barton. "I've seen plenty of them. I've met 'em in camp when they'd just got through with the ring. And plenty of ex-pugs I've poked in the chin and watched 'em drop to sleep. But I couldn't poke this kid. He never was where I wanted him. I tried to rush him and wear him down with weight. That was when he slipped me over his shoulder and heaved me into the side of the barn, and after that, everything begun to get kind of dim. That's all that I know."

100

"Alf, tell me this. Did he ever hit you with his fists?"

"Him?" muttered Barton. "I dunno. But towards the end, it seemed like I remembered something small and light tapping me on the chin, and my brain going black. Something like the tapping of a tack hammer. It put my brain to sleep. It turned me all numb. Then I forgot the rest, till I heard you talkin', Mary. I'm gunna go home."

"Wait till I've fixed you up," she said.

"I won't wait for nothin'," he said. "I ain't gunna run the risk of any of the boys seein' what he done to me! That shrimp! I'll break him in two like a stick of wood, one of these days, I tell you!"

"Of course you will," said she. "But first, let me go and get some water and adhesive tape and —"

"I won't be here when you come back," he said. "I got my hoss right here in the barn. But tell me something before I barge along."

"I'll tell you anything I can, Alf."

"Did you have something agin Doc and Fatty and me that you elected the three of us?"

"Alf!" she cried, in painful protest. "Every time that one of you went out, I was ashamed to send such a man after such a worthless splinter of a boy."

"He ain't a splinter, unless it's a splinter of

101

steel," replied the other. "A splinter like him could slide into a man's heart or brain and leave him dead and not knowin' that nothin' had struck him. I'm gunna go home!"

He heaved himself to his feet. She herself accompanied his unsteady steps into the barn. She was deeply hurt, but she knew that nothing she could say now would persuade him. It was plain that he still nourished a doubt of her honesty in this matter.

And, when he sat in the saddle, he muttered at her through lips increasingly thick and numb:

"Magician, that's what he is. One of these here, now you see it and now you don't. One of them kind of fellows he is. And you knew it, Mary Steyn!"

She started to protest. He merely shook his head, and rode off at a rapid gallop down the slope, a gallop which he was not yet able to sit out easily, for he swayed and reeled wildly in the saddle as the horse raced along.

She looked after him with the feeling that the ground had been cut from under her feet.

And just then she heard the heavy pounding of the piano in the house. She recognized one of the three tunes that Bill Sanson was able to play, and now and again, she heard whoops and stampings, and single yells of joy going up from a delighted crowd.

That was the stranger at work again, no doubt!

She wished that the hobo could be buried in the center of the earth.

She had ordered him from the place; now he had fought his way in, as it were, made a fool of her, shamed her, and established himself in the graces of the crowd.

And she, Mary Steyn, the queen of those ranges, had to go back and try to face him in her own home!

She groaned, the sound making her throat quiver.

Of only one thing was she sure, and this was that she detested the tramp more than she ever had dreamed before that she could loathe any human creature.

However, she had plenty of nerve and courage, and she forced herself to go back to the door of the dining room, where the party was in progress. And there she saw the crowd standing huddled against the walls of the room, while up and down the center of the open space flickered and whirled and bounded the form of the hobo, now doing a buck and wing, and now a soft shoe step or two whose silence threw the crowd into an ecstasy of delight.

Bill Sanson himself, hammering out the tune on the piano, over and over again, could hardly contain himself. He was almost falling from the

103

stool. There was her father also, who rarely even smiled, now wiping tears of childish pleasure from his eyes.

And now the dancer, fiddling with soft shoe steps at one end of the room, announced his imitations — a tipsy man going upstairs in his house, startled by noises on the way, and finally confronting his wife at the head of the steps, and falling all the way down to the starting point.

How realistically it was all done; she found herself smiling, though grimly.

And then, a cat crossing muddy street — earnestly looking and in vain for dry spots, leaping here and there, pausing an instant to shake mud and water from the dainty feet, and finally, with a great bound, coming at last to the safety of the dry sidewalk.

Then he did other things — a boy passing a group of girls gathered on a front porch — with a disastrous stumble in the midst of the passage. An old horse on the trail; a young mustang fighting against the rope; a wise old outlaw bucking with science and yet with an apparent sense of humor, which he showed when the rider was slung to the ground.

At last the boy stopped.

Why, they howled and raised the roof, begging for more; and the tramp, smiling at them, seemed to thank them for their appreciation, and seemed willing to go on forever.

But first he turned with his bow, heels together, and head inclined low, towards the girl.

"Do you want me to go on, Miss Steyn?" said he.

"I know you're tired," said she, grimly.

And then, sullenly, listened to the roar of protest, heard the volleyed entreaties that he should go on. And she watched him delicately, tactfully, declaring that he was really worn out.

It seemed to her that the youth had come there on purpose to discredit her friends and to discredit her. She hated him with far greater bitterness than ever.

12

All the others had come and gone. Even Gentleman Joe Wynne had been there and had departed once more.

She sat, in the tired dark of the evening, after supper, in the kitchen. The dining room was too great a confusion. It would take her half the next day to put it to rights. This should have been a quiet moment, a restful time for her alone with old Arthur Steyn.

But they were not alone. All the others, the old and tried friends, were gone away, but there remained – the stranger!

There he sat, at the right hand of her father, sipping his third cup of coffee and talking on, in a gentle, half dreamy voice.

How consummately, more and more, she hated him!

What was he saying now?

For the waves of her detestation now and then stopped up her ears and prevented her from following the sense of the words. This was where she picked up the thread of the

106

narrative, and the boy was saying:

".. . and when I saw him lying there, and realized that he was dead, I knew what I had to do."

"You went to your father and told him the truth about the blackguard, I hope," said old Steyn, earnestly.

"I couldn't do that," said the boy. "You see, Uncle Tom was a lot younger than my father. He'd raised Tom like a son, and he cared for him a great deal more than he cared for me. It would have broken his heart to think that Tom was really —"

"You mean to say," exclaimed Steyn, "that you let your father think that you had *murdered* your uncle?"

"That was the easiest way for Father," said the boy. "He never thought much of me. I was too much like my mother, and they had separated a few years after their marriage. He never spoke of her, not even after her death. He's a stern man, is my father. He loved only one thing — Uncle Tom. I knew that. And Dad was very ill. He had a heart that wasn't worth a feather. It's better now, I understand."

The girl fixed a stern, doubting gaze upon the boy. And his glance met hers.

Could she believe her eyes?

He deliberately winked at her! Yes, in an instant he seemed to admit that he was talking nonsense to amuse Arthur Steyn and to win the old man's confidence.

She almost gaped with open mouth at the boy.

"And you, my poor lad," said Steyn, his voice troubled, "what did you do?"

"Well," said the boy, "I left home."

"Did they follow you?"

"Yes — I'm sorry to say that Father told the law everything. The police hounded me to the end of South America. Then I managed to slip them and I've worked my way this far to the north."

"And you're bound where?"

"To see Father again, before he dies."

"Suppose that he gives you up to the law?"

"He might," admitted the tramp. "But his face haunts me. You know, since I've been roughing around the world, I've had my share and a little over, of hard knocks. And in the worst times, I've begun to think the most of my father. A man has to grow up a bit before he realizes what a father means."

"It's true," said Steyn, in a voice greatly moved. "It's terribly and profoundly true. My lad, I'm going to help you to —"

"Mr. Steyn," said the boy, pushing back his chair a little from the table, grasping the side of it as though he intended to leap to his feet and leave the room.

"I want to help you," said Steyn, warmly.

"If I'd thought that," said the boy, "I never would have said a word to you. If you think that I've been adroitly begging —"

"No, no," said Steyn.

"It was only," said the hobo, sadly, "that something about you reminded me of Father as he'll be when he comes to your age, if God lets him live that long."

And again, in the midst of this semi-tragic speech, his eye caught the stern glance of the girl, and he winked at her again!

"And so you go on your way," said Steyn, gloomily. "It's a terrible story that you've told me. I want to thank you for speaking as you have. I want to thank you for the confidence that it shows —"

"Mr. Steyn," said the boy, "I imagine that half the world takes its troubles to you!"

And the eyes of Steyn softened and brightened at once.

"There *are* some people who trust me," he admitted, gently.

Then he added:

"You haven't told me your name. Can you do that?"

"You'll see that I can't do that, sir," said the tramp. "My traveling nickname, though, if you want to hear it. They call me Speedy, because I'm never long in one place."

"Hounded as you've been," said Steyn, hotly, "how *could* you remain long in one place? Speedy, if that's what you want me to call you —"

"I'm used to the name," said Speedy.

"Speedy, I want you at least to spend the night here in my house. You know where the bunks are. It's rough hospitality. But I want to have another chat with you, tomorrow."

Speedy hesitated.

Then he said: "I'll stay. I'm glad to stay. You don't want to talk to me half as much as I want to talk to you. You know, Mr. Steyn, that a man who's lived his life knows what life is. And youngsters can't."

Steyn stood up and grasped the hand of the boy, and shook it firmly. Already he had overstepped his usual bedtime by an hour.

"Your story will be with me all night," he said. "In the morning, I hope that I'll have something to say to you."

He kissed the girl goodnight.

"When Speedy wants to turn in," said he, "give him a lantern, there — or a lamp, if he prefers it."

And he left them alone. The girl closed the door after him.

Then, turning, she rested her shoulders against the door and stared with open hostility at Speedy.

"You don't mean that you're going tomorrow," said she.

"No, I don't," said he.

He sat down by the stove, made a cigarette and tilted back in his chair to smoke it, grinning at her through the smoke.

"If poor Dad could see you now!" she exclaimed.

"He won't, though," said Speedy.

"You're intending to settle down and sponge on him for a while, are you?" she demanded.

"Yes, for quite a bit," said the boy. "I like the Sunday parties. I was always partial to beer."

"How long do you think you'll stay in the house after I've told him the truth about you?" she asked.

"He won't believe you," said Speedy.

"He!" she cried. "You mean that he won't believe what I solemnly tell him I know?"

The boy shook his head.

"I wish that you'd explain that," said the girl.

"No man will ever admit that he's been turned into a perfect fool," he answered her.

She could not help admitting that there was much truth in this. But rage was working in her like a ferment.

"Your wretched impudence!" she said. "You won't be here tomorrow night, Speedy!"

"Are you betting on that?" he asked.

"If you were thrown out, you might steal

back and break in — to win the bet!" she suggested, contemptuously.

"I won't break in, because I won't be thrown out," said he.

"I'll make a wager on that!" said she.

"What will you bet?" he asked.

"As much as you wish," she said.

He drew a large roll of bills from his pocket.

"Here's something over three thousand," he said.

"You know I haven't that much," said the girl. "You sham, wearing rags, and carrying that much cash!"

"I'll bet you a thousand that I'm here tomorrow night," said he. "If you lose — you go to the first dance that's given around here — with me."

"With you?" she exclaimed. "Go to a dance with *you?*"

He merely smiled at her.

"Yes," said he, "with me. That's the bet I offer. You have all of tomorrow to work on your father. If you win, I leave a thousand dollars behind me."

"I can imagine you doing that," she sneered.

At this, the smile disappeared from his face.

"I'm the world's champion liar," he admitted, "but my promises are as clean as a hound's tooth."

And she wondered why she knew that now he

was telling her the complete truth.

She studied him in a growing bewilderment that almost overclouded her detestation of him, but she added: "You know, Speedy, that if you begin to pay a lot of attention to me — there may be trouble ahead for you?"

"I know the legend," he said. "The gunmen, and all that — but what do you suppose brought me all this distance, my dear?"

"Don't call me that, if you please," said she.

"You are, though," he said. "I'll tell you, Mary. I came for you, and I'm going to take you."

She laughed; but her teeth hardly parted to let the sound out.

"You're going to marry me and carry me away, are you, young Lochinvar?" said she.

He laughed in turn, easily, confidently.

"That's what I'm going to do," said he.

"Do you know," she replied, quietly, "that I detest you more utterly than I ever have detested a human being in my life? Your lies, your tricks, your vanity — your everything!"

"But I've broken ground with you, Mary," grinned Speedy. "In your whole life you never have thought so much about any man in any one day."

She could not deny it. And her inability to do so choked her. Suddenly she flung from the room, and ran to her own chamber, and there dashed herself down on the bed and lay trembling with fury, her brain spinning, her face hot.

13

Words which have been brooded over during an entire night are powerful words; and the speech of Mary Steyn was filled with hot strength when she saw her adopted father the next morning. Her eye was cold and straight as a bar of steel, and it fixed and held him.

She told him the story in few words.

"Speedy, as he calls himself, is an imposter. He's a sham. He told me so last night. He's the most horrible man that I ever met. He's come here to sponge on you, and to try to marry me. He – he actually told me so!"

Arthur watched her in her fury.

Then he said: "Where's Speedy now?"

"He's outside. I don't know just where – not far from the kitchen, I suspect!"

Said Steyn: "Go call him in here, and you come, too."

She was fired with joy at the prospect. Swiftly she went, and found the boy with his hands in his pockets under the eaves of the woodshed, whistling to a blue jay which alighted on the rooftree. Once, twice and again, as she watched, the blue jay, in alarm, started flapping its wings. Once it actually rose a foot or so for flight, but always it settled down again and regarded the enchanter with one eye and then with the other, amazed, horrified, fascinated to helplessness.

The scene seemed to her neither clever nor common, but horrible; there was some sort of power in this handsome youngster which both beasts and men felt, and she wanted with all her soul to be far from it.

Her voice broke the spell. The blue jay fled in a straight, flashing line through the air, wavering a little up and down in the excess of its zeal to get away. Then Speedy turned to her, and took off his brimless hat, smiling.

"Good morning, Mary," said he. "What is it?"

She looked at him with scorn, and with rage, and with contempt. There was a definite fear in her, also.

She said: "Father wants to talk to you."

"About last night, eh? I hope that you'll be present."

"Oh, I'll be present all right," she answered, grimly. "You don't need to think that I'll miss that little party. When you're unveiled before him, Speedy, I want to be there. I wouldn't miss the picture."

"Poor Mary!" said he. "You'll wish to heaven,

afterwards, that you never had told him a word about it. But if I have to go in there, I'll split you and Arthur Steyn a mile apart."

"You'll split me – and my father – apart?" she said, furiously. *"You* will – half a day after we've first laid eyes on you?"

"Oh, I'm a fast worker, Mary," said he. "Didn't you notice the blue jay, even?"

"You took the blue jay's eye with your tricks for a minute. He'll never come back to lay eyes on you again, so long as he lives."

"You're wrong," declared Speedy. "In half an hour he'll be back there on the crest of the woodshed, wondering what happened, and what it was all about. The same with you, Mary. If I left you, before a day was out you'd be sorry that I had gone away!"

Her angry denial did not reach her lips, since before she uttered it, she saw that he was mocking her with laughter, in expectation of her fury.

Instead, she led the way to where Arthur Steyn now sat, as always, on the eastern side of the house, to enjoy the first brightness of the morning, before the heat became too great.

The boy took off his hat and went cheerfully up to his host.

"Good morning, sir," said he.

"Good morning, Speedy," said Steyn. "Mary

has been telling me a tale about you. What's the truth of it?"

"A tale about me?" asked Speedy, good-naturedly, smiling still. "What sort of a tale, sir?"

"Let me say it over again," urged the girl. "Let me tell him, before your face, Father."

"Very well," said Steyn.

He was not excited. He was merely a little stern, but his old eyes reserved judgment. And Speedy saw this, with relish.

"When you were talking to Father telling him the cock-and-bull yarn about your trouble with your father and the 'murder' of your uncle, you winked at me across the table. D'you deny that?"

"I winked at you?" said the boy.

Her anger almost was stifled by the blank amazement in his face. For an instant she doubted her ability to count against such con-summate acting. But then the strength and outrageousness of her case came over her. She went on: "Do you deny it?"

He glanced at Steyn.

"I don't know what to say to this, sir," said the boy. "If you don't mind, I'll hear out what she has to say. There seems to be more behind this."

"That ought to be the best way," said Steyn. "Mary, don't let your emotions run away with you. Let's have everything as clearly as possible."

"I'll be as clear as glass!" she exclaimed. "Don't doubt that, for a moment. I'll let you look right through his black heart. When you were gone out of the kitchen, Father, he made no attempt to conceal anything. He talked straight out. He's a loafer. He's an idler. You know when he came that he boasted he never had raised a callus by honest work. He admitted that he had arranged everything just in order to sponge on you for a while. He told me in so many words that he had come here for that purpose. He even told me — the contemptible —"

She checked herself.

Then she exploded: "That he would manage it so that he would marry me!"

She paused again, gathering her breath, controlling a tomboy desire to smash her hard, small fist against the blank amazement that was shown on the face of the boy.

"And when just now I told him that you wanted to see him, he said that I'd regret calling him, because he'd split you and me a mile apart — you and me, Dad!"

She ended, trembling; still her eyes shot fire at Speedy.

And he looked back at her, his lips slightly parted. His eyes were big, but that eye which was concealed from the sight of Steyn now suddenly winked at her.

It was the crowning touch; she grew half blind with fury. She could not speak again.

Then Steyn was saying: "Speedy, will you look at me?"

"May I ask her one thing, first?" asked the boy.

"By all means," said Steyn.

And he said: "Mary, is this a practical joke?"

"A practical joke?" she cried. "A practical joke? Oh!"

Then Speedy turned to the wise old man, and met his straight eye.

"She seems to mean it," said the boy. "People dream things pretty vividly, sometimes, but this isn't a dream. I don't know what to call it."

"Neither do I," said Arthur Steyn. "Did you say those things?"

The boy looked at the ground, frowning, seeming to make an effort of memory.

Then he said, as though to himself, slowly, softly: "First, I winked at her, as much to say that my uncle hadn't died and —"

He paused.

He turned from them and walked a few paces away; then he came back. He raised his head and looked at Steyn.

"After that," he said, "I waited until you had left the kitchen, and then I told her that I was a tramp, and a sponger, and that — that I was going to marry her."

He looked back at Mary.

"Wasn't that it? You *did* say the last thing, too, didn't you?"

"You know very well what you said!" she answered.

Arthur Steyn said nothing. He was leaning a little away from his chair, staring steadily at the face of Speedy.

And Speedy said: "People grow hysterical, and I suppose that she was upset by what happened yesterday. I'm sorry that I stayed on. Good-bye, Mary. Good-by, Mr. Steyn. I'll not be forgetting you, for reasons that I told you last night."

He held out his hand, but Steyn shook his head.

"You can't go, Speedy," said he.

"I *have* to go," said the boy. "No, if you want to hear her berate me some more, I'll stay and listen to it. But that's no good, really."

"Mary," said Steyn, "look at me, my dear."

"Dad!" she cried. "Is it true that you're doubting me?"

He drew a soft, long breath.

"I want to make a list of things you say that he told you, Mary," said the old man.

Then he enumerated them:

"First, that he winked at you, while he was

telling me the terrible story of his breach with his father.

"Second, that after I left the room, he admitted that he was a sham.

"Third, that he said he had come here to sponge on me.

"Fourth, that he finally declared that he intended to marry you!

"Now, Mary, that makes a queer conclusion. It doesn't sound like ordinary wooing!"

She was desperate, but out of her desperation she cried: "I didn't add that he swore he would bet me a thousand dollars that I couldn't persuade you to send him away from the house. And I like a fool took the bet. If I lose, I'm to go with him to the first dance in the neighborhood! Will you believe *that?*"

Steyn, after a moment, said gently: "I've thought for a long time that these Sunday parties have been growing too much for your nerves, Mary dear. Now I know it. We've had the last one — for a long time, at least. I hope you'll spread the word around that we've stopped receiving everyone on Sundays."

She cried out in an agony, for she saw how completely she had lost. It was the totality of her true story that had undone her. Part of it might have been believed, but not the staggering whole, and now she exclaimed: "Tell them yourself — let *him* spread the news! I don't care! I don't care! I'm going away from here and I'm never coming back — ever!"

And, with that, sobbing choked her. She turned and fled.

14

She paused in her room long enough to get into boots and spurs, and to jam a hat on her head, jerk a bandanna around her neck. Then she raced on to get to the barn.

But no one was waiting there to prevent her departure.

That was the work of the tramp, too! That was the work of the devil-inspired boy! She turned at the door of the barn and shook her fist at the house.

Then she ran on, snatched a rope from a peg and hurried into the pasture.

She whistled for the gray mare, Whimsy.

Whimsy came to her like a favorite dog to a hunter, as a rule, but this morning she threw up her head, stared at her and fled with a snort.

For a sweating half hour she had to work, the sun growing higher and higher, before she finally caught her in a corner, and as she mounted, finally, with Whimsy under the saddle, she looked back towards the house and saw —

This strange picture: of the tramp done up in one of her own faded blue gingham kitchen aprons in the back yard, holding a small armload of wood, and looking after her?

No, not that. She might not have existed, so far as he was concerned, it appeared. He was lifting his head a little and above him, on the rooftree of the woodshed, was a blue jay, fluttering its wings but never rising into the air, as though held in a trap.

That was too much for her.

She had been consumed with rage before, but now despair, shame, bewilderment all rushed over her, and she sobbed loudly, like a child, as Whimsy carried her headlong over the trail.

She hardly knew what trail it was that she had taken; she only knew that the brown forms of the hills were sliding behind her, and growing bigger and bigger before her, and then, rounding a turn, she almost rode the foaming mare straight into Gentleman Joe Wynne's big-striding black horse.

She swerved Whimsy in a flash; she bowed her head to conceal her tear-stained, swollen face, and cried in a muffled voice: "Hello, Joe!" as she darted by.

She knew that he had turned behind her. She heard the long, rolling beat of the hoofs of the black horse. She was in despair of a new kind, for she knew that Whimsy, even carrying her light weight, could never get away from the long-limbed black racer that Wynne bestrode.

He would think that she had fled to him for help!

Well, and perhaps some instinct had forced her down that trail, urging her towards the one man in the world she came nearest to loving. Certainly he was the one who had her entire and whole-hearted respect, her admiration. To his wisdom and to his power, both, she could look up. He was not rich, but the whole range esteemed Joe Wynne as the first of men!

He came rushing up behind her. Now he was riding at her side. He did not catch at her bridle rein, as any fool would have done.

"Joe, go away! I don't want to talk to you, I don't want to see you!" she shouted.

Even speaking against the wind and the beating of the hoofs his voice remained gentle and controlled.

"I'll go away in an instant," said he. "But you're in trouble of some sort, Mary. I wish you'd tell me what it is!"

She saw, now, that having come this far, she would have to go farther. So she nodded her head. And when their horses were halted, and they faced one another, she was amazed to discover that she really could let him see her reddened face, her swollen eyes, without too much shame. For there was nothing smiling, or sneering about him, there was no concealed air of superiority. He was not looking down at her. He seemed merely waiting, honestly anxious to face her worry with her and help to bear the burden of it.

Suddenly her heart flowed out to him.

"Oh, Joe," said she, "you're the finest fellow in the world. I love you!"

He flushed, but he made no move towards her, even after he had heard the last word.

"Thanks, Mary," said he. "It means something to hear that."

And he was waiting again.

What a man he was! Truly, the lions are gentle in their ways! Like a glorious lion he looked to her, with his wind-bronzed face, his tawny hair and his flawless, clear blue eyes. No shame had ever come upon him, no shame ever would come. True, there was that terrible fighting rage which drove him berserk, more than once, and made the gunmen shun him like the shadow of Satan. But that was the only flaw in the character of Joe Wynne.

Gentleman Joe, the range called him, and there was not a shade of irony in the expression.

The fullness of her problem came over her. It was more than she could deal with. She needed help. She had to have help. And where could she turn, except to Joe Wynne?

And so the story poured out for him — from first to last.

When it ended, he did almost exactly as Steyn had done. He enumerated the points one by one.

And, as he ended, she cried out: "Joe, you don't believe me!"

He answered her, without hesitation: "If anybody else had told me such a yarn, I'd call him a liar, but you've told it — and therefore it's gospel. I believe every word of it."

"God bless you, Joe," said she.

"Now, what shall we do?" he asked her.

"I don't know, Joe," she answered. "I'm trying to think. My mind simply whirls. When I last saw him, he had one of my aprons on, and he was whistling to a blue jay. I suppose it was the very one that he had whistled to before. He was bringing in wood. I think that he's done what he said he would. He's separated Father and me forever. I know that's true! I can't go back, ever! I can't go back!"

"What could he want?" asked Joe Wynne.

"I don't know. Just to make trouble. He hates me because I sent the three of them out to handle him, one after another."

Said Joe Wynne: "A man wouldn't hate you for that. You simply gave him a chance to show his mettle. And there's a lot of mettle in him. That's clear."

They both paused. A mournful lowing came to their ears, and looking up the side of the hill, Mary saw a cow, her head down, standing by a Spanish bayonet, and pouring out her melancholy soul in the foolish way that all cows have, from time to time.

And the whole world seemed tawdry, silly and complicated to her.

"You've got to go back, of course," said Wynne, finally.

"I won't go back," said the girl, "while he's there. Not while that creature is there. I tell you I won't, Joe!"

"You'd better think about your father," said Wynne. "You don't want him left with a trickster like that."

"Poor Dad! But he sided with Speedy against us. He wouldn't listen to me!"

"Your story is pretty hard even for me to swallow," said Wynne, frankly. "I don't know what else to say to you, Mary. But I think that I'd better ride on and see this Speedy. I saw him dancing, the other evening. I couldn't make him out. You say that he smashed up Fat Ginnis and Doc, and even Alf Barton?"

"Yes."

"Alf Barton was one of them?"

"Yes, Alf was one of them."

"Barton is a good man with his hands," said Wynne, shaking his head.

"It's all trickery that Speedy uses," said the girl. "Of course you understand that. It's trickery that gets him along in the world and that's put several thousand dollars in his pocket! He's nothing but cowardly deceit and —"

"Deceit, all right," suggested Wynne, "but not cowardly deceit."

She beat her hands together.

"I'm half mad," she said. "I don't know what can be in his mind. Perhaps there's something about the ranch that he wants. Perhaps he's found pay dirt somewhere in the rocks among the hills. I don't know. I *am* half mad, because I can't understand anything about it!"

Joe nodded at her.

"Perhaps it's something like that," he agreed. "I don't know, either. He's no common hombre. That much is clear as the nose on my face. But I'll tell you what — you're all heated up, Mary."

"I know it," said the girl. "I can't quiet down. I'm shaking."

"Look here," said he, after a moment, "I want you to get down off Whimsy — you've ridden her half to death — and sit down in the shade of the cactus — thank the Lord it's good for something once in its life — and then you're going to stay here a half hour and think things over."

"I don't want to stay here, Joe," said she. "I

want to be a thousand miles away from that — that thing — that devil — that Speedy, as he calls himself!"

He sighed. And then she saw that his face was growing sterner and more set. A ring came into his voice.

"You'd better do what I say," said he.

"Joe," she cried, "are *you* turning against me, too?"

"I?" said Joe Wynne. "Never while I live. But sit down here, will you, Mary? Sit down here and think things over. You need to be alone. Not even with me. I'm going to leave you and come back in a few minutes. Then we can make some sort of head or tail of the thing, I hope."

She nodded. It was against her will, but she felt that if she went counter to his advice, she would be left alone in the world.

So down she slid from the saddle and sat obediently in the shadow of the giant cactus, while Whimsy, still panting and blowing, finally began to crop at the sun-cured grasses, and Gentleman Joe rode up the side of the hill.

At last, the peace of the hills began to pass over her, gently and softly. The familiar touch of the wind on her cheeks, the very sun-drenched blue of the sky, and Whimsy, cropping and snorting nearby, jerking up her head now and then to study the wind against enemies — all of these things soothed the girl.

At last, she was suddenly aware that the half hour had passed, and more than the half hour. For the shadow had moved far beside the cactus, and still Joe had not come back. What did it mean?

Understanding leaped and caught her by the throat.

She had said that she would not return home until the boy was gone; and Gentleman Joe had gone to clear the way!

It meant murder; there was no other way. The tramp would be shot, surely; or Gentleman Joe at this moment lay still in death!

15

Once out of the girl's sight and hearing, Wynne had ridden as fast as the great black horse would carry him, straight for the house of Steyn.

He was not one to waste time over delicate problems. If tact, straightforwardness and honest dealing could not carry the day, there was always the power of the strong right hand, naked − or with a weapon in it.

And he had the strong hand and he had the weapon to fill it. Whether with the bowie knife which was at his right hip, or the six-shooter on his right thigh, worn well down the leg, he was perfectly at home. He did not fight often, but when he did, blood was spilled, and it was not the blood of Joe Wynne. He was one of those proverbially slow, cool, almost sluggish people who, when aroused, are tigers.

He was half a tiger now as he rushed the horse over the hills, but time, and the wind cooling his face altered his temper before he came to the house of Steyn.

He told himself that there were certain factors clear in the case. The tramp was a criminal, and there for a criminal purpose, exactly what, no one could tell. By driving the girl away from the house, he had achieved the first step in his program. And now, God help poor Arthur Steyn, abandoned into such hands as these.

But to combat against such an enemy needed a cool and clever wit, as well as a ready hand and a strong one. So it was a very sober Gentleman Joe who finally arrived at the Steyn house.

As he came near, he saw Arthur Steyn riding down the trail towards town. He knew the man in the far distance by the straightness of his back, the set of his fine head and the gleam of his white hair beneath the hat and through the shadow of the wide brim.

He was glad of the absence of the old man, for what he probably would have to do this day wanted no witness!

So he dismounted, tied his horse to the hitching rack, and knocked at the front door. No answer.

He went around to the rear of the house, and knocked at the kitchen door.

"Come in!" called a cheerful voice.

He opened the door, and there he saw the tramp seated in a chair in front of the sunny window, with a dishpan in his lap, half filled with potatoes. He was peeling the potatoes with a dexterous speed, dropping the peels onto a sheet of newspaper on one side of him, and the crystal shining, naked potatoes into a pan on the other.

"Hello!" said Wynne.

"Hello yourself, Joe," said Speedy, with friendly familiarity. "Sit down and rest your feet."

"You're a cook, eh?" asked Wynne, taking off his hat to cool his hot forehead, and sitting down in an opposite chair that creaked a little under his weight.

"I'm half a cook," said the tramp. "Want the makings?"

"Don't mind if I do."

The boy dipped with the wet tip of thumb and forefinger into an upper vest pocket, extracted a package of Bull Durham and a sheaf of brown papers, and threw them across to his guest. Gentlemen Joe made a cigarette, slowly. He was glad of the time it gave him to arrange his thoughts.

"I thought," he went on, as he folded one end of the cigarette and placed the other between his lips, "I thought that you didn't work, Speedy?"

He threw the papers and the sack of tobacco together towards the boy. They separated in midair, but with one hand, with two movements fast as the pecking head of a sparrow, Speedy picked the articles out of the air and restored them to his pocket.

"I don't raise calluses," he said. "I don't mind work that leaves the hands soft."

"Soft hands are good for cards," said Wynne, tentatively.

"Yes, aren't they?" agreed Speedy. "Or for sleight of hand."

"You know some tricks, I suppose," said Wynne.

"I'm only an amateur. Just a little working knowledge. I pick up a few pennies here and there."

"What I wonder," said the big man, "is that you waste your time here in the Wild West. A fellow like you, Speedy, could dance on the stage, and sing there, too. Easy work, and a lot of easy dough going along with it."

"I couldn't make the grade," answered Speedy. "I'm all right in a bunkhouse or at a schoolhouse dance. The boys and the girls laugh at my little tricks and my dancing steps. But I'm stale compared with the real masters. And you have to be a master to work on the stage."

"I suppose that's true," said Wynne, surprised to find himself rather liking the frankness of the other.

"Besides," said Speedy, "this is my country. That's why I stay here."

"Your country?" exclaimed the other, with surprise. "Born here?"

"Not born here," said the boy. "It's mine by adoption. I did the adopting," he explained, with a grin.

He finished the peeling of the potatoes, scooped up the paper loaded with peels, laid it aside, carried the pan of potatoes to the sink, and washed some water over them from a bucket that stood on the drainboard.

"Here, Joe, be a good fellow and pack in some more water, will you?" he asked.

Joe took the bucket, hardly thinking.

Was it Mary's blue gingham apron that compelled him?

"All right," said he, and strode off to the spring. He came back, wondering at his own docility, and put the bucket down on the floor with a thump; the tramp was building up the fire.

"Kitchen work is pretty snug," commented Speedy, turning.

"Yeah. It's all right when you have somebody to pack the water for you," agreed the other.

"That's right," said the boy. "Carrying water raises calluses."

"Going to keep this job?" asked Wynne.

"Only filling in for Mary."

"Where is she?"

"Where you left her, I suppose," came the astonishing answer.

Wynne rolled his eyes. No, the lad could not have trailed her and overseen anything. He could not have beaten the black horse so much as to get into these togs and this work in time. It was simply one of the lad's acts of mind reading. He must be full of such tricks. Wynne felt full of thumbs.

"What d'you mean by that?" was all he could think of saying.

"I mean," said Speedy, "that she ran to you and asked you to come back here and throw me out of the house. Isn't that right?"

Wynne said nothing. But he bent his brows, for such prescience annoyed him greatly.

"As a matter of fact," he said, bluntly, "you and Mary can't live in the same house."

"Oh, but we're going to," answered the boy.

"You are?"

"Why, yes," said Speedy. "Mary's in a sulk, just now. But she won't leave her poor old white-haired father to the mercy of a rascal like me. She'll come back here and settle down to work like a good fellow. She's not a bad girl. But you people around here have spoiled her a good deal."

Wynne gritted his teeth.

138

"You'll take that out of her, I expect?" he queried.

"In time," said the boy.

Wynne reached out a hand and laid it on the shoulder of the boy. He expected a mass of sinewy muscle; he was surprised to find that his fingers wrapped right around the bone and touched it. He felt that he could crush the joint, if he made an effort.

"It's time for you to start, son," said Gentleman Joe.

"Don't do it," answered the boy. "Don't start anything, Joe."

"Are you warning me?" asked Wynne.

"You've got a hold on me," said Speedy. "That's not a fair break. We're still inside the house, and that's against the rules."

"What rules hold with a rat like you?" said Gentleman Joe, the berserker madness surging suddenly up in him.

He saw the chest of the other heaving. Why, the fellow was a mere wisp, to be broken, or bent out of shape at will!

"Don't do it, Joe," insisted Speedy, with something like pleading in his voice. "Don't hurt me."

"Begging, are you?" said Wynne through his teeth.

"I'm not begging, Joe. I'm telling you not to hurt me. I've been hurt too many times before.

I'm tired of it. If you manhandle me, I'll make you wish that you'd laid your hand on a chunk of living hell fire. I'll burn you to the heart!"

"I'm going to teach you a lesson, you sneak," said Wynne.

"Step outside and let go of me," said the boy, "and I'll read your lesson as far as it goes."

"Go outside, then," said Wynne.

And, stepping in — half maddened by his own sense of power, and with a peculiar relief that the magician had so far showed none of his powers of magic, he caught the boy with his other mighty hand, and heaved him above his head. Even then he wondered a little at the limp, unresisting weight that he lifted. Then he hurled the loose body against the door.

The shock tore the flimsy door from its hinges. Speedy crashed with the door on the porch outside, and then rolled headlong down the steps beyond.

Down them he tumbled, and lay flat on his back in the dust of the backyard.

A little whirlpool of wind came walking across that dust and passed the limp, motionless form of the boy.

Wynne, amazed at the success of his effort, realized now with how taut a sense of expectation he had attacked this enemy, small as he was.

Now he rushed on out, and leaned over the fallen lad.

Straight down into the face of the boy he stared, and suddenly the eyes opened, and one eye winked at Gentleman Joe!

It staggered him. He was so amazed that he was hardly aware of the rapid beat of horse's hoofs approaching, until Mary Steyn rushed up to him, crying out: "Joe! Joe! Oh, for God's mercy, have you killed him?"

"Killed him?" said Joe Wynne. "The rat has just winked at me. He's only playing dead, now!"

"Do you mean it? There's blood on his head! You *have* killed him, Joe!"

And she dropped to her knees beside the limp body.

16

What passed through the mind of the girl, all in a flash, was murder, the trial scene, the witness which she and perhaps her father would have to give, and then, finally, the condemnation of Gentleman Joe Wynne, the blasting of the fame of herself and her father, and finally, the execution of Wynne himself.

For such a train and process of thought, it requires only a fraction of a second. All of the pictures flow through the agile brain, and there is time to spare.

She was convinced before she leaned and applied her ear to the breast of the fallen boy. And she heard what she firmly expected to hear — nothing!

The dreadful conviction almost beat her to the ground. She was barely able to raise her ghostly and accusing face towards Wynne:

And she cried: "You can't say that I told you to do it! You can't say that I wanted you to do it!"

He had practically forgotten that wink

which, as it seemed to him, he had received from the boy. In his turn, he dropped to his knees and bent his ear at the breast of Speedy. Was it the surging of the blood through his ears, the nameless hammer strokes of terror that overwhelmed his sense?

At any rate, he heard no sign of a heartbeat.

He started back, aghast in turn.

He picked up a fallen arm of the boy — and it dropped with a convincing flop into the dust at his side.

"What have I done!" breathed Wynne.

He rose to his feet; he placed a hand before his face. He could remember, now, the brutal emotions, the triumph, the red rage that had been in him when he grappled with the lad and swayed him above his head like a catapult lifting a stone.

Yes, that was the sort of thing out of which murder flowed! Had he not been warned before? Had not his own father, in his childhood, taken him upon his knees, after one of his rages, and said: "Joe, one of these days, you may be stronger in your hands than you are now, and then God and good advice help you to keep that temper of yours!"

Now the thing had happened.

Desperate faces they turned to one another, big Wynne and the girl.

"Bring him into the house!" she gasped.

Wynne snatched up the burden. Head and heels hung down helplessly, and the arms trailed in a horrible way to the ground. The girl, with a low cry, supported the head and shoulders. And, as she did so, cast from her white face a look of horror and reprobation towards the rancher.

So they struggled with the burden into the house, to her own room, and stretched young Speedy on her bed.

She was on her knees again, and pressed her ear against his breast. She could hear not the faintest beat, feel not the least pulsation.

"Do something, Joe," she exclaimed. "Help me to do something!"

"Brandy," he managed to say. "That ought to be good for something."

She fled on wings to get it, and Gentleman Joe looked about the room with the wild and haggard glance of one about to die, peering his last upon the fair world. He noticed the neatness of the white curtains, and the gay rug on the floor, and his own picture standing there on the dressing table beside the photograph of old Arthur Steyn.

Well, that was what he would have expected her room to be like, except that he had not dreamed that his picture would be there. No, he had not guessed that he had already stepped so far into her heart.

But what did that matter — to a murderer — a gallowsbird?

She was back, coming through the door with a rush. It was Wynne who raised the limp head — leadenly heavy! — while Mary Steyn parted the teeth and held the glass.

The lower jaw sagged exactly as she had left it. The liquor which she poured in streamed out again.

She groaned with horror!

Then, pushing the head back, it dropped with a jerk, as though the neck were broken, over the curve of her strong arm. And still the mouth gaped open! Into that mouth she poured the brandy.

"He's swallowed it! He's swallowed it! Oh, thank God, Joe!" she cried. "Put him down at once!"

Gently they lowered him to the pillow, and the loose head turned a little to the side, while the last swallow of the brandy leaked out again onto the cambric.

Mary Steyn collapsed upon a chair, her hands pressed over her face.

As for Gentleman Joe, he could do nothing, think of nothing, except that he had thought he saw the boy wink after falling to the ground — and that he was not dead — dead as a doornail!

Mary was up again.

This time, she caught a mirror from the

dressing table, and held it before the ugly, gaping mouth of Speedy. After a few seconds, she withdrew the glass and looked at it; no trace of moisture appeared — the breath no longer passed those lips, it appeared!

She moaned with terror and grief. There was still another test.

She pushed up the eyelids — dull and glassy the eyes looked back at her — no, not at her, but at eternity, it appeared. And most convincing of all, when her touch was gone, slowly, little by little, the eyelids closed again, as though of their own weight!

Well, that was the final touch.

She turned upon her big companion.

"He'd dead, Joe," she whispered.

"He's dead," said Wynne. "And I've got to run for it!"

"Yes," she said angrily, "run for it, and let the body lie here on my bed! They'll think that I struck him from behind with a club or something. They'll have *me* in jail!"

The selfish injustice of that remark stunned him.

"Except for you, he *wouldn't* be there," said Wynne.

"Ha!" said she. "Are you blaming me?"

"You ran to me and told me a yarn that you knew would make me ripe to murder him!" answered Gentleman Joe, honestly enough.

She was honest, too, at heart, and she answered him: "I know that's true. I shouldn't have gone to you. I told you that, too. You saw I was hysterical. You shouldn't have listened. But you *did* listen. You didn't give him a chance. You caught him where he didn't have a chance to get away. You attacked him without warning there in the kitchen. Answer me! It's true! It's true, isn't it? You began to manhandle him before he ever suspected that you meant to touch him!"

His frank honesty made him answer:

"Yes. I got him by surprise. I knew that he was a tricky snake. Once I had a grip on him, I wouldn't let him go."

"Because you were afraid!" she taunted. "Oh, Joe, you've done a horrible thing! When I saw his poor little limp body flinging through the air and hitting the ground like a limp wet rag and the great bulk of you running out after him! Oh, Joe, when I saw the size of you and the size of him, I felt that he was dead already. That you could smash the life out of him with one stroke! And that's what happened! How could you do it?"

He pushed a hand across his brown forehead.

"I don't know," said Wynne. "I think it was because you'd told me what he did to Ginnis and Doc and Barton. Barton's as big a man as I am, and stronger, if anything. When I met the

147

kid, I sort of expected magic, and tricks, and that sort of thing. I don't know what I expected. I just grabbed him and –"

He paused, shaking his head.

"What did he do?" she gasped.

"He begged me not to hurt him."

"I don't believe you!" she cried.

He looked helplessly at her. Much as she meant to him, there was something besides love of her in his heart, at this moment.

"He begged me not to hurt him," he said. "He asked me to let go of him and fight fair, in the open, outdoors. And he said that if I hurt him without giving him a fair chance, I'd wish that I'd sooner put my hand on a chunk of hellfire, because he'd burn me to the heart!"

"He'd say that. If he lived, he'd do that!" said the girl. "I know he would. He was all fire – and devilish cunning – but he was brave and cool – he was a hero, Joe!"

He shook his head, looking hopelessly at her.

"You're going to get enthusiastic about him now that he's gone and out of the way," said he. "But he was a worthless tramp, when you met me over there on the trail."

"I was just plain hysterical," said she.

"He'd made you that way," insisted the other.

Suddenly she stamped.

"Joe Wynne," she exclaimed, "are you trying to *justify* what we've done?"

"I'm only telling the truth," said he. "You know the shape you were in, when I met you."

"I see," said she, coldly. "You're going to throw the entire blame on me!"

"I didn't say that," he answered her.

"You implied that," said the girl.

"It's not true," he answered, frowning blackly.

"What do I care what you think is true, or untrue?" she cried suddenly. "There he lies — dead! Such a man never came on this range before. Oh, Joe, you've done a terrible, terrible thing! And he was only half your size, too!"

"You've got it well centered on me," said Joe Wynne. "I'm a brute and a bully because I did the job you wanted me to do."

She grew red — then instantly white.

"You did the job that I wanted you to do when I was beside myself," she said. "Now go and save yourself. I've seen enough of you today, Joe Wynne."

"I'll stay here!" said he.

Her anger raged out.

"Leave me alone with him," she commanded. "Go wherever you please — but I don't want you in this house — when the law comes!"

His sense of outrage made him sweep up his hat and stride to the front door.

There he paused and turned.

"You mean it, Mary?" he asked. "You're

sending me out of this house?"

"Yes," she cried, frantically, "and out of my life."

17

Joe Wynne strode out.

The flimsy door of the house trembled a little under the weight of his strides, but then the screen door slammed, she heard him go down the steps from the front porch, and then the jingle of his spurs, a small, ghostly sound, as he went to get his horse.

Last, the black horse and the gallant rider cut across her view through the window.

He had taken her at her word, and ridden out of this trouble, out of her life, indeed!

She was left alone there, with a dead man. And she heard the buzzing of a great blue bottle fly as it thumped audibly against the pane of the closed window, then left the light and went with droning flight, circling around the room.

She ran to the window and jerked it open.

Why did she do that? For reasons that she hardly could have put into words, but it was a ghostly feeling that she dared not remain there alone — imprisoned both with the dead body and the spirit of his vanished life!

Leaning on the windowsill, she drank in the open air with closed eyes — closed because she was seeing herself, turning the glance back upon her soul.

A frail and sinful creature she saw, full of pride, impulse and vanity. What good had she done with her days? No, all the good had been done to her, and she had merely accepted with an open palm!

Here was Speedy gone, because of her.

After all, she wondered, how had he really harmed her? It was she who had cast the challenge down to him, and he had answered her in such a way as she had not dreamed possible. He had beaten her champions, and struck down her strong men of battle. He had laughed his way into the house, and laughingly still, he had jested and smiled her out of the house. He had done as he had said he would do — placed a great gap between her and old Arthur Steyn.

Now, when the old, kind man returned, would he not remember that she was not of his blood, after all? Yes, he would remember that, and she could only blame herself.

She saw a wasted, foolish life behind her; she saw ruin and empty loneliness before her.

And then — a faint groan sounded from the bed!

Was it possible? She turned. She would have

flung herself out of the window to the ground just below, except that there was a dreadful feeling that something would seize her from behind before she got through.

But now, she saw a movement in the horribly open mouth of Speedy; she heard the groan come from him.

She could have dropped to her knees, to give up thanks to God, for that change in the course of events. Straightaway, she ran to him. She took the brandy flask again. She raised his limp head, and as she did so, the eyelids slowly rose, flickering.

She poured a dram down his throat.

"That'll do you good, Speedy!" she stammered.

And again hot thankfulness swept over her as she saw the swallowing muscles of the throat languidly at work.

He coughed and stirred with his whole body. He gasped for air, and began to push himself erect with his hands.

But she put her hand against his breast, and held him down, easily — he who had crushed three strong men, one after another, unscathed by them all! Yes, he was really frail. She could feel the sharp angle of the collar bone through his shirt. He was only a slender boy, but the great spirit in him was what made him significant.

"Lie still, Speedy," she said. "You're all right. You're going to be better, God willing. Lie still, Speedy. You'll be all right — if only — if only —"

Her voice trailed away.

If only his fall had not fractured his skull! That was the sentence which she had been unable to complete!

His eyes were steadily open, now, and clearing. His breath came deeply, regularly.

Suddenly he started up from the bed, up from under her hand.

"You sneaking coward, Wynne!" he gasped.

And reeling, he put out his hands before him, and staggered.

She caught him under the pits of the arms. She steadied him. He was so weak, that his head sagged far over upon one shoulder.

"Joe Wynne has gone," she said. "He won't be back. You're all right, Speedy!"

"He grabbed me!" said Speedy, his breath whistling through his teeth. "And I'll burn him to the heart for it. He didn't give me a fair chance — I'll — here, here, what am I talking about!"

She could see full consciousness return to him, see him collect and gather himself, as it were. Relief and admiration mingled in her. Yes, once this lad took to the trail of great Joe Wynne, she would not give much for the chances of the larger man!

She said: "Are you all right, Speedy?"

"Why, hello, Mary," said he. "Are you back again?"

"I'm back again, Speedy," said she, her voice trembling.

He nodded, frowned a little, and then raised his hand to his head. It came away thick with blood. On her pillow the same bloodstain appeared!

"I remember, now," said he. "It was Joe — well, never mind. Does Wynne happen to be around here?" he asked casually.

She saw the brightness in his eyes.

"He's not here," said she.

"Well — that's all right," he murmured.

She broke in: "I know all about it. I came riding up, just in time to see you fall, Speedy."

"Yes," he said through his teeth. "He slammed me, all right!"

"It's no shame to you," said she. "He had to admit that he didn't give you a fair chance. Speedy, tell me how your head feels? Is there a terrible splitting pain from your hurt?"

"My head's all right," said he. "As right as can be."

"I'll wash the cut," she said. "Let me do that, Speedy."

Said he: "Thanks, Mary. But my head's all right. If you don't mind, though, I'll borrow a horse from you, if I may."

He was quite himself again. She could see that. And the truth came over her.

"You're going to find Joe Wynne," she said.

"Joe? Not at all. I'm just going out to get a little air. I want to see more of the hills around here, Mary. I want to have a look at things and –"

She barred his way at the door, feeling helpless, and therefore all the more desperate.

"You're going to hunt down Wynne," she declared. "And you're going to kill him, Speedy! Admit it! Admit it!"

"Not kill him," said Speedy. "He's a big man – and I suppose that he'll lick me again. But I've got to see Joe Wynne. Mary will you stand out of the way?"

"I won't stir. I don't dare stir, Speedy!"

"I'll slide out the window, then."

"Speedy!" she screamed.

He turned back to her.

"Yes, Mary!" said he.

She wondered at the quiet of his voice. The most terrible raging, roaring accents would have been less terrifying than his calm.

"Speedy," she implored, "listen to me one moment!"

"Certainly," said he. "There's no hurry – about what I have to do. It's simply on my mind, you know."

"If there's somebody who deserves killing, it's I," said the girl. "I went weeping and raging down the trail. I met Joe. I told him about things — the way that they seemed to me. I think I begged him to throw you off our place. And Joe came straight back to do what I'd asked him to do. It's my fault. You'll see that it's my fault? Speedy, for God's sake don't let any more harm come out of miserable, wretched me!"

He stood with his hand resting lightly on the sill of the window.

And he turned his head and looked gravely, considerately at her.

"You wanted to have me killed, Mary?" said he, in the gentle tone that dissolved her with terror.

"I was more than half mad," said she. "I didn't know what I was doing, Speedy. Try to believe that."

"But what had I done to you?" he said. "I'd joked and laughed at you, and told some huge lies, and made a silly bet with you, and I thought that the whole thing was a game between us. And then — you go down the trail to find a man to —"

"To murder you!" she cried. "I know that was what I wanted. God forgive me, Speedy. I never dreamed before today how bad I am! Tell me that *you* forgive me, too! Try to tell me that,

157

Speedy, or else —"

What could she say at the end of that futile sentence?

She heard him saying: "Joe Wynne means a lot to you, doesn't he? And —"

"It isn't Joe, alone. It's the whole wretched business that comes out of my fault! It's all my fault! I'm ashamed. I'm sick about it."

"If it means a lot to you," said he, "I'll stay here. I won't go trailing him. Only, if he comes around the house while I'm here today, or across my trail after I've gone tomorrow —"

His raised voice he checked suddenly.

She was running across the room to him and catching him by the hands.

"That gives me one day of grace," said she. "And now I'm going to try to make the most of it, and ward off trouble that's ahead of us all. Five minutes ago — if anyone had told me that I'd be hoping again so soon, I would have laughed. I thought that you were dead — I thought that Joe Wynne and I were murderers! Oh, Speedy!"

"Stuff," said the boy. "Forget about that, will you?"

"I shall. I'm glad to. Only, you won't go near Joe Wynne?"

"I've told you that I won't," he exclaimed, irritably. "And I mean what I said. I suppose I can swallow what Joe did to me. But now, let's fix things up so that your father won't guess there's been trouble, when he comes home. The back door was knocked off its hinges, as I remember it."

She shook her head, smiling faintly.

"I won't lie to Father," she said. "I've told him lies enough before, but never again, after today. I begin now to tell the truth. He's to know every black thought that was in my heart, and just what happened — every detail!"

18

They had several things to do together, however.

First, she washed the wound in his scalp, and found it a very shallow scratch, to her infinite relief. A sizable bump had grown up around it — that was all. There was not even need of adhesive tape to close the lips of the wound!

After that, they put the door back on its hinges, and tacked into place a panel which had been broken outwards by the shock.

"I'll tell Father," the girl said, "but there's no need why he should know."

They had barely finished this work, when a boy's voice shouted outside the house: "Hey, Mary, are you in?"

She opened the door. A freckle-faced lad slid off his horse and grinned at her.

"Hello, Billy," said she. "What's the news?"

"Ma wants to know will you and Mr. Steyn come over to our house Tuesday night. That's tomorrow. There's some sort of a doings."

She shook her head at once.

"I can't come, Billy," said she. "I'm sorry, but I can't come."

"Ma'll take it hard," said he, indifferently.

"Come in and have a cup of coffee," she invited. "Or some buttermilk. I have some good cold buttermilk, if you like that."

"Not me," said the youngster. "I've gotta get along, anyway. It's a long ways to the Jenkins place and to Wynne's."

"Are you going to Wynne's?"

"Yes."

"Wait a minute, Billy. I want to send a note to Joe."

She hurried to pen and paper and wrote:

"Dear Joe,

He came to a little after you left!

There's only a shallow scratch in the scalp, and a bump, thank heaven!

Forgive me for the way I talked and acted. Everything is my fault.

One thing more, and this is the most important of all. Speedy is going to be here for a few days, I think. And while he's here, please don't come near the place. You can guess why.

He seems to think that he didn't have fair play when he met you, and I think there's blood in his heart on that account. For everybody's sake, stay away.

Thank you with my whole soul for helping, or wanting to help.

Mary."

This she sealed and gave to the boy, who was talking busily to Speedy in the back yard, and Speedy was making five small, bright pebbles dance up from his hands, and shower down through the air again in a mysterious fashion, through many designs.

Billy shouted with joy, and exclaimed with wonder.

He hardly gave the girl a glance, when she handed him the letter.

Then into the saddle he whisked, and off he galloped, waving back at them, and yelling: "You know, Speedy, you don't forget that you're gunna teach me how to do that!"

"I won't forget," said Speedy. "You bet that I won't!"

And he turned and smiled at Mary.

"Billy's a good kid!" he said to her.

And the sudden answer jumped to her lips: "So are you, Speedy!"

All at once, they were laughing together, merrily; and a moment later, she wondered mightily at herself.

It was hardly half an hour or an hour before that she had still thought him the most complicated and complete scoundrel under the wide round of the sky. And now she found him the best of companions!

He was sitting in the kitchen window, later on, swinging his heels, chatting to her, as she went about her work.

"Why did you start doing the kitchen work?" she asked him, looking down at the shining heap of newly peeled potatoes.

"Well, that was to make you suffer a little more. Make you think that the house could get along without you, pretty well. That was the idea, at least."

She nodded, frowning a little.

"And to drive in the wedge between me and Dad?" she asked, without looking at the boy.

"I'd threatened I'd do that," he admitted. "You'd made me pretty hot, Mary."

"Suppose," she asked, looking straight before her — though the wall was only a foot away. "Suppose that you don't feel so angry with me now —?"

"I'm all over that," said he. "Every bit."

"Suppose the other way — that you *hadn't* gotten over being angry at me?" she suggested.

She held her breath, waiting for the answer.

"Why, he loves you, Mary," said the boy. "And you love him, don't you?"

"Father? He's a saint. I worship him!"

"Well," said Speedy, "when two people love

one another, they can't be kept apart, very long."

She looked askance at him.

"You haven't answered me, really," said she.

"About what?"

"About what harm you might have done — if you'd kept on being angry with me."

"I don't intend to answer," said Speedy. "Chiefly because I don't know. I never know very well, from one day to the next, what I'll do."

"I know," said she. "It's the strangeness of every day that you like to have around you."

"Yes, that's part of the idea," he admitted.

"And wandering, and new faces and all of that?"

"Yes, all of that."

"But you're a tremendous liar, Speedy," said she.

"About the greatest in the world," said he, with complacence.

She looked oddly at him. Truly, he was unlike all the other men in the world.

"Well," she said, "you're convincing, too. Even that cock-and-bull story that you told Father last night about your Uncle Tom, and all that rot —"

"Did you believe it?"

"Yes, every word, till you winked at me."

"Yes, that gave things away," said he.

"But why did you wink?"

"I don't know," said he. "It just occurred to me that that would make the job harder and more interesting, to have you scoffing on one side of the table, and yet to make your father believe, on the other side of the table."

"More interesting because it was harder?" she queried.

"That was the idea."

"And afterwards, Speedy, when we were alone in the kitchen, here, and you made the bet — and you talked about —"

She flushed, but she looked straight at him. Then Speedy laughed.

"You know how it is, Mary. I wanted to make you pretty angry, and I was succeeding. I wanted to pay you back for sending those three thugs out after me. That last one was a hard nut to crack — but he fought fair to the finish!" he added, scowling.

"You made me angry enough, Speedy," said she. "I think that I understand you a little better. Not well, but a little better."

"You know, Mary," said he, leaning a trifle towards her, "I don't understand. By the way, it looks as though I might win that bet from you, after all!"

She laughed with the utmost frankness.

"It won't be hard for me to pay," said she.

When Arthur Steyn rode back from town and put up his horse, he heard singing from the kitchen of his house, and coming in, almost on tiptoe, he found Mary working between stove and sink, and the lamp burning brightly on the table, and Speedy, in a corner, working hard at a churn, and keeping time with the strokes to the song that he was singing.

He stood by the door for a moment before he was noticed, for the girl had joined in heartily on the chorus.

Then they both noticed him, and greeted him cheerfully. And he smiled, standing there by the door, leaning his shoulders against the wall, standing as tall and as straight as any youth.

"Time is a great doctor, eh?" said he. "Speedy, you're working that churn too fast. The butter will be rancid, if you don't look out."

Late that night, Speedy sat by lantern light in the big dining-bunk room, and he wrote rapidly:

"Dear Mr. Pierson,
I've arrived, been introduced formally and informally, too, and looked the lay of the land over, and am now stopping for a few days in the Steyn house.

166

Steyn is a charm.

The girl is not a wildcat at all, but gentle as a lamb — when her claws have been trimmed.

As for the terrible gunmen, I see that you've exaggerated. People are not watching her, as you say, and it seems to be the general impression that she's to marry a big handsome fellow called Joe Wynne. Gentleman Joe.

I hope to do away with that impression in a few days.

As for the two thugs who know about the girl's fortune and want to marry her on account of it, I have only met one — Rudy Stern. He's a handy man, they say, with his starboard cannon and his port side, too. However, time will tell which one of us will drop. It will mean a fight to the finish, because he's a devil for punishment and has a long memory.

The second man you told me about, the worst of the lot, has not showed his face around here.

He's not popular. People shiver and look over their shoulders when his name is mentioned. So I'm waiting for him anxiously, and I dare say that he'll call on me when he knows that I'm staying here in the house. When Mr. Six-card Wilson, as they call him here, turns up, I appoint myself a reception committee of one.

I will keep you posted.

My regards to you, respects to Mrs. Pierson and love to Charlotte.

Sincerely yours,
Speedy."

19

Two days later, Mary Steyn paid her debt and went to the dance in the Nixon schoolhouse with Speedy. He was to leave the very next day, he said, but odd words came from old Steyn just before they rode off towards the school-house.

He came out and stood at the head of the boy's horse, a lump-headed mustang which was, nevertheless, well regarded on account of its rocking-chair lope.

Said Arthur Steyn: "Speedy, are you running on a very strict time schedule?"

"No," said the boy.

"Then promise me something."

It was exactly what the boy had wanted.

"I'll do whatever I can," said he.

"Then promise me to stay here another week," said Steyn.

There was so much seriousness in his voice that Speedy leaned a little from the saddle and through the dull twilight looked fixedly at the other.

"All right," he said.

The old man sighed. He seemed to feel such relief that his straight, rigid body drooped a little.

"That's good," he added. "Go have a good time, you youngsters."

They rode off together; the sunset grew tarnished and more dim, the stars began to come out, first Jupiter, blazing when nothing else in the sky had force to show, and immediately afterwards, steel-blue Sirius shone through the mistier lower air, then Arcturus to the east thrust through, and Orion, finally, was printed big in the west.

All things took life about them. The rocks wavered with the swaying lope of the horses, the Spanish bayonets became living silhouettes, like Indians at watch with warspears raised and ready for the charge. In the air there was a faint smell of alkali dust mingling with the breath of spring flowers.

They came to a long rise, very dark, the horses stumbling among broken rocks. So they drew down to a walk.

"It's only five miles more," said the girl.

Speedy laughed.

"I can stand that," he said. "But you see that I'm not much good in the saddle."

"Nobody can do everything," she answered, philosophically.

170

But he could tell from her tone that it was hard for her to make the allowance. In her eyes, if a man could not ride a horse he was hardly a man. Through those first miles, she had been actually fighting to retain some respect for the figure which swayed and jolted even to the easy gait of the roan mustang.

"Horses take learning," said he. "I've ridden the rods or the blind baggage more than I've handled horses."

"You've beaten your way on the railroads?" she translated. "Speedy, why d'you do it? It's not right!"

"You mean," he corrected her, "it's not what most people do. But it's right for me."

"Is it?" she challenged. "Right for you to be a loafer and never lift a hand at work?"

"There are a lot of others like me," he responded. "And the ones who don't drift around a good deal — well, you know, they're apt to explode, now and then, and break things up. Travel is an outlet; safe-cracking, crooked gambling, all kinds of thuggery are outlets, too. I keep myself out of jail by keeping on the road."

She looked closely at him through the darkness.

"Why do you tell me all of these things, Speedy?" said she.

"Why shouldn't I?" asked the boy. "I want you to know me."

171

"You're only showing me a part of the picture," she insisted. "There's a lot more to the picture than what you tell me."

"Well," he answered, "you want to make me a mystery. That's what we do with everyone we first meet. But there's no mystery about me. All of us are a lot alike. You change the wrinkles in the face, or the pitch of the voice, put your high-stepper in a cowpuncher's saddle, or Europe and champagne in a puncher's system, and we all average out about equal."

She digested this thought for a moment.

He seemed serious enough, and yet she had a feeling that he was making game of her. She nearly always had that feeling, when he was talking, unless she could see his eyes, and that was impossible through this dim light.

Finally she said, "You're as different from the rest as a horse is different from a deer. You know it, Speedy. Don't pretend that you don't know it."

"You've known a lot of people," said he, as though making an admission on her side.

"I've known a few. I've seen a lot of punchers and ranchers, and such, about your age. Oh, you're different, Speedy. You know that you're different."

"The other night," he went on, changing the subject a good deal, "you hinted that people who've been fond of you have had a rough time of it. You remember?"

"I said a lot, the other night," she replied. "None of the boys ever gets serious about me now, Speedy."

"Because they're afraid to?"

"It's a hard thing to talk about," said she.

"I'd like to know," he persisted.

"I don't make you out, Speedy," she said with the utmost frankness. "But if you —"

"Why, I'm going to marry you, Mary," said he, and laughed a little, in a way that turned the words into a jest. "And the way to marrying you seems to be dangerous. If you're friendly, I'll expect to be told why."

"It's a queer thing to talk about," said the girl. "But I have to talk to you. I saw you lying dead, once. At least, it was the same to me as though you were dead. Ever since, you're like somebody out of the grave, to me. And I thank heaven that Joe Wynne hasn't a rope around his neck! By the way, Joe will be there tonight, I suppose. How'll you act towards him?"

"The way he acts towards me," said the boy, instantly.

She considered this, found it hard to comment on, and then continued:

"About people who've been pretty close to me — I mean, about what we were talking of —"

"Suitors, eh?" said he.

"Well, boys that took me a lot to dances, and that sort of thing," she answered. "Three years ago, Sid Winchell paid me a lot of attention. Sid was a good fellow – a little wild, but straight as a string. One day there was a shooting scrape at a crossroads. Sid was picked up half dead. When he got out of the hospital, he left the country. He's never come back."

"And never sent you word?"

"He sent word to me, right enough," she answered, grimly. "He wrote me a note when he was out of the hospital. It simply said: 'I hope that I never lay eyes on you again, and God help the next man that gets interested in you!' That was the word he sent to me."

"He was a hound," said the boy.

"No, but he had his walking papers from somebody in a pretty high saddle," she said. "His people live ten miles from here; they've never seen his face since that day. He was told to go, and he went. I don't know who told him, but that must have been what happened."

"That's hard on him," said the boy, carelessly.

She was angered by his indifference.

And she went on: "Toppy Lancaster was pretty interested in me, about a year after that. We went around a lot together. I didn't think about Sid's disappearance so much. Toppy and I went everywhere. I used to see him two or three times a week. And —"

She paused.

"Got engaged?"

"No, but I liked him a lot. And then, one day, Toppy's father heard loud voices in the barn, and one of the voices belonged to Toppy himself. There were several shots fired, and Toppy came walking back to the house holding his right arm against his side; he was dripping blood. And the strange part of it was that he wouldn't say who had had the fight with him. But as soon as he could ride, he left the county — and he's never come back!"

"Hello!" said Speedy.

And he whistled.

"That was pretty bad," went on the girl. "And still I didn't connect him with what had happened to Sid, until I had a note from Toppy Lancaster. He wrote that he was bound for Alaska, but he said that he was not intending to dig gold for me. He said that I'd cut his throat for him, and he only wished me bad luck. That's the last that I've heard from Toppy. Nobody else around here has heard from him, either, except his parents. And they don't speak to me, any more."

"That's two in a row," said Speedy. "Any more? Or were the boys beginning to be pretty suspicious, by this time?"

"They were suspicious," she replied. "Toppy's

175

folks did some talking. They let people think that I was responsible, some way. But only about ten months ago, Red Sam Marvin showed up. I suppose that you've heard of Red?"

"No. Famous man?"

"He's a rough fellow," she said, "but he's all right. He's so rough and tough that he didn't care what the talk was about me. He liked me all the better because there might be some danger. And I liked him. He could talk about all sorts of places and people. He'd been everywhere and done everything. And so we went around together a lot. And then he had the same thing happen to him."

"Shot up?" asked the boy.

She paused. The silence weighted down the air.

Then she said, softly: "Red was shot dead in his own house. His body was found a day or two after the killing. That was the third man."

"And that was enough for the rest of the boys?" asked Speedy.

"That was enough," she agreed.

She went on: "They're nice to me. They dance with me. But nobody calls on me alone, you can be sure. I suppose that's why we've come to the habit of giving the Sunday parties."

They surmounted the slope.

Before them was the thin sickle of a new

moon, and by earth shine the dim, small globe of the moon showed in the arm of the brightness.

"Well," said Speedy, quietly, "I'm putting in my claim, tonight, to be number four on the list!"

20

They got to the schoolhouse at nine-thirty, when the dance was barely beginning. Such affairs have a late start; some of the people come thirty miles to them, over rough mountain trails. However, there was already a good number at the schoolhouse. Saddle horses stood at the hitching rack, drooping their heads, prepared for a long wait. Others were tethered under the shed where the schoolchildren put their ponies in the winter weather, and inside of the building, the orchestra had commenced; the scraping of feet could be heard at a great distance.

When they dismounted, Mary Steyn took a brush out of her saddle bag and brushed off her divided skirts. She passed it to Speedy, and he made himself as fit as he could. The day before, he had bought new clothes in the town, to take the place of his tattered rags, which had been part, and a necessary part, of his role on arrival at the Steyn ranch. Then they dusted off their shoes. Toilets did not have to be elaborate at such a dance as this. Good dancing and good nature were the two requirements.

But, on the way into the schoolhouse, she touched the arm of her escort, and looking vaguely toward the west, where half of Orion's splendor was sinking beneath the horizon, she said: "Why do you do it, Speedy?"

"Do what?" said he.

"Let yourself in for so much trouble? You don't care a rap about me, Speedy. I don't want you in trouble, anyway."

He said: "I care a lot."

"I know," she said. "You care for the game."

She nodded, and walked on again. And he followed her half a pace behind, watching the way she held her head, and the curving line of neck and shoulders. He noticed her walk, too, and the easy spring of it. For his part, he was feeling those eight miles, but she was as fresh as though the day had just begun.

The arrival of a crowd of a dozen or so, all together, covered the entrance of the girl and Speedy, but not entirely. He was aware of bronzed faces of girls and youngsters turned towards him. It seemed to him that the orchestra gave an extra lift to its music, also.

There was a violin, a cornet, a slide trombone and a drummer who had all sorts of appliances for making noise, and for four people, no one could complain of the volume of that orchestra. It whooped and roared and rasped, and for high moments, there were solos by the violin, here and there, and from the nasal, whining cornet, also.

But that did not matter.

Mary Steyn stepped into a whirl of dancing from the start. And never had there been so much conversation with her partners. Sometimes they almost forgot their steps. It was Speedy they wanted to know about.

How long was he staying at the Steyn place?

Where did he come from?

Was he only a tramp?

What had he done to Fat Ginnis, Doc and Alf Barton?

Was he a "good fellow"?

She put these questions off with smiles and half answers.

The longer she watched Speedy circulating in the crowd, the surer she was that she had not made so much as a beginning of his acquaintance. Now he seemed in his element. She watched the happy faces of the girls he danced with. She watched the gliding ease of his dancing. Even big red-faced Ruth Doran seemed graceful when she had the tramp for a partner. And everyone was glad of him. Tramp or not, in that country, in that rough part of the range, a man who was a man was worth any amount of name and gentility.

Then came the first crisis. Big Joe Wynne entered the hall with Maude Willoughby. They danced. He left his partner and went smiling through the crowd, giving a word here and a hand there. No girl would ever have to be ashamed of Joe Wynne, as a husband. And was not that the chief reason for which girls married? To have a man they could be proud of and one they could trust in the making of a home?

So thought Mary Steyn, as she watched Joe.

And then, there he was, bowing in front of her, taking her out to dance.

It was a waltz. Like most very big men who know the step and the rhythm, Joe waltzed well. But she almost forgot the music and the step, for he began to talk seriously, at once.

He said: "Look here, Mary. I had your note and I stayed away. But now I want to know how long I'm to stay off the premises."

She answered: "I don't know. As long as Speedy's with us."

"And how long will that be?"

"He wanted to go tomorrow."

"But?"

"But Father begged him to stay on for a while."

Joe almost stopped in the middle of a step, then went on haltingly.

"Your father likes him, Mary?"

"Father will sit and watch him all through an

evening, as though he never saw that sort of a human being before."

Joe Wynne said: "Tell me why you warned me off the place, Mary."

"Don't command me!" she snapped.

"Don't be ugly," he returned "I have a right to speak short and sharp. What does he mean to you?"

"He's amusing," she said.

"You like him a lot, and he's a tramp!"

"Joe," she said, "let's talk about something else."

"I have to talk about him," said he. "Mary, I love you. I mean to marry you if I can. And when you take up with a fellow like Speedy, it worries me."

"Are you proposing to me, Joe?" she asked him.

"You can call it that."

She wondered at his matter of fact manner, but he added: "You've always known that I'd ask you to marry me, sooner or later."

"You know what trouble it may let you in for?" she demanded.

"I know," he said. "I know about Winchell, and Lancaster, and Red Marvin. I know all about 'em. But I can take care of myself, I think."

She liked him better, at that moment, than she ever had liked him before, and with her usual frankness, she said so.

"There's never been a time," she said, "when you meant so much to me, Joe. But I can't say yes to you. I like you and respect you more than any man I know. But I don't love you enough to marry you."

His answer surprised her.

"Well, I expected that, too," said he. "I don't expect you to say yes at once. We'll see later on. I'm going to have another chance later on and it may turn out better. I'd like to ask you, though, if having Speedy in your house has made any difference?"

"A week ago," she said, "I would have been glad to say yes to you, Joe. But Speedy has turned everything topsy-turvy in my mind. It isn't that I like him such a lot. But he's new. He makes everything seem different. I'm like a person in a foreign country. I want to learn the language before I make up my mind about the people."

He was not angry — only gravely concerned. And just then the music stopped abruptly, and swung into a Spanish dance.

There was only one dancer, and that was Speedy. He had thrown off his coat and vest. He had wrapped a great scarlet sash around his waist, and now, as he whirled with clattering, complicated steps down the hall, the end of the sash stood stiffly out, fluttering like a flag in a strong wind, while the dancer wound himself into the length of it, and out again; never did he allow it to touch the floor.

At each spectacular maneuver, people shouted. Enthusiasm grew tense. People leaned forward and beat time, and swayed with the movements of Speedy, and lifted their feet in a foolish manner as though in sympathy with those lightning steps.

"Is that what you want, Mary," said Joe Wynne. "A professional dancer and entertainer?"

She looked up at him.

"He may be more than that," she said.

"I know that he's a good fighting man, but he's a fox, too," said Joe Wynne.

"Perhaps he is," said she.

She began to be coldly angry with Wynne.

He went on: "Look at his face. He wouldn't be doing anything else in the world. This is heaven for Speedy!"

And, in fact, the face of the boy was flushed, and his eyes were shining. He was fairly laughing with joy as he danced.

She drew in her breath, sharply. And then she shook her head.

"You want me to be ashamed of him," she said. "Well, I like him well enough to be ashamed if he did the wrong thing. But I'm not ashamed. He's this way. He's different from the rest."

"That explains him as a hobo, too," said Wynne.

"You don't understand," said she.

"I don't want to!" answered Wynne.

"Well, Joe," she replied, "I can't be logical. There he is. You see him and hate him; I see him and like him."

"Tell me," he shot at her. "Is he the sort of a man you could marry?"

Perhaps he had overstepped the mark of even a long friendship, but now she looked up slowly and met the eyes of Joe Wynne fairly and squarely.

"Well," she answered, to herself as well as to him, "I don't know. I don't know anything about him, or what I would do."

She saw Wynne turn pale.

"I thought so," he said. "You know about me, but you don't know about him – dancing in his shirt sleeves to please – well, let it go."

"Yes," she said, "we'd better let it go. There's something else to think about, now!"

She nodded towards the door.

"By the Lord," muttered Wynne, "that's too much! He's showing his face again. Something has to be done about it!"

For, in the doorway, stood a man whose face, indeed, did not seem meant for public showing. It was a downward face, long and lean, and yet with profound wrinkles in it that flowed from the eyes and past the mouth, like the wrinkles in the face of a bloodhound. The nose was broken. Half of one ear had been bitten, or shot, or cut away and left a ragged stub. He had lips which showed no red; his eyebrows were so blond that they appeared scalped. And his eyes, like clouded agate, had no color more than a mist. He was tall, very lean, with abnormally narrow shoulders and abnormally long arms and equally long fingers.

That was Six-card Wilson, "Six" for short. And wherever he appeared, trouble was sure to follow.

21

The next moment, Speedy was dancing with Mary. And the first thing he said to her was:

"Who's that beauty who just came in, the fellow with the half ear?"

"Six-card Wilson, the gambler, thug, gunman and general all around crook!" said she.

She felt an electric shock go through him.

"That's Six-card?" said he.

"Yes, that's the man."

"People seem to like him pretty well, then. There's the second nicest girl in the room dancing with him."

"She'll dance with anybody who's exciting. Something may be done about Six tonight."

"Your big friend Joe Wynne may do it," said he.

"Don't sneer at Joe," said she.

"I'm not sneering at him," answered the boy. "I was just thinking what a fine out he'd have with Six, as you call him."

And he laughed.

He was dancing slowly, like silk. To dance

with him was to float downstream. Never before had she known what motion could be.

She said: "Will you keep away from Joe Wynne this evening?"

He answered her: "It's the one thing in the world that I won't do!"

And the anger in her swelled and made her exclaim: "Then I hope that he hurts you!"

"No more than he can hurt a mist in the wind," said the boy, contemptuously.

"You're as sure of yourself as — a murder in the dark!" said she.

And, after saying that, she asked him to take her back to her chair.

He obeyed at once. He stood beside her, smiling, calm, letting no one suspect that there was anything wrong between them.

"D'you want me to leave you for a while?" said he.

"I do," said the girl.

"Thanks," said he, and turned immediately away, as the dance ended.

Why should he have thanked her, she wondered, except to impertinently make out that he was as glad to be away from her as she could be to have him go?

Rage grew hotly in her.

As for Speedy, he went out of the room into the hall where there were many pegs along the walls for the hats and coats of the schoolchildren. On this night, every peg was crowded with three or four hats and coats, one heaped on top of the other.

Through that room went Speedy, and on the outer doorstep he stood, balancing on the sill, while he made and lighted a cigarette.

"Hot, in there," said a husky, whispering voice.

He turned his head a little. A small chill went down his spine before he answered. And there he felt, as much as saw, "Six" Wilson.

Such a sensation went through the boy as he never had known before since once, as a child, he had won a bet by sleeping in a supposedly haunted house.

And, for the first time in his mature life, he could say that he was really afraid of another man.

Yet this was the man whom he should know better. This was the man whom he really had come to find. As for the second fellow who knew the secret of the girl's fortune, Rudy Stern hardly counted. He was no more than a child in a grownup's game.

This was the keystone of the arch. Wrongly handled, the arch might fall, but it would crush all beneath it.

"Yeah," Speedy found himself saying, "it's hot in there, all right."

"Let's go outside and have a smoke, you and me."

"Sure," said Speedy.

And he sauntered down the steps at the side of the tall man.

They stood in the black shade of a group of young pine trees. Another dance had begun. Music, the rushing of feet, the clanging of voices poured out about them, but rather dimly, the sound diffusing like the light from the open doorway, in the greatness of the night.

Six Wilson was making his smoke, then lighting it, and snapping the match away with a flick of his fingers. Half of the arc which it traced was red-streaked; and then it went out.

Said Six: "I ain't introduced myself, kid."

"The world introduces you, Six," said the boy, "and that's a shame."

"Why is it a shame?" asked Six, without emotion.

"Because," said Speedy, "a name's as good as a stone to stumble over, I've noticed."

"You ever stumble that way?" asked the big man.

"Yeah, and bruised my shins, too."

"If that's all you hurt, you're lucky," said Six. "All those suckers in there, they'd like to take a crack at me."

He laughed.

His laughter, like his voice, was no more than a whisper, a raucous whisper, with no sign of vocal cords in it.

Was he a vain, egotistical fool, and no more — except for being an expert crook and gunman?

The boy waited. Two-thirds of his fear already had departed from him.

"Maybe one of them will stand up and take a crack at you," said Speedy.

"Maybe one. Not two," said the thug. "Joe Wynne, he might go to heaven that way. There ain't nobody else made that big."

Speedy said nothing.

"Thinking about yourself?" asked the big man.

"Yes."

"Thinking that maybe *you* might take a crack at me?"

"Maybe."

"Not yet," said Six. "You ain't got over the chill of my face and my voice, yet. It always paralyzes the boys, the first gunsight of me, so to speak."

He laughed again.

Swiftly Speedy revised his opinion. This man was much more than an egotistical fool. Far, far more!

"What's the big idea between you and me?" asked Speedy.

"I thought that we might get acquainted," said Six.

"All right. We're acquainted," said Speedy.

"My line," said Six, "is cards. After that, a little safe-cracking, and after that I got a few side lines. What's your line, kid?"

"My line," said the boy, "is chatter."

"Yeah, chatter for what? Green goods?"

"I'm not particular. I deal a hand, now and then, myself. Trust my hands more than I do my eyes, just like you, Six."

The ghostly laughter of the big man whispered again at the ear of the boy.

"That's pretty good, at that," he declared.

"All right," murmured Speedy. "Besides, I have a few side lines of my own. I've used a jimmy, and I've blown a safe. I can cook well enough to make soup, too, in a pinch. My soup has given a lot of people indigestion."

"I'll bet it has," said Six. "You sound to me like a good kid."

"Good?"

"Yeah, useful."

"I'm useful to myself," said Speedy.

"Never travel double?"

"Never."

"Might make a new habit."

"I don't make new habits."

"You're young. You can learn."

"Can I?"

"Yeah, if you got the right kind of a teacher."

"Like you?"

"Yeah, like me."

"Break the seal, Six," said the boy. "Let's see what the letter's about."

"Good news."

"Money, eh?"

"Big!"

"I like it big," said Speedy. "Go right ahead."

"It's got a tag on it."

"There always is."

"A tag and an even break."

"For you?"

"Yeah, for me."

"Go on, Six. You whistle a pretty good tune. What's the tag?"

"You marry."

"Do I?"

"Yeah, you marry."

The idea was clear enough, now.

"Money?" asked the boy.

"Yeah, a heap."

"What kind of a face?"

"A beauty."

"Why don't you marry it yourself, Six?"

"Because I've got my name wrote on my map. And my map is all wrote all over my name. God never made two faces like mine. He never was so real careless as to do that. He done me for an object lesson, just to make other people feel thankful."

And he laughed again.

He would laugh at death and damnation in the

same way, the boy knew.

"What's the direction of the lady?" asked the boy.

"You want her name? You want all my cards on the table?"

"Sure I do."

"And then do you play with me?"

"If I like her, I might."

"If you don't, Speedy, it'll be hell on you."

"I've been in hell before. I'd rather be there than with most women that I've met."

"This is different. This is the kid inside — Mary Steyn, is what I mean!"

Of course, Speedy was prepared for the name, and still it sent a shiver through him to hear her mentioned by that whispering voice. It was as though something unclean had touched her.

"Without me," said the big man, "you're poorer after marrying her than you were before. With me, I tie you and the kid to a flock of the long green. About nine million bones."

"And you get half?"

"Fifty per cent is all I get. You and her can live on the rest."

"I've got to think," said Speedy.

22

The reason that the boy had to think was because the picture as the crook painted it for him stretched clearly and plainly to the eye as far as the mind could reach.

There would be no difficulty, once Six Wilson was on his side. For Six would take care of Rudy Stern and any other objectors who happened to have more knowledge than was convenient. As for an estate of nine millions, it readily cut into halves each of which was amply big enough to make all concerned happy as kings.

"You could get her," Six Wilson was saying in the same grisly whisper. "You could get her easily enough. No trouble about that. I seen her turning up her nose and getting into a tiff with you a minute ago. She don't often do that. She don't lose her temper. And if she gets mad at you, she'll marry you. That's the way that it always works. I never knew a woman in the world that come anywheres near gettin' real mad at me. Not the way I mean now. But you got an inside track with that girl."

Still the youngster did not answer. Still his thoughts were spinning in a swift circle.

Even Pierson, perhaps, would not be offended. He would get his commission, just the same, for the handling of the big estate as it passed to the heir.

And still the boy could not bring himself to the point of acceding. He had dealt with rough men before this, and men whose hands were far from clean. But never with such a ghoul as Six-card Wilson.

"Mind you," Six was saying, at this point, "if you marry her without getting my tip, it won't do you any good. You'll never collect the boodle. All you'll have on your hands will be a flock of trouble. She's actin' tame, now, but when she kicks over the traces, she smashes things up!"

"Six," said the boy, "it's a big compliment that you're paying me. Why haven't you offered the same thing to other fellows who were interested in Mary Steyn?"

"Because I tried 'em out," said Six Wilson, "and none of them was the right stuff. The sort of a deal that this is, it's gotta be with a man that's able to take care of himself — and that'll keep his word of honor when he's given it once. And you're that kind, I reckon."

"Am I?"

"You are. You'll say yes or no, and you'll mean it."

"I say 'no,' then," said the boy.

"You say no, do you?"

"Yes."

"Then God help your unlucky soul, kid," said Six-card.

"It puts you against me, does it?"

"It puts me against you," said Six, "till you get out of this part of the country. Move off of this range, son, and you'll be healthy, wealthy, and wise. Stay on this range, and worse'n smallpox is likely to take hold on you."

"You'll plug me, eh, the way you plugged three more of Mary's friends?"

"I ain't the only one that's shepherding Mary Steyn," said Six Wilson. "And I ain't the only one to do the shooting. Fact is, shooting is a thing that I hate to do, till I'm drove to it. Don't you go and drive me, son! Gimme a chance to play square with you. Gimme a good chance to help you to a fine slice of loot. You'll find me the best partner in the world, and the worst kind of a burr under the saddle blanket if you say 'no.'"

"I've said it before, and I stick to it," said Speedy.

"You don't like my style?" suggested the big man, his whisper hissing more softly than ever.

"Can't give you reasons," said Speedy. "I play

this game my own way. That's all."

"Well, good for you," said Six Wilson.

He paused. Then he added: "Watch your step. Walk slow. Pick your way. Because there's gunna be a lot of trouble just ahead of you."

"Tell me this," said the boy. "I play a lone hand against you. Do you play a lone hand against me?"

"You're damn right I don't," said Six, "I play with a stacked deck, and a few extras up my sleeve. Now, whacha think about that?"

And he laughed again.

Breaking off that laughter, he said: "You fool, here I've gone and put everything face up on the table in front of you, and you turn your back on it. You got no brains. I'm glad that you didn't agree to make the split. Now, mind you, I leave you be till tomorrow. But tomorrow has gotta see you on the out trail!"

And he walked rapidly away through the darkness, until the silhouette of his moving figure was blotted out behind the corner of the building.

Then Speedy made a new cigarette, and as he scratched a match to light it, realized that perhaps he was a fool to hold a light by which another might shoot safely and accurately out of the blanketing darkness.

He saw that danger and difficulty had increased for him on every side.

In one direction he seemed fairly secure — and that was towards the Steyns. On the other hand, Joe Wynne and Six Wilson were heartily against him, and both of them were names to conjure with.

He went back into the schoolhouse, where the dance was less cheerfully in swing than it had been before, and a small cluster of men, with gloomy, resolved faces, had formed around Joe Wynne in one corner of the room.

Speedy managed to disengage Mary Steyn from a tangle, and she said at once: "Let's get out into the open for a moment."

He took her straight outside, and she began to walk rapidly up and down under the pine trees. Then she said: "D'you know what?"

"Well?"

"They're going to make a pass at Six Wilson, tonight. Joe Wynne and the rest!"

"That's pretty brave," said he.

"Are you sneering?" she asked him.

"Look, Mary," said he. "Don't walk around with a chip on your shoulder all of the time. What's the use of that?"

She disregarded the remark.

"Why don't you go in there and help them?" she asked.

"Because they need guns to handle Six," said he.

"Well, you can help them use the guns," she insisted.

"I never mix in gun plays; I never packed a gun in my life," said Speedy.

At this, he heard her gasp, and then her angry, controlled laughter reached him.

"What a fool you think I am, Speedy," said she. "Do you expect me to believe you?"

"Yes, I do."

She laughed again.

"I'm not a half-wit," she assured him.

"You make me out what?" said he.

"Oh, you know what you are," answered the girl, her anger increasing with the passage of every moment. "You never handled a Colt in your life, I suppose?"

"No," said he.

"That's because you prefer a Smith and Wesson, then," she suggested.

He overlooked her irony.

"You think I'm a killer, Mary, don't you? You're wrong. I never put a man in the hospital in my life."

She had been pacing up and down beside him all of this time, but now she turned about and stamped.

"We can't get on together," she declared. "I thought that you and I could be frank with one another, at least!"

"We ought to be able to be frank," said he.

"But you've tried to read my mind, and you're all wrong about me."

She broke off their talk with another gasp, of a different sort.

"Look!" said she.

The ground on which they stood rose a little above the level of that on which the schoolhouse was placed, and they could look over the edge of the steps, through the two doors and down the middle of the dance floor, with a slightly spreading vista. Into that vista now stepped five men with leveled guns. And in front of them was Six Wilson.

He had raised his great hands above his narrow shoulders, and his ugly face never turned from the place where Joe Wynne stood.

The full flood of the light from the lamp that illumined the room seemed gathering upon the fine brown face of the big man, now. It was the pride of the dance committee that they had managed to get hold of one great lamp with a huge, circular burner, and swinging this from the ceiling of the schoolhouse, they flooded the entire room with light. Speedy could see the glittering pendant at the bottom of this lamp gently oscillating back and forth from where he stood. But nothing else was important inside the place, except the faces of Joe Wynne and of the criminal who had ventured so rashly into the hands of the men who stood for law and order.

And still there was a half sneer upon the face of Six Wilson.

All the place was filled with silence, until Wynne said in a voice that was easily audible to the two listeners outside: "You thought we were a lot of sheep, Wilson, but we're a little better than you expected. We've got you, Wilson, and we're going to put you where you'll keep for a while!"

"Good for you, Joe!" whispered the girl. "Oh, Joe Wynne, you're a man!"

"Yeah. He's a regular hero," commented Speedy, indifferently.

"He's a lion, and you know it," said the girl. "And he's caught Six."

"He and four to back him," said the boy. "They've tagged Six, but don't think that they've caught him yet. The game isn't over, if my guess is worth a rap."

They could see that Wilson made no attempt to answer the words of Joe Wynne. And then they heard Joe Wynne giving orders — two men to fall behind the captive, one to stand on each side of him.

"And don't move those hands of yours, Six Wilson!" he directed, sharply.

The hands were not what Six moved. Instead, he dove straight at the knees of Wynne and the man next to him.

Wynne fired; with what result could not be judged, but he and another went down, rolling with Wilson on the floor. Then another shot boomed heavily, through the screeching of the women and the shouting of the men — and the schoolhouse was blotted with darkness.

23

Out of the black door of the building, a monstrously tall form emerged, bounded to the ground and raced straight at the two.

"Catch him, Speedy!" whispered the girl, through her teeth.

She made no move to run from the danger. And then Six Wilson was upset by sheer bad luck, for his toe caught under a projecting root and he rolled heavily to the ground, crashing into the bushes near the feet of Speedy. One groan from him, and he lay still. The dull night light glimmered upon the revolver which he still clutched loosely. He lay limp, and the weapon was offered freely, as it were, at the feet of the tramp.

Speedy stooped and picked it up, and a whole column of men charged down from the schoolhouse, roaring through the doorway like water through a dam.

"Here he is!" someone yelled, driving straight at Speedy and the girl, then realizing that Speedy did not fulfill the dimensions of the tall bandit, he yelled: "Where'd Wilson go?"

Mary Steyn strove to give the proper answer.

But Speedy had glided behind her, and now, from the rear, he clapped a hand over her lips, while he shouted, loudly: "That way! That way! Around that corner of the school. Hurry like the devil!"

"You yellow hound, why don't you hurry yourself?" shouted the angry questioner. "This way, boys!"

But others, seeing the dim gesture in the distance, already had turned and were running on the false trail.

Up rose, with a stagger and a lurch, big Six Wilson.

"Kid, you're white," he gasped.

And then he bounded straight for the line of tethered horses. Even in his haste, he did not forget to pick and choose. A big shimmering gray was his choice, and leaping into the saddle, he jerked the big horse around with force enough to stagger it. Then off he shot into the night.

The girl bit hard upon the hand of Speedy, but he endured the pain without flinching.

For that matter, there was no need that she should cry out. Others had heard the galloping of the horse, others had seen the vanishing outlaw, and nearly every man at the schoolhouse, young enough for such work, had flung himself on horseback for the pursuit.

Then Speedy unhanded the girl.

She turned upon him, dead silent with fury.

"That's it!" she exclaimed. "That's what you are, at last! You're one of Six Wilson's gang! I'd rather — I'd rather stay at the side of a leper. Speedy, get out of my sight. You poison the air for me!"

"I'm taking you home, first," said he.

"I'll die, first," said she.

"Maybe you will," said he. "But I'm taking you home."

"A Wilson gangster!" she breathed. "Faugh!"

"Mary," he said to her, "you gave me your word that you'd go to this dance with me and go home with me after it. And you'll keep your word if I have to take you by the elbows and throw you on a horse."

He heard her panting, and moaning with helpless rage.

Then she said: "I've given you my promise. Oh, I'm a fool, I'm a fool! But we start now, and we go fast."

"We'll start now," he admitted, "but we'll follow my own pace. Come along!"

The dance was breaking up, but slowly. Someone inside the schoolhouse had found some smaller lamps and candles which were lighted, and by that light the women huddled together, and an excited cackling rose, and flowed away uselessly into the night.

So, unobserved, Speedy and the girl found their horses, mounted and took the return trail.

They rode ten minutes in black silence. Then he began to whistle and kept up the cheerful music for another ten minutes at least.

Then, at last, she said "Speedy, I ought to ask you if you've got any explanation to offer!"

"No," said he.

And he began to whistle again, a tune which was hatefully familiar to her.

"Julia,
    You are peculiar;
Julia,
    You are queer —"

Her blood rose; and it ran hot indeed.

And another mile drifted behind them. He rode in a leisurely fashion. She wanted to eat up the distance quickly, at the full racing speed of her horse. But Speedy dallied along. He paid no heed to her. He kept on the even tenor of his way, and his whistling rose into the night air as sweetly as the song of a bird.

She hated him with a passionate intensity. She hated him as she never before had loathed any living creature.

The horrible face of Six Wilson arose in her mind; and she placed it on the shoulders of the

207

gallant, lithe figure that rode beside her.

Finally, in a choked voice, she said: "D'you mind going on a little faster. I'm not very well. I want to get home."

"You may not be very well, Mary," said he, "but you're a lot better than I am. You know, I never rode this far in my life, before. Sitting down won't be my idea of a good time, for a month."

And he laughed with the utmost cheerfulness as he spoke. She stared at him, feeling suddenly helpless. There was no measuring rod by which she could estimate and judge him. He was a monster quite outside of her ken.

And now a gentle, warm wind came up the valley and brought a sweetness of very distant pines about them. They must have been many miles away, but the scent was unmistakable in the air.

"Speedy," she suddenly exploded, "after all I *don't* believe it! I'll go counter to my own eyes and ears!"

"Will you?" said he.

"Yes!" she cried.

"About what?" he asked her, gently.

She was angered again.

"You know perfectly well," said she. "About Six Wilson and his horrible crew. I don't believe that you're one of them!"

"I didn't say that I was," said he.

"Tell me definitely that you're not!"

"You wouldn't believe me," said he. "I'm a gunman and a killer and a member of Six Wilson's gang. Why, Mary, you're the wildest guesser in the world. I'm a regular lamb, that's what I am!"

She was almost as furious as ever, because of his air of indifference to her opinion. But she had a great desire to laugh.

"Tell me, please, Speedy," said she, "why you didn't let the boys get their hands on that wolf!"

"I'll tell you why," said he. "I don't like a fox very well. It's a sneak and it's a thief, and it's a murderer, too. But when the hounds are running after it, my sympathies are all with the fox!"

"Wilson is the worst man in the world!" she told him.

"He's a bad one," admitted the boy, "but he'd just made a mighty good play. That shooting out the lamp — that dive for the floor — oh, I liked the look of that!"

There was a ring in his voice.

"You admired him?" she asked, coldly.

"Didn't you?" he asked her.

"Ask me if I'd admire the writhings of a boa constrictor!"

"All right, Mary," said he. "You don't like the looks of Six Wilson, and he's not pretty, at that.

But he's got a useful pair of hands, and he's got a useful brain in that ugly head of his. I thought he was a goner; and yet I guessed that he would make a last play, of some sort. I wonder how that stone-headed fellow, that Joe Wynne you like so well, managed to miss a pointblank shot like that?"

"Joe? He was taken by surprise," said the girl.

And she was glad that the night covered the heat that she felt in her face.

"Does he seem such a glorious man to you now?" he asked her.

"I wish that you'd leave Joe alone," said she. "We were talking about you and Six Wilson."

"I couldn't throw that fox to the dogs, not when he lay at my feet, done in by a bad break in the luck after he'd won his way out," said he. "By the way, here's a keepsake for you. Here's Six Wilson's gun."

He passed it to her and she, after a moment, took it, and fingered the notches which had been cut into the stock of the revolver. She shuddered, and yet she was pleased. It was a prize of war and Speedy had won it fairly enough.

"If you wanted him to get away, why did you take his gun?" she asked.

"I wanted him to get away, but not through the door of murder," said the boy.

And suddenly she was silenced again.

Then they came to the house. The moon was up, whitening the old shack, giving it a little grace, ennobling the hills which were its setting.

They put up the horses, stripping the saddles from the sweating backs of the animals. Then they stood by the corral fence and watched them drink, plunging in their heads almost as high as their eyes.

As they stood there, he said to her: "Mary, if I should disappear one of these days — it's not because I'm sliding out; it's because I may be called on business. Understand?"

She looked at him, and saw that he was grave.

"You're afraid of something!" she said.

"Not at all. But there's business in the air."

She said nothing, as they walked back to the house, but at the door he said goodnight, and told her that he was going to stay outside for a walk alone; to watch the moon, he said.

And she, looking at him rather wistfully, put out a hand and touched his arm.

"Speedy," she told him, "I'm through hating you — for tonight!"

"I'm glad of that," said Speedy.

"Do something for me," she begged him.

"Of course I will."

"Be careful, and be good to yourself."

24

He watched the door close after her, and then, turning away, he stood as if irresolute, snapping his fingers together, his head bowed in thought.

For he was in a profound quandary.

It was true that he had befriended Six Wilson, on this night, but Wilson was not a man to be turned from an important object by such an act of kindness.

Now that the bandit had revealed something of his mind to a stranger, the stranger had become a grievance and a danger because he had not fitted himself into the scheme that was in Wilson's mind.

What would Wilson do?

Well, men who have shed blood very often, are likely to turn again to the same method of solving their difficulties. It is a keen knife and severs easily many tough knots.

Now the position was too easy for Six. He was a hunting wolf, and the boy was a quarry that remained in a fixed place. Whenever he pleased, the giant could swoop down on the house of old Steyn with some of his gangsters — and the life of Speedy would be blotted out.

So, revolving the matter deliberately in his mind, the boy saw that there was only one thing remaining for him to do — cut himself adrift from the Steyn house and hunt the hunter until he had disposed of Six Wilson forever.

Now that he had reached a conviction, he started briskly towards the barn. Old Steyn would not grudge him the loan of a horse unasked, he was sure. And a horse he must have to pick up the swift trail of the bandit.

As he passed the corner of the house, he saw a shadow stir behind it — guessed, rather than saw it from the corner of his eye, and his side leap was as swift as the spring of a startled cat. But already there was a hiss at his ear and the falling of a slender shadow. Then his arms were jerked tight against his sides by the pressure of the lariat pulled home. The force of it flung him to the ground.

He did not cry out. There was no one near to bring him help except an old man of seventy, and Mary Steyn herself.

So he lay grimly, and then pushed himself to a sitting posture. Three men stood by him, over him.

"Get up!" growled one, in a subdued voice. He rose.

"Three of us for a job like *this!*" said one voice. "What the devil is the matter with the old man to send out three men for one boy's work?"

"Right about face and march!" snapped another.

Speedy turned obediently about and marched.

He was guided over the rim of the hill to a place where four horses stood, with reins thrown — big, strong-looking animals, standing over plenty of ground.

"Get on that horse, kid," came the order.

"Boss," said Speedy, "if you don't mind, I'll walk. I'm already a little on the raw side!"

A rumble of laughter greeted this remark.

"Don't seem to be such a bad kid," said one. "Hop on that hoss, boy, and stand in the stirrups, if you want to. But we ain't got three men's time to waste on you."

Speedy mounted without further argument, and, as soon as he was in the saddle, a bandanna was tied around his eyes.

"It's no use, boys," said he. "I'm new to all of these mountains. I won't remember the trail, no matter where you take me. Around the corner is lost for me."

"Shut yer face," he was advised. "You got too much lip, kid."

And presently the horse was trotting under

him — a long trot, eased by the silken play of supple fetlock joints. Speedy knew that he had high-priced quality between his knees, now!

Hard rocks rang under the iron-shod hoofs of the animals. Then they scuffed through sand; then they were climbing, climbing, climbing.

After a time, one of his guides said: "Kid, know where we're takin' you?"

"Sure," said the boy, "to a soft bed and a long sleep."

Someone chuckled at this.

"What makes you think it'll be a soft bed?"

"Any bed will be soft for me tonight," said Speedy.

They chuckled again.

"Fresh, ain't he?" was one remark.

"Like paint," said another. "Deacon, does he know why we grabbed him?"

"Kid, you know why we grabbed you?" asked the Deacon.

"Sure," said the boy. "Because I'm a Van Astorbilt in disguise."

They laughed again.

"You're gonna get some of that paint took off of you, kid," said the gruff-voiced Deacon. "But you're makin' a pretty fair start. I like to see 'em start high. They got that much further to fall!"

A few moments later, the horses halted. Someone sang out: "Hello, strangers!"

"Strangers yourself, you wall-eyed, mutton-headed figure four," said the genial Deacon. "Come in here and take these hosses."

"I can't take 'em, Deacon. I'm on the job out here."

"All right, stay there. I hope you catch a hundred degrees of moon-frost, you damn pumpkin-head. Strangers, he says. Strangers, eh! The blind bat, he ain't got the sense of a one-eyed toad. Come on, boy."

A few steps later on, the horses halted again, and this time the boy was told to dismount. He slid gladly to the ground, and stretched himself.

"This way," said the Deacon.

Speedy was led forward. His shoulders rubbed either side of a doorway, and he sensed through the bandanna the shining of a not over-strong light.

"Here he is," said the Deacon. "I dunno why you sent three for this layout. Any pup could of done it as well alone."

Then he added: "Shall I peel this?"

"Yeah, peel it off him," said the expected whisper of big Six Wilson.

The bandanna was jerked forcibly from the head of the boy, and he found himself blinking at a lantern, behind which sat Six Wilson, in the act of attacking a great slab of fried meat. A pint cup of coffee steamed beside his plate, and a huge wedge of cornbread was also at hand.

He was staring out of his clouded, unhuman eyes at the boy.

"They got you easy, did they?" asked he.

"Yeah. They got me," said Speedy. "Any objections if I smoke?"

"Cool and easy right from the start," observed the Deacon.

"Shut up," said Six to the Deacon. "Who told you to shoot off your face, eh? You got him easy, did you?"

The boy was rolling a cigarette. He lighted it as the other said: "Yeah. Just done a stand behind the house, and the fool of a kid walked right in on us, and we doused a rope over him. That was all. He was so scared that when he lay on the ground he didn't even bawl for help!"

He laughed at the memory.

A broad, red man was the Deacon, with immense and beetling brows, and a great hook of a nose. The corners of his mouth twisted upwards when he smiled. He was not handsome, even in the presence of Six Wilson.

"Too scared to bawl out, was he?" asked Six.

"Yeah. I'm telling you."

"You're a fool," said Six. "Is he scared now?"

"He don't know who you are," said the Deacon, "or he'd be on his knees, I'm tellin' you."

"You got sawdust for brains," said Six

Wilson. "This kid knows more about me than you do."

"Yeah?" said the Deacon, dubiously.

"You're all ivory," said the chief. "You oughta be sawed up and sold in chunks for billiard balls. You ain't got no live blood in your bean. That's one of the troubles with you. This is the slickest kid in the country. Fan him."

"I fanned him right off the bat. Whacha think I am?"

"Then gimme the gun that you got off of him."

"I didn't get no gun."

"You lie," said Six, "you beef-faced son of trouble, you lie! Gimme that gun you took off of him!"

"I tell you, I didn't take no gun off of him."

"I tell you again, you lie like a rat!"

"You talk, Six. One of these days, you're gonna shoot off your face too much."

"You'll tame me down — you'll quiet me, will you?" whispered the uncanny voice of the chief.

"I tell you, I didn't find no gun on him!" roared the Deacon.

"Didn't he get no gun off you?" asked Six, pointing his horny finger at the boy.

"No," said Speedy.

"Why didn't you say so before we got into a fight about it?" demanded Six.

"I don't care when you start eating on one another," said Speedy. "You're nothing out of my pantry, either of you."

"No?" murmured Six, with a gleam coming into his dull, whitish eyes.

"No," said the boy, shrugging his shoulders.

"Gimme five minutes alone with him and I'll learn him some manners!" suggested the Deacon.

"Aw, shut up, shut up! How many times I gotta tell you to shut up?" asked Six Wilson.

Then he said in his gasping voice, like the sound that a fish sometimes makes, as it struggles on the shore: "Whatcha do with my gun, kid?"

"Hey, did he have your gun? Where'd he get your gun?" asked the Deacon.

Six Wilson carved off a quarter of a pound of beef and stowed it all in his face by dint of some pushing. Then, his eyes bulging with the effort, he slowly masticated the immense mouthful. His head moved up and down as he worked. And his stare fixed with a painfully thoughtful intensity upon the face of the Deacon.

The latter waited, a little uneasily, until the chief had swallowed a portion of his mouthful.

Then said Six Wilson: "He got it by takin' it out of my hand. Now whacha think of this kid that didn't need three of you to take and hogtie? You're crazy with luck, that's all. The only reason that I sent you three down, was because I expected him to chaw you up. And I wouldn't of missed you none. You only had a pile of luck, damn you!"

25

Speedy had time to look around him, and what he saw was a half ruined shack. The stars peeked through a great rent in the roof. The stove leaned upon rusted and decaying legs, two props of wood helping to support it, and the very flooring was eaten away by time in two large gaps. A single lantern gave the smokey light to the face and the meal of the chief.

"I hear you talk," the Deacon was saying. "Talk don't buy nothin'. I mean, you sent me after the kid; I wished that I'd gone alone!"

"You, kid," said Six Wilson, "whacha do with my gun?"

"Gave it away for a keepsake," said he.

"Gave it — away?" shouted Six.

He half rose from his chair. It was strange to see the grotesque creature moved in this fashion. Sweat actually formed upon his forehead.

"You didn't know," said he, "that that was the fastest and straightest shootin' gat that ever was packed by a man, did you?"

The boy shrugged his shoulders.

"You didn't tell me, Six," said he.

Six Wilson stowed another great carving of meat in his mouth and masticated it with difficulty. Soon the desire to speak came over him and he gave signs of his impatience by glaring at the boy and drumming rapidly upon the table with his bony fingers.

At last partial speech was possible, and it came in a thick, dim roar.

"You been and made a fool of yourself. Know that?" he shouted.

The boy shrugged his shoulders again.

"What's all this lead to?" he asked.

Six Wilson glared at him again, with invincible dislike. Then he said to the Deacon: "What happened, you lucky hound?"

"Aw, just what I said," answered the Deacon. "Just went down there and cached ourselves behind the house and waited for this here tiger, that you'd been tellin' us about. He was talkin' to Mary Steyn in front of the house."

"Was he?"

"Yeah, he was."

"What say?"

"I dunno."

"Take the cotton wool out of your brain and remember!" boomed Six Wilson.

"Well," said the Deacon, "the kid didn't say much. Something about if he disappeared, she was to think that he'd gone on a business trip."

He roared with laughter.

Even Six Wilson smiled, saying: "Yeah, he went on a business trip, all right."

"He sure done that," said Deacon, and they roared in unison.

"What else did she say to him?" said Six.

"Why, she went inside, and the last thing she says is he's to do something for her, and he says he will, and she says, be careful, and be good to himself."

"Is that what she said?" asked Six Wilson, scowling intently on the speaker.

"Take it or leave it. That's what she said."

"She ain't the kind to soft-soap nobody," declared Six Wilson, in deep doubt.

"Take it or leave it," answered the Deacon again, "I heard her say it, with a throb in her voice, too."

"Go on and get out of here," said Wilson. "Get out of here, then. I gotta talk to the kid."

"Where do I chow?"

"You got the whole range to eat in," answered the brutal leader. "Don't bother me. I'm busy."

The Deacon, grumbling loudly, left the shack.

And then, for a time, Six Wilson went on with his meal, watching the boy at times, and at times glancing away in the profundity of his speculation.

Speedy, in the meantime, had found a stool

which he sat upon, uneasily.

But he composed his face and strove to show no doubt or trouble.

The meal of Six Wilson did not occupy a great space in time, to be sure. But the moments dragged, rather naturally, for the boy.

At last, Wilson poured himself his third cup of coffee, and wiped his greasy mouth on the back of his hand. He began to roll a smoke and gather his darkest frown.

"Kid!" said he.

The boy answered nothing.

"Kid," said Wilson, "we gotta talk."

Still Speedy said nothing.

"Dumb?" asked Wilson, his voice lifting to the question.

"Waiting to hear what you'll talk about," said Speedy.

"You couldn't guess, eh?"

"No. I don't care to guess."

"Ain't interested, eh?"

"Look," said the boy, making a gesture. "You've got me. You can slam me with a club or a knife or a gun. All right. That's that. I'm not worrying. The world will get on without me, pretty well, and I'll have to get along without the world. That's all."

He even smiled, and the other regarded him over the rim of the cup as he swallowed down his last, scalding portion of coffee. Then he pushed the cup away, with a rattle.

"You make it simpler than it is, son," said the tall man. "This what I'm talkin' to you about is the difference between heaven and hell."

The boy considered him for a moment.

"You hear me?" roared Six Wilson, suddenly.

"I'll tell you a story," said Speedy.

Wilson nodded and grinned.

"I wanta hear you talk some," he agreed.

He crossed his legs and settled back.

"Make that story damned good, and pronto," said he.

"I'll make it good," said the other. "Open the flap of your ears, will you?"

"They're open."

"How long can a man live without food or water, in hot weather?"

"Four days," said the other, with much certainty.

He even made a wry face. "I could tell you a story about five days on the desert," said he.

"This story is about a boxcar. A refrigerator car that was locked down, and left on a siding, a thousand miles from nothing, with me inside of it."

"You got me interested from the start," remarked the chief.

"You know Arizona in August?"

"Yeah, I know; hell in December, too. Go on."

"It was a brand new car. I guess that was why it had been sidetracked in the middle of nowhere."

"I know," said the bandit. "Got no brains, on railroads. Just meanness."

"That's right," agreed the boy. "Well, there I was inside of the car, and I had along with me one pocket knife. Small blades, but good steel."

"You cut your way through, eh?"

"I cut for five days and five nights," said the boy. "It was slow work. I got dizzy. The knife was always slipping in the blood that ran out of my hands."

"A thing that I've noticed a lot of times," said Six. "The way blood's slippery."

"It's slippery, all right," said Speedy. "Finally, I flopped."

"Went out, eh?"

"Yes. I broke the last blade of the knife, and that made me pretty tired."

"You waked up, though."

"You see me sitting here," said the boy. "I woke up and looked at the work that I'd done. It was easy to see, because it was painted red all around. Only the bottom of the grooves was white where the last cutting had been done. I had no knife, but it seemed to me that those grooves were pretty deep, so I backed up across the width of the car and let drive and hit it with my shoulder — and fell right out into the daylight."

"And found water, eh?"

"I told you that siding was the middle of nowhere. I started hoofing down the track. I was pretty dizzy. It was August, in Arizona."

Six Wilson licked his lips.

"I'm gunna have another whack of that coffee," said he, and was instantly as good as his word.

"Go on," said Six.

"After a while," said the boy, "a train came along. That was the end of the fifth day. I stood in the middle of the track and waved my hands. But the train kept on coming. I saw the engineer leaning out the window and laughing at me. I wasn't very trim in my dressing, just then."

He nodded at the memory.

"Go on!" said Six Wilson.

"Well," said the boy, "when I saw he was coming right on through me, I first thought that I would let the train finish me off, because that way would be so much quicker. But then I decided that I had one good reason for wanting to live."

"To find that engineer, eh?"

"He was a *big* hound," said the boy, "and he laughed till his ears wiggled. So I side-stepped and saw the train go roaring by me, filling my eyes with dust and cinders. Then I humped along down the track. It was ten miles to water."

"Did you ever meet up with that engineer?" asked the other.

"It's a small world," commented Speedy. "I met him in Denver, on the street. I tapped him on the shoulder and asked him if he remembered me. And the surprising thing was that he did, Six, though I was all dressed up at the moment."

"What did you do to him?" asked Six, grinning like a man thirsty for cold drink.

"That crook was fond of cards," said the boy. "That's what I did to him."

"Busted him?"

"I busted everything about him and put him on the bum. He got a gun and came for me, but I had all the luck. That sounds like boasting, though."

"It's all right with me," said Six Wilson. "But what's the point of this little story?"

"I thought you were talking about hell," said Speedy.

Suddenly the other leaned forward and nodded.

"All right," he said. "If I was bluffing, you've called my bluff. Whatever happens between you and me will be fast."

26

He was in no hurry to continue, however. At last he said: "You done me a good turn at the schoolhouse, son."

Speedy watched him, and waited.

"But?" suggested Speedy.

The other grinned.

"I kinda like you, kid," said he. "You're hard-boiled. That's what you are. I like 'em hard-boiled. You been around. That's where you been."

Still Speedy waited, and this time without comment of any kind.

"What I was gunna say," continued the other, "is this. You and me together could get on like nothing at all."

Speedy nodded.

"But agin one another, we couldn't get on at all!"

The boy watched him carefully. Finally he said: "Why not, big boy? It's a fairly big world. I'm not crowding your show, so far as I know."

Six Wilson shrugged his shoulders.

"Listen, kid," said he. "You're crowding Mary Steyn, ain't you?"

"She doesn't care a rap about me."

"She asks you to be careful of yourself."

"I won't argue, if you take that line."

"Speedy," said Six Wilson, "you're a bright kid. You're one of the slickest and the smoothest that ever happened. I never met up with nobody that I could take a real fast likin' to quicker than I could to you. Know what I mean?"

"Thanks," said the boy. "You certainly are the little flatterer, Six. You make me blush!"

Six Wilson laughed with a genuine enjoyment.

"Maybe you think that you'd get along better without me than you would with me," said he. "But you're wrong. I'll tell you how wrong you are."

"Go on and tell me," said the boy. "I've got to listen."

"Keep your first seat," said Wilson. "Don't get five inches nearer to that door, or I'll shoot the brains out of your head, son!"

He laid a revolver on the table as he spoke; but he had not raised his voice.

However, Speedy took his first seat. He knew business when he heard it.

"The kid is soft on you," declared Six Wilson. "She likes you. She tells you to go and be good to yourself. That's what she tells you. She don't never talk to the boys like that. I've heard her, and I've heard reports of her. You've socked her in the right spot. She likes you."

Speedy listened once more without reply. He saw that argument was not invited.

"She'll marry you," said the tall man, nodding with conviction. "And the man that she marries has gotta throw in with me; or else she'll marry him dead!"

He cleared his throat; his husky, whispering, horrible voice went on:

"You dunno, what time I've put in on that case. It took me a whole year of my own money and time to work up the case. When I learned what it was all about, I couldn't go ahead and collect. No, I had to sit still and wait. Three years I waited. Waited for the right man to come along. The man that she'd hook up with. And he never come. Or, if he come, he wasn't the kind that I could work with. He was a slippery sneak, or something. He wasn't the right kind."

"You wanted an honest man, like me," suggested the boy, ironically.

"You're a tough kid," said the other, "but you'd keep your promises. That's what's held you back from your fortune, more'n once. You been too clean in the pinches. Ain't I right?"

Speedy shrugged his shoulders.

"It's the trouble with a lot of good yeggs," said Six Wilson. "It's the trouble with Snapper Dan McGuire, come to that. I ain't got a better man than Snapper Dan. But he's got too much conscience. He lets the under dog up, too many times. Can't make money like that."

"No," agreed Speedy.

"If you gave me your word that you'd split with me, I could trust your promise."

He added: "Ain't I right? No, you don't have to answer that. I know. I can tell a man by what's in his face and his eye. He don't have to talk to me. Now, kid, the girl will marry you; she's the key to nine million; if I let you go free, you marry her, but you don't split with me. Not unless I get the promise out of you. I've got you in my hands now, Mr. Fish. And you don't jump back into the sea. No, not till you've given me your promise that you split the coin with me."

Speedy sighed.

"So you see," said Six Wilson, "you might as well knuckle under. It's a bargain for you. Without me, she ain't worth a nickel. With me, she's worth nine million. I lead you both right by the hand to it. Understand?"

The boy nodded.

"Suppose I say no?" said he.

"You ain't such a fool," said Six Wilson. "But if you should be, you're a dead man, kid!"

"I'll take tonight to think it over," said the boy.

"Is that the way?" whispered Six Wilson. "You're too good to do business with me, are you?"

"I didn't say that."

"You meant it, though! You want a night to think it over? You lie! You want a night to slide out of this!"

He deliberately picked up the revolver and sighted down the barrel. There was no mercy in his relentless eyes.

"Now you talk, Mr. Turkey," said he. "You talk, or you be damned."

"Don't be a fool," said the boy, calmly, looking back at the round, black muzzle of the gun. "You don't throw away four and a half millions like this."

"Don't I?" snarled the other. "I give you five seconds to see if I don't."

"I take tonight to think it over," answered Speedy. "I said that I'd need tonight to think it over, and I'll have tonight. If you don't like that deal, you can be damned, for all I care — and shoot when you're ready, Wilson!"

Slowly, he saw the gun lower.

"You're a tricky young snake," said the other. "I oughta put a slug into you now. But I got a kind of a weakening, just this minute, thinkin' of how you turned that pack of hounds back there at the Nixon school, when they had the taste of me, and was all ready to lap me up like warm milk. I kind of weaken for a minute, but I know that I'm a fool. I ought to take and slam you now. No good'll come out of waiting. Because no matter what you say, you've made up your mind already. But I'm gunna take the chance. Might be you need a sleep under your belt. There's many a man that's a hero after supper that's weak in the knees before breakfast."

He laughed in his soundless way, as he suggested this.

Then, putting two fingers between his lips, he emitted a shrill, ear-cutting whistle.

The Deacon strode through the doorway a moment later.

"Call Snapper Dan," said the chief.

"Yeah; all right."

"You and him has got work together, tonight," said Six Wilson in continuation.

"Him and me? Not him and me!" said the Deacon. "I'll work with anybody else, but I won't work with him."

"You won't?"

"I've told you that before. Him and me, we don't get along. The little runt thinks he's a better man than me. I'm gunna murder him, one of these days. I'm gunna take him apart and see what's wrong with his insides!"

"You beef-faced fool!" said the chief, "call in Snapper Dan!"

The latter still hesitated, but only for a moment. He was crimson with excitement, when he turned to the door and bellowed:

"Snapper! Hey! Come here, runt!"

"That's a good start for the pair of you tonight," said Six Wilson, "but that's the way I want it."

Rapid footfalls came. And then a small man, with a face as lean as a knife and eyes small and black as beads came into the room. He wore the high heels of the dandy, the high heels of the small man who wishes to appear taller than nature made him.

"Who called me runt?" he asked, staring fiercely at the Deacon.

The lip of the big man curled with angry disdain.

"The chief wants you," said he, shortly.

"Who called me runt?" insisted Snapper Dan.

"Shut up!" said the gasping voice of Six Wilson.

Snapper Dan was silent, but his lips moved with inaudible threats as he continued to stare at the Deacon.

"Listen," said Six Wilson. "The pair of you listen, and listen hard, too. You hear me?"

They faced towards him at last.

"The two of you," said the chief, "are gunna spend the night in the shack, here. I'm gunna sleep out. They been too close on my heels, lately. They've offered too big a reward, too. I'll trust you boys when I got my eyes on you, the rest of the time, from now on, I'm sleeping out. Tonight, you move your rolls in here. And you're gunna have company. The company you'll have is the kid, here!"

He pointed at the boy. Neither of them favored Speedy with a glance. Their attention was reserved for one another, still glaring wickedly.

"You'll keep each other awake," said Six Wilson, "and the first fellow to sleep, the other one has my permission to slam him. Slam him hard, and no comeback!"

He laughed and rubbed his hands.

"You'll hear some pretty sweet conversation between these two!" he concluded to the boy. "You two get your things in here!"

They departed at once, and while they were gone, Six Wilson personally tied Speedy hand and foot. It was a good job — not quite enough to paralyze all circulation, and yet enough to make the ropes bite deeply. He tied the ropes with heavy knots. In the meantime, the other two returned, and Wilson went on:

"If the kid so much as takes one roll towards the door, shoot him. If he does anything else funny, salt him away with lead. If he's dead in the morning, when I come in, I ain't gunna call it murder; that's all I gotta say. Mind you, he's slick, mean and worse'n a snake for danger, I tell you. Believe me that I'm right!"

27

At the door, before leaving, Six Wilson turned towards the boy, and said: "Tonight, you think. Or it's your last night! You savvy?"

And he strode off into the darkness, carrying blankets.

There was no regret in Speedy as he watched the chief go. He had known bad men, in his life, but never one who in one evening could return so much evil for good as Six Wilson had done. Humanity was not in the fellow, nor decency, nor any trace of human kindness.

The two who had been chosen as guards now were left alone with Speedy, and regarded one another silently, for some time.

Then the Deacon said: "Go on and roll in and sleep. I'd rather sit out the watch all by myself than have your sneakin' birdeyes open and watchin' me."

"Deacon," said the other, his voice trembling with passion, "there's only one way to do this — with your mouth shut!"

And then he set deliberately about making

down his blankets. The Deacon, after a snarling moment, followed his example. The Snapper, finishing first, put on a pot of coffee. And the Deacon, without asking if there were coffee enough in the pot for two, picked up a rusty pan and began to prepare coffee for himself. No words were heard until the Deacon, crossing the floor in some haste, pretended to find Speedy in the way. Brutally, with the full force of his thick leg, he kicked the limp body out of the way. Speedy was rolled over on his face. He thought, at first, that his hip had been broken by the impact, but gradually the numbness turned into a spreading pain. He rolled over on his back again and was still, smiling a little at the ceiling. Cold hell was in his heart.

The Deacon sat down on a stool at the table with his coffee. The Snapper sat down in the chair, in an opposite corner.

"Snapper," said the boy, "you're Snapper Dan McGuire, aren't you?"

There was a moment of silence.

Then: "What's that to you?" demanded the Snapper.

"I just wondered," said Speedy, half closing his eyes and shaking his head. "I'd heard a lot about you. I didn't think —"

He paused.

"You heard about me, eh? Where'd you hear about me?" asked the Snapper, suspiciously.

"Where? Oh, everywhere! I guess every cop in the land knows about Snapper Dan McGuire."

"He's pulling your leg, Dan," said the Deacon.

"Shut your face," advised the Snapper. "I ain't talkin' to you. I ain't wantin' to talk to you."

The Deacon growled like a sullen dog. Said the Snapper:

"Where you been, to hear about me kid?"

"Montreal," said the boy, "was the first place, I think. I met a fellow called Side-wheel Dugan."

"Hey, you knew Side-wheel, did you?"

"Yes, and a rat he was, but he admired you a lot."

He had struck at random on the name of Dugan, simply because the latter had been over most of the country. It was luck that Snapper really knew of him.

"Yeah, he was a rat," said the Snapper. "But he was kind of funny. I mean to listen to the way he had of talking."

"Yeah, he was funny," said the boy. "That's what surprised me — I mean, after hearing what he said for you."

"What surprised you, kid?"

"Why, he said that you never took a sidestep for the sake of dodging any big thug; nor for the sake of kicking anybody in the face when he was down."

"I don't dodge no big thug," said the other. "If they're big, I whittle 'em down to my own size. And who'd I ever kick in the face when he was down?"

"You kicked me," said the boy.

"That's a lie," said the Snapper. "The Deacon did that."

"It's just the same," said the boy. "You stood by and let the big hound do it — the big, blow-hard!"

The Deacon swayed to his feet.

"You *do* get it in the face, this time," said he.

Speedy laughed.

"Go on. Let him do it, Snapper," said he. "I'll live through it, and I'll tell the boys the truth about you!"

"Hold up, Deacon," said the Snapper.

"He's pulling your leg," said the Deacon.

"Maybe he is."

"You — the Snapper — the gentleman!" sneered Speedy. "The dead-shot Dick, the finest man in the world with a knife! I see the truth about you, now."

"Do you?" asked the Snapper, dangerously.

"Yeah, I see it. You're just a cheap yegg, like that pile of red beef, there!"

"I'm gunna kill him!" choked the Deacon, and strode forward.

The Snapper laid the muzzle of a Colt gently in the pit of the Deacon's stomach.

"Back up, sweetheart," said he.

The big man recoiled.

"You jackass," said he, "are you gunna swaller that soft soap?"

"I'm gunna skin him alive," said the Snapper, "but I'm gunna do it for my own self."

"Go on, then," said the Deacon. "I don't mind watchin' you."

The Snapper, at this, resheathed his gun, and turned a cruel, birdlike face towards the captive.

"By the Lord," exclaimed the boy, "it *is* true, and you're not afraid of 'em, no matter how big they come."

"Who said I was afraid?" asked the Snapper.

"Why," said the boy, "what I always heard was that you were a runt, but that you had the biggest heart in the world. But when I saw the Deacon — I thought that he could open his mouth and swallow you. But I've just seen him back up. He turned green, too, when he did it!"

"You lie!" said the Deacon.

The Snapper laughed with great enjoyment.

"Did he turn green?" he asked of the boy, with the highest good nature.

"I saw him," said Speedy.

"You lie!" shouted the Deacon.

"Oh, that's all right," said the boy, "but I

know what I saw. He's afraid of you, Snapper. I saw his hand jump for his gun, and then come away again. The big yellow-livered tramp!"

"Did he make a move for his gun?" asked the Snapper.

And he laughed again, leering at the Deacon.

"Why, I'm gunna eat you, kid!" said the Deacon. "I'm gunna pulverize you, and then swaller the fragments!"

He started towards the boy again.

"Hold up, leave him be," said the Snapper, with an imperial air. "He kind of interests me, the way that he sort of talks."

"Who are you," asked the Deacon, "to tell me to hold up?"

"I'll tell you who he is!" broke in the boy.

"Shut yer mouth!" shouted the Deacon. "I'm talkin' to you, Snapper. Whacha mean by tellin' me to hold up?"

The Snapper toyed, not with a gun, but with the long handle of a knife that protruded above his belt.

"You tell him, kid, if you got any idea," he said.

"I'll tell him," said Speedy, "because I know. He told you to hold up because he's a better man than you are, Deacon, and in your sneaking heart you know it!"

"By God!" breathed the Deacon.

And his face swelled, and was splotched with

purple. He stood swaying a moment, his hands extended, the fingers stiff, prepared for taking hold of some living thing and throttling and tearing it.

"I ain't hearing straight," said Deacon. "I'm crazy in the head."

"You're not crazy," said the boy. "You're only a big four-flusher, and now I'm seeing your bluff called!"

"Snapper," gasped the big man, "fill your hand!"

And, at the same time, he snatched at his own Colt.

Perhaps passion made his big fingers stumble. At any rate, he was easily and distinctly beaten to the draw. Cleanly and clearly was he beaten by the flashing hand of the Snapper.

The first bullet of the little man hit the Deacon in the middle of his body and doubled him up so quickly that the second, aimed for the head, smashed into the wall, instead.

But, though he was dying on his feet, the Deacon, for all his brutality was a brave man, and determined to live long enough to kill his enemy.

Before a third shot could fly from the Snapper's weapon, the little man was hit, and the weight of the shot knocked him flat.

The Deacon laughed. A red gush of blood cut that laughter short, and he began to sink to his knees, a dreadful sight.

Speedy, in the meantime, had not lost an instant.

One second had not been occupied by that gunplay. The next second, rolling across the floor, the boy had put his teeth in the haft of the Snapper's knife, and still holding it firmly gripped, he drove the point into the floor. That made a secure, firmly held edge, and one brush of the rope against it gave Speedy free hands.

He was reaching for the ropes that held his feet when he saw the big Deacon, now on his knees, his crimsoned face frightfully contorted, one hand gripping his death-wound, lift his revolver and cover the escaping captive.

Understanding was in the face of the dying man; well he knew that his destruction flowed from the talk of the boy, and he meant to pay him in full. But he was blind with the coming of the long night. The gun shook crazily in his hand, and the bullet that he fired was wide of his mark, as Speedy leaped up.

He saw the Deacon pitching forward, like a slowly leaning tower, on his face, and as he went, the boy snatched the gun which lay beside the Snapper.

The little man stirred and groaned at the same time.

Now came a rushing footfall.

"Who's here? What the devil's loose?" gasped

the whispering voice of Six Wilson, thrusting the door open and rushing into the room.

"Yours truly," said the boy, and gave Six the heel of the Snapper's heavy gun full between the eyes.

He pushed the toppling body out of his way, and raced on into the open.

28

He was not alone, as he sprinted out of the shack, with the voice of Six Wilson gasping behind him.

He saw forms running, and the gleam of weapons in their hands, but all very dimly, for a cloud had gathered over the stars and the moon, and the night was thick.

He saw horses, too, and for them he made, wondering why people did not cut in to intercept him. Instead, they all made for the house. A pleasant scene they would find there, something that would make them riper than ever for murder. Well, perhaps necessity had widened his eyes.

As he came closer, he saw the horses fling up their heads from grazing, but they did not run away; they were all hobbled short.

Nearby was a great heap of tackle. He grabbed a bridle that lay on top; there seemed no time for anything else. And then he selected the tallest horse of the lot, one so black that it was more perfectly lost in the night than any of the rest. It closed its teeth hard against the bit. He remembered having seen people put their thumbs inside the mouth of a refractory horse in order to make it yawn for the bit. He tried this with no success.

He had seen others take a cruel turn on the upper lip for the same object. This he tried now, and instantly the black horse admitted the bit.

It was high time, to be sure.

Behind him, from the house, he heard an outbreak of many voices. And, above them, the whining, barking cry of Snapper Dan, yelling curses.

Well, Snapper had plenty of reasons to be irritated; the bullet that had knocked him down was one of them.

And, out of the shack, streamed many forms, one taller than the rest, running ahead of all the others with gigantic strides. That was Six Wilson. He knew the man as well as though a spotlight had been cast upon him, for a sense of loathing reached to the boy even this far through the dark.

He sprang, therefore, on the back of the big horse. He only delayed to open his pocket knife and slash the hobbles. And the instant that its feet were free and the man on its back, the black giant started running.

One jump, and the quivering of its loins

seemed to show that it was settling to its power, and feeling its stride. Another jump, and it thrust out its head and jerked the reins through the hands of Speedy to the very end of them. Lucky for him that they were well knotted! Then the big fellow began to run in such a way as Speedy had never seen, never had ridden, save in wild dreams.

It made straight for a patch of shrubbery and smashed through it. It headed on towards a wilderness of rocks.

"He's crazy mad with fear," thought the boy, and sawed with all his might at the reins.

As well pull at a mountain as strive to influence that mouth of iron and the arching neck behind it!

He considered casting himself to the ground. But the ground was covered with pointed stones that he could see. To throw himself down at that speed would be like flinging himself into the mouth of a dragon. He would be pierced or crushed to death by the fall.

And then they went through the rocks.

They reached for him like spear points, they reached for him like hands, as it seemed, but still he was brought wavering through the peril by the big charger. It was as though water flowed through the interstices, dodging actively, and yet smoothly. There were eyes and brains in the very feet of this flying monster!

Then, through the hedge of rocks, they came into the open, and sped.

He did not know where he was, where they might be bound. Only he saw before him a ragged range of mountains, and in the midst of it two lofty peaks, with a level place between them. They looked to Speedy like the outward canted ears of a donkey, and the round head between the ears. Was it a pass towards which the big horse was running?

Now, it turned sharply to the right. The white ghost of dead cactus of great size had sufficed to make it change its course.

And still it ran as a bird might fly. Without a saddle it was easier to sit that matchless gait, like the blowing of wind, than to stick on the back of an ordinary animal, such as those Speedy had recently ridden.

And now he saw before him, and to the right, very dimly, far in the night, several forms of riders, vaguely silhouetted.

He jerked with all his might against the mouth of the big animal. It was merely to urge him faster ahead.

He looked back over his shoulder.

Others were there behind — three or four, he could not tell.

Well, it was plain that he was lost. If only the black had kept straight on, his matchless speed would have made all well, but his change of direction had enabled the others to follow the beat of hoofs and come up.

A gun cracked behind him — a thin, absurdly small sound, but not absurd was the whiz of the bullet past his ear. They could shoot well even in the dark, these men of Six Wilson!

On went the black.

And then Speedy saw the end of the world, and knew that he was dead.

He had thought that the ground merely dipped down before him, suddenly.

Now he was aware that it dipped indeed — that it was a cliff, in fact, and for the edge of that cliff plunged his horse! Nothing could stop him! Why did not Speedy fling himself, then, to the ground, and give himself broken bones, but a chance of life?

It was because he could see the face of Six Wilson, in vivid prospect, when the monster would lean over him and, perhaps, strike a match to make out the extent of his victim's sufferings. Better to leap the cliff and die swiftly and sweetly in one instant than to endure what Six Wilson might pour out for him in the way of bitterness.

He was not fifty feet from the nearing riders on his right, as he came towards the edge of the rocks.

Why did they not open fire? Because one of them was shouting lustily: "Don't shoot! That's

Coal Tar! Don't shoot or the chief will pull your hides off over your heads!"

He even had time to think of that, to grin faintly at the conception, while the stiff gale of the gallop got inside his mouth and puffed his cheeks.

Then he jerked downwards over the rim of the rock.

Down to quick death, he thought. He relaxed his whole body. His shoulders were loose, and his head rolled a little, his face tilting upwards.

So loose was he on the sweating, hot back of the horse that the first shock almost knocked him to the ground. But true it was that the black had found a footing.

How could he have found it? Never, if he had not been mountain bred, with winged feet, and the wits of a goat. Looking down, aghast, the boy saw what seemed a sheer descent – no, there were here and there dim ridges thrusting out a little; but the angle of the horse's body was such that Speedy had to wind both hands into the wisp of mane above the withers and, so braced, he held himself on with difficulty.

For as a goat goes down a flumelike crevice, bounding from side to side, its nose thrust down almost as low as its feet, its four legs bunched dexterously together to break the shocks of landing, so did the black horse go down the cliff of that great rock.

Despair turned into terror, in the heart of Speedy, and terror into wild hope of life, and that hope into vast exultation.

"I'm riding the king of the world!" he told himself. "I'm riding the only horse in the world. Old Coal Tar! Old hero!"

And, suddenly, as water after a cataract strikes a smooth slope, and straightens, and gathers speed again, and rushes almost soundlessly along, so the big horse gathered his stride, and, flowing noiselessly, over soft ground, swept along a valley that widened, momentarily, to the right and to the left, as smaller ravines dropped down into it.

There was no slackening in the tremendous gallop of the big creature. He went as though he trusted the wind of his gallop to blow the rider from his back.

But fear had left the boy, so long as he was on the back of this magic thing. He merely laughed at the flight of the wind past his face. With one free hand he slapped the wet neck, and he called aloud the name of the horse, and sang it to the sweeping sky above him.

At that, to his surprise, the dead run of Coal Tar changed, drew into a gallop, and finally became an easy, swinging canter.

He was breathing hard. His swelling sides, at every breath, forced out the knees of Speedy; but he ran, now, with his head turned a little, and he seemed to be studying his new rider through the darkness.

In another moment, he was as docile in the hand of Speedy as a family pony with the youngest child of the house on its back!

The same joy, the same trust flowed out of the heart of Speedy towards the gallant fellow.

And then that joy of his turned into a deeper and soberer pleasure. It was a very odd feeling, but as though a voice had spoken at his ear and told him that he was saved for some purpose different from the old course of his life.

Then he drew the black to a halt, and listened. There was no sound behind him. All the danger from Six Wilson and his band of human hornets was far to the rear. Whatever way they followed would not be down the face of that rock he could well guess.

In the meantime, this sea of mountains that surrounded the valley was a mystery to him; the very waves of the ocean could not have been more similar one to another than were these peaks to his unaccustomed eyes.

He rode on again, at a walk, trying to think back to the most likely direction in which he could find the way to the house of Steyn, and in a moment, he caught a flickering of light far away and to his left.

He laughed with the pleasure of that sight, and turned the horse towards it at a trot, at a canter. From this point he could quickly get the proper directions. All worry dropped like a useless cloak from his shoulders.

29

It was the sort of a house he would have expected to find, low, rather long for its height and width, a shed or two nearby, and a tangle of corral fencing. That was all.

A dog ran out and barked at the feet of the big horse; and Coal Tar went straight forward, striking with his forehoofs. The dog fled; Speedy laughed. And in the midst of his laughter the door of the lighted room opened and a man stood in the opening, with the glow from behind surrounding his face with a halo where it struck through a dense brush of hair and beard.

"Who the devil's here?" asked the mountaineer.

"A friend in need," said Speedy, good-naturedly.

"Yeah, everybody's in need. You don't get no handouts here, bum," said the other, and started to close the door.

"Hold on," said Speedy. "I want some directions. I don't want a handout."

The other threw the door wide again.

"You want what?" he asked.

"Directions," said Speedy, and dismounted.

"Directions to what?" asked the man of the mountains.

"Directions to get out of this valley," said Speedy.

"He's lost his way, Pete," said a woman's snarling voice.

"He wants directions, Annie," repeated Pete, helplessly.

"He's lost his way, that's all," said she.

"He's gone and lost his way?" said Pete. "How could anybody lose his way, I wanta know, up here? This ain't a desert or the ocean, is it?"

Said Speedy: "I want to find out the shortest way to get to —"

"Hold on. Are you lost?" asked Pete.

"Yes. I'm lost."

"How come you're lost?" said Pete. "Ain't that Mount Tozer, and ain't that old Baldy, and ain't that Twister Mountain, yonder?"

"I suppose that those are the names," said the boy. "But I couldn't know that. I never saw them before."

"He never seen them before, he says," remarked Pete, over his shoulder.

"I don't know north from south," said Speedy.

"Can't you look at the stars and tell?" asked Pete.

"The stars are covered up behind those clouds," said the boy.

"Well," said Pete, "you're right, for once. Where you wanta go?"

"I want to find the house of a friend of mine."

"What in hell does that help me to know where he lives?" demanded Pete.

"I wanted to tell you his name. He's Arthur Steyn. Do you know him?"

"Steyn? Yeah, I seen Steyn once."

"You don't know where he lives?"

"Well, maybe I don't, but I could find out, if I wanted to."

He said it sullenly. He seemed aggrieved because a name had been mentioned to whose house he did not know the way.

"If he can pay his way, he can stay for the night," said the voice of Annie.

"Yeah, you could stay for the night," said Pete, nodding his head into darkness and swaying it up into the light again. "If you can pay, we'll put you up."

This was not the mountain hospitality to which the boy was growing accustomed. It was not the same breed of which he had heard so many tales.

"I don't want to spend the night," said the boy.

Far indeed was he from that wish, with such pursuers as the Wilson gang somewhere on his trail.

"But," he added, "if you can find out where I can find the right trail, I'll pay you well for that. I have to be moving on."

"Well," said Pete, "you oughta know that you can't buy what a man ain't got to sell."

And he was starting to close the door again when the woman called out:

"Wait a minute, Pete. We got that old map of the county. If he's got a brain in his head, he'll know some place near the Steyn house."

"I can find my way back from the Nixon schoolhouse," said Speedy.

"Well, the schoolhouse would be on the map," said Pete. "Come on in then. Wait a minute. It's a tolerable lot of trouble, to start to readin' a map at this here time of night. It'll cost you fifty cents, about, to find out where the Nixon schoolhouse is."

"Well, that's all right," said the boy.

He tied the reins of the horse to the hitching rack, as he spoke, and then started for the door.

Pete had come out a step or two.

"Darn my socks," said he, "there ain't no saddle on that hoss!"

"I was a little rushed, when I started on this trip," said Speedy, smiling.

"Hey, Annie," said Pete, "doggone me if

there's a saddle on his hoss."

"You don't say!" cried the woman, her voice going up the scale.

"It's a whoppin' biggish hoss, though," said Pete. "Well, come on in."

The boy stepped through the door into a hovel. Behind one partition, he heard cattle munching hay; behind the other, chickens stirred and complained sleepily on their perches, then were quiet again. And in the one occupied room there was a bare, earthen floor, a stove in a corner, two bunks built one above the other. And that was all. Yes, a homemade broom here, worn clothes hanging from pegs, a board across a pair of sawbucks by way of a table, a gun, a fishing rod. Little else. Some greasy tin dishes littered the table.

And in a chair beside the table sat a hag bent with age, but her arm, bare to the elbow, was sinewy with strength, nevertheless. From under a gray mat of hair, perennially bright and youthful eyes looked up at the stranger.

"Come in and rest your feet," said she.

Speedy stood by the table and made himself smile at that face, deformed by long hatred of all the world.

"I don't need to sit down," said he. "I simply want a look at that map of yours, and then I'll go. There's the fifty cents."

She picked up the coin which he put on the

table, frowned at it, spun it in the air, and rang it on the wood.

"Yeah. Maybe that's all right," said she. And she thrust the money into a pocket of her man's coat. It had been brown once. It was chiefly gray-green, now.

"You gone and got yourself all sweated up, ridin' a hoss without a saddle," said she. "Don't you know no better'n that?"

"I had to make a quick start," said the boy.

"I call it kind of disgustin'," said Annie.

And her upper lip curled with distaste, as she looked him over.

"You ain't from these parts, I reckon," said she.

"No," said Speedy.

"I reckoned as how you wasn't," she answered, with a disapproving shake of her head. "What made you start so quick that you couldn't stay for a saddle?"

"It's a long story," said Speedy.

"Well, I got time to listen," said she.

"I haven't time to tell it, though," said Speedy.

He turned impatiently towards the door, wondering what kept Pete so long, but as he waited, Pete in person strode through the door, adjusting the half suspender that held up his greasy overalls and frowning with a very magisterial air. The frown was directed towards the boy.

"Where'd you get that hoss?" asked Pete.

And, as he spoke, he gave a point to his question by drawing out an incredible length of revolver from beneath his ragged coat.

"Where'd you get him?" he demanded.

Speedy was stumped.

And then it seemed to him that there was only one thing for him to do — tell the truth. A theft of a horse, in this region of the world was, as he well knew, an offense as terrible as murder. More grimly punished because more despised, in fact. But a theft from an outlaw was not a theft at all.

"That's Six-card Wilson's horse — or one of his horses," said he.

"Hey!" broke in Annie. "One of Six's hosses? Which one?"

"Not no less'n Coal Tar!" said the man of the house, grimly.

"Coal Tar!" she cried.

She turned on the boy and pointed with her dirt-blackened hand.

"I reckon that you was in a considerable of a hurry when you got on that hoss, you sneakin' thief, you! Fifty cents, eh? Turn out his pockets, Pete. A thief like him, that steals from Six Wilson — what're we gunna do? Let him get away with nothin'? I hope to tell that he ain't gunna get away with nothin'."

"You want me to turn out his pockets?" asked Pete.

"Yeah, ain't I just told you to? D'you know better than me? You fuzzy-headed fool, you!"

Pete ran his thumb under the strap of his suspender and smiled with the superiority of his idea.

"You got a good head on your shoulders, Annie," said he. "You was bright even when you was a girl. Too damn bright, you mighty well know, or we'd be rollin' in money, instead of leadin' not much more'n a dog's life, up here at the end of time. You got a good head on your shoulders, but this time you're wrong."

"You go and tell me why," said Annie, "and stop talkin' about what's done and ended, will you?"

"I'll tell you why," said Pete. "This here — he's gone and stole Wilson's hoss, ain't he?"

"Yes, he has."

"How can a man steal from a thief?" broke in Speedy. "Wilson wanted to murder me —"

"Shut yer face or I'll bash in yer teeth with the butt of the gun," directed Pete. "He wanted to murder you, did he? You hear that, Annie? Six wanted to murder him. Well, then, would Six be kind of pleased or not pleased, if he was to come along down this trail and find his man held here good and safe in our house?"

"I was thinkin' that," said she.

"And if Six got here and found that this here thief hadn't been touched, and that everything about him was just the way we picked him up — I mean, if all of that was pointed out to him, would he be pleased, I ask you, or would he rather find the bird picked?"

"It's true," said the woman. "You got an idea for once in your life. Go out on the hill and swing the lantern, and give the signal ten times over, if you have to, till you get an answer from up the pass."

30

A thousand impulses flashed through the brain of Speedy. He remembered, well enough, the heavy gun he had stolen from Snapper Dan as the latter lay on the floor of Wilson's hut. He might draw that, but the easy and confident way in which Pete handled his own weapon showed that he was a master of it.

Plainly that was a part of the world where one needed a knowledge of guns of all kinds, and of revolvers in particular.

"I'm to go out on the hill, am I?" said Pete. "And let this bird fly out of the coop while I'm gone? You're a fool, Annie. You go out and swing the lantern yourself!"

"I'll see you rot, first," said Annie. "Ain't I got rheumatism or something clean across my back, and you want me to go and stand out there in the night air, do you."

Pete did not debate the point of her rheumatism. He simply said: "Well, how we gunna make sure of this here thief, will you tell me that?"

"Reach me that there shotgun," said the hag.

He side-stepped, keeping a strict eye on Speedy, and handed her the heavy, old-fashioned weapon.

"Is it loaded?" said she.

"Yeah. It's loaded."

"With buckshot?"

"Whacha think? With birdseed?"

"Gimme no more of your flip back talk," said Annie.

She laid the shotgun across the table, pointing the barrels at the breast of the boy. And she curled a capable forefinger around both of the triggers.

"Now go out and swing that lantern, like I was tellin' you to do," said Annie.

"You'll keep care of him?" asked Pete, dubiously.

"Say," said she, "if you was standin' there in his socks, would you think that I was keepin' care of you?"

Pete suddenly laughed.

"Doggone me, you're a card still, Annie. That's what you are. You're a card."

He picked a lantern from a peg on the wall, and pushed up the chimney with a screech of rusted iron against iron. In the meantime, he fixed his scowl upon the old woman.

"If he so much as blinks an eye, blow a hole through the middle of him," said Pete. "I dunno but it's the best way, anyhow. You take Six, he'd be mighty likely to be pleased. It'd show that we was friends of his. A slick and easy life we'd live around here for a while, if Six was a friend of ours."

"There ain't gunna be no killin' unless there's gotta be," said Annie. "He might be safe dead, but we might be safe choked, too, for that matter. You go and do what I told you to do, and if he so much as winks, I'll settle his hash for him. I'll turn him into hash, by jiminy jump-up!"

Pete, lighting the lantern, presently went to the door, and there paused to look doubtfully back upon the scene. But then he smiled, reassured.

"Yeah," said he, "if I was in his socks, I'd feel took care of, all right."

And he went out, his laughter booming heavily and trailing behind him as he walked away.

Speedy stood frozen in place, meeting the hard, steady eye of the woman. He would rather have faced any two men in the world. The Deacon and the Snapper, hard as they were, were nothing, compared with her.

In the meantime, her companion had reached his hill, apparently, and it could not be far away, for presently, across the darkness outside of the door, the boy saw the pale glimmer of light, traveling in three waves — then darkness again. It was clear that the first signal had been sent, calling Wilson and his gang that way.

He could curse his fate; he could grind his teeth and damn his folly for coming to this house. But that would not help him.

It was useless, as he had learned in many a predicament, long before, to stand still while his hair lifted and gooseflesh formed on his body. The cold of the Arctic does not reach the heart so quickly as the icy touch of fear.

And he looked about him, desperately, forcing himself to be cool.

"No," said the woman, "there ain't no hole in the roof for you to jump through, and if you did, I'd shoot you on the wing. I ain't no common woman, boy. I can handle a gun. I'm telling you that. Because it'll be safer for you to wait for Six Wilson than to try to play any monkeyshines around here with me!"

He nodded at her. He even managed a ghost of a smile.

"I feel taken care of," he told her.

And she actually grinned back at him; but her finger remained locked around the triggers of the big gun.

"You're taken care of, all right," said she.

"Who's your musician?" he asked, seeing a guitar that hung from a nail on the wall.

"Him? He's gone," said she. "He's gone, and he ain't comin' back."

268

He stepped to the guitar.

"Stand fast!" said she.

He moved his hand slowly, so that she could not mistake the gesture.

"I'm not reaching for a gun," said he, and took the guitar off the nail.

"Leave that be!" she commanded, angrily.

"I won't hurt it," said Speedy. "Guitars are second nature, for me. Friend of yours have this?"

"He was my boy," said Annie. "Ay, and there was a boy for you. He wasn't no sneakin' hoss thief! Not him! There was one that could jump over a hoss, and rip the innards out of a whole town. When my boy Bill, he got started, he was a hurricane, I tell you. And then he'd come home, and he'd set there in that chair, and he'd lean back his head, and twang that old guitar, and he'd sing me *Annie Laurie* like it would make the tears come into the eyes of a mule to hear him!"

Speedy sat down in the chair.

"Mind what you're doin'!" said she. "And hang that guitar back on the nail. I been and tuned it every day of my life since he died."

"Died?" said Speedy, sympathetically.

"He gone and had a flock of bad luck," said Annie. "He gone and laid out a good plan, and everything was all right and he stood to clean out about a half a million, maybe. But there was a crooked swine of a clerk in that bank that he'd bought, and that hound, he doublecrossed my poor Bill. He goes into that bank, and he lays out his duds, and he starts to work runnin' the soap mold around the door of the safe, and right then and there they up and tell him to hoist his hands."

"Hard luck," said the boy.

He swept the strings, softly; it was amazingly true that they were perfectly in tune.

"My Bill, he wouldn't go and hoist his hands," said Annie. *"He* wasn't the kind that no woman could keep standin' still, no matter whether she had a gun on him, or not. He'd of gone roarin' through the roof, he would. He was that kind of a boy, I tell you."

Speedy nodded.

He swept the strings louder, and still louder.

"And he reached for his guns," said she, "and they took and heaved lead into him, and he died fighting like a man had oughta die, God bless him. One of 'em he killed right out, and paid the score, and two of 'em, he put 'em into the hospital, and somebody else could pay the bill. And that was the end of —"

Her voice died away. Speedy, singing softly into the very train of her voice, began *Annie Laurie,* as he had sung it many a time before. But never had he sung it as he did now. He had sung it for amusement, or on request; now he sang for his life — not too loudly, not loudly enough, he prayed to let the sound of his voice reach to that man on the hill near the house, whose repeated signals were still flashing dimly over the ground beyond the door of the house.

He sang with his head back, his eyes half closed. Only through the lashes of his half-closed eyes did he study the face of Annie, and see her harden and shake her head, and sneer with disapproval. But in a moment, that disapproval was gone.

The song, in fact, was sinking to that moment when the teller would lay him down and die for bonnie Annie Laurie, and if ever Speedy threw melting pathos into his tones, he sent them now.

Ay, and for the best of all reasons — for he heard, far down the valley, the rapid beating of the hoofs of horses.

He did not have to be a prophet to tell that they were the horses of Six Wilson's gangsmen, coming as fast as a gallop would bring them!

The chorus came again; he struck the strings more loudly, his voice flowed out more tenderly than ever.

And suddenly the harsh voice of Annie broke in upon him, as she said:

"You worthless, hoss-stealin' rascal, I see through you and your soft-soap tricks. But — get the devil out of here!" And, tilting the

271

muzzles of the gun towards the ceiling, she pulled the triggers, one after the other.

Speedy saw the table, the gun, the holder of it, also, jarred by the shocks of the roaring explosions. But he only saw these things from the tail of his eye as he leaped through the doorway.

The guitar, unfortunately, fell from his hand as he sprang and smashed upon the floor.

But here he was in the open, with the fresh wind of hope and the night striking his face.

Off to the side, he saw big Pete running, the lantern swinging crazily in his hand, shouting as he strode: "Hey, Annie! What you gone and done, you fool?"

Speedy had unknotted the reins, by that time, his fingers stumbling with haste, and now he flung himself on the back of the tall horse.

And, at that moment, he heard old Annie screeching: "Help! Help! Hey, Pete! He's give me the slip – he's busted the guitar – oh, damn his heart black and blue!"

But Coal Tar was already under way, and sliding like a wind down the valley.

31

Speedy rode far through the night.

The matchless stride of Coal Tar, eventually, dropped the rattle of hoofs behind him into silence.

He struck difficult trails. Even Coal Tar, at last, grew weary and began to stumble, and the boy got off and walked, toiling, it seemed, ever upwards.

The night ended. The mountains grew black. Finally, in the east and then all around the horizon stretched a thin band of pale light. The morning was definitely there. The color began; pink, and purple on the highlands, and rose, and gold. And finally the sun pushed up a rim.

Between a pool and a rock, he found a shepherd's hut, and paused there. His weary black horse stood still behind him. Weary was Speedy, also, and wavering a little even as he stood still, but his voice was hoarse, stern and abrupt, as he called the shepherd to him.

An old man, he came with stumbling steps,

supported by a long knotted staff. He might have been a shepherd out of twenty centuries before, judged by his shapeless rags.

"Where's Nixon?" asked the boy. "I want to find the house of Arthur Steyn!"

The old man turned slowly, like a weather vane in a veering wind, and pointed.

"Right down there," he said. "There's Nixon lyin' under your eyes."

Speedy, dimly, strained his tired vision towards the point, and through the pass in the heart of which he stood, he saw the slope step down, from hill to hill, and the valley widen, until the windows of a little town blinked with red-gold light, far away.

"Nixon?" he said. "Is that Nixon?"

"That's Nixon, as sure as I'm Sam Rogers!" said the shepherd.

And Speedy, with a wave of the hand, by way of greeting and farewell, walked on.

He went on for an endless time. The sun rose hot and high above him. He began to sweat and stumble. At last he lay down in the shade of a rock. Coal Tar made a brief pretense of cropping at the sun-dried grass, and then he lay down in turn, like a dog, and hooked his head around, gave his tail one vain, last flourish at the flies, and went to sleep.

Speedy watched him with a tired grin.

Then he slept, also.

He wakened with the sun in his face, burning him, stinging his nose like an acid.

Coal Tar was already standing, busily eating this time, and his neck arched as of old. He raised his head when his dizzy master stood up, and it seemed to the boy that a new light came into his eyes.

Then Speedy mounted, and rode on.

It was such a short distance, that he wondered how he had given way to weariness, in this manner. In half an hour, he was before the door of the house of Arthur Steyn, and there he dismounted.

Half a dozen horses stood before the door of the house. He thought he recognized the great black horse of Joe Wynne among the rest, but he was not quite sure. He only knew that the place seemed a harbor of infinite refuge to him, just then.

He came to the door, and as he approached, he heard the calm, old, but unwavering voice of Steyn saying: "Of course it was the work of our friend Six Wilson. And I think that the time has come when we have to band together to put an end to him. He has done other murders, my friends. But this time he has taken away a man out of my house, like a tiger taking a child out of an Indian village. I am prepared to ride out by myself and do what I can to stop this man-killer. I have called you together because I think that you are the best fighting men in the district. I talked it over with my girl, and we agreed on you.

"Now, then, I want to hear what one of you is unwilling to ride with me against Six-card Wilson?"

Speedy stepped into the doorway, and he saw at the long table in the dining room, old Steyn, Joe Wynne, Rudy Stern, and four others. He did not know the other four, but they looked like men, one and all.

"Hello, Mr. Steyn," said he.

It was as though he had dropped a bomb among them. They started up, with exclamations. The six men of the range rushed up about him. They even, with their charge, dragged him closer to the door, as though they needed the additional light by which to view him.

But Arthur Steyn ran to an inner door and called, loudly: "Mary! Oh, Mary! Believe it or not, Speedy has come back safe and sound."

Then one of the men cried: "By the Eternal, Joe, there's Coal Tar back again!"

And all the six poured out through the door, bearing Speedy along with them.

Big Joe Wynne stalked up to the head of the black horse.

"That's Coal Tar, all right," said he.

"You can thank Speedy for that," said Rudy

Stern, looking, however, without pleasure upon the boy.

"I'll thank Speedy," said Wynne, "for finding the right horse for himself."

He turned on the boy, smiling a little.

"Where'd you get that horse, son?" said he.

"Am I a horse thief because I have him?" asked Speedy, wearily.

Wynne shook his head.

"That's the best horse I ever bred," said he. "I know him like a book. I knew him even better before Six Wilson stole him. Did you get him from Six?"

"I got him from Six," said Speedy.

"Mind telling me how?" asked Rudy Stern. "Because I reckon that we all of us know that Six would rather lose a couple of eyes than that hoss!"

"Well," said Speedy, reminiscently, "there was a sort of a mixup. The Deacon and the Snapper — you know 'em?"

"Know 'em?" they chorused. "Better'n sin!"

"They had me tied up," said the boy carefully, "but they got into an argument, and the argument led to guns, and when they shot each other up, I borrowed the Snapper's knife, and cut myself loose, and skinned out. This Coal Tar looked bigger than the rest, so I borrowed him from Six Wilson, to help me on my way. That's about all there is to it."

He spoke slowly — so great were the gaps in the narrative which he had slipped over.

"Tied up," said Rudy Stern, "and the Snapper and the Deacon guarding you — and they fight — and you — oh, I see, just a little quiet, ordinary adventure for you, Speedy. Is that all?"

He laughed, in an oddly sharp, high voice.

Said Joe Wynne: "You like that horse, Speedy?"

"Like him?" answered the boy. "Ask me if I like my life! I'd be dead, except for him!"

He went to Coal Tar, and rubbed his nose, and the big stallion nuzzled against the breast of his last rider.

"Look at that," muttered one of the men. "And yet I remember Joe spending three weeks to make him wear a saddle ten minutes at a time."

"Six Wilson tamed him, I suppose," said Speedy. "He ran straight enough for me — and too fast for the rest of Wilson's nags."

Old Arthur Steyn came down the steps and touched his shoulder.

"Speedy," said he, "we've decided to go after Six Wilson, and stay after him until we've washed this section of the range clean of him. Do you ride with us?"

"No," answered Speedy, surprisingly. "I don't ride with you."

"You don't?" echoed the old man.

"I don't have to," said the boy. "Wherever I am, he'll come to find me. And I'm pretty tired of riding!"

He laughed a little.

"I'm tired of everything except a bunk and a blanket," he finished. "I'm going to turn in."

"He wants to turn in," said Arthur Steyn, wagging his head as though he had made a discovery of the profoundest importance.

"The kid is fagged," said Rudy Stern, in a similar tone.

Speedy, with knees that bent uncertainly, found his way into the big room, found a bunk and a crumpled blanket on it, and flung himself down. He made only a feeble gesture at drawing the blanket over him.

Then, to his surprise, he found that other hands had arranged it, carefully.

"The kid's fagged out, and no wonder," said a hushed voice.

"I've got to see Mary," said Speedy, his eyes still closed.

"I'm here," she answered, instantly.

He looked up at her, amazed.

"You here?" he asked, stupidly.

She smiled a little, staring down at him.

"Send the rest away," said he.

She merely waved her hand. He saw only her face, but he heard the retreating footsteps.

"What is it?" she asked. "We're alone, now."

"This is a pinch," said the boy, in a tired voice. "In a pinch, the truth is worth more than a barrel full of lies, eh?"

"Worth a lot more," said she.

She pulled up a chair and sat close to him.

"What's that perfume you're wearing?" he asked, his eyes closing in spite of himself.

"Lavender," said she.

"I hate perfumes," said he.

She said: "Well, I'll drop the lavender, then. You wanted to say something?"

"Yes. I wanted to say something. I'm going to slide out. I'd like to get Six Wilson. But I've got to slide out. He's got a crazy idea. He thinks that you're fond of me. He thinks that you'll marry me. Don't laugh. I'm too tired to listen to laughing."

"I'm not laughing," she answered, quietly.

"He'd rather marry the two of us, than have that happen," said the boy.

"Why?" she asked.

"I can't tell you why. It's a long story. It's a crazy story. You wouldn't believe it. Only, I wanted to tell you, I'm going to breeze along. Understand?"

"I understand," said she.

He opened his eyes and frowned at her.

Steadily he stared up at her face.

"Look here, Mary," said he.

"I'm looking at you, Speedy," she answered.

"Look at my idea, not at me," said the boy.

"Well?" said she.

"You're getting serious," said Speedy. "Don't be serious. Hear me?"

"I hear you," said she.

He went on, painfully: "You think that I'm all right, because I've done a few little things around here that look spectacular. You're wrong. I'm not all right. You hit me off the first time that you laid eyes on me. I'm only a tramp. I'm good for nothing. I'm telling you that because I'm pinched for time, and to save you finding it out for yourself. I'm only a tramp."

She waited a moment, then she said: "You don't think Six Wilson was right, then?"

He answered, half groaning: "Yeah, I think he's right. Every girl's half a fool. She'll step out and marry any loafer that looks like a real man to her. But I'm just the way I look to the naked eye. Don't you make any mistake about that. All I care about in the world is an easy time, and nothing to worry about. A grand husband I'd make. A grand provider for kids, for one thing."

She said, after a moment: "You mean it, Speedy? You don't care about anything else in the world?"

"Nothing else," said he. "I had to tell you the

truth. I'm tired — of everything. Mary, you're all right. You're a grand girl. I had to let you have a look at the truth. Now I'm going to sleep."

"All right, Speedy," said she. "I guess I understand. You sleep tight, will you?"

"Thanks, Mary," said he. "That's just what I'll do."

He reached out his hand, half blindly, and hers closed on it, and then he fell into a profound slumber.

32

When he wakened, it was late in the afternoon.

He knew the time by the dead heat of the air, and by the drowsy buzzing of the flies, as it seemed to him.

Then he sat up, and wiped the beads of sweat from his forehead. The blanket had been too hot and too long upon him. His body, where it had crossed, was wet through the shirt. Now a wave of wind entered the room through the open door. It did not cool him; it simply burned the moisture of the perspiration dry in one gesture, as it were.

Through the doorway, he saw several broad shoulders, several wide sombreros above them. The heads nodded up and down, and hands rose, bearing cards. They were playing poker out there in the shadow of the house, where more air stirred. Perhaps all six of them were playing poker.

"Feeling better, son?" asked the voice of Arthur Steyn.

Speedy looked sharply aside, and saw that

the old man had been sitting like a stone, unobserved.

"I'm a lot better," said Speedy. "But this is a pretty hot place."

"Yes, it's hot," answered Steyn. "Want a drink?"

"A whole well of water," said Speedy, "and a couple of roast beeves."

"Mary's been cooking for hours," said Steyn. "She has a whole table ready to load for you. Let's go into the kitchen. It's a lot cooler out there, in spite of the heat from the stove."

That was true. By a freak of the wind, that end of the house was cooler.

Speedy stood for a moment to appreciate the draught. Then he went outside and pumped a granite basin full of water. He washed his face and hands. Then he shaved. The back of his neck was a little raw and chafed against the flannel collar of his shirt. But he felt fresher and hungrier, every moment. Then he went inside and stood by the door.

The table was literally loaded, and Mary leaned against a chair, red-faced from cookery, her sleeves rolled up to her elbows. She was not the perfect picture of a housewife. Her face was not innocent of perspiration; two or three wisps of hair stuck flat against her forehead, darkened and glistening from the wet. But Speedy looked at her as the jockey looks at a fine horse.

"You could run for my money, Mary," said he. "You're wonderful. Every time I see you, you're more wonderful."

"That's all right," said she. "You don't have to pay before you eat. Sit down and get to work."

He said: "Who's with me? Any of the boys?"

"They've eaten. I'll keep you company," answered Arthur Steyn.

And he sat at the head of the table and passed dishes, and pretended to eat.

Mary went outside, singing, carrying a saddle and a bridle.

Then her father said: "Speedy, you've surprised me."

"Have I?" said Speedy. "You mean that play about Coal Tar and Wilson. I had a lot of luck, that's all."

"I'm not speaking of Wilson," answered Arthur Steyn. "He's far from my mind, just now."

"What's in it?" asked the boy, his mouth full of hot cornbread.

"You are," said Steyn, thoughtfully. "I thought you were a cunning rascal — a worthless thief of time. I find that you're an honest man. All my thoughts about you were wrong!"

Speedy stared in a real astonishment.

"Look here, Mr. Steyn," said he, "right from the first you killed the fatted calf for me."

Steyn smiled.

"You know, Speedy," said he, "that a shrewd man generally tries to play a simple part."

It was Speedy's turn to smile, though for different reasons.

"I see," said he. "Tell me what you thought I was after?"

"There's only one thing I possess that's worth having," said Steyn. "Not my wretched strip of land. I'm the only one in the world who could love these naked hills, I suppose. I thought you wanted Mary."

"You did?" murmured Speedy.

He looked at Steyn with an awe unusual in his hardy soul.

"Yes," said Steyn. "I was sure of it, until you talked to her before you went to sleep."

"Oh, yes, she told you about that, did she?" said the boy.

"She did not have to tell me," said Steyn. "I heard it."

"Hello!" said Speedy. "I didn't know that you were in the room."

"No, I was eavesdropping from the outside. The walls of my house are conveniently thin, Speedy!"

"Ah!" said Speedy.

He stopped eating. He smiled in a friendly way of understanding at the other.

"You listened in," nodded Speedy.

"I've heard nearly every word you've said to

my girl," answered Steyn.

Speedy blinked.

"The first —" he began, and then paused.

"The first night?" said Steyn. "Oh, yes. I had my ear pressed against the door, because I thought that you might talk a little more freely when I was out of the room."

Speedy openly gasped.

"Yes," went on Steyn, smoothly, "pride and honor don't exist for me, where the welfare of my girl is concerned."

"That stops me!" breathed the boy. "But the next day when she accused me in front of you, you seemed to think that she was all wrong and that I —"

Steyn nodded.

"You see, Speedy," said he, "when I listened through the flimsy door to you, the night before, I suddenly realized that I was a very old and dull man, and that you were a very young and clever one. I saw that nothing but diplomacy would help me, then."

"So you let me drive her out of the house?" said Speedy, incredulously.

"You drove her out because you expected her to come back, I think," said Steyn.

Suddenly Speedy smiled.

"That's right," said he. "I was only giving her rope enough to hang herself."

And he added: "I thought I was as deep as

clouded glass and I was as thin as a window-pane, all the while!"

"I thought that I saw your motive," said Steyn, as cautiously as a professor. "Of course, I could not be sure, but I was at least certain that I would be helpless against your youth, your activity, your adroitness, as long as I openly opposed you. So I held my hand and played the part of the fool."

The boy was silent, only murmuring, after a time: "You found me a pretty black rascal, Mr. Steyn."

"The blackest I ever have known," answered Steyn, in his gentle voice, still. "Much blacker than a man-killer like the great Six Wilson. For he only kills with bullets, and you, I thought, with lies. But now, in a moment, I am disarmed. You have put your cards on the table, and told my girl the truth. I thank God and you, Speedy, for doing that! It was a good, shrewd blow at her pride, I daresay, but she'll recover from that. She has agreed with me that you're not like other men, you see!"

He laughed a little.

But there was no laughter in Speedy. He was thinking that never in his life had he known the wisdom of such a man as this.

Then he said: "And now, Mr. Steyn, by telling me frankly what you think, you feel that you've tied my hands for good and all?"

It was the turn of old Steyn to stare for a moment, and then he answered in his gentle way: "Yes, my boy. That was what I hoped. I think that you'll never marry Mary, now."

Speedy bowed his head a little.

She seemed, at that moment, the most gloriously glowing vision that had ever entered his mind.

But old Steyn was saying: "By the way, while you slept, a man was out here to see you, but we sent him back to Nixon because you were asleep, and partly because, although he looked a gentleman, he might have been one of Six Wilson's hired men."

"Who was he?" asked the boy.

"He called himself John Pierson; he seemed rather anxious to talk with you."

"John Pierson!"

"You know him?"

"Yes, I know him. In Nixon now, you say?"

"Yes. In Nixon."

"I've got to start now," said Speedy.

"And returning when?" asked Steyn, gradually rising from the table.

"Never!" said the tramp.

33

When he went outside of the house, he was saying to old Steyn: "Will you sell me a broncho, Mr. Steyn? I want a lift into Nixon."

Big Joe Wynne stood up, at the same moment that Mary Steyn rode her dancing mare around the corner of the house.

"You think that I was joking, Speedy," said he. "But I wasn't. Coal Tar is your horse, if you'll have him."

The upper lip of Speedy curled a little.

He stepped close to Wynne, and said softly: "There's only one thing I'll take — or exchange — with you, Wynne!"

And the big man, frowning, made no answer, and did not repeat his proffer.

The rest, very delicately, referred to it with not a word. Perhaps they could guess at what had passed between the pair in that brief moment.

Old Steyn, without a word, went to the barn and brought back a strongly built pinto.

"This horse will take you to Nixon. If you

want him farther than that, you can pay me fifty dollars. If you change to the railroad from Nixon, give the horse to the hotel keeper. He'll send Pinto back by the first rider that comes out this trail."

Speedy waved his hand.

He had gone to the girl, moved by a freak of fancy.

"Mary," said he, "you've started making a collection of guns, and here's another for you. Take this!"

And he pulled out the long-barreled revolver that he had picked out of the hand of the fallen Snapper.

She received the gun with a studious frown, turned it in her hand, and then rubbed her finger over certain obvious notches that had been either cut or filed into the handle.

"Whose gun?" said she.

And then she gasped, for turning the weapon a little, she saw a name scratched, and the shallow furrow of the scratch was filled with the glint of silver, spelling: "The Snapper"!

"The Snapper!" said she.

They crowded suddenly about her, all of those men, fairly panting with curiosity.

And heard Rudy Stern saying: "He shot up the Snapper and the Deacon all in one party. God knows how! But here's the proof of it. The two of 'em all at once!"

"I tell you," said the boy, "I didn't do it. I didn't shoot up the pair of 'em."

"Sure you didn't," said Rudy Stern, soothingly. "You wouldn't do a thing like that. You're a little doggone shorn lamb, is what you are, and you dunno how to take care of yourself, with all the big rough men of the world around you. Ain't that the fact, kid?"

They all laughed, at this remark. Only Speedy was silent, and Joe Wynne.

He was not free from them even when he had mounted his horse and waved farewell.

But Mary Steyn sent her little mare up beside his pinto and leaning a bit from the saddle, she said: "You think that you're riding out of this, but you'll ride back again, Speedy, take my word for it!"

Then, as he rode off, he saw that four of the six riders had followed him at a short distance; Rudy Stern and big Joe Wynne were among them.

It was not hard to guess the reason why. They had heard what he had reported to Steyn. The great Six Wilson would follow him as that bandit would follow no other bait into a trap. Therefore, they rode behind him, in part as a guard of honor, let us say, and in part hoping to find a pelt and a bounty worth having.

Something over ten thousand dollars was being offered at this time for the arrest or the capture of Six Wilson, dead or alive.

But Speedy made up his mind that he would act as though he were alone, and after the first glance to the rear, he paid not the slightest attention to the others during the entire eight miles to Nixon, and not one of them offered to ride up beside him.

He went to the hotel in Nixon, his horse stepping deep in the liquid white of the dust down the way. And, when he had tethered the pinto and made his way into the lobby, he did not even have a chance to ask for his man. Big John Pierson rose from a corner and strode up to him.

He stood a moment before the tramp, scanning him from head to foot, and then he smiled a little as he shook hands with the boy.

"You've burned the tip of your nose, Speedy," said he.

"To a crisp," said Speedy. "But that's all right!"

"That's all right, if you feel it that way," said Pierson. "Come over here and sit down. No, we'd better go up to my room."

He led the way up creaking stairs to a corner room. The shades were down, but the burning heat had seeped through them until the room was oven-hot.

So they threw off their coats.

"Drinking?" asked Pierson.

"Not with you," said Speedy.

"Not friendly, eh?" asked Pierson, unabashed.

"No, but I need to have my wits about me."

Pierson smiled.

"We'll have some ginger ale and ice," said he. And he was as good as his word.

They sat sipping at the sticky, oversweet, artificial mess, poking at the ice with spoons, deeply and gloomily discontented with such a beverage, and Pierson said: "How do things go?"

"Things have finished," said the boy.

"Finished?" answered Pierson, unconvinced.

"Yes, finished. I'm through."

"That brute of a Wilson turned the trick, eh?" said Pierson, almost sympathetically, although he sighed as he spoke.

"No, not Wilson. I've been in his hands and out again."

"What! In his hands — and out, did you say?"

"It's not Wilson," said the boy. "It's another thing. It's Steyn — and the girl."

"What about them?" snapped Pierson.

"They're too white. I couldn't go on with 'em."

"You liked 'em, eh?"

"Yes, I did."

"Liked 'em too well to introduce 'em to nine

or ten million dollars. Is that the idea?"

In this light, Speedy had never viewed the problem. He could only shake his head, stubbornly.

"I was doing a rotten thing," he insisted. "I wouldn't mind, ordinarily. But I told you before — women are not my line!"

"Oh," said Pierson, "you couldn't get along with Mary Steyn, eh? Well, I don't suppose that I'm surprised. I told you beforehand that she's a hard one to handle."

Speedy stirred in his chair and looked uneasily at the blinded window next to him.

"She's too white," he managed to say. "She's one of the white women of this world, man!"

"So," said the other, "you wouldn't clutter up her fine life with several millions of dollars. Is that it?"

Speedy stared gloomily at the lawyer.

Then he broke out: "Why don't you come clean with her? Why don't you go straight to her and tell her what's what?"

Pierson shook his head.

"No woman under thirty," said he, with sage conviction, "can be trusted. I know that. I haven't been a lawyer for that many years, almost, without learning a little something about women, my lad!"

Speedy watched him with a growing dislike.

"What fetched you down here?" he asked.

295

"Not enough reports from you," said Pierson. "I had to be on the spot, anyway. It's too important. I couldn't leave as big a fish as this to some other fellow's single net."

"Well, I'm through with the game," said Speedy.

"I'm not surprised," said Pierson. "I was only making a cast in the dark, when I picked you out. I knew that you were too young and too inexperienced for the job."

Speedy stirred again in his chair.

Then he stood up.

"I'll be getting along," said he.

Suddenly Pierson leaned back and laughed.

"Sit down, Speedy," said he.

The boy shook his head.

"I'll be moving," he answered, grimly.

"Why, because you're beaten?" asked Pierson.

"Yes," said Speedy, after a moment of thought.

"No," said the other, "but because the game was too easy for you! Isn't that true?"

"What game?" demanded Speedy. "What are you talking about, Pierson?"

"She was tamed to your hand, and came at the call. Am I wrong, Speedy?"

The boy frowned blackly.

"Certainly not," said he.

"Very well," went on Pierson. "What's your next move? New York?"

"My next move? I keep that to myself," said Speedy.

"Don't trust me, Speedy?"

The tramp made a sudden and impatient gesture.

"All right," said he. "I'll tell you, and I'll tell you because I'm going to tell the whole world. I'm going to spend a little time being gotten, myself, or else getting Six Wilson!"

The lawyer whistled, and slowly raised his head, like one peering at a distant, gradually looming object.

"That's it, is it?"

"Yes."

"Six Wilson got under your skin?"

"He did. And I'm going to scratch him out."

"Well," said Pierson, "that's the best job that you could do for me. I'd like to ask for a small promise."

"I make no promises blind to you," said the boy, sullenly.

"It's only this. Spend two or three days with me, because when he knows that I'm here, Six Wilson is going to want to break me open and see what makes me tick. Will you do that?"

Speedy suddenly grinned.

"I might do that," said he. "I'd sort of like to look on and see what he finds!"

34

Here, the door of the room next to theirs opened and shut with a slam and through the paper-thin wall sounded a hearty voice which said:

"Now that we're up here, Sheriff May, I can tell you my name. That thing that I wrote on the hotel register doesn't mean a cipher. I'm Frank Rivera."

"That don't mean a cipher to me, neither," said the blunt voice of Sheriff May.

It meant something to the two who were eavesdropping from the adjoining chamber, however. For they sat up stiffly erect, and looked meaningly at one another. Lawyer Pierson raised a finger to his lips; but he did not need to give the caution, for the boy sat as still as a stone.

"I'm going to make it mean something to you," Frank Rivera was saying. "I'm going to make it mean a thousand dollars hard cash to you."

"What's your game, son?" asked the sheriff, dryly. "Craps?"

"No," said Frank Rivera. "My game is straight. As straight as a string."

"Gunna give me a thousand dollars for luck?" asked the sheriff.

"I'm going to tell you a strange story," said Frank Rivera.

"I'll bet it's strange," said the impolite sheriff, and yawned largely.

"That's all right," answered Rivera, who had the voice of a booster and an optimist. "I'll wake you up before long. I wanta introduce you, Mr. Sheriff, to a southern land by the Rio Grande and the estate of Rivera, the great estate of Rivera."

"With the banana cactus and the beefsteak trees growin' everywhere?" suggested the sheriff.

"Yeah, more or less," said Rivera.

"Thanks," said the sheriff. "But I'm not buying big estates. It ain't my day of the week for that."

"Will you shut up and listen?" asked Rivera, though his tone was still mild and genial. "Or do you kick a thousand dollars in the face every week, on this day?"

"I've seen a thousand dollars pass me in the street," said the sheriff, "but I never had his hand in mine."

"Shall I tell the yarn?"

"I can't stop you, son," said the sheriff. "It's

too hot to move a lot, this time of day. You might ice that breeze through the window, if you don't mind."

"I'm gunna make you forget the climate," said Frank Rivera. "Open your eyes, brother, and look!"

"Beautiful as a dream," yawned the sheriff. "Go on, kid."

"Hill and valley as far as the eye walks," said Frank Rivera, "and God Almighty pullin' the grass up by the roots, it grows so doggone fast. Cattle everywhere. You could tether a calf with a ten foot rope anywhere it was dropped, and without moving outside of the circle, that calf would find so much to eat that it'd grow up and die of fatty degeneration of the heart."

"I believe every word you say," said the sheriff, solemnly. "I'm a Christian, I am. And here's my other ear."

Frank Rivera laughed. It was a contagious chuckle.

He went on: "What's on top of the ground ain't all. Underneath there's a lot of good paying ore."

"Sure," said the sheriff. "You wanta give me a thousand dollars in shares of one of those mines you're gunna uncover, eh?"

"Oh, shut up and listen, will you," said the mild Frank Rivera. "I tell you, some of the coverings has been lifted already. Nothing big found. Just a couple of strikes in pay dirt. Nothing much. Just forty-fifty thousand a year, with old-fashioned methods used. A little thing like that wouldn't make much difference to your way of living, I guess?"

"I could pick my teeth with it," said the sheriff. "Go on."

"There's a little private line to join up with the main railroad. That private line hums, what with beef and hides and tallow and whatnot. I ain't been talking about the sheep. They don't count, hardly. You wouldn't bother with fifteen-twenty thousand sheep, just brushed in around the edges of the picture to make the hills stand out."

"Wouldn't you bother?" said the sheriff. "I can do everything with mutton except eat it. Go on, son. Are you tied to this picture by anything more'n a name?"

"Wait a minute. You ain't seen the heart of the thing, yet. You put a coupla hills in the middle of that paradise, and plant those hills with big cottonwoods, oaks and whatnot, and fill up the hollow with a fine lake, and make the grass green around all year long, and lay out some fine paths wanderin' about high, wide, and handsome, and put blood hosses into the pastures, and blood bulls into the corrals, and build up ten-twelve big barns, and then you set down and sketch out a house that's laid out not in feet but in acres, and you begin to get near the main thing."

"No trouble at all to lay out the acres," said the sheriff. "I'm just putting the gold gilt on the chandeliers and the uniforms on the foot-boys. Now get down to the main thing."

"The main thing is an old man that's eighty plus. He's got eighty years in both eyes, and can't see farther than the end of his nose. He's got five hairs on his head and only one idea in it."

"And what's the idea?"

"That the long lost heir is coming back."

The sheriff yawned.

"You're not the heir, then?" said he.

"No, I'm not. Not in his mind."

"Who is, then?"

"Somebody that's dead as the hills."

"Is he batty, the old boy Rivera?"

"Kind of — on that subject. You wanta hear the story?"

"I wanta hear how you and me and a thousand dollars long and green fit into the yarn."

"I'm gunna tell you, brother. I'm only a third or fourth cousin, or something like that. But I wear the right name by means of leaving off the last half of my name. John Rivers White, I used to be, but White's a hard color to keep where the Chinee laundries ain't so common, and Rivers is harder to say than Rivera, anyway."

"So that's how you got to be a Rivera, eh?"

"That's the way," said Frank Rivera, laughing again, with his amazing and frank good nature.

He went on: "Now all I have is the name, and a lot of good intentions. It ain't that I'm interested in the inheritance. Oh, not at all. But I got a natural affection for the old man, and I can't help showing it every day in every way to make the world bigger and better, if you know what I mean."

"Oh, I know what you mean, all right," said the sheriff. "The old man swallers the guff and puts you into his will."

"He would, if he could make sure that the 'vanished heir' ain't left any trace behind him, but old Rivera still has that dream, so I start out to run it down for him.

"You see, in the old days, Rivera has a son, big as a horse, clean as a whistle and wild as mustard. The old man worships him, and wants to make him king of Mexico or president of North America, or something like that. He would take the backbone out of the Rocky Mountains to make a comb for that kid's hair. He would pour the Mississippi into a bucket to give his hoss a drink, if you know what I mean."

"I gather the idea."

"And then the kid goes off and finds him a little school teacher with no more gold mines in her purse than there is titles onto her name. She says yes to the kid, and his old man says no. But her yes was all that the kid wanted to hear. So he picks up the girl and rides forty miles, and marries her, and keeps right on traveling till he hits California. That California was full of hope and real estate, in those days, and the kid mortgages his four hind teeth and slices off a thousand acres of dobe nearest the rock and a thousand acres more of hope nearest the heart, and he sets down and makes him a home."

"Go on," said the sheriff. "But put in the spurs. Did he catch malaria?"

"No, malaria caught him. He raised ten sacks to the acre; but the mosquitoes beat him to the market. He ups and dies, about five days or so, after his wife gives the world a girl baby and turns up her own toes. He buries his wife today, and the neighbors order a coffin for him, tomorrow. They bury him free of charge, and the bank waits till the first collection day and puts that little old ranch back in its trousers' pockets."

"Yeah, banks has got thousand-acre pockets, all right," observed the sheriff. "I recollect when — but go on with your yarn."

"I go out on the trail of that kid," said Rivera.

304

"Alive, she owns old man Rivera and his cash on hand, and all his futures. I gotta find her. Then I find out that the neighbors had let an Injun woman on the next reservation adopt that white baby, until a Colonel Townsend comes along and decides to raise her white. But she brings everybody bad luck. The Injuns get smallpox, and the colonel gets a busted neck from his favorite ridin' hoss. And when he passes on, the kid passes to a Townsend cousin. But them second-hand Townsends don't know a Rivera from a hole in the ground, and they main manhandle that kid, and one day, when she's nine years old, she picks up and hauls her train, and heads south and west. I follow her trail. Nine-year-old girls don't walk across the Sierras without havin' even the grizzly bears set up and pay attention. I spot her trail. She gets out of the land of hope and real estate and hits the desert, and the last I hear, she's goin' with a limp, and yaller with malaria, and kind of miserable all around. You know what happens to weak kids in this kind of district, with alkali water, and alkali dust? Well, she's dead and gone. There ain't any trace of her, anywhere. That's a good ten, eleven years ago. Things shift pretty fast, around here. For all I know, some old miner or prospector might of took her in, and dug the kid's grave. But that grave is what I wanta find, and dig up the bones, and take them back to old man Rivera. By the time I got them bones properly buried in the village churchyard, and a nice white monument raised, old Rivera will be ready to turn up his toes, bein' long overdue, and if he don't get writer's cramp, I expect to cash in when his will is made. Now, old son, you see where you make a thousand dollars. You find that grave for me, and I pay it in cash. So's you can hear it talk for itself, here's the face of that coin, and this is how it whispers!"

35

The sheriff was more than doubtful.

As he pointed out, the range was full of elements of moving population, all of whom might be willing to take in a sick child, but few of whom could be found, ten years later, and made to give an account of her end.

There were drifting Mexicans, who came north in summer for the roundups; there were Indians — plenty of them, in those days — who enjoyed nothing more than a chance to pick up a white waif and absorb it into the lazy comfort of redskinned ways; there were the prospectors, the squatters, adventurers of all kinds who came into the great land and shrank away from the face of it again, like water from the back of a well-oiled slicker.

However, a thousand dollars made the chance worth looking into. He would do what he could, and after making a few inquiries, he would give whatever answer he had picked up.

With that, Sheriff May stepped out, and Mr. Frank Rivera went along with him, his step short and quick and hurried beside the long and jingling stride of the Southwesterner.

It left Pierson and the boy to stare at one another, Pierson in grim dismay, and the boy smiling.

"There goes your future up the chimney," said young Speedy. "There you are, chief. You go home and get to work in your office. And I'll find the shortest trail to the railroad, and my happy home in the blind baggage."

"You think so?" said Pierson, his forehead gleaming with sweat. "Well, I've had my hand in this deal too far to snatch it out at the last moment. I'm going to try something else."

"Go out and give the good news to the girl, direct," said Speedy. "That's what I'd do, if I were you. You'll have a grateful father and daughter handing you the whole business of the estate, anyway."

"Bah! Just trimmings, trimmings!" said the lawyer. "And I want something off the joint. I'm not through, my lad. But, Speedy, I want you to sleep in this room. There's an extra bed for you. I need you, I think. I might need you, a lot worse than I dream, even. For if I'm right, Big Six will have wind of me, and he may start in this direction."

"I'll be back," said the boy. "I'll be back for dinner time. And then we'll talk about Six Wilson, and the rest of the ghosts."

He went out and down to the lobby, where he spoke to the room clerk.

"Who's the gent in 217?"

"Why?" asked the clerk.

"I was trying to talk to Mr. Pierson in 218, and all that we could hear was the thinking that went on on the other side of the wall."

"We're not soundproof," said the clerk, grinning. "This 217, he's a booster, or a real estate dealer, I guess. He talks like he wanted votes. Wait a minute. Here's his name. Franklin P. Franklin. That's a funny monniker, ain't it?"

"Yeah. That's a funny monniker," agreed the boy. "Funny looking, too."

"Yeah. He's kind of round and red. If he started rolling, he wouldn't stop before he found the bottom. He's in there with the sheriff — right through that door. It's the bar on the far side, if you ain't found the shortest way to the oats."

Speedy went into the barroom.

He saw Joe Wynne, first of all, and Rudy Stern, drinking together at one end of the bar. Closer at hand were the sheriff and the man from the Rio Grande.

As the voice of Mr. Rivera had sounded, so did he look — small, fat, erect, with his chin carried tucked in, and a continual smile that made fat waves rise before his eyes. He looked like a man who had smiled before breakfast and snored all night. He had one hand in a trousers' pocket, jingling coins, while he talked to the sheriff.

Sheriff May, a moment later, left the saloon, and Speedy stepped up beside the other.

"Hello, stranger," said he. "I'm introducing myself."

"You're good news," said Rivera, with his ready grin. "What do you cost a copy?"

"Ice water," said the boy.

"That's cheap," said Rivera. "What headlines you carryin', partner?"

"Something that you'll wanta know, Mr. Franklin Franklin. That sounds like a firm name."

"It only needs an 'and' tucked in the center," said Rivera. "My mother was expecting twins, so she named me twice. That's all."

Speedy grinned.

"I wanted to tell you," said he, "something about this hotel."

"Go right on," said Rivera. "Is it free news?"

"Yes. It's a private printing of an extra. The beds in this hotel are too soft."

"Are they?" said the other. "Yes, for a mule that sleeps standing. I punched my bed upstairs and sprained my wrist."

Speedy shook his head.

"That bed's dangerously soft," said he.

"Is it?"

"Yes."

"You said 'dangerously?' "

"Yes, I said that."

"Look," said Rivera, "the more you talk, the more I see that I met you a long time ago and that we've got a lot of old memories to talk over."

"I guess we have," said Speedy.

"You try first," said Franklin P. Franklin. "I see a lot of memories coming up in your eyes, I think."

"No," said Speedy. "The way it is with me, I'm far-sighted."

"You see the future, eh?"

"Yes. Especially I see tonight."

"What do you see, brother?"

Speedy paused. He was, to be sure, shooting somewhat in the dark, but, after all, the plump little man seemed to have little malice or meanness in him. He was simply one who wanted to take the easiest opportunities that life could afford to him. An attitude with which Speedy had the profoundest sympathy.

"I see you lying on your back, snoring," said he.

"I knew we were old friends," said Rivera. "You've been in hearing distance of me, anyway. I've been the champion of Montana. I've had more boots throwed at me at night than any man in the world. Go on. You see me snoring on my back."

"And in the morning I see you still lying there, without the snore."

"I always lie a while and wiggle my toes," said Franklin P. Franklin.

"You're not wiggling your toes," said the boy, "the way I see you. Your toes are as stiff as a board."

Rivera rose on his toes, and shuddered, as though he had been hit under the chin.

Then he swallowed, and the smile was gone from his face. He looked pouchy with softness, all at once.

"Well, brother?" said he.

"I've said my piece," said Speedy.

He turned. The other caught his arm.

"What's inside the idea?" he asked.

"All I know," said Speedy, "is that Nixon is bad for you, perhaps. About one chance in three, it's bad for you tonight. Two chances out of three, it's bad for you tomorrow. Three chances out of three, you're ready for planting the day after."

The little plump man, his eye darkening, thrust out his jaw.

"You think you can four-flush with me, brother?" he asked.

Speedy sighed.

"I've said too much," said he. "Mind you, it's not my party. I have no hand on either side, except that I think I know the hound who might want to eat you. And he wants to eat me, too."

"Eat me? Eat me?" said the fat man. "I never was in this dump before in my life."

"It'll likely be your last visit, anyway," said Speedy. "I'll tell you what you do. If you spend the night in this hotel, keep your window locked and your door barred. That keeps the snakes out."

Franklin P. Franklin lost his angry air.

"What's your name?" he asked.

"The boys call me Speedy."

"Are you the one they're all talking about?"

"I might have sneaked into the papers," said Speedy, "but I was never in the advertising section."

"You're Speedy," said Rivera, pointing a tubby, quivering forefinger. "And if you're Speedy, you're white."

"Thanks," said the tramp.

"Then, for God's sake tell me what you mean by all this guff!"

"I'm not telling you any more, because I don't know anything," said Speedy. "I'm guessing, and that's all."

The other blinked, and groaned while his eyes were still fast shut.

"Look here," said he, "will you go one step further?"

"If I can."

313

"Will you tell me what it looks like — the man or the snake that might walk into my room tonight and poison me?"

"I haven't time," said Speedy, "and I'm bad at describing, anyway. Any other of these fellows can give you a good idea of him though. Just mention the name of Six-card Wilson, and they'll do the rest for you."

"Six — Wilson?" gasped the fat man.

He grasped the edge of the bar. His face was sick and white.

"I never seen him — I never crossed him!" said he.

"I don't suppose you have," said the boy, in answer, "but he doesn't need much to attract his attention. I've nothing more to say. I may be all wrong about my guess. But I had to tell you what was in my mind."

Speedy turned away, but he heard the other murmur, slowly, softly, to himself: "Where's the sheriff? Where'll I find him? Where'll I find him quick? God help me for comin' to this end of the world!"

36

Franklin P. Franklin could no longer find the sheriff. May had ridden briskly out of town.

He went to the manager of the hotel and said: "Friend, I'm in danger of my life!"

"You're what?" asked the manager, who was suffering from stomach trouble.

"Life!" said the fat man.

"You look like you enjoyed your meals pretty good," said the manager.

"I've been warned."

"About what?"

"That the outlaw, the man killer, Six Wilson, is after my scalp."

"You look out, then," said the cruel hotel man. "Because he mostly gets scalps that he's after."

"I tell you," said Franklin P. Franklin, "I been warned, and by the man that had oughta know!"

"Who?"

"Speedy!"

At this, the manager forgot his ill humor. He

put back his head and laughed.

"Did Speedy tell you that?"

"I'm saying that he told me that!"

The manager laughed again.

"Speedy, he's a joker," said he. "He's a great kid, but he's a joker."

"A joker?"

"Sure. Don't you know anything. He's a scream. He's a regular entertainer."

"He entertained me, all right" said Rivera, his face growing hot at the suspicion that he had been done.

After all, it was a country of practical jokes, and at this moment, Speedy might be telling around the town the jest he had played upon the stranger.

All through the supper hour, Speedy remained in the mind of Rivera, as an object of wrath. One day, he would find a way of entertaining the entertainer, and to good purpose, God willing!

Entertainer indeed!

He worried through his supper, devising expedients, none of which quite fitted the mark, and then he went upstairs to his room, when he had finished looking through some old newspapers that were in the lobby rack.

He was well enough contented with himself and his cigar, when he entered the room, but once in it, his state of mind altered. It seemed to him that the open window yawned at him like the mouth of a cannon. It seemed to him that footsteps were stealing up the hall towards his room.

He jerked the door open, and peered out.

He almost fainted, when he saw, in the hallway, the silhouette of a big man, but, in another moment, he noted that the face was one he had already seen in the barroom. Joe Wynne, that man was named, as he recalled, now.

Joe Wynne turned in at a door just across the hall, giving in silence a keen glance at the fat man before he turned the key in the lock of his door.

Then Franklin P. Franklin retreated into his room.

The face of Speedy no longer appeared, in his imagination, stretched by a widely mocking grin. Instead, it was serious and frowning, and the quiet gravity of the warning voice re-echoed again in the ears of the fat man.

He took his window and drew it down, and turned the two latches.

He drew the shade, and then drew the curtain.

He removed the writing pad from the top of the table and turned the table upside down under the window. That might impede a clever crook who was able, soundless, to enter the room in the middle of the night.

Then he went to the door. He locked it.

There was a bolt inside the door, slender, but better than nothing. It would make a noise, at least, if forced.

That bolt he shot home.

There were two chairs in the room, and these, side by side, he adroitly braced against the door, putting their backs under the strong, solid handle.

After that, he stood for a moment, looking about him.

Fear that had made him cold had nevertheless made him sweat. So he mopped his forehead. It would be hot and close, sleeping in that room.

And the wreaths of smoke from his cigar slowly curled upwards, dimming the ceiling with blue-brown fog.

Regretfully, he stamped out his cigar on a saucer on the washstand.

It was better to go without a smoke than to stifle himself as in a coffin with his own smoke. Darkly, bitterly, he wished that the morning were already there!

He got off his clothes, and stood for a moment, thoughtfully rubbing his swollen stomach, regretting his stale cigar — regretting also the easy target that he made with his prosperous figure.

Someone had said: "A man shot between the neck and the hips — he's done for. Give him a shot of dope to make him die easy.

"That's all you can do, about."

He shuddered. He felt that his own flesh was very delicate, and sensitive.

There was one more preparation that he could make. From his suitcase he took a short-nosed revolver. It was no good for distances, but it threw a forty-four caliber slug hard enough to knock down a man. And he knew that gun. He had used it for years, and he was a good hand with it. Only, he never yet had practiced at a human target. Lucky devils who had early chances at a mark that might shoot back!

He hoped that he would not get deer fever, so to speak.

Then he lay down.

He decided that he would sleep a little, and then rouse himself. Because it was not likely that any attempt would be made before the witching hour of midnight.

Ghosts rise, then — but his ghost might be laid forever!

Then, as he reached for the lamp to turn down the wick, he decided that it was too dangerous to venture to sleep. He might not waken, except when the bullet crashed through his brain. Or might it not be as the deadly knife edge slashed across his throat, and lift him voiceless, his life gushing, to kick one moment in agony, like a headless chicken — and then to die, twisted in his bedclothes as though in red mud!

He felt his throat. It was soft — terribly soft, he thought.

Then he braced himself up in bed with pillows.

Well, it was not the first time he had sat up all night. Only, there had been company, on the other occasions. In this town, this fiendish town, he did not dare to hunt for company. He could not trust what he might find.

And to sit up without smoking!

He crossed his legs under the covers, cleared his throat loudly, and shifted his position in the bed. The springs squeaked noisily under him as he did so. The noise was a comfort. In this old rattletrap of a frame building, every sound could be heard from one end of the place to another.

He picked a magazine out of his suitcase.

It began with a ghost story, progressed to a murder mystery, and ran on to a tale of gang warfare.

He threw that magazine of murders across the room, with a flutter and a crash.

Somebody in the next room beat on the wall. The wall boomed and vibrated like the tympanum of a drum.

"Hey, shut up in there and let a fellow sleep!" called an angry voice.

"Sure!" sang out the fat man.

He was comforted by the nearness of that voice, and the anger in it gave him, somehow, the assurance that an honest man was there. Pity that there were not more honest men in the world — men honest *and* brave!

He looked at his watch.

Only half an hour had passed since he came into the room!

And the long watches of the night lay all ahead!

He folded his arms upon his stomach and bent his eyes upon his thoughts, for he prided himself upon being a man of mind.

And then, though the flare of the lamp was full against his eyes, his sight grew dim.

Once he wakened with a start, and told himself that he had been almost asleep.

But he composed himself again. Somewhere in the hotel a long-drawn snore was resounding. He blessed the homely sound!

Now, and he was unaware of it, the lamp began to smoke. And time passed.

The window stirred slightly. A latch, without visible touch, stirred also, and then, with a slight creak, quite turned from the catch. The second latch was operated with even less sound.

Then the sash of the window began to rise.

That was not an easy operation. But it went on by degrees and degrees. Inch by inch it rose, softly, softly.

Once, the sleeper stirred with a groan, and grasped at his throat with hot hands. And, after that, for five or ten minutes the sash of the window did not stir.

At last the operation began once more.

Finally, when it was half up, a sinewy leg slipped over the sill, cautiously, noiselessly, found and avoided one of the legs of the overturned table, and reached the floor.

Then the curtain parted, with the faintest of whispers, and the face of Speedy looked into the room.

He slipped across the floor without making a sound, and looked for a moment down into the face of the sleeper. He saw the tight, agonized expression, saw the revolver tremble in the grasp of the fat man.

Then he slipped into the corner, and crouched there in the deep shadow behind the chair over which Franklin P. Franklin had thrown his clothes when he undressed.

It took some skill to bunch his body into so small a space, but he managed it to his own satisfaction, and remained there for a long time, gradually flexing muscle after muscle to keep them from cramping.

And then, at length, he heard what he expected — a sound at the window, no louder than the scratching of a cat's paw as it walks on a naked floor.

37

Speedy did not move. Instead, he crouched a little closer into the meager shadow that covered him, but not with his eyes, with hearing only he marked the progress of the second intruder.

He heard the stealthy turning of the catches on the window, which he had been careful to close behind him, and he heard, next, the gradual process by which the window was raised. Next, there was the most delicate of whispers such as might be made, say, by the friction of cloth, very gently rubbed against wood.

The second man, then, was stepping over the windowsill!

Speedy, in his corner, smiled a little, but his lips pressed hard together, like those of a boxer about to deliver a blow.

And then he heard the faintest of creakings. Someone was crossing the floor.

Little by little, Speedy arose. And he saw, as his eyes came over the edge of the clothes on the chair's back, the form of a tall man leaning just over the bed of the sleeper, a great, gaunt body, oddly narrow in the shoulders, and with vast, dangling arms. For a trade mark to identify this midnight prowler, there was the red, ragged remnant of an ear, visible over one shoulder.

His purpose did not seem entirely sinister, however.

First, he leaned close over the sleeper, and as his shadow crossed the face of Franklin P. Franklin, the fat man groaned in his dreams and struck blindly, as though at a mosquito.

At this, Six Wilson slowly re-erected himself, and then, with a gaping grin, moved towards the door.

He moved swiftly, easily, with long steps, and yet the floor, flimsy as it was, did not complain under his weight.

Even cat-footed Speedy wondered as he watched.

Arrived at the door, the big fellow moved the bolt gradually, noiselessly back, and next he turned the lock.

Speedy was crossing the floor in turn, crouching low, hands spread out, as though a cat should partially rise to his hind legs only, while stalking.

The door opened, now, and before he stepped into the hall, Six Wilson drew a revolver, and gripped it twice, flexing his fingers carefully about the handles.

It was plain that he was using the room of Franklin P. Franklin not as a scene for a crime, as the boy had feared, but as an entrance to a more desired place — such a place, for instance, as the chamber where Speedy was supposed to be lying, soundly asleep — where in fact John Pierson was now in deep dreams.

Now, with one long stride, pitching his body low and turning so that his muscled shoulder would be the forward edge of his leap, like the head of a club, he drove straight at the tall man.

He made no sound, even in springing, but perhaps a shadow flew before him, and Six-card turned about, from the waist upwards, not shifting his feet.

It was the worst position he could have been in, to receive a shock. The right hand of Speedy caught the gun; it exploded to send a bullet through the floor. And the shoulder of the boy, at the same time, crashed against the hip of Six-card.

He seemed to break in two, like a slender stick. Then, dropping the gun so that he might use his hands more freely, he grappled with Speedy as he fell.

He reached for the throat of the boy, and only found the head of Speedy, stiffly bent down.

He took that head by the flying hair and, with the power of a gorilla, jerked it up and back.

The spine of Speedy almost snapped, under the shock. Clouds of red sparks flew upward in his brain. And amazement seized him. There was everything about Six Wilson to suggest the incarnate devil, but there was nothing to point to almost superhuman strength. But his muscles seemed to be those of an ape, not those of a human creature.

Yet, though his head was flung back, and the other hand of the thug raised to deliver a stunning blow, the wits and the arms of the boy kept working.

When in doubt, says the prize-ring maxim, work in close and hit as fast as your hands will work. When stung, charge!

Out of the air, half blindly, Speedy caught a thumb and forefinger of the elevated hand. He caught them, and jerked them back with a quick, twisting pressure.

Franklin P. Franklin, at that moment, wakened from a nightmare in dreams to one in reality. He began to scream for help, and shoot at the struggling monsters by the door. But the bullets flew wildly from his trembling hand.

And, through and over that noise, Speedy felt rather than heard a bone snap.

He had a one-handed man against him, to all

intents and purposes, from that moment.

No, now big Six-card jerked the elbow of his free arm around and the blow glanced off the forehead of Speedy.

He felt his knees buckle, and darkness washed across his eyes. But through that darkness he saw the convulsed face of Six Wilson, his lips grinned back from yellow fangs, like a beast about to bite into the throat, and search for the life, and the sight cleared his brain.

His hands had not been idle, and now they found what they wanted. His right hand, working up behind the shoulder of Wilson, now dipped over and to the front, the arm of the boy straining to its uttermost length, until his hand gripped hard around the lean, hard point of Wilson's chin.

He had a leverage, then, that multipled his strength of hand by ten. Even so, it was not easy to bend back the head of Six. It yielded, but only an inch at a time, fighting stubbornly. And, in the meantime, Six Wilson beat with his broken hand into the face of his tormentor.

He was like a great horse, attacked by a wildcat, torn, succumbing, and he struggled valiantly against his fall.

They had risen to their feet, the legs of Wilson lifting the double weight of the entangled bodies. There he stood looking more gigantic than ever, the clinging weight of Speedy appearing less than the body of a child.

If the hand of Wilson had been whole, in two efforts he could have beaten the boy senseless. But, as it was, even from his iron lips groans were wrung as he strove to use the hand as a club.

And, in the meantime, his other arm was tied close to his body by the encircling grip of Speedy, while the lifting shoulder of the tramp worked hard and high into the armpit of the big man, and that small hand seemed to increase and increase its pressure.

And the neck muscles of Six-card, overstrained, wavered, shuddered violently, gave away. Back went his head with a jerk; his mouth came open with a horrible gasping moan. And, close to his breast, he heard the snarl of Speedy, like a fighting animal.

Fat Franklin P. Franklin had rushed towards the door, still screaming, and at the door, he encountered men, big men. One was Joe Wynne; the other was Rudy Stern. But even they could not brush aside the hysterical clawing of the fat man as he strove to get out into the hall, away from the fight. In the instant they were delayed, over the shoulders of Rivera they saw big Six Wilson stagger backward, clawing at the air to get his balance. And they saw his head strained down and down by a remorseless pressure. They saw his whole body arching backwards — and then, like a tower, he crashed.

The weight of the boy was above him. And the force of the doubled body landed fairly upon his head.

He shuddered once, and lay still.

While Speedy, rising, staggered a little, and then he picked up the revolver which the big man, in the fury of the attack, had cast away from him.

"Hello, boys," he said to Wynne and Rudy Stern, as the pair pushed into the room. "Six-card seems to have mixed up the room numbers a little, and you see that he's gone to sleep in the wrong place."

After that, he abandoned the chamber and went to his own room.

The screeching voice of Franklin P. Franklin, in the meantime, was trailing and streaming down the stairs like a comet. And the whole hotel was wakening.

Not many seconds had passed since Speedy first flung himself at the big body of the bandit. But doors were opening, voices were shouting everywhere.

Then he opened the door of his room — to be covered by a revolver held in the hand of John Pierson.

The lawyer, half dressed, with a grim fighting face, glared down the barrel towards the intruder, and it was a long moment before he realized his mistake.

While Speedy said: "Don't be a fool, Pierson."

He crossed with slow, short steps to his own bed and let himself gradually down on it. Then he lay flat on his back. One arm hung over the edge towards the floor.

And every muscle, every tendon through his arms and shoulders seemed strained out of place — pulled thin.

Pierson stood over him, picked up the limp arm, and laid it across his body.

"Speedy, lad," said he, with surprising emotion in his voice, "you've been shot! Where's the hurt?"

"Not shot," muttered Speedy, keeping his eyes tightly shut, while the sparks still flew upwards in his brain. "Only a little tired. Too much noise in this damned hotel. Can't get any sleep."

"Not shot?" said Pierson, nevertheless fumbling anxiously about the breast of the boy, fearful of touching hot blood with his fingers. "What's happened?"

"Oh, nothing," said Speedy. "They're all standing on their heads because Six Wilson is in the next room, there, spread out flat with a bump on the back of his head. You better go and see what they do with him."

"Six Wilson!" breathed the lawyer.

"Six had a bad break," said the boy. "Break in the fingers of his right hand, as a matter of fact. Except for that — well, you go and see what they do with him, will you? If they put him in the jail, see that they keep two fellows guarding him night and day. He's a snake, and he can get out through the fingers of most people, I take it."

He added, as Pierson rushed from the room: "Poor Six! His gun hand, too!"

38

Pierson came back in half an hour. He was jubilant. Everything was easy, now, he said. The great Six Wilson was securely lodged in the jail, and four men had been detailed to keep guard over him in pairs, keeping sailor shifts.

"He'll get out, just the same," said the boy.

"He'll hang," said Pierson. "They're thirsty and hungry to hang him!"

"They're thirsty and hungry," said Speedy. "But he's not meant to die from a rope around the neck. He's not that kind, I tell you! He'll turn up his toes on horseback, filling the air with more lead than language, right up to the end."

Pierson sat down beside the table and stared at the boy, who remained limp, and with his eyes closed, on the bed.

"Are you sick, Speedy?" he said.

"I'm trying to think," said Speedy, "and that's what makes me feel a little sick."

"You'd better not go outside without a body-guard," said the lawyer.

"Why not? Do they want my scalp, too?"

Said Pierson: "Every man in Nixon wants to shake hands with you and pound you on the back. You know the way they are. And they'd like to clip a few souvenirs off you, too, if they have a chance. They'll pull you to shreds, Speedy, if they can!"

"That's good," said Speedy. "Nixon and all the people in it can be damned, as far as I'm concerned. They're not what bothers me."

"I know," suggested the other. "It's because of the rest of Wilson's gang; you think that they'll get on your trail and never leave it till they've polished you off. But I wonder — tell me if it's true that you shot a fellow called the Deacon to death and dropped another celebrated thug named the Snapper in one evening's entertainment?"

"I talked them to death, that was all," said the boy. "I hate gun fights. I told you that I never shot a bullet out of a gun in my life, and I don't intend starting now. It's not the Six Wilson gang that worries me most, just now."

"Go on," said the lawyer. "Tell me if you can."

"It's because something's gone wrong with me and I don't know what to do about it."

"What's gone wrong?"

"Something inside of me; something that I never had before."

"How does it feel?" asked Pierson, anxiously.

"Kind of giddy, Pierson, and a hollow feeling in the pit of the stomach."

"Indigestion," said Pierson. "I know. You've been under too much of a nerve strain."

"I'd call it conscience," said the boy. "It's new to me, but I'd call it conscience."

"You would?"

"Yes. I never had it wrong with me before. But I'd call it conscience, all right. The trouble is that I'm worrying about doing the right thing."

"Don't be foolish," said Pierson. "I'll keep you inside the law in this business, my lad."

"What I'm talking about has nothing to do with the law of the land. It's my law for myself that I'm thinking about."

"Go on, Speedy, and tell me all about it."

The boy opened his eyes and looked up at the ceiling.

"It's the old man that poisons everything," said he.

"What old man?"

"Old Rivera."

"What has he to do with your conscience, Speedy?"

"Ever since I heard that fat-faced fool in the next room talking about the old boy, I've had a picture of him."

"Well, what sort of a picture?"

"Of an old boy on a front veranda, leaning on

a cane and looking down the drive with eyes that he can't see out of. A blind old boy waiting for something to turn up."

"Hello," said Pierson. "Is that troubling you?"

"Yes, that's troubling me."

"I'll cut that trouble out of your mind, well enough," said Pierson. "That old Rivera was the meanest piker that ever rode a horse, when he was a youngster, they say. And he drove his own son away with his meanness."

Speedy shook his head.

"That was twenty years ago," said he. "He's had twenty years to think things over. He's had twenty years to wait. God pity him! I can't get him out of my mind, Pierson."

The lawyer frowned.

"What can you do about it?" he asked.

"Come clean," said Speedy. "You broached the deal to me. Now I suggest that the pair of us come clean."

"A few millions," said the lawyer, "means nothing to you?"

"Oh, hell, Pierson," said the boy, sighing out the words, "you know what money is. It's all right in a daydream. But when you have it once, it doesn't make the sky any bluer or beefsteak any tenderer. You know that?"

Pierson leaned suddenly forward in his chair.

"Do I know that?" he asked, slowly.

And his answer went no farther. He was lost in frowning thought.

"I don't like the job, any more," said the boy. "I told you that I'd go through with it. I want you to let me off the promise and give me a chance to do the white thing."

"What's the white thing?"

The lawyer was talking nervously, his lips and his fingers twitching.

"The white thing," said Speedy, his eyes closed once more, "is to get hold of the girl, and tell her everything straight, and then take her on the jump for the Rivera place. How far is that?"

"Five hundred miles. That's all!"

"We can do that in ten days. If it's that far, we'd better make an early start. You may shake your head and curl the lip at the Wilson boys, but I've nearly been their meat and I'd rather have somebody else digest me. Pierson, have a look at that idea, will you?"

John Pierson sat silent for ten long minutes. Then he swore, not once, but many times. He jumped up from his chair and went to the window, before which he stood with his arms akimbo. Still he swore, from time to time.

"Tough, isn't it?" said the boy. "I've been spending that easy money all the way from Cincinnati to Paris. I've traveled in special cars and raised champagne boils on the end of my nose. I've killed foxes in the galloping counties and smoked a cigar under the chin whiskers of the Sphinx. But it's no good!"

Said Pierson, gloomily: "I've been buying real estate. I've founded a big family fortune. I've been nursing it and building it bigger and stronger in my daydreams, lately. But you're right. It's no good. It's a thing that would make my wife and girl despise me, if they knew the ins and outs."

"Regular Bible talk, Pierson," said the boy.

"Shut up, Speedy," said the other. "You annoy me, when you speak like that. I'm going to chuck the whole business, though."

"And help to put it right?" said the boy.

"How can I help?"

"There's a tidy little job on hand," said Speedy. "Five hundred miles on horseback looks to me like five hundred miles through hell. I'll be worn through to the bone. I'm going to carry air cushions, and carve a hole in the center of my saddle. I'm so sore, Pierson, that I'd hate to ride a rockinghorse on the front veranda; but I've got five hundred miles before me. And I need you, and at least one more. You'll help to make the escort."

"Escort be damned," said Pierson. "I'm going back to my business. I've had enough of this infernal conscience business! Two weeks of riding, when I have cases —"

The slender hand of Speedy rose in the air.

"Think it over, Pierson," said he. "You like hunting. And on this ride, trouble is going to come hunting down the trail of whoever tries to get that girl to her grandfather. There'll be shooting. And I'm no hand with a gun. You know that. I'm just going along to give moral support, if you know what I mean."

He stared up at the ceiling, and the lawyer grinned, sourly.

"You'd even tempt the devil to take a change of air, Speedy," said he.

"You're sold, then," said the boy. "Now, I want to lie here and taste this conscience of mine until I'll know the sour tang of it the next time it gets high in my throat. I want to know what it is, in time to run the other way from it. You send for Mary Steyn and Arthur Steyn. And send for Joe Wynne, too, the big, blue-eyed puncher with the two big guns and the thoroughbred nature. I'll stand here without tying until you arrive again."

Pierson, for a moment, idled up and down the room, trying to find something to say, but he found nothing.

At last, he went out without further speech, and found his way, scowling, down into the lobby. A hum of voices rose from many throats to greet him.

The hotel proprietor rushed to him, sweating, beaming.

"How's the kid?" said he.

"Sound as can be," said Pierson. "You can't put a hole in that armor plate."

The proprietor rubbed his hands together; then he laughed with joy.

"We want him down here," said he. "We want to look at him again and see the sort of skin that handles fire without gloves. The whole town is happy, Mr. Pierson, except Mr. Franklin P. Franklin, and he's in the bar trying to get drunk, but he's still so scared that the liquor won't work on him. If you —"

"I want to get hold of a fellow named Wynne," said Pierson. "Speedy wants to see him."

"Wynne's right outside the door, as big as life. He'll go right up and —"

"And I want to send a message to Mr. Arthur Steyn and his daughter to tell them to come to town at once —"

"They're already in town," said the proprietor.

"Good!" sighed Pierson, his face falling in spite of himself. "Try to collect the whole lot of them, will you? And tell them that Speedy and I are waiting upstairs in hopes of seeing them."

The proprietor agreed, and Pierson took a weary way up the stairs again. Glancing once out the window, when he reached the room, he could hear hoofs beating, and see fresh clouds of dust rising. Other punchers were coming fast to Nixon to see the latest hero of the hour!

And there, on the bed behind him, lay the hero in person — sound asleep, and snoring lightly!

39

Sleep left Speedy only when big Joe Wynne came into the room and stood stiffly, like a soldier at attention, near the door. His eye was straight as ever, but his color was far from high.

"I hear that you want to see me, Speedy," said he.

Speedy slowly rolled to his feet, yawned, and eyed the other up and down. Then he deliberately walked across the room. When he was close to Wynne he thrust out his chin.

"You don't look so doggone big to me," said he.

"I'm big enough, son," said Joe Wynne, with a gleam in his eye.

"Some day we'll see about that," said Speedy.

Most impolitely, he turned on his heel and walked to the window. It was Pierson, a somewhat amused spectator of this scene, who offered a chair to the guest.

"I want to know what Speedy wants to see me about," said Wynne, steadily.

"God knows that I don't want to see you,"

said Speedy, without turning. "All I want to do is to hit you on a corner of your beautiful Greek chin. That's all I want to do. But I've got to talk nice to you about something else. Shut up and sit down, and let me get my wind, will you?"

"You'll understand before long," said Pierson, and got Joe Wynne, reluctantly, to take a chair.

Almost immediately, there was a knock at the door, and Steyn and Mary came in.

She smiled at Wynne, shook hands with Pierson when Speedy introduced her, and then said to the tramp: "What have you been doing, Speedy? Making yourself famous, or just having a good time?"

"Oh, you know," said he, "trouble always comes to him who waits."

"Of course it does," said she, "if it knows the room number so that he can wait in the right spot."

"Sit down, Mary; sit down, Mr. Steyn," said the boy. "I've got a speech coming over me. I need elbow room when I make a speech."

They sat down, all except Pierson, who fidgeted in a corner of the room.

"Hadn't I better explain the thing in detail, Speedy?" said he.

But the boy dominated the room easily.

He answered: "You'd make it too long. The main point is that this is a blue moment for four of the five of us. It's a happy moment for Mary Steyn, yonder."

"Go right on, Speedy," said Steyn. "This isn't one of your jokes, I hope?"

"I wish that it were," said the boy. "But I'll soon rub off all the smiles except from Mary's face. Mr. Steyn, you're going to lose her. Wynne, you and Pierson and I are going to ride five hundred miles with trouble behind us all the way, in order to plant her in the middle of umpteen thousand acres of grass and cows and about nine or ten million bucks."

Wynne sat up higher in his chair. The girl narrowed her eyes and searched the face of Speedy.

"I'll go back and explain a little," said the boy. "Mr. Steyn, about ten-eleven years ago, you picked up in the hills a ragged, nine-year-old brat, on the thin side, and yellow in the eyes from malaria."

"I found Mary in somewhat that way," said Steyn. "Speedy, do you mean it when you say that I'm to lose her?"

"You can't lose her," said Speedy. "She's not the kind to forget anyone she cares a rap about. And she cares a lot of raps about you. Only, you'll be seeing her in Paris models, from now on. And a little while from now you'll be standing on the promenade deck of the Ritz Hotel, steering for bigger and better drinks.

Mary when you found her, had hoofed it all the way from California. She's been kicked around a good bit by some hounds, who had her from Colonel Whatnot, who took her from an Indian squaw, who adopted her when her mother died and also her father, who left home in Texas because *his* father disapproved of the marriage. Does that clear the decks somewhat? The point is that for twenty years grandpa has been sitting on the edge of the Rio Grande, forgetting his bank account and letting his cows multiply regardless, because he wants his darling granddaughter. He's eighty plus, two-thirds blind and hungry to die; but he's hungrier still to give his estate to something nearer home than charity."

Old Steyn stood up and drew in his breath. Then he sat down again, slowly, without a word. The girl came and stood behind him. Her hands rested on his shoulders. Her big, doubting eyes studied the face of Speedy.

"Now, then," said Speedy, "we ride into Six Wilson, who learns about the bank account that's waiting for Mary, and rides off every prospective husband that might not give him a split when the good news breaks. That places Six for you in the game. Enter a hobo, Speedy. He gets wind of the quarry, decides that he wants to be a married man, and comes down the wind to pick up Mary. But she's too hard for him," he said, looking her fairly in the eye, "and so he throws up the sponge and comes to Nixon, where Mr. Pierson persuades him that the best thing is to go straight and tell Mary the whole story."

"Hold on, Speedy," said Pierson, growing very red. "You don't need to save my face, like this. I'll take all the punishment that comes my way."

"Besides Six," went on the boy, waving aside Pierson's protest, "Rudy Stern is also on deck. He doesn't know whether to try to be a power behind the throne or to write himself down as a suitor for the nine millions. Pierson here, has worked out the whole thing from the legal end; so he's in on the know. And there's also another in town who knows the story. He's a little fat pig with a happy eye and more names than you can shake a stick at. So, Mary Rivera, that brings the yarn down to the present. And the future is this: You pack a grip. You get your toughest horse. A pair of 'em, I suppose. And you and Pierson and I start for the Rio Grande."

He turned on Joe Wynne.

"This is where you come in, Joe," said he. "You're the only one of us who's played absolutely straight from the start. I owe you a sock on the chin, but I have to admit for the present that you're the only white man on the range.

You make number three in the escort, with a pair of your best nags, and half a dozen guns guaranteed to shoot straight. Because there's no doubt in my mind that trouble is going to run on our heels. Too many people know that the fat's in the fire the minute that we ride south."

"There's the law, Speedy," said Steyn, "that can give shelter and assure —"

"There are a lot of fourth and fifth cousins," said Speedy, breaking in abruptly, "who know that old Rivera has already made a will and put them down for something better than hope. And if you wait for the law to work, the law will find a dead old man down there by the Rio Grande, a will to be contested and everything tied in a muddle for ten years to come. Mary Rivera will turn into an old maid waiting for hard cash, and the only people to profit will be the lawyers. My way is the only way. Pierson will come. Wynne, will you?"

Joe Wynne stood up and held out his hand, silently. Speedy looked at it, and then up to the blue, honest eyes of the big rancher.

"Not till we're all square," said Speedy.

He raised his hand.

"If there's no more business to come before this meeting," said he, "we're dismissed. I need some sleep before we start."

"There's this much business," said Joe Wynne, who had remained staring at the boy

347

ever since the last rebuff he had received. "I have eight horses that are doing nothing, and one of them is your horse, anyway. You refused him once, but this time you'll have to take Coal Tar."

"Business is business," agreed the boy. "I'll take the nag for the trip, Joe, and a lot of thanks to you — afterwards — well, afterwards can take care of itself."

And he looked hungrily at the fine, strong jaw of the larger man.

Joe Wynne left at once. Mary and Steyn were to return to his house, and there she would pack up. And Speedy and Pierson went down to the head of the stairs, and saw the two go down arm in arm, old Steyn leaning a little against the girl, his head down.

As they disappeared: "He's close to crying," said Speedy, with a sneer which was not what it seemed. "No more chance to spend money on her, and he'll probably have to accept a necktie that he doesn't want every Christmas and birthday. That's the way women are. A man works for 'em all his life, nearly, and right at the end, he starts in sorrowing because they're not on hand to be cried over, anymore, and more worked over, too, and —"

"Be quiet, Speedy," said Pierson, and for once the boy obeyed him.

They were only halfway down the hall, however, when frantic footsteps rushed up the stairs and pursued them.

It was Franklin P. Franklin, who threw himself upon Speedy.

"Keep him off! Keep him off!" he gasped. "You're the only man that can keep him from murdering me!"

"Keep who?" demanded Pierson, helping to push the fat man away.

The white face of Mr. Franklin-Rivera was shaking like soft pudding.

"Six Wilson!" he screamed.

"He's loose already, then," said Speedy, with a resigned nod.

"Loose?" cried Pierson.

And, as though to dismally echo his words, they heard from outside the hotel a confused roar of voices, and a beating of hoofs.

"Yes, he's loose! Six masked men raided the jail, and covered the guards. There's two men shot, and one of 'em likely to die – and Six Wilson – he's gone – he ain't there! He's coming to finish his job and murder me! For God's sake, protect me, Mr. Speedy."

Speedy did not sneer. He merely held up one finger and said: "Listen!"

Franklin P. Franklin was as still as a child at school.

And Speedy said: "You're as safe as a clam in its shell in the bottom of the sea. Six Wilson wants my scalp, and not yours. He was only turning your room into a corridor that led to mine, last night. Now, you go to bed and rest your nerves, and you'll wake up to find that Speedy, and Six, and the whole bad business, have started south!"

40

Far out on the desert, the greasewood flowed like thin smoke in the hollows where water gathered, for a few brief days, in the spring of the year, and then soaked down and down, many yards, the earnest roots of greasewood and mesquite following it. And there was a blur of vegetation covering the ground. In the distance it held out some hope, being a fairly solid dusty green. But the ground over which the four rode was only sparsely set about with grisly forms of cactus, horribly defended, every one, with thorns.

They rode in single file, because the horses went better in this fashion, although the third and fourth man might be bothered, a good deal, by the rising of the alkaline dust. And the sun that beset them was bitterly hot. There had been a severe dust storm, the day before, though it had passed, the air was filled with indescribably fine dust which did not serve, apparently, to ward off any of the rays of the sun, but which blanketed the horizon in a dull and purplish mist.

But under the blast of the sun, which dried the sweat in streaks of salt as soon as it sprang, the horses went on at a good, free-stepping walk. Perhaps they were a little jaded by the work which already lay behind them, but this could not appear in their gait; not for nothing had Joe Wynne bred them for blood and looks, together, and tested his string with the hardest of endurance trials. Now that they were tried, they would not be found wanting.

Joe Wynne himself rode at the head of the line, just now, a magnificent figure of a man, looking nobler and bigger than ever, now that he had the whole setting of the desert around him.

A jack rabbit, long, lean-legged, fast as the flash of a whiplash, jumped from behind a cactus and sped away. Joe Wynne snatched out a revolver and opened fire. Four times the muzzle of his gun jerked up, four times the spray of sand which the bullet kicked up made the rabbit sky-hop high into the air and to the side. Four times, it bleated like a sheep, small and far.

Then Mary Steyn, hurrying her horse up, pulled down the gun-hand of her friend.

"He's run his gauntlet, Joe," said she. "Let him go, poor devil!"

"Four misses — in a row," said Joe Wynne,

"and three this morning."

"Every one of those misses would have killed a man," said John Pierson.

He was red-faced from the extreme heat. It was true that he loved the wilderness and wilderness life, but his choice was the grand, green quiet of the mountains — not that wide-stretched furnace floor.

"Yes," commented Speedy, who was last of the four. "If men were rabbits and ran, seven men would have flopped today, because of you, Joe. You're getting better and better! Pierson, show him some real shooting, will you?"

"Leave Joe alone," commanded the girl.

Wynne put up his revolver, flushing a little, but very little. He was growing accustomed to the badgering which he received from the tramp.

"That's only Speedy," said he. "I don't mind Speedy."

She smiled kindly on him, for a reward. And, since Pierson stopped his horse now to tighten a cinch, and Speedy paused with him, the leading pair were soon out of earshot of their followers.

"Look here," said Joe Wynne, turning half about in the saddle. "I'd like to get a line on something. I ought not to speak about it. But I've got to. It's stuck in my throat."

"What?" said she. "There's nothing in the

world that you can't ask me about."

"Then let me have it straight. I never can make out. Sometimes you go all day and never speak to him. Sometimes you rag and wrangle with one another for an hour at a stretch. How much do you like Speedy?"

She met his glance frankly.

And he hastened to put in: "It's not that I'm trying to push him out of the way. I'm not ambitious about you, Mary. I know that you're out of my horizon. But Speedy's brighter than I am. He's not out of *any* horizon that he cares to step into."

And she said: "I wish that you hadn't asked me. Not that I mind telling you; but it's a thing that makes me a little unhappy to think about. All I know is that I'm a lot more interested in Speedy than he is in me."

The big man stared.

"All right," said he. "But he's top man, isn't he?"

"He's top man with me," said she, firmly. "And then — if you don't mind being second — I think about Joe Wynne."

He grew very hot in the face.

"My God, Mary," he said, "I'm a happy man to hear that! If a horse is in the race it may win — if the leaders fall down!"

She said: "We won't speak about it again, Joe, will we?"

"Never a word," said he.

"There's another thing. Have you tried, really, to make friends with Speedy?"

"Yes," said he. "I've tried. But I might as well try to get close to a winged horse. He hates me. Not because he thinks I'm such a bad lot. Otherwise he never would have asked me to come along on this trip. But it's because I manhandled him, that unlucky day. He'll have to pay me off for that with a broken bone before he feels right about me."

"Oh, Joe," said the girl, "what sort of a man is he? How can anyone make him out?"

"Nobody can," said Wynne. "He's the straightest fellow in the world, and the crookedest. He's has the slipperiest tongue that ever talked; and his promise is a rock of Gibraltar. He's a fighting devil; and he never wore a gun. He'd move mountains to help a friend that he really likes – and he never worked for a dollar in his life!"

She sighed as she thought these things over.

"It's all true," said she. "But whatever he wants to do, he does. He's brought us halfway to the Rio Grande, already, and not a thing has happened."

"Has he done the bringing?" asked Wynne, smiling a little.

"Oh," she answered, "I mean that you all have been wonderful about it. But what keeps enemies at a distance is Speedy. People are afraid of him, once they've seen his teeth!"

"Yes," nodded Wynne, seriously, "he's riding here without a gun, and yet thugs like the Wilsons would be more afraid of him than of all the rest of us put together."

Then the other two came up, the voice of Speedy rising and ringing over the accompaniment that he struck from his guitar. That useless weight and burden added to the expedition!

A more ungraceful horseman never was seen in the Southwest.

He rode to the side, like a Greek muleteer, one stirrup dangling unoccupied, and only the stirrup leather of the other filled, while one foot swung free and bumped against the ribs of Coal Tar. It was an indignity that would have made the big stallion bolt like a streak if any other rider had offered it; but he had learned to endure much from this womanishly helpless, maddeningly reckless rider.

A horse is apt to be like a girl; as long as it is interested it is docile, and Coal Tar would never come to understand this whimsical master.

"Are you singing because you're happy, or because you want to be?" asked Pierson, at last.

"I'm singing," said Speedy, "to make both ends of me forget the middle. Pierson, I haven't got enough skin left to go around me. I walked all day yesterday, and I'd walk again today, but I took the skin off my feet yesterday; and now I'd have to walk on my hands. Pierson, I'd give a thousand dollars for a bread and milk poultice. I'm willing to go to bed and lie on my face for six months. If ever I buy a house, I'll burn all the hard-bottomed chairs in it for the sake of *Auld Lang Syne.*"

They were entering a narrow valley, ragged with rocks that cropped up on both sides, and the trail wound unevenly through the middle.

The sudden voice of big Joe Wynne blasted against their ears: "Ride! Ride like the devil! They're at us! They're at us! Mary, go first!"

The whole valley was ringing, at the same moment. From the rocks along the upper ledges, on the right side of the canyon, the marksmen were placed, in total safety. Ay, and right up the valley itself, behind the four riders, came a swarm of horsemen — four, five, six! They shot as they galloped, letting their horses find their own ways among the rocks.

Speedy was last, as the four got under way.

But he was last for only a second, in that miserable trap.

John Pierson suddenly swayed, lost his stirrups, and lurched to the ground.

Speedy, jerking hard back and shouting to the stallion, leaned down and grasped at the shoulder of the fallen man.

But the lawyer turned a set, blood-stained face towards the tramp.

"I'm only the first cash payment on account," said he. "I don't mind. Ride on, you fool! Get Mary through! Ride like the devil, while I trip up a few of 'em!"

As he spoke, he picked up the rifle that had fallen to the trail beside him, and instantly he was pumping lead at the riders from down the gulch.

And Speedy rode on!

He felt a wrench as though his heart was torn out of his breast. But he knew, in a blinding moment of revelation, that he would have wanted the lawyer to play the same role if he, Speedy, had gone down.

On raced his horse. The gulch vanished behind them, and looking back, he heard the rattling of the rifles far away, where John Pierson must be dying for the sake of the three who remained.

There was no pursuit. And Speedy came up with those who galloped ahead. The immense strides of Coal Tar devoured the distance between.

The girl, as he came up, turned and looked a horrified question at him, and he answered, coldly: "Pierson went down. I thought he'd serve to keep the teeth of the pack busy for a while, so I left him lying there, and came along."

He stared hard at her, and with amazement and bewilderment, he saw that she half believed that he had meant what he said!

41

They went on south for three more days, unhindered, but they were three dark days for Speedy. He never sang so much, so gaily, or so well, seated more like a Greek muleteer than ever in his saddle, but all the while he was black in his heart, for he was sure that both the girl and Joe Wynne blamed him bitterly for having "deserted" John Pierson.

That was the way they would have put it. They drew together more and more. He fell into the habit of lingering a good ways out of earshot to the rear, and he had a sense that when he came up, they talked less, and changed the subject of their conversation, often.

So he smiled and sang all the more, because that was his nature, but the blackness seeped through and through him, like a poison.

And their horses went well. They could see the hills behind which was their goal; in two days they would be there.

So, on the evening of the third day after the

fall of John Pierson, just before the sun set, when they were casting about for a proper place to make the camp, riders swept up out of a shallow draw whose existence they had not even suspected, and came at them in a long line.

The earth was paved with russet and gold from the evening light, and the shadows of the riders fell far before them. Swiftly they came with their guns, and in the center was the unmistakable and grotesque outline of Six Wilson, his narrow shoulders, his sombrero was wider than his shoulders. His right hand hung from his neck in a sling, but he managed his horse with knees and heels, only, like an Indian, and kept the left free for a revolver.

So they came, not yelling to strike terror into the enemy, and raise their own courage, but silently, like people who know their work, each man relying confidently on himself. They seemed to be racing to beat one another.

Speedy saw the girl whip her rifle from its long holster as their horses broke into a sweeping gallop. And then he heard a great, strange shout, that hardly seemed to come from a human throat, and on his right he saw Joe Wynne turn and charge straight at the Wilson gang.

He rode straight in the saddle, the brim of his sombrero curling back from his noble face in the wind of the gallop, and a revolver smoked in either hand. This Speedy saw, and beheld the line of the Wilsonites part in the center, and sway to this side and to that, heard the ringing of their guns, and saw them close around the big man like wolves around an elk.

And that was all.

Waves of swelling ground arose and shut away all view of the melee; he was riding at the side of the girl, now, the guitar giving out a little jingling at every stride, as though the fingers of a ghost were dallying at the strings and striving to begin a tune, but never getting past the first opening chords.

She looked neither to the side nor back, but straight ahead, and he saw that her face was wet.

Well, they were only two days from the Rio Grande. He would be glad when the two days were over!

They galloped into twilight, into darkness. Then they found running water, where the horses drank; they filled their canteens and went on to halt in a mesquite tangle, in a hollow. The girl would have gone on, and she spoke the first time, to say so, but Speedy answered: "They've got Joe Wynne, now, and he's enough to satisfy them, for a little while. Even the Wilsons don't get a Joe Wynne every day in their lives."

He spoke lightly, with a purpose, and then he added with a cheerful briskness: "Pretty good thing, wasn't it, the way old Joe turned around and smashed into 'em!"

She did not answer; then he heard her sobbing, a sad and regular pulse in the darkness.

After that, he waited until he was sure that she slept; then he untwisted his blanket, slipped away, saddled, not Coal Tar but the good bay gelding which was his lead horse, and turned straight back across the desert.

He rode for an hour, and then he found the guiding star that he wanted — a yellow ray shining along the face of the ground. He stalked it closely, left his horse and went on, on foot, stealthily. So he came close to the fire and the three men beside it. Two were faces he did not know; the third man lay some distance from the blaze, very still, his face turned up to the stars. That was big Joe Wynne.

The two were drinking coffee, bending over their tins, smoking cigarettes at the same time. Five horses were picketed nearby, grazing on the scanty grass among the rocks. Bridles, saddles, and packs lay in one confused heap.

Said one of the pair: "Bill's got the idea, Wynne."

"What is it?" asked Wynne, his voice clearly heard in spite of its quiet intonation.

A slight shudder went through the boy. It was like words from the dead.

"We're gunna make a regular rock grave for you, Wynne," said the speaker. "Here, Bill, you up and tell him."

Bill laughed.

He was a short man, with such heavy muscles around the shoulders that his arms were always carried thrusting out a little from his sides. It gave him a jaunty appearance, and now as he laughed, his elbows rose up and down and worked in and out. He looked like a bulldog. His nose and forehead retreated, as though to give his teeth a better chance to bite.

His companion was a bald-headed picture of vice, young, lean, with a crooked throat that looked as though it were broken in the center. He was always smiling.

"All right, Dan," said Bill. "I'll tell him. It's not gunna be any argument about how we finish you off, Joe. When the chief told us off for this job, he gave us a coupla hours to think it over, while he went ahead to rake in Speedy. He told us to think up the best way. Feeding you into a fire, he said would be good enough. He's kind of irritated agin you, Joe. Know that?"

"I can guess that," said the admirably calm voice of Wynne.

"He's mostly irritated because that feller

Pierson crawled off into the bush, and we couldn't afford the time to go and hunt him down. What the chief says is that the luck is rotten, because our guns don't kill, no more, and I says to him, I says: 'Six, you gotta remember that we was doin' all the shootin' off of horseback. That shakes a gun up, considerable.' Which he admitted that I had the rights of it. But now me and Dan, we been thinkin' it all over, and I got this idea. You might as well have dynamite for executioner, and gravedigger, and chief mourner at your funeral, old son."

He laughed again.

"I always pack some powder along with me," went on Bill. "I keep it over there in that saddlebag. Some of the boys, they call me Dynamite Bill, for that reason."

"Naw, that ain't the only reason," said Dan, chuckling.

"Maybe it ain't the only reason neither," said Bill, laughing with a conscious vanity. And he went on: "But it's a funny thing how handy old dynamite will come in, almost every trip. Sometimes they's a door that don't open none too easy, and then it's powder that makes a key to fit the lock — and there you are, inside. And sometimes the path is blocked, and then again old dynamite, he speaks one word, and that path is clear! And there has been a time when we was starvin' on the edge of good fishin' water, and dynamite, it was what killed the fish and drifted the dead of 'em onto the shore, and we ate right plenty, that time. And I recollect, and so does Dan, here, a time when the folks was gettin' thicker'n mosquitoes on our trail, and I just light a short fuse and drop it down the side of the rock onto the trail in the midst of 'em, and they begun to yell, and they pull their hosses around, but the direction that they started in wasn't where they wound up, because they landed in hell, Wynne, if you know what I mean."

Laughter choked him, and he went on, after a moment: "So now, as soon as we finish this here coffee, we're gunna stretch you out there under that high rock, Wynne, and we're gunna put a coupla sticks under the hind end of that rock, and blow it over onto you. This here is a pretty well-traveled trail. Every coupla hours in the day, folks come along, and they'll look at that rock, and they'll say that there must of been an earthquake, or something, and they'll never think that little old dynamite lies on top, and big Joe Wynne, he lies under. Joe, does that sound right to you?"

"That sounds all right to me," said Joe Wynne, as calmly as ever.

"Well," said Dan, "he says that it sounds all right to him. So as long as we got his permission, why shouldn't we do the little job now —

ask dynamite to do it for us, I mean! What's the use of holdin' back, when the crowd is so doggone anxious to see the job done?"

"No reason at all," said Dynamite Bill, and he rose to his feet.

Speedy rose at the same time.

He had reached the designated saddlebag by working along the ground like a snake. He had probed the inside of the bag and found what he wanted, not one stick, but three. One, however, was all that he wanted.

He made careful aim, sighting the distance to the fire, and then he threw the stick well up into the air.

It was some yards away, but Dynamite Bill saw a shadow flick across the corner of his eye, as it were, and whirled with a shout of surprise and anger, snatching out a gun.

There he saw the dim silhouette of the boy standing in the starlight, one hand raised in the completion of the gesture that had thrown the powder.

"Now what in hell d'you want, and who are you?" Bill asked.

"Speedy," said the boy.

And as he spoke, the stick descended from its long arc and struck the fire.

Speedy himself was knocked headlong, staggering, though he had been at such a distance. But when his mind and eyes cleared, he saw a queer heap of something that was neither brush nor stone near the place where the fire had been burning.

And far away, running with blind veerings, ran the tall form of Dan like a snipe flying down the wind, and as he ran, his screaming blew behind him, growing fainter and fainter with his swift strides.

42

It was well before daylight when Speedy wakened the girl.

"It's time to start," he told her.

She got up without a word, and started pulling on her boots. He, beginning to saddle the horses, called over his shoulder: "Joe is all right."

"What!" she cried.

She came running, hobbling, for one high-heeled boot was on, and the other was off.

"He's all right," said Speedy. "He's back there lying in a shady spot, with plenty of food and water, and on a trail where people come along every couple of hours in the day."

"Speedy, Speedy!" cried the girl. "How did you do it? How did you manage to get him away from them? And is he badly hurt? And what happened?"

"They put about a dozen bullets into him," said the boy. "But what do slugs through the arms and legs matter? He might have a stiff shoulder, later on; but every hero ought to have a limp, somewhere or other. He's going to be all right. He's a little weak, but he'll do fine."

"But you haven't said what happened?" insisted Mary Steyn. "You haven't said how you managed —"

"Oh," said the boy, "the Wilson gang changed its mind. They were going to murder him, of course, but they changed their mind. They were too anxious to pick you up, Mary. So we'll just hit the high spots. By the way, they told Joe Wynne, before they left, that Pierson got away from 'em, too. He did it at night, by crawling off into the brush, and he lay so low that they couldn't find him, in the time they could afford to spend searching."

He heard her crying and laughing at once; but he went on cinching up the saddles.

"God had a hand in it!" said the girl. "If there's a God, he had a hand in it. Only, Speedy, I don't believe what you say. You *drove* them away!"

"Look at the guns," said the boy. "Just as much ammunition in them now as there was last night."

She shook her head.

"Your way is magic," said she. "Not guns, but all hand and head."

She began to sing under her breath, and when they mounted, he found her eyes turned constantly towards him, but for his part, he looked straight ahead. The black and bitter poison was still in him.

So they rode into the rose of the morning, and into the brilliant, terrible sunshine.

That day ended. They climbed hills. They came, in the late evening, in sight of a deserted, ruined shack, with massive 'dobe walls, and a growth of poplars crowding together at a little distance from the place. There they halted, and looking down the long slopes, they saw the green of the fields, the rich pasture lands, dull in this faint light, and the thin and curving gleam of a river beyond.

"That's the Rio Grande," said Speedy. "We'll wait here for a while and let the horses rest a bit. Then we'll forge ahead. There's a good moon to the west, now, and we'll make our start and the first hour, or so, by the light of it."

"Is it safe to stop?" she asked him.

"It's not safe," he answered, bluntly. "Nothing's safe, I suppose. But these horses need a rest. We can build a fire in the shack. You make some coffee, and I'll hobble the horses."

He did as he had said, and the coffee was steaming when he came in. They drank some of the night-black, bitter stuff before eating, for they were both weary to death. And, while they were sipping, they heard the first sound of the approach. It was only the popping of a single dead branch. But suddenly they looked up at one another, agape, and each studied the horror of the other in the red firelight, like a thin wash of blood over the face.

Then he said: "I think this is about the finish, Mary."

She got up and gripped a rifle.

"Suppose that we make a break," said she.

"On foot?" said Speedy.

He merely smiled. Then he trod out the fire, kicking dirt over the embers.

Outside, there was a murmer of voices, and one saying, clearly: "There's Coal Tar. The chief'll be glad to see the old devil again! Hey, you inside — Speedy! Speedy! Come out and take your medicine, you sneaking coyote, you poison-faced hound! Come out here and take what's comin' to you!"

He actually made a step towards the door; the girl clung to him with both hands, shuddering, but strong with frenzy.

"If you go out — if you let them murder you — I'll kill myself, Speedy!" said she. "I won't let them take me!"

"They don't want you," said the boy. "What could they do with you? It's me that they want — but I won't go out yet, for a little while. Take your hands off me and stay back in the corner. This is my job."

She shrank from him, and heard him call: "Hello — is Handsome out there?"

"Handsome who?" called the answer.

Speedy paused, saying rather loudly to the girl, "You keep your eye peeled through the slots at the back of the house, will you? And shoot at anything you see moving."

A sudden, hasty rustling answered this speech, from the rear of the house.

"I mean," went on Speedy, "handsome Six-card Wilson. Is he out there?"

A bawling voice answered: "He's here, and he wants me to tell you that he's gunna eat tramp-meat, before sunup. You've made a good play, Speedy. We're gunna remember you, too. It was a good ride and a long ride, but we nailed you in the finish. You can tell the girl that she's not gunna be hurt. She's only gunna be delayed a mite. We'll give our word for that. But you, Speedy, come out and take what's comin', or else, by God, we'll heap up wood and burn out the pair of you."

"That's a lie," said Speedy, calmly. "These walls are 'dobe, there's no roof to hold the smoke, and you can burn wood and be damned, but you'll never smoke me out. There's only one thing that will make me move."

"Speak it out, Speedy," said the spokesman. "What's that?"

"A fair crack at Mr. Six Wilson."

"You fool! Six has only got one hand."

"I'll tie my right hand behind me," said the

373

boy. "I'll meet Six in the moonshine right in front of the shack. You boys can watch from the brush with your rifles, and see there's fair play. The girl will watch from inside with her rifle, and see that there's fair play. I'll wait for Handsome, until he shows his face."

There was murmuring of many voices; several minutes passed, and suddenly the giant stepped forward from the trees. His right arm was crossed behind his back. His left hand dangled empty.

"Speedy, don't go," pleaded Mary Steyn. "I think I'll go mad."

He said nothing. He simply struck her detaining hands away, and she, the rifle shaking in her grip, leaned half fainting in the darkness inside the doorway.

She heard the big man saying: "Now I got you in a fair open place, where there ain't any walls and no surprises to help you, and one hand will be enough to choke you with, you rat!"

Said Speedy, in answer to that ghastly whisper: "From the minute I laid eyes on you, I knew that you'd be my first kill, Six. I've been tasting the death of you all of these days. And tonight's the time."

She heard not so much the words as the voice which uttered them, and her blood congealed.

Then they closed.

The stride, the lofty height of Six, the great, poised hand, made him seem like one of those fierce birds which kill snakes, and snakelike was the wavering, darting approach of the boy. It was not human. It was simply horror past words.

They closed; they parted, they closed again. Six Wilson staggered, and a roar of excitement and dismay went up from his men; and the girl heard a man shrieking: "Six, Six, what's the matter with you? You can break the shrimp's back. What's the matter with you?"

But Speedy like a wildcat had followed in; and they whirled together. The legs of the boy seemed wound into those of the gaunt outlaw, but by his left hand he kept his best hold, and that hold was on the throat of the big man. She saw both their faces, ghastly in the moonlight; one killing, one dying.

But it was not ended, yet. Six Wilson had not come into that battle prepared to trust all to fair combat. Instead, his free hand now jerked up high, with a blade gleaming in it.

Mary Steyn screamed, but only half the scream was uttered as she saw the knife descend and the blade buried in the body of Speedy.

Then the rifle snapped up to her shoulder, and she took aim.

Twice and again the knife struck down, and twice and again her finger curled on the trigger, only to find that the body of Speedy had each time whirled in between her and the target.

She would have to try the head.

Coldly, without a quiver of her body or her nerves, she drew the bead; but the pair collapsed to the ground before she could shoot.

A man ran out, wildly shouting, from the brush. She put a snap shot close to his ear, and he fell backwards to the ground, in his eagerness to get back to safety.

And then — she saw it with eyes that would not close — the pair was twisting on the ground, snakelike, and the throat hold of Speedy was broken. Was he dying? No, the knife was in *his* hand, now.

It drew back, and once, twice, thrice, it went home. Distinctly, on her own heart, she felt the impacts.

Then both bodies lay still.

"They've killed each other. I'm kind of sick," said a groaning voice from the shrubbery. "I'm gunna get out of here."

"And the girl?" said another.

"Only Six would of known what to do with her. Leave her be. She can bury 'em, and be damned to her."

Quickly they went, as men go from a plague spot. The treading of many hoofs died in the distance. And still Mary Steyn, like a statue, stood in the dark of the doorway, and looked at men, and life, and death, and thought such thoughts as she would never think again, in the course of her life.

And so, as she stood, she saw the slender form of Speedy arise, slowly and steadily, and heard him saying, in the calmest of voices: "I had to play 'possum till they left. Must have been hard on your nerves, Mary. But now if you'll do a little bandaging, we'll be starting along, I think."

43

Old Rivera was called, through all the length of the river, Don Alfonso, though his eye was as blue as the next man's. But there was a dignity and a grandeur of living about him that called for a title, and this one was given to him.

Being very old, he kept the hours of a bird, asleep by dark, awake by dawn; and in the heat of the day he slept soundly, for two or three hours. So the fire of life remained in him, perhaps, but clearly burning. He was not changed from his younger self; there was simply less of him in body and in will.

But on this morning, he was having a sop of dark bread in neat wine for breakfast on his veranda. He had eaten just such a breakfast, all the days of his life, when he was at home. The morsel of bread satisfied his hunger. The wine put a warmth in his blood.

And, leaning both his hands upon the round head of his cane, when he had finished his breakfast, he looked fixedly down the avenue under the trees. That was his habit; that was the vista up which the only remaining joy of life could come to him, and down that vista went his thoughts, night and morning. So he lifted his head, a little, when he heard the grinding wheels of the buckboard on the gravel, not in hope, but in interest. Everything that approached the house always gave him that dim, small wave of expectancy, followed by the thin shadow of disappointment.

On the front seat of the wagon there was a Mexican driver, whipping the little pair of mustangs cruelly. In the rear seat of the buckboard a man and a girl were sitting, he with his coat huddled loosely about his shoulders and white bands going around and around his body. He lay back in the seat, his chin on his breast. And the girl beside him was holding one of his hands.

But it was not the youth that held the eye of old Don Alfonso. It was the girl.

As the buckboard came nearer, he rose, helping himself up with a strong push of his hands against the head of the cane. Then he walked to the edge of the steps, and finally halfway down them, staring.

She seemed to pay no heed to him, until she had jumped down to the ground, and even then she did not have a chance to speak. For he called out: "Jose!"

A man jumped out and stood beside him.

"Your mistress has just come home," said Don Alfonso. "Go open the windows of her room."

The moon hung an hour high in the west; four weeks had run since it was there last, at this time, when the sunset and the twilight were meeting.

And old Don Alfonso was saying: "It is better out here on the veranda. The air is sweeter and cooler. You can feel the river moisture in it, on an evening like this, and the mosquitoes are not so bad, this year, Mary. I think we may have to make a screened porch, one of these days.

"Mr. Steyn, will you take this chair on my right? I should live more and happier years, Mr. Steyn, if I could always look forward to having you here at my right hand. But I understand your point of view. A man's home is more than family, more than blood; it is a part of his soul.

"Now, then, Joseph, I think that other chair will bear your weight. And you, Mr. Pierson, try that canvas chair. You'll find your leg more comfortable, while you're in it. And now, I think, we are all together?"

Joe Wynne laughed faintly.

"All except fifty-one per cent of us," said he. "Speedy isn't here."

"Yes," said Don Alfonso, "even Speedy is

here. He'll always be present, when we're together. He can't be absent. And just now I have
a letter from him — a letter written to Mary, for
me to read to her, and explain. But instead, I
am going to read it to all of you because, my
dear friends, in a certain way we are all mem-
bers of one family. Danger and blood have
cemented us together. So, then, if you're ready,
I'll begin. Mary, sit there on the step, where I
can watch your face.

"The letter begins:

" 'Dear Mary,
" 'Last night I talked things over with
your grandfather. We reached an agreement. I'd better say he agreed with me.
" 'The things that make me happiest I
can put first. One is that you're first, with
me, and all the rest of the world is a bad
second. The other is that, the other day, I
think you were about to say that you are
fond of me, too. The reason I wouldn't let
you finish your sentence, that time, was
that an instinct tapped me like a hand on
the shoulder and told me that it was
wrong.
" 'Since then, I've been thinking it over,
for hours, and I've been feeling so sorry for
myself that there have been tears in my

381

eyes and dry bread in my throat. But what I see clearly, now, and what your grandfather agrees, is that a house and a life and a woman's happiness cannot be built on a rolling stone.

" 'This old house, and this whole fine old estate is enough to fill any sensible man's eye. But I'm not sensible, and when I look on the spot where I'm to spend the rest of my life, I feel as though I were already half in the grave.

" 'So I have to see other places, and roll here and there, and go my own way, which is a vagabond's way. I always thought that I was only killing time until a grand opportunity should come my way, but now that the opportunity has come, I see that the devil has been too careful a schoolteacher for me, and I can't forget his lessons.

" 'No, as I see it, a far better man than I ever will be ought to stand first with you. You love him already. And as soon as the tramp is out of the way, you'll see him more clearly. There's no spot on him. He's the one man to whom I'm willing to owe a certain sort of debt and leave it unpaid. There's still a very small bump on the back of my head, and every time I touch it, I'll think of the two of you. It will be a sad business at first, but after a while I know that I'll be happy about it.

" 'I haven't the courage to say good-bye to you, because if I looked in your eyes and saw the least shadow of happiness, I know that I would drop to my knees and beg you to let me try to make you happy the rest of your life.

" 'So, tonight, when the moon begins to shine, I'm going to take my guitar and start out. Tell Pierson that I know he'll be rich before he dies, and give my love to your grandfather and old Joe Wynne, and Mr. Steyn. Three like them never sat together in one room.

" 'Mary, good-bye; and now that I come to the end, I see that I have never given you any name to remember me by except one that will quickly run downhill out of your mind.

Speedy.' "

Now, as the old man finished reading this letter, a great silence came over all of those on the porch. And each one of them looked down, and studied his own thoughts.

So complete grew the stillness, that out of the distance a thin sound of music drifted to them, though so indistinctly that only those who already knew the words could have guessed them:

"Julia,
You are peculiar;
Julia,
You are queer.
Truly,
You are unruly,
As a wild, western steer.
Sweetheart, when we marry,
Dear one, you and I —"

Here the music faded away.

The words of that song were not familiar to Don Alfonso. Besides, he hardly heard the song at all, he was so engaged, now, in watching the girl.

For on the high shoulder of wall beside the steps, she sat just a shade above him, and now the westering moon began to slide down behind her, first catching in a glow of light her hair, and then gliding the curve of her throat, and outlining with infinite tenderness her bowed face.

So it stood, at last, like a great golden shield, and her head the bright boss in the center of it.

She did not stir, and there was no voice along the dark veranda until the wind from the coolness of the river came up through the trees, hushing and whispering at every ear.

te Delicious

5°

ce

rdu

sugar

Almond

Dorothy

Chocolate Pie

5 large or 6 small eggs
2 tablespoons sugar
4 tablespoons cream
1 pkg choc chips
1 tea vanilla
melt chocolate chips in
double boiler. Beat ch
with sugar thoroughly
cream + let cool. Th

BAKING
by Flavor

BAKING

Lisa Yockelson *by Flavor*

FOREWORD BY FLO BRAKER
PHOTOGRAPHY BY BEN FINK

JOHN WILEY & SONS, INC.

A NOTE ABOUT THE EQUIPMENT IN THE PHOTOGRAPHS
All of the materials, including the cookware, bakeware, and linens, both contemporary and antique, are from the author's collection.

Comments about *Baking by Flavor* may be forwarded to the author at fourstarbaking@earthlink.net.

This book is printed on acid-free paper. ∞

Published by John Wiley & Sons, Inc., New York
Published simultaneously in Canada.

This publication is designed to provide accurate and authoritative information in regard to the subject matter covered. It is sold with the understanding that the publisher is not engaged in rendering professional services. If professional advice or other expert assistance is required, the services of a competent professional person should be sought.

Cover and interior design by Vertigo Design, NYC
Cover and interior photography by Ben Fink
Food styling by Lisa Yockelson

Library of Congress Cataloging-in-Publication Data:
Yockelson, Lisa.
    Baking by flavor / by Lisa Yockelson.
        p. cm.
    Includes bibliographical references and index.
    ISBN 0-471-36170-4 (cloth : alk. paper)
        1. Baking. 2. Flavor. 3. Flavoring essences. I. Title.
    TX763.Y628 2001
    641.8'15—dc21   2001046956

PRINTED IN THE UNITED STATES OF AMERICA.

10 9 8 7 6 5 4 3 2 1

this book celebrates the memory of

LILLIAN LEVY YOCKELSON

1899–1969

grandmother, trailblazer, mentor

CONTENTS

ABOUT THE ICONS THAT APPEAR WITH THE RECIPES

The recipes in this book have been evaluated by degree of difficulty: When you see ✳, it means that beginner bakers and cooks should be comfortable with it; ✳✳ means that some moderate kitchen know-how is fundamental to its success (but avocational or occasional bakers should have no trouble with it); and ✳✳✳ indicates that some experienced baking skills are called for (most of the recipes judged ✳✳✳ involve baking with yeast).

FOREWORD

BITE INTO A DECADENT COOKIE, a rich cake, or a sumptuous piece of pie. Consciously or unconsciously, flavors always capture our attention. The art of flavoring requires trial and error as well as an incredible memory bank of tastes that can take years to master. At your fingertips, *Baking by Flavor* represents a wealth of flavor-filled recipes to stimulate your taste buds and expand your knowledge of baking.

Baking by Flavor, with its fresh approach to baking, is destined to be a classic. We're accustomed to thinking about baking in categories such as cakes, pies, and cookies. Lisa Yockelson takes us in another direction by spotlighting not only the ingredient itself but the essence of that ingredient.

The book's mouthwatering recipes show us how to accentuate 18 favorite ingredients in a variety of baked specialties. After more than a decade of research in flavor-baking, Lisa has made home cooks and master pastry chefs the lucky beneficiaries of this carefully assembled information.

Through invaluable, user-friendly charts, Lisa illustrates the intriguing process of developing flavor by using a combination of similar, compatible ingredients in a batter or dough. Lisa dubs this "flavor-layering." Starting with quality ingredients is paramount, but by using unique methods Lisa ensures extraordinarily flavorful results.

Lisa's recipes, with their introductory headnotes, easy-to-follow instructions, and notes, will educate you and give you confidence in your own baking judgment. Lisa's astute insight into the art of baking is apparent on every page of what is certain to become a time-honored reference.

For years Lisa's masterfully written baking books have occupied a very important place in my kitchen. This distinctive volume, with its reassuring voice and original approach, catapults baking into another dimension. Here's a kaleidoscope of taste experiences—from rich chocolate and tangy lemon to spicy ginger and floral vanilla.

You'll never think about flavors in the same way again.

Flo Braker
Author, *The Simple Art of Perfect Baking* and *Sweet Miniatures*
Palo Alto, California

ACKNOWLEDGMENTS

THIS COOKBOOK represents my extensive and cumulative research in the workings of flavor-enhancing baked goods. It was, for many years, a swirling collection of ideas, a way of working in the kitchen with doughs and batters, and a series of baking methods, all swathed in a provocative, sometimes puzzling philosophy. Not until I had a conversation with my longtime childhood friend Lisa Stark, Esq.—by day a notable civil rights attorney—who suggested that I arrange a baking cookbook by favorite flavors in order to define the very scope of my work, did the overall concept crystallize. This is the origin of the organization of *Baking by Flavor*. (And Lisa's chocolate-loving husband, Harvey Rubenstein, M.D., "helped" by test-tasting all of the brownies.)

Mickey Choate, my exceptional literary agent at The Lescher Agency, Inc. (who is both an excellent baker *and* fine cook), forwarded the notion of a book on flavor-baking with a passion equal to, and oftentimes greater than, my own: when I wobbled, he persevered. His own talent is reflected in the pages that follow in the many ways that define the alliance between author and agent—by offering a philosophical overview of the book's theme and his own conceptualization of the recipes. In many ways, *Baking by Flavor* could not have been produced without him. And many sweet thanks to all at The Lescher Agency, Inc. and Lescher and Lescher, Ltd. for ongoing support and guidance—Susan Lescher, Robert Lescher, Carolyn Larson, Barbara Craig, and Richard Prentice. I continue to learn so much from working with you.

My skillful editor on this project, Pamela Chirls, believed in, understood, and respected the concept of *Baking by Flavor* from the very beginning. (And, I confess, the beginning seems like such a long time ago.) Since then, Pam has baked batches of brownies from the manuscript of this book (sometimes along with her enthusiastic helpers, twins Allix and Julia Chirls); mothered the manuscript right along with her newest arrival, Isabelle Chirls; studied recipes and text, and listened to my observations about the book's breadth, design, and defined point of view. Pam's keen interest in the project is apparent on many levels. Sealed between the covers of *Baking by Flavor* is the guidance of an immeasurably competent editor.

Ben Fink's camera lens is a metaphor for his art: focused and sensitive—and, at times, even poignant. And let me tell you about Ben. He photographed all of my bakery sweets, the bakeware (old and new) that I own, and the room where so many of my waking hours are spent, the kitchen. (In my hands, he practically immortalized the Essence of Chocolate Squares.) He did this with grace and style, and a benevolent spirit. While we waited for the sun to rise, and for the day's natural light to creep through my windows, we spoke of many things, and this book is the richer for it.

Flo Braker is a consummate professional and has, for many years, inspired me through her writing of the baking process. Her knowledge of baking and enthusiasm for the subject is vast and impressive, and I am honored to have her presence in the foreword of *Baking by Flavor*.

At John Wiley & Sons, Inc., Jyoti Singla, editorial assistant to Pamela Chirls, kept the schedule for *Baking by Flavor* timely and up-to-date by handling and expediting all of the important notes and materials in a friendly and efficient way. Eileen Chetti, managing editor in the production department, oversaw all the phases of production for *Baking by Flavor* without missing a beat (or a deadline). The fabulous energy of Lucy Kenyon, associate director of publicity; P.J. Campbell, associate director of events; Valerie Peterson, senior marketing manager, culinary and hospitality; Jeff Faust, art director, creative services; and Jean Morley, director, creative services, is evident in all the far-reaching phases through which *Baking by Flavor* has progressed. This thank-you hardly seems enough for all of your time and expertise devoted to this book.

Alison Lew and Renata de Oliveira at Vertigo Design took my prose, detailed recipes, and charts and Ben Fink's luscious art, which comprise *Baking by Flavor*, and turned them into an extraordinarily appealing volume in a way only gifted designers can do. Many chocolate-and-vanilla-wrapped thanks to everyone at Vertigo for your aesthetic sensibilities.

In addition to Pam Chirls, I have been privileged to work with many superb editors over the years, who, in their own way and along with a brand-new band of editors, shaped my thinking about the writing and the baking process: Patricia Brown, editor, consultant, and former cookbook editor at Harper and Row Publishers, edited *Country Pies*, a single-subject baking cookbook that would later spawn a trilogy of country baking books (and lots of baking); Susan Friedland, cookbook author and director of cookbook publishing at HarperCollins Publishers, cultivated my work for years with intelligence and insight; Phyllis C. Richman, author, food critic, and former executive food editor of the *Washington Post*, persuaded me to actually write what I do, step-by-step, in the kitchen; Nancy McKeon, former food editor of the *Washington Post*, nudged me to add special twists to recipes; Pam Anderson, cookbook author and former executive editor of *Cook's Illustrated* magazine, developed my skills for asking all the right questions along the way to recipe refinement, and taught me to "climb a ladder" to review my baking articles from a different perspective; Jeanne McManus, the current (and dynamic!) food editor of the

Washington Post, encourages my cooking and baking by printing the articles that arise from our conversations; Tish Boyle, food editor and test kitchen director of *Chocolatier* magazine and food editor of *Pastry Art & Design* magazine (and friend-in-chocolate), lets me turn my hand—and mixer—to every baking obsession (and there are a lot of them), and write about the results; Timothy Moriarty, former features editor of *Pastry Art & Design* magazine and former managing editor of *Chocolatier* magazine, encouraged me to develop the "flip side" of plated desserts—resulting in baking pans full of sweets—with confidence; and Michael Schneider, publisher of both *Chocolatier* and *Pastry Art & Design* magazines, understands the elements that make a baker's craft so all-involving, and lets my baking flourish in the pages of his magazines.

Many thanks, too, to these professionals who, throughout the years, have cheered on my work in the field of baking and writing about it—Barbara Burtoff, Susan Belsinger, Larissa Berrios, Flo Braker, the late Anne Crutcher, Carol Cutler, Mimi Davidson, Alexandra Greeley, Rebecca Hamill, Marilyn Jarboe, Susan Lindeborg, Quentin Looney, Carol Mason, Kay Nelson, Penelope Pate-Greene, Nancy Pollard, Bunny Polmer, Anna Saint John, Renee Schettler, Carole Sugarman, and Virginia Washburne.

Business associates and longtime friends who encouraged, sampled, counseled, inspired, and on occasion generously unlocked their memories to recall baking favorites from childhood to the present have been, each in his or her own way, an influential part of this book. They are Charles Santos, for his management expertise; Sanford Ain, Esq., and Jeffrey Weinstock, Esq., for their professional presence; Frank Babb Randolph, for his interior design guidance; Daniel Magruder, of Voell Custom Kitchens, for devising such an attractive kitchen that has endured over the years and, since then, for solving some thorny kitchen-equipment predicaments in the most elegant way possible; Marie Romejko, S.N.D.; and my neighbors John George and Peter Maye, for their test-tasting of the absolute mother lode of baked goods deposited under the gate, at the door, in the driveway, and piled on the front seat of their car ("Don't sit on the brownies!") for months on end.

And the course of time has never diminished my admiration for the late Lillian Levy Yockelson, Irene and Bernard Yockelson, and Wilbert Yockelson. You departed much too soon. You are missed.

INTRODUCTION

The Focus and Purpose of Baking by Flavor

IN MANY WAYS, *Baking by Flavor* is a personal baking memoir, a recipe journal that records the way that my own baking style has taken shape. It's also a detailed look into how recipes that underscore specific flavors can be highlighted, then uplifted, intensified, and invigorated. It's important to put these recipes in an evolutionary time frame: a good number of them have evolved in my kitchen over the last 12 years, and many well before then. Although the exact concept had not been codified in my kitchen until a certain time, the idea for packing as much flavor as possible into baked goods has always been a significant consideration in my baking and work in recipe development.

The focus of this book is threefold: (1) to explore how a particular flavor is best developed in a recipe and then imparted to a certain sweet; (2) to elevate the flavor in traditional baking recipes that primarily use doughs and batters, and to deliver them into an up-to-date setting; and (3) to chronicle my research into flavor-baking. *Baking by Flavor* is both a baking cookbook about the hows and whys of bringing out flavor in baked goods and a compendium of recipes that spotlight many appealing flavors.

In researching and formulating the concept of flavor-baking, I found myself sifting through, and ultimately challenging, traditional formulas, procedures, and approaches, and finding ways to introduce taste into baked sweets and their accompanying fillings, glazes, frostings, and sauces. In the beginning I began to inspect recipes through a "taste magnifying glass." As a result, some old recipes seemed quaint. The recipe for Essence of Chocolate Squares on page 282 is a good example of that process. The squares are composed of two layers: a dense and fudgy chocolate cake layer covered completely by a creamy chocolate frosting. My goal was to create, in one bar cookie, an intense chocolate flavor with a bittersweet edge, a moist denseness, a buttery "crumb," and a thick swath of frosting that sweetly contrasts to and merges with the layer beneath. Actually, I was going after something that was part brownie, part confection. Over many months, the composition of this sweet was fine-tuned and ultimately revised to my taste. Many more of my recipes went the route of cultivation and revision, and I worked in this area to satisfy my own contemporary tastes, and to rescue and improve upon recipes that seemed, quite honestly, boring.

The purpose of *Baking by Flavor* is to offer to all cooks whose passion is baking—whether at home or in a restaurant kitchen—some challenging ways to look at and improve recipes in particular flavor categories.

The Organization of the Chapters

PART I OF THIS BOOK, "The Art of Baking by Flavor," is for the conceptual baker, while Part II, "The Flavors," is for the passionate, in-the-kitchen baker. The first four chapters in the book ("The Way to Bake by Flavor," "An Inventory of Baking Equipment," "Creating a Baking Pantry," and "Craft and Technique") illustrate the way you go about making a particular flavor taste dynamic, show you how to make pantry staples that brighten the recipes, survey the kind of equipment used throughout the book, and explain fundamental methods for working with the batters and doughs that are an important element of the recipes. Chapters 5 through 22 (Part II) put all of those notions into recipe form.

The recipes are organized by specific flavor.

The five charts in Part I provide important background material. They've been designed so that home bakers and professionals alike can obtain a range of detailed information about flavors, batters, and doughs at a glance.

Chapter 23, "About Freezing Baked Goods," details the range of baked goods in this book that can be frozen either in their completed state or in dough form, gives recommendations for freezer storage time, and offers suggestions for reheating what you defrost.

About the Recipes

IN MY EXPERIENCE, batters and doughs are the most flexible and responsive to high-intensity flavoring. As a result, the recipes in this book have been developed around specific baked goods that are styled with them: butter cakes, pound cakes, coffee cakes, keeping cakes, tea cakes and loaves, tortes, bar cookies, drop cookies, rolled cookies, press-in-the-pan cookies (such as shortbread), biscuits and scones, muffins, all kinds of yeasted sweet rolls (sticky buns, crumb and streusel buns, and schnecken), pancakes (both flapjacks and crêpes) and waffles. All the fillings, icings, frostings, and glazes that flatter what you bake are included, too.

A typical recipe is composed of an introduction, a list of ingredients, a notation of the bakeware used, and the procedure. Sometimes an "observation line" will appear in the procedure at a critical point in the recipe. The observation line reveals what the dough or batter looks like at a particular (or critical) moment, explains a mixture's consistency or texture, or gives the reason for a certain technique. Essentially, inserting that observation line is my way of hovering over you as you bake.

The recipes are written in some detail, so that an act, function, and process—even a basic one—are defined and described. Each recipe concludes with information on removing the sweet from the baking pan and cooling, and, as appropriate, details about storage.

A variation (or two) is included at the end of selected recipes. Some recipes conclude with a line that begins with "For an extra surge of flavor." This last fillip, which is optional, shows you the way to add a burst of taste to a particular sweet. The extra ingredient may be a scented sugar, a flurry of flavored baking chips, or a topping that would enhance the recipe further. Some recipes also end with the line, "For an aromatic top-note of flavor," or with the line "For a textural contrast." A refined, often subtle, top-note of flavor can be added to a batter or dough, for example, in the form of a scented sugar or dash of liqueur; while dispensable, this ingredient would contribute to the overall taste and flavor aroma of the sweet. And texturally, the crunch of nuts (or splatter of chips) fluttering through a batter or dough would also provide a lively, welcome contrast.

Many recipes contain a note about how long a specific bakery product keeps after baking. The phrase "Freshly baked, the cookies keep for 3 to 4 days" (for example) appears only when the bakery product has sound room-temperature storage life (and can be reheated, as necessary, with good results during that time). For guidance and directions on freezer storage, consult Chapter 23. If the "freshly baked" phrase does not appear at the end of a recipe, plan to use the particular sweet on the day it's made. To keep baked goods at room temperature, store them in an airtight cookie tin or cake keeper. And many recipes conclude with "Best baking advice," a tag line that explains the reason for a certain ingredient, method, or baking strategy.

To bake from this book to its best advantage, be sure to read the introduction to the recipe, which should give you some sense of what to expect: Will the cake be dense or fine-grained and feathery textured? Are the cookies chewy or crispy, thin or chunky? Are the sweet rolls gooey, sticky, and nutty, or are they silky within and topped with a rough and crunchy streusel? Is this a genteel, coffee cake kind of sweet or a mega-chocolate dessert? Then, read through the recipe in its entirety. Preheat the oven, prepare the baking pan, and measure each ingredient as the recipe indicates (allowing enough time for the butter to soften or the chocolate to melt, for example). Set out the important pieces of equipment you'll be using.

Generally, the recipes in this book begin with a batter or dough, but oftentimes include a filling, topping, icing, glaze, or frosting. A multidimensional recipe can be made in stages, with one or more of the elements prepared a day or two ahead of baking. Other recipes can be put together in the time it takes to preheat the oven.

So much of what we use in our daily lives has a consistent, occasionally regimented, almost cookie-cutter style. It's no wonder that we crave a craggy oatmeal cookie, a towering cinnamon bun, or a softly textured slice of chocolate cake, for these are heartening and satisfying. And they look so appealing. Although there's no substitute for the clean lines of an elegant cookie or a beautifully domed loaf cake, the occasional mark of what's handcrafted is welcome in the best of kitchens. While all the recipes in *Baking by Flavor* are about taste, they also demonstrate good design and sound technique. A luxurious slice of pound cake, a jagged dipping cookie, or a crumbly scone may look a bit rustic, but the natural, genuine quality of each is always seductive.

BAKING
by Flavor

PART I

The ART of BAKING by FLAVOR

*t*he process of baking—part alchemy, part flavor—takes basic components such as butter, flour, sugar, eggs, and leavening and transforms them into doughs and batters by using particular methods and techniques. Within the framework of these mixtures a variety of flavors and textures evolve. Imagine almond streusel spirals filled with an almond cream and topped with a buttery crumble or a batch of fudgy brownies deepened by a combination of cocoa and bittersweet chocolate. What preserves these in our memory? In a word, *flavor*; in two words, *flavor intensity.*

The basis for creating sparkling, handmade sweets is the concept I call flavor-layering. The act of flavor-layering ingredients in a recipe is that of building *tiers of similar and compatible flavors* within a cake, or a batch of scones, muffins, cookies, and sweet rolls. Batters and doughs are highly responsive to the infusion of flavoring extracts, seasoned sugars, nut flours and nut pastes, spices, dried and glazed fruit, citrus juice, and chopped candy. What's more, the resulting baked batters and doughs can be amplified by adding streusel or crumble toppings, glazes, glimmery brush-on washes, icings, frostings, and melted-butter-and-spice dips. It's an energetic way to look at baking.

THE WAY TO BAKE BY FLAVOR

Flavor-layering is accomplished by using a combination of compatible ingredients in one recipe. For example, a plain lemon cake can be transformed into a bright, richly luxurious one by performing some baking sleight of hand:

* By marinating grated lemon rind in lemon extract *and* lemon juice for a few minutes before introducing it into the batter.

* By using buttermilk as the liquid ingredient and lemon-flavored granulated sugar as the sweetener to play up the acid jolt of lemon.

* By finishing the cake with both a soaking glaze *and* a buttery, sweetly sharp lemon topping.

Now you've delivered this basic cake, my Ultra-Lemon Cake (see page 402), into a contemporary setting. This goes well beyond adding a splash of lemon extract to a plain cake batter and calling the results lemon cake.

Not every recipe needs this kind of flavor orchestration. Dark chocolate brownies, for example, can be made even richer simply by tossing the chopped nuts that you will stir through the batter first in a little melted butter, vanilla extract, and a light coating of cocoa powder and confectioners' sugar. The nut mixture gives the pan of brownies an enriched, truffle-like texture. It's a simple but indulgent baking stroke in a reasonably direct recipe, and this ploy will win you significant praise for your baking expertise. Look at my Truffled Chocolate-Walnut Brownies on page 258 to see the workings of the recipe.

Once I began reconfiguring the taste of many baking recipes, by instilling vital and vigorous flavor, I realized that many old-time recipes were musty, for their thrifty, subdued use of various spices and extracts produced dreary results. My aim was not only to bring all of my dependable recipes into a contemporary setting but also to develop even more recipes that sing with flavor.

HOW TO FLAVOR-ENHANCE WHAT YOU BAKE

There are many ways to develop identifiable flavors in doughs and batters, and they center on these satellite ingredients, all of which are added to basic elements such as flour, butter, granulated sugar, eggs, leavenings, and liquid or soft dairy items:

* Flavor-accented sugars, such as vanilla-scented or lemon-scented

* Rich and deep, moist or flowing sweetening agents—light brown sugar, dark brown sugar, honey, and molasses

* Chocolate in its varied forms—unsweetened, semisweet, bittersweet, unsweetened, alkalized cocoa powder, and chocolate chips in all sizes

* Whole vanilla beans, plump and moist, for infusing in liquids and scraping the seeds into batters and doughs

* Pure extracts, such as vanilla, lemon, and almond, in addition to flavor-amplified extracts (such as the Intensified Vanilla Extract on page 52)

* An assortment of the "sweet" spices—ground cinnamon, nutmeg, ginger, allspice, cloves, and cardamom

* Citrus, such as lemon juice and freshly grated lemon rind, or a citrus marination that combines juice, extract, and grated rind

* Dried or glazed fruit—apricots, cherries, raisins, cranberries, and blueberries

* An assortment of nuts—almonds, walnuts, pecans, macadamia nuts, and peanuts

* A variety of candy bars and premium chocolate bars—chocolate-covered toffee (buttercrunch); chocolate-covered caramel and vanilla nougat; peanut butter (crunchy/crispy bars or smooth peanut butter cups); chocolate-covered coconut; milk chocolate, peanut, caramel, and peanut butter; milk chocolate; and bittersweet bar chocolate, cut into small or large chunks

To compose baked goods that taste wonderful, use different methods and a mix of ingredients. New and familiar baking ingredients can be used collectively for this "seasoning" process. Here are the basic ways that batters and doughs can be enhanced with flavor.

FLAVOR-ENHANCING A BUTTER CAKE BATTER

The batter for a butter cake, made by the "creamed" method, is ideally suited for developing and expanding flavor. Layers of flavor are added at various stages as the batter is mixed, and the baked cake becomes a delicious composite of all the flavoring elements. In theory and in general, here is how a creamed butter cake batter is endowed with flavor:

* A combination of flour, leavening, and salt is sifted with ground spice(s) or unsweetened, alkalized cocoa

* The softened butter is creamed further with a scented sugar or plain granulated (or superfine) or brown (light or dark) sugar

* After the eggs are blended into the creamed mixture, it is heightened with a flavoring extract, solution of coffee powder and vanilla extract, or melted chocolate

* After addition of the flour and liquid completes the batter, it is embellished with another flavoring enhancement, such as chopped nuts, flavored chips (semisweet chocolate, butterscotch, caramel, cinnamon, cappuccino), chopped candy, flaked coconut, or dried or candied fruit

* The cake batter can be topped or layered with a streusel, nut crumble, or mixture of seasoned nuts, sprinkling of flavored chips and/or nuts, or a spice-seasoned sugar

* The baked cake is finished with an icing, glaze, frosting, sweet liquid syrup, or crackly sugar wash

FLAVOR-ENHANCING A COOKIE DOUGH

A firm drop cookie or press-in-the-pan dough is developed by adding ingredients directly to the dough; pressing ingredients (such as chopped nuts) onto the surface of the formed, unbaked cookie mounds; and/or using a flavored sugar for rolling or sprinkling on the baked cookies. Flavor is introduced into a typical butter cookie dough in this way:

* Flour, in addition to leavening and salt, is whisked or sifted with ground spice(s) or unsweetened, alkalized cocoa

* Butter is creamed with a scented sugar or plain granulated (or superfine) sugar, or brown (light or dark) sugar, then eggs are added to the creamed mixture

* The creamed mixture is expanded with a flavoring extract

* After the flour mixture is incorporated and a dough is formed, ingredients such as bittersweet chocolate chunks, chocolate chips, peanut butter or butterscotch-flavored chips, nuts (in halves, pieces, or chopped), flaked coconut, candy bars cut into chunks, and chopped (or whole, if small) dried or glazed fruit can be worked into the dough

FLAVOR-ENHANCING A SCONE OR BISCUIT DOUGH

A moderately firm dough, such as the type used in making scones, is strengthened with flavor in three components: (1) in the dry ingredients, (2) in the whisked egg and cream mixture, and (3) in the topping that crowns the unbaked wedges of dough. Here is how a scone dough, made by cutting in the fat (breaking down the fat into the flour mixture before adding a whisked liquid mixture to bind the dry ingredients), is enriched with flavor:

❉ Flour, plus leavening and salt, is whisked or sifted with ground spice(s), unsweetened, alkalized cocoa, and/or nut flour before the fat is introduced into the flour

❉ Cream and eggs are whisked together with a flavoring extract and/or another liquid sweetener, such as molasses

❉ The whisked mixture is poured over the butter-flour combination and additional flavoring ingredients, such as flavored baking chips, chopped glazed or seasoned nuts, sweetened flaked coconut, whole or chopped dried fruit, or chopped candy, are added/worked into the dough

❉ Just before baking, the wedges of dough are topped with a streusel mixture, scented sugar, spiced sugar, plain granulated sugar, or turbinado sugar

❉ Baked scones (without a pressed-on or baked-on topping) can be drizzled or spread with an icing or glaze

FLAVOR-ENHANCING A MUFFIN BATTER

A muffin batter is one of the best mediums for mixing in flavorful additions because its texture is reasonably compact. A lighter, cakelike muffin batter is also a good vehicle for flavoring with ground spice, juicy berries, and miniature chips. Typically, a muffin batter receives flavor in this way:

❉ A combination of flour, leavening, and salt is either whisked or sifted with ground spice(s) or unsweetened, alkalized cocoa

❉ If the batter is made by the creamed method, softened butter and a scented sugar, plain granulated sugar, or brown (light or dark) sugar are creamed together before eggs and a flavoring extract are added to the mixture

- ❋ If the batter is made by mixing liquid and dry ingredients, melted (or liquid) fat is whisked with eggs and a flavoring extract; if a scented sugar or other type of sweetener is not combined with the flour mixture as part of the dry ingredients, it's added to the whisked liquid mixture

- ❋ Dry ingredients are added to the creamed or whisked ingredients to form a batter that is accentuated with flavored chips, bittersweet chocolate chunks, chopped nuts, flaked coconut, shredded vegetables or fruit, chopped candy bars, or chopped dried or glazed fruit

- ❋ Unbaked muffins can be topped with a streusel or crumb mixture, spiced or scented sugar, chopped nuts, or flavored chips (especially miniature chips)

- ❋ Baked muffins can be topped with a spiced or scented sugar or dipped in both melted butter and a scented sugar

FLAVOR-ENHANCING A WAFFLE OR PANCAKE BATTER

Given the range in texture and density of pancake and waffle batters (lightly thickened to moderately thick to thick), the batters can handle a variety of flavorings, and additions can be stirred into them at the last moment. One of the best attributes of a pancake or waffle batter is its adaptability, and that flexibility is reflected in the way it can be flavored. Here's how a pancake or waffle batter can be seasoned:

- ❋ A combination of flour, leavening(s), sugar, and salt is whisked together or sifted with ground spice(s), unsweetened, alkalized cocoa powder, or nut flour (such as almond or hazelnut flour)

- ❋ A mixture of eggs, a dairy liquid (such as milk or buttermilk), and/or a soft dairy product (such as sour cream or whole-milk ricotta cheese) is whisked with melted butter and a flavoring extract or grated citrus rind and/or a liquid sweetener such as molasses or honey

- ❋ Liquid ingredients are poured and scraped onto the dry ingredients and a batter is formed by combining the two elements

- ❋ If the beaten egg whites are to be folded into a batter to lighten it further, they are added once the liquid and dry ingredients are combined

- Flavoring ingredients, such as fresh, whole berries, small chunks of soft, ripe fruit (such as banana), chopped dried (but moist) fruit, sweetened flaked coconut, flavored chips, and chopped nuts, are gently blended into the batter. (Flavoring ingredients can also be added before beaten whites are incorporated into the batter.)

FLAVOR-ENHANCING A SWEET YEAST DOUGH

A yeast dough generally derives most of its flavor from butter and eggs that may be an integral part of it, and a filling, frosting, icing, or topping (such as a streusel or crumble mixture). The yeast dough itself, however, can include seasoning agents in its bouncy, silky framework, and these may be flavoring extracts, ground spices, diced dried or glazed fruit, sweetened flaked coconut, or small chunks of bittersweet chocolate. These are examples of how a yeast dough, destined to become sweet rolls, can be accented:

- The mixture of milk, melted butter, eggs, and a swollen, dissolved yeast mixture can be uplifted by the addition of a flavoring extract, liquid sweetener (such as honey), or scented sugar

- The combination of dry ingredients (flour, salt, and occasionally a small amount of nut flour) can include the addition of ground spice(s) or unsweetened, alkalized cocoa

- A filling, to be spread on a sheet of dough, can be made of butter, spice(s), raisins or currants, and sugar; butter and ground semisweet or bittersweet chocolate; flavored pastry cream (especially almond, coconut, or vanilla-flavored); flavored pastry cream blended with a nut paste mixture; or a creamed mixture of butter, sugar, honey, and vanilla extract

- A topping for the rolled and cut unbaked sweet rolls can be made of a plain, coconut, oatmeal, or nut-studded streusel or crumble mixture

- An undercoating for cut, unbaked yeast rolls (usually sticky rolls or sticky-style fruit-based buns), which creates a baked-on caramel topping when the rolls are baked and inverted from the pan, can be made of butter, brown sugar, honey, spices, and vanilla extract

- A topping for fully baked sweet rolls can be a creamy caramel coating, or confectioners' sugar icing or frosting seasoned with a flavoring extract and/or ground spice(s)

THE CHARTS

The following three charts show how a flavor is created within a dough or batter.

The first, the "Flavor Key Compatibility" chart, illustrates what each flavor represented in this book is compatible with, what it is a good contrast to, and how it can be intensified. The second, the "Ways to Intensify and Pyramid Flavor in Baked Goods" chart, shows all the ways to enhance or "pyramid" flavors in baked goods, based on what kind of recipe you are working with. The third, the "Dominant Flavoring Agents and Accessory Flavoring Agents/Ingredients" chart, explains which basic baking ingredients act as either dominant or accessory flavoring agents. Dominant ingredients are those that are bold, intense, strong, forward-tasting, and luxurious. Accessory ingredients are those that bolster, or round out, the taste of the central flavor.

FLAVOR KEY COMPATIBILITY

by flavor category

The primary flavors can be juggled among themselves to arrive at highly flavored composite versions. For example, the taste of buttercrunch is easy to convey in a batter or dough just by adding chopped buttercrunch candy (toffee), but the flavor can be heightened with chopped almonds, almond extract, and chocolate. Two or more flavors can be compatible in a single recipe.

FLAVOR	COMPATIBLE WITH	A GOOD CONTRAST TO	CAN BE INTENSIFIED WITH
CHOCOLATE	vanilla	buttercrunch	butter
	ginger	vanilla	rum
	almond	ginger	ginger
	coconut	coconut	almond
	coffee	apricot	caramel/butterscotch
	buttercrunch	rum	vanilla
	butter	caramel/butterscotch	coffee
	apricot	sweet cheese	buttercrunch
	rum	almond	
	caramel/butterscotch	banana	
	sweet cheese		
	spice		

(continued)

FLAVOR KEY COMPATIBILITY

by flavor category

FLAVOR	COMPATIBLE WITH	A GOOD CONTRAST TO	CAN BE INTENSIFIED WITH
VANILLA	coconut chocolate buttercrunch butter vanilla rum apricot almond caramel/butterscotch blueberry sweet cheese spice cinnamon banana coffee/mocha peanut/peanut butter ginger	chocolate rum blueberry spice almond buttercrunch ginger	butter sweet cheese caramel/butterscotch
ALMOND	vanilla chocolate coconut buttercrunch caramel/butterscotch apricot sweet cheese butter rum spice	chocolate coconut caramel/butterscotch apricot	vanilla caramel/butterscotch butter

(continued)

FLAVOR KEY COMPATIBILITY

by flavor category

FLAVOR	COMPATIBLE WITH	A GOOD CONTRAST TO	CAN BE INTENSIFIED WITH
CINNAMON	spice butter sweet cheese blueberry vanilla coconut almond apricot	sweet cheese vanilla coconut coffee/mocha	butter caramel/butterscotch rum
COCONUT	vanilla butter almond rum chocolate buttercrunch caramel/butterscotch sweet cheese spice	almond chocolate buttercrunch caramel/butterscotch sweet cheese chocolate	rum caramel/butterscotch butter buttercrunch
MOCHA/COFFEE	butter vanilla almond buttercrunch chocolate	almond buttercrunch	butter vanilla
PEANUT/ PEANUT BUTTER	vanilla caramel/butterscotch chocolate butter	chocolate caramel/butterscotch	chocolate butter

(continued)

FLAVOR KEY COMPATIBILITY

by flavor category

FLAVOR	COMPATIBLE WITH	A GOOD CONTRAST TO	CAN BE INTENSIFIED WITH
GINGER	butter apricot vanilla spice chocolate caramel/butterscotch	chocolate caramel/butterscotch apricot	butter
BUTTERCRUNCH	butter almond chocolate caramel/butterscotch coffee/mocha coconut vanilla	sweet cheese coconut caramel/butterscotch	butter caramel/butterscotch almond vanilla
BANANA	spice vanilla coconut rum butter blueberry	vanilla spice cinnamon	vanilla spice rum butter
CARAMEL/ BUTTERSCOTCH	vanilla peanut/peanut butter almond ginger chocolate butter	almond ginger	vanilla

(*continued*)

FLAVOR KEY COMPATIBILITY

by flavor category

FLAVOR	COMPATIBLE WITH	A GOOD CONTRAST TO	CAN BE INTENSIFIED WITH
RUM	banana coconut spice chocolate almond butter vanilla cinnamon	butter vanilla coconut cinnamon almond	butter vanilla
APRICOT	almond vanilla butter spice ginger caramel/butterscotch cinnamon	vanilla spice ginger butter	vanilla
BLUEBERRY	cinnamon spice vanilla butter lemon banana	vanilla butter lemon	vanilla butter lemon cinnamon
SWEET CHEESE	lemon vanilla coconut almond spice butter cinnamon chocolate	lemon almond vanilla	lemon almond butter vanilla

(continued)

FLAVOR KEY COMPATIBILITY

by flavor category

FLAVOR	COMPATIBLE WITH	A GOOD CONTRAST TO	CAN BE INTENSIFIED WITH
SPICE	sweet cheese butter vanilla blueberry banana rum apricot blueberry coconut cinnamon banana ginger	vanilla sweet cheese apricot almond coconut	butter vanilla
BUTTER	spice sweet cheese banana rum apricot caramel/butterscotch blueberry apricot buttercrunch ginger peanut/peanut butter mocha/coffee coconut cinnamon almond vanilla chocolate	sweet cheese spice cinnamon rum	rum vanilla
LEMON	butter sweet cheese blueberry	blueberry sweet cheese	butter

Ways to Intensify and Pyramid Flavor in Baked Goods

by bakery product

Different bakery components (batters, doughs, sauces, frostings, and icings among them) can be fortified with flavor in a variety of ways. Doughs and batters are reasonably sturdy and, for that reason, take to a range of methods for adding and rounding out flavor.

BAKERY PRODUCT (BATTERS, DOUGHS, SAUCES, FROSTINGS, ICINGS)	WAYS TO INTENSIFY AND PYRAMID FLAVOR
BUTTER CAKE BATTERS	Add a citrus infusion
	Use intensified vanilla extract
	Add seed scrapings from a vanilla bean
	Sweeten the batter with scented sugar
	Layer the batter with a flavor swirl based on a combination of sugar and spice, or ground nuts, sugar, and spice
	Swirl a lightly sweetened and flavored cream cheese mixture into the batter
	Layer finely chopped candy bars in the batter
	Layer seasoned nuts in the batter
	Top with a streusel or crumble mixture before baking
	Finish the baked cake with an icing, frosting, glaze, sweet syrup, flavored sugar wash, or sprinklings of scented confectioners' sugar
MUFFIN BATTERS	Add a citrus infusion
	Use intensified vanilla extract
	Sweeten the batter with scented sugar
	Add chopped glazed, seasoned, or candied nuts to the batter
	Stir glazed fruit or chopped, glazed fruit peel into the batter
	Stir fresh whole berries into the batter
	Stir chopped candy bars into the batter
	Top unbaked muffins with a crumble or streusel mixture
	Top unbaked muffins with a spiced nut mixture
	Top unbaked muffins with a spiced sugar mixture
	Top unbaked muffins with flavored chips, such as chocolate, cinnamon, butterscotch, or peanut butter, or stir directly into the batter
	Dip the tops of warm, freshly baked muffins into melted butter and dip again into spiced sugar
	Spoon/brush a sweet syrup onto the tops of warm muffins
	Brush a flavored sugar wash onto the tops of warm muffins

(continued)

WAYS TO INTENSIFY AND PYRAMID FLAVOR IN BAKED GOODS

by bakery product

BAKERY PRODUCT (BATTERS, DOUGHS, SAUCES, FROSTINGS, ICINGS)	WAYS TO INTENSIFY AND PYRAMID FLAVOR
DROP COOKIE DOUGHS	Add a citrus infusion
	Use intensified vanilla extract
	Sweeten the dough with scented sugar
	Add seed scrapings from a vanilla bean
	Mix flavored chips, chopped candy bars, or nuts into the dough
	Mix chopped glazed or candied nuts into the dough
	Mix sweetened flaked coconut into the dough
	Sprinkle the tops of unbaked mounds of dough with a scented sugar, or spiced and sweetened chopped nuts
ROLLED COOKIE DOUGHS	Use intensified vanilla extract
	Add seed scrapings from a vanilla bean
	Sweeten the dough with a scented sugar
	Sprinkle scented sugar on the tops of the unbaked cookies
	Dredge the tops of baked shortbread-style cookies in scented confectioners' sugar
HAND-FORMED AND MOLDED COOKIE DOUGHS	Use intensified vanilla extract
	Add seed scrapings from a vanilla bean
	Sweeten the dough with scented sugar
	Work lightly toasted, finely chopped nuts, finely chopped candy, or miniature flavored chips into the dough
	Roll unbaked cookies in chopped nuts or scented sugar
	Dredge warm, baked shortbread-style cookies in scented confectioners' sugar, confectioners' sugar mixed with ground spice, or confectioners' sugar mixed with unsweetened, alkalized cocoa powder

(continued)

WAYS TO INTENSIFY AND PYRAMID FLAVOR IN BAKED GOODS
by bakery product

BAKERY PRODUCT (BATTERS, DOUGHS, SAUCES, FROSTINGS, ICINGS)	WAYS TO INTENSIFY AND PYRAMID FLAVOR
BAR COOKIE DOUGHS AND BATTERS	Use intensified vanilla extract Sweeten the dough or batter with scented sugar Add seed scrapings from a vanilla bean Work in chopped candy bars, seasoned nuts, or flavored chips Marbleize a thick bar cookie batter with a lightly sweetened cream cheese batter flavored with a compatible extract Sprinkle chopped, glazed, or cocoa-seasoned nuts onto the top of unbaked bar cookies Top a pan of unbaked bar cookies with a crumble or streusel mixture Spread a thick frosting over the pan of baked, uncut bar cookies
SCONE AND BISCUIT DOUGHS	Use intensified vanilla extract Sweeten the dough with scented sugar Use ground spices in the dry ingredients for the dough Create a pocket in each formed biscuit or scone and fill with a sweet mixture (such as almond paste), then pinch the opening seam to close Work chopped candy, whole berries, flavoring chips, and/or flavored or seasoned nuts into the dough Top unbaked biscuits or scones with a streusel or crumble mixture Top unbaked biscuits or scones with turbinado sugar or scented granulated sugar
PANCAKE AND WAFFLE BATTERS	Use intensified vanilla extract Sweeten batter with scented sugar Add ground spices to the dry ingredients Add fresh whole berries or chunks of soft fruit to the batter Add flavoring chips to the batter Add finely ground nuts or nut flour to the batter Add liqueur-marinated, chopped dried or glazed fruit to the batter Serve with a flavor-intense sauce

(continued)

WAYS TO INTENSIFY AND PYRAMID FLAVOR IN BAKED GOODS

by bakery product

BAKERY PRODUCT (BATTERS, DOUGHS, SAUCES, FROSTINGS, ICINGS)	WAYS TO INTENSIFY AND PYRAMID FLAVOR
YEAST DOUGHS	Use intensified vanilla extract Add seed scrapings from a vanilla bean Use ground spices in the dough Use a small amount of nut flour in the dough Work diced glazed fruit, glazed or toasted nuts, flavored chips, or chunks of premium bittersweet chocolate into the dough Spread the rolled-out dough with a spiral of filling (ground nuts; spiced sugar; fruit, nuts, and spiced sugar; fruit preserves and dried fruit); liberally dredge the surface of the rolled-out dough with ground spice (especially cinnamon) Spread the rolled-out dough with a thick pastry cream, nut butter, or paste filling or a combination of nut butter/paste filling and thick pastry cream filling Top unbaked sweet rolls or buns with a streusel or crumble mixture Top warm baked rolls or buns with a flavored icing/frosting or caramel mixture
SWEET DESSERT SAUCES	Use intensified vanilla extract Use seed scrapings from a vanilla bean Sweeten the sauce with scented sugar Use small, flavorful amounts of rum, coffee liqueur, or almond liqueur Stir in slivered or chopped nuts, lightly toasted and cooled, just before serving
FROSTINGS AND ICINGS	Use intensified vanilla extract Add a pinch of salt to bring out the dominant flavor (especially important when making vanilla or chocolate-based frostings/icings) Use seed scrapings from a vanilla bean Use small flavoring amounts of rum, coffee liqueur, or almond liqueur Use scented sugar for up to one-third of the total amount of sugar called for in the recipe

DOMINANT FLAVORING AGENTS AND ACCESSORY FLAVORING AGENTS/INGREDIENTS

by flavor category

The major, or *dominant*, flavor clusters are represented by the ingredients that identify each particular flavor. The dominant flavor can also be described as the primary or the defining flavor/ingredient. The dominant flavor ingredient appears prominently in a recipe. Each primary flavor is enhanced by other ingredients that are an important part of a batter or dough, and they are called *accessory* flavoring agents and/or ingredients. The role of accessory flavoring agents is to supplement, refine, and reinforce the dominant flavor.

For example, chocolate becomes prominent in a batter or dough when bittersweet chocolate, unsweetened chocolate, semisweet chocolate chips, or unsweetened, alkalized cocoa (or a mixture of two or three of these elements) is a component of a recipe. But these ingredients cannot work alone. They usually require the presence of unsalted butter, eggs, and vanilla (and frequently, a soft or liquid dairy product, such as sour cream, whole milk, or buttermilk) to carry the flavor and develop the batter or dough.

FLAVOR	DOMINANT FLAVORING AGENTS	ACCESSORY FLAVORING AGENTS/INGREDIENTS
CHOCOLATE	bittersweet chocolate unsweetened chocolate milk chocolate semisweet or milk chocolate chips unsweetened, alkalized cocoa	unsalted butter vanilla-scented sugar pure vanilla extract vanilla bean seed scrapings unsalted butter sour cream buttermilk whole milk light (table) cream heavy cream whole eggs and/or egg yolks
VANILLA	pure vanilla extract intensified vanilla extract vanilla-scented sugar (granulated, confectioners', superfine) vanilla bean vanilla bean seed scrapings	unsalted butter freshly grated nutmeg sour cream whole milk buttermilk light (table) cream heavy cream cream cheese

(continued)

DOMINANT FLAVORING AGENTS AND ACCESSORY FLAVORING AGENTS/INGREDIENTS

by flavor category

FLAVOR	DOMINANT FLAVORING AGENTS	ACCESSORY FLAVORING AGENTS/INGREDIENTS
ALMOND	pure almond extract slivered, chopped or ground almonds almond flour almond liqueur	unsalted butter pure vanilla extract freshly grated nutmeg vanilla-scented granulated sugar sour cream heavy cream light (table) cream cream cheese
CINNAMON	ground cinnamon	butter pure vanilla extract freshly grated nutmeg ground cloves ground allspice ground cardamom vanilla-scented granulated sugar light brown sugar dark brown sugar unsalted butter sour cream whole milk buttermilk heavy cream light (table) cream cream cheese

(continued)

Dominant Flavoring Agents and Accessory Flavoring Agents/Ingredients

by flavor category

FLAVOR	DOMINANT FLAVORING AGENTS	ACCESSORY FLAVORING AGENTS/INGREDIENTS
Coconut	sweetened flaked coconut coconut milk	unsalted butter freshly grated nutmeg ground cinnamon ground cloves ground allspice ground cardamom pure vanilla extract vanilla-scented granulated sugar vanilla bean seed scrapings light brown sugar dark brown sugar unsalted butter sour cream whole milk buttermilk light (table) cream heavy cream
Mocha/Coffee	*Coffee*: espresso powder, in solution with pure vanilla extract or hot water *Mocha*: combination of espresso powder and bittersweet chocolate, semisweet or milk chocolate chips, or unsweetened chocolate	unsalted butter pure vanilla extract vanilla-scented granulated sugar light brown sugar dark brown sugar unsalted butter sour cream milk heavy cream light (table) cream

(continued)

DOMINANT FLAVORING AGENTS AND ACCESSORY FLAVORING AGENTS/INGREDIENTS

by flavor category

FLAVOR	DOMINANT FLAVORING AGENTS	ACCESSORY FLAVORING AGENTS/INGREDIENTS
PEANUT/PEANUT BUTTER	chopped peanuts peanut butter peanut butter-flavored chips	freshly grated nutmeg ground allspice ground cinnamon ground cloves pure vanilla extract vanilla-scented granulated sugar light brown sugar dark brown sugar semisweet chocolate chips bittersweet chocolate unsweetened, alkalized cocoa chocolate-peanut butter candy heavy cream
GINGER	ground ginger freshly grated gingerroot crystallized ginger ginger preserved in syrup	unsalted butter pure vanilla extract freshly grated nutmeg ground cinnamon ground allspice ground cloves mild, unsulphured molasses sour cream unsweetened, alkalized cocoa bittersweet chocolate
BUTTERCRUNCH	toffee candy bars unsalted butter	unsalted butter pure vanilla extract pure almond extract vanilla-scented granulated sugar

(continued)

DOMINANT FLAVORING AGENTS AND ACCESSORY FLAVORING AGENTS/INGREDIENTS

by flavor category

FLAVOR	DOMINANT FLAVORING AGENTS	ACCESSORY FLAVORING AGENTS/INGREDIENTS
BUTTERCRUNCH (CONTINUED)		light brown sugar dark brown sugar freshly grated nutmeg ground allspice almonds semisweet chocolate chips bittersweet chocolate unsweetened chocolate unsweetened, alkalized cocoa sweetened flaked coconut buttermilk whole milk heavy cream light (table) cream sour cream
BANANA	bananas, mashed or cut into chunks	unsalted butter pure vanilla extract light brown sugar dark brown sugar freshly grated nutmeg ground cinnamon ground ginger ground allspice ground cardamom ground cloves whole milk heavy cream light (table) cream buttermilk

(continued)

DOMINANT FLAVORING AGENTS AND ACCESSORY FLAVORING AGENTS/INGREDIENTS

by flavor category

FLAVOR	DOMINANT FLAVORING AGENTS	ACCESSORY FLAVORING AGENTS/INGREDIENTS
BANANA (CONTINUED)		sour cream
		sweetened flaked coconut
		unsweetened, alkalized cocoa
		semisweet chocolate chips
CARAMEL/BUTTERSCOTCH	unsalted butter	unsalted butter
	light brown sugar	pure vanilla extract
	dark brown sugar	whole milk
	caramel candy	heavy cream
	butterscotch-flavored chips	light (table) cream
	caramel-flavored chips	freshly grated nutmeg
RUM	light rum	unsalted butter
	dark rum	pure vanilla extract
		freshly grated nutmeg
		ground cinnamon
		ground allspice
		ground cloves
APRICOT	dried apricots	unsalted butter
	apricot preserves	pure vanilla extract
	glazed apricots	almond extract
		dark brown sugar
		freshly grated lemon rind
		freshly grated nutmeg
		ground cinnamon
		ground allspice
		ground cardamom

(continued)

DOMINANT FLAVORING AGENTS AND ACCESSORY FLAVORING AGENTS/INGREDIENTS

by flavor category

FLAVOR	DOMINANT FLAVORING AGENTS	ACCESSORY FLAVORING AGENTS/INGREDIENTS
BLUEBERRY	fresh blueberries dried blueberries	unsalted butter pure vanilla extract pure lemon extract freshly grated lemon rind vanilla-scented granulated sugar lemon-scented granulated sugar unsalted butter whole milk buttermilk sour cream heavy cream light (table) cream cream cheese freshly grated nutmeg ground cinnamon ground allspice corn meal
SWEET CHEESE	cream cheese	unsalted butter sour cream heavy cream light (table) cream eggs unsalted butter pure vanilla extract pure almond extract pure lemon extract freshly grated nutmeg

(continued)

DOMINANT FLAVORING AGENTS AND ACCESSORY FLAVORING AGENTS/INGREDIENTS

by flavor category

FLAVOR	DOMINANT FLAVORING AGENTS	ACCESSORY FLAVORING AGENTS/INGREDIENTS
SPICE	freshly grated nutmeg ground cinnamon ground ginger ground allspice ground cloves ground cardamom	unsalted butter heavy cream buttermilk whole milk sour cream pure vanilla extract intensified vanilla extract light brown sugar dark brown sugar molasses
BUTTER	unsalted butter (best quality)	pure vanilla extract freshly grated nutmeg ground mace buttermilk whole milk heavy cream light (table) cream sour cream whole eggs egg yolks
LEMON	lemon rind lemon juice pure lemon extract lemon-scented sugar	unsalted butter whole eggs egg yolks buttermilk whole milk heavy cream light (table) cream sour cream

*f*rom fluted cake pans, to sturdy cookie sheets and muffin pans in all sizes, to festive-looking madeleine plaques, a piece of baking equipment is, by its very nature, the architecturally correct container for a particular batter or dough. Indeed, the container often defines what it will produce in the end. But before a mixture is placed on or turned into a baking pan, it connects with measuring spoons, liquid and dry measuring cups, sifter, hand-held or free-standing electric mixer, rubber spatula, rolling pin, flexible palette knife, and the like in its various phases of production.

The measuring of ingredients is an important phase of a baking recipe, whose success depends on a reasonably precise balance of components. Equally important is how the ingredients are treated in the method. Yet the type and quality of equipment are as important as the balance of ingredients and technique. Mixing bowls should be sturdy and roomy; spatulas flexible enough to sweep the bottom and sides of the mixing bowl and glide through batters; baking pans stable and free of warped spots or nicked interiors; cookie sheets sturdy, level, and durable; wooden spoons or spatulas smooth, well constructed, and comfortable in the hand.

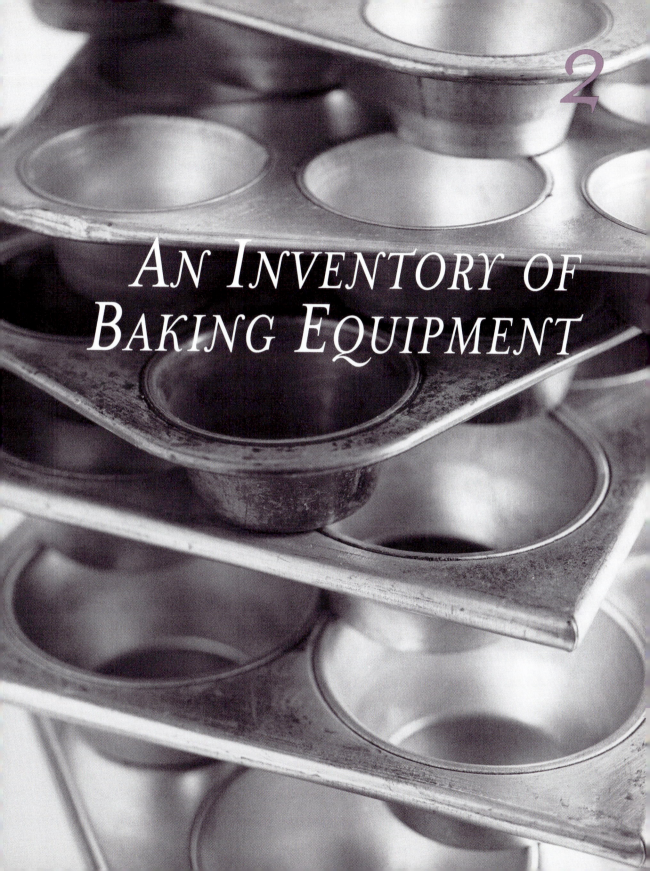

AN INVENTORY OF BAKING EQUIPMENT

Handled and stored properly, well-constructed bakeware should last for years. Most baking pans develop a patina from continual use and require nothing more than a gentle, considerate washing and thorough drying. Cookie sheets, sheet pans, tart pans, pie pans, and springform pans aside, some bakeware benefits from the treatment known as seasoning. Seasoning involves coating the inside of a pan with shortening and "baking" it (in a moderate to moderately low oven) for a certain length of time to create a durable surface that resists sticking. A carbon steel crêpe pan, for instance, comes with a coating to protect it against rusting, so it is imperative that the pan be well scrubbed and seasoned before use. The interiors of most release-surface pans also benefit from seasoning, as do decorative tinned steel baking pans, such as madeleine plaques.

SEASONING BAKEWARE

To season a crêpe pan, preheat the oven to 275° F. Use an abrasive scouring pad to remove the protective coating completely on the inside and outside. Rinse the pan well and dry thoroughly. Thickly coat the inside of the pan with shortening, using a folded paper towel to spread it around. Place the pan in the preheated oven and let it "cure" for 2 hours, then remove it to a heatproof surface (use padded oven mitts to protect your hands) and cool completely. Mop up the shortening with a thick wad of paper towels. The pan is now ready to use. When you make a batch of crêpes, a delicate sizzle of clarified butter that coats the bottom of the pan (before the batter is swirled around) will keep the surface slick—and also add a bit of flavor richness to the thin pancakes. After each crêpe-making session, wipe the pan clean and dry with paper towels before storing it in a dry place.

A crêpe pan may need to be reseasoned from time to time, especially if it has not been used for more than six months; to reseason, follow the procedure above but reduce the oven curing to 1 hour.

To season a Bundt pan, tube pan, madeleine plaques, layer cake pans, square or rectangular baking pans, and muffin pans, wash and completely dry the bakeware. Preheat the oven to 275° F. Thickly coat the inside(s) of the pan(s) with shortening. If the pan has a central tube or clusters of flutes and curves, take particular care to cover all the surfaces with shortening, including the point where the base of the tube meets the bottom of the pan. If you are working with madeleine pans, make sure that all the dips and folds in the depressed shells are greased. Heat the pan(s) for 2½ to 3 hours, turn off the oven, and leave the pans inside for 20 minutes before removing them and cooling completely.

Wipe away all of the shortening, using several thicknesses of paper towels. Even though the bakeware is seasoned, softened butter alone, softened butter and flour, nonstick cooking spray, or shortening and flour is still applied to the interior, depending on the recipe instructions.

The equipment used in this cookbook is classic, in form and function.

MEASURING TOOLS

❋ MEASURING SPOONS: A ring of measuring spoons (¼ teaspoon, ½ teaspoon, 1 teaspoon, and 1 tablespoon amounts) is indispensable for portioning out quantities of baking soda, baking powder, and spices, which are used routinely in small amounts, in addition to smaller amounts of sugar, flour, cocoa, and such. For ardent bakers, it's handy to have three pairs of measuring spoons on hand. Nonstick measuring spoons are wonderful to use when measuring out small quantities of anything sticky—peanut butter, honey, fruit preserves, or molasses.

❋ DRY MEASURING CUPS: Dry measuring cups are available in sets, in amounts of ¼ cup, ⅓ cup, ½ cup, and 1 cup; ⅛-cup (which is handy for measuring 2-tablespoon amounts) and 2-cup measures can usually be purchased singly. Other nesting cups, which include ⅔ cup and ¾ cup (in addition to the standard amounts), are quite useful and worth owning. Dry measures are referred to as such because they are used mostly for portioning out ingredients such as flour or sugar, and occasionally for solid shortening, which is packed into the cup. In order to avoid tedious washing and drying when assembling multiple ingredients for a recipe, avid bakers may want to own two sets of measuring cups.

❋ LIQUID MEASURING CUPS: For reasons of hygiene, durability, and uniformity, liquid measuring cups should be made of heatproof glass and have clear, readable, graduated ounce and cup demarcation lines. Two-cup and 4-cup measures are essential for measuring all liquid and soft dairy products, in addition to such ingredients as honey and molasses.

❋ SCALE: I rely on the Edlund digital scale (Model E-80) for weighing precise amounts. The scale, equipped with the tare function (which allows you to weigh separate ingredients consecutively), has the capacity to weigh ingredients (in ounces and grams) from 0.1 ounce to 80 ounces or 1 gram to 2000 grams. At the push of a button, you can determine the weight of an ingredient in ounces or grams. The scale operates either by battery (it takes one 9-volt alkaline battery) or by the power adaptor supplied with the scale for plugging into an electrical outlet.

AERATING TOOL

❊ SIFTER: A sifter is indispensable for aerating a mixture of flour, leavening(s), ground spices, and salt, although the actual mixing process can be accomplished by whisking the dry ingredients into a bowl. Sifting rids a mixture of any small clumps and helps to create a smooth batter or dough, with a refined texture. Mixtures are usually sifted directly over a large sheet of waxed paper. After you have used the sifter, vigorously tap out any lingering flour dust over the sink, then store the sifter in a plastic bag.

MIXING TOOLS

❊ SPOONS: Made of boxwood or olive wood (both create an elegant surface), mixing spoons should fit comfortably in the hand when stirring batters, doughs, and all kinds of fillings, toppings, and frostings. These will perform a variety of functions.

A high heat-resistant mixing spoon (up to 430° F.) is handy to have for stirring bubbly pudding mixtures and caramel-based sauces. This type of spoon is remarkably sturdy and will withstand constant use in the kitchen. The Exoglass spoon (made of fiberglass) is produced by Matfer (#300).

In general, I prefer mixing spoons with long handles, for they offer better leverage and control.

❊ FLAT WOODEN PADDLE: A flat paddle is one of my favorite tools for mixing a thick, heavy, and chock-full-of-ingredients batter; for working softened butter by hand into a yeast dough; and for putting together dense (but moist) quick bread doughs. A flat paddle is just that, flat—that is, entirely level—with a reasonably narrow handle that crests in a slightly stretched oval (it looks like a large, exaggerated teardrop), which is also flat. Again, as for mixing spoons, boxwood is an excellent choice.

Matfer, of France, produces excellent Exoglass (composed of fiberglass) high-heat flat paddles, and these are wonderful for stirring cooked fillings and glazes (#250 and #300).

❋ ALL KINDS OF SPATULAS: Small and large rubber spatulas, made by Rubbermaid Commercial Products, Inc., make swift and efficient work of combining a batter or soft dough, scraping a mixing bowl, and pressing or pushing a filling or glaze through a fine-meshed sieve (#1901 and #1905). The spatula that finishes with a rounded rubber spoon shape, instead of a flat rubber blade, is also a handy tool to use for mixing batters and spooning them into muffin pans (#1931).

Rubbermaid Commercial Products, Inc., also makes a superlative notched, heat-resistant (up to 500° F.) spatula. It has a reasonably firm, but agile, blade.

A boxwood crêpe spatula, designed specifically for lifting those thin pancakes from the pan, is a wonderful specialty tool to own and use. It's actually a slender-ized, narrow, and elongated paddle, with an ever-so-slightly rounded surface and tip. It looks something like a stylized tongue depressor.

❋ WHISKS: A good, all-purpose, medium-size whisk of 18-8 stainless steel will serve you well for combining a moderate and moderately large quantity of liquid ingredients (such as melted butter, whole milk or buttermilk, light cream, heavy cream, sour cream, eggs, flavorings, and the like) and dry ingredients, which need to be whisked, rather than sifted.

A smaller all-purpose whisk made of stainless steel is an excellent accessory whisk to have for mixing smaller quantities of liquid ingredients.

A balloon whisk is used in tandem with a copper bowl. This type of whisk is essential for beating egg whites expansively to soft, moderately firm, or firm peaks.

❋ FREESTANDING ELECTRIC MIXER (ROTATING MIXING BOWL), EQUIPPED WITH BEATER ATTACHMENT: A freestanding mixer in which *both* the bowl and beaters turn is wonderful to own for making butter cake batters. The benefit of this type of mixer (mine is a Sunbeam) is that you can actually move a spatula along the bottom and sides of the bowl as it revolves to distribute the ingredients and keep the batter even-textured. The large bowl holds 4¼ quarts and the smaller bowl holds 2 quarts.

❋ HEAVY-DUTY FREESTANDING ELECTRIC MIXER (STATIONARY MIXING BOWL), EQUIPPED WITH WHISK, DOUGH HOOK, AND FLAT PADDLE ATTACHMENTS: Beyond purchasing commercial equipment, a fine choice of a heavy-duty, free-standing mixer, which can handle the thorough kneading of a yeast dough (one of the best reasons for owning it), is the KitchenAid Professional KSM50P. It is equipped with an overload reset button, has a 5-quart stainless steel bowl, and has three beaters—a flat paddle, a dough hook, and a whisk. The bowl remains stationary while the beaters revolve.

✱ ELECTRIC HAND MIXER: The nine-speed KitchenAid Mixer (Professional 9) is a sturdy electric mixer that can sail through combining ingredients for a cookie dough, icing, or frosting with superior results. The key pad on the top surface of the handle allows you to increase or decrease the speed.

MIXING BOWLS AND RAMEKINS

✱ MIXING BOWLS: A set of all-purpose, lightweight stainless steel mixing bowls is a kitchen necessity for all the times you mix batters and doughs, streusel mixtures, icings, glazes, frostings, or toppings by hand (or with a hand-held electric mixer). My set of stainless steel, graduated bowls contains four bowls in the following sizes: small (6- to 7-cup capacity), small-medium (10-cup capacity), medium (16-cup capacity), and large (22-cup capacity).

✱ RAMEKINS: Ramekins are handy for combining small mixtures (such as coffee powder, flavoring extract, and water), and do double duty as bake-and-serve containers.
    Over the years, I have amassed a collection of white ovenproof ramekins (made by Apilco), which I've come to rely on for a range of cooking and baking needs: baby ramekins, with 6 tablespoons capacity; small ramekins, with ¾ cup capacity; and large ramekins, with 1½ cups capacity.

TURNING AND LIFTING TOOLS

✱ TONGS: Heavy, high-quality tongs are tailor-made (and the most practical) for turning rusks (twice-baked cookies) as they dry out and rebake in the oven. I use highly durable tongs made by Edlund; the tongs lock in place for easy storage.

✳ OFFSET SPATULAS: With its easy-to-grip wood handle and accommodating offset feature, this sort of spatula can flip pancakes on the griddle, get underneath a big load of drop cookies or scones, slip beneath a batch of crumb buns or brownies snug in the baking pan, and lift up squares of bake-in-the-pan sheet cakes. The distinguishing element of this kind of spatula is that the blade is angled *down and away* from the handle, for better leverage.

My favorite offset spatulas range in size from small to large, the smallest being the most practical for removing brownies from a square baking pan and the largest for detaching big, shapely crumb buns from sheet pans.

SPREADING TOOLS

✳ ICING SPATULAS, ALSO KNOWN AS FLEXIBLE PALETTE KNIVES: An icing spatula can serve a variety of functions. A flexible palette knife is handy for smoothing over and leveling off an icing or cake batter, or spreading a batter along the inside of a tart shell. The blade, usually made of stainless steel, is what I would describe as firmly flexible. These spatulas are all top-quality: Ateco Ultra spatula, with a stainless steel blade and polypropylene handle (#1304 and #1308), and, in the mid-range size, the Dexter flexible spatula.

FLATTENING TOOL

✳ SMOOTH-BOTTOMED STAINLESS STEEL MEAT POUNDER: I have found that using a heavy meat pounder (mine is made in Italy by Rowoco [#130]) to lightly flatten balls of cookie dough, like peanut butter, gets the job done with simple efficiency. One morning, I was pounding veal cutlets for that evening's dinner. The pounder was still on my countertop when I was making a batch of cookies that needed to be flattened lightly before baking; I eyed the pounder, grabbed it, and with a few quick strokes, had several cookie sheets filled with perfectly level, smooth rounds of dough.

CUTTING, GRATING, AND SCRAPING TOOLS

❋ PASTRY BLENDER: In a way, a pastry blender can be identified as a cutting tool because it handily "cuts" the fat into a flour mixture when making a pie crust or streusel mixture. A pastry blender, which is simple to control, can reduce the fat into small or large pieces simply and easily. The pastry blender that I own has a long wood handle and stainless steel wires (*not* interlocking). A pastry blender is a reasonably inexpensive baking implement that should supply you with years and years of good use.

❋ PARING KNIFE: A small paring knife is an integral part of baking—for cutting bar cookies neatly, trimming baked and unbaked doughs, or splitting a vanilla bean to expose the tiny seeds; these are among the many small but important jobs a sharp paring knife can accomplish.

❋ CHEF'S KNIFE: A sturdy, good-sized chef's knife is a necessity for many procedures, such as chopping unsweetened or bittersweet chocolate for melting, for cutting a long, filled yeasted coil into individual buns or rolls, or for cutting round disks of scone dough into wedges. A larger chef's knife is superb for chopping lots of nuts or an ample amount of chocolate, for it can cover a large surface area with ease. I prefer chef's knives with blades made of carbon steel.

❋ SERRATED KNIVES: One of my cherished serrated knives is produced by Victorinox (Swiss-made). It does a matchless job of slicing baked ovals of batter for rusks into individual dipping cookies and for cutting through all kinds of layered cakes and cakes baked in Bundt or tube pans.

An offset serrated knife, with the blade at a counterbalanced, lower level from the handle, is helpful for slicing through firm baked doughs and cakes. An offset serrated knife offers a finer degree of control than the straight version. My offset version of this knife, made by Friedrick Dick (made in Germany), has a "high carbon–no stain" blade (#4055-18).

❋ CAKE KNIFE: My cake knife, made by Friedrick Dick, has an elongated, high carbon–no stain triangular blade (one long edge is serrated and the other has a smooth blade) set in a handle. The knife neatly slices through one- and two-layer cakes and cuts cleanly through tarts.

* **PASTRY/PIZZA CUTTER:** The large PRO LamsonSharp pizza wheel/pastry cutter (10S94) glides through pastry and yeast doughs smoothly and easily. I especially love this tool for cutting squares, strips, and rectangles of flattened, rolled dough. Its handle is large and comfortable. It is a recent, but valued, addition to my baking kitchen and made in the USA (Shelburne Falls, Massachusetts).

* **COOKIE CUTTERS:** Fanciful cookie cutters have always lured me, and I have collected a mix of cutters, many handcrafted, some antique, and some new; these are appealing for their shape and design, and I use them often. Sturdy cutters, with clean, sharp cutting edges, make stamping out sheets of cookie dough a pleasure. Seams should be well soldered, and connecting ends joined together smoothly, without a break.

* **NUTMEG GRATER:** The Microplane (a product of Grace Manufacturing) nutmeg rasp with a wood handle is a phenomenal tool for reducing a whole nutmeg into finely grated (ground) nutmeg quickly and beautifully. Alternatively, a traditional nutmeg grater performs the same function, but with less elegance and a little more work; the benefit of having a classic grater is that you can store a few whole nutmegs in its handy, top open-and-close sliding pocket.

* **CITRUS ZESTER:** The Microplane (a product of Grace Manufacturing) zesting rasp will generate fluffy, feathery shreds of citrus rind. One procedural note: the zester has such a well-honed cutting surface that you need to draw or "rub" the piece of fruit *very lightly* across its surface.

* **SWIVEL-BLADED PEELER:** A peeler that manages to turn here and there over the surface of a lemon (to cut off slender strips of peel) or firm vegetables (carrots and potatoes, in particular) is a requisite kitchen tool. My peeler is stainless steel and measures about 6½ inches in overall length, with a 3-inch blade that moves gently from side to side.

* **PASTRY SCRAPER/DOUGH CUTTER (ALSO KNOWN AS A BENCH KNIFE):** The Matfer Racle Tout (code 82231), a scraper made of strong nylon, has both a rounded and a straight edge. It rests neatly in the hand. A pastry scraper is a vital tool for cleaning the surface of a cutting board after kneading yeast dough (using the flat end), gathering up a mound of chopped nuts from the cutting surface, scraping out a bowl (using the rounded side), or cutting a mass of risen yeast, scone, or biscuit dough into separate portions. I own three scrapers, but the first one I purchased (over 20 years ago) is still in superb shape.

Mashing, Ricing, and Sieving/Straining Tools

❋ POTATO MASHER: An old-fashioned, hand-operated potato masher is the perfect tool for mashing ripe bananas without liquefying them. It maintains the texture and density of the fruit and, consequently, prevents batters and doughs from becoming gummy.

❋ RICER: A stainless steel ricer, with a solid, built-in, medium-fine disk, reduces boiled potatoes to a gossamer consistency, a texture that is all-important if you are incorporating the potatoes into a yeast dough (refer to the potato yeast dough in my recipe for Cinnamon Ripple Rolls on page 312). Chunks of well-drained, cooked potatoes are placed in the bin, and once the handle is closed, an attached round disk on the underside presses against the contents of the bin, which are, in turn, forced through the small holes. (One essential cooking note: Anything that is riced should be thoroughly cooked to *tender softness* or it will remain fibrous and not compress properly or amalgamate smoothly into another mixture.)

❋ STRAINERS/SIEVES: A set of stainless steel fine-meshed sieve/strainers is essential for straining citrus juice for clarity and to remove any pits, and for straining cornstarch mixtures and custard sauces. Although one strainer is just the right size to have for pressing through any kind of mixture, I also find the next two smaller sizes invaluable as well. A tiny strainer is handy for sifting ground spice over a rolled-out sheet of yeast dough, or confectioners' sugar over the expanse of a baked cake.

Saucepans

❋ HEAVY, NONREACTIVE SAUCEPANS: Substantial saucepans should be nonreactive, or impervious to interaction, which means that the surface area that comes in contact with food will not interact with milk- or acid-based ingredients and transfer an off, metallic taste. Enameled cast-iron saucepans with light-colored interiors made by Le Creuset are heavy, long-wearing, and highly resistant to any chemical interaction. In this baking cookbook, the enameled cast-iron saucepans are used exclusively for making sweet sauces (including sensitive custard sauces), delicate fillings (such as the elegant Silky Lemon Cream on page 428), and toppings. I use the following size saucepans constantly: a small saucepan with a 5-cup capacity; a medium-size saucepan with a 6½- to 7-cup capacity; and a large saucepan with an 8-cup capacity.

❊ COPPER (BOTH INTERIOR AND EXTERIOR) SAUCEPAN FOR COOKING SUGAR SYRUP: A copper saucepan is a superb conductor of heat and makes exquisite sugar syrups of all densities. My copper saucepan has a capacity of 1½ quarts and measures about 5½ inches in diameter across the top. Without exception, every time *prior to using the saucepan*, it's important that it be treated to the same vinegar-and-salt scrubdown followed by a tepid water rinse and thorough drying that is necessary for an unlined copper beating bowl used for whipping egg whites. Refer to the directions in "Copper Beating Bowl for Whipping Egg Whites, and Balloon Whisk" on page 46. Use the pan as soon as it is prepared. Use the cooked sugar immediately, and never let it linger in the pan. *Omit the addition of cream of tartar or lemon juice when cooking sugar syrup in a copper saucepan.*

ROLLING DEVICES

❊ STRAIGHT WOODEN ROLLING PIN: Made of solid oak, my absolutely straight (not tapered) wood French rolling pin is one I have used routinely over the last 25 years. The pin, neither exceptionally lightweight nor unusually heavy (it weighs in at about 1 pound), is just the right length—and has just the right heft—for rolling out pie and tart crusts, and cookie doughs.

Once you have purchased this type of pin, wash it lightly and swiftly in cool, sudsy water, rinse again quickly, and dry thoroughly. Let the pin air-dry for about 2 hours longer, then moisten a sheet of paper towel with vegetable oil (such as soybean) and rub down the rolling pin with the oil until the wood just begins to glisten (at first, the pin will absorb a certain amount of oil). Let the rolling pin stand for 12 hours on a sheet pan lined with plastic wrap. Then wipe the pin with a clean, soft cloth and store it away from any direct heat source. After using the rolling pin, dislodge any bits of clinging dough with a nylon dough scraper (do not use a metal scraper or a knife on the rolling pin), rinse it quickly in cool water, and dry thoroughly. Avoid soaking the pin in water. Over time, the wood will develop a smooth, slightly darker patina, so re-oiling the pin is unnecessary unless it seems extremely dry.

❊ HEAVY, BALL-BEARING ROLLING PIN WITH HANDLES: My weighty Thorpe rolling pin, made of maple, has two handles and a rolling surface of 18 inches. It is an ideal pin to use for rolling out all types of yeast dough and the firmer cookie doughs, for the weight of the pin (about 4 pounds) will push out and extend dough with minimal effort on your part. The Thorpe rolling pin, produced in Hamden, Connecticut, is a serious rolling pin and a significant addition to any baking kitchen.

❋ NYLON ROLLING PIN: A nonstick rolling pin, a relatively recent addition to my baking kitchen, proves to be extremely useful for rolling out rich yeast doughs. I love it. Rinse it in cool sudsy water after each use, and store it away from a heat source.

BRUSHING TOOL

❋ PASTRY BRUSH: A pastry brush is necessary for applying washes and some finishing glazes to the tops of cakes and muffins; for brushing off and cleaning away excess flour attached to rolled-out, yeasted sweet doughs; for brushing a flavoring solution over rolled-out doughs; and for applying a simmered preserve to the top of a baked tart. My pastry brush, made by Sparta (432-1 inch), is made of boar bristle.

CAKE PANS

❋ BUNDT PAN: A fluted tube pan 10 inches in diameter, with a capacity of 12 to 14 cups, the pan has full, clearly articulated flutes. Used for baking butter cakes, some pound cakes, and coffee cakes, it will never disappoint. A Bundt-lette pan, six individual baby Bundt pans housed in one pan, creates charming tea cakes. Each baby Bundt measures 4 inches in diameter and a scant 2 inches deep, and has a capacity of 1 cup. Bundt is a registered trademark of Northland Aluminum Products, Inc.

❋ STRAIGHT-SIDED TUBE PAN: A plain tube pan (not false-bottomed) is perfect for baking pound cakes, large coffee cakes, and keeping cakes. This simple but effectively designed cake pan measures 10 inches in diameter and 4½ inches deep, and has a capacity of 18 cups. Another straight-sided tube pan (with the same capacity of 18 cups) that's useful measures 9¾ inches in diameter and 6 inches deep. A pan with a slightly smaller diameter and greater depth produces a tall, especially good-looking cake. I love to use the 6-inch-deep pan for my Grandma Lilly's Butter Pound Cake on page 192.

❊ SWIRLED TUBE PAN: Measuring 10 inches in diameter and 4¾ inches deep, with a capacity of about 13½ cups, this pan makes a pretty butter cake that cuts into nice tall slices. It's is particularly good for baking light, fine-textured pound cake-style batters.

❊ SWIRLED TUBE PAN: A smaller version of the deep pan, 9 inches in diameter and 4¼ inches deep, with a capacity of about 11 cups. It is also terrific to own for baking smaller butter cakes, and fruit-based tube cakes, such as my Cinnamon Apple Cake on page 310.

❊ LAYER CAKE PANS: The layer cake pans used in this book are 9 inches round, with a depth of 1½ inches and capacity of 7 cups. Made of medium-weight aluminum, these pans are a must for baking traditional layer cakes, such as the Heirloom Chocolate Cake on page 284, Vanilla Layer Cake on page 524, and Iced Coffee Chocolate Layer Cake on page 371.

❊ SPRINGFORM PANS: Measuring 8½ inches in diameter and 2½ inches deep (10-cup capacity), and 9 inches in diameter and 2¾ inches deep (12-cup capacity), these pans can accommodate coffee cake and torte batters superbly. A springform pan is used for both tender cakes (such as the Fallen Chocolate Almond Cake, page 115, and the Chocolate-Ginger Soufflé Cake, page 380) and dense cakes (such as the Caramel, Nougat, and Walnut Candy Bar Cake, page 235, and the Espresso and Bittersweet Chocolate Chunk Torte, page 354).

❊ FLUTED DECORATIVE RING MOLD CAKE/BAKING PAN: An ovenproof, fluted decorative ring mold, measuring 11¾ inches in diameter, 3½ inches deep, with a capacity of 12 to 13 cups, is used for the Buttery Glazed Almond Ring on page 118. A decorative ring mold turns out a beautiful cake, although a cake batter can be baked in an unadorned ring mold of the same size, with excellent results.

OTHER BAKING PANS

❊ MADELEINE MOLDS (PLAQUES): Molds or plaques for baking madeleines (*plaques à madeleines*) are the classic shell-shaped forms made of tinned steel in which you bake small tea cakes in various flavors. Each plaque contains twelve 3-inch-long shells and each shell-shaped depression measures 1¾ inches at its widest point. An individual shell has a capacity of 2 tablespoons plus 1 teaspoon. The molds are used for the Delicate Almond Madeleines on page 125 and Double Chocolate Madeleines on page 256.

Other madeleine-style molds, *plaques à madeleinettes* (miniature shells) and *plaques à coques* (fancy, stylized shells slightly wider than the classic shell), also made of tin, can be used for baking madeleine batters. These look fanciful, and are fun to use. The miniature shell plaque holds twenty 1¾-inch-long shells that measure 1⅛ inches at the widest point; each baby shell has a capacity of 1¼ teaspoons. The stylized plaque of shells (which look a bit like scallop shells) holds eight 2½-inch-long shells that measure 2½ inches at the widest point; each shell has a capacity of 2 tablespoons plus 2 teaspoons, slightly more than the traditional madeleine shell.

❋ STRAIGHT-SIDED BAKING PANS: Baking pans with straight sides, which create square corners, come in a variety of sizes and depths. A 2-inch-deep pan is just right for baking bar cookies; a 3-inch-deep pan works perfectly for holding sweet yeast rolls and buns that rise impressively high as they bake. The sizes used in the recipes are not interchangeable, as the volume amounts of the batters and soft doughs were developed to meet the capacities of each particular pan. These are the sizes of the straight-sided pans used in this book: 8 by 8 by 2 inches; 9 by 9 by 2 inches; 10 by 10 by 2 inches; 12 by 8 by 3 inches; 13 by 9 by 2 inches; 13 by 9 by 3 inches; and 12 by 18 by 1 inch. The last pan, which has a large surface area, is a straight-sided rimmed sheet pan. Rimmed sheet pans provide expansive areas for baking scones, cookies, and biscuits, and for holding muffin cup pans that are filled with individual sticky buns to catch any spillovers during baking.

MUFFIN/CUPCAKE PANS

❋ STANDARD MUFFIN PANS: Standard muffin pans are available 12 cups to a pan, and each cup measures 2¾ inches in diameter and 1⅜ inches deep, with a capacity of ½ cup. The muffin cups can be used for baking both muffins and individual sweet rolls.

❋ TEA CAKE/BABY MUFFIN PANS: These small cups, 24 to a pan, each cup measuring 2 inches in diameter and 1³⁄₁₆ inches deep, have a capacity of 3 tablespoons. They make perfectly charming miniature muffins, or tiny sweet rolls and cupcakes.

❋ JUMBO "CROWN TOP" MUFFIN PANS: Large muffin pans with slightly extended tops that form narrow wells are called "crown top" pans. In them, the muffin batter peaks beautifully, creating nice rounded caps. The top of each crown is large and generous. There are six muffin cups in each "crown top" pan; each cup measures 3¼ inches in diameter and 2 inches deep, with a capacity of a scant 1 cup. The pans are nonstick. Although designed to be used for filling with muffin batter, the pans can also accommodate rolled, filled, and cut sweet yeast rolls, such as sticky buns or cinnamon swirls.

❋ JUMBO MUFFIN/CUPCAKE PANS: These capacious, extra-large muffin/cupcake cups flare out slightly and are ideal for holding big yeast-raised buns, plus all kinds of cupcake and muffin batters. Each cup measures 4 inches in diameter and 1¾ inches deep, with a capacity of 1⅛ cups.

❋ SQUARE MUFFIN PANS: The square, release-surface (nonstick) muffin cups, 8 to a pan, measure 2½ inches square and 1½ inches deep, and have a capacity of ⅔ cup each. In these cups, you can bake all kinds of extravagant muffins, cupcakes to be frosted, or nifty quick or yeasted sweet breads. The muffin pans are made by Chicago Metallic.

COOKIE SHEETS, RIMMED SHEET PANS, AND JELLYROLL PAN

❋ COOKIE SHEETS: In general, cookie sheets should be moderately heavy so that cookies, scones, and biscuits bake evenly and thoroughly without scorching on the bottom. If you own lightweight cookie sheets, *double-pan* them—stack one sheet directly on top of the other—to create a solid and stable baking surface for extra protection. Mine are made of aluminum and have two sides with raised rims; each sheet (inclusive of the rim) measures about 14 by 17¾ inches. The two 14-inch sides have the raised rims, which are easy to grip while transferring the cookies into and out of the oven.

Insulated cookie sheets are wonderful for baking tender-textured butter doughs, such as Butter Spritz Cookies (page 195), Butter Crescents (page 188),

Vanilla Crescents (page 522), or Cocoa-Chocolate Chip Pillows (page 266), and are ideal for baking the soft drop cookies that are loaded with chocolate, such as the Mocha Truffle Cookies (page 362). My insulated sheets (made of aluminum) have one raised rim and measure about 14 by 16¼ inches.

❊ RIMMED SHEET PANS: An average-size aluminum sheet pan, with four rimmed sides that flare out slightly, measures 13 by 18 by 1 inches. Oftentimes, you'll find them coated with a release surface on the inside. Flared rimmed sheet pans can serve the same function as the straight-sided rimmed sheet pans (refer to the section on "Straight-Sided Baking Pans," page 42).

❊ JELLYROLL PAN: The overall size (10½ by 15½ by 1¾ inches), weight, and structural form of the jellyroll pan makes it the consummate (and undisputed) shape for baking a lighter-than-light cake batter that, when cool, is spread with a filling and rolled into a spiral. A jellyroll pan, made of aluminum, should be moderately heavy and solidly constructed.

LOAF PANS

❊ LOAF PANS: Apart from being useful for baking yeast breads, metal loaf pans can hold a variety of tea cake and quick bread batters. The size of the loaf pan I use frequently is 9 by 5 by 3 inches, with a capacity of 7½ to 8 cups. The loaf pans I prize among all others have slightly sloping sides: the two long and two short sides slant outward and create a slightly narrower bottom, which bakes a prettier tea cake or quick bread. A loaf pan with angled sides creates a gorgeous crown.

TART PANS

❊ FLUTED TART PANS WITH REMOVABLE BOTTOMS (FALSE-BOTTOMED): Tinned steel tart pans, measuring 8½ inches in diameter and 9½ inches in diameter, have circular bottoms that fit into the frame of each pan. If you carefully set the baked tart on a sturdy ramekin (4 inches in diameter), the outer ring will lift away from the tart, making unmolding easy, and the tart, still on its base, can be transferred to a flat surface for cooling and cutting.

In addition to lining with a crust and filling with a sweet mixture, a tart pan can be used to bake shortbread dough and dough for large, break-apart "sharing" cookies, like A Big Almond, Cornmeal, and Dried Cherry Sharing Cookie on page 117. For years, I've been pressing buttery shortbread dough into tart pans, with excellent results. The design of the pan—the fluted sides and stable, firm base—is the perfect structure for containing the dough; in it the dough bakes an even golden color and cuts into neat triangles with attractively scalloped edges.

With butter as one of the primary components of a tart or shortbread dough, it is oftentimes unnecessary to grease the inside of the tart pan at the outset. But there are exceptions—filming the pan with nonstick vegetable spray is advisable when you're working with a dough that contains cornmeal and/or a sticky ingredient, like dried fruit, such as in the recipe for A Big Almond, Cornmeal, and Dried Cherry Sharing Cookie on page 117, or with any shortbreadlike dough that has a sticky or sugary topping, such as in the recipe for Cinnamon Nut Crunch Shortbread on page 315. When washing the tart pan, do so gently and avoid scraping the inside. Dry both parts of the pan well, independently of each other, then assemble and store in a protected place to prevent the sides from bending. Tart pans of different sizes (graduated) can be nested together for storage.

All tinned steel bakeware should be washed carefully and dried thoroughly. Avoid using a scouring cleaner or an abrasive sponge on the inside of the pans.

❋ TARTE TATIN PAN: Designed specifically for baking the traditional one-crust apple tart, this tin-lined copper pan produces one beautiful tart and measures 9½ inches across the top. The beauty of this pan is in the baking: it renders the apples sublimely tender, allows the caramel to meld nicely with the fruit, and produces a lovely, golden pastry top. (I actually own two 9½-inch *tarte Tatin* pans and one 11-inch pan; the 11-inch pan, a recent acquisition, does double duty as a container for baking a heavy cream-and-cheese-based potato gratin.) As with all of my copper cookware, I treat the inside with consideration, and avoid scrubbing it with anything abrasive, and I keep the outside polished to a shiny gleam. And instead of vigorously scrubbing away stubborn spots from the inside of tin-lined copper pans, I fill the pan with very hot water and let it stand until the cooking particles release themselves; you may need to repeat the process once or twice.

❋ PIE PANS: A sturdy, medium-weight, rimmed aluminum pie pan, 9 inches in diameter, with gently sloping sides and a level bottom, will absorb and diffuse the oven's heat evenly. The scant ½-inch rim that extends outward both stabilizes the sides and edges of the crust and gives you an extended surface to crimp into attractive flutes.

CRÊPE PAN

A crêpe pan, made of carbon steel, is a classic object that has endured over time. Both its figure—a flat bottom and sides that open outward on an angle—and physical composition allow the pan to conduct heat quickly and efficiently, and to turn out crêpes with a tender texture and beautiful color. I admit to owning a stack of crêpe pans because I like the idea of being able to make a variety of pancakes dictated by my mood and what I have on hand in the refrigerator or pantry.

A new crêpe pan needs to be cleaned thoroughly with a scouring pad and seasoned (see page 30) before swirling in a batter. The sizes I own are 5, 5½, 6, 6¾, and 7 inches, in addition to two carbon steel blini pans (measuring about 3¾ inches across the bottom). The carbon steel blini pan has rounded sides that are a jot deeper than those of a crêpe pan. In them I have made doll-size crêpes that are a breakfast delight, in addition to regulation-size blinis (for cushioning dollops of caviar, of course).

COPPER BEATING BOWL FOR WHIPPING EGG WHITES, AND BALLOON WHISK

For beating egg whites to a gossamer texture and expansive volume, a copper bowl is an unrivaled, although expensive, tool. My whisk is not the largest one available, but it fits comfortably in my hand and conforms to the rounded bottom of the bowl.

To prepare a copper bowl for beating egg whites, pour about ¼ cup apple cider vinegar (or distilled white vinegar) into the bottom of the bowl and add 1½ to 2 tablespoons coarse (kosher) salt. Scrub the inside of the bowl thoroughly with the vinegar-salt mixture, using a folded, triple thickness of paper towel. Pour out the vinegar-salt mixture, then rinse the bowl completely (inside and outside) in tepid water and dry thoroughly before using. This treatment must take place *every time* you beat a batch of egg whites. *Note:* Use the copper bowl as soon as it is prepared. And as soon as the egg whites are beaten to the consistency desired (such as the soft or firm peak stage), work with the whites *without delay*, scraping them out of the bowl. Never let the egg whites remain in the bowl. If you are adding the beaten whites to another mixture, do so in a separate, *nonreactive* bowl. *Omit cream of tartar or salt when beating egg whites in a copper bowl.*

PASTRY BAG, TIPS, AND PASTE FOOD COLORS

Embellishing cookies with royal icing (refer to the Spicy Gingerbread Cookies on page 381, Butter Cookie Cut-Outs on page 197, and Royal Icing Made with Meringue Powder on page 384) requires time, patience, and good decorating equipment—such as sturdy 10-inch pastry bags (for small batches of icing), an assortment of tips (with couplers, to let you swap tips without dismantling the pastry bag and its contents), and vibrant paste food colors.

Dedicated cookie decorators will want to own at least six pastry bags for the times when you're using many different colors at once (I use Magic Line, Ateco Flex, and Wilton Featherweight pastry bags); primary paste colors, in addition to all the beautiful pastels and seasonal colors (Wilton, Cake Craft, or Spectrum by Ateco all produce superior paste colors); and a set of tips (made by Ateco, Magic Line, or Wilton). The set of tips, colors, and bags can be basic or comprehensive depending upon how involved your cookie decorating becomes.

COOLING RACKS

Basic and indispensable, proper cooling racks should be completely sturdy, with articulated feet that support the racks at least ½ inch above the countertop and have tight grids that don't buckle under the weight of filled baking pans. It's worthwhile owning several medium-size cooling racks (measuring about 9¼ by 13¾ inches) and one or two large racks (measuring about 13 by 22 inches). Several 9- and 10-inch round racks are handy to have if you bake lots of layer cakes.

WAFFLE IRON

My Belgian-style electric waffle iron (a Vitantonio Premier Belgian Waffler) produces impressive sets of deep-dish waffles. The release-surface grids, the sensitive control which enables you to set the desired darkness of the waffles, and excellent heat distribution are factors that make this iron worth owning.

TEMPERATURE GAUGES

❋ MERCURY THERMOMETERS: A good, reliable thermometer is essential for taking the temperature of water (to be used in dissolving yeast in all the sweet roll and bun recipes), in specific phases in the making of caramel, and such. I use both the Cordon Rose chocolate thermometer and the Cordon Rose candy thermometer. Both thermometers are available at La Cuisine (refer to "Selected Sources for Equipment and Supplies" for the source listing). For detailed information on these thermometers and their use and care, refer to pages 451 through 453 in *The Cake Bible* by Rose Levy Beranbaum (New York: William Morrow, 1988).

PAPER AND PLASTIC PRODUCTS

❋ COOKING PARCHMENT PAPER: Food-safe parchment paper, designed to be used in the oven, is available in 20-square-foot rolls. Paper Maid Kitchen Parchment is an excellent brand, for the paper is sturdy and just the right thickness for lining sheet pans, baking pans, and cookie sheets.

❋ WAXED PAPER: Waxed paper remains one of the best and most economical papers for lining the bottom of cake pans and jelly roll pans. It peels off the bottoms of tube cakes and layer cakes easily. Many of the recipes in this book will direct you to sift a combination of dry ingredients directly onto a large sheet of waxed paper (it's fast and practical), but you can measure sugar and other recipe components, such as cocoa and chopped nuts, onto waxed paper as well.

❋ PLASTIC WRAP AND SELF-SEALING PLASTIC BAGS: For kitchen use, always use food-safe plastic wrap and plastic bags when covering, wrapping, or otherwise enclosing anything edible.

ITEMS PURCHASED AND RESERVED FOR KITCHEN USE ONLY

❋ KITCHEN RULER AND TAPE MEASURE: For the accurate measuring of all bakeware, a sheet of roll-out yeast dough, triangles of shortbread, width and height of drop cookies, disks of scone dough, tart dough rounds, and such, a diligent baker should not be without a standard 12-inch ruler and rolling tape measure. For good kitchen hygiene, buy a rigid plastic ruler that can be washed in hot, soapy water, rinsed clean, and dried thoroughly.

❋ TWEEZERS: Tweezers are necessary for applying edible decorations, which can be minuscule, to cookies coated with royal icing. The tweezers allow you to set the decorations in place without marring the icing's wet surface. A tweezer with a flat and slightly angled, rather than pointed, tip is the easiest to handle.

❋ SHARP SCISSORS: I keep a pair of extra-sharp, stainless scissors (the Fiskars brand) in the kitchen for cutting lengths of parchment paper, waxed paper rounds, and sticky, glazed fruit. The overall length of my scissors measures 6½ inches, and the length of the blades is about 4 inches.

COPPER AND BRASS POLISH

To keep the outside of all of my copper bakeware or saucepans sparkling and brilliant, I use Red Bear copper and brass polish. (It's made in Norway, but is available at cookware shops and some hardware stores in the United States.) This brand of powder keeps copper from tarnishing longer than any other I've tried.

a number of recipes in this book rely on incorporating a scented sugar, potent vanilla extract, finishing syrup, or sugar wash to an unbaked or baked dough or batter. Any one of these adds a layer of flavor. I recommend that you begin by preparing two of the easiest baking accents (or condiments, as I call them) in this chapter, the Intensified Vanilla Extract on page 52 and the Vanilla-Scented Granulated Sugar on page 53. The strengthened vanilla extract and vanilla bean–heightened sugar really glamorize a recipe, and make what you bake even more delicious. The number and type of seasoning agents you prepare depend on your own interests and baking habits, but I hope that you'll be inspired to put together one or two of them.

The basic ingredients used in the baking process—flour, butter, sugar, spices, leavening agents, flavoring extracts, eggs, fluid or soft dairy products (such as milk, buttermilk, and sour cream), nuts, chocolate in all its forms, and so on—eventually determine the type, style, and composition of what gets turned out of a baking pan. The list of essential baking components, which follows the first section on prepared condiments, is an overview of the ingredients used in my recipes. Refrigerated ingredients should be kept tightly closed or sealed to avoid any unpleasant odor absorption or transference. Pantry staples (such as sugar, flour, spices, and leavenings) should be kept cool, dry, and away from a direct heat source (such as an oven or heating register) in tightly sealed containers.

The chapter concludes with a chart on page 74 that explains the roles of the most important staple ingredients used in baking.

3

CREATING A
BAKING PANTRY

Baking Condiments

Intensified Vanilla Extract

One 2-ounce bottle vanilla extract

THE RECIPE FOR A FLAVOR-ELEVATED vanilla extract is fast and easy. And the reward? A cake or batch of cookies, muffins, biscuits, or scones deepened with the taste of vanilla. I use this punched-up extract in baking recipes that call for vanilla flavoring, and in all vanilla-based recipes. Think of the strengthened version as a dramatic and fluid jolt of vanilla goodness.

Half of a small, pliant vanilla bean, split to expose the tiny seeds, using a sharp paring knife
One 2-ounce bottle vanilla extract

Holding one end, dip the split vanilla bean several times in the vanilla to release some of the seeds into the extract. Bend the bean in half to shorten it, then slip it into the bottle. Cap the vanilla tightly, shake several times, and store on a cool, dark pantry shelf for 4 to 5 days before using. This mega-vanilla extract is best used within 6 months, when the flavor is at its boldest best.

✳ *A special vanilla condiment.* This is not a condiment that you make, but rather one that you buy. From Nielsen-Massey Vanillas, Inc., comes Madagascar Bourbon Pure Vanilla Bean Paste; it is a lush, spoonable mixture that will glorify pound cake and cookie batters, yeast doughs, stirred custards, and such. I have found that ¼ to ½ teaspoon of the paste can be added to almost any batter or dough that incorporates 3 to 4 cups of flour in the recipe.

Scented Sugars

Using a flavored sugar in a batter or dough fortifies its flavor. It's easy to make in small or large quantities and stores conveniently in a well-sealed jar.

Vanilla-Scented Granulated Sugar

5 pounds flavored sugar

VANILLA-SCENTED SUGAR is such a congenial ingredient that, apart from the obvious clash with the flavor of citrus, this sweetening agent is at home in almost any batter or dough recipe, topping, icing, glaze, or filling formula. It is, in fact, such a significant and effective flavoring component that I urge you to make a 5-pound quantity to have on hand.

3 moist, aromatic vanilla beans, split down the center to expose the tiny seeds, using a small, sharp knife

5 pounds granulated sugar

OPEN UP THE VANILLA BEANS SLIGHTLY Using a small, flexible palette knife (or tip of a rounded-edged dinner knife), open up the sides of the vanilla bean halves slightly.

LAYER THE VANILLA BEANS IN THE SUGAR Turn about one-third of the granulated sugar into a large storage container. Drop in one of the split vanilla beans. Fill with half of the remaining sugar, and drop in the two remaining vanilla beans. Add the balance of the sugar. Cover the container tightly.

"CURE" THE SUGAR Place the sugar on a pantry shelf, or in a cool place on the kitchen countertop, preferably away from direct sunlight. After 2 days, carefully spoon up the contents of the container to shift the vanilla beans, cover, and let the beans flavor the sugar for at least 2 more days.

TEXTURE OBSERVATION Over time, owing to the moisture content of the vanilla beans, the sugar will be less free-flowing than sugar you dip out of a new 5-pound sack of granulated sugar, and it will compact further as time goes on. To use the flavored sugar, crush or break it up as necessary with a wooden spoon or spatula, and flick aside the vanilla beans when scooping it out. If the sugar is very lumpy, strain it through a medium- to large-mesh stainless steel sieve before measuring.

RECYCLING OBSERVATION When the vanilla beans have given up most of their moistness (in about 4 months), they will turn slightly firm and a bit splintery. The time actually depends on how supple they were initially and the ambient temperature of your kitchen and the storage area. Although the beans are a bit less perfumed now, they can be steeped in a liquid, with excellent results. Heat the beans along with milk, cream, or heavy cream when making a custard or pastry cream for that extra bounce of vanilla taste, then remove and discard the beans.

Variations: Vanilla-scented superfine sugar and vanilla-scented confectioners' sugar can be made in the same way as the granulated sugar. Unless you do an enormous amount of baking, put up the sugar in 3-pound batches. Use three 1-pound boxes of confectioners' sugar or superfine sugar and two split vanilla beans.

LEMON-SCENTED GRANULATED SUGAR

3 pounds flavored sugar

GRANULATED SUGAR ANIMATED with the bold upgrade of citrus peel is a pantry item to use in many lemon-based baked goods. Use a sharp, stainless steel swivel-bladed peeler to remove wide strips of the lemon peel. The flavored sugar refines the taste of creamed cake batters, sweet cheese, and lemon curd fillings, in addition to pourable icings and glazes.

15 strips lemon peel
3 pounds granulated sugar

DRY THE STRIPS OF LEMON PEEL Line a plate or baking sheet with waxed paper. Scatter the strips of lemon peel on the paper in an even layer. Let the peel stand overnight on the kitchen countertop, turning them two or three times. After about 24 hours (or longer, depending upon the atmospheric conditions of your kitchen), the peel should be dry and leathery-textured. If the weather is damp or humid when you are making the peel, you may need to dry them for another 8 hours or so. *Dried peel observation* Make sure to put together the scented sugar with *thoroughly dried peel*; otherwise you risk liquefying the sugar.

BEST BAKING ADVICE
I usually use organic lemons for juicing, and always use them when grating the rind (to be included in batters and doughs) or stripping the peel (for making a batch of scented sugar). A smaller amount of lemon-scented sugar can be made using 1 pound of sugar and 5 strips of lemon peel.

LAYER THE LEMON PEELS IN THE SUGAR Place one-third (1 pound) of the granulated sugar in a large storage container. Scatter over half of the dried lemon peels. Add another third of sugar, top with the remaining lemon peels, and cover with the last pound of sugar, then the lid.

"CURE" THE SUGAR Place the sugar in a cool place for 5 days before using. After 2 days, gently stir the sugar to integrate the peels in it. The lemon-flavored sugar will clump up over time, and should be strained through a sieve or sifted before using to break up any clumps.

SWEET SYRUPS AND WASHES

As glorious final fillips to what you bake, simmered syrups and quickly made liquid-sugar washes add a substantial impact of flavor. The flavored syrups are cooked and the washes are mixed in a bowl. Any one of them enhances the moistness quotient and keeping quality of a cake in a way that a buttercream covering or fluffy icing cannot, for a syrup or wash actually soaks into the "crumb" of the cake.

To apply a syrup or wash, use a pastry brush that's at least 1 inch wide. Dip the brush in the syrup or wash so that it draws up a generous amount of it, then dab-press-pat it onto whatever you're flavoring—such as a pound cake or the tops of a batch of muffins—without actually dragging it over the surface and encouraging crumbs or a fragile top layer to be tousled up. Apply it lightly, in a gentle stroking, pampering, painterly motion.

ALMOND SYRUP

About ½ cup

LUSTROUS AND ALMOND-FLAVORED, two almond derivatives (in the form of liqueur and extract) join with a touch of vanilla extract for balance to make an ideal liquid for moistening tender butter cakes baked in layer and tube pans.

¼ cup granulated sugar

¼ cup plus 2 tablespoons water

½ cup almond liqueur, such as Amaretto

½ teaspoon pure vanilla extract

¼ teaspoon pure almond extract

COOK THE ALMOND SYRUP Place the sugar, water, and almond liqueur in a small, nonreactive saucepan. Cover and set over low heat. When every granule of sugar has dissolved, raise the heat to high and bring the contents of the saucepan to the boil. Cook the liquid at a medium boil for 7 to 8 minutes, until reduced and concentrated-looking. It should measure ½ cup. Stir in the vanilla and almond extracts.

STORE THE SYRUP Pour the syrup into a heatproof storage container and cool completely. Cover tightly and refrigerate. The syrup will keep, refrigerated, for 1 to 2 weeks.

Variation: For rum syrup, substitute dark rum for the almond liqueur, omit the almond extract, and increase the amount of vanilla extract to ¾ teaspoon.

COFFEE SYRUP

About ⅔ cup

THIS LIGHTLY SWEETENED, coffee-endowed syrup will add an elusive richness and mochalike character to chocolate cake layers or chocolate pound cake. The granulated sugar brings out the rounded tones and depth of coffee flavor in the syrup.

¾ cup strong brewed coffee

¼ cup coffee liqueur, such as Kahlúa

¼ cup granulated sugar

¾ teaspoon pure vanilla extract

COOK THE COFFEE SYRUP Place the coffee, coffee liqueur, and sugar in a small nonreactive saucepan. Cover and set over low heat. When the sugar has melted completely and there is no sign of grittiness on the bottom of the saucepan, raise the heat to high and bring the contents of the saucepan to the boil. Cook the liquid at a medium boil for 8 minutes, until reduced to ⅔ cup. Stir in the vanilla extract.

STORE THE SYRUP Pour the syrup into a heatproof storage container and cool completely. Cover tightly and refrigerate. The syrup will keep, refrigerated, for 1 week to 10 days.

LEMON SYRUP

About ⅔ cup

THIS SYRUP IS LESS POTENT than the Lemon-Sugar Wash on page 59; it adds a soft lemon finish rather than a sweet-sharp one. The syrup permeates; the wash settles more on the surface. The syrup's intensity is modulated when the citrus juice and sugar-water mixture is heated and the sugar melts to create a shimmery flavoring liquid. You can use the syrup warm or cool to brush or spoon on cakes or muffins (see my Baby Lemon Muffins on page 405 for a good example of its use) for heightening both moistness and flavor.

½ cup granulated sugar

2 tablespoons water

½ cup freshly squeezed lemon juice

COOK THE LEMON SYRUP Place the sugar, water, and lemon juice in a small nonreactive saucepan. Cover and set over low heat. Cook the mixture slowly to dissolve the sugar thoroughly, about 10 minutes. Uncover, raise the heat to high, and bring to a boil. Adjust the heat so that the mixture cooks at a simmer for 1 to 2 minutes, or until reduced to ⅔ cup.

BEST BAKING ADVICE

For extra pungency, blanch 1 tablespoon of julienned lemon rind in boiling water, drain, and rinse in a sieve under cold water. When cool, pat dry the lemon threads, add to the syrup, and refrigerate for 6 hours or overnight. For a big jolt of flavor, use the the syrup with the threads.

STORE THE SYRUP The syrup, poured into a nonreactive storage container, can be kept in the refrigerator for up to 3 days.

ALMOND-SUGAR WASH

About ½ cup

THE LUSH AND MIGHTY flavor of almond (present in the liqueur and droplets of extract) is present in this wash to brush on Bundt cakes and pound cakes. It has a deep, bold taste.

⅓ cup almond liqueur, such as Amaretto

⅓ cup granulated sugar

¼ teaspoon pure almond extract

MIX THE ALMOND-SUGAR WASH In a small nonreactive bowl, stir together the almond liqueur, sugar, and almond extract. Any sugar that stays undissolved (depending upon how quickly the wash is used) will settle to the bottom of the bowl. The wash can be made up to 2 hours in advance.

LEMON-SUGAR WASH

About ½ cup

QUICK TO MAKE, and exceptionally tangy, this blend is an intense condiment to paint over the top of just-baked (and still oven-hot) fruit muffins, pound and loaf cakes, or sweet tea cakes.

⅓ cup freshly squeezed lemon juice

⅓ cup granulated sugar, preferably lemon-scented (see page 55)

MIX THE LEMON-SUGAR WASH In a small nonreactive bowl, combine the lemon juice and sugar. Stir well. Let stand 10 minutes. Using the wash now will give the surface of a baked tea loaf, pound cake, or batch of muffins a crackly, sugary veneer.

COFFEE-SUGAR WASH

About ¾ cup

LACED WITH COFFEE LIQUEUR, this solution of strong coffee and granulated sugar is a stylish finish to such good things as a chocolate (or chocolate chip) pound or Bundt cake, or dense chocolate fudge cake.

¼ cup plus 2 tablespoons coffee liqueur, such as Kahlúa

2 tablespoons strong coffee, cold

⅓ cup plus 1 tablespoon granulated sugar

MIX THE COFFEE-SUGAR WASH In a small bowl, combine the coffee liqueur, cold coffee, and sugar. Stir well. A good part of the sugar will settle to the bottom of the bowl if the wash is used immediately. This wash can be made up to 30 minutes in advance.

LEMON PEEL INFUSION

Enough to flavor a butter cake batter based on 3 to 3½ cups of flour and ½ pound of butter

A HANDY WAY TO INSTILL optimum flavor in citrus peel is to combine it with a flavoring extract and complementary juice. Once the infusion is mixed, set it aside for the different components to marry. This basic recipe is similar to the lemon rind soak used in the Ultra-Lemon Cake on page 402.

1 tablespoon freshly grated lemon rind

2½ teaspoons freshly squeezed lemon juice

1½ teaspoons pure lemon extract

MAKE THE INFUSION AND ALLOW IT TO BLOOM Combine the lemon rind, lemon juice, and lemon extract in a small nonreactive ramekin. Let the infusion stand for 15 minutes before using.

BEST BAKING ADVICE

When grating lemon rind for the infusion, be sure to remove only the yellow-hued peel. The white pith has a bitter edge, which would make the infusion taste harsh.

BUTTERY SPICED STREUSEL

About 4¼ cups

STREUSEL IS A RICH AND NUBBY topping made of at least three key ingredients: flour, sugar, and butter. My streusels have that and much more, as they include spices, a flavoring extract, nuts, or coconut. A streusel is applied to the top of a cake or pan of sweet rolls just before baking. A delicious variation of streusel, a crunchy oatmeal topping (the Golden Oatmeal Sprinkle on page 65), is scattered over the top of baked and iced or frosted muffins, coffee cakes, or scones.

This is the topping to use on spice and sour cream coffee cakes, to press onto the top of muffins or scones, or to cover any style of kuchen. The streusel can be customized to feature the dominant spice in a batter or dough by adjusting the amounts to highlight a flavor.

1½ cups unsifted bleached all-purpose flour

1 teaspoon freshly grated nutmeg

½ teaspoon ground cinnamon

¼ teaspoon ground allspice

⅛ teaspoon ground cloves

⅛ teaspoon salt

¾ cup firmly packed light brown sugar, sieved if lumpy

½ cup granulated sugar

12 tablespoons (1½ sticks) unsalted butter, cut into chunks, cool, but not cold

1 teaspoon pure vanilla extract

BEST BAKING ADVICE

Using cool (not cold) butter gives the streusel mixture a clumpy, stick-together texture. The light brown sugar adds an earthy edge of sweetness to the streusel, and plays well against the spices.

BLEND THE FLOUR, SPICES, AND SUGARS In a large mixing bowl, thoroughly whisk the flour, nutmeg, cinnamon, allspice, cloves, and salt. Add the light brown sugar and granulated sugar, and combine well with a wooden spoon or rubber spatula.

WORK IN THE BUTTER CHUNKS Scatter the chunks of butter over the flour-sugar mixture, and using a pastry blender (or two round-bladed table knives), cut the butter into the flour mixture until the fat is reduced to pieces about the size of lima beans. Sprinkle over the vanilla extract.

CREATE THE STREUSEL "CURDS" Using your fingertips, crumble-knead-press the mixture together until large and small "curds" or clumps and lumps of streusel are formed. *Texture observation* The streusel mixture should have turned into damp, irregularly shaped nuggets and lumps.

THE STREUSEL CAN BE MADE UP TO 2 DAYS AHEAD; STORE IT IN A TIGHTLY SEALED CONTAINER IN THE REFRIGERATOR. USE THE STREUSEL AT COOL ROOM TEMPERATURE, CRUMBLED INTO LARGE AND SMALL PIECES.

Vanilla Streusel

About 4¼ cups

PLAIN AND BUTTERY, and an inviting coverlet for sweet yeast rolls and coffee cakes.

1½ cups unsifted bleached all-purpose flour

½ teaspoon freshly grated nutmeg

⅛ teaspoon salt

1 cup vanilla-scented granulated sugar (see page 53)

½ cup firmly packed light brown sugar, sieved if lumpy

14 tablespoons (1¾ sticks) unsalted butter, cut into chunks, cool, but not cold

1¼ teaspoons intensified vanilla extract (see page 52)

BLEND THE FLOUR, SPICE, AND SUGAR In a large mixing bowl, thoroughly combine the flour, nutmeg, and salt. Add the granulated sugar and light brown sugar, and mix thoroughly with a wooden spoon or rubber spatula.

WORK IN THE BUTTER CHUNKS Scatter the chunks of butter over the flour-sugar mixture, and using a pastry blender (or two round-bladed table knives), cut the butter into the flour mixture until the fat is reduced to pieces about the size of navy beans. Sprinkle over the vanilla extract.

CREATE THE STREUSEL "CURDS" Using your fingertips, knead-squeeze-press the mixture together until large and small "curds" or lumps of streusel are formed. *Texture observation* The streusel mixture should be clumpy, and not appear grainy or be free-flowing.

Variation: You can make a fine vanilla streusel even if you haven't any vanilla-scented granulated sugar on hand. Increase the vanilla extract to 2 teaspoons. Scrape the tiny seeds from one plump, moist vanilla bean and add it to 1 cup of granulated sugar. Make the streusel as directed in the procedure.

BEST BAKING ADVICE
The streusel can be made up to 2 days ahead; store it in a tightly sealed container in the refrigerator. Use the streusel at cool room temperature, crumbled with your fingertips into large and small irregularly shaped fragments.

NUT STREUSEL

About 4¾ cups

THIS STREUSEL IS BUILT on the usual butter-flour-sugar model, but is deepened by a generous amount of brown sugar (for a lush caramel edge) and a full cup of chopped nuts. This is a bold and crunchy cover for quick breads and creamed-butter coffee cakes, when the topping is as essential, tastewise, as the dough or batter.

1½ cups unsifted bleached all-purpose flour

½ teaspoon freshly grated nutmeg

½ teaspoon ground cinnamon

⅛ teaspoon ground allspice

⅛ teaspoon salt

1¼ cups firmly packed light brown sugar, sieved if lumpy

12 tablespoons (1½ sticks) unsalted butter, cut into chunks, cool, not cold

1 teaspoon pure vanilla extract

1 cup coarsely chopped nuts (walnuts, pecans, macadamia nuts, or blanched and skinned almonds)

BLEND THE FLOUR, SPICES, AND SUGAR In a large mixing bowl, thoroughly whisk the flour, nutmeg, cinnamon, allspice, and salt. Add the light brown sugar, and mix well with a wooden spoon or rubber spatula.

WORK IN THE BUTTER CHUNKS Drop in the chunks of butter, and using a pastry blender (or two round-bladed table knives), cut the butter into the flour mixture until the fat is reduced to pieces about the size of dried lima beans. Sprinkle over the vanilla extract. Mix in the nuts.

CREATE THE STREUSEL "CURDS" Using your fingertips, crumble-knead-press the mixture together until large and small "curds" or clumps of streusel are formed. *Texture observation* After you have worked the streusel, the mixture should form slightly damp, nut-studded lumps of streusel, which are both large and small.

THE STREUSEL CAN BE MADE UP TO 2 DAYS AHEAD; STORE IT IN A TIGHTLY SEALED CONTAINER IN THE REFRIGERATOR. USE THE STREUSEL AT COOL ROOM TEMPERATURE, CRUMBLED INTO LARGE AND SMALL PIECES AS IT IS DISTRIBUTED OVER A BATTER OR ROLLED AND CUT SWEET YEAST ROLLS OR BUNS.

BEST BAKING ADVICE
Keep the nuts evenly and coarsely chopped, which gives the streusel a rough and rugged, nubby character.

COCONUT STREUSEL

About 4 cups

CHARGED WITH COCONUT and reinforced with a few background spices, this is the essential topping for my Coconut Cream Coffee Cake Buns on page 328, but if you want to highlight the taste of coconut, it can also replace nearly any other streusel covering. This is a rich and elegant streusel, which hasn't the stubby quality of one that is nut-based. Use it over chocolate chip, spice, or nut-based coffee cakes; on chocolate, banana, or coconut muffins; and on chocolate, chocolate chip, coconut, or spice-flavored scones. The nutmeg and cinnamon develop the flavor of the coconut in a wonderful way.

1½ cups unsifted bleached all-purpose flour

½ teaspoon freshly grated nutmeg

¼ teaspoon ground cinnamon

⅛ teaspoon salt

½ cup granulated sugar

½ cup firmly packed light brown sugar, sieved if lumpy

1 cup lightly packed sweetened flaked coconut

12 tablespoons (1½ sticks) unsalted butter, cut into chunks, cool, not cold

1¼ teaspoons pure vanilla extract

BLEND THE FLOUR, SPICES, SUGARS, AND COCONUT In a large mixing bowl, thoroughly whisk the flour, nutmeg, cinnamon, and salt. Add the granulated sugar, light brown sugar, and coconut; mix well to blend, using a wooden spoon or spatula.

WORK IN THE BUTTER CHUNKS Drop in the chunks of butter, and using a pastry blender (or two round-bladed table knives), cut the butter into the flour mixture until the fat is reduced to pieces about the size of lima beans. Sprinkle over the vanilla extract.

CREATE THE STREUSEL "CURDS" Using your fingertips, crumble-knead-press the mixture together until large and small "curds" or clumps of streusel are formed. *Texture observation* After working the streusel, the mixture should form moist, irregularly shaped lumps. It should not be granular in consistency.

THE STREUSEL CAN BE MADE UP TO 2 DAYS AHEAD; STORE IT IN A TIGHTLY SEALED CONTAINER IN THE REFRIGERATOR. USE THE STREUSEL AT COOL ROOM TEMPERATURE.

GOLDEN OATMEAL SPRINKLE

About 4 cups

THE SECRET TO DESIGNING a crunchy, durable, and delicious oatmeal topping is to prebake the pebbly rough-textured mixture until lightly crispy and golden. Once baked and cooled, the golden oatmeal-based crisp can be used to top frosted or iced scones, sweet biscuits and yeast rolls, or coffee cakes. This recipe makes a generous amount, which can be halved successfully.

1½ cups old-fashioned rolled oats

½ cup unsifted bleached all-purpose flour

⅛ teaspoon salt

½ teaspoon freshly grated nutmeg

¼ teaspoon ground cinnamon

⅔ cup firmly packed light brown sugar, sieved if lumpy

1½ cups walnuts, macadamia nuts, pecans, roasted cashews, or skinned almonds, coarsely chopped

10 tablespoons (1 stick plus 2 tablespoons) unsalted butter, melted, cooled to tepid, and blended with 1 teaspoon pure vanilla extract

PREHEAT THE OVEN AND PREPARE THE BAKING PAN Preheat the oven to 375° F. Have a jellyroll pan or large rimmed sheet pan at hand.

COMBINE THE TOPPING MIXTURE In a large mixing bowl, thoroughly mix the oats, flour, salt, nutmeg, cinnamon, and brown sugar. Stir in the nuts. Drizzle the melted butter–vanilla mixture over all, and mix thoroughly with your hand to dampen all of the ingredients. Spoon the mixture onto the baking pan, creating an even layer.

BAKE THE TOPPING Bake the topping for 15 to 20 minutes, or until a medium golden color.

COOL THE TOPPING Let the topping stand in the jellyroll pan on a cooling rack for at least 1 hour. When the oatmeal mixture is completely cool, break up any big pieces with your fingertips. The topping should be flaky with very small clumps remaining here and there.

FRESHLY MADE, THE SPRINKLE KEEPS FOR **2** WEEKS; STORE THE TOPPING IN AN AIRTIGHT TIN OR SCREW-TOP GLASS JAR.

CLARIFIED BUTTER

1 cup clarified butter

CLARIFIED BUTTER is a peerless fat to use when greasing a crêpe pan or griddling pancakes. The flavor of clarified butter is pristine and clean. A swipe of clarified butter on a hot crêpe pan or griddle will yield you perfectly browned (and exceptionally light-tasting) pancakes, whether they are the glorious, handkerchief-thin French models (crêpes) or the puffy, leavened all-American flapjacks.

Clarified butter is also a fabulous fat for greasing baking pans. It's slick and pure, and can be put to use in any recipe that calls for buttering or flouring bakeware. The butter can be remelted and painted on the interior.

The process of clarification creates a refined version of the fat, allowing you to cook with it at elevated temperatures without any risk of burning the goods. Clarified butter looks beautiful as it melts and tastes remarkably pure—like the essence of butter—*and* it can withstand high heat, so it's no wonder that it makes an excellent sautéing or griddle-greasing fat. (Clarified butter is also wonderful to use as the fat for frying slices of French toast.)

To make a 1-cup quantity of clarified butter (the amount I usually start out with in the refrigerator), you must begin with ¾ pound of stick or block butter. Use the best—and freshest—unsalted butter you can find.

¾ pound (3 sticks) top-quality unsalted butter

MELT THE BUTTER Cut up the sticks of butter into rough chunks and place the pieces in a heavy, medium-size saucepan (preferably enameled cast iron). Set over moderately low heat. When the butter has melted, in 5 to 7 minutes, remove it from the heat and carefully place on a heatproof surface to cool for 10 minutes. Try not to jiggle the saucepan as you are moving it from burner to heatproof surface.

SKIM THE SURFACE OF THE MELTED BUTTER With the tip of a small teaspoon, drag the white surface foam toward the side of the pan and spoon it up and out in small batches, skimming the top clean. To get up tiny bits that cling to the surface, fold a paper towel several times into the shape of a triangle, dampen one of the tips with cold water, press out any excess moisture, and brush over the surface where the bits are clinging to draw them onto the paper towel. Repeat, as necessary, with a newly dampened towel point. This is tedious work, but does clean up the surface.

TIP THE SAUCEPAN AND DRAW OUT THE CLEAR BUTTER Slant the saucepan to a slight angle by tilting the handle toward you. *Technique observation* Tipping the saucepan so that it slants a bit allows the clear butter to pool up, creating some depth. With a very small (⅛-cup capacity) measuring cup, spoon up the clear, liquified butter and pour into a clean, dry storage container. Drawing off the butter in small amounts lets you keep the milky residue at the bottom behind.

COOL AND STORE THE CLARIFIED BUTTER Cool the clarified butter. Cover the container tightly and store the butter in the refrigerator. Clarified butter keeps for about 1 month.

BASIC INGREDIENTS

BUTTER

Fresh unsalted butter creates baked goods with the cleanest, freshest, and purest flavor. Using unsalted butter gives you the ability to control the precise amount of salt added to a recipe. Store the butter, in its wrappings, on a refrigerator shelf. Avoid using previously frozen and defrosted butter, since freezing and defrosting frequently alter the texture of baked goods by making them heavier. This is especially important when making butter cakes, coffee cakes, and Bundt cakes, or any other type of cake that depends on creaming butter to a smooth and lightened state with sugar, but is not as critical when using butter in its melted state, as you would when making various types of bar cookies, such as brownies.

Butter should be stored in the refrigerator, tightly wrapped, as it readily absorbs any pungent aromas.

CHOCOLATE

In its many forms, chocolate is one of the more dominant flavoring agents available to the baker. As an unabashed fan of this tropical bean, I am pleased to see a dynamic assortment of chocolate at the market, including an impressive selection of the bitter-sweet variety.

❋ *Standard-size semisweet chocolate chips* are available in 6- and 12-ounce bags, *miniature semisweet chips* in 12-ounce bags, and *milk chocolate chips* in 11.5-ounce bags. *Micro-Chips* (available from The Baker's Catalogue) are produced in Germany, available in three varieties—dark, milk, and white chocolate—and packaged in 8-ounce bags; stir a few tablespoons through a layer cake batter, or sprinkle them over the top of a batch of freshly iced or frosted brownies, sheet cake, scones, or cookies. Micro-Chips are the tiniest chips imaginable, and look like very small specks.

❋ *Unsweetened chocolate,* wrapped individually in 1-ounce squares, is available in 8-ounce boxes (Baker's Unsweetened Baking Chocolate Squares); Baker's is the brand of unsweetened chocolate my mother used, and it was such a baking fixture in our kitchen that I still tend to associate its taste with brownies, chocolate cake, and other good things. Scharffen Berger Unsweetened (9.7-ounce bar; 99 percent cocoa) has a deep, complex flavor and makes an exceptional batch of brownies, and a deliriously delicious chocolate fudge or layer cake; with its princely price tag, this is an indulgent baking chocolate.

❋ Top-quality *alkalized* (Dutch-processed) *cocoa,* such as Dröste, is available in 8.8-ounce boxes. In recipes that use cocoa as the primary chocolate ingredient, you may want a deeper, darker look: Dutch-process black cocoa, available in 1-pound bags from The Baker's Catalogue (see "Selected Sources for Equipment and Supplies" at the end of the book), used in small quantities along with regular alkalized cocoa, will intensify the color and chocolate taste in doughs and batters. In testing, I found that you can replace up to one half of the amount of unsweetened, alkalized cocoa called for with the black cocoa, depending upon the recipe.

❋ *Bittersweet chocolate*, to use for melting or cutting into chunks and adding to doughs and batters, is available in bars of all sizes, in varying degrees of chocolate intensity and flavor. Any one of these rich-in-cocoa bittersweet chocolates is wonderful to use in the baking process (the size of the bar and the percentage of cocoa present in the chocolate follow each brand): Lindt Excellence 70% Cocoa Extra Fine (3.5-ounce bar; 70 percent cocoa); El Rey Bucare (14.1-ounce bar; 58.5 percent cocoa) Valrhona Le Noir (3.5-ounce bar; 56 percent cocoa); Valrhona Le Noir Amer (3.5-ounce bar; 71 percent cocoa); Valrhona Le Noir Gastronomie (8.75-ounce bar; 61 percent cocoa); Valrhona Equatoriale (14-ounce bar; 55 percent cocoa), Scharffen Berger Bittersweet (9.7-ounce bar; 70 percent cocoa), Scharffen Berger Semi Sweet (9.7-ounce bar; 62 percent cocoa), and Michel Cluizel Chocolat Amer Brut (3.5-ounce bar; 72 percent cocoa).

EXTRACTS

Alcohol-based extracts, especially vanilla, lemon, and almond, are used routinely to add rounded levels of flavor in batters and doughs, which would taste drab without them. Of the many interesting vanilla extracts available, these are impressive: Nielsen-Massey Organic Madagascar Bourbon Pure Vanilla Extract (35 percent alcohol, 4 fluid ounces), Nielsen-Massey Madagascar Bourbon Pure Vanilla Extract (35 percent alcohol, 4 fluid ounces), and Parker Vanilla Products Pure Vanilla Extract Madagascar Bourbon (4 fluid ounces).

FLAVORING/FLAVORED CHIPS OTHER THAN CHOCOLATE

Butterscotch-flavored chips (available in 11-ounce bags), peanut butter–flavored chips (available in 10-ounce bags), caramel-flavored chips, cappuccino-flavored chips, and cinnamon-flavored chips (all three specialty items are available in 1-pound bags from The Baker's Catalogue) become little pools of flavor in doughs and batters. These add a fanciful, light-hearted taste, and children love them.

FLOUR

❋ *Bleached all-purpose flour*, readily available in 5-pound bags, is the preferred flour to use for making most of the cakes, muffins, cookies, pancakes, waffles, scones, pie, and tart doughs in this book. Bleached, rather than unbleached, flour is preferable to use in baking powder or baking soda-leavened doughs and batters, for it develops an airier, finer texture on baking.

With its slightly higher protein content, *unbleached all-purpose flour*, also available in 5-pound bags, strengthens the composite structure of a sweet yeast dough and makes beautiful, high-rising filled rolls and buns. Depending upon the recipe, however, I use a combination of bleached and unbleached all-purpose flour in a sweet yeast dough, when I want both a finer crumb and a lofty rise, or silkier texture and bit of "pull" to the dough.

Bleached cake flour, available in 2-pound boxes, has a low protein content, and using it creates exceptionally tender, soft-textured baked goods. Sometimes I use a combination of bleached all-purpose flour *and* bleached cake flour in a batter (or dough), the former to develop the structure and integrity of the batter, the latter to relieve the density of the crumb and compose a moister, slightly feathery grain. And in brownies, I love to use a combination of cake flour and all-purpose flour, along with unsweetened cocoa and melted chocolate, to achieve the fudgiest texture possible.

* *Rice flour*, essentially very finely ground rice, is used in this book as an ingredient in shortbread, along with bleached all-purpose flour and/or bleached cake flour. Rice flour tenderizes shortbread dough, while lending an interesting "shear" to the baked cookie. Shortbread made with rice flour has a tender, faintly lightened, crumbly/craggy texture. Use white (not brown) rice flour. Rice flour, if used regularly, should be kept in an airtight container in a cool pantry; otherwise, store it in the freezer.

EGGS

Grade A *large eggs* are used exclusively in this collection of recipes. Eggs, a combination of both protein and fat, are a significant ingredient in most batters and doughs, and serve to add color; contribute to the all-important moistness quotient; strengthen and establish texture; and act as a (nonchemical) leavening agent. Although they are more expensive, I use certified organic eggs in baking, for I love the flavor, golden yolk color, and wonderful taste of baked goods made with eggs gathered from free-roaming chickens. To me, the internal composition, or crumb, of a baked cake is moister, better developed, and softer when organic eggs are used. As eggs are vulnerable to absorbing pesky refrigerator odors (the shells are porous), store them in the covered carton.

FLUID AND SOFT DAIRY PRODUCTS

Liquid and soft dairy products—milk, buttermilk, light (table) cream and heavy cream, half-and-half, or sour cream—are critical to the development of doughs and batters. These are responsible for establishing the structure (the overall density, or lightness, makeup of the internal crumb and texture or color of the crust) and a certain amount of flavor. Sour cream and buttermilk are dairy products, with a gentle tang created by the culturing process, and both produce baked goods with a soft, tender, and ultra-moist texture.

LEAVENING AGENTS

A leavening agent—baking powder or baking soda (which are defined as chemical leaveners) and yeast—creates the "rise" or "lift" in baked goods; clouds of voluminous egg whites and a ribbony, whisked mixture of sugar and eggs (or egg yolks) also act as leavening agents, but are based entirely on the purposeful whipping of ingredients.

❋ *Baking powder* contains bicarbonate of soda, an acid ingredient (calcium acid phosphate), and cornstarch; the cornstarch prevents the baking powder from clumping. For the recipes in this book, use double-acting baking powder, which reacts once as the batter or dough is mixed and a second time during exposure to oven heat. Baking powder should be stored tightly closed, in the pantry; for optimum freshness and the best results in baking, replace baking powder after 6 months.

❋ *Baking soda*, or sodium bicarbonate, works in the presence of an acid ingredient (such as sour cream, buttermilk, or chocolate) along with a liquid; sometimes, more than one acid component is present in a recipe (think of a fudge cake that may include both unsweetened chocolate and sour cream or buttermilk in the batter).

❋ *Yeast*, a natural (some would say organic) source of leavening, is used as the primary leavening agent in my recipes for babka, sweet rolls, sticky buns, and crumb buns. I use active dry yeast in dough making, and for greater accuracy (and to avoid endless confusion), I measure it out in teaspoons; although active dry yeast is considered shelf stable, I store it in the refrigerator.

NUTS, NUT PASTE, AND NUT FLOURS

Almonds, walnuts, unsalted macadamia nuts, peanuts, and pecans are used in recipes throughout this book. Nuts should taste fresh (rather than slightly acrid, which means that they've turned rancid) and snap briskly, with a good crunch. Roasted peanuts can be kept in an airtight tin (not in a plastic container) at room temperature for 2 months; for optimum storage (and the best flavor), refrigerate almonds, walnuts, pecans, and macadamia nuts for up to 6 weeks or freeze them for 5 to 6 months.

A light toasting in the oven brings out the full flavor in nuts to be added directly to a batter or dough, primarily because nuts are oily and the presence of the oil helps to convey—and relay—flavor. *To toast nuts*, spread them out in a baking pan or on a cookie sheet or sheet pan and place in a preheated 325° F. oven for 8 to 10 minutes (the nuts should darken slightly) and cool completely before using.

❋ The nut paste used in this book is *almond paste*, a dense mixture made primarily of blanched almonds, sugar, and water; almond paste adds great flavor to tart fillings, and soft filling mixtures for yeast-raised sweet rolls, crumb buns, and tea rings. In a filling, almond paste is frequently combined with butter, eggs, flavoring extracts, sugar, occasionally flour to build structure and density, and cream cheese for richness.

❊ *Nut flour* is simply a very finely ground (never clumpy) version of the nut powder. It should smell fresh. Measure it as you would all-purpose flour or sugar, in dry measuring cups. Nut flours add a deep, rounded flavor to cookie doughs and cake batters. (La Cuisine, in Alexandria, Virginia [see "Selected Sources for Equipment and Supplies" at the end of the book], carries excellent almond, hazelnut, pistachio, and pecan flours.)

SALT

In batters and doughs, salt is used in small quantities, but it is quite a pivotal ingredient. One of the fundamental functions of salt is to draw out flavor that, in turn, counterbalances spices, makes chocolate taste chocolaty and nuts taste nuttier. A pinch of salt, added to a crumble or streusel topping, or to a frosting or icing, offsets and tempers the sugar. The addition of salt (even as little as ⅛ teaspoon) prevents what you bake from tasting "flat," for it helps to create a rounded dimension of flavor when combined with the other ingredients. For the purest, lightest flavor, I use very fine sea salt in baking recipes; its unadulterated taste delivers a full, clean, and sprightly flavor.

SHORTENING AND VEGETABLE OIL

❊ *Solid shortening*, made from hydrogenated oil (and frequently a combination of oils such as cottonseed and soybean), is used occasionally in a cake batter and cookie or biscuit dough, along with unsalted butter, as a way to lighten (and tenderize) its internal texture by expanding the crumb. Measure shortening by packing it into measuring spoons or dry measuring cups with a flexible spatula, then smooth off and level the top with the straight edge of a palette knife.

❊ *Pure vegetable oil*, measured in a liquid measuring cup, is a fluid fat that contributes a moist and tender quality to baked goods. In batters and doughs, I always use soybean oil, for its clean taste marries well with most flavors.

SPICES

The spices you reach for in those tidy little jars on the grocery shelf emanate from the flavorful seeds and seed pods, berries, bark, and roots of plants, which have been dried and meticulously ground to a powder. The spices used most frequently in this book are cinnamon, nutmeg, allspice, cloves, ginger, and cardamom. Of all the spices mentioned, nutmeg is the only one that should be used freshly grated.

ABOVE Lots of everything, including nuggets of chopped toffee, embellish these Kitchen Sink Buttercrunch Bars (page 209).

TOP RIGHT Mess it up! Break off craggy pieces from A Big Almond, Cornmeal, and Dried Cherry Sharing Cookie (page 117).

MIDDLE RIGHT A curly swirl redolent of spice meanders through slices of Ultra-Cinnamon Pound Cake with Macadamia-Spice Ribbon (page 302).

BOTTOM RIGHT Thick squares of Cocoa-Sour Cream-Chocolate Chip Coffee Cake (page 268) are topped with a chocolate chip crumble.

FACING PAGE A stack of brownies and bar cookies in couture textures and flavors.

ABOVE Tall and regal, and rich beyond belief, Grandma Lilly's Butter Pound Cake (page 192) is an heirloom recipe. Photograph of the author with her grandma (at lower left) is from the personal memorabilia of the late Irene Yockelson.

TOP RIGHT This Apricot and Hazelnut Tart (page 150) is, perhaps, the ultimate jam tart.

MIDDLE RIGHT Retro Peanut Butter Cookies (page 436) and Ginger Cracks (page 392) are sweet tokens of the childhood cookie tin.

BOTTOM RIGHT Sour Cream Blueberry Muffins (page 184), dotted with bright berries, are big and bountiful.

FACING PAGE Mocha Rusks (page 360) await steamy cups of strong coffee.

ABOVE Streusel-topped and flavored with almond through and through, these Almond Pull-Aparts (page 106) are uncommonly distinctive.

TOP RIGHT What makes these Cocoa–Chocolate Chip Pillows (page 266) so irresistible? A cocoa butter dough that traps tiny chocolate chips, of course.

MIDDLE RIGHT A moist Cinnamon Apple Cake (page 310) is baked in a swirly pan.

BOTTOM RIGHT Vanilla Bean Shortbread (page 527), tender and buttery.

ABOVE Double Chocolate Madeleines (page 256) in gentle and natural contrast to Vanilla Madeleines (page 528).

TOP LEFT Chocolate, caramel, and macadamia nuts are a voluptuous threesome in these rich Turtle Squares (page 230).

MIDDLE LEFT Lumpy and bumpy Vanilla Streusel (page 62).

BOTTOM LEFT A basket of Spice Scones (page 482) and Apricot Oatmeal Breakfast Scones (page 134) illuminated by the morning light.

FACING PAGE A sweet invitation: Essence of Chocolate Squares (page 282) are an offering of chocolate heaven.

ABOVE *A jar of sugar graced with vanilla beans, Vanilla-Scented Granulated Sugar (page 53).*

TOP LEFT *Pecan-entangled Cinnamon Sticky Buns (page 296) are grand and oh-so-sticky.*

MIDDLE LEFT *Yum! Yum! Reach into the big jar of Mocha Truffle Cookies (page 362).*

BOTTOM LEFT *Almond Rusks (page 109) are sweet pick-up-sticks.*

SUGAR

⁜ *Granulated sugar*, a classic, and critical, baking ingredient available in 5- and 10-pound bags, not only supplies the sweetness quotient to what you bake but also acts as a tenderizer to a dough or batter. Granulated sugar, and sugar in general, also helps to keep the batter or dough moist, and thus contributes to its keeping qualitites.

⁜ *Superfine sugar* (also known as "bar" sugar), available in 1-pound boxes, is finer and is used in a creamed-butter cake, muffin, or cookie batter when a delicate crumb and tender texture is desired. The fine crumb produced when superfine sugar is used is exemplary. In my experience, spinning regular granulated sugar in a food processor ineffectively approximates the texture of commercially produced superfine sugar.

⁜ *Light* and *dark brown sugar*, available in 1-pound boxes, contains cane caramel color and is soft enough to pack into measuring spoons and dry measuring cups. If there are any small, hard clumps, the sugar should be strained through a medium-mesh sieve. The hardened sugar pellets won't dissolve in a batter or dough as you are mixing it, and they won't disintegrate as the batter or dough bakes in the oven.

⁜ *Confectioners' sugar*, also known as powdered sugar, is very finely processed sugar combined with a bit of cornstarch (3 percent) to inhibit clumping. Although confectioners' sugar is not characterized as a "free-flowing" sugar (like the granulated or superfine variety), cornstarch does keep the sugar reasonably free of bulky lumps.

In hot and balmy weather, sprinklings of confectioners' sugar can quickly disappear on the top of cakes and crumb buns, but using a nonmelting sugar can save the topping from dissolving. Snow White Non-Melting Sugar (available from The Baker's Catalogue; see "Selected Sources for Equipment and Supplies") solves the melting problem and disappearing act. You can sieve or strain nonmelting sugar over the top of a warm pound cake, gooey brownies, or moist buttery streusel topping, without any worry of it decomposing.

THE CHART

Staple baking ingredients incorporated into a dough or batter have, during the baking process, their defining moments. Specific ingredients are responsible for different effects to the character (taste and appearance) of a batter or dough, making it soft, moist, dense, or airy; adding volume or structure; establishing tenderness, and such. The information in the following chart is based solely on conclusions drawn from results generated in the various components and composition of the recipes that make up this book. The chart explains the function of each basic ingredient used in a recipe.

INGREDIENTS AND THEIR CONTRIBUTING CHARACTERISTICS

by ingredient

INGREDIENT	CONTRIBUTING CHARACTERISTICS TO A BATTER OR DOUGH
BUTTER	Enriches and tenderizes the baked crumb; adds to the overall moistness quotient; adds flavor, depth, and rich complexity
SHORTENING	Softens, tenderizes, relaxes the batter or dough; adds volume to the crumb
EGGS	Add liquid richness and moistness; contribute volume (especially in a creamed batter); define and establish the crumb
SUGAR *(free-flowing superfine or granulated)*	Establishes the level of sweetness; adds to the moistness factor; refines and establishes the crumb
SUGAR *(packed light brown or dark brown)*	Establishes the level of sweetness; adds to the moistness factor; creates density in the crumb
HONEY AND MOLASSES	Establishes the level of sweetness; adds significant moisture; colors batter or dough; adds definable flavor (molasses); contributes to keeping quality

(continued)

INGREDIENTS AND THEIR CONTRIBUTING CHARACTERISTICS

by ingredient

INGREDIENT	CONTRIBUTING CHARACTERISTICS TO A BATTER OR DOUGH
FLOUR	Establishes and builds texture and form or structure of the crumb
LIQUID AND SOFT DAIRY PRODUCTS *(whole milk, buttermilk, light [table] cream, heavy cream, half-and-half, thick, cultured sour cream)*	Builds the crumb; establishes density or lightness; adds richness; helps to establish the overall structure
LEAVENING AGENTS *(baking powder and baking soda)*	Develops the overall structure (volume) and crumb, and defines the finished, baked texture and height
FLAVORING EXTRACTS *(liquid, bottled extracts)*	Intensifies and builds flavor; used in small quantities to maintain the balance of liquid to dry ingredients
SPICES *(ground and freshly grated)*	Adds and builds flavor in a batter or dough; depending upon the quantity used, colors a batter, dough, filling, frosting, sauce, or icing
SALT	Seasons a batter or dough, and builds its flavor (especially chocolate-flavored baked goods); in sweet yeast doughs, helps to prevent overfermentation and reinforces the leavened network of dough

*t*he success of a baking recipe depends on two key factors: the balance and interplay of ingredients and the method by which the ingredients are put together. These two components unfold, if not actually converge, in the defining moment when you cut into a divinely tender layer cake, break a buttery scone in half, or bite into a chewy cookie or fudgy brownie.

Creating baked goods that are velvety, moist, creamy, dense, chewy, crunchy, feathery, light, or any combination of these qualities is easy to do if you discover the special characteristics of each dough or batter, and specific ways for assembling them. In this section, I make recommendations about organizing the ingredients before you bake and preparing the bakeware, outline familiar baking terms, and review the kinds of doughs and batters and techniques for making them that you'll come upon frequently in the recipes that appear in *Baking by Flavor*. All of this is followed by a chart that summarizes the qualities of each important dough or batter, called the "Distinguishing Characteristics of Doughs and Batters" chart. Other aspects of baking, such as understanding texture and notes on baking in a summer or winter kitchen, round out this chapter.

4

CRAFT AND TECHNIQUE

BEFORE YOU BAKE

Setting out the ingredients, accurately measured, before you bake is a sensible step toward organizing—and simplifying—the baking process.

In baking, every ingredient is important and must be accounted for in the procedure, from that pinch of salt to the butter, eggs, sugar, spices, leavenings, flavoring extracts, flour, nuts, fruit, and chocolate. Inadvertently omitting one element will upset the recipe. Professional bakers always measure out ingredients before they're combined, and usually line them up on a sheet pan or tray. This concept is called *mise en place* (translated as "put in place"). Using this technique guarantees that items such as softened butter, a sifted flour mixture, chopped chocolate, toasted nuts, and the like are not forgotten or omitted: All of the ingredients are recipe-ready. Even the baking pan is pulled and prepared.

In essence, assembling ingredients and equipment as the oven preheats makes good sense because it streamlines the baking procedure by allowing you to concentrate on the technique of preparing the batter or dough.

MEASURING INGREDIENTS AND PREPARING THE BAKEWARE

All dry ingredients (such as all-purpose or cake flour, nut flour or ground nuts, sugar, spices, cornstarch, leavenings, and cocoa), which are powdery-textured, compact, or free-flowing, are measured in dry measuring cups or in measuring spoons and *leveled off at the surface with the straight edge of a palette knife* or the even, extended *blade of a spatula*. Using rounded measurements will skew a recipe. Liquid and/or other fluid or viscous ingredients (such as milk, cream, water, molasses, honey, and mashed bananas) and flavoring chips or nuts (whole, chopped, or slivered) are measured in clear ovenproof glass measuring cups with quantity lines clearly marked.

Preparing baking pans properly is just as important as measuring ingredients precisely. If your cake has ever fused mercilessly to the pan or a batch of cookies crumbled as you're prodding them from the baking sheet, you already know the importance of preparing bakeware. All of the recipes in *Baking by Flavor* will instruct you how to handle specific bakeware appropriately, *before* the batter or dough is mixed or placed in the pan.

❋ *Cake* or *torte batters* are poured or spooned into pans that are treated in one of the following ways—by filming with nonstick cooking spray, by lightly coating with softened butter and flour, by coating with shortening and flour, by coating with softened butter and cocoa powder, or by coating with softened butter alone; as an extra precaution, the bottom of some layer cake and tube pans are lined with circles of waxed paper.

* *Sweet yeast rolls* are set into baking pans that have been filmed with nonstick cooking spray alone or with cooking spray and softened butter, or just smeared with softened butter.

* A *madeleine batter* is spooned into a set of shell-shaped forms that have been lightly coated with melted, clarified butter and flour.

* *Drop* or *hand-molded cookies* are baked on parchment paper-lined cookie sheets.

* *Bar cookie batters* are baked in pans either coated with cooking spray or lightly buttered and floured.

* Rich, press-in-the-pan *shortbread-style doughs* are patted into unbuttered fluted, false-bottomed tart pans.

* *Muffin batters* are baked in individual cups that have been coated with nonstick cooking spray or softened, unsalted butter and flour.

* *Scones and sweet tea biscuits* are baked on cookie sheets or rimmed baking pans lined with cooking parchment paper; some plain biscuits are baked right on the exposed (untreated) surface of a cookie sheet or baking pan.

* *Tea cakes* are spooned into loaf pans which are coated with shortening and flour, or with nonstick cooking spray.

* A *jellyroll* pan, specifically used for baking a sheet of light, rollable butter cake, is prepared by dabbing shortening in spots on the bottom of the pan, lining the pan with waxed paper, then coating the inside of the paper with softened butter and flour. The shortening keeps the waxed paper intact as the pan is filled with batter and steadies the shape of the sheet of cake as it bakes.

In my kitchen, even release-surface bakeware (such as a Bundt or loaf pan) is lightly covered with nonstick cooking spray or buttered and floured. When butter is used as part of the preparation, make sure to use the unsalted variety, for a veneer of salted butter causes whatever you're baking to bond to the inner surfaces of the pan, especially the bottom and central tube, if there is one.

In addition to preventing whatever sweet you're baking from sticking, preparing the bakeware correctly also preserves the shape and, ultimately, the height and composition of the baked sweet.

THE LANGUAGE OF BAKING

There are a handful of important terms that pertain to and identify a baking process, act, or maneuver within the method of a recipe. Think of them as key phrases that differentiate each technique and phase in the procedure. The following terms appear frequently in the recipes that make up this volume, and here's how I define each when working within the procedure of my recipes:

❋ BEAT: To beat is defined as to work an ingredient actively in a bowl, such as to beat egg whites until firm, puffy peaks are formed or beating sugar into creamy, softened butter until lightened in texture. In general, beat is the act of smoothing or mixing one or more ingredients to combine them thoroughly. You can beat ingredients on a variety of speeds (slow, moderate, moderately high, or high), depending upon the ultimate texture of the batter or dough you want to achieve.

❋ COMPOSE: To compose is to assemble a cake batter and filling, such as when you layer (or intersperse) a pound cake batter with a flavor ribbon of ground nuts and a sugar-and-spice mixture, or a sugar-and-spice mixture alone.

❋ COMPRESS: A technique used in the procedure for making rich yeast dough, to compress is to very lightly deflate the dough after it has risen in volume. Pressing down on the dough softly with either your fingertips or the palms of your hands gets it ready for refrigerator storage or for rolling into a large sheet. It is a gentle motion. Actively punching down the dough with your fist ruins the network of a tender yeast dough, which is rich in sugar, eggs (or egg yolks), sour cream, and butter.

❋ DUST: To dust is to put a fine, glimmery haze on a sweet (such as dusting the top of a baked cake with confectioners' sugar), or a very light coating on a work surface (such as sprinkling a wooden board or marble pastry slab with all-purpose flour), or on a sheet of rolled-out yeast dough (such as topping a buttered sheet of dough with a veneer of ground spice or a spiced sugar). The most effective way to produce a dusting is to place a few spoonfuls of the ingredient to be used for dusting into a small fine-meshed sieve (or small strainer) and to tap it lightly over whatever needs to be coated, moving the sieve around as you go. Just spooning the ingredient over the surface of a baked cake or rolled-out block of dough would result in an unevenly coated surface. For the best effect, hold the sieve about 3 inches above whatever you're dusting.

❋ FILM: To film is to coat with a thin, slick overlay, and is usually referred to when showering nonstick cookware spray on the inside of a baking pan before a batter is spooned in. When filming the inside of a baking pan with the spray, take special care to coat all corners or flutes, sides, and the central tube (especially at the base, where cakes tend to stick), if you're using a tube pan.

✳ FOLD: To fold is to lightly but thoroughly combine two different sets of ingredients and blend them together in the most gentle way possible. Incorporating beaten whites into a butter cake batter to lighten it is a typical folding process. Some bakers use a large, flexible rubber spatula for folding, and others use a large stainless steel spoon; I use a rubber spatula.

The technique I like best for folding two different mixtures together (like a creamed-butter cake batter and egg whites beaten separately until softly firm) is to actually stir a little—about one-quarter—of the lighter mixture (the beaten whites) into the heavier mixture (the cake batter) to loosen it up, then scrape the remaining lighter mixture on top and combine the two.

To unify the ingredients (the whites and lightened batter) into a batter without relinquishing volume, dip the spatula or spoon straight down into the mixture and bring it up and over it. Turn the bowl about 2 inches clockwise, and dip the spatula down and up. Repeat this movement until you've encircled the entire contents of the bowl. Give the mixture a few more up and over turns to create a smooth but buoyant batter, scraping down the sides as you do so. Fold the two mixtures together until just combined and large patches of the lighter mixture disappear; be careful about overmixing, or else you'll deflate the batter.

✳ MELT: To melt is to apply heat to an ingredient so that it becomes fluid. In baking, butter and chocolate are occasionally used in the melted state, especially if you're making brownies or other kinds of bar cookies. I melt butter or chocolate in a heavy saucepan (made of enameled cast iron) over very low heat. To facilitate the melting process, I always cut the butter into rough chunks and coarsely chop the chocolate. If the butter and chocolate are used together in the melted state, both can be heated together in the same saucepan.

✳ MIX: In a procedure, to mix is to combine two or more ingredients by hand or on the lowest speed of an electric mixer. The idea is to blend the ingredients without overworking the batter or dough.

At other times, when the word *mix* appears in the caption within the procedure of a recipe, such as "Mix the chocolate chip butter cake batter," it describes the act of putting together the batter.

✳ PAT: To pat is to level out a baking powder- or baking soda-leavened biscuit or scone dough with your fingertips, or to push a shortbread dough into a baking pan. Do this lightly, with a soft, patting motion.

❋ PRESS: To press (or "pat") is the act of patting a dough into a baking pan. In this baking cookbook, shortbread dough is pressed or patted into the pan. When pressing the dough, use your fingertips and light, even taps.

❋ ROLL: To roll is to both extend the overall size and narrow the thickness of a pie or tart dough, or a mass of sweet, yeast-raised dough.

When rolling a pie or tart dough, use a straight French rolling pin (see Chapter 4, "An Inventory of Baking Equipment"), a light hand, and quick, abbreviated strokes. Begin rolling at the center of the dough and continue to roll outward toward the edge, but avoid rolling over the edge. Roll lightly and gingerly, without bearing down on the dough. Yeast doughs can be handled less cautiously than a sweet shortcrust dough. Use a heavy, ball-bearing rolling pin (see Chapter 4, "An Inventory of Baking Equipment") and roll with even pressure on the dough, beginning at the center and rolling toward the ends. A heavy rolling pin will do most of the work for you, but does require your guiding hands.

Whether you're rolling pie or pastry dough, or a yeast-raised dough, apply steady pressure so that the dough is enlarged in an even layer. A uniform layer of dough will bake (and rise) evenly. A layer of dough that is thick in some places and thin in others will bake unevenly, leaving you with gummy underbaked and dry overbaked spots.

❋ SIEVE: To sieve is to press-and-strain a mixture through a meshed implement. A sieve or strainer with a moderately deep bowl and long handle is easiest to use. I use fine or moderately fine stainless steel sieves in a range of sizes. The most effective way to push through the mixture, whether it's a custard sauce, fruit curd filling, or pastry cream, is to use a flexible rubber spatula to smooth it against the bottom and sides, thus forcing it into a bowl positioned beneath the sieve. The finer the sieve, the slower the process of getting the mixture through, but the results will be so silky and gossamer that your time will be well spent.

❋ SIFT: To sift is to aerate one or a combination of dry ingredients (such as flour, leavening, spices, or cocoa). The sifting process lightens and aerates, rather than actually mixes, the ingredients. (To mix dry ingredients, use a whisk to blend them together in a bowl.)

❋ SPOON: The term to spoon is frequently used to define the act of filling a baking pan. Spooning a batter into a baking pan should not be a careless gesture, but a careful act of filling the pan gently with large spoonfuls of the batter. For this purpose, I normally use a large stainless steel cooking spoon. When filling a cake pan, lightly layer in the batter in even amounts.

❋ SPRINKLE: To sprinkle is to distribute or scatter a mixture over the top of a batter, dough, or frosting. That mixture could be a streusel or sugar-and-spice blend, or simply confectioners' sugar. Sprinkle the mixture evenly over the surface.

❋ STIR: To stir is to mix two or more ingredients, usually with a wooden spoon, spatula, or flat paddle. Stirring is a careful, deliberate process used when you need to be mindful of overbeating or overmixing a batter or soft dough.

❋ SWIRL (OR RIPPLE): To swirl is to combine two mixtures, usually a filling or topping and a cake (or torte) batter, in order to create a ripple-like pattern of curves and spirals within the batter. A round-edged flexible palette knife is by far the best tool for swirling a batter. When swirling two mixtures, take care to avoid scraping the bottom and sides of the baking pan so that you keep the filling within the confines of the batter. If too much of the filling, which is usually sugar-based, is pushed out toward the sides of the baking pan, it could cause the cake to bond to the sides of the pan and make unmolding it difficult.

❋ TOSS: To toss is to mix ingredients in a bowl. Usually, flavored chips (such as chocolate chips), chopped nuts, or fruit (such as chopped dried apricots or blueberries) are tossed with a little of the sifted or whisked dry ingredients to coat them. Coating small ingredients prevents them from sinking to the bottom of the batter during baking. Tossing the ingredients with a few teaspoons of the flour mixture is an extra step, but it does preserve the overall texture of the batter as it bakes. And if fresh berries are added to a cake or muffin batter without being coated first, they'll usually sink to the bottom and create a wet, gummy bottom layer.

❋ WHISK: To whisk is to agitate (using various speeds—slowly but thoroughly to fast-paced) one or more ingredients to mix them completely. Whisking is commonly identified as a lively mixing procedure, frequently with a view toward adding volume or lightness to the mixture, in comparison to stirring, which is a calmer, more methodical process that generally involves using a spoon or flat paddle. Sometimes, however, I use a whisk for combining ingredients such as eggs and sugar (when making brownies, for example) because it's the most efficient mixing tool; when using a whisk for simply blending ingredients (and creating volume is not a consideration), use a lighter hand and a quieter, less vigorous (and more genteel) mixing motion.

❋ WHIP (OR BEAT) EGG WHITES: To whip egg whites is to beat them until they form soft, pillowy mounds or firm, satiny peaks. Begin by beating the whites at a moderately quick speed until frothy, then add the amount of cream of tartar called for in the recipe (cream of tartar is frequently present in a cake or quick bread batter containing two or more whites). The addition of the cream of tartar supports and strengthens the mass of whites during the beating process. *Do not add cream of tartar, however, when beating egg whites in a copper bowl.* Continue to beat the whites according to the degree of firmness that the recipe specifies—soft, moderately soft, or firm (but not stiff) peaks. Sometimes, a portion of sugar (granulated or superfine, but not the light or dark brown variety) is added to the egg whites as they are beaten, before they're incorporated into a batter. The addition of sugar creates firm, shiny, and somewhat glossy-looking peaks.

✳ WORK IN: To work in is to integrate ingredients such as chopped nuts, flavored chips, chopped bar chocolate, flaked coconut, or dried fruit into a particularly dense dough or batter. Sprinkle or scatter the specific ingredient over the dough, then use a wooden spoon or flat wooden paddle to incorporate it.

When working one or more flavoring ingredients into a sweet yeast dough, pat out the dough into a rough rectangle, scatter over the addition(s), roll up the dough into a loose jellyroll, fold in half, and knead the dough until incorporated. At first it will seem that the dough is repelling the addition, but the ingredients will be incorporated after a few minutes more of kneading.

ABOUT TEXTURE: DEFINING "CRUMB" IN BAKED GOODS

The word *crumb* appears in many of the descriptions of the sweets in *Baking by Flavor*. The crumb is the internal grain, or nap, of the baked dough or batter. The variety and style of the ingredients used and way in which they are handled largely determine the texture of the baked sweet.

The crumb can be fine-grained, feathery, moist, dense, velvety, downy, soft, creamy, crumbly, airy, or light, or a combination of these qualities. The texture of a batter or dough, when baked, is established mostly by the type and amount of fat, liquid and soft dairy products, flour, sugar, sweeteners other than sugar, eggs, and leavening used. Other controlling factors include the type and size of the baking pan, oven temperature, and the way that the batter or dough is put together and whether it is treated to a preliminary chilling (pastry doughs, some cookie and scone doughs, and rich yeast doughs are frequently given a cold rest in the refrigerator to establish their texture and facilitate handling).

TECHNIQUES FOR MIXING BATTERS AND DOUGHS

HOW TO MAKE A CREAMED-BUTTER CAKE BATTER

Bundt-style cakes, coffee cakes, pound cakes, keeping cakes, and layer cakes are made from a creamed-butter cake batter. Some drop cookie doughs are also made by the creamed method. Butter cakes are distinguished by their fine, melt-in-your-mouth texture. Butter cakes are mostly light, rather than dense or compact, and delicately downy-textured. Some butter cakes are quite springy, or as I like to call them, pillowy.

A creamed-butter cake batter is supplied structure with flour and eggs; enrichment with butter and eggs; and moistness with eggs, butter, and liquid or soft dairy products. There are five important steps in butter-cake making, and each of these stages has an important technique attached to it:

❋ Creaming the fat

❋ Adding and beating the sugar

❋ Blending in the eggs and flavoring extract

❋ Adding the liquid and dry ingredients

❋ Mixing in any flavoring additions

❋ CREAMING THE FAT: Fat acts as a tenderizing and enriching agent. Butter is usually the primary fat, but sometimes butter and a small amount of shortening are used to add both flavor and volume to a cake batter. In order for the butter to build—and eventually flavor—a cake batter, it must be creamed until soft and smooth. Butter should be creamed in the bowl of a freestanding electric mixer for several minutes.

❋ ADDING AND BEATING IN THE SUGAR: Sugar, in addition to creating the degree of sweetness necessary in a recipe, helps to build the texture or grain of the cake. Add the sugar in small amounts and beat well until incorporated. Creaming the butter with the sugar creates a moist and even, lightened crumb. Underbeating the sugar can create a heavy-textured cake.

❊ BLENDING IN THE EGGS AND FLAVORING EXTRACT: Eggs establish the texture and volume of the batter, form its structure, and impart moisture. Eggs should be added to the creamed butter-sugar mixture *one at a time*, and mixed until just blended; overbeating the batter after each egg is added can, occasionally, produce a tough, rubbery cake. Add the flavoring extract and mix briefly until it blends into the batter.

❊ ADDING THE LIQUID AND DRY INGREDIENTS: The classic, time-honored method of beginning and ending with the dry ingredients creates a downy, even-grained cake. Alternating the sifted mixture with the liquid or soft dairy product (such as sour cream) allows the egg-enriched creamed-butter and sugar mixture to be distributed evenly throughout the batter. Scrape down the sides of the mixing bowl frequently to develop a smooth-textured batter.

❊ MIXING IN ANY FLAVORING ADDITIONS: A completed creamed-butter cake batter is polished and silky-textured, and never grainy-looking. Any addition, such as chopped nuts, flavored chips, flaked coconut, and chopped candy, is stirred into the batter at this point: Blend, do not beat, it into the batter with a rubber spatula, wooden spoon, or flat wooden paddle until just combined.

HOW TO MAKE A QUICK BREAD DOUGH OR BATTER

Quick breads, which range from biscuits and scones to muffins, loaf breads, and coffee cakes, are easy to bake and wonderful to have on hand. An ideal partner to coffee, a scone, muffin, or slice of coffee cake is that perfect buttery, crumbly, and lightly sweetened something that resonates flavor and takes to all kinds of variations.

Although these sweets are quick (that is, leavened with baking powder, baking soda, or a combination of both, rather than yeast), making them still involves thoughtful attention to a procedure that highlights taste, texture, and appearance.

In cataloging quick breads, three specific classifications emerge based on both the finished product and the way the dough or batter is put together:

❊ Combining fat and flour by the cutting-in method, used for biscuits and scones

❊ Combining a whisked liquid mixture and sifted dry ingredients, used for muffins, pancakes, waffles, and some loaf breads/cakes

❊ Creaming fat and sugar, adding eggs, alternating dry and liquid ingredients, used for loaf cakes, coffee cakes, and some muffin batters

Biscuit and scone doughs are moist, but workable; are sturdy enough to cut into decorative shapes; and bake with a dense or feathery crumb, depending upon the recipe. Muffin batters are thick enough to be spooned and mounded into cups, and emerge from the oven with a rugged crumb and beautifully domed cap. Creamed batters are silky-smooth, and generally produce reasonably fine-grained, even-textured baked goods.

Making the dough for *biscuits and scones* requires both a deft hand and a watchful eye during the mixing process. The procedure for the dough begins with whisking or sifting together the essential dry ingredients (flour, salt, spices, and leavenings); sugar is either included in the initial mixing or added after the fat is incorporated into the mixture. Fat is added to the dry ingredients in chunks and reduced, by using either a pastry blender or two round-edged table knives. Sometimes the fat is further reduced to smaller fragments with your fingertips. The size of the fat (in very small flakes, small pea-size bits, larger flakes, or little nuggets) is one of the determining factors of the overall flakiness. At this point, the sugar can be stirred in, if it has not been added to the flour mixture initially. Liquid ingredients (eggs, milk, cream, and flavoring extracts) are whisked together and added, all at once, to the fat-enriched flour. A dough, formed by combining liquid and dry ingredients, should be flexible and tractable, not too sticky or too dry. The dough is finished with a light, short knead in the mixing bowl or on your work surface. Kneading the dough briefly improves the texture of the baked biscuits or scones.

The weather (especially the humidity present in the air) and absorption quality of the flour can affect the amount of flour needed to make the dough reasonably firm, but still moist. If the biscuit or scone dough seems too wet, you can safely add between 1 and 3 tablespoons of additional flour (1 to 2 tablespoons in a recipe that uses 2 cups of flour; 2 to 3 tablespoons for a recipe that uses 3 to 4 cups of flour).

For impressive biscuits and scones, keep these details in mind:

❋ Reduce the butter and/or shortening to pieces about the size of pearls, dried navy or lima beans, or flakes that look like uncooked rolled oats, depending upon what each recipe requires.

❋ Knead the dough for 10 seconds in the bowl, then remove to a work surface, pat into a rough cake, and fold over, repeating this action several times. This builds bulk and causes the dough to rise impressively in the hot oven.

❋ Add shreds or small chunks of fruit, chocolate shards and pieces, coarsely chopped nuts, and such to the dough concurrently with the whisked liquid mixture to avoid overworking the dough.

❋ Cut biscuits and scones with a sharp knife or decorative cutter cleanly and evenly, without twisting or angling the cutting device. To use a floured cutter, rub/smear a tiny scrap of the dough over the cutting surface, then dip in flour.

❋ For crusty-sided biscuits and scones, roll the dough slightly thicker than usual, cut, and arrange 3 inches apart on parchment paper-lined sheet pans. For soft-sided scones, pat dough into 7- to 8-inch round cakes directly on lined sheet pans; cut and disconnect the scones slightly, leaving a space of about ½ inch between each. With this technique, the scones will merge as they bake and the edges will be soft, rather than crusty.

❋ Lightly glaze the tops (only) of the cut biscuits or scones with melted butter (clarified butter is best for flavor and color, if you have it on hand), heavy cream, or a wash of cream, egg, and a dash of flavoring extract, such as vanilla or almond. The glaze is optional, and unnecessary when a topping is added.

The batter for *pancakes, waffles, and some types of muffins* is produced by mixing wet ingredients—the melted fat, liquid (milk or buttermilk), a flavoring extract, and eggs—and sifted or whisked dry ingredients—flour, sugar, spices, and leavening(s)—until combined. (Other muffin batters are made by the creamed method, and these muffins have a finer texture.) Typically, this kind of batter ranges from thick to moderately thick in density, and can support flavored chips, chopped nuts, or shredded fruit. The additions to the batter define the taste and look of the batch of muffins, pancakes, or waffles.

Muffins emerge from the baking pan plump, full, and tender, pancakes from the griddle light and fluffy, and waffles from the iron tender and moist when these points have been observed:

❋ Combine the dry ingredients by whisking or by sifting (to aerate). A thorough mixing dispels the leavening agent evenly and allows the muffins to rise in a balanced way.

❋ Whisk the liquid ingredients well so that the eggs are well blended and thoroughly combined.

❋ To avoid overmixing the batter, add any extras (chopped fruit, nuts, flavored chips) to the batter simultaneously with the whisked liquid mixture.

❋ Use a flat wooden paddle or sturdy rubber spatula to combine liquid and dry ingredients, making sure to reach into the curved bottom edge of the mixing bowl where pockets of the flour mixture can remain. Mix the batter just until the particles of flour are absorbed. Ignore the lumps; they will dissipate during baking.

❋ For muffins, spoon the batter into prepared cups, mounding it lightly toward the center to produce muffins with a curvaceous, rounded cap.

✳ For pancakes, place mounded, even-sized dollops of batter on a hot preheated griddle; the batter will settle down as the pancakes cook.

Some *coffee cakes* are made using the creamed cake batter technique. (See "How to Make a Creamed-Butter Cake Batter" on page 85.) Coffee cakes, served at breakfast, brunch, and throughout the afternoon, are tender-textured, moist, and fragrant with spices. Many are filled or covered with fresh or dried fruit. An unbaked coffee cake batter is an ideal base for sprinkling with a nut-and-spice mixture or buttery crumble.

To make moist, full-flavored coffee cakes, keep this advice in mind:

✳ Bake a coffee cake batter in the pan size recommended in the recipe. A creamed coffee cake batter, especially one filled or topped with a flavor/seasoning mixture, needs enough room to rise.

✳ Spoon half of the batter into the baking pan and sprinkle a flavor band on top. The flavor band can be a spiced sugar mixture (with or without finely chopped nuts), a coconut and nut mixture, a sweetened cocoa mixture, or a toss of chopped dried fruit and nuts. Spoon the remaining batter on top and swirl the layers together. If you are using a sugar-based filling, make a wide channel in the middle of the batter with a small spatula and spoon the mixture into it; the groove contains the filling better than a flat surface would.

✳ Cultured sour cream and buttermilk create coffee cakes with a soft, moist crumb and superb keeping qualities.

HOW TO MAKE COOKIE DOUGHS

Drop cookie dough

Most *drop cookies* are made from a creamed dough, which is similar to a creamed-butter cake batter. A drop cookie dough is somewhat silky and much more dense (in the absence of a significant amount of liquid, there's less volume) than a creamed cake batter. Some cookie doughs are both creamy/velvety-textured and stiff. Using the recipe for the Butterscotch Oatmeal Cookies (page 244) as a guide, here's how a typical cookie dough is assembled:

✳ The dry ingredients (flour, leavenings, and spices) are sifted or whisked together to aerate or mix them.

* The butter is creamed until smooth on low speed for 4 minutes; the sugar is added to the creamed butter and two are mixed for several minutes. Beating the sugar for a total mixing time of about 3 minutes helps to create a tender-textured cookie.

* Eggs are incorporated into the butter-sugar mixture next, followed by a flavoring extract. Minimal liquid is used in drop cookie doughs, but a liquid sweetener (such as honey or molasses) is occasionally used.

* The dry ingredients are added to the butter-sugar-egg-flavoring mixture in two additions, and mixed on low speed only until absorbed into the creamed mixture. The particles of flour should permeate the creamed mixture, creating a soft, medium-firm, or firm dough.

* Additions to the dough, such as the rolled oats, butterscotch-flavored chips, and walnuts, are stirred into the dough.

* Chunks of dough are formed into even-sized mounds, placed on the prepared cookie sheets, and baked.

Drop cookies should lift off from the cookie sheet evenly baked and handsome. Note these hints:

* For even heat distribution, cookie sheets should be moderately heavy; double-pan (stack one sheet directly on top of the other) sheets if they are very light.

* To give chunky drop cookies (made from a dough with lots of chips, nuts, oatmeal, or fruit) that textural, earthy, bakery-style look, keep the edges of the dough mounds slightly rough and jagged, rather than smooth.

* Evenly space the mounds of dough on the cookie sheet, leaving 2 to 2½ inches between each cookie, or as specified in each recipe.

* Cool the cookies on the sheets, as directed in each recipe, to stabilize them.

Rolled cookie dough

A *rolled cookie dough* usually begins as a creamed dough, like a drop cookie dough, but contains more flour and a smaller amount of liquid to bind ingredients in order to make a dough that rolls out smoothly, with minimal stickiness. A very moist rolled cookie dough is rolled between sheets of waxed paper and refrigerated (or frozen) until firm enough to cut. The chilling (or freezing) process sets the dough without using additional flour, which would, inevitably, toughen the baked cookies and ruin their texture.

For the prettiest cut-out cookies made from rolled cookie dough, follow these tips:

* Make sure that the rolled-out dough is thoroughly chilled (or frozen) before cutting.

* Lightly coat the cutting edges of the cookie cutter with nonstick cookware spray to guard against the dough sticking to the cutter; this is more efficient than flouring the cutter. Spraying the cutter is an extra step.

* Begin stamping out cookies from the outer edge of the sheet of dough. Slip an offset spatula underneath each cookie in order to neatly transfer it to the baking sheet.

* Let the baked cookies stand on the baking sheet for at least 1 minute (to firm up) before removing them to cooling racks with a wide offset spatula.

* Use sturdy, balanced cooling racks so that the cookies set without bending or sagging.

Bar cookie dough

A typical *bar cookie dough* is made from either a creamed batter, a combined whisked-and-sifted mixture, or a cookie dough base covered with a layer of batter. Most bar cookie batters are somewhat dense, moderately heavy, and thick. Brownies are a good example of a typical bar cookie, which can be tricky to make properly.

For brownie-style bar cookies, melt the chocolate and butter and mix thoroughly until very smooth. The chocolate-butter mixture should be lustrous. Whisk the eggs until just combined and blended together, add the sugar, and continue whisking until it is just incorporated. *Note:* In a butter- and chocolate-rich brownie batter, it's unnecessary to whisk until the sugar loses its grainy quality and the mixture turns into a voluminous, ribbony mass, as if you're making a sponge cake. If the eggs and sugar are whisked enthusiastically, you'll endow the batter with too much air and cause the top layer of the brownies to rise and separate from the fudgy bottom layer. Blend in the melted chocolate-butter mixture and flavoring extract. At this point, the batter should be chocolate-colored through and through. Stir or whisk in the dry ingredients (frequently the flour mixture is sifted once again over the chocolate-butter-sugar-egg base), mixing until a batter is formed. Overmixing this kind of batter or beating it rapidly at this stage sometimes produces rubbery, slightly gummy bar cookies. Bake the brownies (and all bar cookies) until just set. The meaning of "just set" is different depending on the type of batter you're baking: the brownies will begin to retract around the edges of the baking pan, the top may have a faint puff to it; small, hairline cracks may form here and there. The entire cake will be soft but not liquidy; the chocolate-based batter will settle and firm up on cooling.

For blondie-style bar cookies, dense batters are built around butter, sugar (oftentimes light or dark brown sugar, or a mixture of granulated sugar and brown sugar), eggs, a lightly leavened flour mixture, a liquid flavoring extract, occasionally peanut butter, and additions such as flavoring chips, sweetened flaked coconut, and/or nuts. A melted butter-sugar mixture or creamed butter-sugar mixture forms the base for the addition of one or more eggs, a flavoring extract, and the flour mixture. Additions to the batter, such as nuts or chopped candy, are worked in at the end.

When working with batters for brownies, blondies, and other moist bar cookies, consider these techniques:

❋ Cut or chop sticky or gooey additions (such as candy or glazed fruit) no larger than ½ inch wide, so that the finished sweet can be cut into sleek squares or bars. Nuts can be used finely or coarsely chopped, or in halves and pieces.

❋ Scrape the dense batter into the prepared baking pan, then smooth it evenly into the corners, using a narrow, flexible palette knife or spatula. Level the top.

❋ Let the brownies or other bar cookies cool in the pan on a rack for several hours, making sure that air can freely circulate underneath the pan. With the enriching percentage of melted chocolate and butter in the batter, brownies need to cool completely in order to be cut neatly. In very hot or humid weather, refrigerate the entire cake of baked brownies for 1 to 2 hours so that it cuts into neat squares or bars. This technique also applies to any other kind of moist and tender bar cookie.

HOW TO MAKE A BUTTERY, MOLDABLE COOKIE DOUGH (TO MAKE INDIVIDUAL, HAND-FORMED COOKIES)

A tender, all-butter cookie dough can be formed by hand into all kinds of shapes—crescents, logs, pillows, or buttons. The butter dough used in the Buttercrunch Melt-a-Ways (see page 206) is a good example of this type of moldable dough. This type of dough should be moist but not sticky, and firm but not excessively stiff. It should be a pleasure to handle. Any addition to the dough, such as candy or nuts, needs to be coarsely ground or very finely chopped, so that the cookies can be shaped easily; otherwise, bits of the enriching ingredient would protrude from the edges of the formed cookies.

Typically, this kind of butter-based dough is made by combining a liquid (melted butter) and dry (lightly leavened flour) mixture. For example, in the Buttercrunch Melt-a-Ways, flour, baking powder, and salt are sifted together, and melted butter is blended with confectioners' sugar, vanilla extract, and almond extract. The sifted ingredients are stirred into the butter-sugar-flavoring mixture along with finely chopped toffee to form a dough. The hand-rolled balls of dough are covered in chopped almonds and baked.

Cookies made from this type of dough are rich and exceptionally tender. The lightly sweetened dough can be flavored in any number of ways: with chopped, crystallized ginger; ground nuts (walnuts, almonds, pecans, macadamia nuts); unsweetened alkalized cocoa and miniature semisweet chocolate chips; or finely grated citrus rind.

This kind of lush butter cookie dough should be handled in this way:

* Mix the two basic components (melted butter/dry ingredients) until a manageable dough is formed, but avoid overworking the dough to prevent it from becoming oily.

* Shape cookies out of even-sized chunks of dough so that batches of them bake evenly.

* Form crescent-shaped cookies directly on the baking sheet; form each piece of cookie dough into a log, place on the sheet, bend to create a crescent, and taper the edges.

* Bake the cookies until just set; cookies made from blond-colored dough will be light golden on the bottom, and there may be a few very thin cracks here and there on the tops of the cookies.

* Double-coat the cookies in confectioners' sugar, once while warm and a second time when cool.

HOW TO MAKE A BUTTERY SHORTBREAD DOUGH (TO MAKE ONE WHOLE COOKIE THAT'S CUT INTO PIECES AFTER BAKING)

In shortbread dough, butter is the defining element; in a plain vanilla shortbread dough, it defines the flavor, and in a shortbread dough that is dominated by ground spices and additions such as flavoring chips and/or nuts, butter is the underlying flavor. In any event, butter also establishes that creamy texture and unquestionably moist but dense crumb.

A shortbread dough can be made in two ways: by working the butter into a flour mixture as you would a pastry dough (by the cutting-in technique), or by creaming the butter, then adding the sugar and flour mixture. Of the two techniques, I prefer the creaming method because the baked shortbread made by this procedure seems more delicate and ethereal, with a meltingly tender crumb.

For a creamed shortbread dough, the primary focus is on beating the butter, then adding the rest of the ingredients until they are just absorbed. Beating the butter until very creamy and lightened, about the consistency of thick homemade mayonnaise, makes the dough especially tender. This method for making shortbread will create an exquisite dough that's firm enough to press into a baking pan, but one that creates a tender cookie. Here's how the dough is assembled:

❋ Sift the flour (all-purpose, cake, rice, or a combination of two or more flours) with the leavening and salt. If a spice is part of the recipe, it's sifted along with the dry ingredients.

❋ The butter is creamed in the bowl of a freestanding mixer on low speed for 2 to 3 minutes, to make it ultra-smooth and build its volume.

❋ A small amount of sugar (plus a flavoring extract) is blended into the creamed butter. Additions such as flavoring chips, nuts, or chopped crystallized ginger are usually added at this time, or along with the second portion of the sifted mixture so that the dough is not overworked.

❋ The sifted ingredients are mixed into the butter-sugar-flavoring mixture in two portions, and mixed slowly until assimilated and a soft dough is formed.

❋ The dough is pressed into a baking pan and lightly pricked here and there with the tines of a fork. Pat or press the dough gently and gingerly to avoid compressing it, so that the baked texture remains delicate. A compacted dough may bake into a pasty cookie. Pricking the dough helps to level out the cookie as it bakes and prevents it from buckling in odd areas. If a baked-on topping is part of the recipe, it is applied now.

❋ Once the shortbread is baked, it's cooled for about 10 minutes, unmolded, cooled for an additional 10 to 15 minutes, then cut into wedges, and cooled completely. Sometimes, right after baking, the top of plain shortbread is dusted with granulated sugar or scented granulated sugar. The sugar adds a light, crunchy finish and a bit of agreeable sweetness to the cookie.

❋ When cutting shortbread, use a long chef's knife, and make firm, clean slices, using a single downward cutting motion. Do not use a sawing motion, or the shortbread will shatter and splinter into fragments. It's a good idea to cut the shortbread while still warm, within 25 to 30 minutes after it has been removed from the oven.

All of the yeast doughs in this book—the crumb buns, sticky buns, schnecken—are enriched with varying quantities of butter and eggs. The resulting dough bakes into tender and fine-grained rolls, with a slightly dense or fluffy texture, depending on its composition. The flavor of each batch of sweet rolls is developed by adding a filling and, perhaps, a topping.

The key is to make a rich yeast dough that is smooth and elastic, somewhat glossy and silky. Combine the yeast with a small amount of sugar and warm water, and let it stand, undisturbed, until it foams and swells, 7 to 8 minutes. In the meantime, prepare the liquid ingredient (usually milk) by warming it with sugar; in some recipes, such as the Cream Cheese Schnecken on page 495, the butter is heated with the milk and sugar. Cool the liquid mixture and add the whole eggs and/or egg yolks. Combine a specific amount of flour (the recipe will give the exact amount) with the salt and spice(s). Mix the yeast mixture into the cooled liquid-sugar-egg mixture, pour over the flour, and stir to form a dough. At this point, additional flour is added, as the recipe indicates, or the dough is completed with the addition of pats of softened butter. The dough is then kneaded in the mixer or on a work surface by hand in order to cultivate—or develop—the gluten, the all-important structural network. The kneaded dough is placed in a greased bowl, covered, and set to rise. The risen dough is deflated (preferably compressed with the palms of your hands), formed into rolls, buns, coffee cakes; placed in baking pans; set to rise again; and baked. Each process is important in forming a sweet yeast dough.

* Achieve the correct volume of dough by using the proper amounts of yeast, sugar, fat, liquid, and flour.

* Knead the dough sufficiently, giving it the time each recipe suggests.

* Monitor the dough as it rises in all its stages, to avoid overrising. Overrisen dough will, on baking, taste and smell sour and musty.

* Once the yeast dough has risen, usually to doubled in bulk, it must be patted down to deflate it before rolling and shaping. "Punch down" is a phrase usually used and associated with this process, although I find it both inappropriate and undesirable. Actually punching down the dough with your fist is too aggressive an act for deflating sweet yeast doughs, for it mangles the airy, fine-grained structure of the dough achieved during the rising phase. Instead, lightly and gently pat down the dough

with your fingertips (if it's rich in butter) or with the cupped palm of your hand (if it has only a moderate amount of butter and eggs). This will keep the internal weave of the unbaked dough buoyant and lithe.

❋ Shape and "pan" the dough accurately: improperly shaped dough and/or dough that is crowded into a baking pan will bake unevenly. The dough is rolled, filled, rolled again, and cut into pieces. "Panning the dough" refers to the process of setting the sections of cut, filled, and formed dough into the prepared baking pans. Some rolls are nestled in individual muffin pans, and others are arranged in square or rectangular baking pans.

❋ Bake the sweet rolls or buns in a preheated oven to encourage good "oven spring," the initial booster rise in the oven during the beginning of the baking process.

Sweet yeast doughs are a pleasure to work with, are supple and tractable, and are receptive to fillings and toppings. These recommendations and watchpoints will help you create exceptional sweet rolls:

❋ Measure salt and sugar carefully. Salt, which controls the growth of yeast (and, in part, determines the texture of the crumb), and sugar, which feeds yeast, need to be in the appropriate balance if the dough is to have just the right volume and texture.

❋ Be attentive to the dough during the first rise. Underrisen dough bakes into dense, heavy rolls. Overrisen dough bakes into rolls that can be heavily streaked and coarsely textured, rather than fine-grained. Let the dough rise slowly and shield it from sudden temperature changes.

❋ Cover a bowl of dough or pan of sweet rolls with a sheet of food-safe plastic wrap. Cover the dough bowl tightly and the baking pan of formed rolls or buns loosely but completely.

❋ To accommodate your schedule, a yeast dough, taken through the first rise and compressed or deflated, can be refrigerated overnight in a food-safe, self-sealing plastic bag. Compress the dough lightly three times during the first 6 hours of refrigeration time.

❋ Cool baked sweet rolls in a stable environment, away from an open window or an air conditioning or heating register, to prevent the tops and sides from splitting or sloping.

DISTINGUISHING CHARACTERISTICS OF DOUGHS AND BATTERS

by type of dough or batter

Knowing the structural qualities of batters and doughs in their baked and unbaked states helps in understanding how to flavor them: Thick, substantial types can suspend both light and dense additions, while thin, filmy types can accommodate only lighter, very finely chopped additions.

TYPE OF DOUGH OR BATTER	UNBAKED FEATURES AND QUALITIES	BAKED FEATURES AND QUALITIES
CREAMED-BUTTER CAKE BATTER	Smooth, creamy, fluid, billowy, silky-textured; moderately thin, moderately thick to thick density; capable of suspending chopped nuts, ground nuts, flaked coconut, chopped candy, and miniature flavored chips	Downy, springy, even crumb; feathery, tender texture; moist; fine, medium-grained or dense nap
DROP COOKIE DOUGH	Creamy-textured (even when dense); moderately thick to thick or firm/stiff density; capable of containing nuts, flaked coconut, chopped dried fruit, flavored chips, and chopped candy	Moist; soft and cakelike (tender) or crispy-textured; chewy, crunchy, or crackly
BAR COOKIE DOUGH	Thick but creamy-textured density; capable of containing chopped nuts, flaked coconut, chopped dried fruit, flavored chips, and chopped candy	Tender-textured; soft; chewy; fudgy; crackly/splintery surface

(continued)

DISTINGUISHING CHARACTERISTICS OF DOUGHS AND BATTERS

by type of dough or batter

TYPE OF DOUGH OR BATTER	UNBAKED FEATURES AND QUALITIES	BAKED FEATURES AND QUALITIES
SHORTBREAD DOUGH AND SHAPED BUTTER COOKIE DOUGH	Firm but supple; malleable, moldable, and dense; capable of containing chopped nuts, flaked coconut, flavored chips, chopped candy; can be topped with a flavoring addition, such as pressed-on chopped nuts or finely chopped candy, or sprinkled with scented sugar	Exceptionally buttery; tight and compact grain, close-textured nap; firm but short; meltingly tender-textured
CREAMED MUFFIN BATTER	Smooth, creamy texture; moderately dense to dense; capable of suspending chopped nuts, flaked coconut, chopped dried fruit, whole berries, and diced fresh fruit, candy, and flavored chips	Moist; moderate to moderately dense/compact crumb; feathery-textured and fine-grained
MIXED WET-AND-DRY INGREDIENTS MUFFIN BATTER	Coarse, moderately thick to thick density; lumpy batter; capable of suspending chopped nuts, flaked coconut, chopped dried fruit and candy, flavored chips	Open, relaxed crumb; tender-textured; moist

(continued)

DISTINGUISHING CHARACTERISTICS OF DOUGHS AND BATTERS

by type of dough or batter

TYPE OF DOUGH OR BATTER	UNBAKED FEATURES AND QUALITIES	BAKED FEATURES AND QUALITIES
PANCAKE AND WAFFLE BATTER	Medium, medium-thick, to thick density; lumpy; occasionally lightened with firmly beaten egg whites; capable of suspending ground or chopped nuts, finely chopped dried fruit, whole berries, small chunks of fresh fruit, finely chopped candy, or flavored chips	Tender internal texture, moist and light (both waffles and pancakes); crisp surfaces (waffles)
SCONE/SWEET BISCUIT DOUGH	Pebbly, crumbly, and mealy-textured before the addition of liquid; moist but firm, self-adhering dough with the addition of liquid; capable of containing chopped nuts, chopped dried fruit, fresh whole berries, chunks of firm-fleshed fresh fruit, candy, and flavored chips	Moist and tender; moderately fine or moderately compact crumb (overall texture is defined by how thoroughly the fat is worked into the dough and the type of liquid used); flaky; slightly crusty exterior; plump and well-developed, with a good rise
SWEET YEAST DOUGH	With the richness of eggs and butter, a smooth, supple, and satiny dough; good elasticity; capable of enclosing chopped dried fruit, flaked coconut, chopped nuts, flavored chips, and chopped candy; rolled-out sheets of dough firm enough to be spread with thick pastry cream, butter-nut pastes, or spiced and sweetened butter spreads	Tender, buttery, and rich; structured but feathery, elegantly fine-grained, or slightly opened (airy) nap or close-textured; firm but soft and yielding crumb

Baking in a Summer Kitchen
Baking in a Winter Kitchen

The atmosphere around us, whether it's an icy-cold, damp, or impossibly hot and humid day, can be an upending influence on baking. Doughs and batters are sensitive to temperature (and sudden temperature changes, too) and need to be babied a bit. Here are a few basic guidelines for baking in summer and winter:

In the summer

* Be sure to store flour, leavening, spices, and sugar in tightly sealed containers, in a cool, dry place.

* When softening butter to room temperature in the summer, make sure to use it when slightly cool to the touch; in warm weather, butter can become too soft and, consequently, turn oily very quickly. Greasy butter will spoil the texture of a baked batter or dough.

* If your kitchen is very warm, refrigerate drop cookie dough in the mixing bowl between baking trays of cookies.

* Chill just-cut unbaked scones for 15 to 20 minutes before baking.

* Place a cooled pan of bar cookies in the refrigerator for 45 minutes to 1 hour to firm up before cutting.

* Place a batch of yeast dough in the refrigerator for the last 30 to 45 minutes of the first rise to make it manageable before rolling and shaping.

* On a very hot summer day, refrigerate shortbread dough for 5 to 10 minutes before pressing into the baking pan.

* Place chopped candy (such as toffee, milk chocolate peanut butter cups, or chocolate-covered coconut candy) in the refrigerator for 10 minutes before adding to a cookie dough so that it doesn't make the dough murky.

IN THE WINTER

❋ In very cold weather, cream butter a minute or two longer to make it malleable and receptive to the addition of the sugar and eggs. If butter is used in the softened state, usually for batters produced by the creamed method, it should have the consistency of thick mayonnaise.

❋ If your kitchen is *very* cold, beat frosting in a stainless steel bowl over a tepid water bath.

❋ Check sweet yeast buns, rolls, and schnecken about 5 minutes before the total suggested baking time is up, as cold, dry weather tends to dehydrate formed and risen yeast breads.

❋ Store pound cakes, keeping cakes, and soft/dense bar cookies in sturdy plastic storage containers to retain moisture.

IN THE SUMMER OR WINTER

Cool baked goods on stable metal cooling racks, away from heat or air-conditioning registers, and away from open windows and cascading breezes (put aside that romantic, country notion of cooling a cake or pie on the windowsill).

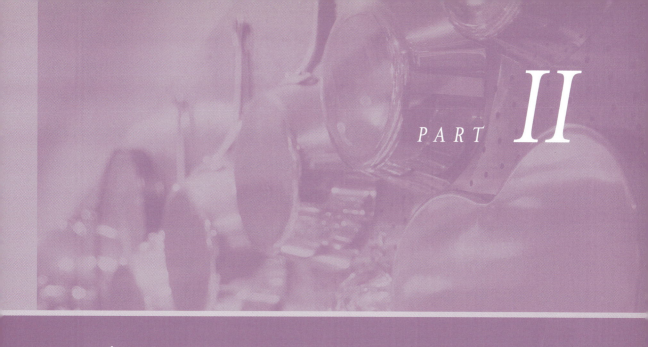

PART II

The Flavors

With its noble, mellow flavor and captivating fragrance, almond is its own flavor package. In essence, the way in which almonds are prepared determines the strength of the flavor they carry and impart—almonds can be used in the form of flour, fine or coarsely ground, chopped, slivered, or turned into a heady paste. Both pure almond extract and almond liqueur, as important ancillary flavoring agents, also contribute mightily to the taste of what you bake.

When you're working with whole almonds, remove the papery brown outer skins for the cleanest taste; skinned almonds can then be chopped, slivered, or ground, either before or after toasting, as each recipe indicates. To detach the skin from almonds, blanch them, 2 cups at a time, in plenty of boiling water for 30 seconds. Then drain in a colander. When they are cool enough to handle, slip off the skins by pressing and squeezing each almond between your thumb and forefinger. Dry the almonds thoroughly by spreading them out on sheets of paper towels. When almonds are to be added directly to a batter or dough, lightly toast them for maximum flavor; if they are to be used as a topping, blanching is sufficient, for the nuts will brown during the baking process. For the sake of time and convenience, you can always purchase blanched and skinned almonds.

Good butter, creamy and unsalted, conveys the flavor of almond in ways that almond extract or liqueur cannot. Butter works in conjunction with the essential oil present in the nut to enrich and expand the taste, as do heavy cream, light (table) cream, and sour cream, but in lesser roles. Almond paste, composed of sugar, water, and blanched almonds, presents a flavor-concentrated form of the nut. Use the paste as a component of a tart or sweet roll filling, or incorporate it into a dense cake batter (especially chocolate) or cookie dough.

5

ALMOND

ALMOND PULL-APARTS

16 sweet roll spirals

*F*OR FESTIVE TIMES, when opulence is the keynote, almond crumb buns are the order of the day. The layering of textures—an expanse of soft, cushiony dough, a dapper almond filling made up of a soft almond paste mixture combined with a silky pastry cream, and an almond crumb topping—is joined together in one hauntingly good, yeasty sweet roll. This recipe has evolved over a period of the last five or six years and now, at last, has achieved the complexity of almond flavor I adore.

What you have here is a recipe in four parts, all of which can be made in manageable stages. The crumb topping can be prepared 2 days in advance and both the almond cream filling and yeast dough 1 day ahead. On baking day, it's just a matter of assembling the large coil of filled dough, cutting it into tidy, swirly buns, and letting the entire pan full of these delectable things rise until puffy. Once covered with the crumb topping, they're ready to be baked. And the fragrance that hovers within the kitchen is almond heaven.

Nonstick cooking spray, for preparing the baking pan

ALMOND, BUTTER, AND EGG YEAST DOUGH

2½ teaspoons active dry yeast

1 teaspoon granulated sugar

¼ cup warm (110° to 115° F.) water

½ cup milk

¼ cup granulated sugar

2 teaspoons pure vanilla extract

1½ teaspoons pure almond extract

4 large eggs

2 large egg yolks

¼ cup thick, cultured sour cream

½ cup almond flour

4 cups unsifted unbleached all-purpose flour, plus about ¼ cup flour for the work surface, or more as needed

1 teaspoon salt

½ pound (16 tablespoons or 2 sticks) unsalted butter, cut into tablespoon chunks, softened

ALMOND CREAM FILLING

2 tablespoons cornstarch

¼ cup superfine sugar

pinch of salt

¾ cup milk

¼ cup light cream

2 large egg yolks

MAKE THE ALMOND, BUTTER, AND EGG YEAST DOUGH
Combine the yeast and 1 teaspoon granulated sugar in a small heatproof bowl. Stir in the warm water and let stand until the yeast is dissolved and the mixture is swollen, 7 to 8 minutes. In the meantime, place the milk and ¼ cup granulated sugar in a small saucepan and set over low heat to dissolve the sugar. Remove from the heat and pour into a heatproof bowl; stir in the vanilla and almond extracts. Cool the mixture to 110° F., then stir in the expanded yeast mixture, the whole eggs, egg yolks, and sour cream.

In a large mixing bowl, combine the almond flour, 4 cups all-purpose flour, and salt. Stir in the yeast-egg mixture. Transfer the

½ teaspoon pure almond extract

½ teaspoon pure vanilla extract

2 teaspoons unsalted butter, softened

ALMOND PASTE FILLING

1 cup (8 ounces) almond paste

2 tablespoons unsalted butter, softened

1 large egg

1 large egg yolk

1½ tablespoons almond liqueur, such
   as Amaretto

2 tablespoons superfine sugar

pinch of salt

1 teaspoon pure vanilla extract

¾ teaspoon pure almond extract

ALMOND CRUMB TOPPING

1½ cups unsifted, bleached all-
   purpose flour

3 tablespoons almond flour

½ teaspoon freshly grated nutmeg

¼ teaspoon ground cardamom

large pinch of salt

¾ cup firmly packed light brown
   sugar, sieved if lumpy

¼ cup granulated sugar

12 tablespoons (1½ sticks) unsalted
   butter, cold, cut into chunks

1¼ teaspoons pure almond extract

½ teaspoon pure vanilla extract

BAKEWARE

15 by 12 by 2-inch baking pan

dough to the bowl of a heavy-duty, freestanding electric mixer fitted with the dough hook. Beat the dough for 2 minutes on moderate speed. Add the softened butter, a tablespoon at a time, beating until incorporated before adding the next chunk. Beat the dough until smooth and very glossy, 2 to 3 minutes longer. During the beating process, the dough should make a slapping noise against the sides of the mixing bowl.

SET THE DOUGH TO RISE Place the dough in a lightly buttered bowl and turn the dough in the bowl to coat all sides in a haze of butter. Cut several deep slashes in the top of the dough. *Technique observation* Slashing the top of the dough helps to boost the rise of a yeast dough rich in eggs and butter. Cover the bowl with a sheet of plastic wrap. Let the dough rise until doubled in bulk, about 1 hour and 45 minutes. (At this point, the dough can be transferred to the refrigerator for a chilled overnight rise. After the first 8 hours, carefully and lightly deflate the dough by pressing down on the top.) In the meantime, cover the dough and refrigerate.

MAKE THE ALMOND CREAM FILLING Sift the cornstarch, superfine sugar, and salt into a small, heavy saucepan (preferably enameled cast iron). Slowly stir in the milk and light cream. Set over moderately high heat and bring to the boil, stirring slowly with a wooden spoon. When the mixture comes to a low boil (large bubbles will appear, and pop here and there over the surface), reduce the heat and simmer the mixture for 1 minute. Beat the egg yolks in a small heatproof bowl and stir in a spoonful of the thickened cream. Remove the saucepan from the heat and slowly mix in the tempered egg yolk mixture. Return the saucepan to the heat and let the mixture bubble slowly for 1 minute, or until nicely thickened.

Strain the filling through a fine-meshed sieve into a heatproof bowl. Slowly stir in the almond and vanilla extracts and softened butter. Immediately place a sheet of plastic wrap directly on top of the filling to prevent a surface skin from forming. Cool the filling for 15 minutes, cover, and refrigerate until needed. (The cream filling can be prepared up to 1 day in advance of filling and baking the spirals.)

PREPARE THE BAKING PAN Film the inside of the baking pan with nonstick cooking spray; set aside.

MAKE THE ALMOND PASTE FILLING Crumble the almond paste into the work bowl of a food processor fitted with the steel knife. Add the softened butter, whole egg, egg yolk, almond liqueur, superfine sugar, salt, and vanilla and almond extracts. Cover and process until very smooth, stopping 2 or 3 times to scrape down the sides of the container. Scrape the filling into a bowl and refrigerate while you are rolling out the dough.

ROLL, FILL, AND CUT THE BUNS With the cupped palms of your hands, softly press down on the dough to flatten it slightly; avoid actively punching down the dough. Roll out the dough on a very lightly floured work surface to a sheet measuring about 17 by 17 inches.

In a medium-size mixing bowl, combine the almond paste filling and the almond cream filling, using a rubber spatula. Spread the filling evenly over the surface of the dough. Roll up the dough into a fat coil as snugly as possible, jellyroll-fashion. *Rolling observation* The filling is quite soft and tends to make the dough a little slippery. Just be sure to roll up the dough as evenly as possible. Pinch closed the long seam end. Gently stretch and pull the coil until it measures about 22 inches in length.

Cut the coil into 16 slices. The filling will ooze as the rolls are cut. Any inconsistencies will be masked later on by the almond crumb topping. Place the slices in the prepared pan, arranging them in four rows of four each.

SET THE BUNS TO RISE Cover the pan loosely with a sheet of plastic wrap. Let the buns rise at cool room temperature until doubled in bulk, about 2 hours and 30 minutes.

PREPARE THE ALMOND CRUMB TOPPING Thoroughly mix the all-purpose flour, almond flour, nutmeg, cardamom, salt, light brown sugar, and granulated sugar in a large mixing bowl. Scatter over the chunks of butter and, using a pastry blender or two round-bladed table knives, cut the fat into the flour until reduced to small chunks about the size of dried lima beans. Sprinkle over the almond extract and vanilla extract. With your fingertips, knead the mixture together until large and small moist, sandy-textured lumps are formed.

PREHEAT THE OVEN, AND TOP AND BAKE THE BUNS Preheat the oven to 375° F. in advance of baking. Remove and discard the plastic wrap covering the spirals. Scatter the streusel mixture in large and small lumps evenly over each bun. Keep the mixture light on top, rather than pressing it down and compacting it. Bake the buns in the preheated oven for 30 to 35 minutes, or until set and the topping is a medium-golden brown color. The buns will pull away slightly from the sides of the baking pan.

COOL THE BUNS Let the buns stand in the pan on a large cooling rack for 20 minutes. Disconnect them here and there at their natural divisions with the tip of a flexible palette knife, and pull apart in blocks of two or four. When they are very fresh, actually cutting into the buns with a knife will compress their fluffy texture. Serve the buns warm or at room temperature.

❋ *For an aromatic topnote of flavor,* use vanilla-scented superfine sugar (see page 54) in place of plain superfine sugar, and intensified vanilla extract (see page 52) in place of plain vanilla extract in the yeast dough.

FRESHLY BAKED, THE PULL-APARTS KEEP FOR 3 TO 4 DAYS.

ALMOND RUSKS

About 34 cookies

EVERY TIME I MAKE THESE SO-GOOD-WITH-COFFEE DIPPING COOKIES, I'm reminded of just how many incarnations one cookie dough can have over time. My mother made a similar type of sweet with vegetable oil, eggs, flour, cinnamon, and leavening, plus two citrus rinds (orange and lemon), fresh orange juice, and a small amount of ground almonds. Her cookies were, perhaps, emblematic of the typical kind of mandelbrot made by Jewish home cooks—reasonably plain but justifiably delicious. I have made those and others like them so many times during numerous baking sessions.

These almond rusks, however, are decidedly not my mother's cookies. They are boldly flavored with almond in the form of coarsely ground (and toasted) slivered almonds, almond liqueur, and almond extract—a result of several years' worth of testing doughs and dense batters. Ultimately, I developed a mixture that baked up firm and crunchy, but with a slight airiness in its internal crumb. Having these rusks around, kept in a tin, is a luxury.

1¾ cups slivered almonds, very lightly toasted and cooled completely

3⅓ cups unsifted bleached all-purpose flour

¼ cup almond flour

1¼ teaspoons baking powder

⅛ teaspoon cream of tartar

1 teaspoon salt

1 teaspoon freshly grated nutmeg

5 large eggs

1¾ cups plus 2 tablespoons vanilla-scented granulated sugar (see page 53)

1 tablespoon plain vegetable oil (preferably soybean)

2 tablespoons almond liqueur, such as Amaretto

2 teaspoons pure almond extract

2 teaspoons pure vanilla extract

About ½ cup slivered almonds, for pressing on the unbaked ovals of dough (optional)

Vanilla-scented granulated sugar (see page 53), for sprinkling on the baked rusks (optional)

BAKEWARE

2 large rimmed sheet pans

PREHEAT THE OVEN AND PREPARE THE SHEET PANS Preheat the oven to 350° F. Line the sheet pans with cooking parchment paper; set aside.

PREPARE THE ALMOND BATTER-DOUGH Place the almonds in the work bowl of a food processor fitted with the steel knife; cover and process until very finely chopped.

In a medium-size mixing bowl, thoroughly whisk together the all-purpose flour, almond flour, baking powder, cream of tartar, salt, and nutmeg. In a large mixing bowl, whisk the eggs to combine. Add the vanilla-scented granulated sugar and whisk rapidly for 2 minutes. Blend in the oil. The mixture should be lightly thickened. Blend in the almond liqueur and almond and vanilla extracts. Pour the flour mixture over the egg mixture and stir to form a batter-like dough. *Batter-dough consistency observation* The mixture will be dense and moderately heavy. Let the dough stand for 2 minutes.

ASSEMBLE THE DOUGH ON THE COOKIE SHEETS With a large, sturdy spoon, spoon half of the dough onto one of the parchment-lined sheet pans and, using a rubber spatula, smooth the length and width into a long oval measuring about 5 by 11 inches. Repeat with the remaining dough, using the second cookie sheet. Moisten your fingertips with cold water. Lightly press and pat the edges of each oval of dough to neaten it.

If you are using the extra slivered almonds, scatter half of them on top of each oval of dough. Press them lightly onto the top of the dough with your fingertips.

BAKE AND COOL THE OVALS OF DOUGH Bake the cakes of dough for about 30 minutes, or until golden on top and completely set. A wooden pick inserted in the center of each oval must withdraw clean, without any flecks of unbaked dough adhering to it. *Baking observation* Fully baking the cakes of dough at this point is critical to the finished crunchiness of the rusks. Underbaked ovals of dough will, during the second baking, become compact, and never achieve the airy crunchiness I prize so much. The dough will expand and rise into a larger oval, about 8¼ inches at its widest point and about 13½ inches long. It doesn't have to be perfectly formed.

Let the ovals stand on the baking pans for 5 minutes. Carefully transfer them (still on their parchment paper bases) to cooling racks. Let stand for 20 to 30 minutes, or until

tepid. *Cooling observation* The ovals of dough must be cool enough to slice evenly and neatly, otherwise they may break, splinter here and there, or crumble at the edges.

Reduce the oven temperature to 275° F.

SLICE THE OVALS OF DOUGH INTO RUSKS Have the cooled sheet pans at hand. Working with one oval at a time, slip a wide, offset metal palette knife under it, and slide it onto a cutting board. With a serrated knife, cut each cooled oval into long ¾-inch-thick slices. Arrange the rusks on unlined cookie sheets, cut side down.

SLOW-BAKE THE RUSKS Bake the rusks again for 15 to 20 minutes to dry them out, or until they are light brown, firm, and dry. Turn the rusks twice during this time. Baking them again at a lower temperature makes them hard, long-keeping, and crunchy without overbrowning them.

COOL THE RUSKS Let the rusks stand on the sheet pans for 10 minutes, then carefully transfer them to racks, using a pair of sturdy tongs. Sprinkle the cut surfaces with a little sugar, if you wish, and cool completely. Store the rusks in an airtight tin.

FRESHLY BAKED, THE RUSKS WILL KEEP FOR 4 TO 6 WEEKS.

PUMPKIN-ALMOND KEEPING CAKE

One 10-inch tube cake, creating about 20 slices

A BEVY OF GROUND SPICES and dark brown sugar form the backdrop to the three-flavor boost of almond (in the form of liqueur, extract, and slivered nuts) in this moist cake. An almond liqueur-based sugar wash, which sinks into the hot cake, is a potent, taste-charging finish.

Shortening and bleached all-purpose flour, for preparing the cake pan

PUMPKIN-ALMOND BUTTER CAKE BATTER

3 cups plus 2 tablespoons unsifted bleached all-purpose flour

1¾ teaspoons baking powder

¼ teaspoon baking soda

⅛ teaspoon cream of tartar

1 teaspoon salt

1½ teaspoons ground cinnamon

1 teaspoon freshly grated nutmeg

½ teaspoon ground ginger

¼ teaspoon ground allspice

¼ teaspoon ground cardamom

½ cup slivered almonds, lightly toasted and cooled completely

½ pound (16 tablespoons or 2 sticks) unsalted butter, softened

2 tablespoons shortening

2 cups granulated sugar

1 cup firmly packed dark brown sugar, sieved if lumpy

4 large eggs

2½ teaspoons pure almond extract

1½ teaspoons pure vanilla extract

PREHEAT THE OVEN AND PREPARE THE CAKE PAN Preheat the oven to 325° F. Grease the inside of the tube pan (do not use a Bundt pan or a tube pan with a removable bottom) with shortening. Line the bottom of the pan with a circle of waxed paper cut to fit, and grease the paper. Dust the inside of the pan with all-purpose flour. Tap out any excess flour; set aside.

MAKE THE PUMPKIN-ALMOND BUTTER CAKE BATTER Sift the flour, baking powder, baking soda, cream of tartar, salt, cinnamon, nutmeg, ginger, allspice, and cardamom. In a small bowl, toss the slivered almonds with 1 teaspoon of the sifted mixture.

Cream the butter and shortening in the large bowl of a free-standing electric mixer on moderate speed for 3 to 4 minutes. Add the granulated sugar in 2 additions, beating for 1 minute after each portion is added. Add the dark brown sugar and beat for 2 minutes longer. Add the eggs, one at a time, beating for 30 seconds after each addition. Blend in the almond and vanilla extracts.

On low speed, alternately add the sifted mixture in three additions with the pumpkin puree in two additions, beginning and ending with the sifted ingredients. Scrape down the sides of the mixing bowl frequently with a rubber spatula to keep the batter even-textured. Blend in the almond liqueur. Stir in the almonds.

Spoon the batter into the prepared tube pan. Lightly smooth over the top with a rubber spatula.

BAKE THE CAKE Bake the cake in the preheated oven for 1 hour and 25 minutes to 1 hour and 30 minutes, or until risen, set, and

One 1-pound can pumpkin puree (not pumpkin pie filling)

3 tablespoons almond liqueur, such as Amaretto

Almond-Sugar Wash (see page 59), for finishing the baked cake

BAKEWARE

plain 10-inch tube pan

a wooden pick inserted in the cake withdraws clean. The baked cake will pull away slightly from the sides of the baking pan.

COOL AND APPLY THE FINISH TO THE CAKE Cool the cake in the pan on a rack for 8 to 10 minutes. Carefully invert the cake onto another cooling rack, peel off the waxed paper circle, then invert again to cool right side up. Place a sheet of waxed paper under the cooling rack to catch any drips of the finishing wash.

Using a sturdy pastry brush, paint the almond-sugar wash on the surface of the cake. Cool completely before slicing. *Slicing observation* Use a serrated knife to cut the cake neatly and cleanly. Store in an airtight cake keeper.

❋ *For an extra surge of flavor,* replace 2 tablespoons of the all-purpose flour with 3 tablespoons almond flour. Sift the almond flour with the all-purpose flour, baking powder, baking soda, cream of tartar, and spices.

❋ *For an aromatic topnote of flavor,* use vanilla-scented granulated sugar (see page 53) in place of plain granulated sugar in the cake batter.

FRESHLY BAKED, THE CAKE KEEPS FOR 1 WEEK.

Variation: For pumpkin-almond keeping cake with dried cherries, toss ½ cup dried tart cherries with the slivered almonds, using 1½ teaspoons of the sifted mixture for tossing the fruit and nuts.

BEST BAKING ADVICE
For the smoothest batter, use thoroughly softened (but not oily) butter.

ALMOND BUTTER CAKE

One 10-inch fluted tube cake, creating 16 slices

To keep the almond flavor pervasive inside and out, you need to highlight the cake batter with freshly grated nutmeg and allspice (to round out the almond taste); boost the batter with almond flour, which is simply a significantly lightened, powdery version of the nut; and complete the cake with lavish brush strokes of almond syrup. In all, this cake has a delicate crumb, inviting flavor, and an alluring moistness that the combination of sour cream, heavy cream, and butter conveys so well.

Nonstick cooking spray, for preparing the cake pan

ALMOND BUTTER CAKE BATTER

2½ cups unsifted bleached all-purpose flour

½ cup unsifted bleached cake flour

¼ teaspoon baking soda

⅛ teaspoon cream of tartar

1 teaspoon salt

¾ teaspoon freshly grated nutmeg

⅛ teaspoon ground allspice

½ pound (16 tablespoons or 2 sticks) unsalted butter, softened

2½ cups superfine sugar

2½ teaspoons pure almond extract

1 teaspoon pure vanilla extract

5 large eggs

½ cup almond flour

1 cup thick, cultured sour cream

2 tablespoons heavy cream

Almond Syrup (see page 56), for brushing over the warm cake

BAKEWARE

10-inch Bundt pan

PREHEAT THE OVEN AND PREPARE THE CAKE PAN Preheat the oven to 325° F. Film the inside of the Bundt pan with nonstick cooking spray; set aside.

MAKE THE ALMOND BUTTER CAKE BATTER Sift the all-purpose flour, cake flour, baking soda, cream of tartar, salt, nutmeg, and allspice onto a sheet of waxed paper.

Cream the butter in the large bowl of a freestanding electric mixer on moderate speed for 3 minutes. Add the superfine sugar in four additions, beating for 1 minute after each portion is added. Blend in the almond and vanilla extracts. Add the eggs, one at a time, beating for 30 seconds after each addition, or until just blended. Scrape down the sides of the mixing bowl after each egg is added. Blend in the almond flour.

On low speed, alternately add the sifted mixture in three additions with the sour cream in two additions, beginning and ending with the sifted mixture. Scrape down the sides of the mixing bowl frequently with a rubber spatula to keep the batter even-textured. Blend in the heavy cream. *Batter texture observation* The batter will be lightly thickened and creamy-textured.

Spoon the batter into the prepared Bundt pan. Lightly smooth over the top with a rubber spatula.

BAKE THE CAKE Bake the cake in the preheated oven for 1 hour and 10 minutes, or until risen, set, a medium golden color on top, and a wooden pick inserted in the cake withdraws clean. The baked cake will pull away slightly from the sides of the baking pan.

COOL AND BRUSH THE ALMOND SYRUP ON THE CAKE Cool the cake in the pan on a rack for 5 to 8 minutes. Carefully invert the cake onto another cooling rack. Place a sheet of waxed paper under the cooling rack to catch any drips of syrup.

Immediately, while the cake is still oven-hot, brush the syrup over the top and sides of the cake, using a 1-inch-wide pastry brush. Cool completely before slicing. *Slicing observation* Use a serrated knife to cut the cake neatly and cleanly. Store in an airtight cake keeper.

✳ *For an aromatic topnote of flavor,* use vanilla-scented superfine sugar in place of plain superfine sugar (see page 54) in the cake batter.

✳ *For a textural contrast,* stir ⅔ cup slivered almonds, lightly toasted and cooled completely, into the cake batter after the heavy cream is added.

FRESHLY BAKED, THE CAKE KEEPS FOR 4 DAYS.

FALLEN CHOCOLATE ALMOND CAKE

One 9-inch cake, creating about 8 to 10 slices

*T*HIS CAKE IS DELICIOUSLY DECEPTIVE. As an almond version of a chocolate soufflé cake, the flavor will (at first) appear delicate and weightless, but as you linger over the cake, the chocolate-and-almond intensity comes through solidly.

Softened unsalted butter, for preparing the cake pan

CHOCOLATE AND ALMOND CAKE BATTER

9 ounces bittersweet chocolate, melted and cooled

PREHEAT THE OVEN AND PREPARE THE CAKE PAN Preheat the oven to 350° F. Lightly butter the inside of the springform pan; set aside.

MIX THE CHOCOLATE AND ALMOND CAKE BATTER Whisk the melted chocolate and melted butter in a small mixing bowl until thoroughly blended.

9 tablespoons (1 stick plus 1 tablespoon) unsalted butter, melted and cooled

5 large eggs, separated

½ cup granulated sugar

1 tablespoon almond liqueur, such as Amaretto

1¼ teaspoons pure almond extract

¾ teaspoon pure vanilla extract

3 tablespoons almond flour blended with 1½ tablespoons unsweetened, alkalized cocoa

⅛ teaspoon cream of tartar

Vanilla Custard Sauce (see page 531) or Vanilla Whipped Cream (see page 530), to accompany the cake

BAKEWARE

9-inch springform pan, 2¾ inches deep

In a large mixing bowl, whisk the egg yolks and granulated sugar for 1 to 2 minutes, until combined and very lightly thickened. Blend in the almond liqueur and almond and vanilla extracts. Thoroughly stir in the melted chocolate-butter mixture, then the almond flour-cocoa mixture. *Batter color observation* The mixture should be evenly colored, without any streaks of the yolk mixture trailing through the batter.

Beat the egg whites in a clean, dry bowl until foamy, add the cream of tartar, and continue beating until firm (but not stiff) peaks are formed. Stir 2 large spoonfuls of the beaten whites into the chocolate-almond batter, then fold in the remaining whites, combining the two mixtures lightly but thoroughly so that no streaks of the beaten whites remain.

Spoon the batter into the prepared springform pan. Gently smooth over the top with a flexible palette knife or rubber spatula.

BAKE AND COOL THE CAKE Bake the cake in the preheated oven for 35 minutes, or until set. The cake must be gently set, not shaky or wobbly with a liquid core.

Cool the cake completely in the pan on a rack. The cake will fall on cooling. Open the hinge on the side of the springform pan and remove the outer ring, allowing the cake to stand on the base. (The cake must be thoroughly cooled for it to cut cleanly.) Serve the cake, cut into slices for serving, with a spoonful or two of custard sauce or whipped cream. Store in an airtight cake keeper.

❋ *For an extra surge of flavor,* toss 3 tablespoons chopped, blanched almonds, lightly toasted and cooled completely, with 1 teaspoon of the almond flour-cocoa mixture and fold into the batter along with the beaten egg whites.

❋ *For an aromatic topnote of flavor,* use vanilla-scented granulated sugar (see page 53) in place of plain granulated sugar and intensified vanilla extract (see page 52) in place of plain vanilla extract in the cake batter.

FRESHLY BAKED, THE CAKE KEEPS FOR 2 DAYS.

A Big Almond, Cornmeal, and Dried Cherry Sharing Cookie

One large, 9½-inch cookie, creating about 15 casual, irregularly shaped pieces

THE BUTTER IN THE DOUGH forms a backdrop for the flavor interchange of the cornmeal, almonds, and dried cherries. The texture of the cookie is at once slightly gritty (good cornmeal makes it so), firm-crunchy, and slightly chewy with fruit. This textural cookie, broken off in irregular pieces, is an easygoing sweet to make and serve—it's marvelous with a glass of wine or a cup of espresso.

Nonstick cooking spray, for preparing the tart pan

ALMOND AND DRIED CHERRY COOKIE DOUGH

1 cup plus 1 tablespoon unsifted bleached all-purpose flour

⅓ cup plus 2 tablespoons fine yellow cornmeal

¼ teaspoon baking powder

⅛ teaspoon salt

12 tablespoons (1½ sticks) unsalted butter, softened

⅓ cup plus 2 tablespoons superfine sugar

1 tablespoon ground almonds

1½ teaspoons pure almond extract

¼ teaspoon pure vanilla extract

⅔ cup dried tart cherries

⅓ cup slivered almonds, lightly toasted and cooled

About 2 tablespoons granulated sugar, for sprinkling on top of the unbaked cookie

BAKEWARE

fluted 9½-inch round tart pan (with a removable bottom)

PREHEAT THE OVEN AND PREPARE THE TART PAN Preheat the oven to 350° F. Film the inside of the tart pan with nonstick cooking spray; set aside.

MIX THE ALMOND AND DRIED CHERRY COOKIE DOUGH Sift the flour, cornmeal, baking powder, and salt onto a sheet of waxed paper.

Cream the butter in the large bowl of a freestanding electric mixer on low speed for 3 to 4 minutes. Add the superfine sugar, ground almonds, and almond and vanilla extracts, and continue creaming for 2 minutes. Add the sifted mixture and mix on low speed until the particles of flour are absorbed and a soft dough is formed. Scrape down the sides of the mixing bowl frequently with a rubber spatula to keep the dough even-textured. *Dough texture observation* The dough will be moderately soft. Scatter the dried cherries and almonds over the dough and work them in with your fingertips, wooden spoon, or flat wooden paddle.

PRESS THE DOUGH INTO THE PREPARED PAN Turn the dough into the prepared tart pan. Press and pat the dough into an even layer, using your fingertips. Prick the dough here and there with the tines of a fork.

BAKE AND COOL THE COOKIE Bake the cookie for 30 minutes, or until golden on top and set. Let the cookie stand in the pan on a cooling rack. Immediately sprinkle the granulated sugar evenly over the top. Cool for 10 minutes. Carefully remove the outer ring, leaving the shortbread on its round base. Cool completely, then slip the shortbread off the base, sliding a narrow, offset metal spatula between the cookie and the base. Serve the big cookie whole, letting your guests break it into informal, uneven pieces. Store any leftover pieces in an airtight tin.

❋ *For an aromatic topnote of flavor,* blend 2 teaspoons almond liqueur (such as Amaretto) into the cookie dough before the sifted mixture is added.

FRESHLY BAKED, THE COOKIE KEEPS FOR I WEEK.

Variation: For a big almond, cornmeal, and dried cranberry sharing cookie, substitute dried, sweetened cranberries for the cherries.

BUTTERY GLAZED ALMOND RING

One 11- to 12-inch decorative ring cake,
creating about 20 slices

*T*HE BATTER FOR THIS DELICATELY FLAVORED, light-textured cake bakes into a handsome and plump ring cake. The cake looks charming baked in a large fluted ring mold, with the scalloped indentations forming a swirled pattern across the bottom of the pan.

Shortening and bleached all-purpose flour, for preparing the ring mold

ALMOND BUTTER CAKE BATTER

2⅔ cups unsifted bleached all-purpose flour

¼ cup plus 2 tablespoons unsifted bleached cake flour

PREHEAT THE OVEN AND PREPARE THE RING MOLD BAKING PAN Preheat the oven to 350° F. Grease the inside of the ring mold with shortening. Dust the inside of the pan with all-purpose flour. Tap out any excess flour; set aside.

MIX THE ALMOND BUTTER CAKE BATTER Sift the all-purpose flour, cake flour, baking powder, salt, nutmeg, and cardamom onto a sheet of waxed paper.

2 teaspoons baking powder

½ teaspoon salt

¾ teaspoon freshly grated nutmeg

¼ teaspoon ground cardamom

16 tablespoons (1¾ sticks) unsalted
butter, softened

2 cups superfine sugar, divided into
1¾ cups and ¼ cup amounts

4 large eggs

2 large egg yolks

¼ cup ground almonds

1¼ teaspoons pure almond extract

¾ teaspoon intensified vanilla extract
(see page 52)

1 cup heavy cream blended with
3 tablespoons milk

3 large egg whites

pinch of cream of tartar

ALMOND-BUTTER GLAZE

4 tablespoons (½ stick) unsalted
butter, cut into chunks

2 tablespoons almond liqueur, such as
Amaretto

3 tablespoons mild honey, such as clover

BAKEWARE

11¾-inch fluted decorative ring mold
with a 12- to 13-cup capacity

BEST BAKING ADVICE

*Bake the cake until just-baked and
springy; the combination of baking
powder and egg white-raised batter
overbakes easily.*

Cream the butter in the large bowl of a freestanding electric mixer on moderate speed for 3 to 4 minutes. Add the 1¾ cups superfine sugar in three additions, beating for 1 minute after each portion is added. Blend in the whole eggs, one at a time, beating for 30 to 45 seconds after each addition. Blend in egg yolks and ground almonds. Blend in the almond and vanilla extracts.

On low speed, alternately add the sifted mixture in three additions with the heavy cream-milk mixture in two additions, beginning and ending with the sifted mixture. Scrape down the sides of the mixing bowl frequently with a rubber spatula to keep the batter even-textured.

Beat the egg whites in a clean, dry bowl until frothy, add the cream of tartar, and continue beating until soft peaks are formed. Gradually beat in the remaining ¼ cup sugar and continue to beat until the egg whites are firm (but not stiff) and shiny. Stir a large spoonful of the whites into the batter, then fold in the remaining whites.

Pour and scrape the batter into the prepared ring mold baking pan. Smooth over the top with a rubber spatula.

BAKE AND COOL THE CAKE Bake the cake for 45 to 50 minutes, or until risen, set, and a wooden pick inserted in the cake withdraws clean or with a few moist crumbs adhering to it.

Cool the cake in the pan on a rack for 5 minutes, then invert onto another cooling rack. Place a sheet of waxed paper underneath the cooling rack to catch any drips of glaze.

MAKE THE ALMOND-BUTTER GLAZE AND APPLY TO THE WARM CAKE While the cake is cooling, combine the butter, almond liqueur, and honey in a small, heavy saucepan (preferably enameled cast iron), place over moderately low heat, and cook until the butter and honey are completely dissolved, stirring the mixture occasionally with a wooden spoon or flat wooden paddle.

Bring the mixture to a low boil, remove from the heat, and whisk very well to combine. Brush the hot glaze on the top and sides of the cake, using a soft, 1-inch-wide pastry brush. Cool completely before slicing. *Slicing observation* Use a serrated knife to cut the cake neatly and cleanly. Store in an airtight cake keeper.

FRESHLY BAKED, THE CAKE KEEPS FOR 3 DAYS.

BUTTER ALMOND PANCAKES

About 20 pancakes

*T*HE ACCENT FLAVOR OF ALMOND, present in the delicate crunch of a few table-spoons of slivered almonds and the mellow taste of almond liqueur and almond extract, dominates these pancakes. The melted butter in the batter establishes the background flavor of the pancakes and allows the almond taste to flourish.

BUTTER ALMOND PANCAKE
BATTER

1 cup unsifted bleached all-purpose
    flour

1½ teaspoons baking powder

pinch of salt

¼ teaspoon freshly grated nutmeg

3 tablespoons granulated sugar

2 tablespoons almond flour

1 large egg

4 tablespoons (½ stick) unsalted
    butter, melted and cooled to tepid

1 tablespoon almond liqueur, such as
    Amaretto

¾ teaspoon pure vanilla extract

½ teaspoon pure almond extract

¾ cup plus 1½ tablespoons milk

3 tablespoons slivered almonds, lightly
    toasted and cooled

Clarified butter (see page 66), for the
    griddle

Confectioners' sugar, for sprinkling on
    the pancakes (optional)

MIX THE BUTTER ALMOND PANCAKE BATTER Sift the flour, baking powder, salt, nutmeg, and granulated sugar into a medium-size mixing bowl. Whisk in the almond flour.

Whisk the egg, melted butter, almond liqueur, vanilla extract, almond extract, and milk in a small mixing bowl. Pour the butter-egg-milk blend over the sifted ingredients and stir to form a batter, using a wooden spoon or flat wooden paddle. *Batter texture observation* The batter will be lumpy and moderately thick. Lightly stir in the slivered almonds.

GRIDDLE THE PANCAKES Heat a griddle and lightly coat the surface with clarified butter, using several thickness of paper toweling to apply a thin coating. The griddle should be hot enough so that the batter sizzles and cooks, but not so hot that it burns the bottom of the pancakes before they've had the chance to set up.

Spoon 2-tablespoon amounts of batter onto the griddle, placing them about 3 inches apart. Cook the pancakes for about 45 seconds, or until set and a few bubbles appear on the tops; flip the pancakes, using a wide, offset metal spatula, and griddle for about 45 seconds longer, or until cooked through. Continue to griddle pancakes with the remaining batter, cooking them in batches, and filming the griddle with more butter as needed. If the batter becomes very thick, thin it with an extra tablespoon or so of milk.

Serve the pancakes as quickly as they are lifted from the griddle, and sprinkle them with confectioners' sugar, if you wish.

BITTERSWEET ALMOND CHUNK BROWNIES

16 brownies

*I*N THIS BAR COOKIE, chocolate and almond blend in a temperate way, with bits of chopped nuts flecking the batter and enough almond extract to identify the flavor. The fusion of chocolate and almond, here in a bar cookie, is a classic one.

Nonstick cooking spray, for preparing the baking pan

BITTERSWEET ALMOND BROWNIE BATTER

1¼ cups unsifted bleached all-purpose flour

¼ cup unsifted bleached cake flour

2 tablespoons unsweetened, alkalized cocoa

¼ teaspoon baking powder

½ teaspoon salt

7 ounces bittersweet chocolate, chopped into chunks

¾ cup coarsely chopped skinned almonds, lightly toasted and cooled completely

½ pound (16 tablespoons or 2 sticks) unsalted butter, melted and cooled to tepid

3 ounces bittersweet chocolate, melted and cooled to tepid

5 ounces (5 squares) unsweetened chocolate, melted and cooled to tepid

4 large eggs

2 cups plus 2 tablespoons granulated sugar

1¼ teaspoons pure almond extract

¾ teaspoon pure vanilla extract

PREHEAT THE OVEN AND PREPARE THE BAKING PAN Preheat the oven to 325° F. Film the inside of the baking pan with nonstick cooking spray; set aside.

MIX THE BITTERSWEET ALMOND BROWNIE BATTER Sift the all-purpose flour, cake flour, cocoa, baking powder, and salt onto a sheet of waxed paper. In a medium-size mixing bowl, toss the chopped bittersweet chocolate and almonds with 2½ teaspoons of the sifted mixture.

Whisk the melted butter, melted bittersweet chocolate, and melted unsweetened chocolate in a medium-size mixing bowl until thoroughly blended. Whisk the eggs in a large mixing bowl until frothy, about 1 minute. Add the granulated sugar and whisk lightly until just combined, about 30 seconds to 1 minute. Blend in the almond and vanilla extracts. Blend in the melted butter and chocolate mixture. Sift over the sifted ingredients and mix with a rubber spatula (or whisk) until all particles of flour are completely absorbed, making sure to catch any pockets of flour along the bottom and sides of the bowl. *Batter texture observation* The batter will be dense. Stir in the bittersweet chocolate chunks and almonds.

Scrape the batter into the prepared baking pan. Smooth over the top with a rubber spatula.

BAKE AND COOL THE BROWNIES Bake the brownies for 35 to 38 minutes, or until set. Let the brownies stand in the pan on a cooling rack for 3 hours, then refrigerate for 45 minutes, or until firm enough to cut. (In hot or humid weather, or in a warm kitchen, freeze the pan of brownies for 20 minutes before cutting,

Confectioners' sugar, for sifting over
the top of the brownies (optional)

BAKEWARE
10 by 10 by 2-inch baking pan

or until firm enough to cut.) Cut the entire cake of brownies into four quarters, then cut each quarter into four squares, using a small, sharp knife. Remove the brownies from the baking pan, using a small, offset metal spatula. Sprinkle the top of the brownies with confectioners' sugar, just before serving, if you wish. Store in an airtight tin.

❊ *For an extra surge of flavor,* decrease the amount of cake flour to 1 tablespoon and blend ¼ cup almond flour into the beaten eggs along with the granulated sugar.

❊ *For an aromatic topnote of flavor,* use intensified vanilla extract (see page 52) in place of plain vanilla extract in the brownie batter.

FRESHLY BAKED, THE BROWNIES KEEP FOR 3 TO 4 DAYS.

Variation: For bittersweet almond chunk brownies with Dutch-process black cocoa, use 1 tablespoon Dutch-process black cocoa and 1 tablespoon unsweetened, alkalized cocoa.

ALMOND SHORTBREAD

One 9½-inch shortbread, creating 12 triangular pieces

THE MINGLING OF GROUND ALMONDS, almond extract, and slivered, lightly toasted almonds develops the almond theme in this buttery cookie. To keep its shape, the shortbread is baked in a fluted tart pan and cut into wedges while still warm.

ALMOND SHORTBREAD DOUGH

1¼ cups unsifted bleached all-purpose
    flour

¼ cup rice flour

¼ teaspoon baking powder

large pinch of salt

2 tablespoons ground almonds

PREHEAT THE OVEN AND PREPARE THE TART PAN Preheat the oven to 325° F. Have the tart pan at hand.

MAKE THE ALMOND SHORTBREAD DOUGH Sift the all-purpose flour, rice flour, baking powder, and salt into a medium-size bowl. Whisk in the ground almonds.

Cream the butter in the large bowl of a freestanding electric mixer on low speed for 3 to 4 minutes, or until smooth. Add the

12 tablespoons (1½ sticks) unsalted butter, softened

⅓ cup plus 2 tablespoons unsifted confectioners' sugar

1 teaspoon pure almond extract

¾ teaspoon pure vanilla extract

⅔ cup slivered almonds

About 2 tablespoons granulated sugar, for sprinkling on top of the baked shortbread

BAKEWARE

fluted 9½-inch round tart pan (with a removable bottom)

confectioners' sugar and beat on moderately low speed for 2 minutes. Blend in the almond and vanilla extracts. On moderately low speed, blend in the sifted dry ingredients, mixing until the particles of flour are absorbed and a smooth dough is created. Scrape down the sides of the mixing bowl frequently with a rubber spatula to keep the dough even-textured. *Dough texture observation* The dough will be soft.

PAT THE DOUGH INTO THE PREPARED PAN Transfer the dough to the tart pan, and lightly press it into an even layer. Prick the shortbread with the tines of a fork in about 15 random places. Scatter over the slivered almonds and press them lightly on the top of the dough.

BAKE AND COOL THE SHORTBREAD Bake the shortbread in the preheated oven for 40 minutes, or until set and an overall medium tan color on top. The shortbread must be baked through. Place the pan of shortbread on a cooling rack and immediately dust the top with the granulated sugar. Cool for 10 minutes.

CUT THE SHORTBREAD Carefully unmold the shortbread, leaving it on its round base. After 10 minutes, cut into even-sized wedges, using a sharp chef's knife. Or serve the cookie whole, communal style, and let each person break off his or her own portion. Store the shortbread in an airtight tin.

FRESHLY BAKED, THE SHORTBREAD KEEPS FOR 1 WEEK.

BEST BAKING ADVICE
Lightly press the dough into the tart pan.

Sweet Almond and Chocolate Chip Drop Biscuits

About 1½ dozen biscuits

*T*ENDER AND CRUMBLY, moist and chocolate-spattered, these are the biscuits to have with coffee or tea anytime during the day.

ALMOND AND CHOCOLATE CHIP DROP BISCUIT DOUGH

2 cups unsifted bleached all-purpose flour

3¼ teaspoons baking powder

¼ teaspoon cream of tartar

¼ teaspoon salt

6 tablespoons (¾ stick) unsalted butter, cold, cut into tablespoon pieces

2 tablespoons shortening, cold, cut into small chunks

¼ cup granulated sugar

1 cup miniature semisweet chocolate chips

½ cup slivered almonds, lightly toasted and cooled

1 cup milk blended with 1 teaspoon pure almond extract and ½ teaspoon pure vanilla extract

3 to 4 tablespoons granulated sugar, for sprinkling over the top of the unbaked biscuits

BAKEWARE

2 heavy cookie sheets or rimmed sheet pans

PREHEAT THE OVEN AND HAVE THE BAKING SHEET AT HAND Preheat the oven to 425° F. Have the cookie sheets or rimmed sheet pans at hand. The baking sheets need to be heavy to prevent the bottoms of the biscuits from scorching. Double-pan the sheets, if necessary.

MIX THE ALMOND AND CHOCOLATE CHIP DROP BISCUIT DOUGH Whisk the flour, baking powder, cream of tartar, and salt. Drop in the chunks of butter and shortening and, using a pastry blender, reduce the fat to small pea-sized bits. Stir in the granulated sugar, chocolate chips, and almonds. Pour over the milk-vanilla and almond extract blend. Mix to form a dough, using a wooden spoon or flat wooden paddle. Mix lightly for 5 to 6 seconds. *Dough texture observation* The dough will come together and unify into a soft, slightly sticky mass.

FORM THE DROP BISCUITS Drop rounded 2-tablespoon-size portions of dough, about 2½ inches apart, in high (not flat) mounds, on the cookie sheet or sheet pan. Place 9 mounds of dough on each sheet. Sprinkle the tops of the biscuits with the granulated sugar.

BAKE AND COOL THE BISCUITS Bake the biscuits in the preheated oven for 13 to 15 minutes, or until set, with golden spots and patches here and there on top. The bottoms of the biscuits will be a medium golden brown color. Remove the biscuits to a cooling rack, using a wide, offset metal spatula. Serve the biscuits very fresh, slightly warm or at room temperature.

DELICATE ALMOND MADELEINES

17 small cakes

THESE MADELEINES HAVE AN ETHEREAL ALMOND TASTE and fine-grained crumb; the combination of mixing method and use of superfine sugar creates the delicate texture. A sponge cake batter is usually spooned into madeleine molds rather than this light, somewhat fragile butter cake batter (and the batter for my Double Chocolate Madeleines on page 256), but the results are even more delicious. In fact, I prefer to use this creamed batter in these small cakes, for they bake up moister and texturally more interesting. The shell-shaped cakes are baked in the classic *plaques à madeleines* molds.

Melted clarified butter (see page 66) and bleached all-purpose flour, for preparing the madeleine molds

ALMOND MADELEINE BATTER

½ cup unsifted bleached all-purpose flour

¼ cup unsifted bleached cake flour

¼ teaspoon baking powder

⅛ teaspoon salt

⅛ teaspoon freshly grated nutmeg

6 tablespoons (¾ stick) unsalted butter, softened

⅓ cup plus 2 tablespoons superfine sugar

2 large eggs

2 tablespoons ground almonds

1 teaspoon pure almond extract

½ teaspoon pure vanilla extract

Confectioners' sugar, for sifting over the tops of the baked madeleines

BAKEWARE

2 *plaques à madeleines* (twelve 3-inch shells to each plaque)

PREHEAT THE OVEN AND PREPARE THE MADELEINE PANS
Preheat the oven to 350° F. Film the inside of 17 madeleine molds with clarified butter, using a soft pastry brush. Let stand for 5 minutes, or until completely set, then dust the inside of each shell with all-purpose flour. Tap out any excess flour; there should be a very thin coating. Set aside.

MIX THE ALMOND MADELEINE BATTER Sift the all-purpose flour, cake flour, baking powder, salt, and nutmeg onto a sheet of waxed paper.

Using an electric hand mixer, cream the butter in a medium-size mixing bowl on moderate speed for 1 to 2 minutes. Add the superfine sugar and beat for 1 minute longer. Beat in the eggs, one at a time, mixing for 30 to 45 seconds after each addition. Scrape down the sides of the mixing bowl frequently with a rubber spatula to keep the batter even-textured. Blend in the ground almonds and almond and vanilla extracts. Add the sifted ingredients and mix on low speed until the particles of flour are absorbed. Scrape down the sides of the mixing bowl frequently to keep the batter even-textured. *Batter texture observation* The batter will be creamy-textured and velvety.

FILL THE MADELEINE PANS Fill the prepared molds with the batter, dividing it evenly among them. Mound the batter down the length of the center of each shell. *Batter position observation* Placing the batter in a slight mound keeps the shape of the batter stable and even as the cakes bake. *Batter amount observation* Dividing the batter among the 17 shell-shaped cavities will produce rounded, well-developed madeleines that, when baked, fill the molds correctly. Some shell-shaped molds are just under 3 inches in length, and if you own these, you may need to fill one or two extra molds.

BAKE AND COOL THE MADELEINES Bake the cakes in the preheated oven for 13 minutes, or until plump, set, and a wooden pick inserted in the middle of a madeleine withdraws clean. The edges of the fully baked cakes will be golden-colored.

Cool the madeleines in the pans on racks for 1 minute, then nudge them out of the pan at one side, using the rounded tip of a flexible palette knife. Place the madeleines, rounded (shell-side) side up, on cooling racks. Cool completely.

Just before serving, sift confectioners' sugar over the tops of the madeleines. The madeleines are best served very fresh, within 4 hours of baking.

❋ *For an aromatic topnote of flavor,* use intensified vanilla extract (see page 52) in place of plain vanilla extract in the madeleine batter.

ALMOND AND DRIED CHERRY TART

One 9-inch tart, creating 8 slices

*T*HE FILLING FOR THIS TART is made with almond paste, almond liqueur, almond extract, and chopped almonds (for flavor), plied with enough butter and eggs (to enrich it) and sufficient cake flour (to build its structure)—the alliance of ingredients creates a mixture that bakes up tender-textured, with a complex almond flavor and the deep, fruity "chew" of dried cherries.

TART DOUGH

Almond Tart Dough, prepared and prebaked (see page 128)

PREPARE THE TART DOUGH AND PREBAKE THE TART SHELL Make the almond tart dough, line the tart pan, and prebake the crust as directed in the recipe for Almond Tart Dough on page 128.

One 8-ounce can almond paste

½ cup unsifted confectioners' sugar

7 tablespoons unsifted bleached cake
flour

1 tablespoon unsalted butter, melted
and cooled

2 large eggs

2 large egg yolks

2 teaspoons almond liqueur, such as
Amaretto

pinch of salt

¾ teaspoon pure almond extract

½ teaspoon pure vanilla extract

⅔ cup very coarsely chopped dried
cherries, preferably the tart variety

¼ cup coarsely chopped, skinned
almonds, lightly toasted and cooled

Confectioners' sugar, for sprinkling on
the baked tart (optional)

BAKEWARE

fluted 9½-inch tart pan (with a
removable bottom)

PREHEAT THE OVEN Preheat the oven to 350° F.

*MIX THE ALMOND PASTE AND DRIED CHERRY TART FILL-
ING* Prepare the filling while the tart shell is baking. Crumble the
almond paste into the work bowl of a food processor fitted with
the steel knife. Cover and process for 10 seconds, using on-off
pulses, to break up the paste into small bits. Add the confectioners' sugar and cake flour, cover, and process, using quick 2-second
on-off pulses, for 10 to 15 seconds or until the ingredients are
combined. Uncover, and add the melted butter, whole eggs, egg
yolks, almond liqueur, salt, and almond and vanilla extracts. Cover
and process for 25 to 30 seconds, or until thoroughly combined
and smooth, stopping once or twice to scrape down the sides
of the container with a rubber spatula to keep the filling
even-textured.

Scrape the almond and egg mixture into a mixing bowl. Stir
in the dried cherries and almonds.

*FILL THE TART SHELL WITH THE ALMOND AND CHERRY
FILLING* Spoon the filling into the tart shell. Smooth over the
top, using a small, flexible palette knife.

BAKE AND COOL THE TART Bake the tart in the preheated oven
for 30 minutes, or until firmly soft and set. Transfer to a cooling
rack. Cool completely. Carefully release the tart from the outer
ring, leaving it on its base. Sprinkle the tart crust edge with confectioners' sugar, if you
wish. Cut the tart into pie-shaped wedges for serving.

BEST BAKING ADVICE

*Process the tart filling until just smooth. It
must be smooth, but not over-processed,
so that the filling bakes evenly. Bake the
tart as soon as it is filled to preserve the
texture of the filling.*

ALMOND TART DOUGH

One 9½-inch tart crust

A̲N EGG YOLK-ENRICHED COOKIE DOUGH makes a tender tart crust for enclosing all kinds of fillings. This one, endowed with ground almonds and almond
extract, acts as a flavoring "envelope" for the almond and dried
cherry tart filling on page 127. The dough can be made in the
work bowl of a food processor fitted with the steel knife or by
hand, and the method for each is outlined below.

ALMOND TART DOUGH

1¼ cups unsifted bleached all-purpose
flour

⅛ teaspoon salt

⅛ teaspoon freshly grated nutmeg

½ cup ground almonds

¼ cup plus 1 tablespoon
confectioners' sugar

¼ pound (8 tablespoons or 1 stick)
unsalted butter, cool but still firm,
cut into tablespoon chunks

3 large egg yolks

½ teaspoon pure vanilla extract

½ teaspoon pure almond extract

BAKEWARE

fluted 9½-inch tart pan (with a
removable bottom)

TO MAKE THE ALMOND TART DOUGH IN A FOOD PROCES-
SOR Place the flour, salt, and nutmeg in the work bowl of a food
processor fitted with the steel knife. Cover and process, using a few
quick on-off pulses, until combined, 3 to 4 seconds. Uncover, add
the almonds and confectioners' sugar, cover, and process for 4 to 5
seconds to incorporate the ingredients. Uncover, add the chunks
of butter, cover, and process for about 30 seconds, using quick on-
off pulses, until the fat is reduced to small bits about the size of
dried lentils.

In a small mixing bowl, whisk the egg yolks, vanilla extract,
and almond extract. Pour the egg yolk mixture over the tart dough
base, cover, and process for 15 to 30 seconds longer, using on-off pulses, or until the
dough comes together in small, most clumps. Do not process further, or the dough will
be overworked.

Remove the dough from the work bowl of the processor and place on a clean, dry
work surface. Lightly work the large and small clumps of dough into a cohesive cake with
your fingertips, gently kneading it together.

TO MAKE THE ALMOND TART DOUGH BY HAND Combine the flour, salt, and nutmeg in a medium-size mixing bowl. Stir in the ground almonds and sugar. Drop in the
chunks of butter and, using a pastry blender, cut the fat into the almond-flour mixture
until reduced to bits about the size of dried navy beans.

In a small mixing bowl, whisk the egg yolks, vanilla extract, and almond extract. Pour
the egg yolk mixture over the tart dough mixture, and mix lightly with a rubber spatula.

When putting together the dough, work it
lightly until cohesive after adding the egg
yolk–vanilla extract–almond extract–milk
mixture. This dough is modeled after the
Butter Cookie Tart Dough on page 423;
both are buttery and slightly dense, like a
cookie dough, but to preserve the textural
integrity of the dough, the almond version
has more butter and uses confectioners'
sugar to sweeten it.

With your fingertips, work the mixture until it forms a cohesive dough by pressing portions together. *Technique observation* The most effective way to create this cookie-dough style crust is to dip into the mixing bowl, bring up sections of the mixture between your fingertips, and rub it together lightly. If you work lightly, the dough will stay cool; if you are too forceful it will be overworked and greasy.

Turn the fragments of dough onto a work surface. Gather them together into a cake by lightly compressing them.

ROLL OUT THE DOUGH AND REFRIGERATE Place the dough between two sheets of waxed paper and roll into a circle 10 to 10½ inches in diameter. Carefully place the sheet of dough on a cookie sheet and refrigerate for 15 minutes.

LINE THE TART PAN WITH THE DOUGH Remove the sheet of dough from the refrigerator, and peel away the top sheet of waxed paper.

Invert the dough onto the tart pan. Quickly peel off the sheet of waxed paper. Press the dough lightly on the bottom of the pan, then up the fluted sides of the pan. With your thumb, press back a scant ⅛-inch ridge of dough (using the dough that extends past the rim) all around the perimeter of the pan. Roll over the top of the dough with a rolling pin to cut away the excess tart dough (the overhang). Remove the excess dough. Now press on the tucked-in ⅛-inch of dough—all around the pan—to create a slightly thicker reinforcing bottom and top edge.

Prick the bottom of the crust lightly with the tines of a fork in about 10 random places.

REFRIGERATE THE DOUGH-LINED TART PAN Refrigerate the crust for 1½ to 2 hours. (The tart shell can be made in advance and stored in the refrigerator for up to 2 days. To do so, after 1 hour, slide the dough into a large, self-sealing plastic bag and refrigerate.)

PREBAKE THE TART SHELL Preheat the oven to 375° F. Place a cookie sheet on the oven rack about 5 minutes before you are ready to prebake the tart shell.

Line the dough-lined tart pan with a sheet of aluminum foil, pressing the foil very lightly against the bottom and sides of the dough. Firmly pressing the foil against the tart crust would actually bond a thin layer of the crust to the foil, and when you remove the foil insert, some of the crust would cling to it and peel away from the surface. Use a gentle touch.

Fill the lined tart pan with raw rice to about a scant ⅛ inch of the rim. Place on the cookie sheet and bake for 15 minutes. Remove the shell from the oven. Reduce the oven temperature to 350° F. Carefully spoon out about one-third of the rice (or beans), then *gently* lift away the foil with the remaining rice. (Cool the rice completely, then store it for another baking day.)

Return the tart shell to the oven and continue baking for 10 minutes longer, or until light golden around the edges of the tart and set on the bottom. Transfer the tart shell to a cooling rack and let stand for 5 minutes. The tart shell is now ready to be filled.

✳ *For an aromatic topnote of flavor,* use vanilla-scented confectioners' sugar (see page 54) in place of plain confectioners' sugar in the tart dough

ALMOND AND BITTERSWEET CHOCOLATE NUGGET COOKIES

About 33 cookies

THE FLAVORING FRAMEWORK OF BROWN SUGAR, vanilla extract, almond extract, and slivered almonds forms the basis for these intensely rich, candy bar-like cookies.

ALMOND AND BITTERSWEET CHOCOLATE NUGGET COOKIE DOUGH

1⅓ cups plus 3 tablespoons unsifted bleached all-purpose flour

⅛ teaspoon baking soda

⅛ teaspoon cream of tartar

¼ teaspoon salt

¼ pound (8 tablespoons or 1 stick) unsalted butter, softened

2 tablespoons plus 2 teaspoons shortening

⅔ cup firmly packed light brown sugar, sieved if lumpy

⅓ cup granulated sugar

1 large egg

1 teaspoon pure almond extract

¾ teaspoon pure vanilla extract

12 ounces bittersweet chocolate, cut into ½- to ¾-inch nuggets

1 cup lightly packed sweetened flaked coconut

⅔ cup slivered almonds, lightly toasted and cooled completely

BAKEWARE

several cookie sheets

PREHEAT THE OVEN AND PREPARE THE COOKIE SHEETS
Preheat the oven to 325° F. Line the cookie sheets with lengths of cooking parchment paper; set aside.

MIX THE ALMOND AND BITTERSWEET CHOCOLATE NUGGET COOKIE DOUGH Whisk the flour, baking soda, cream of tartar, and salt in a small mixing bowl.

Cream the butter and shortening in the large bowl of a free-standing electric mixer on moderately low speed for 2 minutes. Add the light brown sugar and beat for 1 minute. Add the granulated sugar and beat for a minute longer. Blend in the egg, almond extract, and vanilla extract. Scrape down the sides of the mixing bowl with a rubber spatula to keep the dough even-textured. On low speed, add the whisked flour mixture in two additions, beating just until the particles of flour are absorbed. Work in the chocolate nuggets, coconut, and almonds, using a wooden spoon or flat wooden paddle.

SPOON THE DOUGH ONTO THE PREPARED COOKIE SHEETS
Spoon rounded (not flat) 2-tablespoon-size mounds of dough onto the lined cookie sheets, spacing the mounds about 3 inches apart. Place nine mounds of dough on each sheet.

BAKE AND COOL THE COOKIES Bake the cookies in the pre-heated oven for 16 to 18 minutes, or until just set and pale golden around the edges. Let the cookies stand on the sheets for 2 minutes, then remove them to cooling racks, using a sturdy offset metal spatula. Store the cookies in an airtight tin.

FRESHLY BAKED, THE COOKIES KEEP FOR 3 DAYS.

*a*t once sweet, tart, and fruity, the tang of apricot comes through in doughs and batters as a bright stir-in mixture, filling, spread, or glaze. Dried apricots, glazed apricots, and apricot preserves, used alone or in combination with each other, contribute the most intense accent of flavor. Nuts, particularly almonds and walnuts, and butter, as background ingredients, strengthen and round out the apricot taste.

The concentrated flavor present in dried apricots (and in good glazed apricots) makes them ideal for adding to a moist scone dough and bar cookie batter, or to simmer, puree, and combine with preserves to use as a vigorous filling mixture. Australian glazed apricots and dried California apricots, specifically the Blenheim variety, are superb examples of the fruit that glamorizes what you bake. Both are tender, full of flavor, and best of quality.

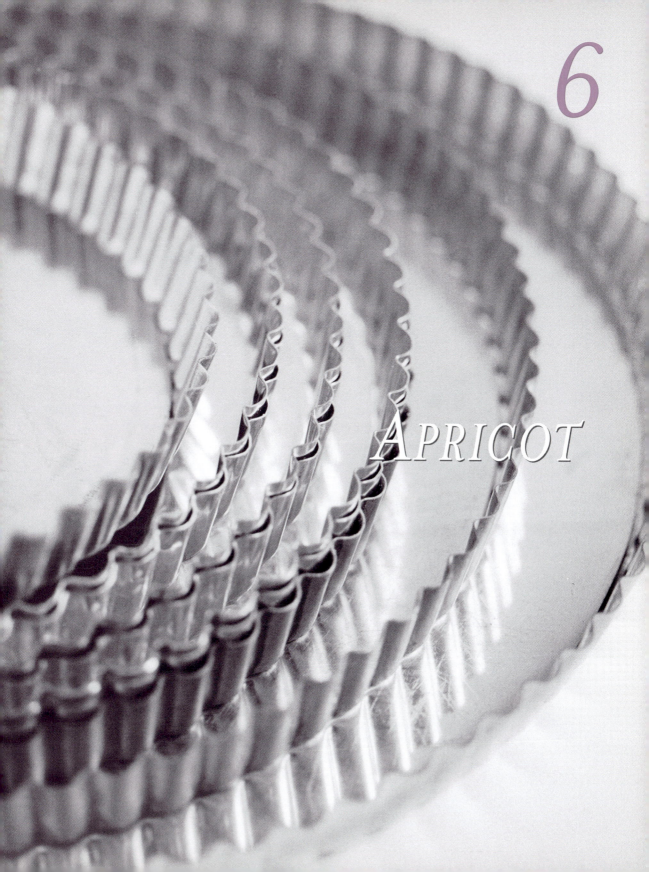

6

APRICOT

APRICOT OATMEAL BREAKFAST SCONES

16 scones

*T*HESE BRIMMING-WITH-OATMEAL-AND-FRUIT SCONES look rugged and taste sublime. The sweet-and-sharp addition of chopped dried apricots is the ingredient that both defines this batch of scones and energizes it, and the apricot glaze is a lustrous, sweetly tart overlay for the breakfast quick bread. On another level, a teaspoon of almond extract, in addition to vanilla extract, sharpens the flavor of the dough by developing the intensity of the fruit.

APRICOT-OATMEAL
SCONE DOUGH

4¼ cups unsifted bleached all-purpose flour

3½ teaspoons baking powder

½ teaspoon baking soda

¾ teaspoon salt

1 teaspoon ground cinnamon

1 teaspoon freshly grated nutmeg

½ teaspoon ground allspice

½ teaspoon ground ginger

¾ cup granulated sugar

¼ cup firmly packed dark brown sugar, sieved if lumpy

1⅓ cups plus 3 tablespoons quick-cooking rolled oats

12 tablespoons (1½ sticks) unsalted butter, cold, cut into tablespoon pieces

4 large eggs

1 cup heavy cream

2 teaspoons pure vanilla extract

1 teaspoon pure almond extract

1½ cups diced moist, dried apricots

⅓ cup golden raisins

About ⅓ cup turbinado sugar, for sprinkling the tops of the unbaked scones (optional, if not using the glaze)

MIX THE APRICOT-OATMEAL SCONE DOUGH Thoroughly whisk the flour, baking powder, baking soda, salt, cinnamon, nutmeg, allspice, ginger, granulated sugar, and dark brown sugar in a large mixing bowl. Stir in the rolled oats. Add the pieces of butter, and using a pastry blender, reduce the butter to small bits about the size of dried lima beans.

In a medium-size mixing bowl, whisk the eggs, heavy cream, and vanilla and almond extracts. Pour the egg-cream blend over the oat mixture, add the diced apricots and raisins, and stir to form a moist, somewhat sticky dough, using a sturdy wooden spoon or flat wooden paddle.

KNEAD THE SCONE DOUGH Turn the dough onto a well-floured work surface and knead very lightly for about 1 minute (about 12 to 15 turns), dusting the dough with flour as necessary to keep it from sticking.

CHILL THE DOUGH Divide the dough into two even portions, place each on a large sheet of waxed paper, and pat into a 7½- to 8-inch round cake. Refrigerate the dough cakes for 30 minutes, or until firm enough to cut.

PREHEAT THE OVEN AND PREPARE THE BAKING SHEETS Preheat the oven to 400° F. Line the cookie sheets or rimmed sheet

APRICOT GLAZE

1 cup apricot preserves

1 teaspoon water

½ teaspoon pure vanilla extract

BAKEWARE

large cookie sheets or rimmed
    sheet pans

BEST BAKING ADVICE

*Knead the dough on a well-floured work
surface until it is easy to handle. Chilling
the cakes of dough before cutting and
baking establishes their texture and shape.*

pans with cooking parchment paper; set aside. The pans need to be heavy to prevent the bottoms of the scones from overbrowning. Double-pan the sheets, if necessary.

FORM THE DOUGH INTO SCONES With a chef's knife, cut each round of dough into eight plump wedges. Using a wide, offset metal spatula, transfer the scones to the lined baking sheets, placing them 3 inches apart and eight to a sheet. If necessary, press back any apricot chunks sticking out of the cut edges. Sprinkle the turbinado sugar evenly over the tops of the scones, if you are using it in place of the apricot glaze.

BAKE AND COOL THE SCONES Bake the scones for 17 to 20 minutes, or until risen, plump, and set. Let the scones stand on the baking sheets for 2 minutes, then remove them to cooling racks, using a wide, offset metal spatula.

MAKE THE APRICOT GLAZE Combine the apricot preserves and water in a small, heavy nonreactive saucepan (preferably enameled cast iron). Bring to the simmer and let the apricot mixture bubble slowly for a minute or two. Remove from the heat and stir in the vanilla extract.

GLAZE THE SCONES Brush the tops of the scones with the warm apricot glaze, using a 1-inch pastry brush. Let the glaze set, which will take about 1 hour. Serve the scones very fresh.

❋ *Turbinado sugar note:* Turbinado sugar, sprinkled on top of the unbaked scones, is a quick and effective topping, if you're not using the apricot glaze. The raw sugar crystals are a beautiful amber color, and they retain their shape and texture during the baking process.

❋ *For an aromatic topnote of flavor,* use vanilla-scented granulated sugar (see page 53) in place of plain granulated sugar, and intensified vanilla extract (see page 52) in place of plain vanilla extract in the scone dough.

❋ *For a textural contrast,* add ⅔ cup coarsely chopped walnuts to the dough mixture along with the diced apricots and raisins.

FRESHLY BAKED, THE SCONES KEEP FOR **2** TO **3** DAYS.

GLAZED APRICOT, ALMOND, AND CHOCOLATE TORTE

One 9-inch cake, creating 8 slices

BITS OF TART AND CHEWY GLAZED APRICOTS are scattered throughout this dense chocolate torte—the cake batter itself is draped in butter and chocolate, and tempered with dashes of slivered, toasted almonds.

Softened unsalted butter, for preparing the cake pan

GLAZED APRICOT STIR-IN

¾ cup diced glazed apricots (cut the sticky apricots with sharp kitchen scissors)

1 teaspoon unsweetened, alkalized cocoa

CHOCOLATE TORTE BATTER

1 cup unsifted bleached all-purpose flour

⅓ cup unsifted bleached cake flour

¼ teaspoon baking powder

½ teaspoon salt

½ pound (16 tablespoons or 2 sticks) unsalted butter, melted and cooled to tepid

4 ounces (4 squares) unsweetened chocolate, melted and cooled to tepid

3 ounces bittersweet chocolate, melted and cooled to tepid

4 large eggs

1¾ cups granulated sugar

2 teaspoons pure vanilla extract

½ teaspoon pure almond extract

PREHEAT THE OVEN AND PREPARE THE CAKE PAN Preheat the oven to 325° F. Butter the inside of the springform pan.

MAKE THE GLAZED APRICOT STIR-IN Scatter the apricot pieces on a sheet of waxed paper, sprinkle over the cocoa to coat the fruit lightly, and set aside.

MIX THE CHOCOLATE TORTE BATTER Sift the all-purpose flour, cake flour, baking powder, and salt onto a sheet of waxed paper.

Whisk the melted butter, melted unsweetened chocolate, and melted bittersweet chocolate in a medium-size bowl until the ingredients are completely combined. In a large mixing bowl, whisk the eggs until lightly beaten. Add the granulated sugar and continue whisking for 1 minute, or until just combined; blend in the whisked butter-chocolate mixture. Blend in the vanilla and almond extracts. Whisk in the sifted flour mixture, until absorbed. *Batter observation* At this point, the batter will be moderately thick and slightly shiny. Stir in the cocoa-dusted apricot pieces and almonds.

Scrape the batter into the prepared cake pan. Smooth over the top with a rubber spatula.

BAKE AND COOL THE TORTE Place the torte on a cookie sheet (or rimmed sheet pan) and bake in the preheated oven for 45 to 50 minutes, or until set. There will be a few hairline cracks on the top of the torte. Cool the cake in the pan on a rack. Release the sides when completely cool. Place a sheet of waxed paper under the cooling rack to catch any drips of glaze.

⅓ cup slivered almonds, lightly toasted and cooled completely

¾ cup plus 2 tablespoons apricot preserves

¼ teaspoon pure almond extract

BAKEWARE

9-inch springform pan, 2¾ inches deep

MAKE THE GLAZE Place the apricot preserves in a small, heavy nonreactive saucepan (preferably enameled cast iron). Set over moderately high heat and bring to a rapid simmer, stirring occasionally. Strain the preserves through a medium-size, fine-meshed sieve into a heatproof bowl. Stir in the almond extract. Use the glaze immediately. (If made in advance, pour and scrape the glaze back into the rinsed and dried saucepan and reheat to a gentle simmer.)

GLAZE THE TORTE Using a 1-inch-wide pastry brush, daub the warm glaze onto the top and sides of the torte. Let the glaze set for at least 1 hour before cutting the torte into slices for serving. *Slicing observation* Use a serrated knife to cut the torte neatly and cleanly.

❋ *For an aromatic topnote of flavor,* use vanilla-scented granulated sugar (see page 53) in place of plain granulated sugar in the cake batter.

APRICOT SANDWICH COOKIES

About 4 dozen cookies

FOR ME, THE FINEST SANDWICH COOKIE is composed of nut butter cookie rounds held together by a sweet-tart apricot preserve filling. For any baker who loves a project, consider this recipe. A butter dough needs to be mixed, rolled, and chilled (or frozen) before cutting and baking. Half of the dough is cut into precise scalloped rounds, and the other half into the same size rounds with smaller rounds cut out of the centers, in order to reveal the filling when the cookies are formed. The cooled rounds are then filled and assembled. To complete your handiwork, dust the rim of each sandwiched cookie with a little confectioners' sugar just before serving.

After many afternoons of baking, I learned the secret to making sandwich cookies that don't turn soggy once they've been filled: The key is to apply a warm, previously simmered filling over the surface of the cooled bottom cookies, for this technique keeps them firm, tender, and fresh-tasting.

For more than 15 years now, Apricot Sandwich Cookies have remained one of my very favorite sweets to pile into my Christmas cookie tins.

PECAN BUTTER COOKIE DOUGH

4½ cups unsifted bleached all-purpose flour

1 teaspoon baking soda

1¼ teaspoons salt

¾ teaspoon ground cinnamon

¾ teaspoon freshly grated nutmeg

1 pound (4 sticks) unsalted butter, softened

1 cup less 1 tablespoon granulated sugar

2½ teaspoons pure vanilla extract

2 cups coarsely ground pecans

APRICOT FILLING

One 18-ounce jar apricot preserves

2 teaspoons lemon juice

1 tablespoon water

½ teaspoon pure vanilla extract

Confectioners' sugar, for sifting over the tops of the assembled cookies (optional)

BAKEWARE

several cookie sheets

MIX THE PECAN BUTTER COOKIE DOUGH Sift the flour, baking soda, salt, cinnamon, and nutmeg onto a sheet of waxed paper.

Cream the butter in the large bowl of a freestanding electric mixer on low speed for 3 minutes. Add the granulated sugar in three additions, beating for 30 seconds on moderate speed after each portion is added. Blend in the vanilla extract and pecans. On low speed, mix in the sifted mixture in three additions, beating just until the particles of flour are absorbed. *Dough texture observation* The dough will be moderately soft.

DIVIDE AND ROLL THE COOKIE DOUGH Cut the dough into four equal parts. Roll each portion of dough between two sheets of waxed paper to a thickness of a scant ¼ inch. *Rolling observation* The cookie dough must be rolled out smoothly and evenly if it is to bake properly. Stack the lengths of rolled-out dough on a cookie sheet; refrigerate overnight or freeze for 3 to 4 hours, or until firm enough to handle. (The cookie dough can be refrigerated, enclosed in plastic wrap once firm, for up to 3 days before cutting and baking.)

MAKE THE APRICOT FILLING Spoon the preserves into a medium-size nonreactive saucepan. Stir in the lemon juice, water, and vanilla extract. Bring to the boil, stirring often. Boil slowly for 1 minute. Strain the preserves through a fine-meshed stainless steel sieve, firmly pressing down on the solids with a rubber spatula. (The apricot filling can be made 2 to 3 weeks in advance; refrigerate it in a tightly covered container.) Use the filling warm, as described below.

PREHEAT THE OVEN AND PREPARE THE COOKIE SHEETS Preheat the oven to 350° F. Line the cookie sheets with lengths of cooking parchment paper.

ROLL AND CUT THE DOUGH One rolled-out portion of chilled dough at a time, quickly and carefully peel away both sheets of waxed paper. Place the dough on a lightly floured work surface and, using a 2-inch scalloped cookie cutter, cut the dough into rounds. Place the rounds, about 2 inches apart, on the lined sheets.

BAKE THE COOKIE ROUNDS Bake the cookies for 12 to 14 minutes, or until firm, set, and light golden. Let the cookies stand on the sheet for 3 to 5 minutes, then remove them to cooling racks, using a wide, offset metal spatula. Cool completely.

FILL AND ASSEMBLE THE COOKIES Reheat the strained apricot filling slowly until bubbly in a small- to medium-size nonreactive saucepan. Remove from the heat and cool to warm. Using a flexible palette knife, spread a little of the warm apricot filling carefully over the surface of a baked cookie and place another cookie round on top, pressing down lightly. Let the filled cookies stand on a cooling rack to firm up. *Filling observation* Always spread warm apricot filling over the baked cookie rounds; bring it to the simmer again, as necessary. The warm filling won't create soggy cookies; room-temperature (or cold) filling will dampen the wonderfully tender cookie rounds. Store the cookies in an airtight tin, with waxed paper separating the layers. Just before serving, lightly sift confectioners' sugar over the tops of the cookies, if you wish.

❋ *For an aromatic topnote of flavor,* use vanilla-scented granulated sugar (see page 53) in place of plain granulated sugar in the cookie dough.

FRESHLY BAKED, THE COOKIES KEEP FOR 5 TO 7 DAYS.

Variation: The dough for the apricot sandwich cookies can be made with ground walnuts instead of ground pecans.

APRICOT BABKA

Three coffee cakes, each measuring about 6½ inches in diameter

*D*ICED DRIED APRICOTS and an apricot glaze are the defining flavor presence in these gorgeous coffee cakes. Baking the babkas in deep, swirled pans gives the individual cakes a regal look, and the crowning finish of a shiny glaze makes them so inviting.

Softened unsalted butter, for preparing the baking pans

RUM-SUFFUSED DRIED
FRUIT MIXTURE

1 cup lightly packed dried (but moist) apricots, diced

¾ cup golden raisins

½ cup dried cherries, very coarsely chopped if large

3 tablespoons light rum

SPICED YEAST DOUGH

1 tablespoon plus 2½ teaspoons active dry yeast

1¼ teaspoons granulated sugar

⅓ cup warm (110° F.) water

1 cup milk

¾ cup granulated sugar

1 tablespoon pure vanilla extract

8 large egg yolks, lightly beaten in a small bowl

6 cups unsifted unbleached all-purpose flour, plus extra for kneading

1¼ teaspoons freshly grated nutmeg

¾ teaspoon ground cinnamon

¾ teaspoon ground cardamom

¼ teaspoon ground allspice

MARINATE THE DRIED FRUIT IN RUM Place the diced apricots, raisins, and cherries in a medium-size nonreactive bowl. Toss with the rum and let the fruit marinate, uncovered, for at least 1 hour or up to 6 hours.

MAKE THE SPICED YEAST DOUGH Combine the yeast and 1¼ teaspoons granulated sugar in a small heatproof bowl. Stir in the water and let stand for 8 minutes, or until the yeast foams and swells.

In the meantime, place the milk and ¾ cup granulated sugar in a small saucepan and set over moderately low heat. When the sugar has melted, remove from the heat and stir in the vanilla extract; cool to 110° F. Blend the egg yolks and swollen yeast mixture into the milk mixture.

Place 2 cups of flour in a large mixing bowl. Pour the yeast-milk-egg yolk mixture over the flour. Stir to form a batter.

SET THE BATTER TO RISE AND GENTLY DEFLATE Cover the bowl with plastic wrap and let stand in a cozy spot for 45 minutes. This batter mixture should be lightly bubbly and increased a little less than doubled in volume. Creating a preliminary batter helps to develop the internal texture and keeping qualities of the coffee cake. Gently deflate the risen batter by stirring it down with a sturdy wooden spoon or flat wooden paddle.

COMPLETE THE DOUGH Combine 2 cups of flour with the nutmeg, cinnamon, cardamom, allspice, and salt. Stir into the yeast mixture, ½ cup at a time. Stir in 1 cup of the flour, making this a

¾ teaspoon salt

½ pound (16 tablespoons or 2 sticks) unsalted butter, cut into chunks, softened

1 12-ounce jar apricot preserves

2 teaspoons fresh lemon juice

1½ teaspoons water

1 large egg

2 teaspoons milk

¼ teaspoon pure vanilla extract

Whole glazed apricots, for decorating the top of the babkas (optional)

three 6½-inch by 3½-inch-deep fluted tube pans with 5-cup capacity

full 5 cups of flour in the dough. *Dough texture observation* The dough will be shaggy-textured at this point.

With a sturdy wooden spoon, vigorously work in the softened butter, 2 tablespoons at a time. Alternatively, place the dough in a heavy-duty, freestanding electric mixer fitted with the dough hook and add the butter, a few pieces at a time, while beating the dough on moderate speed. Add the last cup of flour, ¼ cup at a time, mixing with a wooden spoon and your hands; the dough should be slightly sticky.

Turn out the dough onto a very lightly floured work surface. Knead the dough for 7 to 10 minutes, or until smooth-textured, supple, and bouncy. Use a dough scraper to lift up the dough as it is kneaded.

SET THE DOUGH TO RISE Turn the dough into a large buttered bowl and turn to coat in the butter. Cut several deep slashes in the dough with a clean pair of kitchen scissors. Cover the bowl tightly with plastic wrap and let rise at room temperature for 1 hour and 30 minutes, or until doubled in bulk.

DEFLATE THE DOUGH AND WORK IN THE MARINATED FRUIT Deflate the dough by gently pressing down on the middle and sides with the cupped palms of your hands. Turn out the dough onto a lightly floured work surface and press into a rough square, about 16 by 16 inches. Scatter the fruit onto the dough, pressing it down gently. Roll up the dough into a loose jellyroll, fold in half, and knead lightly to distribute the fruit, about 3 minutes. *Dough texture observation* Initially, as you are kneading the dough, it will feel slightly slick, and the fruit will break through here and there.

Leave the dough on the work surface, cover with plastic wrap, and let stand for 15 minutes to relax the dough. *Dough resting time observation* Allowing the dough to rest makes it easier to roll and form into coffee cakes without it recoiling or shrinking in the pans.

MAKE THE APRICOT GLAZE Place the apricot preserves, lemon juice, and water in a medium-size nonreactive saucepan, and heat until the preserves melt down. Stir occasionally. Bring the contents of the saucepan to a low boil; boil for 2 minutes. Strain the preserves through a fine-meshed sieve into a small nonreactive saucepan; set aside.

PREPARE THE BAKING PANS AND FORM THE BABKAS Lightly butter the inside of the tube pans.

Divide the dough into three even portions. Roll each into a cylinder measuring 10 to 12 inches long, form into a circle, and pinch together the ends. Place each cylinder in a prepared pan, pressing down lightly. Cover each pan loosely with a sheet of plastic wrap and let rise at room temperature for 1 hour and 30 minutes, or until the dough rises to the top (or slightly above) of each baking pan.

MAKE THE VANILLA-SCENTED EGG GLAZE Whisk the egg, milk, and vanilla extract in a small mixing bowl.

GLAZE AND BAKE THE BABKAS Preheat the oven to 350° F. in advance of baking. Gently brush the egg glaze over the tops of the risen babkas.

Bake the babkas for 35 to 40 minutes, or until plump and the top sounds hollow when carefully tapped with a wooden spoon. If the babkas appear to be browning too quickly midway through baking, place a loose tent of aluminum foil over the top of each.

COOL, UNMOLD, AND GLAZE THE BABKAS Let the babkas stand in the pans on cooling racks for 5 to 7 minutes.

Carefully invert the babkas onto cooling racks and unmold them. Bring the glaze to a simmer, and simmer for 2 minutes. Using a 1-inch-wide pastry brush, paint the top and sides of each warm babka with the warm glaze.

While the glaze is still warm and sticky, garnish the top of each babka with a concentric ring of glazed apricots, if you wish. Let the babkas stand until completely cool and the glaze has set, about 2 hours, before slicing. *Slicing observation* Use a serrated knife to cut the babka neatly and cleanly. Store the babkas in airtight containers.

❊ *For a textural contrast,* just before scattering the rum-suffused fruit on the dough, toss ⅔ cup coarsely chopped walnuts with the fruit.

FRESHLY BAKED, THE BABKAS KEEP FOR **2** DAYS.

Brown Sugar–Apricot Bars

2 dozen bar cookies

Nonstick cooking spray, for preparing the baking pan

Preserve-sweetened apricots

1 cup coarsely chopped dried apricots

1½ tablespoons apricot preserves

Brown sugar-coconut-walnut batter

½ cup unsifted bleached all-purpose flour

¼ cup plus 2 tablespoons unsifted cake flour

¼ teaspoon baking powder

¼ teaspoon salt

½ teaspoon freshly grated nutmeg

¼ teaspoon ground cinnamon

⅛ teaspoon ground cardamom

¼ pound (8 tablespoons or 1 stick) unsalted butter, melted and cooled to tepid

⅔ cup firmly packed light brown sugar, sieved if lumpy

¼ cup plus 1 tablespoon granulated sugar

2 large eggs

2 teaspoons pure vanilla extract

½ cup lightly packed sweetened flaked coconut

⅔ cup chopped walnuts, lightly toasted and cooled

Bakeware

9 by 9 by 2-inch baking pan

Best baking advice

Combine the dried apricots with the apricot preserves to coat the fruit thoroughly.

Dried apricots, chopped and seasoned with apricot preserves, turn a buttery, coconut-charged bar cookie batter into a tart, chewy-with-fruit sweet. The technique of coating the apricots in a light veneer of preserves is a good way to underscore the flavor of the fruit.

Preheat the oven and prepare the baking pan Preheat the oven to 350° F. Film the inside of the baking pan with nonstick cooking spray; set aside.

Make the preserve-sweetened apricots In a small nonreactive mixing bowl, mix the chopped apricots and apricot preserves. Set aside.

Make the brown sugar-coconut-walnut batter Sift the all-purpose flour, cake flour, baking powder, salt, nutmeg, cinnamon, and cardamom onto a sheet of waxed paper.

Combine the melted butter, light brown sugar, and granulated sugar in a large mixing bowl, using a flat wooden paddle. Blend in the eggs and vanilla extract. Add the sifted flour mixture and stir to form a batter, using a rubber spatula. Blend in the coconut, walnuts, and dried apricot-apricot preserves mixture.

Scrape the batter into the prepared baking pan. Smooth over the top with a rubber spatula.

Bake, cool, and cut the bars Bake the sweet in the preheated oven for 25 minutes, or until golden on top and just set. Transfer the pan to a cooling rack. Cool completely. Cut the entire cake into four quarters, then cut each quarter into six bars, using a small, sharp knife. Remove the bars from the baking pan, using a small, offset metal spatula. Store in an airtight tin.

Freshly baked, the bar cookies keep for 3 days.

APRICOT THUMBPRINT COOKIES

About 4½ dozen cookies

THE LITTLE POOLS OF BAKED-IN APRICOT PRESERVES distinguish these pretty walnut and butter tea cookies. The dough is seasoned lightly with cinnamon and nutmeg, which accentuate the taste of both the nuts and the preserves. I've used this recipe for years and years, and fill up Christmas cookie tins with batches of this homey cookie.

WALNUT BUTTER COOKIE DOUGH

2½ cups unsifted bleached all-purpose flour

½ teaspoon baking powder

½ teaspoon salt

½ teaspoon freshly grated nutmeg

¼ teaspoon ground cinnamon

½ pound (16 tablespoons or 2 sticks) unsalted butter, softened

¾ cup superfine sugar

2 large egg yolks

2½ teaspoons pure vanilla extract

¾ cup finely chopped walnuts

EGG WHITES AND WALNUTS FOR ROLLING THE BALLS OF DOUGH

3 large egg whites, lightly beaten to mix, in a small, shallow bowl

About 1½ cups finely chopped walnuts, in a small, shallow bowl

About 1 cup apricot preserves, for filling the thumbprints

Confectioners' sugar, for sprinkling over baked cookies

BAKEWARE

several cookie sheets

PREHEAT THE OVEN AND PREPARE THE COOKIE SHEETS Preheat the oven to 375° F. Line the cookie sheets with lengths of cooking parchment paper; set aside.

MIX THE WALNUT BUTTER COOKIE DOUGH Sift the all-purpose flour, baking powder, salt, nutmeg, and cinnamon onto a sheet of waxed paper.

Cream the butter in the large bowl of a freestanding electric mixer on low speed for 2 minutes. Add the superfine sugar and beat for 2 to 3 minutes on moderately low speed. Blend in the egg yolks and vanilla extract. Blend in the ¾ cup chopped walnuts. On low speed, add the sifted flour mixture in two additions, beating until the particles of flour are absorbed and large and small curds of dough are formed. Scrape down the sides of the mixing bowl frequently with a rubber spatula to keep the dough even-textured.

Remove the bowl from the mixing stand. Using a rubber spatula, work the mixture until it forms a cohesive dough. Knead the dough lightly in the bowl for 30 to 45 seconds. *Dough consistency observation* The dough should be workable, buttery, and moist but not sticky.

FORM AND FILL THE THUMBPRINT COOKIES Have the beaten egg whites, chopped walnuts, and apricot preserves at hand. Spoon up heaping 2-teaspoon quantities of dough and roll into plump balls. Roll the balls very lightly into the beaten egg whites, then generously into the chopped walnuts, and place them, 2½ to 3 inches apart, on the lined cookie sheets. Arrange 10 to 12 cookies on each sheet. With your thumb (or the rounded end of a wooden dowel or rounded handle-end of a small wooden spoon), make even, deep, and round indentations in the center of the cookies. Fill the depressions with apricot preserves, using a demitasse spoon.

BAKE AND COOL THE COOKIES Bake the cookies for 12 to 14 minutes, or until set and golden in color. Remove the cookies to cooling racks, using a small, metal offset spatula. Cool completely. Store in an airtight tin. Just before serving, sprinkle the confectioners' sugar over the nut-encrusted edges of the cookies.

BAKED COOKIE APPEARANCE OBSERVATION You will find that once the cookies are baked, the apricot preserve filling actually sinks in a bit, although it looks full before baking. The full look can be restored by heating about ½ cup apricot preserves to a rapid simmer for about 1 minute. While the cookies are still warm, and on the cooling rack, carefully refill the slight cavities by carefully spooning in a little of the warm preserves. *Preserve temperature observation* The reason for using hot, previously simmered preserves is to avoid making the cookies soggy. The simmered preserves set correctly, just as if baked, and can't seep into the cookies and dampen them. Filling the slight cookie depressions is an optional, but visually enhancing, step.

❋ *For an aromatic topnote of flavor,* use vanilla-scented superfine sugar (see page 54) in place of plain superfine sugar in the cookie dough.

FRESHLY BAKED, THE COOKIES KEEP FOR 3 TO 4 DAYS.

Variation: The apricot thumbprint cookies can be made with finely chopped pecans instead of walnuts. Substitute the same amounts of pecans in the butter cookie dough and in the quantity of finely chopped nuts used for rolling the cookies.

APRICOT SCHNECKEN

About 3 dozen sweet rolls

Schnecken, or snails, are small, rich pastries filled with cinnamon, spices, and chopped nuts, and occasionally, a creamy cheese spread or fruit butter (or preserves), raisins, and generous sprinklings of spiced sugar. These sweet yeast rolls are made with a moderately dense but buttery yeast dough that first rises at cool room temperature, then overnight in the refrigerator. The longer, slower rise in the refrigerator builds the texture of the pastries, and, coupled with the finishing rise once the schnecken are assembled, keeps them moist and beautifully textured.

Nonstick cooking spray, for preparing the muffin cups

BUTTER AND SOUR CREAM YEAST DOUGH

3 teaspoons active dry yeast

¾ teaspoon granulated sugar

¼ cup warm (110° to 115° F.) water

¼ cup milk

⅓ cup granulated sugar

1 cup thick, cultured sour cream

1 tablespoon pure vanilla extract

4 large egg yolks

4¾ cups plus 1 tablespoon unsifted unbleached all-purpose flour

¾ teaspoon salt

14 tablespoons (1¾ sticks) unsalted butter, softened, cut into tablespoon chunks

APRICOT, CINNAMON, AND GOLDEN RAISIN FILLING FOR SPREADING ON THE ROLLED-OUT YEAST DOUGH

Luxurious Apricot Spread (see page 149)

⅓ cup granulated sugar blended with 2 teaspoons ground cinnamon

1 cup golden raisins

HONEY-BUTTER UNDERCOATING

½ pound (16 tablespoons or 2 sticks) unsalted butter, softened

MAKE THE BUTTER AND SOUR CREAM YEAST DOUGH Combine the yeast and ¾ teaspoon granulated sugar in a small heatproof bowl. Stir in the warm water and let stand until the yeast dissolves and the mixture is swollen, 7 to 8 minutes.

Place the milk and ⅓ cup sugar in a small, heavy saucepan set over low heat to dissolve the granulated sugar. Remove from the heat and cool to 115° F. Combine the sour cream, cooled sugar-milk mixture, vanilla extract, and egg yolks in a medium-size mixing bowl. Stir in the swollen yeast mixture.

Combine 3 cups flour and the salt in a large mixing bowl. Add the yeast-sour cream mixture and stir well, using a sturdy wooden spoon or flat wooden paddle. At this point, the mixture will be a thick, heavy, very elastic batter. Work in the butter, 2 tablespoons at a time, kneading it in with your fingers. Sprinkle over 1 cup flour, ¼ cup at a time, mixing it in with a spatula or paddle. The dough will be very soft at this point.

Transfer the dough to the bowl of a heavy-duty, freestanding electric mixer fitted with the dough hook. Sprinkle over ¾ cup of flour, ¼ cup at a time, mixing on low speed until the flour is

½ cup granulated sugar

½ cup firmly packed light brown sugar, sieved if lumpy

1 tablespoon ground cinnamon

⅓ cup mild honey (such as clover)

1 cup walnut halves and pieces, for scattering on top of the honey-butter undercoating

BAKEWARE

3 standard (12-cup) muffin pans, each cup measuring about 2¾ inches in diameter and 1⅜ inches deep

absorbed into the dough. Knead the dough for 5 minutes, or until very smooth and elastic.

Remove the bowl from the mixer, sprinkle over the remaining 1 tablespoon flour, and lightly knead the dough in the bowl with your hands for 1 minute. *Dough texture observation* The dough will be soft, smooth, and supple.

SET THE DOUGH TO RISE AT COOL ROOM TEMPERATURE Place the dough in a self-sealing 1-gallon plastic bag. Let the dough rise at cool room temperature for 2½ hours, or until puffy. With your fingertips, lightly compress the dough to deflate.

CHILL THE DOUGH OVERNIGHT Refrigerate the dough overnight, compressing the dough two or three times during the first 5 hours of chilling.

ASSEMBLE THE APRICOT SPREAD, SPICED SUGAR, AND GOLDEN RAISINS On baking day, place the apricot spread, cinnamon-sugar, and golden raisins in separate work bowls, and have at hand.

MAKE THE HONEY-BUTTER UNDERCOATING Beat the butter, granulated sugar, light brown sugar, cinnamon, and honey in a medium-size mixing bowl until smooth and spreadable. Set aside.

PREPARE THE MUFFIN PANS Film the inside of the muffin cups with nonstick cooking spray; set aside. Have the 1 cup walnut halves and pieces at hand.

COAT THE MUFFIN CUPS WITH THE HONEY-BUTTER MIXTURE AND DOT THE FILLING WITH THE WALNUTS Place a spoonful of the honey butter mixture on the bottom of each muffin cup, dividing it evenly among all the cups. Scatter the walnuts on the butter mixture, pressing them down as you go.

ROLL THE DOUGH, FILL, AND CUT THE SCHNECKEN Place the chilled dough on a floured work surface. Lightly flour a rolling pan. Roll out the dough into a sheet measuring about 17 by 17 inches. Smooth the apricot spread on the surface of the dough, using a flexible palette knife or rubber spatula. Sprinkle over the cinnamon sugar. Scatter over the raisins. With the underside of a firm, metal offset spatula (or your fingertips), press down the raisins lightly so that they adhere to the dough. Roll the dough into a long jellyroll. Pinch the long seam and two ends closed. Shape the roll into a coil measuring 4½ inches wide and 17 inches long, by patting it with the cupped palms of your hands.

Best baking advice
Let the butter and sour cream yeast dough rise at cool room temperature, long and slow, for the best texture. Mix the honey-butter mixture for the undercoating thoroughly so that the honey mixture bakes smoothly and doesn't bead up. Form each chunk of filled schnecken dough into a round, pinching the edges together so that the filling is contained. Bake the schnecken until nicely golden to avoid centers that are gummy or sticky.

Cut the dough in half down the length, using a sharp chef's knife. Cut the strips into a total of 36 chunks. Lightly form each chunk into a round spiral by pressing the cut ends together.

Place each slice, cut side down, into a prepared muffin cup, and press down lightly.

Set the schnecken to rise Cover each pan loosely with a sheet of plastic wrap. Let the pastries rise at cool room temperature for 1 hour and 45 minutes to 2 hours and 15 minutes. *Risen schnecken observation* The schnecken should look puffy and full.

Preheat the oven and bake the schnecken Have three rimmed baking sheets or jellyroll pans at hand. Preheat the oven to 375° F. in advance of baking. Remove and discard the sheets of plastic wrap covering the pans. Place each pan of pastries on a baking sheet (to catch any drips of the bubbly honey butter) and bake for 30 to 35 minutes, or until set and golden. To bake the pastries in shifts (depending upon oven space), keep one pan of risen schnecken in the refrigerator while the first two pans bake.

Cool the schnecken Let the schnecken stand in the pans on cooling racks for 8 to 10 minutes. Carefully lift out each pastry, using the rounded tip of a flexible palette knife, and place on a rimmed sheet pan, bottom side up. Make sure your hands are protected (wear food-safe protective gloves) when handling the hot schnecken, for the honey-butter undercoating turns into a very hot glaze. With a flexible spatula, spread any glaze (and nuts) lingering on the bottom of the muffin cups onto the tops of the schnecken. Cool for 30 minutes. Serve the schnecken very fresh, slightly warm or at room temperature.

❊ *For an aromatic topnote of flavor,* use vanilla-scented granulated sugar (see page 53) in place of plain granulated sugar and intensified vanilla extract (see page 52) in place of plain vanilla extract in the yeast dough.

Freshly baked, the schnecken keep for 3 to 4 days.

LUXURIOUS APRICOT SPREAD

2 cups

Schnecken in particular, and sweet yeast doughs in general, want aggressively seasoned fillings. To build the intensity of an apricot spread, worthy of slathering over an opulent butter and sour cream yeast dough, you must mix a concentrated dried apricot mixture with apricot preserves, and illuminate the mixture with lemon peel and vanilla extract.

DRIED APRICOT AND APRICOT PRESERVES SPREAD

½ pound moist, dried apricots

3 slender strips lemon rind

¾ cup water

¼ cup plus 1½ tablespoons superfine sugar

1 cup apricot preserves

½ teaspoon pure vanilla extract

COOK AND COOL THE DRIED APRICOTS Combine the dried apricots, lemon rind strips, water, and superfine sugar in a medium-size nonreactive saucepan. Cover and cook over moderate heat until the sugar dissolves completely, 3 to 4 minutes. Bring the contents of the saucepan to a simmer, simmer 1 minute uncovered, then cover and simmer for 20 minutes, or until the apricots are very tender.

Spoon the apricot mixture, including the syrup liquid left in the saucepan, into a nonreactive bowl and cool for 15 minutes. *Cooked apricots appearance observation* The apricots will be glossy and soft.

PUREE THE DRIED APRICOT MIXTURE Turn the contents of the saucepan (including the strips of lemon peel) into the work bowl of a food processor fitted with the steel knife. Cover and process, using short on-off bursts, for 1 minute, or until pureed. *Texture observation* Very small chunks of fruit will remain, here and there, in the puree. There should be about 1½ cups of puree.

COMBINE THE DRIED APRICOT MIXTURE WITH THE PRESERVES AND FLAVORING EXTRACT TO CREATE THE SPREAD Thoroughly blend together the apricot puree, apricot preserves, and vanilla extract. Scrape the spread into a storage container, cover tightly, and cool for 30 minutes. Refrigerate for at least 2 hours before using. (The spread may be made up to 1 week in advance and stored in the refrigerator. Remove the spread from the refrigerator about 20 minutes before using; use cool, but not cold.)

APRICOT AND HAZELNUT TART

One 8½-inch tart, creating 8 slices

A LIGHTLY LEAVENED HAZELNUT COOKIE DOUGH forms the buttery base for a top coat of apricot preserves and cut-outs of dough. The combination of nutty dough and tangy, sweet-tart preserves is delicious. This is one of my favorite tarts to bake during the winter holidays.

HAZELNUT BUTTER COOKIE DOUGH

1⅓ cups plus 2 teaspoons unsifted bleached all-purpose flour

2 tablespoons unsifted bleached cake flour

½ teaspoon baking powder

⅛ teaspoon salt

¼ teaspoon ground cinnamon

¼ teaspoon freshly grated nutmeg

¼ pound (8 tablespoons or 1 stick) unsalted butter, softened

¾ cup granulated sugar

2 large egg yolks

2 teaspoons pure vanilla extract

⅓ cup hazelnut flour

APRICOT PRESERVES LAYER

⅔ cup plus 2 tablespoons apricot preserves

¼ teaspoon pure vanilla extract

Confectioners' sugar, for sifting on top of the baked tart (optional)

BAKEWARE

fluted 8½-inch round tart pan (with removable bottom)

PREHEAT THE OVEN AND PREPARE THE BAKING PAN Preheat the oven to 350° F. Have the tart pan and cookie sheet or rimmed sheet pan at hand.

MIX THE HAZELNUT BUTTER COOKIE DOUGH Sift the all-purpose flour, cake flour, baking powder, salt, cinnamon, and nutmeg onto a sheet of waxed paper.

Cream the butter in the large bowl of a freestanding electric mixer on moderate speed for 2 minutes. Add the granulated sugar and beat for 1 to 2 minutes. Blend in the egg yolks and vanilla extract. Scrape down the sides of the bowl with a rubber spatula to keep the mixture even-textured. Blend in the hazelnut flour.

On low speed, add the sifted mixture in two additions, beating until the dough comes together in large and small curds. Remove the bowl from the stand. With a rubber spatula, work the dough until it comes together into a dough, pressing sections of it together. Using your hands, lightly knead the dough on a work surface for 1 minute. *Dough texture observation* The dough should be buttery and firm, but workable.

Divide the dough into two equal portions. Lightly form each portion into a rounded cake.

FREEZE ONE PORTION OF THE DOUGH Roll one portion of dough between two sheets of waxed paper to a round about 9½ inches in diameter. Place the dough on a cookie sheet and freeze (for 5 to 10 minutes) while you work with the other half of the dough.

LINE THE TART PAN WITH THE REMAINING PORTION OF DOUGH Roll out the remaining portion of the dough between sheets of waxed paper to a round measuring about 9 inches in diameter. Peel off the top sheet of waxed paper and invert the dough disk onto the bottom of the tart pan. Peel off the second sheet of waxed paper.

Lightly press the dough onto the bottom of the tart pan and halfway up the sides, making the sides slightly thicker.

MIX THE APRICOT FILLING AND FILL THE TART SHELL Combine the apricot preserves and vanilla extract in a small bowl.

Spoon the preserves on the layer of dough. Spread the preserves on the bottom of the dough, using a small offset palette knife.

CREATE THE COOKIE DOUGH CUT-OUTS AND COVER THE TART WITH THE CUT-OUTS Place the sheet of dough on a work surface. Peel off the top sheet of waxed paper.

Using a 1½-inch cookie cutter (such as a heart or scalloped round cutter), stamp out 33 pieces of dough as close as possible to each other.

Place the cut-outs around the perimeter of the tart (at the edge of the dough), then follow with a second ring of cut-outs in the middle of the tart, and, finally, fill in the center with three cut-outs. Overlap the remaining cut-outs attractively in the middle.

BAKE THE TART Place the tart on the cookie sheet (or sheet pan) and bake for 40 minutes, or until the apricot preserves are bubbly and the cut-outs are a medium golden color on top. As the tart bakes, the dough will rise to fill the tart pan. The tart must be fully baked and golden or it will be pasty-textured in the center.

Carefully transfer the tart pan to a cooling rack. Cool completely. Carefully release the tart from the outer ring, leaving it on its base. Place the tart in a storage container, cover tightly, and let stand for at least 4 hours (or overnight). *Resting time observation* The resting time tenderizes the texture of the tart dough and unifies the flavor.

Sift confectioners' sugar lightly over the top of the tart, if you wish. Serve the tart cut into wedges. *Slicing observation* Use a serrated knife to cut the tart neatly and cleanly.

❊ *For an aromatic topnote of flavor,* use vanilla-scented granulated sugar (see page 53) in place of plain granulated sugar in the butter cookie dough.

FRESHLY BAKED, THE TART KEEPS FOR 4 DAYS.

Variation: For apricot and walnut tart, substitute walnut flour for the hazelnut flour.

*t*he direct flavor of banana is concentrated in baked goods by using the fruit—mashed, crushed, or cut into chunks. Bananas that are ripe (but not mushy) lend the best texture and taste to batters and doughs: the skin of the fruit should be a tawny yellow with random blackish spotting and speckling, the flesh tender and submissive but not at all slippery. And, above all, bananas should be redolent. Overly ripe mashed bananas frequently turn a baked batter or dough waxy-textured, with an unsavory acrid flavor.

The flavor of banana is emphasized by the use of vanilla extract; butter, heavy cream, sour cream, and buttermilk; all the sweet spices (nutmeg, cinnamon, allspice, ginger, and cardamom); chocolate in the form of semisweet chips and unsweetened, alkalized cocoa; macadamia nuts or walnuts; and the occasional use of light brown sugar and sweetened flaked coconut.

Banana-based recipes frequently specify mashing them, and the most sensible way to crush the fruit is by using the old-fashioned (but entirely practical) potato masher. Break the peeled bananas into segments, place them in a large nonreactive bowl, and mash to a soft, pulpy mass. Bananas treated in this way retain a little bit of texture and enough body to build the textural crumb of the batter. Crushing the banana flesh in a food processor liquidates the fruit more than needed and, frequently, this mixture will skew the recipe. So, the traditional method is best—mash the bananas by hand.

7

BANANA

Sweet Banana and Chocolate Chip Scones

8 scones

THE WINNING FLAVORS OF BANANA AND CHOCOLATE are paired in these delicately textured sweet tea biscuits, so good as a morning or mid-afternoon partner to coffee. Oven-fresh scones that aren't eaten on the day that they're baked are best wrapped individually and frozen. Reheat the biscuits (thawed in their freezer wrappings, unwrapped and nestled in an aluminum foil bundle) in a moderate oven for about 10 minutes, to revive the texture and bring out the flavor of the fruit.

BANANA AND CHOCOLATE CHIP SCONE DOUGH

2½ cups unsifted bleached all-purpose flour

2¾ teaspoons baking powder

¼ teaspoon cream of tartar

½ teaspoon salt

⅓ cup unsifted confectioners' sugar

6 tablespoons (¾ stick) unsalted butter, cold, cut into chunks

2 large eggs

6 tablespoons heavy cream

2 teaspoons pure vanilla extract

½ cup mashed ripe bananas

¾ cup miniature semisweet chocolate chips

½ cup sweetened flaked coconut

5 tablespoons miniature semisweet chocolate chips, for pressing on top of the unbaked scones

BAKEWARE

large cookie sheet or rimmed sheet pan

PREHEAT THE OVEN AND PREPARE THE BAKING SHEET Preheat the oven to 400° F. Line the cookie sheet or rimmed sheet pan with a length of cooking parchment paper; set aside. *Bakeware observation* The baking sheet must be heavy, or the chip-laden dough will scorch on the bottom as the scones bake. Double-pan the sheets, if necessary.

MIX THE BANANA AND CHOCOLATE CHIP SCONE DOUGH Whisk the flour, baking powder, cream of tartar, salt, and confectioners' sugar in a large mixing bowl. Add the chunks of butter, and using a pastry blender (or two round-bladed table knives), reduce the butter to small bits about the size of dried lima beans.

In a small mixing bowl, whisk the eggs, heavy cream, and vanilla extract. Blend in the mashed bananas. Pour the banana-egg-heavy cream mixture over the dry ingredients, add the chocolate chips and coconut, and stir to form a dough. *Dough texture observation* The dough will be pliant, slightly sticky, but shapeable.

FORM THE DOUGH INTO SCONES Knead the dough lightly on a well-floured work surface for 10 seconds. Kneading the dough on the floured work surface will relieve it of some of the stickiness. Pat into an 8½- to 9-inch round disk. Cut into eight wedges with

Adding the chocolate chips and coconut to the dough along with the banana–egg–heavy cream mixture assures you that the additions will wind their way through the entire mass of dough. Before baking, refrigerate the scones to preserve the internal structure and stability.

a chef's knife. With a wide, offset metal spatula, transfer the scones to the lined cookie sheet, placing them about 3 inches apart. Refrigerate the scones for 15 minutes.

TOP THE SCONES Press the miniature chocolate chips on the tops of the scones, using about a scant 2 teaspoons to top each scone.

BAKE AND COOL THE SCONES Bake the scones in the preheated oven for 17 to 20 minutes, or until set. Remove the scones to a cooling rack, using a wide, offset metal spatula. Cool. Serve the scones very fresh, barely warm or at room temperature.

❋ *For an extra surge of flavor,* press lightly crushed banana chips on top of the scones in place of or along with the miniature semisweet chocolate chips. Use 1 tablespoon of banana chips (½ cup in total) to top each scone.

❋ *For an aromatic topnote of flavor,* use vanilla-scented confectioners' sugar (see page 54) in place of plain granulated sugar in the scone dough.

FRESHLY BAKED, THE SCONES KEEP FOR 2 TO 3 DAYS.

Variations: For sweet banana and chocolate chip-walnut scones, add ⅓ cup chopped walnuts (lightly toasted and cooled completely) to the dough along with the semisweet chocolate chips and flaked coconut.

For sweet banana and chocolate chip-almond scones, add ⅓ cup slivered almonds (lightly toasted and cooled completely) to the dough along with the semisweet chocolate chips and flaked coconut. Reduce the vanilla extract to 1 teaspoon and add 1 teaspoon of pure almond extract.

TEXAS-SIZE BANANA MUFFINS

13 muffins

THESE ARE BIG AND GLORIOUS BANANA MUFFINS, fragrant with the direct, fruity taste of banana and a range of spices. The brown sugar in the batter develops and uplifts the banana flavor, while conveying a hint of caramel, and the spices add warm, accenting grace notes. This recipe creates a splendid batch of weekend muffins, perfect for Sunday brunch or as an afternoon treat with tea or coffee.

Nonstick cooking spray, for preparing the muffin pans

BANANA MUFFIN BATTER

4 cups unsifted bleached all-purpose flour

3 teaspoons baking powder

½ teaspoon baking soda

⅛ teaspoon cream of tartar

1 teaspoon salt

1 teaspoon freshly grated nutmeg

¾ teaspoon ground cinnamon

¼ teaspoon ground allspice

¼ teaspoon ground cloves

⅛ teaspoon ground cardamom

½ pound (16 tablespoons or 2 sticks) unsalted butter, softened

½ cup granulated sugar

½ cup firmly packed light brown sugar, sieved if lumpy

4 large eggs

1 tablespoon pure vanilla extract

1½ cups plus 2 tablespoons mashed ripe bananas

¾ cup thick, cultured sour cream

1½ cups lightly packed sweetened flaked coconut

1¼ cups coarsely chopped walnuts

PREHEAT THE OVEN AND PREPARE THE MUFFIN PANS Preheat the oven to 375° F. Film the inside of 13 jumbo, crown top muffin cups with nonstick cooking spray; set aside.

MIX THE BANANA MUFFIN BATTER Sift the all-purpose flour, baking powder, baking soda, cream of tartar, salt, nutmeg, cinnamon, allspice, cloves, and cardamom onto a sheet of waxed paper.

Cream the butter in the large bowl of a freestanding electric mixer on moderately high speed for 2 minutes. Add the granulated sugar and beat for 1 minute; add the light brown sugar and beat for a minute longer. Beat in the eggs, one at a time, mixing for 30 seconds after each addition. Blend in the vanilla extract and mashed bananas, mixing well.

On low speed, alternately add the sifted ingredients in three additions with the sour cream in two additions, beginning and ending with the sifted mixture. Scrape down the sides of the mixing bowl with a rubber spatula after each addition to keep the batter even-textured. Blend in the coconut and walnuts.

FILL THE MUFFIN CUPS WITH THE BATTER Divide the batter evenly among the prepared muffin cups, mounding it slightly in the center of each cup.

BAKE AND COOL THE MUFFINS Bake the muffins for 25 minutes, or until risen and set. When baked, a wooden pick inserted

13 jumbo, crown top muffin cups
(three pans, each holding 6
individual muffin cups), each cup
measuring about 3¼ inches in
diameter, with a capacity of scant
1 cup

in the center of a muffin should withdraw clean, or with a few moist crumbs attached to it.

Place the muffin pans on cooling racks and let stand for 30 minutes. Carefully remove the muffins from the pans and place on other cooling racks. Serve the muffins freshly baked, barely warm or at room temperature.

❋ *For an extra surge of flavor,* sprinkle coarsely crushed banana chips, ¾ cup in total, on top of the unbaked muffins.

❋ *For an aromatic topnote of flavor,* use vanilla-scented granulated sugar (see page 53) in place of plain granulated sugar and intensified vanilla extract (see page 52) in place of plain vanilla extract in the muffin batter.

FRESHLY BAKED, THE MUFFINS KEEP FOR 3 DAYS.

Variation: For Texas-size chocolate chip banana muffins, omit the nutmeg, cinnamon, allspice, cloves, and cardamom. Reduce the amount of sweetened flaked coconut to 1 cup and the chopped walnuts to ¾ cup. Toss 2 cups miniature semisweet chocolate chips with 1 tablespoon of the sifted mixture and stir into the batter along with the coconut and walnuts.

BEST BAKING ADVICE
Mounding the batter in the center of each baking cup helps to form high, elevated crowns on the baked muffins.

Spiced Banana Breakfast Loaf

One 9 by 5-inch loaf, creating about 12 slices

Slices of this tender morning cake envelop the taste of banana, spice (particularly cinnamon), and butter in its moist, creamy-textured crumb.

Shortening and bleached all-purpose flour, for preparing the loaf pan

CINNAMON AND WALNUT RIPPLE

¾ cup chopped walnuts

1 tablespoon firmly packed light brown sugar

¾ teaspoon ground cinnamon

SPICED BANANA BATTER

2 cups unsifted bleached all-purpose flour

1 teaspoon baking powder

½ teaspoon salt

1 teaspoon ground cinnamon

¾ teaspoon freshly grated nutmeg

¼ teaspoon ground ginger

⅛ teaspoon ground cloves

¼ pound (1 stick or 8 tablespoons) unsalted butter, melted and cooled

⅔ cup plus 2 tablespoons granulated sugar

2 large eggs

1½ cups mashed ripe bananas

1½ teaspoons pure vanilla extract

¾ cup chopped walnuts, lightly toasted and cooled completely

BAKEWARE

9 by 5 by 3-inch loaf pan

PREHEAT THE OVEN AND PREPARE THE LOAF PAN Preheat the oven to 350° F. Lightly grease the loaf pan with shortening, then dust the inside with all-purpose flour. Tap out any excess flour; set aside.

MAKE THE CINNAMON AND WALNUT RIPPLE Combine the walnuts, brown sugar, and cinnamon in a small bowl. Set aside.

MAKE THE SPICED BANANA LOAF CAKE BATTER Whisk the flour, baking powder, salt, cinnamon, nutmeg, ginger, and cloves in a large mixing bowl.

Whisk the melted butter, granulated sugar, eggs, mashed bananas, and vanilla extract in a medium-size mixing bowl. Pour the banana-egg mixture over the dry ingredients, add the walnuts, and using a flat wooden paddle or flexible rubber spatula, stir to form a batter, mixing until the particles of flour are absorbed. Take care to scrape the sides and the bottom of the mixing bowl well to break up any pockets of flour.

LAYER THE BATTER WITH THE CINNAMON AND WALNUT RIPPLE MIXTURE Spoon a little more than half the batter into the prepared loaf pan. Make a wide, but shallow (about ⅛ inch deep) trench down the center of the batter. Spoon the ripple mixture evenly over the surface and top with the remaining batter. Using a narrow, flexible palette knife, swirl the filling into the batter (this can be accomplished in five or six strokes), taking care not to scrape the bottom or sides of the loaf pan.

BAKE AND COOL THE LOAF Bake the loaf for 55 minutes, or until risen, set, and a wooden pick inserted in the center of the loaf withdraws clean, or with a few moist crumbs. Cool the loaf in the pan on a rack for 5 to 8 minutes, remove carefully to another rack, and cool completely. Enclose the loaf completely in a large sheet of plastic wrap and allow it to ripen for at least 3 hours before slicing and serving. *Slicing observation* Use a serrated knife to cut the loaf neatly and cleanly. Store in an airtight cake keeper.

❋ *For an extra surge of flavor,* sprinkle the top of the unbaked loaf with ⅓ cup coarsely crumbled banana chips.

FRESHLY BAKED, THE LOAF KEEPS FOR 4 DAYS.

FEATHERY BANANA PANCAKES

About 2 dozen pancakes

A PLATE OF FRUIT-FILLED PANCAKES makes a weekend breakfast rosy, for they are simply one of the easiest quick-from-scratch breakfast batters to put together. Both the cake flour and beaten egg white tenderize the texture of the pancakes, and the undertone of nutmeg and allspice dovetails neatly with the forward taste of the banana chunks.

BANANA PANCAKE BATTER

¾ cup unsifted bleached all-purpose flour

¼ cup unsifted bleached cake flour

1¼ teaspoons baking powder

3 tablespoons granulated sugar

⅛ teaspoon salt

¼ teaspoon freshly grated nutmeg

¾ cup small ripe banana chunks

3 tablespoons unsalted butter, melted and cooled to tepid

1 large egg, separated

2 teaspoons pure vanilla extract

¾ cup milk

pinch cream of tartar

Clarified butter (see page 66), for the griddle

MAKE THE BANANA PANCAKE BATTER Sift the all-purpose flour, cake flour, baking powder, granulated sugar, salt, and nutmeg into a medium-size mixing bowl.

Place the banana chunks on a plate and crush lightly with a potato masher (or table fork) to flatten slightly.

Whisk the melted butter, egg yolk, vanilla extract, and milk in a small mixing bowl. Beat the egg white in a small, clean, dry bowl, using a rotary egg beater, until frothy and just beginning to mound. Add the cream of tartar and continue beating until firm (not stiff) peaks are formed.

Pour the whisked liquid mixture over the sifted ingredients, and stir to form a batter. Fold in the beaten egg white along with the crushed bananas. Let stand 2 minutes. *Batter texture observation* The chunky banana batter will be lightly thickened, with a soft-creamy texture.

GRIDDLE THE PANCAKES For each pancake, place 2 heaping tablespoon-size puddles of batter on a hot griddle greased with a film of clarified butter. Cook the pancakes until the bottoms are golden, about 1 minute, then flip them with a wide, offset metal spatula, and continue cooking until the pancakes are completely set and cooked through, about 45 seconds longer.

Serve the pancakes piping hot, with warmed maple syrup flavored with a few gratings of nutmeg, if you wish.

Variation: For feathery banana pancakes with coconut, add ¼ cup (firmly packed) sweetened flaked coconut to the batter along with the crushed banana chunks.

For feathery banana-walnut pancakes, add ⅓ cup chopped walnuts (lightly toasted and cooled completely) to the batter along with the crushed banana chunks.

BANANA AND DRIED CRANBERRY TEA CAKE

One 9 by 5-inch loaf, creating about 12 slices

THE DRIED CRANBERRIES ADD A TART FLAVOR rush to this light, banana-based batter. The sour cream produces a soft acid tang, which lets the spices come through in a vibrant way while creating a tea cake with a supple texture.

Shortening and bleached all-purpose flour, for preparing the loaf pan

DRIED CRANBERRY AND BANANA TEA CAKE BATTER

2 cups unsifted bleached all-purpose flour

1¼ teaspoons baking powder

½ teaspoon baking soda

½ teaspoon salt

PREHEAT THE OVEN AND PREPARE THE LOAF PAN Preheat the oven to 375° F. Lightly grease the inside of the loaf pan with shortening, then dust the inside with all-purpose flour. Tap out any excess flour; set aside.

MIX THE DRIED CRANBERRY AND BANANA TEA CAKE BATTER Sift the flour, baking powder, baking soda, salt, nutmeg, cinnamon, and cardamom onto a sheet of waxed paper. In a small mixing bowl, toss the cranberries with 1 teaspoon of the sifted mixture.

½ teaspoon freshly grated nutmeg

¼ teaspoon ground cinnamon

¼ teaspoon ground cardamom

¾ cup dried cranberries, very coarsely chopped

¼ pound (8 tablespoons or 1 stick) unsalted butter, softened

2 tablespoons shortening

1 cup granulated sugar

2 large eggs

2 teaspoons pure vanilla extract

½ teaspoon almond extract

1⅓ cups mashed ripe bananas blended with ¼ cup sour cream

BAKEWARE

9 by 5 by 3-inch loaf pan

Cream the butter and shortening in the large bowl of a free-standing electric mixer on moderate speed for 2 minutes. Add the granulated sugar and beat for 2 minutes longer. Beat in the eggs, one at a time, blending well after each addition. Blend in the vanilla and almond extracts. Scrape down the sides of the mixing bowl frequently with a rubber spatula to keep the batter even-textured.

On low speed, alternately add the sifted mixture in three additions with the mashed bananas-sour cream blend in two additions, beginning and ending with the sifted mixture. Stir in the cranberries.

Spoon the batter into the prepared loaf pan, mounding it slightly in the center.

BAKE AND COOL THE TEA CAKE Bake the tea cake for 55 minutes, or until risen, set, and a wooden pick inserted in the center of the loaf withdraws clean or with a few moist crumbs attached to it. Cool the loaf in the pan on a rack for 5 minutes, remove to another rack, and cool completely. Let the tea cake mellow for at least 2 hours before cutting into slices for serving. *Slicing observation* Use a serrated knife to cut the cake neatly and cleanly. Store in an airtight cake keeper.

❋ *For an extra surge of flavor,* sprinkle the top of the unbaked tea cake with ⅓ cup lightly crushed banana chips.

❋ *For an aromatic topnote of flavor,* use vanilla-scented granulated sugar (see page 53) in place of plain granulated sugar in the tea cake batter.

FRESHLY BAKED, THE TEA CAKE KEEPS FOR 4 TO 5 DAYS.

BEST BAKING ADVICE

Mixing the mashed bananas with the sour cream helps to guard against a waxy-textured batter and overly compact texture.

Banana, Walnut, and Chocolate Chip Waffles

5 deep, Belgian-style 2-sided waffles,
each waffle section measuring 4½ by 4½ inches

THIS LIGHT AND TENDER WAFFLE BATTER is composed of mashed bananas, enough vanilla extract to punctuate the fruit flavor, and a dashing stir-in of miniature semisweet chocolate chips and walnuts. The mashed bananas both moisten and define the flavor of the batter.

BANANA, WALNUT, AND CHOCOLATE CHIP WAFFLE BATTER

2 cups unsifted bleached all-purpose flour

2 teaspoons baking powder

¼ teaspoon baking soda

¼ teaspoon salt

⅓ cup granulated sugar

3 large eggs, separated

6 tablespoons (¾ stick) unsalted butter, melted and cooled to tepid

1 cup mashed ripe bananas

1 cup milk

2 teaspoons pure vanilla extract

¾ cup miniature semisweet chocolate chips

½ cup chopped walnuts

¼ teaspoon cream of tartar

Confectioners' sugar, for sprinkling on the waffles

MAKE THE BANANA, WALNUT, AND CHOCOLATE CHIP WAFFLE BATTER Sift the flour, baking powder, baking soda, salt, and granulated sugar into a large mixing bowl. In a medium-size mixing bowl, whisk the egg yolks, butter, bananas, milk, and vanilla extract. Pour the liquid ingredients over the sifted mixture and stir to form a batter. Stir in the chocolate chips and walnuts. *Batter texture observation* The batter will be thick.

In a medium-size bowl, beat the egg whites until frothy, add the cream of tartar, and continue beating until firm (but not stiff) peaks are formed. Stir 2 large spoonfuls of the beaten whites into the batter, then fold in the remaining whites. The egg whites should be completely mixed into the batter. *Batter texture observation* The batter will be moderately thick, and will thicken slightly as it stands.

MAKE THE WAFFLES Preheat a deep-dish waffle iron. Spoon about ½ cup of batter onto each square of the preheated iron. For evenly shaped waffles, pour the batter on the upper third section of each square, slightly above the middle; as you fold down the iron, the batter will flow down toward the bottom. Cook the waffles until golden, 1 minute to 1 minute and 15 seconds. Serve the waffles sprinkled with confectioners' sugar, if you wish, and softened sweet butter.

COCOA BANANA LOAF

One 9 by 5-inch loaf, creating about 12 slices

*T*HE FRUITY RICHNESS OF RIPE, mashed bananas combines with a buttery double chocolate batter (composed of cocoa and semisweet chocolate chips) to compose an especially delicious loaf cake. The chocolate chip stir-in adds a lush quality to the cake. And if you're in an extravagant mood, substitute 6 ounces of bittersweet chocolate, chopped into small chunks, for the semisweet chips.

Nonstick cooking spray, for preparing the loaf pan

COCOA-BANANA BUTTER CAKE BATTER

1¾ cups plus 2 tablespoons unsifted bleached all-purpose flour

¼ cup unsweetened, alkalized cocoa

1¼ teaspoons baking powder

¼ teaspoon salt

1 cup semisweet chocolate chips

¼ pound (8 tablespoons or 1 stick) unsalted butter, softened

1 cup granulated sugar

2 large eggs

1½ teaspoons pure vanilla extract

1⅓ cups mashed ripe bananas

Confectioners' sugar, for sifting on top of the baked loaf cake (optional)

BAKEWARE

9 by 5 by 3-inch loaf pan

PREHEAT THE OVEN AND PREPARE THE LOAF PAN Preheat the oven to 350° F. Film the inside of the loaf pan with nonstick cooking spray; set aside.

MIX THE COCOA-BANANA BUTTER CAKE BATTER Sift the flour, cocoa, baking powder, and salt onto a sheet of waxed paper. In a small mixing bowl, toss the chocolate chips with 1½ teaspoons of the sifted mixture.

Cream the butter in the large bowl of a freestanding electric mixer on moderate speed for 2 minutes. Add the granulated sugar and beat for 2 minutes longer. Beat in the eggs, one at a time, blending well after each addition. Blend in the vanilla extract. Scrape down the sides of the mixing bowl frequently with a rubber spatula to keep the batter even-textured. Blend in the mashed bananas. *Batter texture observation* After the bananas are added, the mixture will curdle a bit, but will smooth out in the next step when the sifted flour mixture is added to the batter.

On low speed, add the sifted mixture in two additions, mixing just until the particles of flour are absorbed. Stir in the chocolate chips.

Spoon the batter into the prepared loaf pan, mounding it slightly in the center.

BAKE AND COOL THE LOAF CAKE Bake the loaf cake for 1 hour and 5 minutes, or until risen, set, and a wooden pick inserted in the center of the loaf withdraws clean. If

The mashed ripe bananas furnish most of the moisture in the loaf, and for that reason, the fruit should be fully (but not overly) ripe.

the loaf seems to be darkening around the edges as the loaf bakes, lightly tent a sheet of aluminum foil over the top.

Cool the loaf in the pan on a rack for 5 minutes, remove to another rack, and cool completely. If you wish, sift confectioners' sugar over the top of the cooled cake before cutting into slices for serving. *Slicing observation* Use a serrated knife to cut the loaf neatly and cleanly.

FRESHLY BAKED, THE LOAF KEEPS FOR 3 DAYS.

BANANA LAYER CAKE

One two-layer, 9-inch cake, creating about 12 slices

*T*HIS IS A SOFT-TEXTURED LAYER CAKE, with a rounded banana flavor. The cake layers are cloaked in chocolate frosting—a good and sweet contrast.

Shortening and bleached all-purpose flour, for preparing the layer cake pans

BANANA LAYER CAKE BATTER

2⅓ cups plus 3 tablespoons unsifted bleached cake flour

1 teaspoon baking powder

¾ teaspoon baking soda

½ teaspoon salt

½ teaspoon freshly grated nutmeg

¼ pound (8 tablespoons or 1 stick) unsalted butter, softened

2 tablespoons shortening

1½ cups granulated sugar

2 large eggs

2 teaspoons pure vanilla extract

PREHEAT THE OVEN AND PREPARE THE LAYER CAKE PANS Preheat the oven to 350° F. Lightly grease the cake pans with shortening. Line the bottom of each pan with a circle of waxed paper, grease the paper, and dust the inside with all-purpose flour. Tap out any excess flour; set aside.

M THE BANANA LAYER CAKE BATTER Sift the flour, baking powder, baking soda, salt, and nutmeg onto a sheet of waxed paper.

Cream the butter and shortening in the large bowl of a free-standing electric mixer on moderate speed for 3 minutes. Add half of the granulated sugar and beat for 2 minutes; add the remaining granulated sugar and beat for 1 to 2 minutes longer. Blend in the eggs, one at a time, beating for about 1 minute after each addition. Blend in the vanilla extract and mashed bananas.

On low speed, add half of the sifted mixture, the buttermilk, then the balance of the sifted mixture. Scrape down the sides of

1¼ cups mashed ripe bananas

½ cup buttermilk, whisked well

Chocolate Cream Frosting (see page 272), for spreading on the baked cake layers

BAKEWARE

two 9-inch round layer cake pans, 1½ inches deep

the mixing bowl frequently with a rubber spatula to keep the batter even-textured.

Spoon the batter into the cake pans, dividing it evenly between them. Using a flexible palette knife or rubber spatula, smooth over the top of each layer to spread the batter evenly.

BAKE AND COOL THE CAKE LAYERS Bake the layers for 25 to 30 minutes, or until set and a wooden pick inserted 1 inch from the center of each cake layer withdraws clean. Cool the layers in the pans on racks for 5 minutes.

Invert each layer onto another cooling rack, peel off the waxed paper round, then invert again to cool right side up. Cool completely.

ASSEMBLE AND FROST THE CAKE Tear off four 3-inch-wide strips of waxed paper. Place the strips in the shape of a square around the outer 3 inches of a cake plate. Center one cake layer on the plate (partially covering the waxed paper square; the strips should peek out at least by 1 inch), and spread the top with some of the frosting, using a flexible palette knife. Carefully place the second layer on top, then ice the entire cake (top and sides) by swirling over the frosting. When the frosting has set, in about 45 minutes, gently slide out and discard the waxed paper strips.

Cut the cake into slices for serving. Store in an airtight cake keeper.

❋ *For an extra surge of flavor,* slice 1 ripe, medium-size banana and arrange the slices on the first frosted layer of the cake. Top with the remaining layer and frost the outside of the cake.

Variation: For spiced banana layer cake, sift ½ teaspoon ground cinnamon, ¼ teaspoon ground allspice, ⅛ teaspoon ground cloves, and ⅛ teaspoon ground cardamom with the flour, baking powder, baking soda, salt, and nutmeg.

*b*lueberries, fresh or dried, interspersed within a butter cake, pancake, or waffle batter, or clinging to a quick bread dough, add an identifiably fruity quality to bakery sweets. The fresh berries form pools that moisten the surrounding batter in a lush, luxurious way, while dried berries introduce a stronger, more concentrated and intense flavor.

Lemon (in the form of freshly grated lemon rind and lemon extract in addition to a lemon wash, syrup, or icing), freshly grated nutmeg, and vanilla can highlight the taste of blueberries, acting as a contrast or accentuating flavor. Dairy ingredients, such as sour cream, whole milk, buttermilk, and light (table) cream, present in the batter or dough develop a rich crumb that acts as a perfect backdrop for the berries.

Blueberries are usually lightly floured (using a bit of the sifted or whisked dry ingredients present in the recipe) before they are introduced into a creamy-textured batter. This tactic helps to keep the berries suspended in the batter; otherwise, they would sink to the bottom and form a soggy layer rather than appear in beautiful, fruity dots throughout. When you are adding the berries to a biscuit dough, it is unnecessary to flour them first, as the dough's moist density will trap the berries in a sweeping, random pattern.

When selecting fresh blueberries at the market, look for lustrous berries with a slight silvery complexion; the berries should appear firm and plump. Blueberries should be picked over to remove small stems and leaves, rinsed in cool water, and blotted dry on paper towels.

8

BLUEBERRY

TENDER, CAKELIKE BLUEBERRY MUFFINS

14 jumbo muffins

BLUEBERRY MUFFIN-LOVERS—and I am one of them—can never have too many recipes: This batter is creamy-textured and somewhat plain, but it bakes up into the most sublime muffins that really spotlight the flavor of the juicy berries. These muffins are tender, with a fine, cakelike quality to them.

Nonstick cooking spray, for preparing the muffin pans

SWEET MILK BLUEBERRY MUFFIN BATTER

3½ cups unsifted bleached all-purpose flour

½ cup unsifted bleached cake flour

3 teaspoons baking powder

1 teaspoon salt

1 teaspoon freshly grated nutmeg

¼ teaspoon ground cardamom

2¼ cups fresh blueberries

½ pound (16 tablespoons or 2 sticks) unsalted butter, softened

1⅓ cups plus 2 tablespoons superfine sugar

4 large eggs

1 tablespoon pure vanilla extract

1⅓ cups milk

About ⅓ cup granulated sugar, for sprinkling on the tops of the warm muffins

PREHEAT THE OVEN AND PREPARE THE MUFFIN PANS Preheat the oven to 375° F. Generously coat the insides of 14 jumbo, crown top muffin cups with nonstick cooking spray; set aside.

MIX THE SWEET MILK BLUEBERRY MUFFIN BATTER Sift the all-purpose flour, cake flour, baking powder, salt, nutmeg, and cardamom onto a sheet of waxed paper. In a medium-size bowl, toss the blueberries with 1½ tablespoons of the sifted flour mixture.

Cream the butter in the large bowl of a freestanding electric mixer on moderate speed for 2 to 3 minutes. Add the superfine sugar in two additions, and beat for 1 to 2 minutes after each portion is added. Beat in the eggs, one at a time, mixing for 30 seconds after each addition. Blend in the vanilla extract.

On low speed, alternately add the sifted mixture in three additions with the milk in two additions, beginning and ending with the sifted mixture. Scrape down the sides of the mixing bowl frequently with a rubber spatula to keep the batter even-textured. Carefully but thoroughly, stir in the blueberries.

FILL THE MUFFIN CUPS WITH THE BATTER Spoon the batter into the prepared muffin cups, dividing it evenly among them. Mound the batter lightly in the center of each cup. *Batter mounding observation* Heaping drifts of batter toward the center creates nice domed (and full-figured) baked muffins.

BAKE THE MUFFINS Bake the muffins in the preheated oven for 25 minutes, or until risen, light golden, plump, and set. A wooden pick will withdraw from the center of a muffin clean, although it may be berry-stained.

14 jumbo, crown top muffin cups
(three pans, each holding 6
individual muffin cups, each cup
measuring about 3¼ inches in
diameter and 2 inches deep, with a
capacity of scant 1 cup)

COOL THE MUFFINS Place the muffin pans on cooling racks. Immediately sprinkle the granulated sugar over the tops of the muffins. Cool the muffins in the pans for 30 minutes. *Cooling observation* The muffins are quite tender and fragile, and they should cool in the pans until the oven heat diminishes in order to hold their shape; otherwise the muffins will sag. Remove the muffins to cooling racks. Serve the muffins freshly baked.

❋ *For an extra surge of flavor,* serve the muffins with blueberry preserves.

❋ *For an aromatic topnote of flavor,* use vanilla-scented superfine sugar (see page 54) in place of plain superfine sugar and intensified vanilla extract (see page 52) in place of plain vanilla extract in the muffin batter.

FRESHLY BAKED, THE MUFFINS KEEP FOR 2 DAYS.

BEST BAKING ADVICE
Using superfine sugar as the sweetening agent makes the finest-textured muffins, with a meltingly tender crumb.

SWEET BLUEBERRY BREAKFAST BISCUITS

8 biscuits

*E*ARLY MORNING IS BRIGHTENED when you're greeted with one of these cheery blueberry biscuits: radiant, sweet berries drift through a butter-and-cream dough, and just before baking, each triangular biscuit gets a sprinkle of granulated sugar mixed with freshly grated nutmeg.

BLUEBERRY BISCUIT DOUGH

2 cups plus 2 tablespoons unsifted bleached all-purpose flour

2½ teaspoons baking powder

¼ teaspoon salt

½ teaspoon freshly grated nutmeg

¼ teaspoon ground cinnamon

⅛ teaspoon ground cloves

⅓ cup granulated sugar

6 tablespoons (¾ stick) unsalted butter, cold, cut into tablespoon chunks

2 large eggs

½ cup heavy cream

2 teaspoons pure vanilla extract

1 cup fresh blueberries, cold

3 tablespoons granulated sugar blended with ¼ teaspoon freshly grated nutmeg, for sprinkling on the unbaked biscuits

BAKEWARE

large, heavy cookie sheet or rimmed sheet pan

PREHEAT THE OVEN AND PREPARE THE BAKING SHEETS Preheat the oven to 400° F. Line the cookie sheet or rimmed sheet pan with cooking parchment paper; set aside. *Bakeware observation* The baking sheet must be heavy, or the dough will scorch on the bottom as the biscuits bake. Double-pan the sheets, if necessary.

MIX THE BLUEBERRY BISCUIT DOUGH Whisk the flour, baking powder, salt, nutmeg, cinnamon, cloves, and granulated sugar in a medium-size mixing bowl. Drop in the chunks of butter, and using a pastry blender, cut the butter into small, pearl-size bits. Lightly and quickly, crumble the mixture between your fingertips until the butter is reduced to smaller flakes, 30 seconds to 1 minute.

In a small mixing bowl, whisk the eggs, heavy cream, and vanilla extract. Pour the egg-cream mixture over the dry ingredients, scatter over the blueberries, and stir to form the beginning of a dough, using a rubber spatula. With lightly floured hands, bring the mixture together into a workable (but slightly moist) dough. Knead the dough lightly in the bowl for 10 to 15 seconds, about eight light pushes. *Dough mixing observation* Using the blueberries while cold helps to maintain their shape, but you must knead the dough lightly in order to keep the berries intact. The dough will be somewhat soft, but shapeable and flexible.

FORM THE DOUGH INTO BISCUITS On a well-floured work surface, pat the dough into an 8- to 8½-inch disk. Cut into eight wedges with a sharp chef's knife. With a wide, offset metal spatula, transfer the biscuits to the lined cookie sheets, placing them about

Cold blueberries (or berries spread out on a baking pan and frozen for 10 minutes) are easier to incorporate into the dough, and because they are slightly firmer, they are less likely to crush or break down during baking.

2½ inches apart. *Unruly blueberries observation* If some of the blueberries pop or peek out of the dough as you are shaping and/or cutting the biscuits, firmly press them back in with your fingertips.

TOP THE BISCUITS WITH THE NUTMEG-SUGAR SPRINKLE Sprinkle a little of the nutmeg-sugar on top of each biscuit.

BAKE AND COOL THE BISCUITS Bake the biscuits in the preheated oven for 16 to 17 minutes, or until set and golden on top. Remove the biscuits to a cooling rack, using a wide metal spatula. Serve the biscuits very fresh.

❋ *For an extra surge of flavor,* add ¼ cup dried blueberries to the dough ingredients along with the fresh berries.

❋ *For an aromatic topnote of flavor,* use vanilla-scented granulated sugar (see page 53) in place of plain granulated sugar and intensified vanilla extract (see page 52) in place of plain vanilla extract in the biscuit dough.

FRESHLY BAKED, THE BISCUITS KEEP FOR 2 DAYS.

BLUEBERRY LOAF

One 9 by 5 by 3-inch loaf, creating about 12 slices

A SWEET LOAF, LIGHTLY PERFUMED with vanilla and catching blueberries here and there, is the perfect morning bread to slice and serve with softened sweet butter. As a flavor variation, substitute lemon-scented granulated sugar (see page 55) and lemon extract for the vanilla variety of each, add 2 teaspoons freshly grated lemon rind to the batter after the eggs are incorporated, and top the warm loaf with lemon-sugar wash (see page 59).

Shortening and bleached all-purpose flour, for preparing the loaf pan

BLUEBERRIES AND CREAM LOAF CAKE BATTER

2 cups unsifted bleached all-purpose flour

1¼ teaspoons baking powder

½ teaspoon salt

½ teaspoon freshly grated nutmeg

1 cup fresh blueberries

¼ pound (8 tablespoons or 1 stick) unsalted butter, softened

1 cup granulated sugar

2 large eggs

2 teaspoons pure vanilla extract

¾ cup light (table) cream

BAKEWARE

9 by 5 by 3-inch loaf pan

PREHEAT THE OVEN AND PREPARE THE LOAF PAN Preheat the oven to 350° F. Lightly grease the loaf pan with shortening. Dust the inside of the pan with all-purpose flour. Tap out any excess flour; set aside.

MAKE THE BLUEBERRIES AND CREAM LOAF CAKE BATTER Sift the flour, baking powder, salt, and nutmeg onto a sheet of waxed paper. In a small mixing bowl, toss the blueberries with 1½ teaspoons of the sifted mixture. *Blueberry flouring observation* The blueberries must be well floured to stay suspended in the batter as the loaf bakes.

Cream the butter in the large bowl of a freestanding electric mixer on moderate speed for 2 to 3 minutes. Add the granulated sugar in three additions, beating for about 45 seconds after each portion is added. Beat in the eggs, one at a time, mixing for about 45 seconds after each is added. Blend in the vanilla extract. Beat on moderate speed for 45 seconds.

On low speed, add the sifted mixture in three additions with the cream in two additions, beginning and ending with the sifted mixture. Scrape down the sides of the mixing bowl frequently with a rubber spatula to keep the batter even-textured. *Batter texture observation* The batter will be moderately thick and creamy. Stir in the blueberries. Spoon the batter into the prepared loaf pan.

Using light (table) cream contributes to the dreamy, almost pound-cake-like quality to the crumb of the baked loaf. Half-and-half can be substituted for the cream, but the texture will be slightly fluffier.

BAKE AND COOL THE LOAF Bake the loaf for 1 hour, or until risen, set, and a wooden pick inserted in the cake withdraws clean. When baked, the loaf will pull away slightly from the sides of the baking pan.

Let the cake stand in the pan on a cooling rack for 10 minutes, then carefully remove it to another cooling rack. Stand the loaf right side up. Cool completely before slicing and serving. *Slicing observation* Use a serrated knife to cut the loaf neatly and cleanly.

❋ *For an extra surge of flavor,* toss 3 tablespoons moist, dried blueberries with the fresh berries and 2 teaspoons of the sifted mixture, then fold into the batter.

❋ *For an aromatic topnote of flavor,* use vanilla-scented granulated sugar (see page 53) in place of plain granulated sugar and intensified vanilla extract (see page 52) in place of plain vanilla extract in the loaf cake batter.

FRESHLY BAKED, THE LOAF KEEPS FOR 2 TO 3 DAYS.

BLUEBERRY-BANANA TEA LOAF

One 9 by 5 by 3-inch loaf, creating about 12 slices

*T*HE MOISTNESS OF THE BANANA-ENRICHED BATTER becomes a softly scented, tropical backdrop for the blueberries that decorate the loaf.

Nonstick cooking spray, for preparing the loaf pan

BANANA-BLUEBERRY TEA CAKE BATTER

2 cups unsifted bleached all-purpose flour

1 teaspoon baking powder

¾ teaspoon baking soda

½ teaspoon salt

¼ teaspoon freshly grated nutmeg

1 cup fresh blueberries

8 tablespoons (¼ pound or 1 stick) unsalted butter, softened

¾ cup granulated sugar

¼ cup firmly packed light brown sugar, sieved if lumpy

2 large eggs

1½ teaspoons pure vanilla extract

1¼ cups mashed ripe bananas

BAKEWARE

9 by 5 by 3-inch loaf pan

BEST BAKING ADVICE

Remove the just-baked, warm loaf from the pan carefully because it's tender.

PREHEAT THE OVEN AND PREPARE THE LOAF PAN Preheat the oven to 350° F. Film the inside of the loaf pan with nonstick cooking spray; set aside.

MAKE THE BANANA-BLUEBERRY TEA CAKE BATTER Sift the flour, baking powder, baking soda, salt, and nutmeg onto a sheet of waxed paper. In a small mixing bowl, toss the blueberries with 1½ teaspoons of the sifted mixture. *Blueberry flouring observation* The blueberries must be thoroughly tossed with flour in order not to sink toward the bottom of the cake.

Cream the butter in the large bowl of a freestanding electric mixer on moderate speed for 2 minutes. Add the granulated sugar and beat for 1 minute. Add the light brown sugar and beat for another minute. Beat in the eggs, one at a time, mixing for about 45 seconds after each is added. Blend in the vanilla extract and mashed bananas.

On low speed, add the sifted mixture in two additions, blending until the particles of flour are absorbed. Scrape down the sides of the mixing bowl frequently with a rubber spatula to keep the batter even-textured. Carefully but thoroughly, stir in the blueberries.

Spoon the batter into the prepared loaf pan.

BAKE AND COOL THE TEA LOAF Bake the cake for 1 hour, or until risen, set, and a wooden pick inserted in the cake withdraws clean.

Let the cake stand in the pan on a cooling rack for 10 minutes, then carefully remove it to another cooling rack. Stand the cake right side up. Cool completely before slicing and serving. *Slicing observation* Use a serrated knife to cut the loaf neatly and cleanly.

FRESHLY BAKED, THE TEA CAKE KEEPS FOR 2 TO 3 DAYS.

BLUEBERRY CORNMEAL WAFFLES

6 deep, Belgian-style 2-sided waffles, each waffle section measuring 4½ by 4½ inches

A CORNMEAL-ENRICHED BATTER produces robust and pleasantly gritty-crunchy waffles. The batter, lightly flavored with lemon rind and extract, needs to be tempered with sour cream to tenderize the crumb and fortified with enough eggs to build the structure. The blueberries distinguish the batter, making it sweetly fruity.

BLUEBERRY CORNMEAL WAFFLE BATTER

2 cups unsifted bleached all-purpose flour

¾ cup fine yellow cornmeal

2 teaspoons baking powder

¾ teaspoon baking soda

¼ teaspoon salt

¼ cup granulated sugar

1 cup fresh blueberries

½ cup thick, cultured sour cream

1½ cups milk

3 large eggs, lightly beaten

6 tablespoons (¾ stick) unsalted butter, melted and cooled

2 teaspoons freshly grated lemon rind

¾ teaspoon pure lemon extract

Confectioners' sugar, for sprinkling on the waffles (optional)

Blueberry preserves, for serving with the waffles

BEST BAKING ADVICE

Using a finely milled cornmeal keeps the texture of the waffles light and tender.

MAKE THE BLUEBERRY CORNMEAL WAFFLE BATTER Sift the flour, cornmeal, baking powder, baking soda, salt, and granulated sugar into a large mixing bowl. In a medium-size bowl, toss the blueberries with 1½ teaspoons of the sifted mixture.

Place the sour cream in a medium-size mixing bowl; slowly whisk in the milk. Blend in the eggs, melted butter, lemon rind, and lemon extract. Pour the liquid ingredients over the dry ingredients and stir to form a batter, using a wooden spoon, flat wooden paddle, or rubber spatula. Fold in the blueberries.

MAKE THE WAFFLES Preheat a deep-dish waffle iron. Spoon a scant ½ cup of batter onto each square of the preheated iron, placing it in the center of each grid section. Cook the waffles until golden, about 1 minute to 1 minute and 15 seconds, and sprinkle with confectioners' sugar, if you wish. Serve the waffles with dollops of blueberry preserves and pats of sweet butter.

❋ *For an extra surge of flavor,* toss the fresh blueberries and ¼ cup moist, dried blueberries with 2 teaspoons of the sifted mixture.

❋ *For an aromatic topnote of flavor,* use lemon-scented granulated sugar (see page 54) in place of plain granulated sugar in the waffle batter.

BLUEBERRY COFFEE CAKE

One 9 by 9-inch cake, creating 16 squares

THIS CAKE IS, PERHAPS, one of the best ways to enclose blueberries in a batter—its feathery texture and lightened crumb forms a peerless base for a cup of blueberries. Mixing one of the leavening agents (the baking soda) into the sour cream in advance is the secret to creating the cake batter's soft and incomparably delicate nap. It's exceptional served freshly baked, with coffee or tea.

Nonstick cooking spray, for preparing the baking pan

CINNAMON AND SUGAR TOPPING

¼ cup granulated sugar

¼ cup firmly packed light brown sugar, sieved if lumpy

2 teaspoons ground cinnamon

BLUEBERRY COFFEE CAKE BATTER

1 cup thick, cultured sour cream

½ teaspoon baking soda

1½ cups plus 2 tablespoons unsifted bleached all-purpose flour

¼ cup unsifted bleached cake flour

¾ teaspoon baking powder

¼ teaspoon salt

½ teaspoon ground cinnamon

½ teaspoon freshly grated nutmeg

1 cup fresh blueberries

¼ pound (8 tablespoons or 1 stick) unsalted butter, softened

1 cup superfine sugar

2 large eggs

2 teaspoons pure vanilla extract

BAKEWARE

9 by 9 by 2-inch baking pan

PREHEAT THE OVEN AND PREPARE THE BAKING PAN Preheat the oven to 350° F. Film the inside of the baking pan with nonstick cooking spray; set aside.

MIX THE CINNAMON AND SUGAR TOPPING In a small mixing bowl, thoroughly combine the granulated sugar, light brown sugar, and cinnamon; set aside.

MIX THE BLUEBERRY COFFEE CAKE BATTER Combine the sour cream and baking soda in a medium-size mixing bowl. *Sour cream texture observation* The mixture will swell and puff a bit as it stands.

Sift the flours, baking powder, salt, cinnamon, and nutmeg onto a sheet of waxed paper. In a small mixing bowl, thoroughly toss the blueberries with 1½ teaspoons of the sifted mixture. *Blueberry flouring observation* The blueberries must be well coated with the flour mixture, so that they remain suspended in the cake batter.

Cream the butter in the large bowl of a freestanding electric mixer on moderately low speed for 2 minutes. Add the superfine sugar and beat for 1 to 2 minutes. Beat in the eggs, one at a time, blending well after each addition. Mix in the vanilla extract.

On low speed, add half of the sifted ingredients, the sour cream–baking soda blend, then the remaining sifted mixture. Scrape down the sides of the mixing bowl frequently with a rubber spatula to keep the batter even-textured. *Batter texture observation* The batter will be moderately thick. Fold in the blueberries.

Along with the baking soda–sour cream blend, the superfine sugar gives the baked coffee cake a gossamer texture. Add only the baking powder, not the baking soda, to the dry ingredients.

Scrape the batter into the prepared baking pan. Smooth over the top with a rubber spatula or flexible palette knife.

SPRINKLE THE CINNAMON AND SUGAR TOPPING OVER THE COFFEE CAKE BATTER Sprinkle the topping evenly over the surface of the batter.

BAKE AND COOL THE COFFEE CAKE Bake the cake in the preheated oven for 35 minutes, or until set and a wooden pick inserted in the cake withdraws clean. Cool the cake in the pan on a rack for at least 20 minutes before cutting into squares for serving. Serve the cake warm or at room temperature.

❊ *For an extra surge of flavor,* toss 2 tablespoons moist, dried blueberries with the fresh berries and 2 teaspoons of the sifted mixture and fold into the batter.

❊ *For an aromatic topnote of flavor,* use vanilla-scented superfine sugar (see page 54) in place of plain superfine sugar in the coffee cake batter.

FRESHLY BAKED, THE COFFEE CAKE KEEPS FOR 2 TO 3 DAYS.

BLUEBERRY TEA CAKE

One 10-inch fluted tube cake, creating 16 slices

A WONDERFUL BLUEBERRY FLAVOR is imparted to this light butter cake by using a mixture of fresh and dried blueberries. The fresh berries give the batter a certain bursting-with-juice lushness, while the dried variety add a bold, intense quality to the batter. The blueberries are suspended in a luxurious vanilla-heightened sour cream batter, which offsets the fruit nicely.

Nonstick cooking spray, for preparing the cake pan

SOUR CREAM-BLUEBERRY BUTTER CAKE BATTER

3 cups unsifted bleached all-purpose flour

1¼ teaspoons baking powder

½ teaspoon baking soda

1 teaspoon salt

1 teaspoon freshly grated nutmeg

¼ teaspoon ground cinnamon

⅛ teaspoon ground cardamom

1¼ cups fresh blueberries

3 tablespoons moist, dried blueberries

½ pound (16 tablespoons or 2 sticks) unsalted butter, softened

2 cups vanilla-scented granulated sugar (see page 53)

4 large eggs

2½ teaspoons pure vanilla extract

1 cup thick, cultured sour cream

3 tablespoons buttermilk

Vanilla-scented confectioners' sugar (see page 54), for sifting over the baked cake

BAKEWARE

10-inch Bundt pan

PREHEAT THE OVEN AND PREPARE THE CAKE PAN Preheat the oven to 350° F. Film the inside of the Bundt pan with nonstick cooking spray; set aside.

MIX THE SOUR CREAM-BLUEBERRY BUTTER CAKE BATTER Sift the flour, baking powder, baking soda, salt, nutmeg, cinnamon, and cardamom onto a sheet of waxed paper. In a medium-size mixing bowl, thoroughly but lightly toss the fresh and dried blueberries with 2½ teaspoons of the sifted mixture.

Cream the butter in the large bowl of a freestanding electric mixer on moderate speed for 3 minutes. Add the vanilla-scented granulated sugar in three additions, beating for 1 minute after each portion is added. Beat in the eggs, one at a time, mixing for 45 seconds after each addition. Blend in the vanilla extract.

On low speed, alternately add the sifted ingredients in three additions with the sour cream in two additions, beginning and ending with the sifted mixture. Scrape down the sides of the mixing bowl frequently with a rubber spatula to keep the batter even-textured. Add the buttermilk and beat on low speed for 1 minute. Stir in the fresh and dried blueberries.

Spoon the batter into the prepared pan. Shake the pan lightly from side to side, once or twice, to level the top, or smooth over the top with a flexible palette knife.

The combination of sour cream and buttermilk guarantees a moist and fine-grained batter. The sour cream creates a soft textural density and the buttermilk a light creaminess. Do not substitute whole milk for the buttermilk, for the presence of two acidic ingredients is necessary to build the crumb of the tea cake.

Bake and cool the cake Bake the cake in the preheated oven for 50 minutes or until risen, set, and a wooden pick inserted in the cake withdraws clean. The baked cake will be golden brown on top and pull away slightly from the sides of the pan.

Cool the cake in the pan on a rack for 5 to 10 minutes, then invert onto another cooling rack. Cool completely. Dredge the top of the cake with confectioners' sugar just before slicing and serving. *Slicing observation* Use a serrated knife to cut the cake neatly and cleanly.

Freshly baked, the cake keeps for 2 to 3 days.

BABY BLUEBERRY CORN MUFFINS

28 teacake-size muffins

Amuffin batter built on yellow cornmeal becomes an excellent "baking canvas" for the addition of ripe blueberries. Both extracts (vanilla and almond) add a soft flavoring touch to the batter and, in an elusive way, elevate the flavor of the fruit.

Nonstick cooking spray, for preparing the muffin pans

BLUEBERRY CORN MUFFIN BATTER

2 cups unsifted bleached all-purpose flour

1 cup fine yellow cornmeal

3 teaspoons baking powder

¾ teaspoon salt

½ cup granulated sugar

1¼ cups fresh blueberries

4 large eggs

½ cup milk

½ pound (16 tablespoons or 2 sticks) unsalted butter, melted and cooled

¼ teaspoon pure vanilla extract

¼ teaspoon pure almond extract

BAKEWARE

28 teacake-size miniature muffin cups (each pan contains 24 muffin cups), each cup measuring 2 inches in diameter by 1³⁄₁₆ inches deep, with a capacity of 3 tablespoons

BEST BAKING ADVICE

For the puffiest muffins, mix the batter lightly, taking care to thoroughly incorporate any pockets of the flour and cornmeal mixture.

PREHEAT THE OVEN AND PREPARE THE MUFFIN PANS
Preheat the oven to 400° F. Film the inside of the muffin cups with nonstick cookware spray; set aside.

MIX THE BLUEBERRY CORN MUFFIN BATTER Sift the flour, cornmeal, baking powder, salt, and granulated sugar into a large mixing bowl. Add the blueberries and toss lightly. In a medium-size bowl, whisk together the eggs and milk; blend in the melted butter and vanilla and almond extracts, whisking thoroughly. Pour the liquid ingredients over the dry ingredients and stir to form a batter, using a wooden spoon, flat wooden paddle, or rubber spatula. Mix the ingredients lightly but thoroughly to dispel all pockets of flour lingering at the bottom of the bowl.

Divide the batter among the 28 muffin cups, mounding the batter in the center.

BAKE THE MUFFINS Bake the muffins for 13 to 15 minutes, or until risen, plump, set, and golden in spots on top. A wooden pick inserted in a muffin will withdraw clean, but if you pierce a berry, the pick will be stained.

Place the muffin pans on cooling racks. Let the muffins cool in the pans for 4 to 5 minutes. Carefully remove muffins from the pans and place on another cooling rack. Serve the muffins very fresh, warm or at room temperature.

❋ *For an extra surge of flavor,* add 3 tablespoons dried blueberries to the sifted flour mixture along with the fresh berries.

FRESHLY BAKED, THE MUFFINS KEEP FOR 2 DAYS.

BLUEBERRIES AND CREAM BREAKFAST CAKE

One 9 by 9-inch cake, creating 16 squares

DENSE BUT SOFT, AND VERY MOIST, this plainly flavored blueberry butter cake is finished with a generous sprinkling of granulated sugar. Freshly baked, it's divine with your morning tea or coffee.

Nonstick cooking spray, for preparing the baking pan

BLUEBERRIES AND CREAM CAKE BATTER

2¼ cups unsifted bleached all-purpose flour

¼ cup unsifted bleached cake flour

2 teaspoons baking powder

¾ teaspoon salt

½ teaspoon freshly grated nutmeg

1 cup fresh blueberries

14 tablespoons (1¾ sticks) unsalted butter, softened

2 tablespoons shortening

1¼ cups superfine sugar

2 large eggs

2 teaspoons pure vanilla extract

⅔ cup heavy cream blended with ½ cup milk

2 to 3 tablespoons granulated sugar, for sprinkling over the top of the warm, baked cake

BAKEWARE

9 by 9 by 2-inch baking pan

PREHEAT THE OVEN AND PREPARE THE BAKING PAN Preheat the oven to 350° F. Film the inside of the baking pan with nonstick cooking spray; set aside.

MIX THE BLUEBERRIES AND CREAM CAKE BATTER Sift the flours, baking powder, salt, and nutmeg onto a sheet of waxed paper. In a small mixing bowl, thoroughly toss the blueberries with 2 teaspoons of the sifted mixture. *Blueberry flouring observation* The blueberries must be thoroughly tossed with the flour mixture, so that they don't sink to the bottom of the cake as it bakes; if the blueberries settle during baking, the bottom of the cake will be wet and gummy.

Cream the butter and shortening in the large bowl of a free-standing electric mixer on moderate speed for 2 to 3 minutes. Add the superfine sugar in two additions, beating for 1 minute after each portion is added. Beat in the eggs, one at a time, blending well after each addition. Mix in the vanilla extract.

On low speed, alternately add the sifted mixture in three additions with the heavy cream–milk blend in two additions, beginning and ending with the sifted mixture. Scrape down the sides of the mixing bowl frequently with a rubber spatula to keep the batter even-textured. *Batter texture observation* The batter will be moderately thick and creamy-textured. Carefully but thoroughly, stir in the blueberries.

Scrape the batter into the prepared baking pan and spread it evenly into the pan, using a rubber spatula. Smooth over the top with a rubber spatula or flexible palette knife.

Lightly stir the blueberries into the batter so that the fruit remains whole and uncrushed. Crushed (or mashed) berries would weaken the consistency of the batter.

BAKE, TOP, AND COOL THE BREAKFAST CAKE Bake the cake in the preheated oven for 50 minutes, or until set and a wooden pick inserted 2 inches from the center of the cake withdraws clean. (If you run into a berry, the pick will be stained.) Immediately sprinkle the granulated sugar on top of the cake. Cool the cake in the pan on a rack. Cut into squares for serving directly from the pan. *Texture observation* The texture of the cake is best if cut and served at room temperature. If the cake is cut while hot or warm, the crumb will compact a bit.

❈ *For an aromatic topnote of flavor,* use vanilla-scented superfine sugar (see page 54) in place of plain superfine sugar and intensified vanilla extract (see page 52) in place of plain vanilla extract in the cake batter.

FRESHLY BAKED, THE CAKE KEEPS FOR 2 TO 3 DAYS.

SWEET MILK BLUEBERRY PANCAKES

About 28 pancakes

THESE GRIDDLE CAKES ARE THE ESSENCE OF SUMMER—the berries are caught up in a tender, cozy batter that is lightly sweetened and rounded out by vanilla extract. The hint of vanilla boosts the blueberry flavor.

SWEET MILK BLUEBERRY
PANCAKE BATTER

1¼ cups unsifted bleached all-purpose flour

¼ cup unsifted bleached cake flour

1½ teaspoons baking powder

⅛ teaspoon salt

¼ teaspoon freshly grated nutmeg

MIX THE SWEET MILK BLUEBERRY PANCAKE BATTER Whisk the all-purpose flour, cake flour, baking powder, salt, nutmeg, and granulated vanilla-scented sugar in a medium-size mixing bowl. In a small bowl, toss the blueberries with 1 teaspoon of the whisked flour mixture.

In a small mixing bowl, whisk the egg, egg yolk, melted butter, vanilla extract, and milk. Pour the whisked milk mixture over the dry ingredients and stir to form a batter, using a wooden spoon, flat wooden paddle, or rubber spatula. *Batter texture obser-*

¼ cup vanilla-scented granulated sugar (see page 53)

1 cup fresh blueberries

1 large egg

1 large egg yolk

5 tablespoons (½ stick plus 1 tablespoon) unsalted butter, melted and cooled

¾ teaspoon pure vanilla extract

1 cup milk, plus more as needed

Clarified butter (see page 66), for the griddle

Confectioners' sugar, for sprinkling on the pancakes (optional)

vation The batter will be lumpy and moderately thick. Stir the blueberries through the batter.

GRIDDLE THE PANCAKES Heat a griddle and when hot, film the surface with a little of the clarified butter, using two folded-over paper towels to apply it. The griddle should be hot enough so that the batter sizzles.

Spoon 2-tablespoon-size puddles of batter onto the griddle, placing them 2½ to 3 inches apart. Cook the pancakes for 45 seconds to 1 minute (or until just set), flip the pancakes using a sturdy, wide, offset metal spatula, and griddle for about 45 seconds longer, or until cooked through. With the remaining batter, cook the pancakes in batches, greasing the griddle with clarified butter as necessary. *Batter consistency observation* This batter has the tendency to thicken as it stands; thin it with extra milk as necessary, 2 teaspoons at a time, then continue to griddle the pancakes.

Serve the pancakes right off the griddle, sprinkled with confectioners' sugar, if you wish.

❊ *For an extra surge of flavor,* serve the pancakes with blueberry preserves or blueberry syrup.

BEST BAKING ADVICE

The small amount of cake flour tenderizes the griddled crumb of the pancakes.

SOUR CREAM BLUEBERRY MUFFINS

12 jumbo muffins

WHEN PINTS OF GORGEOUS BLUEBERRIES ABOUND, it's time to stir them through a moist and tender muffin batter. These enormous muffins are brimming with enough berries to please, and accented with cinnamon, nutmeg, and cardamom, all the better to showcase the berries. The topping—a simple mixture of granulated sugar and cinnamon—is a quick and flavorsome cap for the baked muffins.

Nonstick cooking spray, for preparing the muffin pans

SOUR CREAM BLUEBERRY MUFFIN BATTER

2¾ cups unsifted bleached all-purpose flour

¼ cup unsifted bleached cake flour

2½ teaspoons baking powder

1 teaspoon baking soda

¾ teaspoon salt

¾ cup plus 2 tablespoons granulated sugar

1 teaspoon freshly grated nutmeg

½ teaspoon ground cinnamon

⅛ teaspoon ground cardamom

2 cups fresh blueberries

1½ cups thick, cultured sour cream

¼ cup plus 2 tablespoons milk

2 large eggs

1 tablespoon pure vanilla extract

¼ pound (8 tablespoons or 1 stick) unsalted butter, melted and cooled

CINNAMON-SUGAR SPRINKLE

½ cup granulated sugar blended with ½ teaspoon ground cinnamon

PREHEAT THE OVEN AND PREPARE THE MUFFIN PANS Preheat the oven to 375° F. Generously coat the insides of 12 jumbo, crown top muffin cups with nonstick cooking spray; set aside.

MIX THE SOUR CREAM BLUEBERRY MUFFIN BATTER Sift the all-purpose flour, cake flour, baking powder, baking soda, salt, granulated sugar, nutmeg, cinnamon, and cardamom in a large mixing bowl. In a medium-size bowl, toss the blueberries with 2½ teaspoons of the sifted flour mixture.

In a medium-size mixing bowl, whisk the sour cream and milk together; blend in the eggs, vanilla extract, and melted butter.

Pour the whisked ingredients over the dry ingredients and stir to form a batter, using a rubber spatula. Make sure to scrape the bottom of the sides of the mixing bowl to dispel any pockets of flour as you are combining the batter. *Batter consistency observation* The batter will be thick. Carefully, but thoroughly, fold through the blueberries.

FILL THE MUFFIN CUPS WITH THE BATTER Divide the batter among the prepared muffin cups, mounding it lightly in the center.

TOP THE MUFFINS WITH THE CINNAMON-SUGAR SPRINKLE Sprinkle the cinnamon-sugar evenly over the tops of the muffins.

**12 jumbo, crown top muffin cups
(two pans, each holding 6 individual
muffin cups), each cup measuring
about 3¼ inches in diameter and 2
inches deep, with a capacity of scant
1 cup**

BAKE THE MUFFINS Bake the muffins for 25 to 30 minutes, or until risen, plump, and completely set. When the muffins are baked, a wooden pick inserted in the center will withdraw clean, or with a few moist crumbs attached to it.

COOL THE MUFFINS Place the muffin pans on cooling racks and let stand for 30 minutes to cool down and firm up. *Cooling observation* The muffins are quite tender and fragile at this point, and they should cool in the pans until the oven heat diminishes in order to hold their shape, otherwise the muffins will slouch. Carefully remove the muffins to cooling racks. Serve the muffins freshly baked.

❊ *For an extra surge of flavor,* add 3 tablespoons moist, dried blueberries to the fresh berries when tossing with the sifted flour mixture.

❊ *For an aromatic topnote of flavor,* use vanilla-scented granulated sugar (see page 53) in place of plain granulated sugar and intensified vanilla extract (see page 52) in place of plain vanilla extract in the muffin batter.

FRESHLY BAKED, THE MUFFINS KEEP FOR 2 TO 3 DAYS.

BEST BAKING ADVICE
Make sure that the blueberries are well coated with the flour mixture and thoroughly folded through the batter, so that they don't drop to the bottom of the cups as the muffins bake. You can also bake the batter in 11 jumbo muffin/cupcake pans (4 inches in diameter and 1¾ inches deep).

*t*he natural flavor of unsalted butter is not only one of the indispensable underpinnings of good baking, it is also an identifiable flavor in and of itself. The taste of butter is supported by various pivotal ingredients—sugar, egg yolks, whole eggs, milk, buttermilk, light cream, heavy cream, freshly grated nutmeg, and a touch of vanilla or almond extract. Unsalted butter has the freshest, purest, and clearest flavor and is preferable to the salted variety for use in baking. The most forward quality is its smooth creaminess, and for that reason butter blends well with all dairy products, flavoring agents (such as extracts), and scented sweeteners.

Of the brands available, I use Keller's European Style Butter, Kate's Homemade Butter, Land O Lakes, and Breakstone's. For a creamy presence, I use The Organic Cow of Vermont, Celles sur Belle, Vermont Cultured Butter, Président, Isigny Ste Mère Beurre Cru de Normandie, and Beurre d'Isigny Extra-Fin.

For the specifics of baking, I regularly use Land O Lakes and Breakstone's (and frequently The Organic Cow of Vermont) for cake, muffin, and quick bread batters; for cookie doughs; and in frostings, icings, and toppings. I use The Organic Cow of Vermont, Keller's European Style Butter, or Kate's Homemade Butter for pastry doughs, in sweet yeast doughs, for brownie and other dense bar cookie batters, and in flourless chocolate cakes. For shortbread doughs, for hand-formed butter cookies, and for madeleine batters, I use Celles sur Belle, Président, Isigny Ste Mère Beurre Cru de Normandie, and Beurre D'Isigny Extra-Fin, for any one of these is substantial and flavorful. To make clarified butter, I melt down the unsalted varieties of The Organic Cow of Vermont, Keller's European Style Butter, or Kate's Homemade Butter.

9

BUTTER

BUTTER CRESCENTS

2½ to 3 dozen cookies

IN THIS TYPE OF COOKIE, the flour seems to dissolve into the pecan-flecked dough, at once creating and releasing the taste of butter. The small amount of nutmeg and vanilla extract serves to enhance and build the butter flavor. The cookies' texture can be described as "short," or tenderly buttery, made with just enough leavening to have them crumble deliciously as you eat them.

BUTTER COOKIE DOUGH

2¼ cups unsifted bleached all-purpose flour

¾ teaspoon baking powder

⅛ teaspoon salt

¼ teaspoon freshly grated nutmeg

½ pound (16 tablespoons or 2 sticks) unsalted butter, melted and cooled

⅓ cup plus 2 tablespoons superfine sugar

¾ teaspoon pure vanilla extract

⅓ cup very finely chopped pecans

About 3 cups confectioners' sugar, for dredging the baked cookies

BAKEWARE

several cookie sheets

PREHEAT THE OVEN AND PREPARE THE COOKIE SHEETS Preheat the oven to 350° F. Line the cookie sheets with cooking parchment paper; set aside.

MIX THE BUTTER COOKIE DOUGH Sift the flour, baking powder, salt, and nutmeg onto a sheet of waxed paper.

In a large mixing bowl, combine the melted butter, superfine sugar, and vanilla extract, using a wooden spoon or flat wooden paddle. Stir in the pecans. Stir in the sifted ingredients in three additions, mixing thoroughly before adding the next portion. *Dough texture observation* The dough will be soft but firm, and shapeable.

SHAPE THE CRESCENTS Spoon out scant tablespoon-size quantities of dough and roll into pudgy logs about 2¼ to 2½ inches long. Arrange the cookie dough logs, about 2 inches apart, on the lined cookie sheets, placing 12 to 16 to a sheet (depending on the size of the sheet). Bend the logs into crescents, narrowing the ends very slightly.

BAKE AND COOL THE CRESCENTS Bake the cookies in the preheated oven for 13 to 15 minutes, or until set, with light golden bottoms. *Cookie appearance observation* The tops of the baked cookies will crack slightly, which is typical of this kind of rich butter cookie.

Let the cookies stand on the sheets for 3 minutes, then remove them to cooling racks, using a sturdy, offset metal spatula.

COAT THE BUTTER CRESCENTS IN THE CONFECTIONERS' SUGAR Line a work surface with waxed paper. Place the confectioners' sugar in a shallow bowl. After 5 to 8 minutes, and while the cookies are still warm, carefully roll them, a few at a time, in the sugar to coat, and place on the waxed paper. After 30 minutes, coat the cookies again.

FRESHLY BAKED, THE COOKIES KEEP FOR 1 WEEK.

BUTTER LAYER CAKE

One two-layer, 9-inch cake, creating about 12 slices

IN PRINCIPLE, a good butter cake contains enough egg yolks to enrich and color the batter, in addition to the primary flavor-fat, unsalted butter. The bottom cake layer is coated with a thick pastry cream that, in its own way, strengthens the rounded taste of butter. The composed layers are swaddled in chocolate frosting.

Shortening and bleached all-purpose flour, for preparing the layer cake pans

BUTTER LAYER CAKE BATTER

2 cups unsifted bleached all-purpose flour

¼ cup unsifted bleached cake flour

1¾ teaspoons baking powder

¼ teaspoon salt

¼ teaspoon freshly grated nutmeg

¼ pound (8 tablespoons or 1 stick) unsalted butter, softened

1½ cups granulated sugar

6 large egg yolks

PREHEAT THE OVEN AND PREPARE THE LAYER CAKE PANS Preheat the oven to 350° F. Lightly grease the cake pans with shortening. Line the bottom of each pan with a circle of waxed paper, grease the paper, and dust the insides with all-purpose flour. Tap out any excess flour; set aside.

MIX THE BUTTER LAYER CAKE BATTER Sift the all-purpose flour, cake flour, baking powder, salt, and nutmeg onto a sheet of waxed paper.

Cream the butter in the large bowl of a freestanding electric mixer on moderate speed for 2 minutes. Add half of the granulated sugar and beat for 1 minute; add the balance of the sugar and continue beating for 1 minute longer. Add the egg yolks and beat for 2 minutes on moderate speed, or until the mixture is creamy-textured. Blend in the vanilla extract.

2 teaspoons intensified vanilla extract (see page 52)

¾ cup milk blended with ½ cup light (table) cream

Cream Cake Filling (see page 191), for assembling the baked cake layers

Buttery Chocolate Frosting (see page 285) or Chocolate Cream Frosting (see page 272), for spreading on the baked cake layers

BAKEWARE

two 9-inch round layer cake pans (1½ inches deep)

BEST BAKING ADVICE
The combination of egg yolks and milk-cream blend makes for the richest cake batter, one that supports and emphasizes the flavor of the butter.

On low speed, add the sifted ingredients in three additions with the milk-light cream mixture in two additions, beginning and ending with the sifted mixture. Scrape down the sides of the mixing bowl frequently with a rubber spatula to keep the batter even-textured.

Spoon the batter into the layer cake pans, dividing it evenly between them. Smooth over the batter with a rubber spatula or flexible palette knife.

BAKE AND COOL THE CAKE LAYERS Bake the layers for 30 minutes, or until set and a wooden pick inserted 1 inch from the center of each cake layer withdraws clean. Each baked layer will pull away slightly from the sides of the cake pan. Cool the cake layers in the pans on racks for 5 to 8 minutes. Invert each layer onto another rack, peel off the waxed paper round, then invert again to cool right side up. Cool completely.

ASSEMBLE AND FROST THE CAKE Have the cream filling and frosting at hand. Tear off four 3-inch-wide strips of waxed paper. Place the strips in the shape of a square around the outer 3 inches of a cake plate. Center one cake layer on the plate (partially covering the waxed paper square; at least 1 inch of the strip should be visible). Spread the filling on the cake layer in an even layer, using a flexible palette knife. Carefully place the second layer on top, then ice the entire cake in drifts of frosting. When the frosting has set, in about 45 minutes, gently slide out and discard the waxed paper strips.

Cut the cake into slices for serving. Serve the cake very fresh, within 2 hours of filling and frosting. The cream-filled cake is fragile and must be refrigerated after 2 hours. Refrigerate any leftover cake.

CREAM CAKE FILLING

About 1 cup

FILLING ROUNDS OF LAYER CAKE with a creamy, egg yolk-endowed pastry cream is a luxurious way to connect them. The cream builds a sweet "sandwich" of the soft layers, and is one way to add extra moistness to the buttery rounds of cake.

RICH CREAM FILLING

½ cup heavy cream

½ cup milk

¼ cup granulated sugar

2 tablespoons cornstarch

pinch of salt

3 large egg yolks

1 teaspoon intensified vanilla extract (see page 52)

1½ teaspoons unsalted butter, softened

MAKE THE RICH CREAM FILLING Combine the heavy cream and milk in a small 1-quart saucepan (preferably enameled cast iron) and heat until warm. Set aside.

Sift the granulated sugar, cornstarch, and salt into a small (5-cup), heavy saucepan (preferably enameled cast iron). Whisk the sugar-cornstarch mixture well to combine; it must be thoroughly blended if the cream is to thicken properly. Slowly blend in the egg yolks.

Place a small fine-meshed sieve over the saucepan and dribble in about 1 tablespoon of the tepid cream-milk mixture and immediately stir it in. Add 2 to 3 more tablespoons of the liquid in this way to avoid shocking the egg yolks. Add the remaining liquid in three more additions, mixing well. *Straining technique observation* Straining the liquid into the yolk mixture through a sieve prevents any particles of filmy cream-milk that may have formed over or on the sides of the liquid from incorporating into the filling.

Bring the filling mixture to a boil slowly, over gentle heat, stirring constantly all the while with a wooden spoon. Do not use a whisk. Do not beat the mixture. As soon as the thickened cream comes to a low boil, regulate the heat so that it bubbles gently for about 1 minute and 30 seconds. *Cream texture observation* The cream filling will be thickened and smooth if you supervise the cooking carefully and bring the mixture to a boil very slowly; otherwise it will form small lumps. Since the cream filling is strained (in the next step), any small lumps can be smoothed out and the texture restored.

STRAIN AND FLAVOR THE CREAM Press the cream through a fine-meshed sieve into a heatproof bowl, using a rubber spatula.

Slowly stir in the vanilla extract and butter.

Immediately press a sheet of plastic wrap directly over the surface of the cream. Cool. Refrigerate the cream in an airtight container for at least 6 hours before using. The cream can be made one day in advance and stored in the refrigerator.

GRANDMA LILLY'S BUTTER POUND CAKE

One 9¾-inch tube cake, creating about 18 slices

MY PATERNAL GRANDMOTHER, LILLY YOCKELSON, just adored pound cake. In fact, a pound cake sitting inside a cake keeper on top of her long stainless-steel kitchen countertop remains one of my earliest childhood images. The formula for this reasonably light but very buttery cake comes from my grandmother's small, loose-leaf book of handwritten recipes. Her recipe uses all cake flour, which produces a cake with a heavenly texture, but for a cake with a slightly firmer texture, you can use half bleached all-purpose flour and half bleached cake flour (1½ cups of each).

The cake is plain but elegant and straightforward—adjectives that could also be used to describe my grandma. Its utter simplicity will impress you.

Unsalted butter and all-purpose flour, for the cake pan

BUTTER CAKE BATTER

3 cups unsifted bleached cake flour

1½ teaspoons baking powder

½ teaspoon salt

½ teaspoon ground mace

1 pound (4 sticks) unsalted butter, softened

2⅔ cups confectioners' sugar

8 large eggs, separated

2 teaspoons pure vanilla extract

BAKEWARE

plain 9¾-inch tube pan (6 inches deep), with a capacity of 18 cups

PREHEAT THE OVEN AND PREPARE THE CAKE PAN Preheat the oven to 350° F. Butter the inside of the tube pan. Dust the inside of the pan with all-purpose flour. Tap out any excess flour; set aside.

MAKE THE BUTTER CAKE BATTER Sift the flour, baking powder, salt, and mace.

Cream the butter in the large bowl of a freestanding electric mixer on moderately low speed for 5 minutes. Add the confectioners' sugar in two additions, beating for 1 minute after each portion is added. Add the egg yolks, two at a time, beating for 15 seconds after each addition, or until just incorporated. Blend in the vanilla extract.

On low speed, add the sifted mixture in three additions, mixing just until the flour particles are absorbed. Scrape down the sides of the mixing bowl frequently with a rubber spatula to keep the batter even-textured. *Batter consistency observation* At this point, the batter will be relatively thick.

Using an electric hand mixer (or rotary egg beater), beat the egg whites in a clean, dry bowl until firm peaks are formed. Remove the mixing bowl from the mixer stand. Vigorously stir one-third of the beaten egg whites into the batter, then add the remain-

BEST BAKING ADVICE
Overbeating the egg yolks would toughen
the crumb of the baked cake. Using a deep
tube pan creates an impressive and
beautifully tall pound cake.

ing whites. Stir for 1 minute, or until somewhat combined. Return the bowl to the base of the freestanding mixer and beat on low speed for 1 minute. *Method observation* Beating the egg white–endowed batter in the mixer is an unusual step, but it works to establish the fine-grained texture of the baked pound cake, and actually improves the finished crumb. *Batter texture observation* The batter should be smooth and even-textured.

Spoon the batter into the prepared pan. Lightly smooth over the top with a rubber spatula.

BAKE AND COOL THE CAKE Bake the cake in the preheated oven for 1 hour to 1 hour and 10 minutes, or until risen, set, and a wooden pick inserted in the cake withdraws clean. The baked cake will be a medium golden color on top.

Cool the cake in the pan on a rack for 10 minutes. Carefully invert the cake onto a cooling rack, then invert again onto another rack to cool right side up. Cool completely before slicing and serving. *Slicing observation* Use a serrated knife to cut the cake neatly and cleanly.

FRESHLY BAKED, THE CAKE KEEPS FOR 4 DAYS.

Variations: For Grandma Lilly's butter pound cake with nutmeg, omit the mace and substitute 1 teaspoon freshly grated nutmeg.

For Grandma Lilly's butter pound cake with three extracts, reduce the vanilla extract to 1¾ teaspoons and along with it add ¾ teaspoon pure almond extract and ¾ teaspoon pure lemon extract. The combination of extracts adds a soft, floral undertone to the cake batter.

BUTTER BISCUITS

14 to 16 biscuits

ESTABLISHING THE DEPTH OF BUTTER FLAVOR in baking powder biscuits is accomplished by using buttermilk as the liquid, incorporating both butter and shortening in the dough, and brushing the tops with melted butter. Using a blend of butter and shortening generates a dough with a good, buttery taste and lightened texture, as shortening creates volume, rather than density, and a certain airy lightness.

Freshly baked and blushing from the heat of the oven, these biscuits are a simple indulgence. Serve them with butter and honey, or bursting-with-fruit preserves.

BUTTER AND BUTTERMILK BISCUIT DOUGH

3 cups unsifted bleached all-purpose flour

3 teaspoons baking powder

¾ teaspoon baking soda

¼ teaspoon cream of tartar

1 teaspoon salt

3 tablespoons granulated sugar

¼ pound (8 tablespoons or 1 stick) unsalted butter, cold, cut into tablespoon pieces

4 tablespoons shortening, cold

1 cup buttermilk

3 tablespoons unsalted butter, melted and cooled, for brushing on the tops of the unbaked biscuits

BAKEWARE

large rimmed sheet pan or cookie sheet

PREHEAT THE OVEN AND HAVE THE BAKING SHEET AT HAND
Preheat the oven to 425° F. Have a sheet pan or cookie sheet at hand.

MAKE THE BUTTER AND BUTTERMILK BISCUIT DOUGH
Whisk the flour, baking powder, baking soda, cream of tartar, salt, and granulated sugar in a large mixing bowl. Drop in the chunks of butter and shortening. Using a pastry blender, cut the butter and shortening into the flour until reduced to small pieces about the size of dried lima beans. Crumble the mixture between your fingertips for a minute or so, to further reduce the butter-shortening to smaller bits and flakes, bringing the mixture up onto the surface as you go. Pour over the buttermilk and stir to form a slightly moist, but malleable, dough.

KNEAD THE BISCUIT DOUGH Knead the dough briefly in the bowl about 12 times by pushing it lightly from side to side and top to bottom.

ROLL AND CUT THE BISCUITS Turn the dough onto a very lightly floured work surface. With a lightly floured rolling pin, roll the dough into a generous 1-inch-thick slab (or pat the dough to an even thickness with your fingertips).

Stamp out biscuits, using a lightly floured 2-inch square or round cutter. (Using a square cutter keeps the scraps down to a minimum because you can cut closely edge-to-edge.) *Cutting observation* When cutting the biscuits, make sure to press straight down into the dough and lift the cutter straight up; use even pressure and avoid twisting the cutter or the biscuits will rise unevenly and bake lopsided. Place the biscuits, 2 inches apart, on the baking sheet, using a small, offset metal spatula.

GLAZE THE UNBAKED BISCUITS WITH THE COOLED, MELTED BUTTER Brush the tops of the biscuits with the melted butter. For the loftiest biscuits, with the highest rise possible, don't let the melted butter dribble down the sides.

BAKE AND COOL THE BISCUITS Bake the biscuits for 13 to 15 minutes, or until set and golden. Remove the biscuits to a cooling rack, using a offset metal spatula. Serve the biscuits very fresh and warm.

BUTTER SPRITZ COOKIES

2½ to 3 dozen cookies

THE DOUGH FOR THESE TENDER, fine-crumbed tea cookies is buttery and lightly seasoned with nutmeg and vanilla extract. The spice and flavoring extract, along with a bit of salt, bring out the substantial richness—and vitality—of the butter. The small amount of baking powder present (and not often a part of many spritz cookie dough recipes) tenderizes the crumb of the dough, without completely diminishing its baked shape and pattern. The soft dough is loaded into a pastry bag fitted with a star tip and piped into S-shaped cookies. For the best overall taste and most delicate crumb, refrigerate the formed cookies for 20 minutes before baking, and bake them until golden all over, with slightly darker edges.

BUTTER COOKIE DOUGH

2¼ cups plus 2 teaspoons sifted bleached all-purpose flour

¼ teaspoon baking powder

¼ teaspoon salt

¼ teaspoon freshly grated nutmeg

½ pound (16 tablespoons or 2 sticks) unsalted butter, softened

⅔ cup superfine sugar

3 large egg yolks

1½ teaspoons pure vanilla extract

FIT A PASTRY BAG WITH THE DECORATIVE TIP Fit a large pastry bag with a coupler and star tip (such as Ateco #4 or

Plain granulated sugar, colored or white sanding sugar, or sprinkles, for sprinkling on the unbaked cookies

BAKEWARE
several cookie sheets

Ateco #5). Twist and tuck about 1 inch of the bag into the tip and a bend a collar on the bag. Set aside.

PREPARE THE COOKIE SHEETS Line the cookie sheets with cooking parchment paper; set aside.

MIX THE BUTTER COOKIE DOUGH Resift the flour with the baking powder, salt, and nutmeg onto a sheet of waxed paper.

Cream the butter in the large bowl of a freestanding electric mixer on low speed for 5 minutes. Add the superfine sugar and beat on moderately low speed for 3 to 4 minutes longer, or until lightened and a creamy white color. *Butter-sugar texture observation* The butter and sugar should be creamed thoroughly to dispel any of the sugar's grittiness.

Blend in the egg yolks and vanilla extract. On low speed, add the sifted ingredients in two additions, beating just until the particles of flour are absorbed. Scrape down the sides of the mixing bowl with a rubber spatula to keep the dough even-textured.

FILL THE PASTRY BAG WITH THE DOUGH AND PIPE THE COOKIES Holding the pastry bag by the inside of the turned-down collar, fill with about one-third of the dough. Flip up the collar and press the dough down with your fingertips. Twist the top. Pipe S-shaped cookies, 2 inches apart, on the lined cookie sheets, placing 10 cookies to a sheet. Refill the pastry bag as necessary, and continue piping cookies.

BEST BAKING ADVICE
Use superfine sugar to make a fragile crumb, and egg yolks, rather than whole eggs, for richness. On baking, a small amount of baking powder expands the dough slightly, lightening and tenderizing it.

REFRIGERATE THE COOKIES Chill the piped cookies on the cookie sheets for 15 minutes.

PREHEAT THE OVEN, TOP, BAKE, AND COOL THE COOKIES Preheat the oven to 375° F. Lightly sprinkle sugar on the tops of the cookies. Bake the cookies for 10 to 14 minutes, or until light golden all over, with slightly darker edges. Cool the cookies on the sheets for 1 minute, then remove them to cooling racks using a sturdy, offset metal spatula. Cool completely.

FRESHLY BAKED, THE COOKIES KEEP FOR 3 TO 4 DAYS.

BUTTER COOKIE CUT-OUTS

About twenty 5-inch cookies or about 3 dozen 3-inch cookies or about forty-five 2-inch cookies

Cookie cut-outs made from this dough bake up with smooth, level surfaces, making them ideal for decorating with Royal Icing (see page 384). The cookie dough handles well and is delicious, too. You can pipe colored royal icing on baked and cooled cookies in whimsical designs according to the shape and style of the cookies, or simply dust the tops of the unbaked cookies with plain, coarse sugar or brilliantly colored sanding sugar.

BUTTER COOKIE DOUGH

4 cups unsifted bleached all-purpose flour

1½ teaspoons baking powder

¼ teaspoon cream of tartar

1¼ teaspoons salt

½ pound (16 tablespoons or 2 sticks) unsalted butter, softened

¼ cup plus 2 teaspoons shortening

1½ cups granulated sugar

2 large eggs

3 teaspoons pure vanilla extract

2 tablespoons evaporated milk

About 1 cup granulated sugar, coarse sugar, or sanding sugar, for sprinkling on the tops of the unbaked cookies, or Royal Icing Made with Meringue Powder (see page 384), for applying on the tops of the baked cookies

BAKEWARE

several cookie sheets

MAKE THE BUTTER COOKIE DOUGH Sift the flour, baking powder, cream of tartar, and salt onto a sheet of waxed paper.

Cream the butter and shortening in the large bowl of a freestanding electric mixer on moderate speed for 2 to 3 minutes. Add the granulated sugar in two additions, beating for 1 minute after each portion is added. Blend in the eggs, one at a time, beating for about 45 seconds after each addition. Blend in the vanilla extract and evaporated milk.

On low speed, add the sifted ingredients in three portions, beating just until the particles of flour have been absorbed. Scrape down the sides of the mixing bowl frequently with a rubber spatula to keep the cookie dough even-textured.

ROLL THE DOUGH Divide the dough into four portions and roll each between two sheets of waxed paper to a thickness of a scant ¼ inch. Layer the sheets of dough on a cookie sheet. Refrigerate the dough overnight.

PREHEAT THE OVEN AND PREPARE THE COOKIE SHEETS Preheat the oven to 375° F. Line the cookie sheets with lengths of cooking parchment paper; set aside.

FREEZE THE COOKIE DOUGH BEFORE BAKING Place the dough in the freezer 30 minutes before cutting out the cookies and baking them.

CUT OUT THE COOKIES Remove one sheet of dough at a time from the freezer. Carefully peel off both sheets of waxed paper and place the dough on a lightly floured work surface. Stamp out cookies with the desired cookie cutter and place them, 2 inches apart, on the lined cookie sheets. Sprinkle coarse sugar or colored sanding sugar on top of the baked cookies, or leave the cookies plain, if you are decorating them with royal icing later on.

BAKE AND COOL THE COOKIES Bake the cookies for 10 to 12 minutes, or until set and light brown around the edges. Let the cookies rest on the sheet for 1 minute, then remove them to a cooling rack using a wide, offset metal spatula. Cool completely before storing or decorating with icing.

FRESHLY BAKED, THE COOKIES KEEP FOR 5 TO 7 DAYS.

BUTTERMILK BUTTER POUND CAKE
One 10-inch fluted tube cake, creating 16 slices

*T*HE TEMPERATE TANG OF BUTTERMILK, along with the unsalted butter, keeps this fine-grained pound cake batter moist. The full, rounded dimension of butter, in all its creaminess, comes through and is balanced by the nutmeg and cardamom.

Nonstick cooking spray, for preparing the cake pan

BUTTERMILK BUTTER CAKE BATTER

3 cups unsifted bleached all-purpose flour

¼ teaspoon baking soda

1 teaspoon salt

½ teaspoon freshly grated nutmeg

⅛ teaspoon ground cardamom

½ pound (16 tablespoons or 2 sticks) unsalted butter, softened

PREHEAT THE OVEN AND PREPARE THE CAKE PAN Preheat the oven to 350° F. Film the inside of the Bundt pan with nonstick cooking spray; set aside.

MIX THE BUTTERMILK BUTTER CAKE BATTER Sift the flour, baking soda, salt, nutmeg, and cardamom onto a sheet of waxed paper.

Cream the butter in the large bowl of a freestanding electric mixer on moderate speed for 2 to 3 minutes. Add the superfine sugar in three additions, beating for 1 minute after each portion is added. Beat in the eggs, one at a time, mixing for 45 seconds to 1 minute after each addition. Blend in the vanilla extract.

2½ cups superfine sugar

4 large eggs

2 teaspoons pure vanilla extract

1 cup buttermilk, whisked well

Confectioners' sugar, for sifting on top
of the baked cake (optional)

BAKEWARE

10-inch Bundt pan

On low speed, alternately add the sifted mixture in three additions with the buttermilk in two additions, beginning and ending with the sifted mixture. Scrape down the sides of the mixing bowl frequently with a rubber spatula to keep the batter even-textured. *Batter texture observation* The batter will be lightly thickened and very creamy.

Spoon the batter into the prepared pan. Gently shake the pan (once or twice) from side to side to level the top.

BAKE AND COOL THE CAKE Bake the cake in the preheated oven for 50 to 55 minutes, or until risen, set, and a wooden pick inserted in the center of the cake withdraws clean. The baked cake will pull away slightly from the sides of the baking pan.

Cool the cake in the pan on a rack for 5 to 10 minutes. Invert the cake onto another cooling rack. Cool completely. Sift confectioners' sugar over the top of the cake just before slicing and serving, if you wish. *Slicing observation* Use a serrated knife to cut the cake neatly and cleanly.

❋ *For a textural contrast,* stir 1 cup chopped walnuts or pecans, lightly toasted and cooled completely, into the cake batter after the last addition of flour has been incorporated.

FRESHLY BAKED, THE CAKE KEEPS FOR 1 WEEK.

BEST BAKING ADVICE
Use fresh buttermilk, not powdered buttermilk and water, for the best-tasting cake. Use superfine sugar to keep the internal grain of the cake fine and gossamer.

BUTTER SHORTBREAD

One 9½-inch shortbread, creating 12 triangular pieces

SHORTBREAD DOUGH MADE WITH RICE FLOUR bakes into a crumbly-tender, grainy cookie. Its meltingly delicate texture does emphasize the flavor of the butter, so use the freshest, highest quality unsalted butter you can find, such as Kate's Homemade Butter or Keller's European Style Butter, also known as Plugrá.

Nonstick cooking spray, for preparing the tart pan

BUTTER SHORTBREAD DOUGH

1¼ cups unsifted bleached all-purpose flour

¼ cup rice flour

¼ teaspoon baking powder

⅛ teaspoon salt

12 tablespoons (1½ sticks) unsalted butter, softened

⅓ cup superfine sugar

½ teaspoon pure vanilla extract

About 2 tablespoons granulated sugar, for sprinkling on the top of the baked shortbread

BAKEWARE

fluted 9½-inch tart pan (with a removable bottom)

PREHEAT THE OVEN AND PREPARE THE TART PAN Preheat the oven to 325° F. Film the inside of the tart pan with nonstick cooking spray; set aside.

MIX THE BUTTER SHORTBREAD DOUGH Sift the all-purpose flour, rice flour, baking powder, and salt onto a sheet of waxed paper.

Cream the butter in large bowl of a freestanding electric mixer on low speed for 3 to 4 minutes, or until smooth. Blend in the superfine sugar and vanilla extract and beat for 2 minutes longer on low speed. Blend in the sifted flour mixture in two additions, mixing slowly until the particles of flour are absorbed and a soft, smooth dough is created. Scrape down the sides of the mixing bowl with a rubber spatula to keep the dough even-textured. *Dough texture observation* The dough will be soft and lightly sticky.

PAT THE DOUGH INTO THE PREPARED PAN Transfer the dough to the tart pan, and lightly press it into an even layer. Prick the shortbread with the tines of a fork in about 15 random places.

BAKE AND COOL THE SHORTBREAD Bake the shortbread in the preheated oven for 40 to 45 minutes, or until set, and an all-over medium tan color on top. The shortbread must be baked through, otherwise the core will be tacky.

Place the pan of shortbread on a cooling rack and immediately dust the top with granulated sugar. Cool for 10 minutes.

The rice flour adds a pleasantly gritty edge to the internal structure of the baked shortbread. Sprinkling the top of the fully baked shortbread with granulated sugar adds an interesting dimension to the cookie, which is both lightly sweet and pleasingly sandy.

CUT THE SHORTBREAD Carefully unmold the shortbread, leaving it on its round base. After 10 to 15 minutes, cut into even-sized wedges, using a sharp chef's knife. *Cutting observation* To slice cleanly and neatly, the shortbread must be cut while still warm. Cool completely.

FRESHLY BAKED, THE SHORTBREAD KEEPS FOR 1 WEEK TO 10 DAYS.

GOLDEN BUTTER CAKE

One 10-inch swirled tube cake, creating 14 slices

With the light support of vanilla extract and nutmeg, and enough eggs for fortification, the buttery flavor in this plain cake really glows. The crumb is close-textured and lush, so slices of the cake pair nicely with fresh berries and whipped cream, or ice cream and hot fudge sauce, the Caramel Custard Sauce on page 229, or the Buttery Caramel Sauce on page 237.

Nonstick cooking spray, for preparing the cake pan

BUTTER CAKE BATTER

2⅔ cups unsifted bleached all-purpose flour

⅓ cup unsifted bleached cake flour

½ teaspoon baking powder

¾ teaspoon salt

¾ teaspoon freshly grated nutmeg

¾ pound (3 sticks) unsalted butter, softened

2⅔ cups superfine sugar

5 large eggs

1¾ teaspoons pure vanilla extract

1 cup milk

Confectioners' sugar, for sifting on top of the baked cake (optional)

BAKEWARE

deep 10-inch swirled tube pan, 4¾ inches deep, with a capacity of about 13½ cups

PREHEAT THE OVEN AND PREPARE THE CAKE PAN Preheat the oven to 325° F. Film the inside of the tube pan with nonstick cooking spray; set aside.

MIX THE BUTTER CAKE BATTER Sift the all-purpose flour, cake flour, baking powder, salt, and nutmeg onto a sheet of waxed paper.

Cream the butter in the large bowl of a freestanding electric mixer on moderate speed for 3 to 4 minutes. Add the superfine sugar in four additions, beating for 1 minute after each portion is added. Add the eggs, one at a time, beating well after each addition. Blend in the vanilla extract.

On low speed, alternately add the sifted mixture in three additions with the milk in two additions, beginning and ending with the sifted mixture. Scrape down the sides of the mixing bowl frequently with a rubber spatula to keep the batter even-textured.

Spoon the batter into the prepared cake pan. Gently shake the pan (once or twice) from side to side to level the top. *Batter texture observation* The batter will be medium-thick and very creamy.

BAKE AND COOL THE CAKE Bake the cake in the preheated oven for 1 hour and 5 minutes, or until risen, set, and a wooden pick inserted in the cake withdraws clean. The baked cake will pull away slightly from the sides of the baking pan.

Cool the cake in the pan on a rack for 5 to 10 minutes. Invert the cake onto another cooling rack. Cool completely. Sift confectioners' sugar over the top of the cake before slicing and serving, if you wish. *Slicing observation* Use a serrated knife to cut the cake neatly and cleanly.

FRESHLY BAKED, THE CAKE KEEPS FOR 3 TO 4 DAYS.

*t*he playful flavor that is called buttercrunch (also known as toffee)—made up of butter, nuts, and caramelized sugar, generally enclosed in a scrumptious wrap of chocolate—is an excellent "sweet seasoning" agent for batters and doughs. Just adding the chopped-up candy bars supplies intensity to a plain cookie or biscuit dough, tea cake batter, or buttery yeast dough. Buttercrunch is simply packed with crunchy, butter-and-nut-infused taste.

Toffee is usually produced in small, flat, rectangular blocks. Reducing the candy to large or small nuggets, finely chopped pieces, or chunks is easy to do: line up the blocks touching each other on a sturdy chopping board and, with a large chef's knife, cut each in half lengthwise, then cut vertically into chunks ranging from pebbly-small to large. At this point, the chunks can be finely chopped. Inevitably, when chopping the candy, small shards will be produced; these are the tiny odd-shaped fragments that usually break off here and there—be sure to add these splinter-like pieces into the dough or batter, too.

Chopped candy in general, and toffee in particular, gets very hot when exposed to the intense heat of an oven, and for that reason, bakery items containing toffee should not be directly touched or consumed until the heat subsides completely. Remove all baked goods that are filled or laced with toffee (such as biscuits, buns, or cookies) from baking pans or cookie sheets with a sturdy, offset metal spatula to durable cooling racks.

10

BUTTERCRUNCH

BUTTERCRUNCH MELT-A-WAYS

About 2½ to 3 dozen

SPOTTED WITH FRAGMENTS OF TOFFEE, bathed in butter, and covered in chopped almonds, these cookies nearly vaporize in the mouth. I find them totally irresistible.

BUTTERCRUNCH BUTTER COOKIE DOUGH

2¼ cups unsifted bleached all-purpose flour

¾ teaspoon baking powder

⅛ teaspoon salt

½ pound (16 tablespoons or 2 sticks) unsalted butter, melted and cooled

⅓ cup plus 1 tablespoon unsifted confectioners' sugar

1½ teaspoons pure vanilla extract

1 teaspoon pure almond extract

4 packages (1.4 ounces each) milk chocolate-covered toffee (Heath Milk Chocolate English Toffee Bar), finely chopped (see Chopping Note below)

About 1½ cups finely chopped almonds, for rolling the balls of cookie dough

About 2½ cups confectioners' sugar, for dredging the baked cookies

BAKEWARE

several cookie sheets

PREHEAT THE OVEN AND PREPARE THE COOKIE SHEETS Preheat the oven to 350° F. Line the cookie sheets with cooking parchment paper; set aside.

MIX THE BUTTERCRUNCH BUTTER COOKIE DOUGH Sift the flour, baking powder, and salt onto a sheet of waxed paper.

In a large mixing bowl, stir the melted butter, confectioners' sugar, and vanilla and almond extracts, using a wooden spoon or flat wooden paddle. *Butter and sugar mixture observation* At this point, the sugar will form small speckled clumps in the butter mixture, but as soon as you add the flour, the sugar will disperse.

Stir in half of the flour mixture and the chopped candy. Stir in the remaining flour and mix to form a cohesive dough. Let the dough stand for 5 minutes to allow the butter to be absorbed into it. *Dough texture observation* The dough will be moist but reasonably firm and manageable.

SHAPE AND COAT THE MELT-A-WAYS Place the almonds in a shallow bowl. Spoon out scant tablespoon-size quantities of dough and roll into balls. Roll the balls into the chopped almonds, pressing the nuts in lightly as they are rolled. Arrange the cookie dough balls about 2 inches apart on the lined cookie sheets, placing 12 to 16 on each sheet (depending on the size of the sheet).

BAKE AND COOL THE COOKIES Bake the cookies in the preheated oven for 13 to 15 minutes, or until set, with light golden bottoms. There will be a few thin cracks in the tops. Little bits of chopped candy will puddle at the base of the cookies, here and there.

Let the cookies stand on the sheets for 30 seconds, then remove them to cooling racks, using a sturdy, offset metal spatula. As you are removing them, detach any melted bits of candy from the base of the cookies, using a flexible palette knife or tip of a teaspoon. Cool the cookies for 5 to 8 minutes.

COAT THE COOKIES WITH THE CONFECTIONERS' SUGAR Line a work surface with waxed paper. Place the confectioners' sugar in a shallow bowl. Wearing food-safe rubber gloves to protect your hands, carefully roll the cookies, a few at a time, in the sugar to coat, and place on the waxed paper. After 30 minutes, coat the cookies again.

❋ *Chopping Note:* The toffee should be chopped into bits tiny enough to allow the candy to be fully enclosed in the dough. This helps to keep the candy contained in the dough.

FRESHLY BAKED, THE COOKIES KEEP FOR 4 TO 5 DAYS.

BUTTERCRUNCH FLATS

About 3 dozen cookies

CHOCKABLOCK WITH CHOPPED TOFFEE, these crisp-on-the-edge and chewy-in-the-middle cookies have a delicate, buttercrunchy caramel flavor and exceptionally buttery taste.

TOFFEE-BROWN SUGAR
COOKIE DOUGH

2 cups unsifted bleached all-purpose flour

¼ teaspoon baking soda

½ teaspoon salt

½ pound (2 sticks or 16 tablespoons) unsalted butter, softened

½ cup granulated sugar

PREHEAT THE OVEN AND PREPARE THE COOKIE SHEETS Preheat the oven to 350° F. Line the cookie sheets with lengths of cooking parchment paper; set aside.

MIX THE TOFFEE-BROWN SUGAR COOKIE DOUGH Sift the flour, baking soda, and salt onto a sheet of waxed paper.

Cream the butter in the large bowl of a freestanding electric mixer on low speed for 3 to 4 minutes. Add the granulated sugar and beat for 1 minute on moderate speed. Add the light brown sugar and beat for a minute longer. Beat in the egg. Blend in the

½ cup firmly packed light brown
   sugar, sieved if lumpy

1 large egg

2 teaspoons pure vanilla extract

½ teaspoon pure almond extract

10 packages (1.4 ounces each) milk
   chocolate-covered toffee (Heath
   Milk Chocolate English Toffee Bar),
   chopped into ½- to ¾-inch chunks

BAKEWARE

several cookie sheets

vanilla and almond extracts. Scrape down the sides of the mixing bowl frequently to keep the batter even-textured. On low speed, add the sifted mixture in two additions, beating just until the particles of flour are absorbed. Work in the chopped toffee, using a wooden spoon or flat paddle.

PLACE BALLS OF DOUGH ONTO THE PREPARED COOKIE SHEETS Spoon up rounded 2-tablespoon mounds of dough. Place the dough mounds, 4 inches apart, on the lined cookie sheets, arranging six to eight to a sheet (depending upon the size of the cookie sheet). Firmly press in any pieces of toffee that stick out on the rounded edges.

BAKE AND COOL THE FLATS Bake the cookies in the preheated oven for 12 to 14 minutes, or until just set. As the cookies bake, they will flatten out, swell lightly, and still be slightly puffy (even though set). Let the cookies stand on the sheets for 1 minute, then remove them to cooling racks, using a wide, offset metal spatula. Remove and detach any bits of candy that may have puddled around the base of the baked cookies. Cool completely.

❋ *For an aromatic topnote of flavor,* use intensified vanilla extract (see page 52) in place of plain vanilla extract in the cookie dough.

FRESHLY BAKED, THE COOKIES KEEP FOR 3 DAYS.

Variation: For almond buttercrunch flats, work ¾ cup coarsely chopped blanched almonds (lightly toasted and cooled completely) into the dough along with the chopped toffee.

BEST BAKING ADVICE

The brown sugar in the cookie dough
supports the taste of the toffee candy.

KITCHEN SINK BUTTERCRUNCH BARS

24 bars

THE BAR COOKIE BATTER, which is more like a dense but soft dough, is intensified with both vanilla extract and almond extract, and becomes an excellent canvas for an abundant stir-in of chopped toffee, chips, and nuts.

Softened unsalted butter and bleached all-purpose flour, for preparing the baking pan

TOFFEE BAR COOKIE BATTER

¾ cup plus 2 tablespoons unsifted bleached all-purpose flour

¼ teaspoon baking soda

⅛ teaspoon salt

¼ teaspoon freshly grated nutmeg

¼ pound (8 tablespoons or 1 stick) unsalted butter, melted and cooled to tepid

¾ cup firmly packed light brown sugar, sieved if lumpy

¼ cup granulated sugar

1 large egg

1 teaspoon pure vanilla extract

½ teaspoon pure almond extract

4 packages (1.4 ounces each) milk chocolate-covered toffee (Heath Milk Chocolate English Toffee Bar), chopped into ½-inch chunks

¾ cup coarsely chopped skinned almonds, lightly toasted and cooled completely

¾ cup semisweet chocolate chips

BAKEWARE

9 by 9 by 2-inch baking pan

PREHEAT THE OVEN AND PREPARE THE BAKING PAN Preheat the oven to 350° F. Lightly butter and flour the inside of the baking pan. Tap out any excess flour; set aside.

MIX THE TOFFEE BAR COOKIE BATTER Sift the flour, baking soda, salt, and nutmeg onto a sheet of waxed paper.

Whisk the melted butter, light brown sugar, and granulated sugar in a medium-size mixing bowl. Blend in the egg and vanilla and almond extracts. Stir in the sifted mixture, mixing until all particles of flour are absorbed, using a wooden spoon or flat wooden paddle. Stir in the chopped toffee, almonds, and chocolate chips. *Batter/dough texture observation* The batter/dough will be dense but creamy-textured.

Scrape the batter/dough into the prepared baking pan. Spread the batter/dough evenly in the pan, using a flexible palette knife.

BAKE, COOL, AND CUT THE BARS Bake the sweet for 25 minutes, or until set. Transfer the pan to a cooling rack. Cool for 30 minutes. Using a small, sharp knife, cut the entire cake into four quarters, then cut each quarter into six bars. *Cutting observation* Dividing the cake into bars after 30 minutes lets you cut through the toffee neatly. Cool completely. Recut the bars and remove them from the baking pan, using a small, offset metal spatula.

FRESHLY BAKED, THE BARS KEEP FOR 3 DAYS.

BEST BAKING ADVICE
Baking the bars until just set keeps them chewy and moist. For a thicker bar cookie (my favorite version), use an 8 by 8 by 2-inch baking pan, and increase the baking time by 5 to 7 minutes.

BUTTERCRUNCH BUTTER BUNS

18 sweet rolls

Completely outrageous, these soft sweet rolls have lots of chopped toffee rolled up in the dough. The dough itself picks up the almond and butter flavors in the candy, and thus the taste is unified. These are sumptuous, great fun to make, and a wonderful excuse to put candy in a yeast dough.

Softened unsalted butter, for preparing the baking pans

BUTTER-ALMOND YEAST DOUGH

4½ teaspoons active dry yeast

1 teaspoon granulated sugar

½ cup warm (110° to 115° F.) water

¼ cup granulated sugar

⅔ cup milk

2 teaspoons pure vanilla extract

2 teaspoons pure almond extract

5 large eggs

5⅓ cups unsifted unbleached all-purpose flour, plus ½ cup to add in process, plus ¼ cup to finish, and extra as needed for the work surface

1½ teaspoons freshly grated nutmeg

¼ teaspoon ground allspice

1¼ teaspoons salt

¾ pound (3 sticks) unsalted butter, lightly softened but cool, cut into tablespoon chunks

BUTTERCRUNCH ALMOND FILLING

4 tablespoons (½ stick) unsalted butter, softened

10 packages (1.4 ounces each) milk chocolate-covered toffee (Heath Milk Chocolate English Toffee Bar), chopped

MAKE THE BUTTER-ALMOND DOUGH Stir the yeast, 1 teaspoon granulated sugar, and warm water in a small heatproof bowl. Let stand until the yeast dissolves and the mixture is swollen, 7 to 8 minutes. In the meantime, place the ¼ cup granulated sugar and the milk in a small saucepan and warm to dissolve the sugar. Pour the milk-sugar mixture into a medium-size heatproof bowl and cool to 110° to 115° F.; whisk in the vanilla and almond extracts and the eggs. Blend in the yeast mixture.

Mix 4 cups of flour with the nutmeg, allspice, and salt in a large mixing bowl. Using a sturdy wooden spoon or flat wooden paddle, stir in the yeast-milk-egg mixture. Mix well. Stir in the remaining 1⅓ cups of flour, a little at a time.

Transfer the dough to the bowl of a heavy-duty, freestanding electric mixer fitted with the flat paddle. Beat the dough for 3 minutes on moderately low speed. Add 1 stick (8 tablespoons) of the butter, 2 tablespoons at a time, beating constantly until it has assimilated into the dough before adding the next piece. Remove the flat paddle, scraping the dough off the sides. Put the dough hook in place. Add the remaining 2 sticks (16 tablespoons) of butter, 2 tablespoons at a time, beating on moderately low speed to incorporate each portion.

Continue to beat the dough on low speed, sprinkling over the ½ cup of flour. Beat for 3 minutes longer. *Dough texture observation* The dough should be elastic and glossy.

SET THE DOUGH TO RISE Scrape the dough into a large mixing bowl. Sprinkle over the ¼ cup of flour and knead lightly in the

¾ cup slivered almonds, lightly
toasted and cooled

3 tablespoons heavy cream

1 large egg yolk

½ teaspoon pure almond extract

Confectioners' sugar. for sprinkling on
top of the baked rolls (optional)

BAKEWARE

two 9 by 9 by 3-inch baking pans

BEST BAKING ADVICE
*For the best texture, incorporate the butter
into the dough 2 tablespoons at a time,
and mix until completely absorbed before
adding the next portion. Letting the
completed dough stand, bagged, at cool
room temperature for 30 minutes,
initiates the rise and begins to develop the
dough's texture. The remainder of the
rising should be done in the refrigerator
because the dough is so rich in butter.*

bowl for 2 minutes, or until the flour is absorbed into the dough. Transfer the dough to a gallon-size, food-safe self-locking plastic bag and seal. Let the dough stand at cool room temperature for 30 minutes.

PREPARE THE DOUGH FOR REFRIGERATION Lightly deflate the dough and place on a floured work surface. Gently press the dough into a 12 by 12-inch square. Fold the dough in half and roll lightly with a rolling pin to compress it. Return the dough to the plastic bag and refrigerate. After 1 hour, compress the dough to deflate lightly. Flatten the dough with your fingertips to deflate again two more times over the next 3 hours. Refrigerate the dough overnight. *Dough texture observation* After an overnight refrigeration, the dough will be moderately firm.

PREPARE THE BAKING PANS Lightly butter the inside of the baking pans; set aside.

ROLL, FILL, AND CUT THE BUNS Have all the ingredients for the buttercrunch almond filling at hand. Remove the dough from the refrigerator and place on a floured work surface. Pat the dough into a cake and dust both sides with flour. Flour a rolling pin.

Roll out the dough into a sheet measuring about 16 by 22 inches. Spread the surface with the softened butter. Sprinkle over the chopped toffee and slivered almonds. Roll up the dough into a long jellyroll, pinching closed the ends as you go. Pinch close the long seam to seal. Pull-and-roll the coil gently to lengthen it to about 28 inches long.

Cut the coil in half, then cut each half into nine slices, using a sharp chef's knife. Place nine rolls, cut side up, in rows of three each, in each buttered pan.

SET THE ROLLS TO RISE Cover each pan loosely with a sheet of plastic wrap. Let the buns rise until doubled in bulk at cool room temperature, 2 hours to 2 hours and 30 minutes. *Rising observation* A leisurely rise will create fine-textured, light buns.

MAKE THE ALMOND CREAM WASH AND GLAZE THE BUNS Just before baking the buns, whisk the heavy cream, egg yolk, and almond extract in a small mixing bowl. Lightly brush the tops of the risen buns with a coat of the wash.

PREHEAT THE OVEN AND BAKE THE BUNS Preheat the oven to 375° F. in advance of baking. Remove and discard the sheets of plastic wrap covering the pans. Bake the buns for 30 minutes, or well risen, set, and golden on top.

COOL THE BUNS Let the sweet rolls stand in the pans on cooling racks for 45 minutes. Remove the rolls individually, or in rows of three. The toffee in the rolls gets quite hot during baking; the buns must cool to room temperature before they are consumed. Serve the buns freshly baked, their tops sprinkled with confectioners' sugar, if you wish.

❊ *For an extra surge of flavor and texture,* omit the almond cream wash. Sprinkle Nut Streusel, made with almonds (see page 63) evenly over the tops of the buns just before baking.

❊ *For an aromatic topnote of flavor,* use vanilla-scented granulated sugar (see page 53) in place of plain granulated sugar and intensified vanilla extract (see page 52) in place of plain vanilla extract in the butter-almond yeast dough.

FRESHLY BAKED, THE BUNS KEEP FOR 2 DAYS.

BUTTERCRUNCH ALMOND TEA CAKE
One 10-inch fluted tube cake, creating 16 slices

W**HEN A CREAMY, BUTTERY BATTER** is interrupted by lots of chopped chocolate-covered toffee and slivered almonds, a great snacking cake is the happy consequence. The texture of the cake is fine-grained and moist, and the flavoring power of the candy is further developed by using light brown sugar as part of the sweetening agent (along with granulated sugar), and both vanilla and almond extract.

Nonstick cooking spray, for preparing the cake pan

BUTTERCRUNCH ALMOND BUTTER CAKE BATTER

2¾ cups unsifted bleached all-purpose flour

⅓ cup unsifted bleached cake flour

2 teaspoons baking powder

¼ teaspoon baking soda

½ teaspoon salt

PREHEAT THE OVEN AND PREPARE THE CAKE PAN Preheat the oven to 350° F. Film the inside of the Bundt pan with nonstick cooking spray. *Pan preparation observation* Using nonstick cookware spray to coat the inside of the cake pan helps to detach any bits of buttercrunch candy in the batter that may fuse to the sides of the baking pan as the cake bakes. Set aside.

MIX THE BUTTERCRUNCH ALMOND BUTTER CAKE BATTER Sift the all-purpose flour, cake flour, baking powder, baking soda, salt, nutmeg, and allspice onto a sheet of waxed paper. In a

½ teaspoon freshly grated nutmeg

⅛ teaspoon ground allspice

8 packages (1.4 ounces each) milk chocolate-covered toffee (Heath Milk Chocolate English Toffee Bar), chopped into ¼-inch chunks

¼ cup slivered almonds, lightly toasted and cooled

½ pound (16 tablespoons or 2 sticks) unsalted butter, softened

1⅔ cups granulated sugar

¼ cup plus 2 tablespoons firmly packed light brown sugar, sieved if lumpy

4 large eggs

1½ teaspoons pure almond extract

1 teaspoon pure vanilla extract

¾ cup milk blended with ¼ cup light (table) cream

Confectioners' sugar, for sprinkling on top of the baked cake (optional)

BAKEWARE

10-inch Bundt pan

medium-size mixing bowl, toss the chopped toffee and almonds with 1 tablespoon of the sifted mixture.

Cream the butter in the large bowl of a freestanding electric mixer on moderate speed for 3 to 4 minutes. Add the granulated sugar and beat for 2 minutes; add the light brown sugar and beat for a minute longer. Beat in the eggs, one at a time, mixing for 45 seconds after each addition. Blend in the almond extract and vanilla extract.

On low speed, alternately add the sifted ingredients in three additions with the milk-cream blend in two additions, beginning and ending with the sifted mixture. Scrape down the sides of the mixing bowl frequently with a rubber spatula to keep the batter even-textured. Stir in the chopped toffee.

Spoon the batter into the prepared Bundt pan. Shake the pan gently from side to side, once or twice, to level the top.

BAKE AND COOL THE CAKE Bake the cake in the preheated oven for 55 minutes to 1 hour, or until risen, set, and a wooden pick inserted in the cake withdraws clean, or with a few moist crumbs adhering to it. The baked cake will pull away slightly from the sides of the pan.

Cool the cake in the pan on a rack for 5 to 6 minutes, then invert onto another cooling rack. Cool completely. Before slicing and serving, dust the top of the cake with confectioners' sugar, if you wish. *Slicing observation* Use a serrated knife to cut the cake neatly and cleanly.

❋ *For an aromatic topnote of flavor,* use vanilla-scented granulated sugar (see page 53) in place of plain granulated sugar and intensified vanilla extract (see page 52) in place of plain vanilla extract in the cake batter.

FRESHLY BAKED, THE CAKE KEEPS FOR 3 TO 4 DAYS.

CHEWY BUTTERCRUNCH SQUARES

16 squares

Stuffed with toffee and slivered almonds, these squares are reminiscent of blondies, the golden-colored, butterscotch-flavored version of the brownie. The chopped toffee is reinforced by vanilla and almond extracts, brown sugar, coconut, and slivered almonds, ingredients that also help flavor the dense bar cookie batter.

Softened unsalted butter and bleached all-purpose flour, for preparing the baking pan

ALMOND AND TOFFEE BAR COOKIE DOUGH

1 cup unsifted bleached all-purpose flour

2 tablespoons unsifted bleached cake flour

¼ teaspoon baking soda

¼ teaspoon salt

¼ teaspoon freshly grated nutmeg

¼ pound (8 tablespoons or 1 stick) unsalted butter, softened

7 tablespoons firmly packed light brown sugar, sieved if lumpy

¼ cup granulated sugar

1 large egg

1 teaspoon pure vanilla extract

¾ teaspoon pure almond extract

1 cup sweetened flaked coconut

6 packages (1.4 ounces each) milk chocolate-covered toffee (Heath Milk Chocolate English Toffee Bar), chopped into ½-inch chunks

⅔ cup coarsely chopped skinned almonds, lightly toasted and cooled

BAKEWARE

9 by 9 by 2-inch baking pan

PREHEAT THE OVEN AND PREPARE THE BAKING PAN Preheat the oven to 350° F. Lightly butter and flour the inside of the baking pan. Tap out any excess flour; set aside.

MIX THE ALMOND AND TOFFEE BAR COOKIE DOUGH Whisk the all-purpose flour, cake flour, baking soda, salt, and nutmeg in a small mixing bowl.

Cream the butter in the large bowl of a freestanding electric mixer on moderately low speed for 2 to 3 minutes. Add the light brown sugar and beat for 2 minutes; add the granulated sugar and beat for a minute longer. Blend in the egg and vanilla and almond extracts. Scrape down the sides of the mixing bowl with a rubber spatula to keep the batter even-textured. On low speed, add the whisked dry ingredients, beating just until the particles of flour are absorbed. Work in the coconut, chopped toffee, and almonds, using a sturdy wooden spoon or flat wooden paddle. *Bar cookie texture observation* The buttery mixture will be thick and firm, and bulky with coconut, candy, and nuts.

Scrape the bar cookie dough into the prepared baking pan. Using a rubber spatula (or flexible palette knife), lightly push the dough into the pan in an even layer, pressing it into the corners as you go along.

BAKE, COOL, AND CUT THE SQUARES Bake the sweet in the preheated oven for 25 minutes, or until just set and a light golden color around the edges of the square. Transfer the pan to a cooling

The bar cookie dough is chunky and somewhat stiff, but it must be pushed into the sides of the baking pan. For even baking, smooth over the surface of the unbaked dough with a flexible palette knife or rubber spatula to level it.

rack. Cool for 30 minutes. Using a small, sharp knife, cut the entire cake into four quarters, then cut each quarter into four squares. *Cutting observation* Dividing the entire cake into squares after 30 minutes lets you cut through the toffee neatly before it firms up completely. Cool completely. Remove the squares from the baking pan, using a small, offset metal spatula.

FRESHLY BAKED, THE BAR COOKIES KEEP FOR 3 DAYS.

BROWN SUGAR BUTTERCRUNCH COFFEE CAKE WITH CARAMEL BUTTERCRUNCH TOPPING

One 10-inch fluted tube cake, creating 16 slices

CHOPPED TOFFEE—locked into the batter and sprinkled on a caramel topping—makes a coffee cake batter resonate with flavor. The combination of butter and brown sugar develops the background flavor of the batter, and the buttermilk and sour cream keep the crumb of the cake moist and soft.

Nonstick cooking spray, for preparing the cake pan

BUTTERMILK BUTTERCRUNCH COFFEE CAKE BATTER

3 cups unsifted bleached all-purpose flour

1½ teaspoons baking powder

1 teaspoon baking soda

½ teaspoon salt

½ teaspoon freshly grated nutmeg

8 packages (1.4 ounces each) milk chocolate-covered toffee (Heath Milk Chocolate English Toffee Bar), chopped into ¼-inch chunks

½ cup slivered almonds, lightly toasted and cooled

½ pound (16 tablespoons or 2 sticks) unsalted butter, softened

1¼ cups firmly packed light brown sugar, sieved if lumpy

¼ cup granulated sugar

4 large eggs

1½ teaspoons pure vanilla extract

PREHEAT THE OVEN AND PREPARE THE CAKE PAN Preheat the oven to 350° F. Film the inside of the Bundt pan with nonstick cooking spray; set aside.

MIX THE BUTTERMILK BUTTERCRUNCH COFFEE CAKE BATTER Sift the flour, baking powder, baking soda, salt, and nutmeg onto a sheet of waxed paper. In a medium-size mixing bowl, toss the chopped toffee and almonds with 2½ teaspoons of the sifted mixture.

Cream the butter in the large bowl of a freestanding electric mixer on moderate speed for 3 minutes. Add the light brown sugar and beat for 2 minutes; add the granulated sugar and beat for 1 minute longer. Beat in the eggs, one at a time, mixing for 45 seconds after each addition. Blend in the vanilla extract.

On low speed, alternately add the sifted ingredients in three additions with the buttermilk in two additions, beginning and ending with the sifted mixture. Blend in the sour cream. Scrape down the sides of the mixing bowl frequently with a rubber spatula to keep the batter even-textured. Stir in the chopped toffee and slivered almonds.

Spoon the batter into the prepared Bundt pan. Shake the pan gently from side to side, once or twice, to level the top.

1 cup buttermilk, whisked well

2 tablespoons thick, cultured sour cream

CARAMEL AND BUTTERCRUNCH TOPPING

Caramel Nut Topping (see page 232), using ½ cup slivered almonds (lightly toasted and cooled completely)

3 packages (1.4 ounces each) milk chocolate-covered English toffee, coarsely chopped

BAKEWARE

10-inch Bundt pan

BAKE AND COOL THE CAKE Bake the cake in the preheated oven for 55 minutes or until risen, set, and a wooden pick inserted in the cake withdraws clean, or with a few moist crumbs adhering to it. The baked cake will pull away slightly from the sides of the pan. Cool the cake in the pan on a rack for 5 to 6 minutes, then invert onto another cooling rack. Cool for 1 hour.

FINISH THE CAKE WITH THE CARAMEL AND BUTTERCRUNCH TOPPING Drizzle the warm caramel topping on the top of the Bundt cake, letting it flow down the sides in a casual way. Immediately sprinkle the chopped toffee on the rounded, caramel-coated top flutes of the cake. Let the topping set for at least 2 hours, or until completely set and cool, before cutting into slices for serving. *Slicing observation* Use a serrated knife to cut the cake neatly and cleanly.

FRESHLY BAKED, THE COFFEE CAKE KEEPS FOR 2 TO 3 DAYS.

BEST BAKING ADVICE

To underscore the creamy texture of the baked cake, use fully softened (but not oily) butter.

BUTTERCRUNCH TEA BISCUITS

1 dozen biscuits

*T*HE RANGE OF FLAVORINGS IN THESE TALL, ample biscuits is wide and definitive: the topping consists of a lightly fragrant, sweetened crumble mixture and the biscuit dough is buttery, considerately spiced, and showered with chopped toffee. The almond crumble topping meshes with the flavor of the toffee, and keeps each bite of biscuit interesting.

ALMOND AND BUTTERCRUNCH STREUSEL TOPPING

⅔ cup unsifted bleached all-purpose flour

¼ cup ground almonds

⅔ cup firmly packed light brown sugar, sieved if lumpy

½ teaspoon freshly grated nutmeg

pinch of ground allspice

pinch of salt

7 tablespoons (1 stick less 1 tablespoon) unsalted butter, cold, cut into cubes

½ teaspoon pure almond extract

½ teaspoon pure vanilla extract

⅓ cup chopped almonds

2 packages (1.4 ounces each) milk chocolate-covered toffee (Heath Milk Chocolate English Toffee Bar), chopped into ¼-inch chunks

BUTTERCRUNCH TEA BISCUIT DOUGH

4⅓ cups unsifted bleached all-purpose flour

5 teaspoons baking powder

1 teaspoon salt

1 teaspoon freshly grated nutmeg

PREHEAT THE OVEN AND SET OUT THE BAKING SHEETS
Preheat the oven to 400° F. Line the cookie sheets or sheet pans with lengths of cooking parchment paper; set aside. *Bakeware observation* The baking sheets must be heavy, or the dough will scorch on the bottom as the biscuits bake. Double-pan the sheets, if necessary.

MAKE THE ALMOND AND BUTTERCRUNCH STREUSEL TOPPING In a medium-size mixing bowl, thoroughly combine the flour, ground almonds, light brown sugar, nutmeg, allspice, and salt. Scatter over the cubes of butter and, using a pastry blender (or 2 round-bladed table knives), reduce the butter to small bits about the size of dried navy beans. Drizzle over the almond extract and vanilla extract; stir in the chopped almonds and toffee. Crumble the mixture between your fingertips to form large and small nuggets. *Streusel topping texture observation* The crumble mixture should be moist; if it's still sandy textured and somewhat free-flowing, it hasn't bonded together enough, and needs to be compressed/kneaded/rubbed together for a minute or two longer. Set aside.

MIX THE BUTTERCRUNCH TEA BISCUIT DOUGH In a large mixing bowl, whisk together the flour, baking powder, salt, nutmeg, cinnamon, allspice, and granulated sugar. Drop in the cold chunks of butter, and using a pastry blender, cut the fat into the flour mixture until reduced to large pearl-size pieces. Lightly stir in the chopped toffee.

½ teaspoon ground cinnamon

¼ teaspoon ground allspice

⅔ cup vanilla-scented granulated sugar (see page 53)

12 tablespoons (1½ sticks) unsalted butter, cold, cut into tablespoon-size chunks

4 packages (1.4 ounces each) milk chocolate-covered English toffee (Heath Milk Chocolate English Toffee Bar), chopped into ½-inch chunks

4 large eggs

1½ teaspoons pure vanilla extract

1½ teaspoons pure almond extract

1 cup heavy cream

BAKEWARE

2 heavy cookie sheets or rimmed sheet pans

In a medium-size mixing bowl, whisk the eggs and vanilla and almond extracts. Whisk in the cream.

Pour the egg and cream mixture over the flour mixture and stir to form the beginning of a dough. *Dough texture observation* At this point, the dough will form sandy-textured clumps. Knead the dough in the bowl until it comes together firmly. It will be slightly moist.

FORM THE TEA BISCUITS Divide the dough in half. On a lightly floured work surface, pat and press each piece into a round disk, 7 to 8 inches in diameter. With a sharp chef's knife lightly dipped in flour, cut each round into six pie-shaped wedges. As the biscuits are cut, poke in any bits of toffee that may stick out of the sides.

TOP THE TEA BISCUITS Press some of the crumble mixture on top of each biscuit, dividing the mixture among the scones. Use all of the crumble topping. Carefully transfer the biscuits to the lined cookie sheet, placing them 3 inches apart from each other. Assemble six biscuits on each sheet.

BAKE AND COOL THE BISCUITS Bake the biscuits in the preheated oven for 18 to 20 minutes, or until set and the topping is golden. Transfer the baking sheets to cooling racks. Let the biscuits stand on the sheets for 2 minutes, then carefully remove them to cooling racks, using a wide, offset metal spatula, detaching any small puddles of firm toffee that might have melted down during baking. Cool completely. Serve the biscuits at room temperature.

FRESHLY BAKED, THE BISCUITS KEEP FOR 3 TO 4 DAYS.

BEST BAKING ADVICE
Using ground almonds in the streusel topping gives it the perfect essence of almond; using chopped almonds would lessen the significance of the chopped toffee candy and produce a texture that detracts from the candy.

TEXAS-SIZE BUTTERCRUNCH-PECAN-CHIP MUFFINS

10 muffins

BIG, BOLD, AND BEAUTIFUL—these must be the toffee-est muffins around. Already loaded up with chopped candy, the batter also supports miniature semisweet chocolate chips and juggles two flavoring extracts—vanilla and almond. The presence of the brown sugar creates a soft caramel undertone, a taste that mingles nicely with the chocolate, toffee, and pecans, and the small amount of cocoa powder in the batter underscores the chocolate flavor present in the coating of the toffee.

Nonstick cooking spray, for preparing the muffin pans

TOFFEE-PECAN-CHIP TOPPING

3 packages (1.4 ounces each) milk chocolate-covered toffee (Heath Milk Chocolate English Toffee Bar), chopped into ¼- to ½-inch chunks

¾ cup chopped pecans

⅓ cup miniature semisweet chocolate chips

TOFFEE-MINIATURE CHOCOLATE CHIP MUFFIN BATTER

2¾ cups unsifted bleached all-purpose flour

¼ cup unsifted bleached cake flour

2¼ teaspoons baking powder

¼ teaspoon baking soda

1 teaspoon salt

1 tablespoon unsweetened, alkalized cocoa

4 packages (1.4 ounces each) milk chocolate-covered toffee (Heath Milk Chocolate English Toffee Bar), chopped into ¼-inch chunks

¾ cup miniature semisweet chocolate chips

10 tablespoons (1 stick plus 2 tablespoons) unsalted butter, softened

PREHEAT THE OVEN AND PREPARE THE MUFFIN PANS
Preheat the oven to 375° F. Film the inside of the muffin cups with nonstick cooking spray; set aside.

MAKE THE TOFFEE-PECAN TOPPING Mix the chopped toffee, pecans, and chocolate chips in a small bowl; set aside.

MIX THE TOFFEE-MINIATURE CHOCOLATE CHIP MUFFIN BATTER Sift the all-purpose flour, cake flour, baking powder, baking soda, salt, and cocoa. In a medium-size mixing bowl, toss the chopped toffee and chocolate chips with 1 tablespoon of the sifted mixture.

Cream the butter and shortening in the large bowl of a freestanding electric mixer on moderately high speed for 2 to 3 minutes. Add the light brown sugar and beat for 1 minute; add the granulated sugar and beat for a minute longer. Blend in the vanilla and almond extracts. Beat in the eggs, one at a time, mixing for 30 seconds after each addition.

On low speed, alternately add the sifted ingredients in three additions with the half-and-half in two additions, beginning and ending with the sifted mixture. Scrape down the sides of the mix-

2 tablespoons shortening

⅔ cup firmly packed light brown sugar, sieved if lumpy

⅓ cup plus 1 tablespoon granulated sugar

1½ teaspoons pure vanilla extract

1 teaspoon pure almond extract

3 large eggs

1 cup half-and-half

BAKEWARE

10 jumbo, crown top muffin cups (two pans, each holding 6 individual muffin cups)

ing bowl frequently with a rubber spatula to keep the batter even-textured. Stir in the chopped toffee and chocolate chips.

FILL THE MUFFIN CUPS WITH THE BATTER AND SPRINKLE ON THE TOPPING Divide the batter among the prepared muffin cups. Sprinkle a little of the topping on top of the muffins.

BAKE AND COOL THE MUFFINS Bake the muffins for 25 minutes, or until risen and set. When muffins are baked, a wooden pick inserted in the center of a muffin will withdraw clean, or with a few moist crumbs attached to it.

Place the muffin pans on cooling racks and let them stand for 20 minutes. Carefully remove the muffins and place on cooling racks. Serve the muffins at room temperature.

FRESHLY BAKED, THE MUFFINS KEEP FOR 3 DAYS.

Variation: For Texas-size buttercrunch-walnut-chip muffins, substitute walnuts for pecans in the topping, above.

BEST BAKING ADVICE

Sprinkle the toffee-pecan-chip topping on the surface of the batter, keeping it away from the outermost edges; this will make the muffins easier to lift from the baking pans.

ALMOND FUDGE
BUTTERCRUNCH BROWNIES

16 brownies

Moist and fearlessly candy-laden, these are the brownies to make when the craving for something sweet and extravagant takes over.

Nonstick cooking spray, for preparing the baking pan

ALMOND AND TOFFEE FUDGE BROWNIE BATTER

1 cup unsifted bleached all-purpose flour

7 tablespoons (½ cup less 1 tablespoon) unsifted bleached cake flour

1 tablespoon unsweetened, alkalized cocoa

¼ teaspoon baking powder

½ teaspoon salt

7 packages (1.4 ounces each) milk chocolate-covered toffee (Heath Milk Chocolate English Toffee Bar), chopped into ¼- to ½-inch chunks

½ pound (16 tablespoons or 2 sticks) unsalted butter, melted and cooled

6 ounces (6 squares) unsweetened chocolate, melted and cooled to tepid

3 ounces bittersweet chocolate, melted and cooled to tepid

5 large eggs

1¾ cups plus 2 tablespoons granulated sugar

2 teaspoons pure vanilla extract

1½ teaspoons pure almond extract

½ cup slivered almonds, lightly toasted and cooled

PREHEAT THE OVEN AND PREPARE THE BAKING PAN Preheat the oven to 325° F. Film the inside of the baking pan with nonstick cooking spray; set aside.

MIX THE ALMOND AND TOFFEE FUDGE BROWNIE BATTER Sift the all-purpose flour, cake flour, cocoa, baking powder, and salt onto a sheet of waxed paper. In a medium-size mixing bowl, toss the chopped toffee with 1 tablespoon of the sifted mixture.

In a medium-size mixing bowl, whisk the melted butter, melted unsweetened chocolate, and melted bittersweet chocolate until well blended. Whisk eggs in a large mixing bowl for 1 minute; add the granulated sugar and vanilla and almond extracts, and whisk slowly for 1 minute, or until the ingredients are just combined. Blend in the melted butter and chocolate mixture. Sift over the flour mixture and whisk to form a batter, mixing just until the particles of flour are absorbed, but making sure to dispel any lingering pockets or small clumps of flour. *Batter texture observation* The batter will be moderately thick and glossy. Stir in the toffee and almonds.

Scrape the batter into the prepared baking pan; smooth over the top with a flexible palette knife or rubber spatula, pushing the batter evenly into the corners as you do so.

BAKE AND COOL THE BROWNIES Bake the brownies in the preheated oven for 30 minutes, or until just set. The brownies should be slightly soft (but not liquidy).

Cool the brownies in the pan on a rack for 45 minutes. Carefully cut the cake of brownies into squares, using a small,

Vanilla-scented confectioners' sugar (see page 54), for sprinkling over the baked brownies (optional)

BAKEWARE

10 by 10 by 2-inch baking pan

sharp knife. *Pre-cutting observation* Dividing the the brownies into squares within the first hour of cooling lets you cut through the chopped toffee neatly. Cool completely. Recut the brownies and remove them from the baking pan, using a small, offset metal spatula. Just before serving, sprinkle the top with confectioners' sugar, if you wish.

❊ *For an aromatic topnote of flavor,* use vanilla-scented granulated sugar (see page 53) in place of plain granulated sugar in the brownie batter.

FRESHLY BAKED, THE BROWNIES KEEP FOR 4 TO 5 DAYS.

BEST BAKING ADVICE

Using a combination of unsweetened chocolate and bittersweet chocolate makes a creamy-textured brownie batter, with a complex flavor that heightens the taste of the buttercrunch candy.

*t*he twin flavors of caramel and butterscotch have in common the basic ingredient of sugar. In its elemental form, caramel is simply sugar melted and cooked until it turns a golden tea-colored brown. Clear, amber-colored caramel is made by first dissolving the sugar completely (with or without water, as the recipe specifies), then boiling it to achieve a rich depth of color. A liquid is added to convert the caramel into a sauce, if the sugar has not been cooked initially with water. Occasionally, caramel is fortified with enrichments such as butter, heavy cream, and vanilla extract, and that is called a caramel cream.

As a related flavoring, butterscotch is a cooked mixture of caramel, butter, heavy cream, and vanilla extract. The caramel flavoring is sometimes set into place by the addition of brown sugar, and this is used to jump-start a sauce, rather than beginning with a cooked sugar caramel mixture.

Frequently, caramel and butterscotch are generic flavor labels that are used interchangeably to refer to a creamy, buttery, cooked sugar mixture lightly seasoned with vanilla extract. The caramelizing flavor can be achieved by initially cooking sugar until a tawny brown, or by using light or dark brown sugar. The taste of caramel and butterscotch can be sharpened by adding certain pivotal ingredients to batters, doughs, coatings, sauces, and toppings. These are pure vanilla extract; light or dark brown sugar; a combination of spices such as nutmeg, cinnamon, allspice, cloves, and cardamom; freshly grated nutmeg; vanilla-scented granulated sugar; or mild honey.

11

CARAMEL AND BUTTERSCOTCH

CARAMEL AND BUTTERSCOTCH CHIP POUND CAKE

One 10-inch cake, creating about 20 slices

T HE BROWN SUGAR, MOLASSES, and butterscotch-flavored chips in the batter, teamed with the rounded flavor of the Caramel Basting Sauce, builds the flavor in this cake. The chopped walnuts add a note of crunch, and the sour cream develops a tender crumb that, later on, readily absorbs the brush-on caramel basting sauce. If you wish, the chopped walnuts in the cake batter can be replaced with the same amount of pecans or macadamia nuts, or omitted entirely.

Shortening and bleached all-purpose flour, for preparing the cake pan

BROWN SUGAR AND BUTTERSCOTCH CHIP CAKE BATTER

3 cups unsifted bleached all-purpose flour

½ teaspoon baking powder

¼ teaspoon baking soda

1 teaspoon salt

½ teaspoon freshly grated nutmeg

½ teaspoon ground allspice

½ teaspoon ground cinnamon

⅛ teaspoon ground cloves

⅛ teaspoon ground cardamom

1¼ cups butterscotch-flavored chips

½ pound (16 tablespoons or 2 sticks) unsalted butter, softened

1 tablespoon mild, unsulphured molasses

2¼ cups firmly packed dark brown sugar, sieved if lumpy

2½ teaspoons pure vanilla extract

6 large eggs

1 cup thick, cultured sour cream

¾ cup chopped walnuts

PREHEAT THE OVEN AND PREPARE THE CAKE PAN Preheat the oven to 325° F. Grease the inside of the tube pan with shortening. Line the bottom with a circle of waxed paper cut to fit, and grease the paper. Dust the inside of the pan with all-purpose flour and set aside.

MIX THE BROWN SUGAR AND BUTTERSCOTCH CHIP CAKE BATTER Sift the flour, baking powder, baking soda, salt, nutmeg, allspice, cinnamon, cloves, and cardamom onto a sheet of waxed paper. In a small mixing bowl, toss the butterscotch chips with 1½ teaspoons of the sifted mixture.

Cream the butter and molasses in the large bowl of a freestanding electric mixer on moderate speed for 3 minutes. Add the dark brown sugar in three additions, beating for 1 minute after each portion is added. Blend in the vanilla extract. Beat in the eggs, one at time, blending for 30 seconds after each is added. *Mixture texture observation* At this point, the creamed butter-sugar, egg-molasses mixture will look slightly curdled.

On low speed, alternately add the sifted ingredients in three additions with the sour cream in two additions, beginning and

Caramel Basting Sauce (see page 228), for applying to the baked cake

Caramel Custard Sauce (see page 229), for serving with the cake (optional)

plain 10-inch tube pan

ending with the sifted mixture. Scrape down the sides of the mixing bowl frequently with a rubber spatula to keep the batter even-textured. *Batter texture observation* The batter will be moderately thick and creamy. Stir in the butterscotch chips and walnuts.

Spoon the batter into the prepared tube pan. Shake the pan gently from side to side, once or twice, to level the top.

BAKE THE CAKE Bake the cake in the preheated oven for 1 hour and 15 minutes, or until risen, set, and a wooden pick inserted in the cake withdraws cleanly.

Cool the cake in the pan on a rack for 10 minutes. Carefully invert the cake onto another cooling rack, peel off the waxed paper circle, and invert again to stand right side up.

COAT THE TOP AND SIDES OF THE CAKE WITH THE WARM CARAMEL BASTING SAUCE Place a sheet of waxed paper under to cooling rack to catch any drips of the basting sauce. With a pastry brush, paint the sauce over the top and sides of the hot cake, coating the cake thoroughly. Use all of the sauce.

BEST BAKING ADVICE

To use all of the basting sauce, wait 2 to 3 minutes before applying each coating. The short waiting time gives the sauce the opportunity to sink in, so the cake can absorb the next coating.

COOL THE CAKE Cool the cake for at least 2 hours before cutting into slices for serving. *Slicing observation* Use a serrated knife to cut the cake neatly and cleanly. Serve the cake with a spoonful of the caramel custard sauce.

❋ *For an aromatic topnote of flavor,* use intensified vanilla extract (see page 52) in place of plain vanilla extract in the cake batter.

FRESHLY BAKED, THE CAKE KEEPS FOR 4 TO 5 DAYS.

CARAMEL BASTING SAUCE

About 1 cup

THINK OF THIS SAUCE, intended to add a sweet and luminous quality to a baked cake, as part soaking solution and part glaze. It's scrumptious brushed over a brown sugar-based pound cake, vanilla or coconut butter cake, or dense chocolate cake that's been sweetened with brown sugar. For the best taste effect, use the sauce warm, and apply it over the warm cake with a pastry brush, so that every drop of it gets absorbed.

CARAMEL BASTING SAUCE

4 tablespoons (½ stick) unsalted butter

½ cup plus 2 tablespoons firmly packed dark brown sugar, sieved if lumpy

½ cup heavy cream

pinch of salt

½ teaspoon pure vanilla extract

⅛ teaspoon freshly grated nutmeg

MAKE THE CARAMEL BASTING SAUCE Place the butter, dark brown sugar, heavy cream, and salt in a small, heavy, nonreactive saucepan. Set over moderately low heat and cook until the sugar has dissolved, 5 to 8 minutes, stirring occasionally with a wooden spoon or flat wooden paddle. Bring the mixture to a vigorous simmer, then simmer until lightly thickened, 1 to 2 minutes.

STRAIN AND FLAVOR THE SAUCE Remove the saucepan from the heat and strain the basting sauce through a fine-meshed sieve into a nonreactive bowl. Stir in the vanilla extract and nutmeg.

Use the basting sauce warm, to paint over the top of a just-baked and unmolded cake. (The basting sauce can be made in advance, poured into a sturdy storage container, covered, and refrigerated for up to 2 days. Reheat the sauce slowly in a saucepan until bubbly.)

CARAMEL CUSTARD SAUCE

About 1⅔ cups sauce

*T*HE BASE FOR THIS potent custard sauce begins as a tea-colored caramel fortified with both heavy and light cream. The sauce is formed by using this wildly concentrated, creamy caramel mixture as a luxurious base to season a custard mixture. The resulting sauce, which has depth and complexity, makes a flavorful accompaniment to slices of butter cake in a rainbow of flavors—caramel, rum, vanilla, coconut, or chocolate.

CARAMEL AND CREAM MIXTURE

⅓ cup granulated sugar

½ cup water

¼ cup heavy cream

½ cup light (table) cream

CUSTARD MIXTURE

5 large egg yolks

2 tablespoons granulated sugar

pinch of salt

¾ cup heavy cream

½ cup milk

2 teaspoons pure vanilla extract

MAKE THE CARAMEL AND CREAM MIXTURE Place the granulated sugar and water in a heavy, medium-size saucepan (2-quart), preferably enameled cast iron. Cover the saucepan, set over low heat, and cook until the sugar dissolves completely. Uncover, raise the heat to moderately high, and cook until the sugar syrup turns a medium tea-colored brown. *Syrup color observation* Watch the syrup carefully as it begins to take on color, regulating the heat so that you can control the darkening process. *Caramel color observation* If the syrup is too dark, the custard sauce will taste bitter; if the syrup is undercooked and too pale, the sauce will lack flavor.

Note: The next step must be taken carefully. Put on a pair of long heatproof oven mitts or gloves to protect your hands and forearms. Carefully remove the saucepan of syrup away from the heat source. Step back from the saucepan, and immediately add the ¼ cup heavy cream; stir in the cream, using a long wooden spoon. The sauce will bubble up, releasing hot steam. There will be small splotches of caramel floating about; these will dissolve as the sauce cooks. Stir in the light cream and set aside to cool to warm (about 115° F.), stirring now and again. Pour into a heatproof bowl.

ASSEMBLE THE CUSTARD MIXTURE AND COOK THE SAUCE Whisk the egg yolks and granulated sugar in a clean, heavy, medium-size (2-quart) saucepan, preferably enameled cast iron, until lightly thickened, about 1 minute. Blend in the salt, heavy cream, and milk, using a medium-length wooden spoon. Whisk in the warm caramel cream mixture. Cook the custard mixture over low heat until it coats the back of a wooden spoon, 10 to 12 minutes, stirring slowly and constantly.

STRAIN AND FLAVOR THE SAUCE Strain the sauce through a fine-meshed sieve into a heatproof storage container. Lightly smooth the mixture through the strainer with a rubber spatula. Stir in the vanilla extract. Immediately press a sheet of plastic wrap directly over the surface of the sauce to prevent a skin from forming. Cool. Cover the storage container tightly with the lid and refrigerate for 3 hours.

⁂ *Note:* For the best texture and flavor, the sauce is best served within 3 to 5 hours, but can be refrigerated overnight. The sauce will thicken during storage and, for serving, should be thinned by stirring in 2 to 3 tablespoons of milk.

TURTLE SQUARES

16 squares

*H*ERE'S A CHOCOLATE FUDGE bar cookie layer, languishing beneath a caramel and nut topping. This sweet is easy to make and difficult to resist. You can cut the confections in good-size squares—or smaller bars, if you must.

Nonstick cooking spray, for preparing the baking pan

CHOCOLATE FUDGE BAR
COOKIE BATTER

1 cup unsifted bleached all-purpose flour

2 tablespoons unsweetened, alkalized cocoa

¼ teaspoon baking powder

¼ teaspoon salt

¾ cup miniature semisweet chocolate chips

½ pound (16 tablespoons or 2 sticks) unsalted butter, melted and cooled to tepid

PREHEAT THE OVEN AND PREPARE THE BAKING PAN Preheat the oven to 325° F. Film the inside of the baking pan with nonstick cooking spray; set aside.

MIX THE CHOCOLATE FUDGE BAR COOKIE BATTER Sift the flour, cocoa, baking powder, and salt onto a sheet of waxed paper. In a small mixing bowl, toss the chocolate chips with 1 teaspoon of the sifted mixture.

Whisk the melted butter and melted unsweetened chocolate in a medium-size mixing bowl until thoroughly blended. Whisk the eggs in a large mixing bowl until frothy, about 1 minute. Add the granulated sugar and whisk until just combined, about 1 minute. Blend in the vanilla extract. Blend in the melted butter and chocolate mixture. Sift over the sifted ingredients and mix with a wooden spoon or rubber spatula (or whisk) until the particles of flour are completely absorbed, making sure to scrape along

4 ounces (4 squares) unsweetened chocolate, melted and cooled to tepid

4 large eggs

1¾ cups plus 2 tablespoons granulated sugar

2 teaspoons pure vanilla extract

Caramel Nut Topping (see page 232), using chopped walnuts, pecans, or macadamia nuts for sprinkling, for applying to the baked cake of brownies

BAKEWARE

9 by 9 by 2-inch baking pan

the bottom and sides of the mixing bowl. *Batter texture observation* The batter will be moderately thick. Stir in the chocolate chips.

Scrape the batter into the prepared baking pan. Smooth over the top with a rubber spatula.

BAKE AND COOL THE FUDGE BAR COOKIE LAYER Bake the sweet for 33 to 38 minutes, or until set. Let the sweet stand in the pan on a cooling rack for 1½ hours.

APPLY THE CARAMEL TOPPING ON THE BAKED FUDGE BAR COOKIE LAYER Puddle the warm caramel topping on the top of the bar cookie layer, using a small teaspoon, or lightly spread it in patches, using a flexible palette knife. Immediately sprinkle the nuts on the caramel.

LET THE SWEET SET AND CUT INTO SQUARES Let the caramel set for 45 minutes to 1 hour. Cut the entire cake into four quarters, then cut each quarter into four squares, using a small, sharp knife. Remove the turtle squares from the baking pan, using a small, offset metal spatula.

❋ *For an aromatic topnote of flavor,* use vanilla-scented granulated sugar (see page 53) in place of plain granulated sugar and intensified vanilla extract (see page 52) in place of plain vanilla extract in the cookie batter.

FRESHLY BAKED, THE SQUARES KEEP FOR 2 DAYS.

Variation: For turtle squares with Dutch-process black cocoa: To integrate this type of cocoa into the fudge bar cookie batter layer, substitute 1 tablespoon Dutch-process black cocoa for 1 tablespoon of the regular unsweetened, alkalized cocoa, using 1 tablespoon of the black cocoa and 1 tablespoon of the unsweetened, alkalized cocoa.

CARAMEL NUT TOPPING

About ⅞ cup sauce, without the nut sprinkle

*T*HIS IS CHILD'S PLAY TO MAKE. It is a swift topping to consider for lavishing over baked brownies, triangles of shortbread, big chewy cookies, and the tops of scones or muffins, and creamed butter or yeast-risen coffee cakes. With a bag of caramels in the pantry, you can add a tasty and whimsical touch to almost any freshly baked sweet.

CARAMEL TOPPING

25 vanilla-flavored caramels (about 8.2 ounces)

2 tablespoons milk

1 tablespoon light (table) cream

pinch of salt

½ teaspoon pure vanilla extract

¾ cup chopped roasted peanuts, walnuts, pecans, almonds (almonds can be chopped or slivered) or macadamia nuts

MAKE THE CARAMEL TOPPING Place the caramels, milk, cream, and salt in a small, heavy saucepan (preferably enameled cast iron). Set over moderately low to moderate heat and cook for 10 to 13 minutes, until the caramels melt down, stirring occasionally with a wooden spoon. *Texture observation* At first, it appears as if the candy won't ever dissolve into a creamy, smooth, and flowing mixture, but it will.

When the caramels begin to melt, stir the mixture continuously until completely smooth. Simmer the mixture for 30 seconds to 1 minute, or until lightly bubbly, then stir in the vanilla extract. Immediately and quickly, spread, spoon, or thickly drizzle the topping over the thoroughly baked and cooled sweet.

Sprinkle the chopped, toasted nuts to the caramel-covered surface as soon as the topping is applied and still warm.

BEST BAKING ADVICE

For the most flavorful result, lightly toast— and completely cool—the walnuts, pecans, almonds, or macadamia nuts before using.

CARAMEL UPSIDE-DOWN APPLE TART

One 9½-inch upside-down tart, creating 6 to 8 servings

THIS FRAGRANT TART is baked in the classic tarte Tatin pan—copper outside, with a tin lining and outwardly sloping sides. Since copper retains and disperses heat so well, the pan cooks the apples and pastry to a tender conclusion. The tart is composed of three elements: a caramel mixture that forms the bottom layer; a covering of seasoned, sweetened apple slices; and a round of buttery dough that conceals the top tier of apples. As the apples bake, their sweet juices mingle with the caramel, and the caramel in turn is absorbed into the apples. Served warm with whipped cream, caramel sauce, or crème fraîche, it's unforgettable.

Nonstick cooking spray, for preparing the tarte Tatin pan

LIGHTLY SWEETENED BUTTER DOUGH

- 1½ cups unsifted, bleached all-purpose flour
- 2 tablespoons granulated sugar blended with ⅛ teaspoon ground cinnamon
- ¼ teaspoon salt
- 9 tablespoons (1 stick plus 1 tablespoon) unsalted butter, cut into tablespoon chunks, removed from the refrigerator for 10 minutes
- 3 tablespoons plus 1¾ teaspoons ice-cold water blended with ¼ teaspoon pure vanilla extract

CARAMEL AND BUTTER MIXTURE

- 6 tablespoons granulated sugar
- 4 tablespoons plus ¾ teaspoon water
- 1 tablespoon unsalted butter, cut into small bits, for dotting the cooked, poured caramel in the baking pan

SEASONED APPLES

- 7 firm cooking (Rome Beauty, Jonathan, Empire, or Stayman) apples (3 pounds 5 ounces total weight), peeled, cored, trimmed, halved, and cut into generous ⅛-inch-thick slices
- 1 tablespoon fresh lemon juice

MAKE THE LIGHTLY SWEETENED BUTTER DOUGH Place the flour, cinnamon-sugar, and salt in the bowl of a food processor fitted with the steel knife. Cover and process, using five to six quick on-off pulses, until combined. Uncover, toss in the chunks of butter, cover, and process, using about 12 on-off pulses, or until the butter is reduced to small pieces about the size of large pearls. Uncover, add the ice-cold water-vanilla extract blend, cover, and process, using on-off pulses, until the mixture begins to adhere to itself in very small pellets, 30 to 45 seconds. *Dough texture observation* Process the mixture until the dough comes together in small clumps. Carefully turn out the clumps of dough onto a work surface and gather together, lightly pressing the dough into a flat cake with your fingertips.

Roll out the dough between two sheets of parchment paper to a round measuring about 11 inches in diameter. Refrigerate the dough on a cookie sheet for 4 to 6 hours. The dough should be reasonably firm. The dough can remain in the refrigerator at this stage for up to 2 days; when firm, enclose in plastic wrap.

CUT OUT A CIRCLE OF DOUGH On baking day, remove the sheet of pastry dough from the refrigerator. Peel off one sheet of

10 tablespoons granulated sugar blended with ½ teaspoon ground cinnamon, ¼ teaspoon freshly grated nutmeg, and ⅛ teaspoon ground cardamom

3 tablespoons unsalted butter, melted and cooled slightly

2 teaspoons granulated sugar, for sprinkling over the pastry top

Vanilla Whipped Cream (see page 530), Buttery Caramel Sauce (see page 237), or crème fraîche, for serving with the tart

BAKEWARE

9½-inch tin-lined copper tarte Tatin pan

BEST BAKING ADVICE

For the best result, I like to work with dough that has been refrigerated overnight. Sprinkling the pastry cover of dough with granulated sugar gives it a lightly crunchy, textural top crust, which helps to keep it firm. When developing the density of caramel for covering the bottom of the baking pan, I found the best ratio to be 6 tablespoons of sugar to a little more than 4 tablespoons of water.

parchment paper. Using the inverted tarte Tatin pan as your guide, trace and cut a circle of chilled dough, using a small, sharp knife. Strip away the extra dough. Peel off the remaining piece of parchment paper. Using a very small cookie cutter (½ or ¾ inch in diameter), stamp out three to five pieces of dough on the top near the center to create steam vents. Return the round of dough to the refrigerator.

PREHEAT THE OVEN AND PREPARE THE TARTE TATIN PAN Preheat the oven to 375° F. Have a rimmed baking pan or jellyroll pan at hand.

Film the bottom and sides the tarte Tatin pan with nonstick cooking spray. Set aside.

MAKE THE CARAMEL MIXTURE Place the sugar and water in a small, heavy saucepan, preferably enameled cast iron. Set over low heat and cook slowly, undisturbed, until the sugar has melted down completely. There should be no visible grains of sugar or grittiness. Bring the sugar-water to a boil, then boil slowly undisturbed until it turns a rich, tea-colored brown, about 8 minutes.

POUR THE CARAMEL INTO THE TARTE TATIN PAN Protecting your hands with long, heatproof mitts, immediately pour the caramel randomly into the prepared baking pan. The caramel will blanket most of the bottom of the pan in a large puddle. Let stand for 15 minutes, then dot the top with the bits of butter.

PREPARE THE SEASONED APPLES Lightly toss the apple slices in a large mixing bowl with the lemon juice, spiced sugar, and melted butter.

ASSEMBLE THE TART Remove the pastry dough circle from the refrigerator.

Arrange a layer of apple slices on the bottom of the tart pan in a pretty pattern for an architectural look, or just place a layer of them casually on the bottom for a rustic look. Then top with the remaining apples. Press down lightly on the slices. Place the circle of dough on the top of the apples and pat it down, pressing it firmly against the top layer of apples. Sprinkle the top of the tart with 2 teaspoons of sugar.

BAKE THE TART Place the tart on the baking pan to catch cooking juices that may bubble over and bake for 55 to 60 minutes, or until the apples are tender and the pastry top is golden. The juices that trickle up at the sides will look condensed when the tart is fully baked.

COOL THE TART Keeping the tart in its pan, transfer it to a cooling rack and let it stand for 20 to 30 minutes to allow the sweet juices to settle down and reabsorb. *Cooling observation* If you cool the tart for less than 20 minutes, the baking juices will flow and swirl around the pastry base when the tart is inverted, saturate it, and make it soggy.

UNMOLD THE TART Place a flat, heatproof serving plate on top of the tart pan. Carefully invert the tart onto the serving dish and lift off the baking pan. To lift off the baking pan, carefully wedge a flexible palette knife under an edge to give you enough room to elevate the pan. Cool for an additional 15 to 20 minutes. Slice into wedges and serve.

CARAMEL, NOUGAT, AND WALNUT CANDY BAR CAKE

One 9½-inch round cake, creating 8 pie-shaped wedges

THE CARAMEL ENCASED in chocolate-covered caramel and nougat candy bars adds waves of goodness to this fudgelike, single-layer cake. Using candy bar chunks develops the flavor in a quick and easy way. To unify the caramel taste further, set a slice of cake on a puddle of warm, homemade caramel sauce.

Nonstick cooking spray, for preparing the cake pan

CHOCOLATE CANDY BAR
CAKE BATTER

3 bars (1.76 ounces each) dark chocolate, caramel, and vanilla nougat candy bars (Milky Way Midnight bars), cut into ½-inch chunks

¾ cup unsifted bleached cake flour

PREHEAT THE OVEN AND PREPARE THE CAKE PAN Preheat the oven to 350° F. Film the inside of the springform pan with nonstick cooking spray; set aside.

MIX THE CHOCOLATE CANDY BAR CAKE BATTER Place the candy bar chunks on a sheet of waxed paper. Squash them very gently, using the bottom of an offset metal spatula, rolling pin, or flat side of a cleaver.

Sift the cake flour, all-purpose flour, cocoa, and salt onto a sheet of waxed paper. In a small mixing bowl, lightly and carefully

6 tablespoons unsifted bleached all-
  purpose flour

1 tablespoon unsweetened, alkalized
  cocoa

¼ teaspoon salt

⅔ cup chopped walnuts, lightly
  toasted and cooled completely

9 tablespoons (1 stick plus 1
  tablespoon) unsalted butter, melted
  and cooled

4 ounces (4 squares) unsweetened
  chocolate, melted and cooled

4 large eggs

1⅔ cups plus 2 tablespoons vanilla-
  scented granulated sugar (see
  page 53)

2½ teaspoons pure vanilla extract

Buttery Caramel Sauce (see page 237),
  as an accompaniment

BAKEWARE

9½-inch round springform pan

toss the walnuts and candy bar pieces with 2 teaspoons of the sifted mixture.

In a medium-size mixing bowl, whisk the melted butter and melted unsweetened chocolate until well blended. Beat the eggs in a large mixing bowl. Add the vanilla-scented granulated sugar and whisk lightly for 1 minute, or until just combined. Blend in the vanilla extract. Add the melted butter-chocolate mixture and whisk to combine. Sift over the sifted mixture. Whisk until all particles of flour are absorbed. Stir in the candy bar chunks and walnuts.

Scrape the batter into the prepared springform pan. Smooth over the top with a rubber spatula.

BAKE AND COOL THE CAKE Bake the cake for 10 minutes, reduce the oven temperature to 325° F., and continue baking for 20 to 25 minutes longer, or until just set. The center will be slightly soft.

Cool the cake in the pan on a rack. Remove the outer ring from the pan. Cut the cake into wedges, and serve with a spoonful of the warm caramel sauce, if you wish. *Slicing observation* Use a serrated knife or long chef's knife to cut the cake neatly and cleanly.

FRESHLY BAKED, THE CAKE KEEPS FOR 2 TO 3 DAYS.

Variation: For caramel, nougat, and pecan candy bar cake, substitute chopped pecans for the walnuts.

Buttery Caramel Sauce

1½ cups

WITH ITS CREAMY COUNTERPOINT, here is a sauce that, with a few ingredients, becomes a celebrated accompaniment to a slice of cake or pie. Think of this sauce as a sweet canvas that's adaptable to flavoring with a splash of bourbon or almond liqueur: If you are using any of these, spoon 2 to 3 teaspoons into the sauce with the vanilla extract after it's removed from the heat.

CARAMEL SAUCE

6 tablespoons (¾ stick) unsalted butter

¾ cup firmly packed dark brown sugar, sieved if lumpy

1 tablespoon granulated sugar

⅔ cup plus 1 tablespoon heavy cream

pinch of salt

2 tablespoons light (table) cream

1¼ teaspoons pure vanilla extract

pinch of freshly grated nutmeg

MAKE THE CARAMEL SAUCE Place the butter, dark brown sugar, and granulated sugar in a heavy, medium-size (2-quart capacity) saucepan, preferably enameled cast iron. Place over low heat and cook for about 4 minutes, stirring occasionally, to dissolve the sugar.

Stir in the heavy cream and salt. Raise the heat to moderate and cook for 2 minutes, stirring occasionally with a wooden spoon. Bring the contents of the saucepan to a boil over moderately high heat (bubbles will begin appearing around the edge of the saucepan, just before the whole surface fills with bubbles), stirring with a wooden spoon or flat wooden paddle. Watch carefully to avoid scorching the mixture. Reduce the heat and let the sauce cook at a moderate boil for 3 minutes. Add the light cream, stir to combine, and boil for 1 to 2 minutes longer. *Consistency observation* The sauce should be lightly thickened, well amalgamated, and smooth, and lightly coat the back of a wooden spoon. If it doesn't seem dense enough, simply simmer it for a minute longer to concentrate.

Remove the saucepan from the heat and add the vanilla extract and nutmeg. *Bubbling observation* The sauce will bubble up in the spot where you've added the vanilla extract. Stir well. Cool the sauce to lukewarm before using. *Note:* Any caramel sauce, as well as caramel-candy-based baked goods (and toffee candy), should never be touched or consumed while hot.

Use the sauce freshly made, while it is still lukewarm, or pour into a heatproof container, cover, and refrigerate for up to 1 week.

❋ *To use the refrigerated sauce,* heat the sauce in a heavy saucepan until smooth and liquified, bring to a simmer, simmer 1 minute, then cool to lukewarm before spooning over and around a dessert.

CARAMEL-WALNUT STICKY ROLLS

18 rolls

*T*HE DOMINATING TASTE in these ample, shapely sweet rolls is caramel, which is in the topping. It sinks into the rolls, and the rest puddles here and there on top. The mashed-potato dough in the recipe for Cinnamon Ripple Rolls (on page 312) produces exceptionally moist and generously sized rolls, with an appealingly fluffy texture.

Potato butter dough in the recipe for the Cinnamon Ripple Rolls (page 312)

Nonstick cooking spray and softened unsalted butter, for preparing the baking pans

NUTMEG-CINNAMON BUTTER, SUGAR, AND RAISIN FILLING

6 tablespoons (¾ stick) unsalted butter, softened

⅔ cup granulated sugar blended with 1½ teaspoons freshly grated nutmeg and 1½ teaspoons ground cinnamon

2 teaspoons pure vanilla extract

1 cup dark raisins

CARAMEL MIXTURE FOR SPREADING ON TOP OF THE BAKED SWEET ROLLS AND WALNUTS FOR SPRINKLING

Creamy Caramel Sticky Coat (see page 240)

1 cup coarsely chopped walnuts, lightly toasted and cooled completely

BAKEWARE

two 9 by 9 by 3-inch baking pans

MAKE THE YEAST DOUGH Prepare the potato butter dough through the first rise.

ASSEMBLE THE NUTMEG-CINNAMON BUTTER, SUGAR, AND RAISIN FILLING Cream the butter in a small mixing bowl and blend in the sugar-nutmeg-cinnamon mixture and vanilla extract, mixing well. Have the raisins at hand in a small bowl.

PREPARE THE BAKING PANS Film the inside of the baking pans with nonstick cooking spray. Thickly butter the inside of the pans; set aside.

ROLL, FILL, AND CUT THE STICKY ROLLS With the palms of your hands, compress the dough to deflate it. Place the dough on a well-floured work surface, cover, and let stand for 10 minutes.

Roll out the dough to a sheet measuring 17 by 20 inches. Spread the nutmeg-cinnamon butter evenly on the surface of the dough. Sprinkle over the raisins. Lightly press down on the raisins with your fingertips or with the underside of a small, metal offset spatula so that they stick to the butter.

Roll the dough tightly into a coil, jellyroll-style, tucking the ends inside and pressing them down as you roll. Brush the excess flour away from the dough as you roll, using a soft pastry brush. If necessary, use a pastry scraper to guide you in lifting the dough as you roll it. Seal closed the long seam by pinching it tightly. Carefully lengthen the roll by rolling it until it is about 25 inches long. With a sharp chef's knife, cut the roll into 18 even slices.

ASSEMBLE THE ROLLS IN THE PREPARED BAKING PANS Place the rolls in the prepared baking pans, cut side down, in three rows of three, nine to a pan.

SET THE ROLLS TO RISE Cover each pan of rolls loosely with a sheet of plastic wrap and let rise for 2 to 2½ hours or doubled in bulk and very puffy. The rolls should rise to about ½ inch above the top of the baking pans.

PREHEAT THE OVEN AND BAKE THE ROLLS Preheat the oven to 375° F. in advance of baking the rolls. Remove and discard the sheets of plastic wrap covering the rolls. Bake the rolls in the preheated oven for 30 minutes, or until golden on top and set.

COOL THE ROLLS Place the baking pans on cooling racks and let the rolls stand for 5 to 10 minutes. Invert each pan onto another cooling rack and reinvert onto a rimmed sheet pan. Cool the rolls for 20 minutes.

TOP THE CAKE OF ROLLS WITH THE COOLED CARAMEL COAT Place a sheet of waxed paper underneath the cooling rack to catch any drips of the caramel coating. Spoon the caramel coating on top of the rolls, letting some of it flow down the sides. *Caramel sticky coat puddling observation* The topping will naturally puddle here and there, in the dips and crevices on the top of the rolls. Sprinkle the walnuts on top of the caramel. Cool completely.

Carefully detach and remove the rolls from the pan, and serve fresh.

Variation: For caramel-pecan sticky rolls, substitute pecans for the walnuts for sprinkling over the caramel topping.

CREAMY CARAMEL STICKY COAT

About 1 cup

WHETHER SPOONED OVER a block of sweet rolls, or poured over a pound cake or Bundt cake, this creamy, wonderfully sticky spread is caramel-flavored nirvana. The caramel coating is roughly based on the caramel cream component in the Caramel Custard Sauce on page 229.

Use a heavy saucepan with a light-colored interior so that you can easily see how the darkening process, or caramelization, of the sugar-water mixture is progressing. Any utensils that come in contact with the hot sugar mixture or hot, finished sauce should be heatproof, and you must protect your hands at all times.

CREAMY CARAMEL COATING

1⅓ cups plus 2 tablespoons granulated sugar

6 tablespoons water

⅔ cup heavy cream blended with 2 tablespoons milk, warmed

large pinch of salt

large pinch of freshly grated nutmeg

3 tablespoons unsalted butter, cut into chunks

½ teaspoon intensified vanilla extract (see page 52)

CARAMELIZE THE SUGAR Place the granulated sugar and water in a heavy, medium-size saucepan (preferably enameled cast iron). Cover, set over low heat, and cook slowly until the sugar dissolves completely. The liquid mixture must be free of any granules of sugar.

Bring the mixture to a boil and boil until it turns a rich, tea-colored brown, without scorching the sugar. This will take about 15 minutes.

INTEGRATE THE HEAVY CREAM-MILK MIXTURE INTO THE CARAMEL Carefully remove the saucepan from the heat and place on a heatproof surface. Protecting your hands and forearms with long, padded oven mitts, stir in a little less than half of the warmed cream-milk mixture. As soon as the cream is added, the mixture will boil up furiously. Stir in the remaining warm cream. *Mixture texture observation* At this point, the mixture will be very sticky and clumpy, and appear inadequately combined. Add the salt, nutmeg, and butter. The consistency will improve during the next step.

COOK THE CREAMY CARAMEL MIXTURE UNTIL THICKENED Return the pan to moderately low heat and cook the mixture until the caramel dissolves completely, stirring all the while. When the mixture is an even, tawny-colored brown, raise the heat and bring to the boil for 5 to 7 minutes, or until it thickly coats a wooden spoon. The mixture will bubble as it cooks. Remove from the heat, stir in the vanilla extract, and scrape into a heatproof bowl.

COOL THE CARAMEL STICKY MIXTURE Cool down the caramel coating until it is thick but still pourable, about 20 minutes at room temperature. The timing on this can be tricky, for you need the mixture to be fluid enough to spoon over the sweet rolls, but not too fluid, or it will sink into, not settle over, the tops of the rolls.

To hasten the cooling process, you can set the bowl containing the caramel mixture in a larger bowl filled with ice cubes and cold water, and cool down the mixture for 5 minutes or until thickened, stirring frequently, then remove the bowl from the ice bath.

Use the caramel coating now, spooning it over the top of a baked cake or batch of sweet rolls.

CARAMEL CHIP CAKE

One 10-inch fluted tube cake, creating 16 slices

LITTLE CARAMEL-FLAVORED CHIPS, snared in a buttery cake batter, are an amusing change from the typical semisweet chocolate variety that frequently dots a butter cake. The light brown sugar adds depth to the batter and reinforces the flavor of the chips.

Nonstick cookware spray, for
   preparing the cake pan

CARAMEL CHIP
BUTTER CAKE BATTER

2¾ cups unsifted bleached all-purpose
   flour

¼ cup unsifted bleached cake flour

2 teaspoons baking powder

¾ teaspoon baking soda

1 teaspoon salt

½ teaspoon freshly grated nutmeg

2 cups caramel-flavored chips

½ pound (16 tablespoons or 2 sticks)
   unsalted butter, softened

1½ cups firmly packed light brown
   sugar, sieved if lumpy

⅓ cup granulated sugar

4 large eggs

2½ teaspoons pure vanilla extract

1 cup buttermilk, whisked well

Confectioners' sugar, for sprinkling
   over the top of the baked cake

BAKEWARE

10-inch Bundt pan

PREHEAT THE OVEN AND PREPARE THE CAKE PAN Preheat the oven to 350° F. Film the inside of the Bundt pan with nonstick cooking spray; set aside.

MIX THE CARAMEL CHIP BUTTER CAKE BATTER Sift the all-purpose flour, cake flour, baking powder, baking soda, salt, and nutmeg onto a sheet of waxed paper. In a medium-size mixing bowl, toss the caramel-flavored chips with 1 tablespoon of the sifted mixture.

Cream the butter in the large bowl of a freestanding electric mixer on moderate speed for 2 to 3 minutes. Add the light brown sugar and beat for 1 minute; add the granulated sugar and beat for 1 to 2 minutes longer. Beat in the eggs, one at a time, blending well after each addition. Blend in the vanilla extract.

On low speed, alternately add the sifted ingredients in three additions with the buttermilk in two additions, beginning and ending with the dry ingredients. Scrape down the sides of the mixing bowl frequently with a rubber spatula to keep the batter even-textured. *Batter texture observation* The batter will be creamy-textured. Stir in the caramel-flavored chips.

Spoon the batter into the prepared Bundt pan. Smooth over the top with a rubber spatula.

BAKE AND COOL THE CAKE Bake the cake in the preheated oven for 50 to 55 minutes, or until risen, set, and a wooden pick inserted in the cake withdraws clean. The baked cake will pull away slightly from the sides of the baking pan. Let the cake stand in the pan on a cooling rack for 5 to 8 minutes. Invert the cake onto another cooling rack. Cool completely. Sprinkle flurries of confectioners' sugar on top of the baked cake, just before slicing and serving. *Slicing observation* Use a serrated knife to cut the cake neatly and cleanly.

✳ *For an extra surge of flavor,* omit the final sprinkling of confectioners' sugar and apply the Caramel Basting Sauce (see page 228) to the top and sides of the warm cake. Or, sprinkle the cake with confectioners' sugar and serve with Buttery Caramel Sauce (see page 237).

✳ *For an aromatic topnote of flavor,* use intensified vanilla extract (see page 52) in place of plain vanilla extract in the cake batter.

FRESHLY BAKED, THE CAKE KEEPS FOR 4 DAYS.

Variations: For caramel chip-walnut cake, stir ⅔ cup chopped walnuts (lightly toasted and cooled completely) into the batter along with the caramel chips.

For caramel chip-macadamia nut cake, stir ⅔ cup unsalted, coarsely chopped macadamia nuts (lightly toasted and cooled completely) into the batter along with the caramel chips. Add ½ teaspoon ground cinnamon and ¼ teaspoon ground allspice to the dry ingredients before sifting.

Butterscotch Oatmeal Cookies

About 3½ dozen cookies

THE BUTTERSCOTCH FLAVOR, in the form of brown sugar and flavored chips, envelops this oatmeal cookie dough in the most wonderful of ways. The combination of butter, nutmeg, and allspice makes the butterscotch taste resonate.

BUTTERSCOTCH OATMEAL
COOKIE DOUGH

2 cups unsifted bleached all-purpose
flour

2 teaspoons baking powder

¾ teaspoon baking soda

1 teaspoon salt

¾ teaspoon freshly grated nutmeg

⅛ teaspoon ground allspice

½ pound (16 tablespoons or 2 sticks)
unsalted butter, softened

1 cup firmly packed light brown sugar,
sieved if lumpy

½ cup granulated sugar

2 large eggs

2½ teaspoons pure vanilla extract

1 tablespoon hot water

1½ cups quick-cooking (not instant)
rolled oats

2 cups butterscotch-flavored chips

¾ cup chopped walnuts

BAKEWARE

several cookie sheets

PREHEAT THE OVEN AND PREPARE THE COOKIE SHEETS
Preheat the oven to 375° F. Line the cookie sheets with lengths of cooking parchment paper; set aside.

MIX THE BUTTERSCOTCH OATMEAL COOKIE DOUGH Sift the flour, baking powder, baking soda, salt, nutmeg, and allspice onto a sheet of waxed paper.

Cream the butter in the large bowl of a freestanding electric mixer on low speed for 4 minutes. Add the light brown sugar in two additions, beating on moderate speed for 1 minute after each portion is added. Add the granulated sugar and beat for 1 minute longer. Blend in the eggs, one at a time, beating for 1 minute after each is added. Blend in the vanilla extract and hot water. On low speed, add the flour mixture in two additions, beating just until the particles of flour are absorbed. Scrape down the sides of the mixing bowl with a rubber spatula to keep the dough even-textured. Blend in the rolled oats. *Dough texture observation* The dough will be thick and moderately stiff. Work in the butterscotch chips and walnuts, using a wooden spoon or flat wooden paddle.

SPOON THE DOUGH ONTO THE PREPARED COOKIE SHEETS
Drop rounded 2-tablespoon-size mounds of dough, 3 inches apart, onto the lined cookie sheets. Place nine mounds of dough on each sheet.

BAKE AND COOL THE COOKIES Bake the cookies in the preheated oven for 10 to 12 minutes, or until softly set and light golden in small patches here and there on the surface or edges of the cookies. Let the cookies stand on the sheets for 1 minute, then transfer them to cooling racks, using a wide, offset metal spatula. Cool completely.

✳ *For an extra surge of flavor,* top the baked cookies with drizzles of the Caramel Nut Topping (see page 232), using chopped walnuts for the nut sprinkle.

✳ *For an aromatic topnote of flavor,* use intensified vanilla extract (see page 52) in place of plain vanilla extract in the cookie dough.

FRESHLY BAKED, THE COOKIES KEEP FOR 2 TO 3 DAYS.

Variation: For butterscotch oatmeal cookies with coconut, stir ½ cup sweetened flaked coconut into the dough along with the butterscotch-flavored chips and walnuts.

CHOCOLATE-COVERED CARAMEL AND PEANUT CANDY BAR BROWNIES

16 brownies

*T*o BRING THIS SWEET into the mega-caramel realm, you'll be obscuring the surface of the baked brownies with the Caramel Nut Topping on page 232 and pressing whole roasted peanuts onto the warm caramel drizzle. For the best results, add the topping when the entire cake of baked brownies has cooled to lukewarm, in about 1 hour, then cool for another hour before cutting into squares.

Nonstick cooking spray, for preparing the baking pan

FUDGY CARAMEL AND PEANUT BUTTER CANDY BROWNIE BATTER

1½ cups unsifted bleached cake flour

¼ teaspoon baking powder

½ teaspoon salt

1 tablespoon unsweetened, alkalized cocoa

10 snack-size bars (.6 oz each) milk chocolate, peanut, caramel and peanut butter (Reese's NutRageous snack-size bars), each bar cut into 4 to 6 pieces

½ pound (16 tablespoons or 2 sticks) unsalted butter, melted and cooled to tepid

4 ounces (4 squares) unsweetened chocolate, melted and cooled to tepid

2 tablespoons smooth peanut butter

2½ teaspoons pure vanilla extract

4 large eggs

2 cups superfine sugar

Caramel Nut Topping (see page 232), using whole roasted peanuts for sprinkling, for applying to the baked cake of brownies

BAKEWARE

9 by 9 by 2-inch baking pan

PREHEAT THE OVEN AND PREPARE THE BAKING PAN Preheat the oven to 325° F. Film the inside of the baking pan with nonstick cooking spray; set aside.

MIX THE FUDGY CARAMEL AND PEANUT BUTTER CANDY BROWNIE BATTER Sift the flour, baking powder, salt, and cocoa onto a sheet of waxed paper. In a small mixing bowl, toss the candy bar chunks with 2 teaspoons of the sifted mixture.

In a medium-size mixing bowl, whisk the melted butter, melted unsweetened chocolate, peanut butter, and vanilla extract for 1 to 2 minutes, or until very smooth.

In a large mixing bowl, whisk the eggs to blend, add the superfine sugar, and whisk for 1 minute to combine. Blend in the melted butter-melted chocolate-peanut butter mixture. Sift over the sifted ingredients and mix to form a batter, using a whisk or flat wooden paddle. *Batter texture observation* The batter will be thick. Stir in the chunks of candy, using a wooden spoon or flat wooden paddle.

Scrape the batter into the prepared baking pan and spread it into an even layer, using a flexible palette knife (or rubber spatula).

BAKE AND COOL THE BROWNIES Bake the brownies in the preheated oven for 40 to 45 minutes, or until set. Let the brownie cake cool in the pan on a rack for 1 hour and 30 minutes.

APPLY THE CARAMEL TOPPING ON THE BAKED BROWNIES
Drizzle the warm caramel topping on the top of the brownie cake using a small teaspoon, or lightly spread it in patches using a flexible palette knife. Immediately sprinkle the peanuts on the warm caramel so that they stick.

LET THE CARAMEL SET AND CUT THE BROWNIES Let the caramel set for 45 minutes to 1 hour before cutting the brownie cake into squares with a small, sharp knife. Remove the squares from the baking pan, using a small, offset metal spatula.

FRESHLY BAKED, THE BROWNIES KEEP FOR 4 DAYS.

BUTTERSCOTCH SOUR CREAM COFFEE CAKE

One 10-inch fluted tube cake, creating 16 slices

CURLS OF SPICED AND SWEETENED walnuts snake through this butterscotch-flavored, sour cream–enriched batter. This cake is especially moist. For an added bounce of flavor, cover the top of the cake with the Caramel Basting Sauce on page 228 while it's still warm.

Nonstick cooking spray, for preparing the cake pan

SPICED WALNUT SWIRL

¾ cup finely chopped walnuts

¼ cup granulated sugar

2 tablespoons firmly packed light brown sugar, sieved if lumpy

½ teaspoon ground cinnamon

½ teaspoon freshly grated nutmeg

⅛ teaspoon ground allspice

BUTTERSCOTCH SOUR CREAM CAKE BATTER

3 cups unsifted bleached all-purpose flour

2 teaspoons baking powder

¾ teaspoon baking soda

1 teaspoon salt

½ teaspoon ground cinnamon

½ teaspoon freshly grated nutmeg

⅛ teaspoon ground allspice

1½ cups butterscotch-flavored chips

½ pound (16 tablespoons or 2 sticks) unsalted butter, softened

1¾ cups firmly packed light brown sugar, sieved if lumpy

PREHEAT THE OVEN AND PREPARE THE CAKE PAN Preheat the oven to 350° F. Film the inside of the Bundt pan with nonstick cooking spray; set aside.

MAKE THE SPICED WALNUT SWIRL Thoroughly combine the walnuts, granulated sugar, light brown sugar, cinnamon, nutmeg, and allspice in a small mixing bowl.

MIX THE BUTTERSCOTCH SOUR CREAM CAKE BATTER Sift the flour, baking powder, baking soda, salt, cinnamon, nutmeg, and allspice onto a sheet of waxed paper. In a medium-size bowl, toss the butterscotch chips with 2 teaspoons of the sifted mixture.

Cream the butter in the large bowl of a freestanding electric mixer on moderate speed for 3 minutes. Add the light brown sugar and beat for 1½ to 2 minutes; add the granulated sugar and beat for a minute longer. Beat in the eggs, one at a time, blending well after each addition. Blend in the vanilla extract.

On low speed, alternately add the sifted mixture in three additions with the sour cream in two additions, beginning and ending with the sifted ingredients. Scrape down the sides of the mixing bowl frequently with a rubber spatula to keep the batter even-textured. Stir in the butterscotch chips and walnuts.

LAYER THE SPICED WALNUT SWIRL AND BUTTERSCOTCH SOUR CREAM CAKE BATTER Spoon a little more than half of the cake batter into the prepared pan. Sprinkle over the walnut mix-

3 tablespoons granulated sugar

4 large eggs

2 teaspoons pure vanilla extract

1 cup plus 2 tablespoons thick, cultured sour cream

½ cup chopped walnuts

BAKEWARE

10-inch Bundt pan

ture, keeping it within ¼ inch of the sides of the baking pan. Spoon over the remaining batter. Using a narrow, flexible palette knife, swirl the batter, making slightly exaggerated waves by placing the palette knife down into the batter and dragging it through and around in curves. Avoid scraping the bottom and sides of the baking pan.

BAKE AND COOL THE CAKE Bake the cake in the preheated oven for 55 minutes, or until risen, set, and a wooden pick inserted in the cake withdraws clean. The baked cake will pull away slightly from the sides of the baking pan. Cool the cake in the pan on a rack for 10 minutes, then invert onto another cooling rack. Cool completely before slicing and serving. *Slicing observation* Use a serrated knife to cut the cake neatly and cleanly.

❋ *For an extra surge of flavor,* serve with Buttery Caramel Sauce (see page 237), and/or apply the Caramel Basting Sauce (see page 228) to the top and sides of the warm cake.

FRESHLY BAKED, THE CAKE KEEPS FOR 3 DAYS.

BUTTERSCOTCH PECAN BARS

2 dozen bars

REMINISCENT OF PECAN PIE, these bars are composed of two layers—a buttery cookie base and a sweet, chewy-nutty pecan topping. The butter-brown sugar match appears in the dough and topping, accented by vanilla extract and a flutter of spice.

Nonstick cooking spray, for preparing the baking pan

BROWN SUGAR–BUTTER DOUGH

1½ cups unsifted bleached all-purpose flour

¼ teaspoon baking powder

⅛ teaspoon salt

½ teaspoon freshly grated nutmeg

12 tablespoons (1½ sticks) unsalted butter, softened

⅓ cup firmly packed light brown sugar, sieved if lumpy

1 teaspoon pure vanilla extract

HONEY-PECAN TOPPING

2 large eggs

⅛ teaspoon ground allspice

1 teaspoon pure vanilla extract

½ cup firmly packed light brown sugar, sieved if lumpy

½ cup mild honey, such as clover

3 tablespoons unsalted butter, melted and cooled

1½ cups coarsely chopped pecans

BAKEWARE

9 by 9 by 2-inch baking pan

PREHEAT THE OVEN AND PREPARE THE BAKING PAN Preheat the oven to 350° F. Film the inside of the baking pan with non-stick cooking spray; set aside.

MAKE THE BROWN SUGAR–BUTTER DOUGH Sift the flour, baking powder, salt, and nutmeg onto a sheet of waxed paper.

Cream the butter in the large bowl of a freestanding electric mixer on low speed for 2 minutes. Add the light brown sugar and vanilla extract; beat for 1 to 2 minutes longer. On low speed, add the sifted mixture and beat just until the particles of flour are absorbed into the mixture and a dough is formed. *Dough consistency observation* The dough will be somewhat soft and smooth.

FORM AND BAKE THE FIRST LAYER Press the butter dough into the prepared baking pan in an even layer. Prick the dough with the tines of a fork in 10 to 15 random places. Bake the layer until a medium golden color, about 25 minutes.

Place the baking pan on a cooling rack and let stand for 10 minutes. Leave the oven on.

MIX THE HONEY-PECAN TOPPING, TOP THE BAKED BROWN SUGAR–BUTTER CRUST LAYER, AND BAKE THE SWEET Place the eggs, allspice, and vanilla extract in a medium-size mixing bowl and whisk lightly to blend. Whisk in the light brown sugar, honey, and melted butter. Mix in the pecans. Spoon the pecan mixture over the brown sugar-butter crust layer.

Bake the sweet for 20 to 25 minutes, or until firm, set, and golden.

COOL AND CUT THE SWEET INTO BARS Transfer the baking pan to a cooling rack. Cool 20 to 30 minutes. With a small, sharp knife, cut the entire cake into four quarters, then cut each quarter into six bars. Let stand for 20 to 30 minutes longer, then remove the bars from the baking pan, using a small, offset metal spatula.

✳ *For an extra surge of flavor,* drizzle the entire cake of uncut bars with the Caramel Nut Topping (see page 232), using chopped pecans for sprinkling (or chopped walnuts, if you're making the variation, butterscotch walnut bars).

FRESHLY BAKED, THE BARS KEEP FOR 3 DAYS.

Variation: For butterscotch walnut bars, substitute chopped walnuts for the pecans in the topping.

*e*ver since the Aztecs crushed, pounded, and pulverized the bean known as *Theobroma cacao* (translated as "food of the gods"), thus creating a bitter but drinkable brew, chocolate—satiny, smooth, and lush—has been glorified in its many forms in batters and doughs. Long before the tropical beans were processed into solid chocolate or cocoa powder, they were used as valued legal tender, but once it was converted into substances known as milk, semisweet, and bittersweet chocolate, it became the prized currency of the baking world.

The motif of chocolate winds through both opulent and simple bakery sweets, highlighting itself or complementing other flavors. Chocolate sings in a buttery cake or muffin batter, or a scone, cookie, or yeast dough; it's rounded out by pure vanilla extract and vanilla-scented sugar, and flourishes in the presence of unsalted butter, sour cream, heavy cream, whole milk, and buttermilk.

The key to using chocolate in the baking process, to take advantage of its velvety flavor and extensive taste-intensity and structural integrity, is, in a word, balance. Enough butter, sugar, eggs, soft (such as sour cream) and/or liquid (such as whole milk, heavy cream, or buttermilk) dairy products, and flavoring extract must be present to offset whatever form of chocolate is used in the batter or dough—be it unsweetened cocoa, semisweet chips (miniature, regular, or mega-size), melted unsweetened squares, or chopped bittersweet bar chocolate. Salt, a prime seasoning agent, should be integrated in most recipes that contain chocolate, for it uplifts the flavor and prevents the baked dough or batter from tasting flat.

12

CHOCOLATE

CHOCOLATE CHIP BUTTER CAKE

One 10-inch fluted tube cake, creating 16 slices

I T'S THE SOUR CREAM IN THE BATTER that enriches the texture, plays against the little bits of semisweet chocolate, and helps frame the soft bouquet of vanilla extract. The small amount of shortening adds a certain lightness to the creamy structure of the cake and is the secret ingredient to its composition. This sweet is simple and good, and easy to put together.

Nonstick cooking spray, for preparing the baking pan

CHOCOLATE CHIP BUTTER CAKE BATTER

3 cups unsifted bleached all-purpose flour

¾ teaspoon baking soda

⅛ teaspoon cream of tartar

1 teaspoon salt

2 cups miniature semisweet chocolate chips

½ pound (16 tablespoons or 2 sticks) unsalted butter, softened

2 tablespoons shortening

2 cups vanilla-scented granulated sugar (see page 53)

1 tablespoon pure vanilla extract

4 large eggs

2 large egg yolks

1¼ cups thick, cultured sour cream

2 tablespoons milk

Vanilla-scented confectioners' sugar (see page 54), for sprinkling over the top of the baked cake, optional

BAKEWARE

10-inch Bundt pan

PREHEAT THE OVEN AND PREPARE THE CAKE PAN Preheat the oven to 350° F. Film the inside of the Bundt pan with nonstick cooking spray; set aside.

MIX THE CHOCOLATE CHIP BUTTER CAKE BATTER Sift the all-purpose flour, baking soda, cream of tartar, and salt onto a sheet of waxed paper. In a medium-size mixing bowl, toss the chocolate chips with 1 tablespoon of the sifted mixture.

Cream the butter and shortening in the large bowl of a free-standing electric mixer on moderate speed for 3 minutes. Add the granulated sugar in four additions, beating on moderate speed for 45 seconds after each portion is added. Blend in the vanilla extract. Beat in the eggs, one at a time, mixing for 30 seconds after each addition. Beat in the egg yolks. Scrape down the sides of the mixing bowl frequently with a rubber spatula to keep the batter even-textured.

On low speed, alternately add the sifted mixture in three additions with the sour cream in two additions, beginning and ending with the sifted mixture. Blend in the milk. *Batter texture observation* The batter will be moderately dense and creamy-textured. Stir in the chocolate chips.

Scrape the batter into the prepared Bundt pan. Lightly smooth over the top with a rubber spatula.

BAKE THE CAKE Bake the cake in the preheated oven for 50 to 55 minutes, or until risen, golden brown on top, set, and a

Coat the miniature chocolate chips in the sifted mixture to keep them suspended throughout the batter; they should have a fine surface haze of flour on them. This is especially important when the chips are a part of a butter-enhanced sour cream cake batter, which tends to be quite silky.

wooden pick inserted in the cake withdraws clean, or with a few moist crumbs clinging to it.

COOL THE CAKE Cool the cake in the pan on a rack for 5 to 10 minutes. Invert the cake onto another cooling rack and cool completely. Just before slicing and serving, dust the top of the cake with the confectioners' sugar, if you wish. *Slicing observation* Use a serrated knife to cut the cake neatly and cleanly.

❋ *For an extra surge of flavor,* omit the confectioners' sugar topping. Spoon freshly made, very warm Chocolate Glaze (see page 479) over the completely cooled cake.

❋ *For an aromatic topnote of flavor,* use intensified vanilla extract (see page 52) in place of plain vanilla extract in the cake batter.

FRESHLY BAKED, THE CAKE KEEPS FOR 2 DAYS.

Variations: For chocolate chip butter cake with walnuts or pecans, stir ½ cup chopped walnuts or pecans (lightly toasted and cooled completely) into the batter along with the miniature semisweet chocolate chips.

For chocolate chip butter cake with coconut, stir ¾ cup (lightly packed) sweetened flaked coconut into the batter along with the miniature semisweet chocolate chips.

DOUBLE CHOCOLATE MADELEINES

2 dozen small cakes

Bittersweet, plump, and entirely endearing, these little shell-shaped cakes are a delight to make and exceptionally good to eat. The intensity of the chocolate flavor is created by using alkalized cocoa, a bit of melted bittersweet chocolate, and baby semisweet chocolate chips. The trick to keeping the cakes moist is to let the batter stand for 1 minute before filling the molds; in this way, the molds can be filled with a bit more batter than you would usually use because it has had the opportunity to set and firm up slightly. You must be scrupulous about the size of the eggs, for larger eggs add too much liquid to the batter and cause it to run past the sides of the molds as the madeleines bake. The cakes are baked in the classic *plaques à madeleines* molds (see page 41).

Melted clarified butter (see page 66) and bleached all-purpose flour, for preparing the madeleine molds

DOUBLE CHOCOLATE MADELEINE BATTER

½ cup plus 1 tablespoon unsifted bleached cake flour

⅓ cup plus 2 tablespoons unsweetened, alkalized cocoa

¼ teaspoon baking powder

⅛ teaspoon salt

⅓ cup plus 1 tablespoon miniature semisweet chocolate chips

7 tablespoons (1 stick less 1 tablespoon) unsalted butter, softened

⅓ cup plus 3 tablespoons superfine sugar

3 large eggs

1¼ teaspoons pure vanilla extract

1 ounce bittersweet chocolate, melted and cooled to tepid

SUGAR AND COCOA TOPPING FOR FINISHING THE MADELEINES

3 tablespoons confectioners' sugar

½ teaspoon unsweetened, alkalized cocoa

PREHEAT THE OVEN AND PREPARE THE BAKING MOLDS Preheat the oven to 350° F. Film the inside of the madeleine molds with clarified butter, using a soft pastry brush. Let stand for 5 minutes, or until completely set, then dust the inside of each shell with all-purpose flour. Tap out any excess flour; there should be a very thin coating. Set aside.

MIX THE DOUBLE CHOCOLATE MADELEINE BATTER Sift the cake flour, cocoa, baking power, and salt onto a sheet of waxed paper. In a small mixing bowl, toss the chocolate chips with 1 teaspoon of the sifted mixture.

Using an electric hand mixer, cream the butter in a medium-size mixing bowl on moderate speed for 2 minutes. Add the superfine sugar and beat for 1 minute longer. Beat in the eggs, one at a time, mixing for 30 to 45 seconds after each addition. Scrape down the sides of the mixing bowl frequently with a rubber spatula to keep the batter even-textured. Blend in

2 *plaques à madeleines* (madeleine molds, twelve 3-inch shells to each plaque)

the vanilla extract and melted bittersweet chocolate. *Batter texture observation* At this point, the mixture will look slightly curdled.

On low speed, add the sifted ingredients in two additions, mixing just until the particles of flour and cocoa are absorbed. *Batter texture observation* The batter will be thick, dense, and creamy-textured. Stir in the chocolate chips. Let the batter stand for 3 minutes.

FILL THE MADELEINE MOLDS Fill the prepared molds with the batter, dividing it evenly among them. Mound the batter lightly down the length of the center of each shell. *Batter position observation* Placing the batter in a slight mound helps to maintain the shape of the baked cake and prevent it from baking unevenly. *Batter amount observation* Dividing the batter among the 24 shell-shaped molds will produce rounded, well-developed madeleines that, when baked, fill the molds to capacity without overflowing the rims.

BAKE AND COOL THE MADELEINES Bake the cakes in the preheated oven for 12 minutes, or until plump, set, and a wooden pick inserted in the middle of a madeleine withdraws clean. Underbaked madeleines will be gummy-textured.

Cool the madeleines in the pans on racks for 1 minute, then lightly prod them out of the pan at one long side, using the rounded tip of a flexible palette knife. Place the madeleines, ridged side up, on cooling racks. Cool completely.

MAKE THE CONFECTIONERS' SUGAR AND COCOA TOPPING Sift the confectioners' sugar and cocoa into a small bowl. Whisk the two mixtures together to blend well.

Just before serving, resift the mixture of confectioners' sugar and cocoa over the rounded tops of the madeleines. Serve the madeleines fresh, within 1 to 2 hours of baking.

BEST BAKING ADVICE

Let the completed madeleine batter stand for 3 minutes. It will thicken slightly as it stands. The slightly thicker batter bakes richly and evenly, and tends to hold its shape better in the shell-shaped baking forms.

FOR AN AROMATIC TOPNOTE OF FLAVOR, use vanilla-scented superfine sugar (see page 54) in place of plain superfine sugar in the batter.

Variation: For double chocolate madeleines with Dutch-process black cocoa, substitute 2 tablespoons Dutch-process black cocoa for the unsweetened, alkalized cocoa, and use ⅓ cup unsweetened, alkalized cocoa.

TRUFFLED CHOCOLATE–WALNUT BROWNIES

16 brownies

*T*HESE ARE DREAMY BROWNIES, damp, fudgy, and dark as midnight. The batter locks in an immoderate amount of chocolate in the form of cocoa powder, unsweetened squares, and a bittersweet candy bar. This excess of chocolate is eclipsed only slightly by walnuts that have been tossed in melted butter and a powdery mixture of cocoa and confectioners' sugar. The seasoned nuts make the brownies even richer, and help to define the structure of the baked sweet. For a brownie that's chocolate through and through, without the interruption of nuts, make the Truffled Double Chocolate Brownies in the variation that follows.

With or without nuts, the brownies are pure bliss when eaten freshly baked and nudged right out of the baking pan when they're cool enough to maneuver. And sometimes it's really hard to wait until the blush of the oven's heat has diminished, and then you're on your own.

Nonstick cooking spray, for preparing the baking pan

DARK CHOCOLATE BROWNIE BATTER

1 cup unsifted bleached all-purpose flour

⅓ cup unsifted bleached cake flour

⅓ cup unsweetened, alkalized cocoa

¼ teaspoon baking powder

¼ teaspoon salt

½ pound (16 tablespoons or 2 sticks) unsalted butter, melted and cooled to tepid

5 ounces (5 squares) unsweetened chocolate, melted and cooled to tepid

3 ounces bittersweet chocolate, melted and cooled to tepid

5 large eggs

2 cups superfine sugar

2¾ teaspoons pure vanilla extract

TRUFFLED WALNUTS

1 cup walnut halves and pieces, lightly toasted and cooled completely

1 tablespoon unsalted butter, melted, cooled to tepid and blended with ¼ teaspoon pure vanilla extract

PREHEAT THE OVEN AND PREPARE THE BAKING PAN Preheat the oven to 325° F. Film the inside of the baking pan with nonstick cooking spray; set aside.

MIX THE DARK CHOCOLATE BROWNIE BATTER Sift the all-purpose flour, cake flour, cocoa, baking powder, and salt onto a sheet of waxed paper.

Whisk the melted butter, melted unsweetened chocolate, and melted bittersweet chocolate in a medium-size mixing bowl until thoroughly blended. Whisk the eggs in a large mixing bowl for 1 minute. Add the superfine sugar and whisk for 1 minute, or until just combined. *Whisking observation* Once the sugar is added, whisking the mixture too vigorously or for a prolonged period of time will beat too much air into the brownie base, ruining the creamy texture of the baked brownies. Whisk in the tepid melted

½ teaspoon unsweetened, alkalized cocoa sifted with 2 teaspoons unsifted confectioners' sugar

Confectioners' sugar, for sprinkling over the baked brownies (optional)

BAKEWARE
10 by 10 by 2-inch baking pan

chocolate-butter mixture. Blend in the vanilla extract. Sift over the sifted ingredients. Whisk slowly until the particles of flour are completely absorbed, taking care to catch any pockets of flour along the bottom and sides of the bowl. *Batter texture observation* The batter will be thick and heavy.

MAKE THE TRUFFLED WALNUTS In a medium-size mixing bowl, toss the walnuts with the melted butter-vanilla extract mixture. Sprinkle over the sifted cocoa-confectioner's sugar mixture and toss thoroughly. *Coated nuts observation* The nuts will look a bit glossy.

COMBINE THE TRUFFLED WALNUTS WITH THE BROWNIE BATTER Mix the truffled walnuts into the brownie batter with a rubber spatula. Scrape the batter into the prepared baking pan, taking care to spread it evenly and into the corners. Smooth over the top with a rubber spatula.

BAKE AND COOL THE BROWNIES Bake the brownies for 30 to 33 minutes, or until softly set (but not at all liquid). Cool the brownies in the pan on a rack for at least 4 to 5 hours before cutting into squares with a small, sharp knife. (In hot or humid weather, or if your kitchen is warm, refrigerate the cooled brownies for 1 hour—or until firm—before cutting.) Remove the brownies from the baking pan, using a small, offset metal spatula. Sprinkle the top of the brownies with confectioners' sugar just before serving, if you wish.

❈ *For an aromatic topnote of flavor,* use vanilla-scented superfine sugar (see page 54) in place of plain superfine sugar in the brownie batter.

FRESHLY BAKED, THE BROWNIES KEEP FOR 4 DAYS.

Variations: For truffled double chocolate brownies, a version of this recipe without nuts, omit the walnuts and confectioners' sugar and reduce the butter to 2 teaspoons in the *truffled walnuts* section of the recipe. Instead, toss 1 cup semisweet chocolate chips or 6 ounces bittersweet chocolate (coarsely chopped) with the melted butter-vanilla extract mixture, combine with the cocoa-sugar, and stir into the batter along with the sifted ingredients.

BEST BAKING ADVICE
Using tepid melted butter and chocolate helps to create a fudgy brownie. The all-purpose flour, cake flour, and cocoa (in combination with the small amount of baking powder) contribute to the structure of the baked brownie batter.

For truffled double chocolate brownies with Dutch-process black cocoa, substitute 1 tablespoon Dutch-process black cocoa for the regular unsweetened, alkalized cocoa. Use ¼ cup plus 1 teaspoon unsweetened, alkalized cocoa.

SOUR CREAM FUDGE CAKE

One 13 by 9-inch cake, creating 20 squares

THE CHOCOLATE TASTE IN THIS CAKE is expansive, and extends from the cake batter, darkened with unsweetened chocolate and rounded out with sour cream and buttermilk, to an ultra-thick layer of chocolate frosting. Actually, the cake and the frosting compete for your attention, which means that the cake definitely packs in enough chocolate, even for me.

Nonstick cooking spray, for preparing the baking pan

SOUR CREAM FUDGE CAKE BATTER

1¾ cups unsifted bleached cake flour

¼ cup unsifted bleached all-purpose flour

¾ teaspoon baking soda

¼ teaspoon baking powder

¾ teaspoon salt

½ pound (16 tablespoons or 2 sticks) unsalted butter, softened

1¾ cups vanilla-scented granulated sugar (see page 53)

4 large eggs

4 ounces (4 squares) unsweetened chocolate, melted and cooled

1¾ teaspoons intensified vanilla extract (see page 52)

¾ cup plus 2 tablespoons thick, cultured sour cream whisked with ½ cup buttermilk

Fudge Cake Frosting (see page 262), for topping the baked fudge cake

Vanilla Whipped Cream (see page 530), to accompany the cake (optional)

BAKEWARE

13 by 9 by 3-inch baking pan

PREHEAT THE OVEN AND PREPARE THE BAKING PAN Preheat the oven to 350° F. Film the inside of the baking pan with nonstick cooking spray; set aside.

MIX THE SOUR CREAM FUDGE CAKE BATTER Sift the cake flour, all-purpose flour, baking soda, baking powder, and salt onto a sheet of waxed paper.

Cream the butter in the large bowl of a freestanding electric mixer on moderate speed for 2 minutes. Add the vanilla-scented granulated sugar in three additions, beating 1 minute after each portion is added. Beat in the eggs, one at a time, mixing for 30 seconds after each addition. Blend in the melted unsweetened chocolate and vanilla extract, mixing until the batter is a uniform color. Scrape down the sides of the mixing bowl frequently with a rubber spatula to keep the batter even-textured.

On low speed, add the sifted mixture in three additions with the sour cream-buttermilk blend in two additions, beginning and ending with the sifted mixture.

Spoon the batter into the prepared baking pan. Lightly smooth over the top with a rubber spatula.

BAKE THE CAKE Bake the cake in the preheated oven for 40 minutes, or until set and a wooden pick inserted 1 to 2 inches from the center of the cake withdraws clean.

MAKE THE FROSTING WHILE THE CAKE IS BAKING Have the frosting ready about 10 minutes before the cake is baked.

*A chocolate cake batter turns positively
exquisite in the presence of sour cream
(and buttermilk, too). The dairy
component tenderizes the crumb and
builds the chocolate flavor.*

FROST AND COOL THE CAKE Cool the cake in the pan on a rack for 5 minutes. Carefully place generous spoonfuls of the frosting over the surface of the cake, and gently spread it over the top of the cake, using a flexible palette knife. (Spread the frosting carefully to prevent dislodging small patches of cake on the surface.) The frosting will smooth out as the heat of the cake softens it. As the cake cools, the frosting will set.

Cool the cake completely before cutting into squares directly from the pan. Serve with dollops of whipped cream, if you wish.

❋ *For an extra surge of flavor,* toss ½ cup miniature semisweet chocolate chips with ¾ teaspoon of the sifted mixture. Stir the chips into the cake batter after the dry ingredients have been added.

FRESHLY BAKED, THE CAKE KEEPS FOR **2** TO **3** DAYS.

FUDGE CAKE FROSTING

About 4 cups

I N MY KITCHEN, a deeply flavored fudge cake requires a bountiful amount of soft and creamy frosting to keep it company. This one will do nicely.

FUDGE CAKE FROSTING

6¾ cups plus 2 tablespoons unsifted confectioners' sugar

⅛ teaspoon salt

12 tablespoons (1½ sticks) unsalted butter, melted and cooled to tepid

3 ounces (3 squares) unsweetened chocolate, melted and cooled to tepid

2 teaspoons pure vanilla extract

½ cup milk

MAKE THE FUDGE CAKE FROSTING Place the confectioners' sugar and salt in a large mixing bowl. In a medium-size mixing bowl, whisk together the melted butter, melted unsweetened chocolate, and vanilla extract. Blend the ingredients well to create a smooth mixture. *Texture observation* If the butter and chocolate are not well mixed, the finished frosting will form tiny, glossy puddles of butter on the top.

Pour and scrape the chocolate mixture over the confectioners' sugar. Add the milk. Using an electric mixer, combine the ingredients together on moderately low to moderate speed until thoroughly mixed and very smooth. Scrape down the sides of the mixing bowl two or three times to keep the frosting even-textured. *Texture observation* The frosting should be smooth, thick, and creamy. If it's too dense, add an additional tablespoon of milk, 1 teaspoon at a time, to correct the consistency. Place a sheet of plastic wrap directly over the surface of the frosting, and set aside to use on the freshly baked cake.

MUD CAKE

One 13 by 9-inch cake, creating 20 squares

*T*HIS MUD CAKE IS NONSTOP CHOCOLATE: A chocolate sheet cake is covered with a dreamy, thick, and creamy chocolate frosting. It's the properly muddy frosting that distinguishes this kind of cake. As with some iced mud cakes or pies, it's essential to apply the frosting (or topping) over the cake just minutes after you pull it from the oven—then the frosting melts onto the top surface of the cake, and once it's firm, wraps the top in fabulous fudge.

Nonstick cooking spray, for preparing the baking pan

CHOCOLATE MUD CAKE BATTER

2 cups plus 1 tablespoon unsifted bleached cake flour

⅓ cup plus 1 tablespoon unsifted bleached all-purpose flour

1½ teaspoons baking soda

½ teaspoon salt

¼ pound (8 tablespoons or 1 stick) unsalted butter, softened

3 tablespoons shortening

1¾ cups granulated sugar

3 large eggs

2 teaspoons pure vanilla extract

4 ounces (4 squares) unsweetened chocolate, melted and cooled

1 cup buttermilk whisked with ¼ cup milk

Mud Cake Frosting (see page 265), for topping the baked mud cake

2½ cups walnut or pecan halves and pieces, lightly toasted and cooled completely

BAKEWARE

13 by 9 by 3-inch baking pan

PREHEAT THE OVEN AND PREPARE THE BAKING PAN Preheat the oven to 350° F. Film the inside of the baking pan with nonstick cooking spray; set aside.

MIX THE MUD CAKE BATTER Sift the cake flour, all-purpose flour, baking soda, and salt onto a sheet of waxed paper.

Cream the butter and shortening in the large bowl of a freestanding electric mixer on moderate speed for 3 minutes. Add the granulated sugar in three additions, beating for 45 seconds to 1 minute after each portion is added. Beat in the eggs, one at a time, mixing for 45 seconds to 1 minute after each addition. Blend in the vanilla extract and melted unsweetened chocolate, mixing until the batter is a uniform color. Scrape down the sides of the mixing bowl frequently with a rubber spatula to keep the batter even-textured.

On low speed, alternately add the sifted mixture in three additions with the buttermilk-milk mixture in two additions, beginning and ending with the sifted mixture. Spoon the batter into the prepared baking pan. Lightly smooth over the top with a flexible spatula.

BAKE THE CAKE Bake the cake in the preheated oven for 35 to 40 minutes, or until set and a wooden pick inserted in the cake withdraws clean.

MAKE THE FROSTING Make the frosting while the cake is baking. It must be ready 5 minutes after you remove the cake from the oven.

FROST AND COOL THE CAKE Cool the cake in the pan on a rack for 5 minutes. While the cake is still oven-hot, spoon dollops of the frosting evenly and gently over the surface of the cake, using a flexible palette knife. The frosting will melt down as it comes in contact with the heat of the cake, then firm up as it cools; frosting that is in direct contact with the cake will fuse into it in a delicious way. As soon as you've spread the frosting on the cake, scatter the nuts on top.

Cool the cake completely before cutting into squares for serving.

✻ *For an extra surge of flavor,* toss ¾ cup miniature semisweet chocolate chips with 1 teaspoon of the sifted mixture. Stir the chips into the cake batter after the dry ingredients have been added.

✻ *For an aromatic topnote of flavor,* use vanilla-scented granulated sugar (see page 53) in place of plain granulated sugar in the cake batter.

FRESHLY BAKED, THE CAKE KEEPS FOR 2 TO 3 DAYS.

MUD CAKE FROSTING

About 2½ cups

CREAMY YET FIRM (like fudge), this frosting sets up into a dense chocolate covering, sheltering the cake beneath.

MUD FROSTING

4 cups less 2 tablespoons unsifted confectioners' sugar

¼ pound (8 tablespoons or 1 stick) unsalted butter, melted and cooled to tepid

2 ounces (2 squares) unsweetened chocolate, melted and cooled to tepid

1 teaspoon pure vanilla extract

⅓ cup plus 1 tablespoon light (table) cream

large pinch of salt

BEST BAKING ADVICE

Using tepid butter and chocolate keeps the frosting fudgelike.

MAKE THE MUD FROSTING Sift the confectioners' sugar into a large mixing bowl. Add the melted butter, melted unsweetened chocolate, vanilla extract, cream, and salt. Using an electric hand mixer, mix the ingredients on low speed until smooth and creamy, like very soft fudge. Scrape down the sides of the mixing bowl once or twice with a rubber spatula to keep the frosting even-textured. *Texture observation* The frosting should be creamy-thick (not billowy or fluffy), but not excessively stiff.

Place a sheet of plastic wrap directly over the surface of the frosting and set aside briefly (and not more than about 15 minutes in advance, or it will be too dense). Use the frosting on the hot cake, as directed on page 264.

COCOA-CHOCOLATE CHIP PILLOWS

About 3 dozen cookies

*T*ENDER AND ALTOGETHER SUFFUSED with chocolate, these are buttery mouthfuls. The coarsely ground walnuts and chocolate chips add a certain texture and body to the butter cookies. This highly workable dough is easily made in a mixing bowl and is pleasing to handle: you can shape it into pillows as I've described below, or into crescents or logs.

COCOA-CHOCOLATE CHIP COOKIE DOUGH

2 cups unsifted bleached all-purpose flour

¼ cup plus 1 tablespoon unsweetened, alkalized cocoa

1 teaspoon baking powder

⅛ teaspoon cream of tartar

⅛ teaspoon salt

½ pound (16 tablespoons or 2 sticks) unsalted butter, melted and cooled

½ cup plus 2½ tablespoons unsifted vanilla-scented confectioners' sugar (see page 54)

2 teaspoons pure vanilla extract

¼ cup plus 1 tablespoon ground walnuts

⅔ cup miniature semisweet chocolate chips

CONFECTIONERS' SUGAR AND COCOA ROLLING MIXTURE

1¾ cups unsifted confectioners' sugar

1 teaspoon unsweetened, alkalized cocoa

BAKEWARE

several heavy cookie sheets

PREHEAT THE OVEN AND PREPARE THE COOKIE SHEETS Preheat the oven to 350° F. Line the cookie sheets with cooking parchment paper; set aside. The cookie sheets need to be heavy to prevent the bottoms of the cookies from overbaking or scorching. Double-pan the sheets, if necessary.

MIX THE COCOA-CHOCOLATE CHIP COOKIE DOUGH Sift the flour, cocoa, baking powder, cream of tartar, and salt onto a sheet of waxed paper.

Place the melted butter in a large mixing bowl. Sift over ½ cup vanilla-scented confectioners' sugar and mix it in with a wooden spoon or flat wooden paddle. *Consistency observation* The melted butter-sugar mixture will have small lumps of confectioners' sugar. Blend in the vanilla extract and walnuts. Stir in half of the sifted mixture and all of the chocolate chips. Stir in half of the remaining sifted mixture, then the balance of it. The dough will be malleable and workable.

FORM THE COOKIE PILLOWS Spoon up scant-tablespoon quantities of dough and roll into chubby balls. Place the balls of dough about 2 inches apart on the lined cookie sheets. Place 12 to 16 balls of dough on each sheet (the actual number depends upon the size of your cookie sheets).

BAKE AND COOL THE COOKIES Bake the cookies for 13 to 15 minutes, or until set. *Texture observation* The tops of the baked cookies will crack slightly here and there. Let the cookies stand on

By adding the chocolate chips along with the first half of the sifted mixture, you virtually guarantee that the chips will be evenly mixed into the dough, because the chips are most easily integrated into the dough while it is still very soft.

the sheets for 1 minute, then carefully remove them to cooling racks, using an offset metal spatula. Cool for 5 to 8 minutes.

MIX THE CONFECTIONERS' SUGAR AND COCOA ROLLING MIXTURE, AND DREDGE THE COOKIES Sift the 1¾ cups of confectioners' sugar with the cocoa into a mixing bowl. While the cookies are still warm, carefully dredge them, a few at a time, in the sugar-cocoa mixture to coat, then transfer them to a sheet of waxed paper to cool completely. Dredge lightly again, if you wish. A second roll in the sugar mixture makes the prettiest cookies.

FRESHLY BAKED, THE COOKIES KEEP FOR 5 DAYS.

Variation: For cocoa-chocolate chip pillows with Dutch-process black cocoa, use 1 tablespoon Dutch-process black cocoa and ¼ cup unsweetened, alkalized cocoa in the cookie dough.

Cocoa–Sour Cream– Chocolate Chip Coffee Cake

One 13 by 9-inch cake, creating 20 squares

Sometimes, in the morning, you just need to be consoled by chocolate. To oblige that, here is a coffee cake to indulge in. It soothes in the sweetest of ways. And the morning will seem much brighter.

Nonstick cooking spray, for preparing the baking pan

Chocolate chip–pecan crumble

1½ cups unsifted bleached all-purpose flour

¾ cup granulated sugar

¾ cup firmly packed light brown sugar, sieved if lumpy

big pinch of salt

12 tablespoons (1½ sticks) unsalted butter, cold, cut into small chunks

1 cup coarsely chopped pecans

¾ cup miniature semisweet chocolate chips

Cocoa–sour cream–chocolate chip coffee cake batter

3 cups unsifted bleached all-purpose flour

2 tablespoons unsweetened, alkalized cocoa

1½ teaspoons baking powder

¾ teaspoon baking soda

1 teaspoon salt

2¼ cups miniature semisweet chocolate chips

½ pound (16 tablespoons or 2 sticks) unsalted butter, softened

PREHEAT THE OVEN AND PREPARE THE BAKING PAN Preheat the oven to 350° F. Film the inside of the baking pan with non-stick cooking spray; set aside.

MAKE THE CHOCOLATE CHIP–PECAN CRUMBLE Thoroughly mix the flour, granulated sugar, light brown sugar, and salt in a medium-size mixing bowl. Scatter over the chunks of butter and, using a pastry blender, cut the butter into the flour until reduced to small pieces. Stir in the pecans and chocolate chips. Work the mixture boldly with your fingertips until it comes together in large and small moist, sandy-textured lumps. Set aside.

MIX THE COCOA SOUR CREAM CHOCOLATE CHIP COFFEE CAKE BATTER Sift the all-purpose flour, cocoa, baking powder, baking soda, and salt onto a sheet of waxed paper. In a medium-size mixing bowl, toss the chocolate chips with 1 tablespoon of the sifted mixture.

Cream the butter in the large bowl of a freestanding electric mixer on moderate speed for 4 minutes. Add the granulated sugar in three additions, beating for 1 minute after each portion is added. Beat in the eggs, one at a time, blending for 45 seconds after each addition. Blend in the vanilla extract.

On low speed, add the sifted mixture in three additions with the sour cream in two additions, beginning and ending with the sifted mixture. As the ingredients are added, scrape down the sides of the mixing bowl with a rubber spatula to keep the batter even-textured. Stir in the chocolate chips.

2 cups granulated sugar

3 large eggs

2 teaspoons pure vanilla extract

1½ cups thick, cultured sour cream

BAKEWARE

13 by 9 by 3-inch baking pan

BEST BAKING ADVICE
Cover the top of the coffee cake batter with a thick layer of the crumble mixture. Sprinkle it over lightly and don't compress it; otherwise the crumble may turn pasty and/or greasy.

Scrape the batter into the prepared baking pan. Smooth over the top with a flexible rubber spatula.

TOP THE COFFEE CAKE WITH THE CRUMBLE MIXTURE Sprinkle the crumble mixture evenly over the top of the cake batter. *Sprinkling technique observation* Placing the crumble evenly over the top prevents the mixture from forming pools of butter and the cake batter from baking unevenly. Use all of the crumble, creating a generous topping.

BAKE THE COFFEE CAKE Bake the coffee cake for 55 minutes to 1 hour, or until set and a wooden pick inserted in the cake withdraws clean, or with a few moist particles clinging to it. *Top texture observation* The surface will have natural and pretty dips and peaks. This is typical of how a sour cream butter cake batter topped with streusel behaves. The baked cake will pull away slightly from the sides of the baking pan.

COOL THE COFFEE CAKE Cool the cake in the pan on a rack. Serve the cake, warm or at room temperature, cut into squares, using a sturdy, offset metal spatula.

❉ *For an aromatic topnote of flavor,* use vanilla-scented granulated sugar (see page 53) in place of plain granulated sugar in the coffee cake batter.

FRESHLY BAKED, THE CAKE KEEPS FOR 5 DAYS.

MEMORIES-OF-CHILDHOOD CHOCOLATE CAKE

One 13 by 9-inch cake, creating 20 squares

My chocolate memories probably began with a version of this soft chocolate cake, covered with lots of creamy chocolate frosting. As the years have progressed, I keep going back to this kind of cake, which is full of depth and draws you in at every bite. I've charged up the batter by escalating the amount of vanilla, adding a bit of cocoa to deepen the focus of the chocolate, and combining all-purpose flour and cake flour to get just the right softness to the crumb. It's a cake to remember, and its honest goodness never disappoints.

Nonstick cooking spray, for preparing the baking pan

CHOCOLATE BUTTER CAKE BATTER

1⅔ cups unsifted bleached all-purpose flour

¼ cup plus 2 tablespoons unsifted bleached cake flour

2 tablespoons plus 1 teaspoon unsweetened, alkalized cocoa

1 teaspoon baking powder

¼ teaspoon baking soda

½ teaspoon salt

12 tablespoons (1½ sticks) unsalted butter, softened

1¾ cups superfine sugar

3 large eggs

5 ounces (5 squares) unsweetened chocolate, melted and cooled

2¼ teaspoons intensified vanilla extract (see page 52)

½ cup heavy cream blended with ½ cup milk

2 tablespoons thick, cultured sour cream

Chocolate Cream Frosting (see page 272), for spreading on the baked cake layers

PREHEAT THE OVEN AND PREPARE THE BAKING PAN Preheat the oven to 350° F. Film the inside of the baking pan with nonstick cooking spray; set aside.

MIX THE CHOCOLATE BUTTER CAKE BATTER Sift the all-purpose flour, cake flour, cocoa, baking powder, baking soda, and salt onto a sheet of waxed paper.

Cream the butter in the large bowl of a freestanding electric mixer on moderate speed for 2 to 3 minutes. Add the superfine sugar in three additions, beating for 1 minute after each portion is added. Blend in the eggs, one at a time, beating for 45 seconds after each addition.

On low speed, beat in the melted unsweetened chocolate and vanilla extract. Scrape down the sides of the mixing bowl frequently with a rubber spatula to keep the batter even-textured.

On low speed, alternately add the sifted ingredients in three additions with the heavy cream-milk blend in two additions, beginning and ending with the sifted mixture. Scrape down the sides of the mixing bowl often to keep the batter even-textured. Blend in the sour cream.

Vanilla Whipped Cream (see page 530), to accompany the cake (optional)

BAKEWARE
12 by 8 by 3-inch baking pan

Spoon the batter into the prepared baking pan. Smooth over the top with a rubber spatula.

BAKE AND COOL THE CAKE Bake the cake for 45 minutes, or until set and a wooden pick inserted in the center of the cake withdraws clean. The baked cake will pull away slightly from the sides of the baking pan. Let the cake stand in the pan on a cooling rack. Cool completely.

FROST THE COOLED CAKE Place spoonfuls of frosting on top of the cooled cake and spread it in swirls and waves, using a flexible palette knife. Let the cake stand for at least 2 hours before cutting into squares for serving. Serve the cake with dollops of whipped cream, if you wish.

FRESHLY BAKED, THE CAKE KEEPS FOR 2 DAYS.

❋ *For an aromatic topnote of flavor,* use vanilla-scented superfine sugar (see page 54) in place of plain superfine sugar in the cake batter.

CHOCOLATE CREAM FROSTING

About 3¾ cups

THIS ABUNDANTLY RICH FROSTING is the perfect creamy counterpoint to a downy, soft-crumbed cake.

CHOCOLATE CREAM FROSTING

4⅓ cups plus 2 tablespoons unsifted confectioners' sugar

large pinch of salt

4 ounces (4 squares) unsweetened chocolate, melted and cooled to tepid

1½ ounces bittersweet chocolate, melted and cooled to tepid

6 tablespoons (¾ stick) unsalted butter, cut into tablespoon chunks, softened

¾ cup plus 3 tablespoons heavy cream

2¼ teaspoons pure vanilla extract

MAKE THE CHOCOLATE CREAM FROSTING Place the confectioners' sugar and salt in a large mixing bowl. Add the melted unsweetened chocolate, melted bittersweet chocolate, butter, cream, and vanilla extract. Using an electric hand mixer, beat for 1 minute on low speed to combine the ingredients; continue beating for 2 minutes on high speed, or until very smooth and creamy, scraping down the sides of the mixing bowl several times with a rubber spatula to keep the frosting even-textured. *Frosting texture observation* The frosting should be thick but creamy; if it seems too dense, lighten it with a little more heavy cream, added a teaspoon at a time. Use the frosting immediately.

CHOCOLATE, COCONUT, AND CHOCOLATE CHIP BAR COOKIES

2 dozen bar cookies

WITH THE BASIC PANTRY INGREDIENTS on the shelf, these bar cookies—chewy-crunchy and undeniably rich—are a snap to make.

Nonstick cooking spray, for preparing the baking pan

COCONUT-CHOCOLATE CRUMB COOKIE BASE

¼ pound (8 tablespoons or 1 stick) unsalted butter, melted and cooled to tepid

½ teaspoon pure vanilla extract

1⅓ cups plus 3 tablespoons chocolate cookie wafer crumbs

¼ cup lightly packed sweetened flaked coconut

COCONUT-CHOCOLATE CHIP-WALNUT TOPPING

1⅓ cups sweetened flaked coconut

1¼ cups semisweet chocolate chips

1¼ cups coarsely chopped walnuts

One 14-ounce can sweetened condensed milk

BAKEWARE

9 by 9 by 2-inch baking pan

BEST BAKING ADVICE
Thoroughly combine the chocolate wafer crumbs and flaked coconut.

PREHEAT THE OVEN AND PREPARE THE BAKING PAN Preheat the oven to 350° F. Film the inside of the baking pan with nonstick cooking spray; set aside.

MAKE THE COCONUT-CHOCOLATE CRUMB COOKIE BASE In a small bowl, whisk the melted butter and vanilla extract. In another bowl, combine the chocolate wafer crumbs and flaked coconut. Pour the butter mixture into the prepared baking pan. Sprinkle the cookie crumb mixture in an even layer over the butter. Using a small, offset metal spatula, lightly press down the cookie crumbs.

COVER THE COOKIE BASE WITH THE TOPPING Sprinkle the coconut over the cookie base, then top with the chocolate chips. Scatter the chopped walnuts over all. Pour the sweetened condensed milk evenly over everything, making sure to drizzle it along the edges. *Technique observation* So that the bars are moist throughout, it's important that the condensed milk be evenly distributed.

BAKE THE BAR COOKIES Bake the bar cookies in the preheated oven for 25 to 30 minutes, or until just set and light golden on top.

COOL AND CUT THE BAR COOKIES Cool the entire cake of bar cookies in the pan on a cooling rack. With a small, sharp knife, cut the cake into quarters, then cut each individual quarter into six bars. Remove the bars, using a small, offset metal spatula.

FRESHLY BAKED, THE BARS KEEP FOR 3 DAYS.

BITTERSWEET CHOCOLATE STOLLEN

4 stollen

THIS FESTIVE TURN ON A traditional holiday yeast bread has you kneading chopped bittersweet chocolate into a lightly sweetened and buttery yeast dough. To make this a truly extraordinary chocolate experience, I use nearly a pound of bittersweet bar chocolate. The dough that catches the chunks of chocolate is thoroughly flavored with vanilla—it's graceful and plush.

CHUNKY BITTERSWEET
CHOCOLATE DOUGH

4½ teaspoons active dry yeast

1½ teaspoons granulated sugar

⅓ warm (110° to 115° F.) water

¾ cup milk

⅔ cup vanilla-scented granulated sugar
    (see page 53)

Half of a moist, supple vanilla bean,
    split down the center to expose the
    tiny seeds

1½ tablespoons pure vanilla extract

3 large eggs

1 large egg yolk

5 cups unsifted unbleached all-purpose
    flour, plus ⅓ to ½ cup additional
    for kneading, or as needed

1¼ teaspoons salt

½ pound (16 tablespoons or 2 sticks)
    unsalted butter, cut into 2
    tablespoon-size chunks, softened
    but cool

15 ounces bittersweet chocolate,
    coarsely chopped

MAKE THE BITTERSWEET CHOCOLATE STOLLEN DOUGH
Combine the yeast and plain granulated sugar in a small bowl; stir in the warm water and let stand for 7 to 8 minutes, or until foamy and swollen. In the meantime, heat the milk, the vanilla-scented granulated sugar, and vanilla bean in a small saucepan over low heat until the sugar dissolves. Remove from the heat and cool to 115° F. Remove the vanilla bean with a pair of tongs. With a flexible palette knife, carefully scrape out the vanilla bean seeds into the milk mixture. Discard the section of vanilla bean. Beat the eggs and egg yolk into the milk mixture; stir in the swollen yeast mixture.

In a large mixing bowl, mix half of the flour with the salt. Pour over the yeast-milk-egg mixture and stir it in. Blend in all the remaining flour, a little at a time, using a wooden spoon or flat wooden paddle. *Texture observation* The dough will have a rough, slightly shaggy texture. Work in the butter with your fingertips, 2 tablespoons at a time, smearing it into the dough and slapping the dough against itself. Alternatively, you can place the butter-free dough in the bowl of a heavy-duty, freestanding electric mixer fitted with the flat paddle, and incorporate the butter into it, 2 tablespoons at a time, on moderate speed. *Texture observation* In the beginning, as the butter is added, the dough will become slippery and a bit loose-textured, but will smooth out when all of the butter is beaten in and the dough is kneaded.

KNEAD THE STOLLEN DOUGH Dust a work surface generously with ⅓ cup flour, working in enough of the flour to keep the dough from sticking. Knead the dough for

VANILLA-BUTTER WASH

¼ pound (8 tablespoons or 1 stick) unsalted butter, melted and cooled to tepid

2 teaspoons intensified vanilla extract (see page 52)

Confectioners' sugar or vanilla-scented confectioners' sugar (see page 54), for dredging on the tops of the baked stollen

BAKEWARE

2 large, rimmed baking pans

BEST BAKING ADVICE

It's easy to overbake stollen because they are somewhat flat and tend to bake quickly. Check on them toward the end of baking, beginning at 25 minutes.

8 to 10 minutes, adding extra sprinkles of flour as necessary to keep the dough from bonding to the kneading surface; the dough, however, should not be stiff. (The amount of additional flour used in the kneading process really depends on the absorption quality of the flour, humidity of the day, and atmospheric conditions of your kitchen.) Use a dough scraper to lift up the dough as you knead it. *Texture observation* When kneaded sufficiently, the dough will be smooth and satiny. Alternatively, knead the dough in the bowl of a freestanding mixer fitted with the dough hook for 5 minutes on moderate speed.

SET THE DOUGH TO RISE Place the dough in a large, lightly buttered bowl, turn to coat all sides in the butter, and cut a large cross in the dough with a clean pair of kitchen scissors to facilitate the rising process. Cover the bowl with a sheet of plastic wrap and let stand at room temperature for 1 hour and 45 minutes to 2 hours, or until doubled in bulk.

INTEGRATE THE BITTERSWEET CHOCOLATE CHUNKS INTO THE RISEN STOLLEN DOUGH With the cupped palms of your hands, or your fingertips, lightly compress the dough and turn it onto a lightly floured work surface. *Dough texture observation* The dough will still be slightly puffy. Pat (or roll out) the dough into a large sheet, about 15 by 15 inches. Don't worry about the exact size of the dough sheet; all you need is a large enough surface area for scattering the chocolate.

Strew the chocolate over the dough and pat down the chocolate pieces lightly with your fingertips. Roll up the dough into a casual jellyroll. Fold the roll in half and knead the dough until the chocolate is incorporated. While kneading the dough initially, the chocolate will separate out from the dough slightly, and occasionally shear through it, but will work back in after about 2 to 3 minutes of light kneading.

If it is difficult to knead the dough (that is, if it gives you too much resistance and begins to fight back), leave it as is on the work surface and cover with a linen towel or sheet of plastic wrap. Let the dough rest for 10 to 15 minutes, then continue kneading.

PREPARE THE BAKING PANS Line the baking pans with cooking parchment paper; set aside.

MIX THE VANILLA-BUTTER WASH Whisk the melted butter and vanilla extract in a small mixing bowl. Keep the mixture in a warm place to prevent it from solidifying.

FORM THE STOLLEN Cut the dough into four even-sized pieces, cover with a sheet of plastic wrap, and let stand for 15 minutes. Working with one piece of dough at a time, pat it into a 9-inch-long oval. Brush the top with a film of the vanilla-butter wash. Fold one long side to the center and press down lightly. Fold over the other side, overlapping it and extending it over the center edge by about ¾ inch. Form three more stollen with the remaining pieces of dough. Place the stollen, two to a sheet, on the parchment paper-lined baking pans, carefully arranging them (on a slight diagonal) on the upper and lower third sections.

SET THE FORMED STOLLEN TO RISE Brush the tops of the stollen with another film of the vanilla-butter wash. Cover the stollen loosely with plastic wrap and let rise at room temperature until almost doubled in bulk, about 1 hour to 1 hour and 15 minutes.

PREHEAT THE OVEN AND BAKE THE STOLLEN Preheat the oven to 375° F. in advance of baking. (If necessary, rewarm the vanilla-butter wash to its liquid state.) Brush the stollen again very lightly with the vanilla-butter wash. Bake the stollen for 30 minutes, or until golden on top and baked through. (Check the stollen after 25 minutes.) As soon as the stollen are baked, brush again with the vanilla-butter wash.

COOL THE STOLLEN Let the stollen cool on the baking pans for 4 to 5 minutes, then carefully remove them to cooling racks, using two wide, offset metal spatulas. Just before slicing and serving, dust the tops of the stollen with confectioners' sugar. *Slicing observation* Use a serrated knife to cut the sweet neatly and cleanly.

FRESHLY BAKED, THE STOLLEN KEEPS FOR 2 TO 3 DAYS.

Variation: For bittersweet chocolate stollen with walnuts, work ½ cup chopped walnuts into the dough along with the chunks of bittersweet chocolate.

DOUBLE CHOCOLATE SCONES

1 dozen scones

Delightfully and deeply chocolate, there's significant richness in this quick bread dough—the taste-fusion of butter and heavy cream sets up just the right dairy background to the cocoa and nuggets of bittersweet chocolate. These scones are large, tall, and moist.

DOUBLE CHOCOLATE SCONE DOUGH

4 cups plus 2 tablespoons unsifted bleached all-purpose flour

½ cup plus 1 tablespoon unsweetened, alkalized cocoa

5 teaspoons baking powder

1 teaspoon salt

¾ cup superfine sugar

12 tablespoons (1½ sticks) unsalted butter, cold, cut into chunks

4 large eggs

1 cup heavy cream

1 tablespoon pure vanilla extract

12 ounces bittersweet chocolate, chopped into small chunks, or 2 cups semisweet chocolate chips

BAKEWARE

2 large, heavy cookie sheets or rimmed baking pans

PREHEAT THE OVEN AND PREPARE THE COOKIE SHEETS Preheat the oven to 400° F. Line the cookie sheets or rimmed baking pans with cooking parchment paper. *Bakeware observation* The baking sheets must be heavy, or the chocolate dough will scorch on the bottom as the scones bake. Double-pan the sheets, if necessary.

MIX THE DOUBLE CHOCOLATE SCONE DOUGH Whisk the flour, cocoa, baking powder, salt, and superfine sugar into a large mixing bowl.

Scatter over the chunks of butter, and using a pastry blender (or two round-bladed table knives), cut the fat into the flour until reduced to small nuggets about the size of dried lima beans.

In a medium-size mixing bowl, whisk the eggs until blended. Whisk in the heavy cream and vanilla extract. Pour the whisked mixture over the sifted ingredients, add the chunks of bittersweet chocolate (or chocolate chips), and stir to form a dough, using a wooden spoon or flat wooden paddle. *Dough consistency observation* The dough will be stiff but moist. You may need to work a few tablespoons of the dry ingredients into the dough by hand.

Flour your hands and knead the dough in the bowl for about 15 seconds. Divide the dough in half. On a floured work surface, pat each piece of dough into a cake measuring 7 to 8 inches in diameter.

FORM THE CAKES OF DOUGH INTO SCONES With a chef's knife, cut each cake of dough into six wedges. Using an offset metal spatula, arrange the scones 3 inches apart on the lined baking sheets, placing six scones on each sheet.

BAKE AND COOL THE SCONES Bake the scones for 20 minutes, or until set. Let the scones stand on the baking sheets for 1 minute, then remove them to cooling racks using an offset metal spatula. Serve the scones very fresh, at room temperature.

❈ *For an aromatic topnote of flavor,* use vanilla-scented superfine sugar (see page 54) in place of plain superfine sugar and intensified vanilla extract (see page 52) in place of plain vanilla extract in the scone dough.

FRESHLY BAKED, THE SCONES KEEP FOR **2** DAYS.

Variations: For double chocolate scones with walnuts or pecans, add ½ cup chopped walnuts or pecans to the dough along with the chopped bittersweet chocolate or chocolate chips.

For double chocolate scones with Dutch-process black cocoa, use 3 tablespoons Dutch-process black cocoa and 6 tablespoons unsweetened, alkalized cocoa.

CHOCOLATE COCONUT CREAM BATTER PIE
One 9-inch pie, creating 8 slices

NO PIE CRUST NEEDED HERE—this lissome batter pie is sustained with chocolate, plus a creamy coconut and miniature chocolate chip mixture that shapes a baked-on topping.

Softened unsalted butter, for preparing the pie pan

COCONUT CREAM TOPPING

4 ounces (one 3-ounce package plus one-third of a 3-ounce package) cream cheese, softened

3 tablespoons vanilla-scented granulated sugar

1 large egg yolk

PREHEAT THE OVEN AND PREPARE THE PIE PAN Preheat the oven to 350° F. Lightly butter the inside of the pie pan; set aside.

MAKE THE COCONUT CREAM TOPPING Using an electric hand mixer, beat the cream cheese and granulated sugar in a medium-size bowl on moderately high speed for 1 minute. On low speed, blend in the egg yolk, flour, vanilla, and salt. Scrape down the sides of the mixing bowl two or three times with a rubber spatula to keep the batter even-textured. Beat on high speed for 30 seconds.

1 teaspoon unsifted bleached all-purpose flour

1¼ teaspoons pure vanilla extract

big pinch of salt

½ cup miniature semisweet chocolate chips

⅓ cup lightly packed sweetened flaked coconut

CHOCOLATE FUDGE
BROWNIE BATTER

½ cup unsifted bleached all-purpose flour

¼ teaspoon salt

¼ pound (8 tablespoons or 1 stick) unsalted butter, melted and cooled

3 ounces (3 squares) unsweetened chocolate, melted and cooled

2 large eggs

1 cup vanilla-scented granulated sugar (see page 53)

2 teaspoons pure vanilla extract

¾ cup chopped walnuts (or pecans), lightly toasted and cooled

BAKEWARE

9-inch pie pan

Batter texture observation The batter will be smooth and creamy. Stir in the chocolate chips and coconut.

MAKE THE CHOCOLATE FUDGE BROWNIE BATTER Whisk the flour and salt in a small bowl. In a medium-size mixing bowl, whisk the melted butter and melted unsweetened chocolate until thoroughly combined. In a large mixing bowl, whisk eggs for 1 minute to blend, add the vanilla-scented granulated sugar and vanilla extract, and continue whisking for 1 to 2 minutes, or until lightly thickened. Add the flour mixture, and mix until all particles of flour are absorbed into the batter, using a wooden spoon or flat wooden paddle. Stir in the walnuts (or pecans).

ASSEMBLE THE TOPPING AND BATTER TO CREATE THE PIE Scrape the chocolate batter into the pan. Spoon the coconut cream topping in patches over the chocolate batter and, using the tip of a round-bladed table knife (or a flexible palette knife), lightly swirl the topping through the chocolate.

BAKE THE PIE Bake for 25 to 30 minutes, or until just set. The center of the pie will be somewhat soft, with slightly firmer edges. Cool the pie on a cooling rack. Serve the pie plain, or with whipped cream or vanilla ice cream. Refrigerate any leftover pie (or any pie not eaten within 2 to 3 hours of baking) in an airtight container.

FRESHLY BAKED, THE PIE KEEPS FOR **2** DAYS.

BEST BAKING ADVICE

When swirling the chocolate fudge brownie batter and coconut cream topping together, remember that just a few swirls are effective. Overswirling the batter can give it a muddy look.

Simply Intense Chocolate Brownies

16 brownies

The clear and direct flavor of chocolate dazzles in this brownie.

Nonstick cooking spray, for preparing the baking pan

INTENSELY CHOCOLATE
BROWNIE BATTER

¾ cup unsifted bleached all-purpose flour

⅓ cup unsifted bleached cake flour

3 tablespoons unsweetened, alkalized cocoa

¼ teaspoon baking powder

¼ teaspoon salt

½ pound (16 tablespoons or 2 sticks) unsalted butter, melted and cooled to tepid

4 ounces (4 squares) unsweetened chocolate, melted and cooled to tepid

4 large eggs

2 cups superfine sugar

1½ teaspoons pure vanilla extract

Confectioners' sugar, for sifting over the top of the brownies (optional)

BAKEWARE
9 by 9 by 2-inch baking pan

PREHEAT THE OVEN AND PREPARE THE BAKING PAN Preheat the oven to 325° F. Film the inside of the baking pan with nonstick cooking spray; set aside.

MIX THE BROWNIE BATTER Sift the all-purpose flour, cake flour, cocoa, baking powder, and salt onto a sheet of waxed paper.

Whisk the melted butter and melted chocolate in a medium-size mixing bowl until thoroughly combined.

Whisk the eggs in a large mixing bowl to blend well, about 45 seconds, then add the superfine sugar and whisk for 45 seconds to 1 minute, or until just combined. Blend in the melted chocolate–butter mixture. Blend in the vanilla extract. Sift over the sifted mixture and mix until all particles of flour are absorbed into the batter, using a wooden spoon or flat wooden paddle.

Scrape the batter into the prepared baking pan. Smooth over the top with a rubber spatula.

BAKE AND COOL THE BROWNIES Bake the brownies for 30 to 33 minutes, or until just set. Let the brownies stand in the pan on a cooling rack for 3 to 4 hours, then refrigerate for 30 to 45 minutes, or until firm enough to cut. (In hot or humid weather, or in a warm kitchen, you can freeze the pan of brownies for 15 to 20 minutes before cutting, or until solid enough to cut.) Cut the entire cake of brownies into four quarters, then cut each quarter into four squares, using a small, sharp knife. Remove the brownies from the baking pan, using a small offset spatula. Just before serving, sift confectioners' sugar on top of the brownies, if you wish.

✳ *For an aromatic topnote of flavor,* use intensified vanilla extract (see page 52) in place of plain vanilla extract in the brownie batter.

FRESHLY BAKED, THE BROWNIES KEEP FOR 3 DAYS.

The combination of all-purpose flour and cake flour, and the use of superfine (rather than plain granulated) sugar in the brownie batter, keep the baked texture of the brownies tender and softly moist. To make the brownies remain fudgy-moist throughout, be careful about overbaking them—the top, specifically the middle section, should be softly set, without any liquidy patches.

Variations: For simply intense chocolate brownies with chocolate chips, stir ¾ cup miniature semisweet chocolate chips, tossed with 1 teaspoon of the sifted flour mixture, into the brownie batter after the sifted mixture has been added.

For simply intense chocolate brownies with bittersweet chocolate chunks, stir 4 ounces chopped bittersweet chocolate, tossed with 1 teaspoon of the sifted flour mixture, into the brownie batter after the sifted mixture has been added.

For simply intense chocolate brownies with Dutch-process black cocoa, use 1 tablespoon Dutch-process black cocoa and 2 tablespoons unsweetened, alkalized cocoa in the brownie batter.

ESSENCE OF CHOCOLATE SQUARES

16 squares

THE DOUBLE DOSE OF CHOCOLATE, in two contrasting but harmonious layers, is uninterrupted by nuts or anything else. These are provocative and candylike, and one of the most thoroughly chocolate-flavored bar cookies I've ever baked.

Nonstick cooking spray, for preparing the baking pan

FUDGY CHOCOLATE BAR COOKIE BATTER

1¼ cups unsifted bleached all-purpose flour

2 tablespoons plus 2 teaspoons unsweetened, alkalized cocoa

¼ teaspoon baking powder

½ teaspoon salt

½ pound (16 tablespoons or 2 sticks) unsalted butter, melted and cooled to tepid

4 ounces (4 squares) unsweetened chocolate, melted and cooled to tepid

4 large eggs

2 cups vanilla-scented granulated sugar (see page 53)

1½ teaspoons intensified vanilla extract (see page 52)

DENSE CHOCOLATE FROSTING FOR TOPPING THE FUDGE CHOCOLATE LAYER

3¾ cups plus 2 tablespoons unsifted confectioners' sugar

⅛ teaspoon salt

¼ pound (8 tablespoons or 1 stick) unsalted butter, melted and cooled to tepid

PREHEAT THE OVEN AND PREPARE THE BAKING PAN Preheat the oven to 325° F. Film the inside of the baking pan with nonstick cooking spray; set aside.

MIX THE FUDGY CHOCOLATE BAR COOKIE BATTER Sift the all-purpose flour, cocoa, baking powder, and salt onto a sheet of waxed paper.

Whisk the melted butter and melted unsweetened chocolate in a medium-size mixing bowl until thoroughly combined.

Whisk the eggs in a large mixing bowl to blend well, about 1 minute, then add the vanilla-scented granulated sugar and whisk slowly for 1 minute, or until just combined. Whisk in the tepid melted chocolate-butter mixture. Blend in the vanilla extract. Sift over the dry ingredients and mix until all particles of flour are absorbed into the batter, using a whisk, wooden spoon, or flat wooden paddle.

Scrape the batter into the prepared baking pan. Smooth over the top with a rubber spatula.

BAKE THE FUDGY CHOCOLATE BAR COOKIE LAYER Bake the cake layer for 35 to 37 minutes, or until just set. Cool the cake layer in the pan on a rack for 5 minutes while you make the frosting.

MIX THE DENSE CHOCOLATE FROSTING Place the confectioners' sugar and salt in a large mixing bowl. Whisk the melted butter and melted unsweetened chocolate in a small mixing bowl until thoroughly combined. Add the milk, light cream, and vanilla extract. Using an electric hand mixer, beat the frosting on moderately low speed until creamy and completely combined. Scrape

2 ounces (2 squares) unsweetened chocolate, melted and cooled to tepid

¼ cup milk

2 tablespoons light (table) cream

1 teaspoon intensified vanilla extract (see page 52)

(see page 52)

BAKEWARE

9 by 9 by 2-inch baking pan

down the sides of the mixing bowl two or three times to keep the frosting even-textured. *Frosting texture and frosting mixing observation* Do not beat the frosting on high speed or it will become airy and fluffy, instead of creamy and dense.

TOP THE FUDGY CHOCOLATE BAR COOKIE LAYER WITH THE FROSTING Immediately and carefully, place large dollops of the frosting evenly over the surface of the hot bar cookie base and spread it, using a flexible offset spatula. Spread it smoothly and lightly, to keep the bar cookie layer intact.

COOL THE SWEET Let the sweet cool in the pan on a rack for to 3 to 4 hours, or until cooled and completely set. The cooling time is especially important in hot, humid, or damp weather. Cut the cake into four quarters, then cut each quarter into four squares, using a small, sharp knife. Remove the chocolate squares from the baking pan, using a small, metal offset spatula.

FRESHLY BAKED, THE SQUARES KEEP FOR 4 TO 5 DAYS.

Variation: For essence of chocolate squares with Dutch-process black cocoa, use 1 tablespoon Dutch-process black cocoa and 1 tablespoon plus 2 teaspoons unsweetened, alkalized cocoa. You can sprinkle the top of the fudge frosting with Dark Micro-Chips (see page 68).

BEST BAKING ADVICE

Spreading the frosting on the top of the hot bar cookie layer can be tricky. Place spoonfuls of frosting in rows across and down the bar cookie layer, wait a minute, then begin to spread it. The heat of the bar cookie layer will begin to melt the frosting enough to make it spreadable. Don't panic if the bottom layer of the frosting seems soft; it will firm up as it cools.

HEIRLOOM CHOCOLATE CAKE

One two-layer, 9-inch cake, creating about 12 slices

TENDER AND DOWNY, with a velvety texture, these cake layers are moist and plump.

Shortening and bleached all-purpose
    flour, for preparing the layer
    cake pans

BUTTERMILK CHOCOLATE
LAYER CAKE BATTER

2¼ cups sifted bleached cake flour

¾ teaspoon baking soda

¼ teaspoon baking powder

½ teaspoon salt

10 tablespoons (1 stick plus 2
    tablespoons) unsalted butter,
    softened

1⅓ cups plus 3 tablespoons superfine
    sugar

3 large eggs

3 ounces (3 squares) unsweetened
    chocolate, melted and cooled

1¾ teaspoons pure vanilla extract

1 cup plus 1 tablespoon buttermilk,
    whisked well

Buttery Chocolate Frosting (see
    page 285), for spreading on the
    baked cake layers

Vanilla Whipped Cream (see page 530),
    to accompany the cake (optional)

BAKEWARE

two 9-inch round layer cake pans

PREHEAT THE OVEN AND PREPARE THE LAYER CAKE PANS
Preheat the oven to 350° F. Lightly grease the inside of the cake pans with shortening. Line the bottom of each pan with a circle of waxed paper, grease the paper, and dust the inside with all-purpose flour. Tap out any excess flour; set aside.

MIX THE BUTTERMILK CHOCOLATE LAYER CAKE BATTER
Sift the flour with the baking soda, baking powder, and salt onto a sheet of waxed paper.

Cream the butter in the large bowl of a freestanding electric mixer on moderate speed for 3 minutes. Add the superfine sugar in three additions, beating for 1 minute after each portion is added. Beat in the eggs, one at a time, blending for 30 to 45 seconds after each addition. Blend in the melted unsweetened chocolate and vanilla extract.

On low speed, alternately add the sifted mixture in three additions with the buttermilk in two additions, beginning and ending with the sifted mixture. Scrape down the sides of the mixing bowl frequently with a rubber spatula to keep the batter even-textured.

Spoon the batter into the layer cake pans, dividing it evenly between them. Using a flexible palette knife, smooth over the top of each layer to spread the batter evenly.

BAKE AND COOL THE CAKE LAYERS Bake the layers for 30 minutes, or until set and a wooden pick inserted 1 inch from the center of each cake layer withdraws clean. Cool the cake layers in the pans on racks for 5 to 8 minutes.

Invert each layer onto another rack, peel off the waxed paper round, then invert again to cool right side up. Cool completely.

ASSEMBLE AND FROST THE CAKE Tear off four 3-inch-wide strips of waxed paper. Place the strips in the shape of a square around the outer 3 inches of a cake plate. Center one cake layer on the plate partially covering the waxed paper square; the strips should peek out by at least 1 inch. Using a flexible palette knife, spread a thin layer of frosting over the cake layer. Carefully place the second layer on top, then ice the entire cake in pretty swirls of frosting. When the frosting has set, in about 45 minutes, gently slide out and discard the waxed paper strips. Cut the cake into slices for serving. Serve with spoonfuls of the whipped cream, if you wish.

❊ *For an aromatic topnote of flavor,* use intensified vanilla extract (see page 52) in place of plain vanilla extract in the cake batter.

FRESHLY BAKED, THE CAKE KEEPS FOR 2 DAYS.

BUTTERY CHOCOLATE FROSTING
About 3⅔ cups

INCORPORATING THE SLIGHTLY WARM melted chocolate with the sugar, butter, and flavorings creates the creamiest frosting, which swirls over layers of cake so smoothly.

CHOCOLATE FROSTING

7 tablespoons (1 stick less 1 tablespoon) unsalted butter, softened

5 ounces (5 squares) unsweetened chocolate, melted and cooled to tepid

large pinch of salt

1½ teaspoons intensified vanilla extract (see page 52)

4⅓ cups plus 2 tablespoons unsifted confectioners' sugar

½ cup plus 2 tablespoons milk

MIX THE CHOCOLATE FROSTING Using an electric hand mixer, blend the butter, melted unsweetened chocolate, salt, vanilla extract, half of the confectioners' sugar, and all of the milk in a large mixing bowl. Blend in the remaining confectioners' sugar and continue beating the frosting on moderate speed for 1 to 2 minutes, or until very smooth. Scrape down the sides of the mixing bowl once or twice with a rubber spatula to keep the frosting even-textured. Raise the speed to high and beat for 1 minute. *Frosting texture observation* The frosting should be thick and creamy-textured. If the frosting seems at all dense after the minute of beating on high speed, add a little more milk, a teaspoon at a time, to lighten the frosting. Use the frosting immediately.

BIG CHOCOLATE-
CHOCOLATE CHIP MUFFINS

9 jumbo muffins

BURDENED IN THE MOST DELICIOUS WAY possible with chocolate and chopped pecans, this recipe makes a glorious batch of muffins. The buttery, cakelike texture of the batter reveals the flavor of chocolate directly, in the melding of alkalized cocoa and a fearless amount of semisweet chocolate chips.

Softened unsalted butter and bleached all-purpose flour, for preparing the muffin pans

CHOCOLATE-CHOCOLATE
CHIP MUFFIN BATTER

2¾ cups unsifted bleached all-purpose flour

6 tablespoons unsweetened, alkalized cocoa

2 teaspoons baking powder

¾ teaspoon salt

1⅓ cups semisweet chocolate chips

¾ cup chopped walnuts

10 tablespoons (1 stick plus 2 tablespoons) unsalted butter, softened

3 tablespoons shortening

½ cup firmly packed light brown sugar, sieved if lumpy

½ cup granulated sugar

3 large eggs

2½ teaspoons pure vanilla extract

1 cup milk

PREHEAT THE OVEN AND PREPARE THE MUFFIN/CUPCAKE PANS Preheat the oven to 375° F. Lightly butter and flour the muffin/cupcake cups. Tap out any excess flour; set aside.

MIX THE CHOCOLATE-CHOCOLATE CHIP MUFFIN BATTER Sift the flour, cocoa powder, baking powder, and salt onto a sheet of waxed paper. In a medium-size mixing bowl, toss the chocolate chips and walnuts with 1 tablespoon of the sifted mixture.

Cream the butter and shortening in the large bowl of a free-standing electric mixer on moderate speed for 3 minutes. Add the light brown sugar and beat for 1 minute; add the granulated sugar and beat for a minute longer. Blend in the eggs, one at a time, beating for 30 seconds after each addition. Blend in the vanilla extract. Scrape down the sides of the mixing bowl frequently with a rubber spatula to keep the batter even-textured.

On low speed, add the sifted mixture in three additions with the milk in two additions, beginning and ending with the sifted mixture. Stir in the floured chocolate chips and walnuts.

Spoon the batter into the muffin cups, filling each a little more than three-fourths full.

BAKE AND COOL THE MUFFINS Bake the muffins in the preheated oven for 25 to 30 minutes, or until risen, set, and a wooden pick inserted in the center of a muffin withdraws clean or with a few moist crumbs clinging to it.

9 jumbo muffin/cupcake cups (two pans, each holding six individual muffin cups), 4 inches in diameter by 1¾ inches deep (with a capacity of about 1⅛ cups)

Transfer the muffin pans to cooling racks. Let the muffins stand in the pans for 15 minutes, then carefully remove them to another cooling rack. Take care as you are removing the muffins, for they are exceptionally tender and fragile when freshly baked. Cool completely.

❋ *For an extra surge of flavor,* sprinkle miniature semisweet chocolate chips, ⅓ cup in total, on top of the unbaked muffins.

❋ *For an aromatic topnote of flavor,* use intensified vanilla extract (see page 52) in place of plain vanilla extract in the muffin batter.

FRESHLY BAKED, THE MUFFINS KEEP FOR 2 DAYS.

Variation: For big chocolate-chocolate chip muffins with Dutch-process black cocoa, use 2 tablespoons Dutch-process black cocoa and ¼ cup unsweetened, alkalized cocoa.

BEST BAKING ADVICE
The small amount of shortening in the batter provides textural relief and opens up the crumb of the baked muffins.

BITTERSWEET CHOCOLATE BROWNIES WITH PECANS

16 brownies

THESE ARE DRAMATIC BROWNIES, with melted bittersweet chocolate and chopped bittersweet chocolate chunks linked in a buttery, vanilla-scented batter.

Nonstick cooking spray, for preparing the baking pan

BITTERSWEET CHOCOLATE BROWNIE BATTER

1¼ cups unsifted bleached cake flour

¼ cup unsifted bleached all-purpose flour

1 tablespoon unsweetened alkalized cocoa

¼ teaspoon baking powder

½ teaspoon salt

6 ounces bittersweet chocolate, cut into small chunks

14 tablespoons (1¾ sticks) unsalted butter, melted and cooled to tepid

5 squares (5 ounces) unsweetened chocolate, melted and cooled to tepid

3 ounces bittersweet chocolate, melted and cooled to tepid

4 large eggs

2 cups plus 1 tablespoon superfine sugar

2 teaspoons pure vanilla extract

⅔ cup coarsely chopped pecans, lightly toasted and cooled completely

Confectioners' sugar, for sifting over the top of the brownies (optional)

BAKEWARE

10 by 10 by 2-inch baking pan

PREHEAT THE OVEN AND PREPARE THE BAKING PAN Preheat the oven to 325° F. Film the inside of the baking pan with nonstick cooking spray; set aside.

MIX THE BITTERSWEET CHOCOLATE BROWNIE BATTER Sift the cake flour, all-purpose flour, cocoa, baking powder, and salt onto a sheet of waxed paper. In a small mixing bowl, toss the bittersweet chocolate chunks with 2½ teaspoons of the sifted mixture.

Whisk the melted butter, melted unsweetened chocolate, and melted bittersweet chocolate in a medium-size mixing bowl until thoroughly combined.

Whisk the eggs in a large mixing bowl to blend well, about 45 seconds, then add the superfine sugar and whisk for 1 minute, or until just combined. Blend in the melted chocolate-butter mixture. Blend in the vanilla extract. Sift over the sifted mixture and mix until all particles of flour are absorbed into the batter, using a wooden spoon or flat wooden paddle. Stir in the bittersweet chocolate chunks and pecans.

Scrape the batter into the prepared baking pan. Smooth over the top with a rubber spatula.

BAKE AND COOL THE BROWNIES Bake the brownies for 35 to 38 minutes, or until set. Let the brownies stand in the pan on a cooling rack for 3 hours, then refrigerate for 45 minutes, or until firm enough to cut. (In hot or humid weather, or in a warm kitchen, you can freeze the pan of brownies for 20 minutes before cutting, or until firm enough to cut.) Cut the entire cake of

*The little pools of bittersweet chocolate
make this bar cookie ultra-moist.*

brownies into four quarters, then cut each quarter into four squares, using a small, sharp knife. Remove the brownies from the baking pan, using a small offset spatula. Just before serving, sift confectioners' sugar on top of the brownies, if you wish.

❋ *For an aromatic topnote of flavor,* use vanilla-scented superfine sugar (see page 54) in place of plain superfine sugar and intensified vanilla extract (see page 52) in place of plain vanilla extract in the brownie batter.

FRESHLY BAKED, THE BROWNIES KEEP FOR 4 DAYS.

Variation: For bittersweet chocolate brownies with walnuts or macadamia nuts, substitute chopped walnuts or chopped, unsalted macadamia nuts for the pecans.

*t*he aroma of cinnamon may just be one of the most beguiling bakery scents around. As a breakfast or brunch flavor, it is inviting and irresistible. It works in a forward and resonant way to permeate batters, fillings, toppings, and glazes with the very essence of flavor. Hardly a timid spice, cinnamon thrives in the company of unsalted butter, sour cream, whole milk, and buttermilk. It is balanced by nutmeg, allspice, cloves, and cardamom; builds a taste-alliance with all kinds of nuts (especially walnuts, pecans, and macadamia nuts); is strengthened by sweeteners such as light brown and dark brown sugar; and expands when vanilla extract (or vanilla-scented sugar) is present. Cinnamon-based toppings, such as buttery streusel and dipping mixtures, combine cinnamon and sugar to a tasty conclusion.

Korintje cassia cinnamon (see "Selected Sources") brings an excellent cinnamon presence to baked goods; its all-around tempered taste comes forward in batters and doughs in a rounded way. Ceylon cinnamon, which is beautifully aromatic, also stands up to batters and doughs and delivers the direct taste of cinnamon.

13

CINNAMON

LAVISH CINNAMON BRUNCH CAKE

One 13 by 9-inch cake, creating 20 squares

CRUMBLES OF CINNAMON BUTTER STREUSEL covering a texturally light, spiced batter produces one of the best Sunday-morning cakes imaginable. The cinnamon flavor is present in both the topping and the batter, and is supported by freshly grated nutmeg and a good dose of vanilla extract.

Nonstick cooking spray, for preparing the baking pan

CINNAMON BUTTER STREUSEL

1½ cups unsifted bleached all-purpose flour

pinch of salt

1½ teaspoons ground cinnamon

1 cup firmly packed light brown sugar, sieved if lumpy

½ cup granulated sugar

12 tablespoons (1½ sticks) unsalted butter, cold, cut into chunks

1¼ teaspoons pure vanilla extract

1 cup coarsely chopped walnuts (or pecans)

CINNAMON BUTTER CAKE BATTER

2⅔ cups unsifted bleached all-purpose flour

⅓ cup unsifted bleached cake flour

2 teaspoons baking powder

¾ teaspoon baking soda

¾ teaspoon salt

2 teaspoons ground cinnamon

¾ teaspoon freshly grated nutmeg

⅛ teaspoon ground allspice

PREHEAT THE OVEN AND PREPARE THE BAKING PAN Preheat the oven to 350° F. Film the inside of the baking pan with nonstick cooking spray; set aside.

MAKE THE CINNAMON BUTTER STREUSEL Thoroughly combine the flour, salt, cinnamon, light brown sugar, and granulated sugar in a large mixing bowl. Drop in the chunks of butter, and using a pastry blender, cut the fat into the flour until reduced to marble-size lumps. Sprinkle over the vanilla extract. Add the chopped walnuts (or pecans) and blend them in. With your fingertips, crumble the mixture until it comes together into small and large sandy-textured lumps. You can knead the ingredients together without overworking the topping at all. *Streusel consistency observation* The streusel mixture should be moist and somewhat firm, and should hold together in large and small nuggets. If it's the least bit powdery-textured, continue working it between your fingertips.

MIX THE CINNAMON BUTTER CAKE BATTER Sift the all-purpose flour, cake flour, baking powder, baking soda, salt, cinnamon, nutmeg, and allspice onto a sheet of waxed paper.

Cream the butter in the large bowl of a freestanding electric mixer on moderate speed for 4 minutes. Add the light brown sugar and beat for 1 minute; add the granulated sugar, and continue beating for a minute longer. Beat in the eggs, one at a time, mixing for 30 seconds after each addition. Blend in the vanilla extract.

½ pound (16 tablespoons or 2 sticks)
   unsalted butter, softened

¾ cup firmly packed light brown
   sugar, sieved if lumpy

½ cup granulated sugar

3 large eggs

2½ teaspoons pure vanilla extract

1 cup buttermilk

BAKEWARE
13 by 9 by 2-inch baking pan

Scrape down the sides of the mixing bowl frequently with a rubber spatula to keep the batter even-textured.

On low speed, alternately add the sifted mixture in three additions with the buttermilk in two additions, beginning and ending with the sifted mixture. Scrape down the sides of the mixing bowl after a portion of each ingredient is added.

Spoon the batter into the prepared baking pan and smooth over the top with a rubber spatula. Break up the streusel mixture into small clumps. Sprinkle the streusel as evenly as possible over the surface of the cake batter, taking care to cover the four corners and long edges. *Sprinkling technique observation* If the topping is sprinkled over unevenly, a few buttery pools will form as the cake bakes, but will be reabsorbed as it cools. Use all of the streusel.

BAKE AND COOL THE CAKE Bake the cake in the preheated oven for 45 minutes, or until the topping is set and firm, and a wooden pick inserted in the center of the cake withdraws clean. The baked cake will pull away from the sides of the baking pan.

Let the cake stand in the pan on a cooling rack for at least 1 hour before cutting into squares for serving.

❋ *For an extra surge of flavor,* toss ¾ cups cinnamon-flavored chips with 1 teaspoon of the sifted mixture in the cinnamon butter cake batter. Stir the chips into the batter after the last portion of the sifted flour mixture has been added.

FRESHLY BAKED, THE CAKE KEEPS FOR 3 DAYS.

BEST BAKING ADVICE
Brown sugar helps to create a moist and clumpy streusel topping. The buttermilk in the batter opens up the internal grain somewhat, and keeps the cake moist and tender.

CINNAMON CHIP CINNAMON CAKE

One 10-inch fluted tube cake, creating 16 slices

CINNAMON IN ALL THE RIGHT PLACES: a drift of ground walnuts and cinnamon running through a cinnamon and brown sugar-colored cake batter speckled with tiny cinnamon-flavored chips—this spice blossoms through the baked cake in a mellow way.

Nonstick cooking spray, for preparing the cake pan

CINNAMON-WALNUT STREAK

⅓ cup ground walnuts

1½ teaspoons ground cinnamon

¼ teaspoon freshly grated nutmeg

3 tablespoons granulated sugar

CINNAMON CHIP BUTTER CAKE BATTER

3 cups unsifted bleached all-purpose flour

2¼ teaspoons baking powder

¾ teaspoon salt

2 teaspoons ground cinnamon

1½ cups miniature cinnamon-flavored chips

½ pound (16 tablespoons or 2 sticks) unsalted butter, softened

1 cup granulated sugar

⅔ cup firmly packed light brown sugar, sieved if lumpy

4 large eggs

2 teaspoons pure vanilla extract

1 cup milk

BAKEWARE

10-inch Bundt pan

PREHEAT THE OVEN AND PREPARE THE CAKE PAN Preheat the oven to 350° F. Film the inside of the Bundt pan with nonstick cooking spray; set aside.

MAKE THE CINNAMON-WALNUT STREAK Mix the ground walnuts, cinnamon, nutmeg, and granulated sugar in a small mixing bowl. Set aside.

MIX THE CINNAMON CHIP BUTTER CAKE BATTER Sift the flour, baking powder, salt, and cinnamon onto a sheet of waxed paper. In a small mixing bowl, toss the cinnamon chips with 1 tablespoon of the sifted mixture.

Cream the butter in the large bowl of a freestanding electric mixer on moderate speed for 3 minutes. Add the granulated sugar and beat for 2 minutes; add the light brown sugar and beat for a minute longer. Beat in the eggs, one at a time, mixing for 30 seconds after each addition. Scrape down the sides of the mixing bowl frequently to keep the batter even-textured. Blend in the vanilla extract.

On low speed, alternately add the sifted mixture in three additions with the milk in two additions, beginning and ending with the sifted mixture. Scrape down the sides of the mixing bowl frequently with a rubber spatula to keep the batter smooth and even-textured. *Batter texture observation* The batter will be moderately thick and creamy. Stir in the cinnamon chips.

ASSEMBLE THE BATTER WITH THE CINNAMON-WALNUT MIXTURE Spoon a little more than half of the batter into the prepared Bundt pan. Make a slight depression or well in the batter around the middle. Spoon over the cinnamon-walnut mixture. Scrape the remaining batter over the top. Using a flexible palette knife, swirl the batter in bold, curly ripples (about eight foldover swirls) without touching the bottom of the baking pan. *Technique observation* Creating too many swirls and waves in the batter will muddy the inner pattern. Shake the pan gently from side to side once or twice to level the top of the batter.

BAKE AND COOL THE CAKE Bake the cake for 55 minutes, or until set and a wooden pick inserted in the cake withdraws clean. The baked cake will pull away slightly from the sides of the baking pan.

Let the cake stand in the pan on a cooling rack for 7 to 10 minutes, then invert the cake onto another cooling rack. Cool completely before cutting into slices for serving. *Slicing observation* Use a serrated knife to cut the cake neatly and cleanly.

FRESHLY BAKED, THE CAKE KEEPS FOR 2 TO 3 DAYS.

CINNAMON STICKY BUNS

13 jumbo sticky buns

*A*PLUMP STICKY BUN, with pecans embedded in a cinnamon glaze and spiraled in cinnamon-sugar, is one of those delights entirely available to those who love to bake. How else would you get a bun like this loaded with all the good stuff? The buns are baked in individual jumbo muffin cups, which, I've discovered, is the best way to get maximum coverage of nuts and glaze.

As with all sweets made of yeast, this is a project, but one that can be handled over several days. The soft, enriched yeast dough can be refrigerated up to 36 hours after the initial rise (compressed several times during the first 6 hours, or until well chilled, to stabilize the rising and thus prevent overfermenting), and the ingredients for the sticky mixture can be creamed together and stored in the refrigerator in a tightly sealed container for up to 2 days.

Nonstick cookware spray, for preparing the muffin pans

CINNAMON YEAST DOUGH

1 tablespoon active dry yeast

¾ teaspoon granulated sugar

⅓ cup warm (110° to 115° F.) water

¾ cup milk

1 small cinnamon stick

6 tablespoons (¾ stick) unsalted butter, cut into chunks

1 tablespoon solid shortening

5 tablespoons granulated sugar

2½ teaspoons pure vanilla extract

1 large egg

1 large egg yolk

3¾ cups unsifted unbleached all-purpose flour, plus ¼ cup flour for dusting the work surface, or more as needed

1 teaspoon ground cinnamon

¾ teaspoon salt

CINNAMON-BROWN SUGAR-NUT (OR RAISIN) FILLING

½ cup granulated sugar blended with 1 tablespoon ground cinnamon and ¼ teaspoon freshly grated nutmeg

3 tablespoons firmly packed dark brown sugar, sieved if lumpy

3 tablespoons firmly packed light brown sugar, sieved if lumpy

MAKE THE CINNAMON YEAST DOUGH Combine the yeast and ¾ teaspoon granulated sugar in a small heatproof bowl. Pour over the warm water, stir, and let the yeast soften in the water for 7 to 8 minutes, or until swollen.

Place the milk, cinnamon stick, butter, shortening, and 5 tablespoons granulated sugar in a medium-size saucepan and set over low heat. When the sugar has melted down completely, in about 8 minutes, pour the mixture into a medium-size heatproof bowl. Stir in the vanilla extract and cool to 110° to 115° F. Remove and discard the cinnamon stick. Whisk in the whole egg and egg yolk, then the swollen yeast mixture.

In a large mixing bowl, combine 2½ cups of flour with the ground cinnamon and salt. Pour the milk-egg-yeast mixture over the flour and stir well, using a flat wooden paddle or firm spat-

¾ cup chopped pecans (or walnuts), or raisins (dark or golden)

5 tablespoons unsalted butter, softened

¼ pound (8 tablespoons or 1 stick) unsalted butter, softened

½ cup firmly packed dark brown sugar, sieved if lumpy

¼ cup firmly packed light brown sugar, sieved if lumpy

3 tablespoons mild honey (such as clover)

1½ teaspoons ground cinnamon

¼ teaspoon freshly grated nutmeg

2 teaspoons pure vanilla extract

1⅔ cups pecan halves and pieces (or walnuts)

BAKEWARE

13 jumbo muffin/cupcake cups (three pans, each holding six individual muffin cups), each cup measuring 4 inches in diameter and 1¾ inches deep (with a capacity of about 1⅛ cups)

3 rimmed sheet pans

ula. Work in the remaining 1¼ cups flour to form a slightly sticky dough.

Turn the dough onto a lightly floured work surface and knead for 8 minutes, using as much of the extra ¼ cup flour as needed to keep the dough from sticking too much. The dough, however, should be smooth and soft, and may stick to the work surface here and there in patches. Use a dough scraper to move the dough as necessary and use enough flour to keep the dough from adhering to the work surface.

SET THE DOUGH TO RISE Place the dough in a large buttered bowl and turn to coat all sides in the butter. Cover the bowl tightly with a sheet of plastic wrap and let rise in a warm, cozy place for 1 hour, or until doubled in bulk.

PREPARE THE JUMBO MUFFIN/CUPCAKE PANS Film the inside of the muffin/cupcake cups with nonstick cooking spray. Have three rimmed sheet pans at hand.

MAKE THE CINNAMON-BROWN SUGAR-NUT (OR RAISIN) FILLING In a small mixing bowl, combine the granulated sugar-spice mixture, dark brown sugar, light brown sugar, and pecans (or walnuts) or raisins. Have the softened butter at hand.

MAKE THE CINNAMON-NUT STICKY MIXTURE Cream the softened butter, dark brown sugar, light brown sugar, honey, cinnamon, nutmeg, and vanilla extract in a medium-size mixing bowl with a hand-held electric mixer; if the butter is softened enough, you can do this with a sturdy wooden spoon or flat wooden paddle. Set aside. Have the pecan halves (or walnuts) at hand in a small bowl.

ROLL, FILL, AND CUT THE STICKY BUNS Softly press down on the dough to deflate it. Roll out the dough on a lightly floured work surface to a sheet measuring 16 by 16 inches. Beginning with the filling ingredients, spread the 4 tablespoons butter over the surface of the dough. Sprinkle the combined filling mixture evenly over the surface of the buttered dough; press it down, quickly and lightly, with the palms of your hands.

Roll the dough into a thick coil, tucking the ends inside and pressing them down as you roll. Plump the roll with the palms of your hands and seal the long seam end by pinching it tightly. Gently elongate the roll by pulling it out slightly until it is about 21 inches long. With a sharp knife, cut the roll into 13 even slices.

BEST BAKING ADVICE
To maintain the gentle but sturdy framework of the yeast dough, deflate the dough as softly as possible, and roll it quicky and lightly. Using light, but controlling strokes will help to keep the baked sticky buns tender-textured. The cinnamon sticky mixture should be well mixed so that the honey doesn't "weep out" in small beads as the buns bake.

ASSEMBLE THE STICKY BUNS IN THE PREPARED MUFFIN/CUPCAKE CUPS Place big dollops of the cinnamon-nut sticky mixture on the bottom of each muffin/cupcake cup, dividing it evenly among them. Press the pecans on top of the sticky mixture. Place each bun in a prepared muffin cup, cut side (spiral side) down, pressing it lightly on the sticky mixture.

SET THE STICKY BUNS TO RISE Cover each pan of sticky buns loosely with a sheet of plastic wrap, and let rise in a cozy spot for about 1 hour, or until almost doubled in bulk.

PREHEAT THE OVEN AND BAKE THE STICKY BUNS Preheat the oven to 375° F. in advance of baking the sticky buns. Remove and discard the sheets of plastic wrap covering the baking pans. Place the pans on the rimmed sheet pans (to help catch any of the sticky mixture that may bubble up and over). Bake the sticky buns in the preheated oven for 30 minutes, or until golden brown on top, and set.

COOL THE STICKY BUNS Place the muffin pans on cooling racks and let the buns stand for 7 or 8 minutes. Place a jellyroll pan (or rimmed sheet pan) on top of each pan of buns and carefully invert. Some of the sticky mixture and pecans will lodge on the bottom; spoon it out onto the tops of the buns. The sticky mixture will set and the nuts will bond to it. Transfer the buns to a large baking sheet with a wide, offset metal spatula, then invert the next batch using the jellyroll pan. The sticky bun glaze is very hot; make sure your hands are protected when handling the hot buns.

Let the buns cool for at least 1 hour before serving.

✳ *For an extra surge of flavor,* add ¾ cup cinnamon-flavored chips to the cinnamon-brown sugar-nut filling.

FRESHLY BAKED, THE STICKY BUNS KEEP FOR 2 DAYS.

CINNAMON RAISIN PANCAKES

About 14 pancakes

A PLATE OF THESE GENTLY WHEATY, cinnamon-scented pancakes is a breakfast or brunch delight. The earthy flavor is created by replacing part of the all-purpose flour with whole wheat flour. Adding ¼ cup miniature cinnamon-flavored chips to the batter would put these flapjacks near the category of confection.

BUTTERMILK CINNAMON
PANCAKE BATTER

¾ cup unsifted bleached all-purpose flour

¼ cup unsifted whole wheat flour

½ teaspoon baking soda

⅛ teaspoon cream of tartar

⅛ teaspoon salt

½ teaspoon ground cinnamon

¼ teaspoon freshly grated nutmeg

3 tablespoons granulated sugar

1 large egg

3 tablespoons unsalted butter, melted and cooled to tepid

¾ cup plus 2 tablespoons buttermilk

½ teaspoon pure vanilla extract

¼ cup chopped walnuts

¼ cup dark raisins

Clarified butter (see page 66), for the griddle

MIX THE BUTTERMILK CINNAMON PANCAKE BATTER Whisk the all-purpose flour, whole wheat flour, baking soda, cream of tartar, salt, cinnamon, nutmeg, and granulated sugar in a medium-size mixing bowl.

In a small mixing bowl, whisk the egg, melted butter, buttermilk, and vanilla extract. Pour the whisked liquid mixture over the dry ingredients, add the walnuts and raisins, and stir to form a batter, using a rubber spatula. As you are mixing the batter, make sure that you break up any pockets of flour along the bottom and sides of the bowl. *Batter texture observation* The batter will be moderately thick.

GRIDDLE THE PANCAKES Heat a griddle and when hot, film the surface with a little of the clarified butter, using a paper towel to spread it on. The griddle should be hot enough so that the batter sizzles on contact.

Spoon 2-tablespoon-size puddles of batter onto the griddle, placing them 2½ to 3 inches apart. Cook the pancakes for about 45 seconds (the tops should be set and bubbles will appear here and there). Flip the pancakes, using a wide, offset metal spatula, and griddle for about 45 seconds longer, or until cooked through. Using the remaining batter, cook the pancakes in batches, greasing the griddle with clarified butter as necessary. *Batter consistency observation* The batter will thicken as it sits; stir in an extra tablespoon or two of buttermilk, as necessary, to restore its consistency.

Serve the pancakes right off the griddle, with dollops of apple butter, honey-butter, or warmed maple syrup.

Cinnamon Chip Scones with Cinnamon–Pecan Streusel

10 scones

The (endearing) baby cinnamon chips look positively charming in these coffee cake–styled scones. If you wish, ¼ cup of the chips may also be added to the streusel mixture, making it even more deluxe.

Cinnamon-pecan streusel

¾ cup unsifted bleached all-purpose flour

½ teaspoon ground cinnamon

⅓ cup plus 3 tablespoons firmly packed light brown sugar, sieved if lumpy

pinch of salt

6 tablespoons (¾ stick) unsalted butter, cold, cut into chunks

¾ teaspoon pure vanilla extract

¾ cup chopped pecans

Cinnamon chip scone dough

3 cups plus 2 tablespoons unsifted bleached all-purpose flour

3½ teaspoons baking powder

⅛ teaspoon cream of tartar

½ teaspoon salt

1½ teaspoons ground cinnamon

¾ teaspoon freshly grated nutmeg

⅓ cup plus 1 tablespoon granulated sugar

¼ pound (8 tablespoons or 1 stick) unsalted butter, cold, cut into chunks

1 tablespoon shortening, cold

Preheat the oven and prepare the baking sheets Preheat the oven to 400° F. Line the cookie sheets or sheet pans with a length of cooking parchment paper. *Bakeware observation* The baking sheets must be heavy, or the cinnamon dough will scorch on the bottom as the scones bake. Double-pan the sheets, if necessary.

Mix the cinnamon-pecan streusel Thoroughly combine the flour, cinnamon, light brown sugar, and salt in a medium-size mixing bowl. Scatter over the butter chunks and drizzle over the vanilla extract. Using a pastry blender or two round-bladed table knives, cut the butter into the flour-sugar mixture until reduced to marble-size bits. Scatter over the chopped pecans and mix them in. With your fingertips, work the mixture until moist clumps of streusel are formed, pressing and crumbling it into large and small lumps.

Make the cinnamon chip scone dough Whisk the flour, baking powder, cream of tartar, salt, cinnamon, nutmeg, and granulated sugar in a large mixing bowl. Drop in the chunks of butter and tablespoon of shortening. Using a pastry blender or two round-bladed table knives, cut the fat into the flour until reduced to small nuggets. Further crumble the mixture between your fingertips for 30 seconds to 1 minute. Mix in cinnamon chips.

Whisk the heavy cream, eggs, and vanilla extract in a medium-size mixing bowl. Pour the liquid ingredients over the

1¼ cups miniature cinnamon-flavored chips

⅔ cup heavy cream

2 large eggs

2½ teaspoons pure vanilla extract

BAKEWARE

2 heavy cookie sheets or rimmed sheet pans

BEST BAKING ADVICE

Press the streusel topping as firmly as possible on top of the unbaked scones without squashing them. If the scones become misshapen, place them on a work surface and plump up the sides with your fingertips.

flour mixture and combine to form the beginnings of a dough, using a sturdy wooden spoon or flat wooden spatula. *Dough texture observation* At this point, the dough will be crumbly. Knead the dough together in the bowl with your hands until it forms a firm dough, 1 to 2 minutes. If the dough seems very dry, you can add an additional tablespoon of heavy cream, although it should be firm enough to form a stable base for the topping.

CUT THE SCONE DOUGH Turn out the dough onto a very lightly floured work surface, divide in half, and pat each piece into a 6- to 6½-inch round cake. With a chef's knife, cut each cake into five wedges. *Cinnamon chip observation* If a chip protrudes from any cut section of the scone dough, just press it back in.

TOP THE SCONES WITH THE STREUSEL MIXTURE Press some of the streusel topping on top of each triangle of dough, patting it down with your fingertips or the palm of your hand, dividing the topping evenly among all of the scones. Use all of the topping.

Place the scones on the lined cookie sheets, spacing them about 3½ inches apart. Arrange five scones on each sheet.

BAKE AND COOL THE SCONES Bake the scones for 17 to 18 minutes, or until risen and set. Transfer the scones to cooling racks, using a wide, offset metal spatula. Serve warm or at room temperature.

FRESHLY BAKED, THE SCONES KEEP FOR 2 DAYS.

ULTRA-CINNAMON POUND CAKE WITH MACADAMIA-SPICE RIBBON

One 10-inch cake, creating about 20 slices

*T*HE PRESENCE OF NUTMEG, allspice, cardamom, and cloves in the batter actually refines, rather than overwhelms, the taste of cinnamon in the batter. Some of the spices are repeated in an inner ribbony pattern of nuts and sugar, and this design adds great flavor to the cake.

Shortening and bleached all-purpose flour, for preparing the cake pan

MACADAMIA-SPICE RIBBON

¾ cup very finely chopped macadamia nuts

2 tablespoons granulated sugar

1 teaspoon ground cinnamon

½ teaspoon freshly grated nutmeg

¼ teaspoon ground allspice

CINNAMON POUND CAKE BATTER

3 cups unsifted bleached all-purpose flour

1½ teaspoons baking powder

1 teaspoon baking soda

1 teaspoon salt

2 tablespoons ground cinnamon

1¼ teaspoons freshly grated nutmeg

¾ teaspoon ground allspice

½ teaspoon ground cardamom

¼ teaspoon ground cloves

½ pound (16 tablespoons or 2 sticks) unsalted butter, softened

1½ cups granulated sugar

PREHEAT THE OVEN AND PREPARE THE CAKE PAN Preheat the oven to 350° F. Grease the inside of the tube pan with shortening. Line the bottom of the pan with a circle of waxed paper cut to fit, and grease the paper. Dust the inside of the pan with all-purpose flour. Tap out any excess flour; set aside.

MAKE THE MACADAMIA-SPICE RIBBON In a small mixing bowl, thoroughly combine the macadamia nuts, granulated sugar, cinnamon, nutmeg, and allspice.

MIX THE CINNAMON POUND CAKE BATTER Sift the flour, baking powder, baking soda, salt, cinnamon, nutmeg, allspice, cardamom, and cloves onto a sheet of waxed paper.

Cream the butter in the large bowl of a freestanding electric mixer on moderate speed for 2 to 3 minutes. Add the granulated sugar in two additions, beating for 1 minute after each portion is added. Add the light brown sugar and continue beating for a minute longer. Blend in the eggs, one at a time, beating for 45 seconds after each addition. Blend in the vanilla extract.

On low speed, alternately add the sifted ingredients in three additions with the sour cream in two additions, beginning and ending with the sifted mixture. Scrape down the sides of the mixing bowl frequently with a rubber spatula to keep the batter even-textured.

½ cup firmly packed light brown
sugar, sieved if lumpy

4 large eggs

2 teaspoons intensified vanilla extract
(see page 52)

1½ cups thick, cultured sour cream

BAKEWARE

plain 10-inch tube pan

COMPOSE THE POUND CAKE WITH THE FLAVOR RIBBON
Spoon about one-third of the batter into the prepared tube pan.
Sprinkle half of the macadamia nut ribbon mixture over the surface and spoon over half of the remaining batter. Sprinkle the
rest of the ribbon mixture on top. Spoon over the balance of
the batter.

Using a sturdy, flexible palette knife, swirl the layers together,
creating large, curly waves. *Swirling technique observation* Keep the
palette knife within the confines of the batter, rather than scraping
the bottom and/or sides of the tube pan. This will keep the filling as contained as possible, and protect the preliminary pan coating of shortening and flour.

BAKE AND COOL THE POUND CAKE Bake the cake in the preheated oven for 1 hour
and 5 minutes to 1 hour and 10 minutes, or until set and a wooden pick inserted in the
cake withdraws clean. The baked cake will pull away slightly from the sides of the pan.

Cool the cake in the pan on a rack for 10 minutes. Carefully invert the cake onto
another cooling rack, peel off the waxed paper circle, then invert again to cool right side
up. Cool completely before slicing and serving. *Slicing observation* Use a serrated knife
to cut the cake neatly and cleanly.

FRESHLY BAKED, THE CAKE KEEPS FOR 4 TO 5 DAYS.

BEST BAKING ADVICE

*For the best look, and prettiest waves, the
flavor ribbon should be contained within
the edges of the batter before swirling.*

Cinnamon Butter Rosebuds

10 coffee cake–style pastries

EVERY ELEMENT OF THESE YEASTY, buttery sweet pastries is stroked with cinnamon. The twisty spirals of the spiced dough (rolled up with a cinnamon butter filling) are coated with melted butter and more cinnamon-sugar to give them an appealingly light and crunchy wrap. Straight from the oven—warm and heavenly scented—these are gorgeous.

Nonstick cooking spray, for preparing
   the muffin pans

BUTTERY YEAST DOUGH

2½ teaspoons active dry yeast

¼ teaspoon granulated sugar

¼ cup warm (110° to 115° F.) water

¼ pound (8 tablespoons or 1 stick)
   unsalted butter, cut into chunks

⅔ cup milk

¼ cup granulated sugar

2 teaspoons pure vanilla extract

2 large egg yolks

3 cups unsifted unbleached all-purpose
   flour, plus more for the work
   surface

½ teaspoon ground cinnamon

½ teaspoon freshly grated nutmeg

½ teaspoon salt

CINNAMON BUTTER FILLING

5 tablespoons unsalted butter, softened

⅔ cup granulated sugar blended with
   2 teaspoons ground cinnamon

CINNAMON-SUGAR AND
VANILLA-BUTTER BATH

¼ pound (8 tablespoons or 1 stick)
   unsalted butter, melted and cooled
   to tepid, poured into a shallow bowl
   and blended with ¼ teaspoon pure
   vanilla extract

MAKE THE BUTTERY YEAST DOUGH Combine the yeast, ¼ teaspoon granulated sugar, and warm water in a small heatproof bowl, and let stand until the yeast mixture is swollen, 7 to 8 minutes. In the meantime, place the butter, milk, and ¼ cup granulated sugar in a small saucepan and set over low heat to dissolve the sugar, stirring once or twice. Remove from the heat, pour into a medium-size heatproof bowl, stir in the vanilla extract, cool to 110° to 115° F., then whisk in the egg yolks. Slowly stir in the puffy yeast mixture.

In a large mixing bowl, thoroughly mix 2½ cups flour, the cinnamon, nutmeg, and salt. Pour over the milk-egg-yeast mixture and stir well, using a wooden spoon or flat wooden paddle. Add the remaining ½ cup flour, ¼ cup at a time, to create a soft but cohesive, buttery dough.

Dust a work surface with flour. Knead the dough for 7 to 10 minutes, or until supple, adding extra sprinkles of flour, as necessary, to make the dough manageable for kneading (but not stiff).

SET THE DOUGH TO RISE Turn the dough into a lightly buttered bowl and roll the ball of dough around in the bowl to cover with a film of butter. Cut several slashes in the dough with a pair of kitchen scissors. Cover the bowl tightly with a sheet of plastic wrap and let rise until doubled in bulk, 1 hour to 1 hour and 15 minutes.

PREPARE THE BAKING PANS Coat the inside of the muffin/cupcake cups with nonstick cooking spray; set aside.

1 cup granulated sugar blended with 1 tablespoon ground cinnamon, in a shallow bowl

10 jumbo muffin/cupcake cups (two pans, each holding 6 individual muffin cups), each cup measuring 4 inches in diameter by 1¾ inches deep (with a capacity of about 1⅛ cups)

2 rimmed sheet pans

ROLL THE DOUGH INTO A SHEET, FILL AND FORM THE ROSEBUDS Have the cinnamon butter filling ingredients at hand. Lightly compress the dough with the palms of your hands, place on a lightly floured work surface, cover, and let stand for 10 minutes. Roll out the dough on a sheet measuring about 13 by 15 inches. Spread the 8 tablespoons softened butter on the dough; there will be a generous coating of butter. Sprinkle on the cinnamon-sugar mixture. Lightly press down on the cinnamon-sugar with the bottom of an offset spatula. *Pressing procedure observation* Pressing down on the cinnamon-sugar to compact it helps to set the filling.

Carefully pick up the bottom half of the dough and fold it to the top of the dough; the filling will shift. Press the three edges together to seal, then press down on the top surface of the dough. Roll the dough lightly to set the filling. Using a sharp chef's knife, cut the dough into 10 even-sized strips.

One at a time, pick up a strip, stretch it slightly, and twist. Form the dough into a ring around your index and middle finger, and bring one end up, over, and through the center to form a bud. Tuck the end under the formed pastry and pinch to seal.

COAT THE ROSEBUDS IN THE CINNAMON-SUGAR AND VANILLA-BUTTER BATH Have the melted butter–vanilla extract mixture, cinnamon-sugar, and prepared muffin pans at your work surface. Dip each rosebud in the vanilla extract-melted butter mixture to coat lightly, then into the cinnamon-sugar to coat thickly. Place each pastry, as it's coated, in a prepared muffin cup. Drizzle any remaining melted butter over the pastries.

SET THE ROSEBUDS TO RISE Cover each muffin pan with a sheet of plastic wrap and let rise until nearly doubled in bulk, about 1 hour.

BAKE AND COOL THE ROSEBUDS Preheat the oven to 375° F. in advance of baking. Remove and discard the plastic wrap covering the muffin pans. Have two rimmed sheet pans at hand.

Set each pan of pastries on a rimmed sheet pan (to catch any buttery drips that may trickle over during baking). Bake the pastries for 25 minutes, or until puffed, set, and golden. The tops will have a crunchy cinnamon-sugar coating. Place the pans of pastries on cooling racks and let stand for 35 to 45 minutes, or until tepid and stable. The rosebuds are tender at this point, and should remain in the pans for at least 30 minutes; otherwise they may lean to one side.

Carefully remove the pastries to cooling racks, using the tip of a flexible palette knife to edge them out of the muffin cups. Serve the pastries very fresh, warm or at room temperature.

Variation: For cinnamon butter rosebuds styled as pull-aparts, coat the inside of a 12 by 8 by 3-inch baking pan with nonstick cooking spray; set aside. Cut the dough into eight even-sized strips following the directions in the section "Roll the dough into a sheet, fill and form the rosebuds" above. Place the eight rosebuds in four rows of two each in the prepared baking pan. There will be spaces between the rosebuds, but as the pastries rise they'll converge into a solid panful. Cover the baking pan with a sheet of plastic wrap and let rise until nearly doubled in bulk, about 1 hour. Remove and discard the plastic wrap covering the baking pan. Bake the pull-aparts in the preheated oven for 25 to 30 minutes, or until set. (It is unnecessary to place the pan on a rimmed sheet pan, as you would do with the individually formed rosebuds.) Place the baking pan on a rack to cool.

CINNAMON-WALNUT MUFFINS WITH SPICED SUGAR-BUTTER DUNK

1 dozen muffins

SERVED AT BREAKFAST OR BRUNCH, these muffins have a fine, cakelike texture and tempting cinnamon bouquet. While the baked muffins are still warm, they are treated to a dip of flavor. The dunk is what makes the muffins so distinctive: A quick plunge into melted butter and second one into a cinnamon and nutmeg-heightened sugar creates the alluring topping.

Softened unsalted butter and bleached all-purpose flour, for preparing the muffin pan

CINNAMON MUFFIN BATTER

1½ cups unsifted bleached all-purpose flour
½ cup unsifted bleached cake flour
¾ teaspoon baking powder
½ teaspoon baking soda

PREHEAT THE OVEN AND PREPARE THE MUFFIN PAN Preheat the oven to 400° F. Lightly butter and flour the muffin cups. Tap out any excess flour; set aside.

MIX THE CINNAMON MUFFIN BATTER Sift the all-purpose flour, cake flour, baking powder, baking soda, salt, cinnamon, nutmeg, and allspice onto a sheet of waxed paper.

Cream the butter and shortening in the large bowl of a freestanding electric mixer on moderate speed for 3 minutes. Add the

½ teaspoon salt

1½ teaspoons ground cinnamon

½ teaspoon freshly grated nutmeg

¼ teaspoon ground allspice

6 tablespoons (¾ stick) unsalted butter, softened

2 tablespoons shortening

⅔ cup granulated sugar, preferably vanilla-scented (see page 53)

2 large eggs

1½ teaspoons pure vanilla extract

1 cup thick, cultured sour cream

½ cup chopped walnuts, lightly toasted and cooled (optional)

CINNAMON AND NUTMEG-SPICED SUGAR-BUTTER DUNK

5 tablespoons unsalted butter, melted and still warm, placed in a small, deep heatproof bowl

1 cup granulated sugar blended with 1 tablespoon ground cinnamon and ⅛ teaspoon freshly grated nutmeg, in a small, deep bowl

BAKEWARE

standard (12-cup) muffin pan, each cup measuring 2¾ inches in diameter and 1⅜ inches deep (with a capacity of ½ cup)

BEST BAKING ADVICE

The sour cream in the batter (in addition to the fact that the batter is made by the creamed method) makes these baked muffins tender. Handle them carefully when dipping the tops into the melted butter and cinnamon-spice blend.

granulated sugar and continue beating for 2 minutes longer. Beat in the eggs, one at a time, blending for 30 to 45 seconds after each addition. Blend in the vanilla extract.

On low speed, add half of the sifted ingredients, all of the sour cream, then the balance of the sifted ingredients. Scrape down the sides of the mixing bowl frequently to keep the batter even-textured. Stir in the walnuts, if you are using them.

Spoon the batter into the prepared muffin cups, dividing it evenly among them.

BAKE THE MUFFINS Bake the muffins in the preheated oven for 16 to 19 minutes, or until a wooden pick inserted in the center of a muffin withdraws clean. The baked muffins will pull away slightly from the sides of the cups. Place the muffin pans on cooling racks and let the muffins stand for 5 minutes. Carefully remove the muffins to cooling racks.

ASSEMBLE THE CINNAMON AND NUTMEG-SPICED SUGAR-BUTTER DUNK Have the bowls of melted butter and cinnamon and nutmeg-spiced sugar at hand. Dip the top of each muffin first into the melted butter, then into the spiced sugar. Place the muffins on cooling racks as you are coating them. Serve the muffins very fresh, warm or at room temperature.

❈ *For an extra surge of flavor,* toss ½ cup of cinnamon-flavored chips with ¾ teaspoon of the sifted flour mixture in the cinnamon muffin batter. Stir the chips into the muffin batter (along with the walnuts, if you are using them) after the balance of the sifted mixture has been added.

CINNAMON SOUR CREAM COFFEE CAKE

One 10-inch coffee cake, creating about 20 slices

THE BUTTER, CREAM CHEESE, AND SOUR CREAM—all ingredients that heighten the flavor of cinnamon—create a moist-beyond-the-imagination coffee cake, with a velvety, fine-grained crumb, welcome at Sunday brunch. The absence of chopped nuts makes the batter fluid and very elegant, and serves to spotlight the cinnamon taste.

Shortening and bleached all-purpose flour, for preparing the cake pan

CINNAMON-SUGAR FILLING

¼ cup firmly packed light brown sugar, sieved if lumpy

¼ cup granulated sugar

2½ teaspoons ground cinnamon

⅛ teaspoon freshly grated nutmeg

pinch of ground cardamom

CINNAMON SOUR CREAM COFFEE CAKE BATTER

3 cups unsifted bleached all-purpose flour

¼ teaspoon baking soda

1 teaspoon salt

1 tablespoon ground cinnamon

½ teaspoon freshly grated nutmeg

⅛ teaspoon ground allspice

⅛ teaspoon ground cardamom

½ pound (16 tablespoons or 2 sticks) unsalted butter, softened

One 3-ounce package cream cheese, softened

2¾ cups plus 2 tablespoons granulated sugar

PREHEAT THE OVEN AND PREPARE THE CAKE PAN Preheat the oven to 325° F. Grease the inside of the tube pan with shortening. Line the bottom of the pan with a circle of waxed paper cut to fit, and grease the paper. Dust the inside of the pan with all-purpose flour. Tap out any excess flour; set aside.

MAKE THE CINNAMON-SUGAR FILLING Thoroughly combine the light brown sugar, granulated sugar, cinnamon, nutmeg, and cardamom in a small mixing bowl; set aside.

MIX THE CINNAMON SOUR CREAM COFFEE CAKE BATTER Sift the all-purpose flour, baking soda, salt, cinnamon, nutmeg, allspice, and cardamom *twice* onto a sheet of waxed paper.

Cream the butter and cream cheese in the large bowl of a free-standing electric mixer on moderate speed for 2 to 3 minutes. Add the granulated sugar in three additions, beating for 1 minute after each portion is added. Blend in the eggs, one at a time, beating for 30 seconds after each addition. Blend in the vanilla and almond extracts.

On low speed, alternately add the sifted ingredients in three additions with the sour cream in two additions, beginning and ending with the sifted mixture. Scrape down the sides of the mixing bowl frequently with a rubber spatula to keep the batter even-textured. *Batter texture observation* The batter will be soft and creamy-textured.

6 large eggs

1 tablespoon pure vanilla extract

¼ teaspoon pure almond extract

1 cup thick, cultured sour cream

BAKEWARE

plain 10-inch tube pan

BEST BAKING ADVICE

Sifting the dry ingredients twice helps to aerate them sufficiently to be absorbed by the creamed butter–sugar mixture and sour cream.

COMPOSE THE COFFEE CAKE WITH THE CINNAMON-SUGAR FILLING Spoon half of the batter into the prepared tube pan. Sprinkle the cinnamon-sugar mixture over the surface. Spoon over the remaining batter, making sure to cover the cinnamon filling.

Using a flexible palette knife, swirl the two layers of batter and filling together, making wide, looping waves. *Swirling technique observation* Keep the palette knife in the batter and avoid scraping the sides and bottom of the tube pan.

BAKE AND COOL THE COFFEE CAKE Bake the cake in the preheated oven for 1 hour and 20 minutes to 1 hour and 30 minutes, or until set and a wooden pick inserted in the cake withdraws clean. The baked cake will pull away slightly from the sides of the pan.

Cool the cake in the pan on a rack for 10 minutes. Carefully invert the cake onto another cooling rack, peel off the waxed paper round, then invert again to cool right side up. Cool completely before slicing and serving. *Slicing observation* Use a serrated knife to cut the cake neatly and cleanly.

✳ *For an extra surge of flavor,* toss 1 cup cinnamon-flavored chips with 1½ teaspoons of the sifted flour mixture from the cake batter. Stir the chips into the cake batter after the last portion of the sifted mixture is added.

FRESHLY BAKED, THE COFFEE CAKE KEEPS FOR 4 TO 5 DAYS.

CINNAMON APPLE CAKE

One 10-inch fluted tube cake, creating 16 slices

IN ONE PLUMP AND PRETTY FLUTED RING, apple cake marries all the polished flavors of autumn. Nearly a poetic diversity of apples abounds during the breezy months of September, October, and November, and many are ideal to use in this sweet. This cake is a sublime, classic union of spicy and tempered, sweet and gently tart. The finishing glaze is a fresh, contemporary addition.

Despite its complex set of tastes, the sweet is simple to make and one that mellows wonderfully over time. The shreds of apple practically melt into the moist, cinnamon-spiced batter, creating a wonderful everyday kind of cake that's delicious served plain as a coffee cake or, with whipped cream or vanilla ice cream, as dessert.

Nonstick cookware spray, for preparing the cake pan

CINNAMON APPLE CAKE BATTER

3 cups unsifted bleached all-purpose flour

1½ teaspoons baking powder

¾ teaspoon baking soda

1 teaspoon salt

2½ teaspoons ground cinnamon

¾ teaspoon freshly grated nutmeg

¼ teaspoon ground allspice

¼ teaspoon ground cardamom

1⅔ cups granulated sugar

⅓ cup firmly packed dark brown sugar, sieved if lumpy

3 large eggs

1 cup plain vegetable oil (such as soybean)

6 tablespoons (¾ stick) unsalted butter, melted and cooled

1 tablespoon pure vanilla extract

3¼ cups peeled and shredded apples, preferably Jonathan, Stayman, Empire, Gala, Paula Red, Rome Beauty, or Granny Smith, about 3 large or 1⅓ pounds (for grating, use the large holes of a 4-sided box grater)

¾ cup chopped walnuts, lightly toasted and cooled completely (optional)

PREHEAT THE OVEN AND PREPARE THE CAKE PAN Preheat the oven to 350° F. Film the inside of the pan with nonstick cooking spray; set aside.

MIX THE CINNAMON APPLE CAKE BATTER Sift the all-purpose flour, baking powder, baking soda, salt, cinnamon, nutmeg, allspice, and cardamom onto a sheet of waxed paper.

Place the granulated sugar, dark brown sugar, and eggs in the large bowl of a free-standing electric mixer. Mix on moderately high speed for 2 minutes, or until lightened, creamy-textured, and slightly billowy. The mixture will be a creamy coffee color. Add the oil, butter, and vanilla extract, and continue beating for 2 minutes longer. The batter will be moderately thin.

On low speed, beat in the sifted mixture in two additions, blending until the particles of flour are completely absorbed. Scrape down the sides of the bowl frequently to keep the batter even-textured. Stir in the shredded apples and walnuts, if you are using them.

½ cup unsweetened, pasteurized apple
   juice

¼ cup honey

¼ teaspoon ground cinnamon

3 tablespoons butter, softened

¼ teaspoon pure vanilla extract

BAKEWARE

10-inch Bundt pan (or 9-inch-deep
   swirled tube pan; see Variation
   below)

BEST BAKING ADVICE

*Cook the syrupy glaze for the full 5 minutes,
or until reduced to 5 tablespoons—you want
a concentrated flavor because a watery glaze
tastes dreary. This glaze is also a delight
brushed over any warm, cinnamon-
flavored pound cake.*

Spoon the batter into the prepared Bundt pan. Gently shake the pan (once or twice) from side to side to level the top.

BAKE AND COOL THE CAKE Bake the cake for 55 minutes, or until a wooden pick withdraws clean or with a few moist crumbs attached. The baked cake will pull away slightly from the sides of the baking pan. Let the cake stand in the pan on a cooling rack for 5 to 8 minutes, then invert onto another rack. Place a sheet of waxed paper under the rack to catch any droplets of glazing syrup.

MAKE THE BUTTERY CINNAMON–APPLE JUICE SYRUP Stir the apple juice, honey, and cinnamon in a small, heavy nonreactive saucepan (preferably enameled cast iron). Place over high heat and cook 1 minute to dissolve the honey. Simmer the mixture for 5 minutes, or until reduced to 5 tablespoons.

Remove the saucepan from the heat, and add the softened butter and vanilla extract. Whisk until the butter has melted down completely.

GLAZE THE CAKE WITH THE HOT SYRUP Using a soft pastry brush, apply the hot glaze generously over the top and sides of the cake. Cool completely before slicing and serving. *Slicing observation* Use a serrated knife to cut the cake neatly and cleanly.

❋ *For an extra surge of flavor,* toss ⅔ cup cinnamon-flavored chips with ½ teaspoon of the sifted flour mixture. Stir the chips into the cake batter after the apples (and optional walnuts) have been added.

Variation: This cake can also be baked in a 9-inch-deep, 4¼-inch-tall, swirled tube pan (with a capacity of 11 cups). In it, the batter will bake into a plumper cake. If you are using this pan, increase the baking time by 5 to 7 minutes.

FRESHLY BAKED, THE CAKE KEEPS FOR 4 DAYS.

CINNAMON RIPPLE ROLLS

1½ dozen rolls

Softened unsalted butter, for preparing
  the baking pans

POTATO BUTTER DOUGH

3 teaspoons active dry yeast

¾ teaspoon granulated sugar

¼ cup warm (110° to 115° F.) water

6 tablespoons (¾ stick) unsalted
  butter, cut into chunks

¾ cup milk

⅓ cup granulated sugar

1½ cups cooked, unseasoned, riced
  potatoes

1 large egg

2 teaspoons pure vanilla extract

2 cups unsifted bleached all-purpose
  flour

3½ to 4 cups unsifted unbleached all-
  purpose flour, plus extra for
  kneading, as necessary

2 teaspoons salt

CINNAMON-SUGAR-RAISIN
RIPPLE FILLING

4 tablespoons (½ stick) unsalted
  butter, softened

1 cup granulated sugar blended with
  2 tablespoons ground cinnamon

1 cup dark raisins

Creamy Cinnamon Roll Icing (see
  page 314), for spreading on the
  warm, baked cinnamon rolls

BAKEWARE

two 9 by 9 by 3-inch baking pans

THE COMBINATION OF FLUFFY DOUGH, a simple cinnamon-sugar and raisin filling, and creamy icing makes a tempting batch of sweet rolls. The lightest, softest, and coziest yeast dough conceivable is made by using plain, freshly mashed potatoes as the essential ingredient, and allowing the dough to rise twice to refine the texture of the baked rolls. The texture of the cooked potatoes is integral to the success of the dough. Boil peeled potatoes, preferably Russets, in salted water until soft and completely yielding; drain them well, return to the saucepan, and toss briefly over moderate heat to evaporate any lingering water. Now, pass the cooked potatoes through a ricer or a food mill fitted with the fine disk. Use the potatoes while they are still warm, for the best amalgamation into the liquid mixture, dissolved yeast, and flour.

MAKE THE POTATO BUTTER DOUGH Combine the yeast and ¾ teaspoon granulated sugar in a small heatproof bowl. Pour over the warm water, stir, and let the yeast dissolve in the water for 7 to 8 minutes, or until swollen and puffy.

Place the butter, milk, and ⅓ cup granulated sugar in a medium-size saucepan and set over low heat. Stir occasionally. Place the riced potatoes in a medium-size heatproof bowl. When the sugar has dissolved in the milk, in about 8 minutes, pour the liquid over the potatoes and stir well. Cool to 110° F., then blend in the egg and vanilla extract. Blend in the swollen yeast mixture.

In a large mixing bowl, thoroughly combine the bleached flour, 3 cups unbleached flour, and salt. Pour the potato-milk-egg-yeast mixture over the flour and stir well, using a flat wooden paddle or wooden spoon. Work in ½ cup unbleached flour.

Turn the dough onto a work surface sprinkled with the remaining ½ cup unbleached flour and knead for 10 minutes, incorporating as much of the flour as necessary to keep the dough from sticking. Sprinkle the work surface with additional flour, as needed. *Dough texture observation* After 10 minutes, the dough should be soft and bouncy, hold its shape, and knead away from the work surface without bonding to it. Depending upon the absorption quality of the flour and humidity present in the air, the dough may require extra flour.

SET THE DOUGH TO RISE FOR THE FIRST TIME Place the dough in a large buttered bowl and turn to coat all sides in the butter. Cover the bowl tightly with a sheet of plastic wrap and let rise in a warm, cozy place, away from drafts, until doubled in bulk, about 1 hour and 30 minutes.

SET THE DOUGH TO RISE FOR THE SECOND TIME Compress the dough to deflate, cover tightly with a sheet of plastic wrap, and let rise again until doubled in bulk, about 1 hour and 15 minutes.

SET OUT THE CINNAMON-SUGAR-RAISIN RIPPLE FILLING INGREDIENTS Place the butter near the work surface, along with the cinnamon-sugar mixture and raisins.

PREPARE THE BAKING PANS Butter the inside of the baking pans.

ROLL, FILL, AND CUT THE CINNAMON ROLLS Deflate the dough gently by compressing it with your hands. It will be bouncy and blistery. Let the dough stand for 5 to 10 minutes. Roll out the dough on a well-floured work surface to a sheet measuring 12 by 15 inches. Spread the 4 tablespoons butter over the surface of the dough. Sprinkle the cinnamon-sugar evenly over the surface of the buttered dough. Scatter over the raisins, pressing them down lightly with your fingertips.

Roll the dough into a long coil, tucking the ends inside and pressing them to seal as you roll. Pinch closed the long seam end. Carefully stretch the roll by pulling/rolling it out slightly until it measures about 24 inches long. With a sharp knife, cut the roll into 18 even slices.

ASSEMBLE THE CINNAMON ROLLS IN THE PREPARED BAKING PANS Place rolls, spiral side down, in the prepared baking pans, smoothing them into rounds as you go. Arrange the rolls in three rows of three, nine in each prepared baking pan.

SET THE CINNAMON ROLLS TO RISE Cover each pan of rolls loosely with a sheet of plastic wrap, and let rise at cool room temperature for about 1 hour and 20 minutes, or until doubled in bulk.

PREHEAT THE OVEN AND BAKE THE CINNAMON ROLLS Preheat the oven to 375° F. in advance of baking the cinnamon rolls. Remove and discard the sheets of plastic wrap covering the baking pans. Bake the cinnamon rolls in the preheated oven for 35 minutes, or until golden brown on top and set.

COOL AND ICE THE ROLLS Place the baking pans on cooling racks and let the rolls stand for 8 to 10 minutes. Have the icing at hand. Place a jellyroll pan or rimmed sheet pan on top of each pan of rolls and carefully invert. Invert again onto cooling racks to stand right side up. Place a sheet of waxed paper under each cooling rack to catch any drips of icing.

Using a flexible palette knife, lightly spread half of the icing over each block of warm cinnamon rolls, letting it flow naturally on the tops of the rolls. Let the rolls stand until the icing firms up before pulling apart individual rolls for serving. Serve the rolls fresh.

CREAMY CINNAMON ROLL ICING

About 1 cup

THIS CLASSIC CONFECTIONERS' ICING is thick and pearly, but melts down beautifully when swept on top of the warm cinnamon rolls.

CINNAMON ROLL ICING

2 tablespoons unsalted butter, softened

2 cups unsifted confectioners' sugar

2 tablespoons plus 2 teaspoons light (table) cream

½ teaspoon pure vanilla extract

pinch of salt

MAKE THE CINNAMON ROLL ICING Place the butter and confectioners' sugar in a medium-size mixing bowl. Add the cream, vanilla extract, and salt. Using an electric hand mixer, beat the ingredients on low speed until smooth, about 1 minute, scraping down the sides of the mixing bowl once or twice with a rubber spatula to keep the icing even-textured. Immediately press a sheet of plastic wrap directly over the surface of the icing.

Spread the icing over the tops of warm cinnamon rolls, letting it melt down slightly as it flows over the surface.

CINNAMON NUT CRUNCH SHORTBREAD

One 9½-inch shortbread, creating 12 triangular pieces

T O UPLIFT THIS CINNAMON-FRAGRANT round of shortbread, chopped nuts—lightly sweetened, spiced, and glossed with a bit of melted butter—are scattered over and pressed onto the surface of the cookie just before baking. To bring out the sparkle of cinnamon in the dough, the usual amount of sugar is increased by a few tablespoons; the extra sugar also heightens the creamy-rich flavor of the butter.

Nonstick cooking spray, for preparing the tart pan

CINNAMON SHORTBREAD DOUGH

1¼ cups unsifted bleached all-purpose flour

¼ cup rice flour

¼ teaspoon baking powder

⅛ teaspoon salt

1¼ teaspoons ground cinnamon

¼ teaspoon freshly grated nutmeg

12 tablespoons (1½ sticks) unsalted butter, softened

⅓ cup unsifted confectioners' sugar

1½ teaspoons pure vanilla extract

NUT CRUNCH TOPPING

¾ cup coarsely chopped walnuts (or pecans)

2 tablespoons granulated sugar

½ teaspoon ground cinnamon

Confectioners' sugar, for sifting over the baked and cooled shortbread (optional)

BAKEWARE

fluted 9½-inch round tart pan (with a removable bottom)

PREHEAT THE OVEN AND PREPARE THE TART PAN Preheat the oven to 350° F. Film the inside of the tart pan with nonstick cooking spray; set aside.

MIX THE CINNAMON SHORTBREAD DOUGH Sift the all-purpose flour, rice flour, baking powder, salt, cinnamon, and nutmeg onto a sheet of waxed paper.

Cream the butter in the large bowl of a freestanding electric mixer on low speed for 2 to 3 minutes. Add the confectioners' sugar and vanilla extract, and continue beating for 1 to 2 minutes longer. Add the sifted mixture in two additions, mixing until the particles of flour are absorbed and a smooth soft dough is created. Scrape down the sides of the mixing bowl once or twice with a rubber spatula to keep the dough even-textured. *Dough texture observation* The shortbread dough will be shapeable and supple.

PRESS THE DOUGH INTO THE PREPARED PAN Turn the dough into the prepared tart pan. Lightly press and pat the dough into an even layer, using your fingertips. Lightly prick the dough with the tines of a fork in 12 to 15 places.

MIX THE NUT CRUNCH TOPPING Combine the chopped nuts with the granulated sugar and cinnamon. Sprinkle the topping evenly over the top of the shortbread dough. With the underside of a small, offset metal spatula (or your fingertips), lightly press the nut topping on top of the dough.

BAKE AND COOL THE SHORTBREAD Bake the shortbread for 45 minutes, or until set. The baking time on this shortbread is a little longer than usual because the topping adds an extra dimension of thickness to the cookie. The shortbread must be completely baked through. (If the nut topping appears to be browning too fast after 30 minutes, place a sheet of aluminum foil lightly on top of the cookie.)

Let the cookie stand in the tart pan on the cooling rack for 10 minutes, then unmold carefully, leaving it on its round base. Cool for 10 to 15 minutes longer. With a sharp chef's knife, cut into even-sized wedges. Cool completely. Just before serving, sieve a light coating of confectioners' sugar over the top of the shortbread triangles, if you wish.

✳ *For an extra surge of flavor,* add ⅓ cup cinnamon-flavored chips to the shortbread dough along with the second portion of the sifted mixture.

FRESHLY BAKED, THE SHORTBREAD KEEPS FOR 4 DAYS.

CINNAMON WALNUT BAKLAVA

One 13 by 9-inch pan of baklava, creating 20 square pieces or about 40 triangular pieces

MY FLAVOR-HEIGHTENED TRAY of baklava is constructed in this way: a cinnamon-spiced walnut filling is layered on well-buttered layers of phyllo; once the entire panful is scored, baked, and cut, you bathe it with a cinnamon, clove, and lemon-based honey syrup. It's a wonderfully intense sweet that, once all the different elements are assembled, is great fun to create. The beauty of baklava is that you can design it with nuts such as almonds and pistachios, alter the cut shape from traditional to whimsical, and customize the honey flavoring syrup. This recipe is not built around a batter or dough, as are the others in this volume. It's the soft scent of cinnamon in the filling that puts it into the flavor-development category. And it's an exception that's worth baking.

Nonstick cooking spray, for preparing
the baking pan

1 pound (4 sticks) unsalted butter, cut
into chunks

CINNAMON-WALNUT FILLING

1 pound walnuts, very finely chopped

⅔ cup plus 2 tablespoons granulated
sugar

1 tablespoon plus 1 teaspoon ground
cinnamon

¼ teaspoon ground cloves

¼ teaspoon ground allspice

One 16-ounce package phyllo pastry
dough leaves (about twenty 14 by
18-inch sheets), defrosted slowly in
the refrigerator for 2 days

CINNAMON-CLOVE-LEMON
HONEY SYRUP

1¾ cups water

¾ cup granulated sugar

4 strips lemon peel, blanched and
refreshed in cold water

4 whole cloves

2 cinnamon sticks

1 cup mild honey (such as clover)

BAKEWARE

13 by 9 by 2-inch baking pan

Using the correct equipment is important to the process of both creating and assembling baklava. Choose a straight-sided 13 by 9 by 2-inch baking pan in order to achieve architecturally straight sides to the finished sweet, to keep the filling in a steady, even layer, and to avoid losing precious sections of the dessert. Use a sturdy pastry brush, with well-set bristles (preferably boar), for brushing the melted butter over the many layers of phyllo dough; the bristles of a high-quality, substantial brush won't drop out as you are glazing the surface of the phyllo with butter. A sharp paring knife is necessary for marking the pattern on the top of the unbaked baklava and for cutting through the baked and scored baklava just before spooning on the syrup.

PREHEAT THE OVEN AND PREPARE THE BAKING PAN Preheat the oven to 350° F. Adjust the oven racks to the middle and lower third positions. Film the inside of the baking pan with nonstick cookware spray; set aside.

CLARIFY THE BUTTER Clarify the butter according to the directions in the recipe for Clarified Butter on page 66, using 1 pound of butter in place of the ¾ pound listed in that recipe. Keep the butter tepid—in the clear, liquid state.

MAKE THE CINNAMON-WALNUT FILLING Thoroughly combine the chopped walnuts, granulated sugar, cinnamon, cloves, and allspice in a medium-size mixing bowl.

SET UP THE PHYLLO LEAVES AND CONSTRUCT THE BAKLAVA Place two sheets of plastic wrap overlapping each other on a flat work surface. The sheets of plastic wrap should be large enough to be an adequate base for the 17½ by 13½-inch sheets of phyllo. Unwrap and open up the phyllo sheets; carefully place the stack of them on the plastic wrap. If any edges look wadded together, cut them loose with a sharp paring knife or small pair of kitchen scissors. Loosely cover the pile of phyllo with two more sheets of plastic wrap overlapping each other. *Phyllo covering technique observation* Covering the phyllo with plastic wrap keeps the moisture in the sheets for the short amount of time you're working with them. A damp towel, the time-honored covering for preventing the phyllo from drying out, actually adds too much moisture and creates gummy, self-adhesive sheets.

Place one sheet of phyllo on the bottom of the baking pan, brush with butter by passing the brush on the bottom edges of the pans, then over the entire sheet, creating long and short end flaps resting up the sides of the baking pan.

Turn one end flap down, brush with butter, and make a square corner by folding down an adjacent side, then "butter down" the remaining flaps of phyllo in this way. Make sure that you lightly brush down the end flaps, glossing over the tops of the flaps with the butter. Put down and butter five more sheets of phyllo in this way, for a total of six layers.

Place one sheet of phyllo in the pan, butter the sheet, but don't butter down the sides yet. Sprinkle over about ½ cup of the nut mixture in an even layer. Carefully butter down the sides, keeping the butter on the phyllo (and not on the nuts).

Now put down two sheets of phyllo in this way: Butter the next sheet and butter down the sides. Butter the next sheet, leaving the sides unbuttered for the moment. Sprinkle over another ½ cup of the nut mixture, then butter down the sides. Continue to build the phyllo layers, two sheets at a time, until you have four sheets of phyllo remaining, ending with an exposed layer of nuts.

To create the top of the baklava, place the first sheet on top of the nut layer; brush with butter, but don't butter down the end flaps. Instead, brush butter along the edges of the pan, leaving the ends to ruffle up the sides a bit, then brush the entire sheet with the butter. Repeat with the remaining three sheets of phyllo. With a small, sharp paring knife, cut along the inside edge of the baking pan evenly to trim off the end flaps of phyllo. The edges should be neat and clean.

SCORE THE PREPARED PAN OF BAKLAVA With a clean kitchen ruler and paring knife, measure and cut the top of the baklava into squares or diamonds. Divide the tray into squares or diamonds by scoring the baklava in even lines, using the ruler as your guide. When cutting the lines, cut about ⅛ inch deep into the baklava, keeping the top of the knife against the edge of the ruler in order to maintain a straight line.

BAKE THE BAKLAVA Fill a 9 by 9 by 2-inch baking pan (or its equivalent) three-fourths full with boiling water and place on the lower third rack of the preheated oven. *Water pan technique observation* The water keeps the baklava moist during baking. Place the baklava on the middle rack and bake for 30 minutes. Reduce the oven temperature to 325° F. and continue baking for 1 hour longer, or until the baklava is golden and has retracted slightly from the sides of the baking pan.

PREPARE THE CINNAMON-CLOVE-LEMON HONEY SYRUP About 35 minutes before the baklava is completed, place the water, granulated sugar, strips of lemon peel, cloves, and cinnamon sticks in a heavy, nonreactive, medium-size saucepan (preferably enameled cast iron). Cover, set over low heat, and cook until the granules of sugar are completely dissolved. Uncover, raise the heat, and boil the mixture for 10 minutes. Stir in the honey and bring to the boil. Lower the heat to moderate and boil slowly until lightly thickened and dense, about 12 minutes. Strain the syrup through a fine-meshed sieve into a heatproof bowl. Cool for 15 minutes. You can use the syrup warm or tepid.

CUT THE BAKLAVA AND DOUSE WITH SYRUP Transfer the pan of baklava to a cooling rack. Let stand for 5 minutes. Following the scoring marks, cut the baklava into the shapes as marked, using a small, sharp paring knife. *Cutting technique observation* To cut the pieces most effectively, put the tip of the knife at the edge of a long scoring line and cut the baklava, using slightly exaggerated up and down motions. This technique keeps the baked phyllo sheets in shape.

Spoon the prepared syrup over the warm baklava. Cool completely.

Remove the pieces of baklava from the baking sheet to storage containers (lined with cooking parchment paper), using a small offset spatula. Arrange the baklava in single layers and cover tightly.

FRESHLY BAKED, THE BAKLAVA KEEPS FOR 1 WEEK TO 10 DAYS.

*S*tirred through batters or kneaded into sweet yeast doughs, sweetened coconut is a dramatic flavor. It's derived from the firm, fleshy interior of rough and thick pods, the fruit of the coconut palm tree. Sweetened flaked coconut conveys a direct, rounded taste that is so appealing in cakes, cookies, scones, and sweet rolls. This ingredient also contributes considerable moistness. The sweetened variety is preferable in flavor and texture to the unsweetened, desiccated style.

The flavor of coconut is, first and foremost, strengthened by the presence of sugar (granulated, vanilla-scented, or light brown), for sugar brings out the fruit's tropical savor and rounded essential oils. Once underpinned by sugar, coconut is magnified by the presence of sour cream, milk, heavy cream, light (table) cream, or coconut milk; chocolate, vanilla and almond extracts; spices such as cinnamon, nutmeg, allspice, cloves, and cardamom; crushed pineapple; and chocolate-covered coconut candy chunks. Avoid using coconut flavoring, which adds a vaguely antiseptic taste-scent to a batter or dough.

14

Coconut

TROPICAL CARROT AND COCONUT CAKE

One 13 by 9-inch cake, creating 20 squares

THE MOIST CRUMB OF THIS CARROT CAKE is the direct result of incorporating crushed pineapple and coconut into the batter, and by using a combination of oil and melted butter that, together, underscores the taste of the ground spices. Oil keeps the crumb of the cake nicely soft, but butter (in the melted state) helps to develop the flavor of the batter.

Nonstick cooking spray, for preparing the baking pan

CARROT AND COCONUT
CAKE BATTER

2 cups unsifted bleached all-purpose flour

1 teaspoon baking powder

1 teaspoon baking soda

½ teaspoon salt

2 teaspoons ground cinnamon

1 teaspoon freshly grated nutmeg

½ teaspoon ground allspice

½ teaspoon ground cloves

4 large eggs

2 cups superfine sugar

1 cup plain vegetable oil (preferably soybean)

¼ pound (8 tablespoons or 1 stick) unsalted butter, melted and cooled

2 teaspoons pure vanilla extract

One 8-ounce can crushed pineapple, in natural juices, well drained

2⅓ cups lightly packed grated carrots (use the large holes of a 4-sided box grater)

1⅓ cups lightly packed sweetened flaked coconut

PREHEAT THE OVEN AND PREPARE THE BAKING PAN Preheat the oven to 350° F. Film the inside of the baking pan with nonstick cooking spray; set aside.

MIX THE CARROT AND COCONUT CAKE BATTER Sift the flour, baking powder, baking soda, salt, cinnamon, nutmeg, allspice, and cloves onto a sheet of waxed paper.

Beat the eggs in the large bowl of a freestanding electric mixer on moderate speed for 1 minute. Blend in the superfine sugar and beat for 1 minute. Blend in the oil and melted butter. Beat in the vanilla extract and drained pineapple. Scrape down the sides of the mixing bowl frequently with a rubber spatula to keep the batter even-textured.

On low speed, add the sifted flour mixture in two additions, beating just until the particles of flour are absorbed. Stir in the carrots and coconut. *Batter texture observation* The batter will be soupy-chunky, and lightly thickened.

Scrape the batter into the prepared baking pan.

BAKE AND COOL THE CAKE Bake the cake for 40 to 45 minutes, or until risen, golden brown on top, set, and a wooden pick inserted in the cake withdraws clean. The baked cake will pull away slightly from the sides of the baking pan. Let the cake stand in the pan on a cooling rack. Cool completely.

FROST THE CAKE Place large spoonfuls of the frosting on top of the cake and, using a flexible palette knife, spread it in an even

Coconut Cream Cheese Frosting (see page 324), **for topping the baked cake**

BAKEWARE

13 by 9 by 2-inch baking pan

layer. Let the frosting set for 1 hour before cutting the cake into squares for serving. Refrigerate any leftover cake in an airtight cake keeper.

❋ *For an extra surge of flavor,* sprinkle an additional 1 cup sweetened flaked coconut on top of the coconut-embellished frosting.

❋ *For a textural contrast,* stir ½ cup chopped pecans or walnuts into the cake batter along with the grated carrots and flaked coconut.

FRESHLY BAKED, THE CAKE KEEPS FOR 3 DAYS.

BEST BAKING ADVICE

Carrots grated on the large holes of a box grater keep the texture of the cake from turning too dense; the larger shreds float through the batter and disperse evenly throughout.

COCONUT CREAM CHEESE FROSTING

About 4½ cups

DAPPLED WITH FLAKED COCONUT and seasoned with vanilla extract, this frosting complements a square of carrot cake in a sweet and creamy way. The addition of sweetened coconut adds textural contrast to the frosting and buffers the soft tang of the cream cheese. The frosting is also fabulous spread generously over banana, vanilla, spice, or coconut-flavored cupcakes.

CREAM CHEESE AND
COCONUT FROSTING

- 12 ounces (one and one-half 8-ounce packages) cream cheese, softened
- 5 tablespoons (¼ stick plus 1 tablespoon) unsalted butter, softened
- 2½ teaspoons pure vanilla extract
- 3 tablespoons heavy cream
- ⅛ teaspoon freshly grated nutmeg
- 5½ cups unsifted confectioners' sugar
- ¾ cup lightly packed sweetened flaked coconut

BEST BAKING ADVICE

The cream cheese and butter should be beaten until very smooth (to dispel any pebbly bits of cream cheese) so that the mixture readily—and uniformly—accepts the confectioners' sugar.

MIX THE CREAM CHEESE AND COCONUT FROSTING Using an electric hand mixer, beat the cream cheese and butter in a large mixing bowl on moderate speed for 1 minute, or until creamy and well combined. Blend in the vanilla extract, heavy cream, and nutmeg. On low speed, add the confectioners' sugar in three additions, beating until throughly combined before adding the next batch. Scrape down the sides of the mixing bowl frequently with a rubber spatula to keep the frosting even-textured. Blend in the coconut.

If you are preparing the frosting in advance, press a sheet of food-safe plastic wrap over the surface of the frosting and set aside. Use the frosting within 30 minutes of mixing. All baked goods topped with cream cheese frosting should be kept refrigerated after the frosting has set.

COCONUT-CHOCOLATE CHIP COOKIES

20 to 22 cookies

*T*HE COMBINATION OF LIGHT BROWN SUGAR and butter accentuates the flavor of the chocolate chips that roam throughout this cookie dough, which is nubby with the addition of flaked coconut. The texture of the cookies is dependent upon using butter both in the softened and melted state. This dough keeps beautifully in the refrigerator for up to 4 days, so you can bite into a soft, chewy, coconut-laced sweet as soon as the oven is preheated and the cookie sheets are assembled.

COCONUT-CHOCOLATE CHIP
COOKIE DOUGH

⅓ cup quick-cooking (not instant)
    rolled oats

2 cups plus 3 tablespoons unsifted
    bleached all-purpose flour

½ teaspoon baking soda

¾ teaspoon salt

¼ pound (8 tablespoons or 1 stick)
    unsalted butter, softened

1¼ cups firmly packed light brown
    sugar, sieved if lumpy

¼ cup granulated sugar

2½ teaspoons pure vanilla extract

5 tablespoons (½ stick plus 1
    tablespoon) unsalted butter, melted
    and cooled to tepid

2 large eggs

2¼ cups semisweet chocolate chips

⅔ cup sweetened flaked coconut

BAKEWARE

several heavy cookie sheets

PREHEAT THE OVEN AND PREPARE THE COOKIE SHEETS
Preheat the oven to 350° F. Line the cookie sheets with cooking parchment paper; set aside. The baking sheets need to be heavy to prevent the bottoms of the cookies from overbrowning. Double-pan the sheets, if necessary.

PROCESS THE ROLLED OATS Place the rolled oats in a food processor fitted with the steel knife. Cover and process, using 3-second on-off bursts, until reduced to a moderately fine bits, like a coarse-textured powder. Set aside.

MIX THE COCONUT-CHOCOLATE CHIP COOKIE DOUGH
Whisk the flour, baking soda, and salt in a medium-size mixing bowl.

Cream the softened butter in the large bowl of a freestanding electric mixer on moderately low speed for 2 minutes. Add the light brown sugar and beat for 1 minute. Add the granulated sugar and beat for 1 minute. Blend in the vanilla extract and melted, tepid butter. Blend in the eggs. Remove the mixing bowl from the stand. Mix in the processed oats. Add the whisked flour mixture, chocolate chips, and coconut, and stir to form a dense but somewhat sticky dough, using a wooden spoon or flat wooden paddle.

SPOON THE DOUGH ONTO THE PREPARED COOKIE SHEETS Take up generous 3 tablespoon-size mounds of dough and form into rough mounds about 1¾ inches in diameter by 2 inches tall. *Dough height observation* The height of the mounds is important if the cookies are to bake up pudgy and chewy-textured.

Place the mounds on the lined cookie sheets, spacing them about 3 inches apart. Place nine mounds of dough on each sheet.

BAKE AND COOL THE COOKIES Bake the cookies in the preheated oven for 13 to 15 minutes, or until softly set, pale golden around the edges, and a spotty pale golden on top. The bottoms of the cookies will be light golden-colored. Let the cookies stand on the sheets on cooling racks for 10 minutes, then remove them to sheets of parchment paper, using a wide, offset metal spatula. Cool completely.

✳ *For an aromatic topnote of flavor,* use intensified vanilla extract (see page 52) in place of plain vanilla extract in the cookie dough.

FRESHLY BAKED, THE COOKIES KEEP FOR 2 DAYS.

Variation: For coconut chocolate chip cookies with walnuts, pecans, or macadamia nuts, stir ⅔ cup coarsely chopped walnuts, pecans, or unsalted macadamia nuts into the dough along with the chocolate chips and coconut.

LAYERED COCONUT AND PECAN BARS

2 dozen bar cookies

PAVING THE TOP OF THIS SWEET COCONUT and nut confection is a generous blanket of pecans. The coconut taste is rounded out in each layer by adding coconut to the graham cracker base along with the cinnamon and nutmeg, and by centering a thick overlay of flaked coconut in between the chocolate chips and nuts. These are rich, and utterly luscious.

PREHEAT THE OVEN AND PREPARE THE BAKING PAN Preheat the oven to 350° F. Film the bottom of the baking pan with nonstick cooking spray.

Nonstick cooking spray, for preparing the baking pan

GRAHAM CRACKER–
COCONUT LAYER

¼ pound (8 tablespoons or 1 stick) unsalted butter, melted

¼ teaspoon pure vanilla extract

1⅓ cups plus 3 tablespoons graham cracker crumbs

⅛ teaspoon ground cinnamon

⅛ teaspoon freshly grated nutmeg

¼ cup lightly packed sweetened flaked coconut

COCONUT AND PECAN TOPPING

½ teaspoon pure vanilla extract

One 14-ounce can sweetened condensed milk

1 cup plus 2 tablespoons semisweet chocolate chips

1⅓ cups lightly packed sweetened flaked coconut

1 cup coarsely chopped pecans

BAKEWARE

9 by 9 by 2-inch baking pan

MAKE GRAHAM CRACKER–COCONUT LAYER Whisk the melted butter and vanilla extract in a small bowl and pour into the prepared baking pan. Thoroughly combine the graham cracker crumbs, cinnamon, nutmeg, and coconut in a small mixing bowl. Scatter the coconut-flecked crumbs evenly over the bottom of the butter mixture. Using a small, offset metal spatula (or your fingertips), lightly press the crumbs into the butter.

PREPARE THE TOPPING AND ASSEMBLE THE SWEET WITH THE CHOCOLATE CHIPS, COCONUT, AND PECANS In a small mixing bowl, stir the vanilla extract into the sweetened condensed milk. Sprinkle the chocolate chips onto the graham cracker crumb base, then scatter over the coconut. Top with the pecan pieces. Press down lightly on the pecan pieces.

Spoon-and-drizzle the vanilla-flavored sweetened condensed milk evenly over the top of the pecans, making sure that it moistens the sides and corners.

BAKE THE BARS Bake the sweet for 25 to 30 minutes, or until set. *Baking observation* The fully baked bars will be light golden on top. Overbaking the bars will make them tough, rather than moist and chewy.

COOL AND CUT THE BARS Let the cake of bar cookies stand in the baking pan on a rack until completely cool. With a small, sharp knife, cut the cake into four quarters, then each quarter into six bars. Remove the bars with a small, offset metal spatula.

FRESHLY BAKED, THE BARS KEEP FOR 3 DAYS.

COCONUT CREAM COFFEE CAKE BUNS

16 buns

*T*HE ROUNDED FLAVORS of both butter and coconut dominate in these rich, pull-apart buns. The sour cream yeast dough (graced with flaked coconut) that forms the basis for the buns is styled after the almond, butter, and egg yeast dough in the recipe for Almond Pull-Aparts on page 106, but it is sour cream–based butter and egg coffee cake dough that has some of the attributes of brioche but, although tender, is less fluffy.

To enlarge upon the creamy crumb of the yeast dough, the pastry cream filling that's slathered onto twice-risen and well-chilled dough is smooth, thick, and jammed with coconut. Just before baking, the buns are covered in coconut streusel. What emerges from the oven is sublime: a pan full of moist and buttery, crumb-topped sweet rolls.

Nonstick cooking spray, for preparing the baking pan

SOUR CREAM AND COCONUT YEAST DOUGH

4½ teaspoons active dry yeast

¾ teaspoon granulated sugar

¼ cup warm (110° to 115° F.) water

2 large eggs

1 tablespoon pure vanilla extract

⅓ cup granulated sugar

1 cup sour cream

About 4⅔ cups unsifted unbleached all-purpose flour, plus more as needed

1 teaspoon salt

1½ teaspoons freshly grated nutmeg

¼ teaspoon ground cinnamon

⅓ cup lightly packed sweetened flaked coconut

½ pound (16 tablespoons or 2 sticks) unsalted butter, softened, cut into chunks

Coconut Pastry Cream (see page 331), for spreading on the sheet of yeast dough

Coconut Streusel (see page 64), to cover the unbaked buns

BAKEWARE

12 by 15 by 2-inch baking pan

MAKE THE SOUR CREAM AND COCONUT YEAST DOUGH
Mix the yeast, ¾ teaspoon granulated sugar, and warm water in a small heatproof bowl. Let stand until the yeast is dissolved and the mixture is swollen, 7 to 8 minutes. While the yeast is dissolving, whisk the eggs, vanilla extract, ⅓ cup granulated sugar, and the sour cream in a large mixing bowl. Stir in the yeast mixture.

Combine 3½ cups of the flour, the salt, nutmeg, and cinnamon in a large mixing bowl. Stir in the coconut and the yeast mixture. Blend in ½ cup flour. Drop over the chunks of butter, a few at a time, and work them into the dough with a sturdy, flat wooden paddle. *Dough texture observation* With 4 cups of flour, the dough will be sticky. Work in another ⅓ cup of flour. Lightly knead the dough in the bowl for 5 minutes, adding the remaining ⅓ cup of flour to create a soft, manageable dough. Add sprinkles of flour, as needed, to keep the dough from sticking too much, but remember that it should be moist and soft.

An overnight refrigeration of the once-risen yeast dough develops its flavor, and makes it easier to roll and form the buns.

BAG THE DOUGH AND SET TO RISE Place the dough in a heavy, self-closing, food-safe gallon-size plastic bag. Let rise at cool room temperature for 1½ hours.

COMPRESS AND REFRIGERATE THE DOUGH Lightly compress the dough by patting the outside surfaces of the bag with the palms of your hands. Refrigerate the dough overnight, compressing the dough two times more in the next 4 hours.

PREPARE AND CHILL THE COCONUT CREAM FILLING Make the Coconut Pastry Cream and refrigerate overnight.

PREPARE THE BAKING PAN Film the inside of the baking pan with nonstick cooking spray; set aside.

ROLL, FILL, AND CUT THE BUNS Compress the chilled dough with your fingertips. Place the dough on a well-floured work surface and roll it into a sheet measuring about 17 by 21 inches. Spread the cold coconut pastry cream filling over the surface of the dough. Roll up the dough into a coil as tightly as possible, jellyroll fashion. As you are rolling, sweep off any excess flour with a soft pastry brush. *Rolling observation* The creaminess of the filling may cause the dough to slide a bit as you roll it. Roll slowly, pinching together the edges as you go. Pinch closed the long seam end.

Gently stretch and pull the coil until it measures about 16 inches in length. Cut the coil into 16 thick slices with a sharp chef's knife. Gently pat and press the slices into slightly flattened ovals. Place buns in the prepared pan, arranging them in four rows of four each.

SET THE BUNS TO RISE Cover the pan loosely with a sheet of plastic wrap. Let the spirals rise at room temperature until doubled in bulk, light, and puffy-looking, 2 hours to 2 hours and 15 minutes. *Bun rising observation* Although the buns are not connected initially, the edges will join as the dough the rises. *Buns touching observation* Ultimately, you want the buns to touch each other, for that is one way to maintain moistness in sweet roll dough.

MIX THE COCONUT STREUSEL Make the coconut streusel topping and have at hand.

PREHEAT THE OVEN AND TOP THE BUNS WITH THE COCONUT STREUSEL Preheat the oven to 375° F. in advance of baking. Once the buns are risen, remove and discard the plastic wrap covering them. Distribute the streusel mixture in large and small lumps evenly over each bun, crumbling it lightly as you go, using all of the streusel. *Streusel sprinkling observation* Sprinkling the streusel topping lightly, rather than packing it on top, will create moister sweet rolls and a richly crumbly (rather than pasty) topping.

BAKE AND COOL THE BUNS Bake the buns for 35 minutes, or until set and the topping is a medium-golden brown color.

Let the buns stand in the pan on a cooling rack for 20 minutes. Remove them, individually or in blocks of two or four, using a wide, offset metal spatula, dividing them where the sides have attached during baking. Serve the buns barely warm or at room temperature.

❀ *For an aromatic topnote of flavor,* use vanilla-scented granulated sugar (see page 53) in place of plain granulated sugar in the yeast dough.

FRESHLY BAKED, THE BUNS KEEP FOR 2 DAYS.

COCONUT PASTRY CREAM

About 2 cups

WHEN AN ELEGANT PASTRY CREAM is enclosed in a spiral of rich yeast dough, it both moistens and flavors the finished composition. The coconut coffee cake buns benefit from such a treatment, and this pastry cream is an important element that distinguishes the dough.

COCONUT PASTRY CREAM

1 cup light (table) cream

¾ cup milk

2 tablespoons cornstarch

⅓ cup granulated sugar

pinch of salt

4 large egg yolks

¾ cup lightly packed sweetened flaked coconut

1 teaspoon pure vanilla extract

1 tablespoon unsalted butter, softened

COOK THE PASTRY CREAM Combine the light cream and milk in a small saucepan and heat until warm.

Sift the cornstarch, granulated sugar, and salt into a small (5-cup), heavy saucepan (preferably enameled cast iron). Whisk the sugar-cornstarch mixture well to combine. Slowly blend in the egg yolks. Place a fine-meshed sieve over the saucepan and dribble in 1 tablespoon of the warm cream-milk mixture. Stir it in. Add 5 additional tablespoons of the warm liquid in this fashion, to temper the egg yolks. Add the remaining liquid slowly, mixing well. *Straining observation* Straining the liquid into the yolk mixture prevents any patches of skin formed on the liquid from being incorporated into the filling.

Bring the filling mixture to a boil slowly, stirring constantly with a wooden spoon. Do not use a whisk. Do not beat the mixture. As soon as the mixture comes to a low boil, regulate the heat so that it bubbles gently for about 1 minute and 30 seconds. *Pastry cream texture observation* The filling will be smooth-textured if you watch the cooking carefully, and bring the mixture to a boil slowly; otherwise it will form small lumps. If lumps do form, the pastry cream will be strained and the texture smoothed out.

STRAIN AND FLAVOR THE PASTRY CREAM Using a rubber spatula, press the cream through a medium-size, fine-meshed sieve into a heatproof bowl. Slowly stir in the coconut, vanilla extract, and butter. Immediately press a sheet of plastic wrap directly over the surface of the cream. Cool. Refrigerate the pastry cream for 5 hours. (The cream can be made 1 day in advance; refrigerate the pastry cream in an airtight container.)

❋ *For an aromatic topnote of flavor,* use intensified vanilla extract (see page 52) in place of plain vanilla extract in the pastry cream.

Coconut Washboards

About 4½ dozen cookies

M EANT FOR THE COOKIE JAR, these old-time treats are packed with coconut. Tablespoonfuls of dough are formed by hand into ovals and flattened with a table fork to impress the cookies with the traditional striated shape. This is my grandmother's recipe that is her version of the washboards in *Betty Crocker's Picture Cook Book* (Minneapolis: General Mills, Inc., 1950). Grandma Lilly used all butter (rather than both butter and solid shortening), a combination of granulated sugar and light brown sugar, and a higher ratio of coconut (for a coconut-loving family). I accent the cookie dough with the shadowy spice seasonings of nutmeg and cinnamon, increase the vanilla extract, and replace the water with heavy cream. All of this flavor-orchestrating helps to bring out the appealing bouquet of coconut.

COCONUT BUTTER COOKIE DOUGH

3 cups sifted bleached all-purpose flour

1 teaspoon baking powder

½ teaspoon baking soda

¼ teaspoon salt

¾ teaspoon freshly grated nutmeg

½ teaspoon ground cinnamon

12 tablespoons (1½ sticks) unsalted butter, softened

1 cup firmly packed light brown sugar, sieved if lumpy

½ cup granulated sugar

1 large egg

1 large egg yolk

2 teaspoons pure vanilla extract

3 tablespoons heavy cream

1⅔ cups lightly packed sweetened flaked coconut

BAKEWARE

several heavy cookie sheets

PREHEAT THE OVEN AND PREPARE THE COOKIE SHEETS Preheat the oven to 400° F. Line the cookie sheets with cooking parchment paper; set aside. The baking sheets need to be heavy to prevent the bottoms of the cookies from over-browning. Double-pan the sheets, if necessary.

MIX THE COCONUT BUTTER COOKIE DOUGH Sift the flour, baking powder, baking soda, salt, nutmeg, and cinnamon onto a sheet of waxed paper.

Cream the butter in the large bowl of a freestanding electric mixer on low speed for 2 minutes. Add the light brown sugar in two additions, beating for 1 minute after each portion is added. Add the granulated sugar and beat for a minute longer. Beat in the whole egg, egg yolk, vanilla extract, and heavy cream. Mix in the coconut.

On low speed, blend in the sifted mixture in two additions, mixing until the particles of flour are absorbed and the mixture forms a dough. Scrape down the sides of the mixing bowl frequently with a rubber spatula to keep the dough even-textured. *Dough texture observation* The dough will be buttery and firm, pliable and moldable.

FORM AND "CORRUGATE" THE WASHBOARD COOKIES Spoon out the dough by rounded tablespoons and form into oval-shaped logs. Place the logs of dough 3 inches apart on the lined cookie sheets, arranging them nine to a sheet. Flatten the balls slightly with the palm of your hand or the lightly floured, smooth bottom of a juice glass. With the tines of a fork, make rows of striated impressions to flatten each ball of dough into a rounded oval. The surface of each cookie should look corrugated—lightly grooved and ridged.

BAKE AND COOL THE COOKIES Bake the cookies in the preheated oven for 8 to 10 minutes, or until set. The bottom of the cookies will be golden, as will the edges and the top of the striated ridges. (As the cookies bake, though, the clarity of the ridges will diminish a bit owing to the leavening in the dough.) Remove the cookies to cooling racks, using a wide, offset metal spatula. Cool completely.

❋ *For an aromatic topnote of flavor,* use intensified vanilla extract (see page 52) in place of plain vanilla extract in the cookie dough.

FRESHLY BAKED, THE COOKIES KEEP FOR 2 TO 3 DAYS.

In-Love-with-Coconut Chocolate Cake

One 13 by 9-inch cake, creating 20 squares

Fanciful and generously jammed with coconut, this is a richly moist, tempting cake. The cake batter bakes into a downy, chocolate-flavored cushion, a pillowy layer that serves as a base for a buttery coconut and walnut frosting.

Nonstick cookware spray, for preparing the baking pan

COCONUT-FLECKED CHOCOLATE CAKE BATTER

2 cups unsifted bleached cake flour

¼ cup unsifted bleached all-purpose flour

2 teaspoons baking powder

¾ teaspoon salt

10 tablespoons (1 stick plus 2 tablespoons) unsalted butter, softened

1¾ cups plus 2 tablespoons granulated sugar

2 large eggs

2 teaspoons pure vanilla extract

4 ounces (4 squares) unsweetened chocolate, melted and cooled

1 cup milk blended with ⅓ cup light (table) cream

1 cup lightly packed sweetened flaked coconut

Coconut Frosting (see page 336), for topping the baked cake

BAKEWARE

13 by 9 by 3-inch baking pan

PREHEAT THE OVEN AND PREPARE THE BAKING PAN Preheat the oven to 350° F. Film the inside of the baking pan with nonstick cooking spray; set aside.

MIX THE COCONUT-FLECKED CHOCOLATE CAKE BATTER Sift the cake flour, all-purpose flour, baking powder and salt onto a sheet of waxed paper.

Cream the butter in the large bowl of a freestanding electric mixer on moderate speed for 2 minutes. Add half of the granulated sugar and beat for 1 minute; add the balance of the granulated sugar and beat for 1 to 2 minutes longer. Beat in the eggs, one at a time, mixing for 45 seconds to 1 minute after each addition. Blend in the vanilla extract and melted unsweetened chocolate. Scrape down the sides of the mixing bowl frequently with a rubber spatula to keep the batter even-textured.

On low speed, alternately add the sifted mixture in three additions with the milk-table cream blend in two additions, beginning and ending with the sifted mixture. *Batter texture observation* The batter will be creamy and lightly thickened. Mix in the coconut.

Spoon the batter into the prepared baking pan. Gently shake the pan from side to side, two or three times, to level the top or smooth over the top lightly with a rubber spatula.

BAKE AND COOL THE CAKE Bake the cake in the preheated oven for 40 minutes, or until risen, set, and a wooden pick inserted in the cake withdraws clean. The baked cake will pull away slightly from the sides of the baking pan. Let the cake stand in the pan on a cooling rack. Cool completely.

FROST THE CAKE Place large spoonfuls of the frosting on top of the cooled cake and, using a flexible palette knife, spread the frosting over the surface of the cake. Cool completely.

❋ *For an aromatic topnote of flavor,* use intensified vanilla extract (see page 52) in place of plain vanilla extract in the cake batter.

FRESHLY BAKED, THE CAKE KEEPS FOR **2** DAYS.

COCONUT FROSTING

About 3⅓ cups

AT ONCE CREAMY, BUTTERY, and ruffled with sweetened flaked coconut, this frosting has a delicious caramel-like taste that is reinforced with vanilla extract. The pivotal point to remember when cooking this frosting is to thicken it properly, so that it retains its shape on the baked cake.

BROWN SUGAR-COCONUT-WALNUT FROSTING

¾ cup heavy cream

¾ cup plus 2 tablespoons firmly packed light brown sugar, sieved if lumpy

¼ cup granulated sugar

3 large egg yolks, lightly beaten

large pinch of salt

2 cups lightly packed sweetened flaked coconut

1½ cups coarsely chopped walnuts, lightly toasted and cooled

7 tablespoons (1 stick less 1 tablespoon) unsalted butter, cut into tablespoon chunks

1½ teaspoons pure vanilla extract

BEST BAKING ADVICE
The frosting should be cooked until thickened properly, or the top layer of the cake will absorb too much of it.

MAKE THE BROWN SUGAR-COCONUT-WALNUT FROSTING Combine the heavy cream, light brown sugar, granulated sugar, egg yolks, salt, coconut, and walnuts in a heavy, medium-size saucepan (preferably enameled cast iron). Add the butter chunks. Set over moderately high heat and cook, stirring frequently with a wooden spoon or flat paddle, until the butter melts down entirely and the mixture comes to a low boil. Cook the frosting mixture at a low boil for 8 to 10 minutes, or until thickened, stirring continually. *Frosting appearance observation* The thickened frosting will look somewhat shiny.

COOL THE FROSTING Remove the saucepan from the heat. Stir in the vanilla extract. Carefully spoon the frosting into a large heatproof bowl. Cool for 15 to 20 minutes, stirring occasionally. The frosting is now ready to be used.

❊ *For an aromatic topnote of flavor,* use intensified vanilla extract (see page 52) in place of plain vanilla extract in the frosting.

COCONUT AND CHOCOLATE CHIP PICNIC CAKE

One 10-inch fluted tube cake, creating 16 slices

THICKSET WITH CHOCOLATE, entwined with coconut, and buttery enough to please, this cake has a soft crumb and classic flavor. The texture of the cake is developed by using superfine sugar and a combination of sour cream and light cream, which creates its tender-moist quality. Four bars (3 ounces each) of top-quality bittersweet chocolate, chopped by hand into small bits, can be substituted for the miniature semisweet chocolate chips.

Nonstick cookware spray, for preparing the cake pan

COCONUT AND CHOCOLATE CHIP CAKE BATTER

3 cups unsifted bleached all-purpose flour

1 teaspoon baking powder

¼ teaspoon baking soda

1 teaspoon salt

2 cups miniature semisweet chocolate chips

½ pound (16 tablespoons or 2 sticks) unsalted butter, softened

2 cups superfine sugar

4 large eggs

2 teaspoons pure vanilla extract

⅓ cup sour cream whisked with ¾ cup plus 2 tablespoons light (table) cream

1 cup lightly packed sweetened flaked coconut

BAKEWARE

10-inch Bundt pan

PREHEAT THE OVEN AND PREPARE THE CAKE PAN Preheat the oven to 350° F. Film the inside of the Bundt pan with nonstick cooking spray; set aside.

MIX THE COCONUT AND CHOCOLATE CHIP CAKE BATTER Sift the all-purpose flour, baking powder, baking soda, and salt onto a sheet of waxed paper. In a medium-size mixing bowl, toss the chocolate chips with 1 tablespoon of the sifted mixture.

Cream the butter in the large bowl of a freestanding electric mixer on moderate speed for 3 to 4 minutes. Add the superfine sugar in three additions, beating for 1 minute after each portion is added. Beat in the eggs, one at a time, mixing on moderate speed for 45 seconds after each is added. Blend in the vanilla extract.

On low speed, alternately add the sifted ingredients in three additions with the sour cream–table cream mixture in two additions, beginning and ending with the sifted mixture. Scrape down the sides of the mixing bowl frequently with a rubber spatula to keep the batter even-textured. *Batter texture observation* The batter will be thick and creamy. Blend in the chocolate chips and coconut.

Spoon the batter into the prepared Bundt pan. Lightly smooth over the batter with a flexible palette knife.

Bake the cake Bake the cake for 55 minutes to 1 hour, or until risen, set, and a wooden pick inserted in the cake withdraws clean. The baked cake will pull away slightly from the sides of the baking pan.

Cool the cake Let the cake stand in the pan on a cooling rack for 5 to 8 minutes. Carefully invert the cake onto another cooling rack. Cool completely before cutting into slices for serving. *Slicing observation* Use a serrated knife to cut the cake neatly and cleanly.

❋ *For an aromatic topnote of flavor,* use vanilla-scented superfine sugar (see page 54) in place of plain superfine sugar in the cake batter.

FRESHLY BAKED, THE CAKE KEEPS FOR 2 DAYS.

COCONUT JUMBLES
About 4 dozen cookies

*E*VERY BITE OF THIS CRISP COCONUT COOKIE stirs memories of my childhood. These thinly rolled sugar cookies, topped with sweetened flaked coconut, appeared as a staple at Christmastime, closed snugly in a cluster of old and new cookie tins. The recipe, which belonged to my late mother, requires some patience. The cookie dough is made with cake flour—so it's exceptionally tender—but bakes up into crisp cookies, with a nice snap-and-crunch. The jumbles have a deliciously rounded, buttery flavor.

To stamp out cookies, my mother used (of all things) a doughnut cutter, so the baked cookies looked like large, wide, round rings. The cookies' physical shape is so nostalgically pressed into my consciousness that it's sometimes difficult for me to imagine using any other cutter, although I have cut the dough with a scalloped round and fancy heart cutter.

Mix the butter cookie dough Sift the flour, baking powder, salt, and nutmeg onto a sheet of waxed paper.

Cream the butter in the large bowl of a freestanding electric mixer on moderate speed for 2 minutes. Add the granulated sugar in two additions, beating for about 1 minute after

5 cups unsifted bleached cake flour

3 teaspoons baking powder

1 teaspoon salt

½ teaspoon freshly grated nutmeg

½ pound (16 tablespoons or 2 sticks) unsalted butter, softened

2 cups granulated sugar

2 large eggs

2 teaspoons pure vanilla extract

¼ cup milk

About 3 cups lightly packed sweetened flaked coconut, for sprinkling on the unbaked cookies

BAKEWARE

several cookie sheets

each portion is added. Blend in the eggs, one at a time, beating for 30 seconds after each one is added. Blend in the vanilla extract. On low speed, blend in half of the sifted mixture, the milk, then the remaining sifted mixture. Scrape down the sides of the mixing bowl frequently with a rubber spatula to keep the batter even-textured. *Dough texture observation* The dough will be moist and sticky at this point.

DIVIDE THE DOUGH AND ROLL BETWEEN SHEETS OF WAXED PAPER Divide the dough into three portions. Roll each portion of dough between sheets of waxed paper to a thickness of a scant ¼ inch. Stack the sheets of dough on a large cookie sheet and refrigerate overnight.

FREEZE THE SHEETS OF COOKIE DOUGH On baking day, transfer the stacks of rolled-out dough, still on the cookie sheet, to the freezer. Freeze for 1 hour, or until very firm.

PREHEAT THE OVEN AND PREPARE THE COOKIE SHEETS Preheat the oven to 400° F. Line several cookie sheets with cooking parchment paper; set aside.

CUT AND TOP THE COOKIES Working with one sheet of dough at a time, remove it from the freezer, peel off the waxed paper, and place on a lightly floured work surface. Using a lightly floured 3-inch cookie cutter, stamp out cookies from the dough. Place the cookies, 2 inches apart, on the lined cookie sheets. Sprinkle the tops of the cookies with the coconut.

BAKE AND COOL THE COOKIES Bake the cookies in the preheated oven for 10 minutes, or until golden and set. Let the cookies stand on the sheets for 1 minute, then remove them to cooling racks, using a wide, offset metal spatula. Cool the cookies completely.

❋ *For an aromatic topnote of flavor,* use vanilla-scented granulated sugar (see page 53) in place of plain granulated sugar in the cookie dough.

FRESHLY BAKED, THE COOKIES KEEP FOR 1 WEEK.

SOFT COCONUT OATMEAL COOKIES WITH DRIED FRUIT

About 4 dozen cookies

*F*OR A DROP COOKIE, this one is certainly sumptuous, with a luxurious assortment of dried fruit and coconut caught up in the dough. On baking, the coconut and rolled oats seem to meld together, creating an accommodating backdrop for the tart and tangy chew of the dried cranberries, cherries, and apricots.

OATMEAL AND COCONUT COOKIE DOUGH

1½ cups unsifted bleached all-purpose flour

¼ teaspoon baking soda

⅛ teaspoon cream of tartar

1 teaspoon salt

1 teaspoon freshly grated nutmeg

¾ teaspoon ground cinnamon

¼ teaspoon ground cloves

¼ teaspoon ground cardamom

½ pound (16 tablespoons or 2 sticks) unsalted butter, softened

5 tablespoons shortening

1¼ cups granulated sugar

1 cup firmly packed light brown sugar, sieved if lumpy

2 large eggs

1 tablespoon plus 1 teaspoon pure vanilla extract

2½ cups quick-cooking (not instant) rolled oats

2 cups lightly packed sweetened flaked coconut

1 cup coarsely chopped walnuts

1 cup moist, dried cherries

PREHEAT THE OVEN AND PREPARE THE COOKIE SHEETS Preheat the oven to 325° F. Line the cookie sheets with cooking parchment paper.

MAKE THE OATMEAL AND COCONUT COOKIE DOUGH Sift the flour, baking soda, cream of tartar, salt, nutmeg, cinnamon, cloves, and cardamom onto a sheet of waxed paper.

Cream the butter and shortening in the large bowl of a free-standing electric mixer on moderately low speed for 3 to 4 minutes. Add half of the granulated sugar and beat on moderate speed for 1 minute. Add the remaining granulated sugar and light brown sugar and beat for 2 minutes on low speed. Add the eggs and vanilla extract. Beat for 30 to 45 seconds, or until just blended. Scrape down the sides of the mixing bowl frequently with a rubber spatula to keep the mixture even-textured.

On low speed, add the flour mixture in two additions, beating just until the particles of flour are absorbed, then blend in the rolled oats and coconut. With a sturdy wooden spoon or flat wooden paddle, work in the walnuts, cherries, cranberries, and apricots.

FORM THE COOKIES Drop even 3-tablespoon-size mounds of dough onto the lined sheets, spacing the mounds about 3 inches apart.

BAKE AND COOL THE COOKIES Bake the cookies for 16 minutes, or until light golden here and there on top. *Cookie appear-*

¾ cup moist, dried cranberries

¾ cup coarsely chopped moist, dried
apricots

BAKEWARE
several cookie sheets

ance observation The surface of the baked cookies will no longer
look like wet, unbaked dough, and will be slightly soft and just set.

Let the cookies stand on the sheets for 2 to 3 minutes (they
are tender), then remove them to cooling racks, using a wide, offset metal spatula. Cool completely.

❄ *For an aromatic topnote of flavor,* use vanilla-scented granulated sugar (see page 53)
in place of plain granulated sugar in the cookie dough.

BEST BAKING ADVICE
*Mix the sifted dry ingredients into the
mixture until absorbed, but avoid
overbeating the dough at this point or the
texture of the cookies will be too compact,
rather than softly lush and moist.*

FRESHLY BAKED, THE COOKIES KEEP FOR **3** DAYS.

COCONUT AND OATMEAL SHORTBREAD

One 9½-inch shortbread, creating 10 triangular pieces

THERE ARE MANY FLAVORS and textures circulating within this crunchy and tender shortbread: the caramel taste of brown sugar, the soft chew of flaked coconut, the crunch of walnuts, the whiff of cinnamon and nutmeg, and the tenderizing effect of the rice flour. The dough itself is very buttery and simple to work with, and presses into a tart pan with ease.

COCONUT AND OATMEAL
SHORTBREAD DOUGH

¾ cup unsifted bleached all-purpose flour

¼ cup rice flour

¼ teaspoon baking powder

pinch of salt

½ teaspoon freshly grated nutmeg

⅛ teaspoon ground cinnamon

½ cup plus 2 tablespoons quick-cooking (not instant) rolled oats

½ cup lightly packed sweetened flaked coconut

12 tablespoons (1½ sticks) unsalted butter, softened

⅓ cup plus 2 tablespoons firmly packed light brown sugar, sieved if lumpy

1 teaspoon pure vanilla extract

⅓ cup coarsely chopped walnuts

1½ tablespoons granulated sugar, for sprinkling on top of the baked shortbread

BAKEWARE

fluted 9½-inch round tart pan (with a removable bottom)

PREHEAT THE OVEN AND PREPARE THE TART PAN Preheat the oven to 350° F. Have the tart pan at hand.

MIX THE COCONUT AND OATMEAL SHORTBREAD DOUGH In a medium-size mixing bowl, whisk the all-purpose flour, rice flour, baking powder, salt, nutmeg, and cinnamon to mix. Blend in the rolled oats and coconut, mixing thoroughly with a rubber spatula.

Cream the butter in the large bowl of a freestanding electric mixer on low speed for 3 minutes. Add the light brown sugar and vanilla extract, and beat for 2 minutes on low speed. Blend in the oat mixture and mix until the particles of flour are absorbed. Scrape down the sides of the mixing bowl once or twice with a rubber spatula to keep the dough even-textured. *Dough texture observation* The dough will be soft and buttery.

PRESS AND PAT THE DOUGH INTO THE PREPARED PAN Place the dough in the tart pan. Lightly dip your fingertips in flour, then press the dough into an even layer. Prick the dough in 12 to 15 random places, using the tines of a fork.

TOP THE SHORTBREAD WITH THE NUTS Scatter the chopped nuts on top of the unbaked shortbread and press them lightly on the surface.

BAKE, COOL, AND CUT THE SHORTBREAD Bake the shortbread for 40 minutes, or until firm, set, and golden on top. The baked shortbread will have risen and filled the entire tart pan. Immediately sprinkle the granulated sugar on the surface of the large cookie.

The brown sugar needs to be sieved to
remove any small, hard lumps, for these
won't dissolve in the shortbread dough,
even as it bakes.

Cool the shortbread in the pan on a rack for 15 minutes. Carefully unmold the shortbread, keeping it on the base. Cut the shortbread into wedges. Cool completely.

✳ *For an aromatic topnote of flavor,* use intensified vanilla extract (see page 52) in place of plain vanilla extract in the shortbread dough.

FRESHLY BAKED, THE SHORTBREAD KEEPS FOR 5 TO 7 DAYS.

COCONUT AND ALMOND FUDGE SQUARES

16 squares

*T*HE SWEETENED FLAKED COCONUT in this high-intensity, exceedingly buttery chocolate batter adds to its candy bar–like quality and contributes its own mark of flavor. You can top squares of the sweet with light sprinklings of plain confectioners' sugar, or 2 tablespoons confectioners' sugar sifted with ½ teaspoon of unsweetened, alkalized cocoa.

Nonstick cookware spray, for preparing the baking pan

COCONUT AND ALMOND FUDGE
BAR COOKIE BATTER

1 cup unsifted bleached all-purpose flour

½ cup unsifted bleached cake flour

2 tablespoons unsweetened, alkalized cocoa

⅛ teaspoon baking powder

½ teaspoon salt

½ pound (16 tablespoons or 2 sticks) unsalted butter, melted and cooled to tepid

4 ounces (4 squares) unsweetened chocolate, melted and cooled to tepid

PREHEAT THE OVEN AND PREPARE THE BAKING PAN Preheat the oven to 325° F. Film the inside of the baking pan with nonstick cooking spray; set aside.

MIX THE COCONUT AND ALMOND FUDGE BAR COOKIE BATTER Sift the all-purpose flour, cake flour, cocoa, baking powder, and salt onto a sheet of waxed paper.

Whisk the melted butter, melted unsweetened chocolate, and melted bittersweet chocolate in a medium-size mixing bowl. Whisk the eggs in a large mixing bowl for 1 minute. Add the granulated sugar and whisk for 1 minute, or until just combined. Blend in the vanilla and almond extracts. Blend in melted chocolate-butter mixture.

3 ounces bittersweet chocolate, melted
and cooled to tepid

5 large eggs

2 cups granulated sugar

1½ teaspoons pure vanilla extract

½ teaspoon pure almond extract

1 cup lightly packed sweetened flaked
coconut

½ cup slivered almonds, lightly
toasted and cooled

BAKEWARE

9 by 9 by 2-inch baking pan

Sift over the sifted ingredients and whisk until all particles of flour are absorbed. Stir in the coconut and almonds, using a wooden spoon or flat wooden paddle. *Batter texture observation* The batter will be moderately thick.

Scrape the batter into the prepared baking pan. Spread the batter evenly in the pan, using a rubber spatula or flexible palette knife.

BAKE, COOL, AND CUT THE FUDGE SQUARES Bake the fudge squares for 30 to 35 minutes, or until just set. There will be a few hairline cracks on the top and the entire cake will pull away slightly from the sides of the baking pan. Thoroughly cool the fudge squares in the baking pan on a rack. Even when cool, the fudge squares will be soft-fudgy, and damp.

Cut the block of fudge squares into quarters with a small, sharp knife, then cut each quarter into four pieces. (In hot and humid weather, or in a warm kitchen, refrigerate the entire cake of brownies in the pan for 1 to 2 hours before attempting to cut them.) Carefully remove them from the baking pan, using a small, offset metal spatula.

❊ *For an aromatic topnote of flavor,* use intensified vanilla extract (see page 52) in place of plain vanilla extract in the brownie batter.

FRESHLY BAKED, THE FUDGE SQUARES KEEP FOR 4 DAYS.

BEST BAKING ADVICE
Mix the flaked coconut, which adds a dimension of flavor and richness, completely through the batter, making sure to break up any small pockets that might remain at the bottom or sides of the mixing bowl.

Toasted Coconut and Macadamia Nut Scones

1 dozen scones

*T*HE CANDY-GLAZED MACADAMIA NUTS and sweetened coconut make a lively, perfectly delightful scone dough. A full 1½ cups of Mauna Loa Coconut Candy-Glazed Macadamia Nuts (see page 545) and 1⅓ cups of toasted coconut are the prominent flavoring agents.

TOASTED COCONUT AND MACADAMIA NUT SCONE DOUGH

4 cups unsifted bleached all-purpose flour

4¾ teaspoons baking powder

1¼ teaspoons salt

1 teaspoon freshly grated nutmeg

¼ teaspoon ground allspice

½ cup granulated sugar

12 tablespoons (1½ sticks) unsalted butter, cold, cut into tablespoon pieces

4 large eggs

1 cup heavy cream

2½ teaspoons pure vanilla extract

1½ cups coconut candy-glazed macadamia nuts, very coarsely chopped

1⅓ cups lightly packed sweetened flaked coconut, lightly toasted and cooled

BAKEWARE

2 large cookie sheets or rimmed sheet pans

PREHEAT THE OVEN AND PREPARE THE BAKING SHEETS Preheat the oven to 400° F. Line the cookie sheets or sheet pans with cooking parchment paper; set aside.

MIX THE TOASTED COCONUT AND MACADAMIA NUT SCONE DOUGH Whisk the flour, baking powder, salt, nutmeg, allspice, and granulated sugar into a large mixing bowl. Add the chunks of butter, and using a pastry blender, reduce the butter to small bits about the size of dried lima beans. With your fingertips, crumble the mixture until the bits of butter are reduced to slightly smaller flakes.

In a medium-size mixing bowl, whisk the eggs, cream, and vanilla extract. Pour the egg-cream mixture over the dry ingredients, add the macadamia nuts and coconut, and stir to form a dough, using a wooden spoon or flat paddle.

FORM THE DOUGH INTO SCONES Knead the dough lightly in the bowl for about 30 seconds (about 10 push and turns). *Dough texture observation* The dough will be soft and moist. On a lightly floured work surface, divide the dough in half and form into two 7-inch disks. If necessary, sprinkle the dough and the work surface with a little extra flour. With a chef's knife, cut each round into six wedges. With a wide, offset metal spatula, transfer the wedges to the lined cookie sheets, placing them 3 inches apart, and six to a sheet. Refrigerate the scones for 15 minutes.

B A K E A N D C O O L T H E S C O N E S Bake the scones in the preheated oven for 18 minutes, or until golden and set. Remove the scones to a cooling rack, using a wide metal spatula. Serve the scones warm or at room temperature.

❊ *For an aromatic topnote of flavor,* use vanilla-scented granulated sugar (see page 53) in place of plain granulated sugar and intensified vanilla extract (see page 52) in place of plain vanilla extract in the scone dough.

FRESHLY BAKED, THE SCONES KEEP FOR 2 DAYS.

JUMBO COCONUT CUPCAKES
8 jumbo frosted cupcakes

*T*HESE ARE GRAND, IMPOSING CUPCAKES, loaded with flaked coconut in the batter, covered in cream cheese frosting, and topped with more coconut. The best-tasting cupcakes are capped with a very thick layer of frosting, so thick that it stands over an inch above the cake's surface.

Nonstick cookware spray, for
   preparing the muffin/cupcake pans

SOUR CREAM COCONUT
CUPCAKE BATTER

2½ cups plus 2 tablespoons unsifted
   bleached all-purpose flour

½ teaspoon baking soda

¾ teaspoon salt

¾ teaspoon freshly grated nutmeg

12 tablespoons (1½ sticks) unsalted
   butter, softened

1½ cups superfine sugar

3 large eggs

2½ teaspoons pure vanilla extract

¾ cup thick, cultured sour cream

PREHEAT THE OVEN AND PREPARE THE MUFFIN/CUPCAKE PANS Preheat the oven to 375° F. Film the inside of the muffin/cupcake cups with nonstick cooking spray. Set aside.

MIX THE SOUR CREAM COCONUT CUPCAKE BATTER Sift the flour, baking soda, salt, and nutmeg onto a sheet of waxed paper.

Cream the butter in the large bowl of a freestanding electric mixer on moderate speed for 3 minutes. Add half of the superfine sugar and beat for 1 minute; add the balance of the superfine sugar and beat for 2 minutes longer. Beat in the eggs, one at a time, mixing for 45 seconds after each addition. Blend in the vanilla extract. Scrape down the sides of the mixing bowl frequently with a rubber spatula to keep the batter even-textured.

On low speed, alternately add the sifted mixture in three additions with the sour cream in two additions, beginning and ending

1 cup lightly packed sweetened flaked
   coconut

Coconut Cream Cheese Frosting (see
   page 324), without the addition of
   the sweetened flaked coconut, for
   topping the baked cupcakes

About 1½ cups sweetened flaked
   coconut, to top the frosted cupcakes

BAKEWARE

8 jumbo muffin/cupcake cups (two
   pans, each holding six individual
   muffin cups), each cup measuring
   4 inches in diameter, 1¾ inches
   deep, with a capacity of about
   1⅛ cups

with the sifted mixture. *Batter texture observation* The batter will be smooth, moderately thick, and buttercream-like. On low speed, blend in the coconut.

FILL THE MUFFIN/CUPCAKE CUPS WITH THE BATTER Divide the batter among the prepared muffin/cupcake cups, mounding it lightly in the center.

BAKE THE CUPCAKES Bake the cupcakes for 30 to 35 minutes, or until risen and completely set. When baked, a wooden pick inserted in the center of a cupcake will withdraw clean.

COOL THE CUPCAKES Cool the cupcakes in the pans on racks for 15 minutes. Carefully remove the cupcakes to cooling racks. Cool completely.

FROST AND TOP THE CUPCAKES Using a flexible palette knife, spread the frosting as thickly as possible on top of the cooled cupcakes, making a thick 2-inch cap on top. Sprinkle the frosted surfaces of the cupcakes with the coconut. Refrigerate any cupcakes not served within 2 hours.

❋ *For an aromatic topnote of flavor,* use intensified vanilla extract (see page 52) in place of plain vanilla extract in the cupcake batter.

FRESHLY BAKED, THE CUPCAKES KEEP FOR **2** DAYS.

DOUBLE CHOCOLATE AND
COCONUT BROWNIES

16 large brownies

A PANFUL OF BROWNIES for those who dote on the combination of coconut and chocolate. The batter is strengthened with cocoa and unsweetened chocolate, and flecked with chocolate chips and soft wisps of coconut.

Nonstick cooking spray, for preparing the baking pan

DOUBLE CHOCOLATE AND COCONUT BROWNIE BATTER

1¼ cups unsifted bleached cake flour

3 tablespoons unsweetened, alkalized cocoa

¼ teaspoon baking powder

¼ teaspoon salt

¾ cup miniature semisweet chocolate chips

½ pound (16 tablespoons or 2 sticks) unsalted butter, melted and cooled to tepid

6 ounces (6 squares) unsweetened chocolate, melted and cooled to tepid

4 large eggs

2 cups plus 2 tablespoons superfine sugar

2 teaspoons pure vanilla extract

1¼ cups lightly packed sweetened flaked coconut

BAKEWARE

10 by 10 by 2-inch

PREHEAT THE OVEN AND PREPARE THE BAKING PAN Preheat the oven to 325° F. Film the inside of the baking pan with nonstick cooking spray; set aside.

MIX THE DOUBLE CHOCOLATE AND COCONUT BROWNIE BATTER Sift the cake flour, cocoa, baking powder, and salt onto a sheet of waxed paper. In a bowl, toss the chocolate chips with 1 teaspoon of the sifted mixture.

Whisk the melted butter and melted unsweetened chocolate in a medium-size mixing bowl until thoroughly combined. Whisk the eggs in a large mixing bowl for 1 minute, then add the superfine sugar and whisk for 1 minute, or until just combined. Blend in the melted chocolate-butter mixture and vanilla extract. Sift over the sifted ingredients and whisk until all particles of flour are absorbed into the batter. Stir in the coconut and chocolate chips.

Scrape the batter into the prepared baking pan. Smooth over the top with a rubber spatula.

BAKE, COOL, AND CUT THE BROWNIES Bake the brownies for 35 to 40 minutes, or until set. Let the brownies stand in the pan on a cooling rack for 3 hours, then refrigerate for 45 minutes, or until firm enough to cut. (In hot or humid weather, or in a warm kitchen, freeze the pan of brownies for 20 minutes before cutting, or until firm enough to cut.) Cut the entire cake of brownies into four quarters, then cut each quarter into four squares, using a small, sharp knife. Remove the brownies from the pan, using a small offset spatula.

❋ *For an aromatic topnote of flavor,* use intensified vanilla extract (see page 52) in place of plain vanilla extract in the brownie batter.

FRESHLY BAKED, THE BROWNIES KEEP FOR 4 DAYS.

COCONUT TEA CAKE

One 10-inch fluted tube cake, creating 16 slices

WITH ITS SOFT TEXTURE AND LIGHTENED CRUMB, this cake tastes simply of coconut and butter. It's plain and delicious, and very good served with a spoonful of the Caramel Custard Sauce on page 229 or a seasonal berry compote (especially a mixture of raspberries, blackberries, and blueberries).

Nonstick cookware spray, for preparing the cake pan

COCONUT BUTTER CAKE BATTER

2¾ cups unsifted bleached all-purpose flour

⅓ cup unsifted bleached cake flour

¾ teaspoon baking powder

¼ teaspoon baking soda

1 teaspoon salt

½ teaspoon freshly grated nutmeg

½ pound (16 tablespoons or 2 sticks) unsalted butter, softened

2 tablespoons shortening

2 cups granulated sugar

1 tablespoon pure vanilla extract

4 large eggs

PREHEAT THE OVEN AND PREPARE THE CAKE PAN Preheat the oven to 350° F. Film the inside of the Bundt pan with nonstick cooking spray.

MIX THE COCONUT BUTTER CAKE BATTER Sift the all-purpose flour, cake flour, baking powder, baking soda, salt, and nutmeg onto a sheet of waxed paper.

Cream the butter and shortening in the large bowl of a free-standing electric mixer on moderate speed for 3 minutes. Add the granulated sugar in three additions, beating for 1 minute after each portion is added. Blend in the vanilla extract. Beat in the eggs, one at a time, beating on moderate speed for 30 seconds after each is added. Whisk the coconut milk and whole milk in a measuring cup.

On low speed, alternately add the sifted ingredients in three additions with the whole milk–coconut milk mixture in two addi-

½ cup canned coconut milk, whisked well before measuring

½ cup whole milk

2 tablespoons thick, cultured sour cream

1⅔ cups lightly packed sweetened flaked coconut

Vanilla-scented confectioners' sugar (see page 54), for sifting over the top of the baked cake (optional)

BAKEWARE

10-inch Bundt pan

tions, beginning and ending with the sifted mixture. Scrape down the sides of the mixing bowl frequently with a rubber spatula to keep the batter even-textured. Add the sour cream and beat on low speed for 30 seconds. Stir in the coconut.

Spoon the batter into the prepared Bundt pan. Gently shake the pan from side to side to level the top.

BAKE THE CAKE Bake the cake for 55 minutes, or until risen, set, and a wooden pick inserted in the cake withdraws clean. The baked cake will pull away slightly from the sides of the baking pan.

COOL THE CAKE Let the cake stand in the pan on a cooling rack for 5 to 8 minutes. Carefully invert the cake onto another cooling rack. Cool completely. Sift confectioners' sugar over the top, if you wish, just before cutting into slices. *Slicing observation* Use a serrated knife to cut the cake neatly and cleanly.

❋ *For an aromatic topnote of flavor,* use vanilla-scented granulated sugar (see page 53) in place of plain granulated sugar in the cake batter.

FRESHLY BAKED, THE CAKE KEEPS FOR 2 DAYS.

DOUBLE COCONUT–CHOCOLATE CHIP–BROWN SUGAR SQUARES

16 squares

Bursting with coconut, and supporting enough chocolate to please, these bar cookies are especially buttery and chewy, and simply blooming with chunks of chocolate-covered coconut candy.

Nonstick cooking spray, for preparing the baking pan

COCONUT-CHOCOLATE CHIP-BROWN SUGAR BATTER

½ cup plus 2 tablespoons unsifted bleached all-purpose flour

½ cup unsifted bleached cake flour

¼ teaspoon baking powder

¼ teaspoon salt

¼ pound (8 tablespoons or 1 stick) unsalted butter, melted and cooled to tepid

⅔ cup firmly packed light brown sugar, sieved if lumpy

2 large eggs

1½ teaspoons intensified vanilla extract (see page 52)

4 packages (1.9-ounces each) chocolate-covered coconut candy (Peter Paul Mounds), cut into small chunks about ½ inch wide

⅓ cup lightly packed sweetened flaked coconut

¾ cup semisweet chocolate chips

BAKEWARE

9 by 9 by 2-inch pan

PREHEAT THE OVEN AND PREPARE THE BAKING PAN Preheat the oven to 350° F. Film the inside of the baking pan with nonstick cooking spray; set aside.

MAKE THE COCONUT–CHOCOLATE CHIP–BROWN SUGAR BATTER Sift the all-purpose flour, cake flour, baking powder, and salt onto a sheet of waxed paper.

Whisk the melted butter and light brown sugar in a medium-size mixing bowl, using a wooden spoon or whisk. Blend in the eggs and vanilla extract. Stir in the sifted mixture with a wooden spoon, mixing just until the particles of flour are absorbed. Stir in the coconut candy chunks, flaked coconut, and chocolate chips. *Batter texture observation* The batter will be dense and quite chunky.

Scrape the batter into the prepared pan. Spread the batter evenly in the pan, using a rubber spatula or flexible palette knife. Make sure that you nudge it into the corners.

BAKE AND COOL THE SWEET Bake the sweet for 24 minutes, or until softly set. The edges will be a light golden color. Transfer the pan to a rack and cool completely. Cut the entire cake into quarters with a small, sharp knife, then cut each quarter into four squares. Carefully remove the squares from the pan, using a small, offset metal spatula.

FRESHLY BAKED, THE BAR COOKIES KEEP FOR 3 DAYS.

*t*he flavor of coffee can wind its way into bakery sweets by the addition of strong, rich, and full-bodied brewed coffee to a batter or dough, or a slaked mixture of instant espresso powder and vanilla extract (or instant coffee blended with vanilla extract and a very small amount of hot water) into a batter or dough. Mocha, the flavor developed by blending chocolate and coffee (and occasionally including milk, light cream, or heavy cream into the mix), is both a chocolate and a coffee lover's dream, for its taste is deep, dark, and satisfying.

In an indirect way, the flavors of coffee and mocha are complemented and enhanced by the use of auxiliary ingredients such as pure vanilla extract, light brown sugar, freshly grated nutmeg, and coffee liqueur.

15

COFFEE AND
MOCHA

ESPRESSO AND BITTERSWEET CHOCOLATE CHUNK TORTE

One 9-inch cake, creating 10 slices

Pieces of bittersweet chocolate infiltrate a boldly chocolate, tinged-with-coffee batter. The combination of butter with unsweetened and bittersweet chocolate makes this a fudgy sweet.

Softened unsalted butter and unsweetened alkalized cocoa, for preparing the cake pan

ESPRESSO-CHOCOLATE TORTE BATTER

2 teaspoons instant (not granular) espresso powder

2 teaspoons pure vanilla extract

1½ cups unsifted bleached cake flour

¼ teaspoon baking powder

¼ teaspoon salt

3 tablespoons unsweetened, alkalized cocoa

8 ounces bittersweet chocolate, cut into small chunks

½ pound (16 tablespoons or 2 sticks) unsalted butter, melted and cooled

4 ounces (4 squares) unsweetened chocolate, melted and cooled

4 large eggs

1¾ cups plus 2 tablespoons granulated sugar

1 tablespoon heavy cream

Confectioners' sugar, for sifting over the top of the baked torte

Vanilla Whipped Cream (see page 530), to accompany the torte (optional)

PREHEAT THE OVEN AND PREPARE THE CAKE PAN Preheat the oven to 325° F. Lightly butter the inside of the springform pan and dust with unsweetened alkalized cocoa. Tap out any excess cocoa; set aside. Have the sheet pan or jellyroll pan at hand.

MAKE THE ESPRESSO-CHOCOLATE TORTE BATTER Combine the espresso powder and vanilla extract in a small ramekin; set aside.

Sift the flour, baking powder, salt, and cocoa onto a sheet of waxed paper. In a small mixing bowl, toss the bittersweet chocolate chunks with 2½ teaspoons of the sifted mixture.

In a medium-size mixing bowl, thoroughly blend the melted butter and melted unsweetened chocolate. Whisk the eggs in a large mixing bowl to blend; add the granulated sugar and whisk lightly for 1 minute longer, or until just combined. Blend in the coffee-vanilla extract mixture and melted chocolate-butter mixture, mixing well. Sift over the sifted ingredients and mix until the particles of flour are thoroughly absorbed, using a wooden spoon, flat wooden paddle, or whisk. Blend in the heavy cream. *Batter texture observation* The batter will be moderately thick. Stir in the chopped bittersweet chocolate.

Scrape the batter into the prepared cake pan. Smooth over the top with a rubber spatula.

BAKE AND COOL THE TORTE Place the torte on the sheet pan (or jellyroll pan) and bake for 45 minutes, or until set. There will

9-inch springform pan (2¾ inches deep)

rimmed sheet pan or jellyroll pan

be a few faint hairline cracks on the surface of the torte, mostly within 1 to 1½ inches of the circular edge. Cool the torte in the pan on a rack. When completely cool, release the sides and slice. Just before slicing and serving, sift confectioners' sugar over the top of the torte. *Slicing observation* Use a serrated knife or long chef's knife to cut the cake neatly and cleanly. Serve slices of the torte with dollops of whipped cream, if you wish.

❋ *For an aromatic topnote of flavor,* use intensified vanilla extract (see page 52) in place of plain vanilla extract in the torte batter.

FRESHLY BAKED, THE TORTE KEEPS FOR 2 DAYS.

BEST BAKING ADVICE

The small fillip of heavy cream smooths out the chocolate–coffee flavor.

Variation: For espresso and bittersweet chocolate chunk torte with walnuts, pecans, or macadamia nuts, stir ¾ cup chopped walnuts, pecans, or macadamia nuts (lightly toasted and cooled completely), tossed with 1 teaspoon of the sifted flour mixture, into the batter after the sifted mixture has been mixed in.

MOCHA BARS

2 dozen bar cookies

A FLAVORING SOLUTION OF COFFEE and vanilla extract combines with un-sweetened chocolate and semisweet chocolate chips to develop and expand the taste of mocha in these bar cookies. They are moist and luxurious, and simple to make.

Nonstick cooking spray, for preparing the baking pan

BUTTERY MOCHA BAR COOKIE BATTER

2 teaspoons instant (not granular) espresso powder

2 teaspoons pure vanilla extract

1 cup unsifted bleached all-purpose flour

3 tablespoons unsifted bleached cake flour

PREHEAT THE OVEN AND PREPARE THE BAKING PAN Preheat the oven to 325° F. Film the inside of the baking pan with non-stick cooking spray.

MIX THE BUTTERY MOCHA BAR COOKIE BATTER Combine the espresso powder and vanilla extract in a small ramekin.

2 tablespoons unsweetened, alkalized
  cocoa

¼ teaspoon baking powder

¼ teaspoon salt

1 cup semisweet chocolate chips

14 tablespoons (1¾ sticks) unsalted
  butter, melted and cooled to tepid

4 ounces (4 squares) unsweetened
  chocolate, melted and cooled to tepid

3 large eggs

1¾ cups plus 2 tablespoons superfine
  sugar

1 tablespoon heavy cream

¾ cup chopped walnuts (or pecans),
  lightly toasted and cooled

Confectioners' sugar, for sifting on top
  of the baked bars (optional)

BAKEWARE

9 by 9 by 2-inch baking pan

Sift the all-purpose flour, cake flour, cocoa, baking powder, and salt onto a sheet of waxed paper. In a small mixing bowl, toss the chocolate chips with 1½ teaspoons of the sifted mixture.

Whisk the melted butter and melted unsweetened chocolate in a medium-size mixing bowl. Whisk in the eggs in a large mixing bowl for 45 seconds. Add the superfine sugar and whisk slowly for 1 minute, or until just combined. Blend in the coffee-vanilla extract mixture. Sift over the sifted ingredients and whisk to form a batter, mixing just until the particles of flour are absorbed. Blend in the heavy cream. *Batter texture observation* The batter will be thick and somewhat glossy. Stir in the chocolate chips and walnuts (or pecans), using a wooden spoon or flat wooden paddle.

Scrape the batter into the prepared baking pan. Smooth over the top with a flexible palette knife or rubber spatula.

BAKE, COOL, AND CUT THE BARS Bake the bars for 35 minutes, or until just set. Place the pan on a rack and cool completely. Cut the cake into quarters and cut each quarter into six bars, using a small, sharp knife. Remove the bars from the baking pan, using a small, offset metal spatula. Just before serving, sift confectioners' sugar on top of the bars, if you wish.

❊ *For an aromatic topnote of flavor,* use intensified vanilla extract (see page 52) in place of plain vanilla extract in the bar cookie batter.

BEST BAKING ADVICE
The superfine sugar refines the crumb of the baked bars, and the heavy cream smooths out the coffee and chocolate flavor.

FRESHLY BAKED, THE BAR COOKIES KEEP FOR 3 TO 4 DAYS.

Variation: For mocha bars with Dutch-process black cocoa, use 1 tablespoon Dutch-process black cocoa and 1 tablespoon unsweetened, alkalized cocoa in the bar cookie batter.

ICED MOCHA SWEET ROLLS

18 buns

A YEAST-RAISED CHOCOLATE and coffee dough, filled with bittersweet chocolate butter and chocolate chips, bakes into soft and alluring sweet rolls. The tops of the warm, pull-apart buns are blanketed with a coffee liqueur icing, forming another layer of flavor that distinguishes the yeast bread. The mocha rolls are worth lingering over with good coffee.

Softened unsalted butter, for preparing the baking pans

MOCHA-COCOA YEAST DOUGH

4½ teaspoons active dry yeast

1 teaspoon granulated sugar

⅓ cup warm (110° to 115° F.) water

¾ cup milk

2 tablespoons instant (not granular) espresso powder

⅓ cup granulated sugar

¼ pound (8 tablespoons or 1 stick) unsalted butter, cut into tablespoon pieces

2½ teaspoons intensified vanilla extract (see page 52)

1 large egg

2 large egg yolks

4 cups unsifted unbleached all-purpose flour, plus more as needed

⅔ cup unsweetened, alkalized cocoa

¼ teaspoon cream of tartar

1 teaspoon salt

¾ teaspoon ground cinnamon

CHOCOLATE BUTTER FILLING

3 ounces bittersweet chocolate, cut into pieces

6 tablespoons (¾ stick) unsalted butter, softened

¼ cup confectioners' sugar

MAKE THE MOCHA-COCOA YEAST DOUGH Combine the yeast, 1 teaspoon granulated sugar, and the water in a heatproof 2-cup bowl. Let stand until the yeast softens and swells, 7 to 8 minutes. Place the milk and espresso powder in a medium-size saucepan and set over low heat. When the coffee powder dissolves, add the ⅓ cup granulated sugar and butter pieces, raise the heat to moderately low, and cook until the sugar and butter melt down, stirring occasionally with a wooden spoon. Remove from the heat and pour into a heatproof bowl. Stir in the vanilla extract. Let stand until warm, about 115° F., then whisk in the whole egg and egg yolks; stir in the puffy yeast mixture.

In a large mixing bowl, thoroughly combine 3 cups of the all-purpose flour, cocoa, cream of tartar, salt, and cinnamon. Pour over the yeast-milk-egg mixture and combine the ingredients with a flat wooden paddle. Work in the remaining cup of flour, ¼ cup at a time, to create a soft dough. *Dough texture observation* Depending upon the absorption quality of the flour, you'll need more or less than the designated amount of flour. The dough should be soft and supple, not dry or craggy. Knead the dough on a floured work surface for 8 to 10 minutes.

SET THE DOUGH TO RISE Place the dough in a lightly buttered bowl, and turn to coat all sides in a film of butter. With a clean pair of kitchen scissors, cut four or five slashes in the dough. *Technique observation* Cutting the dough in this fashion bolsters

½ teaspoon intensified vanilla extract (see page 52)

1⅓ cups semisweet chocolate chips

Coffee Liqueur Icing (see page 359), for covering the warm, baked rolls

BAKEWARE

two 9 by 9 by 3-inch square baking pans

its rise and encourages an expansive lift. Cover the bowl with a sheet of plastic wrap and let rise in a cozy place (away from drafts) until doubled in bulk, about 2 hours.

MAKE THE CHOCOLATE BUTTER FILLING Place the pieces of bittersweet chocolate in the work bowl of a food processor fitted with the steel knife. Cover and process, using 3-second on-off bursts, until the chocolate is very finely chopped. In a small mixing bowl, blend together the softened butter, confectioners' sugar, and vanilla extract. Blend in the chopped chocolate and vanilla extract; cover with plastic wrap and set aside. Have the chocolate chips at hand in a small bowl.

PREPARE THE BAKING PANS Lightly butter the inside of the baking pans; set aside.

ROLL, FILL, AND CUT THE CHOCOLATE BUNS Compress the dough with your fingertips to deflate slightly. Place the dough on a lightly floured work surface and roll into a sheet measuring about 16 by 16 inches. Spread the chocolate butter on the sheet of dough, using a small spreader or spatula, taking care not to tear into the surface. Sprinkle the chocolate chips evenly over the chocolate butter.

Roll up the dough, jellyroll style, tucking in and pinching the edges as you go along. Gently stretch the coil of dough to a length of about 26 inches. Cut the coil into 18 slices, using a sharp chef's knife. Arrange the sweet roll spirals cut side up in the prepared baking pans, nine to a pan, placing them in three rows of three each.

SET THE SWEET ROLLS TO RISE Cover each pan loosely with a sheet of plastic wrap. Let the rolls rise until doubled in bulk, about 1 hour and 30 minutes.

MAKE THE ICING Make the Coffee Liqueur Icing, press a sheet of plastic wrap directly over the surface, and set aside.

PREHEAT THE OVEN AND BAKE THE SWEET ROLLS Preheat the oven to 375° F. Remove the sheets of plastic wrap covering the baking pans. Bake the spirals for 10 minutes, reduce the oven temperature to 350° F., and continue baking for 12 to 14 minutes longer, or until just set. The baked rolls will pull away ever-so-slightly from the sides of the baking pan. Let the rolls stand in the pans on racks for 10 minutes.

ICE AND COOL THE SWEET ROLLS Spoon the icing on the surface of the sweet rolls, here and there. If the icing has been made in advance, it will firm up slightly; if you are using firmer icing, scoop it up with a flexible palette knife rather than a spoon.

Using a small, flexible palette knife, spread the icing. *Icing flow observation* The asymmetric melting pattern is pretty, so let it flow naturally.

Let the iced rolls cool in the pans. Remove the rolls with a offset metal spatula, breaking them apart where they've connected during the rising and baking process. Serve the sweet rolls while they're fresh and downy.

Variation: For iced mocha sweet rolls with Dutch-process black cocoa, use 2 tablespoons plus 2 teaspoons Dutch-process black cocoa and ½ cup unsweetened, alkalized cocoa in the yeast dough.

COFFEE LIQUEUR ICING

1 cup

A TOUCH OF COFFEE LIQUEUR adds fragrance and depth to this confectioners' sugar icing.

COFFEE ICING

2 cups unsifted confectioners' sugar

2 tablespoons unsalted butter, softened

1½ tablespoons coffee liqueur, such as Kahlúa

1 tablespoon plus 1 teaspoon milk

½ teaspoon pure vanilla extract

BEST BAKING ADVICE

Mix the icing on low speed until creamy and smooth, but not fluffy, so that it melts smoothly over the top of the baked sweet rolls.

MIX THE COFFEE ICING Place the confectioners' sugar, butter, coffee liqueur, milk, and vanilla extract in a medium-size mixing bowl. Using an electric hand mixer, beat the ingredients together on low speed to blend, scraping down the sides of the mixing bowl with a rubber spatula to keep the icing even-textured. Mix only until the icing is smooth, about 1 minute. Cover the icing by pressing a sheet of plastic wrap directly on the top. Use the icing as directed.

MOCHA RUSKS

About 38 dipping cookies

CRISP BUT TENDER, and especially chocolaty, these coffee-scented, filled-with-chips dipping cookies are made from a moist dough. I have been making these rusks for more than seven years and worked out a dough as good as the Almond Rusks on page 109, replacing butter for the oil, using both cocoa and flour to build its bulk, and stirring in chocolate chips to add pockets of flavor. The significant difference in the styling of the dough is that this one is made by the creamed method (like the procedure for mixing a butter cake) and the technique creates a batch of rusks that are pleasantly crisp.

The flavor-essence of coffee infuses the batter in two forms—in a solution of coffee powder, vanilla extract, and hot water, and in a splash of coffee liqueur.

MOCHA CHIP BATTER/DOUGH

2¼ teaspoons instant (not granular) espresso powder

1½ teaspoons pure vanilla extract

¼ teaspoon hot water

3 cups unsifted bleached all-purpose flour

⅔ cup plus 2 tablespoons unsweetened, alkalized cocoa

1½ teaspoons baking powder

¾ teaspoon salt

12 tablespoons (1½ sticks) unsalted butter, softened

1½ cups granulated sugar

3 large eggs

1 ounce (1 square) unsweetened chocolate, melted and cooled to tepid

1 tablespoon plus 2 teaspoons coffee liqueur, such as Kahlúa

1½ cups semisweet chocolate chips

BAKEWARE

three cookie sheets or rimmed sheet pans

PREHEAT THE OVEN AND PREPARE THE BAKING PANS
Preheat the oven to 350° F. Line the cookie sheets or rimmed sheet pans with cooking parchment paper; set aside.

PREPARE THE MOCHA CHIP BATTER/DOUGH Mix the espresso powder, vanilla extract, and hot water in a small ramekin; cool.

Sift the all-purpose flour, cocoa, baking powder, and salt onto a sheet of waxed paper.

Cream the butter in the large bowl of a freestanding electric mixer on moderately low speed for 2 minutes. Add the granulated sugar in two additions, beating for 1 minute on moderate speed after each portion is added. Blend in the eggs, one at a time, beating for 45 seconds after each addition. Blend in the cooled coffee-vanilla extract mixture, melted unsweetened chocolate, and coffee liqueur.

On low speed, add the sifted ingredients in two additions, mixing until the flour is absorbed. Scrape down the sides of the mixing bowl with a rubber spatula to keep the dough even-textured. Blend in the chocolate chips. *Dough texture observation* The dough will be heavy, dense, and damp.

Bake the ovals of dough fully, so that later on the rusks will be tender–crunchy rather than doughy–tough.

ASSEMBLE THE DOUGH ON THE COOKIE SHEETS Using a sturdy rubber spatula, place one-third of the dough in a rough elongated oval on one of the lined cookie sheets or sheet pans. Moisten your fingers with cold water. Shape and smooth the mass of dough into a slightly elongated oval, measuring about 4½ inches wide and 8 inches long. Pat the sides of the dough to neaten it. Place half of the remaining dough on the second cookie sheet, and the remainder on the third sheet. Shape and level the dough.

BAKE AND COOL THE OVALS OF DOUGH Bake the ovals of dough for 34 to 38 minutes, or until completely set. A wooden pick inserted in the center of each baked oval will withdraw clean. Each oval of dough will expand somewhat as it bakes.

Let the ovals stand on the baking sheets for 5 minutes. Carefully transfer them, still on their parchment paper bases, to cooling racks. Cool for 25 to 30 minutes, or until tepid. Cool the cookie or baking sheets. *Cooling observation* The ovals of dough must be cool enough to slice evenly and neatly.

Reduce the oven temperature to 300 degrees F.

SLICE THE OVALS OF DOUGH INTO RUSKS Have the cooled cookie sheets or sheet pans at your work surface. Working with one oval at a time, slip an offset flexible palette knife under it and slide it onto a cutting board. With a serrated knife, cut each cooled oval into long ¾-inch-thick slices. Arrange the rusks on cooled, unlined cookie or baking sheets, cut side down.

SLOW-BAKE AND COOL THE RUSKS Bake the rusks for about 15 minutes (in total) to dry them out, or until they are firm and dry. Turn the rusks twice during this time. Baking them again at a low temperature makes them rigid and crunchy.

Let the rusks stand on the baking sheets for 10 minutes, then carefully transfer them to cooling racks, using a pair of sturdy tongs. Cool completely.

❅ *For an aromatic topnote of flavor,* use intensified vanilla extract (see page 52) in place of plain vanilla extract in the batter/dough.

❅ *For a textural contrast,* blend ⅓ cup chopped walnuts into the batter/dough along with the chocolate chips.

FRESHLY BAKED, THE RUSKS KEEP FOR 2 TO 3 WEEKS.

Variations: For mocha rusks with Dutch-process black cocoa, use 2 tablespoons Dutch-process black cocoa and ⅔ cup unsweetened, alkalized cocoa in the rusk batter/dough.

For mocha rusks with bittersweet chocolate chunks, substitute 9 ounces bittersweet chocolate, coarsely chopped, for the semisweet chocolate chips.

MOCHA TRUFFLE COOKIES

About 4 dozen cookies

SOFT, SOPHISTICATED, AND RICH, these tinged-with-coffee, packed-with-pecans-and-bittersweet-chocolate cookies are tender, intense, and easy to make.

This cookie dough is chunky. Pieces of chopped bittersweet chocolate and nuts ramble throughout, and the soft, creamy dough melds beautifully with the flavoring agents. The combined amount of flour along with cocoa powder binds the ingredients correctly; cocoa, which is a starch, helps to set, color, and flavor the dough. Mounds of cookie dough are baked in an oven preheated to 325° F. The low oven temperature helps to establish the texture of the cookies and bake them until softly firm throughout, without overbaking the interiors, muddying the taste of the chocolate, or drying out the edges.

This recipe was inspired by three sources: from one of my paternal grandmother's brownie recipes, which was reasonably light on cake flour and positively jam-packed with butter and chocolate; and from two of my mother's recipes, one for a dense French chocolate cake, the other for a Southern fudge-nut cookie. A creamy, dark chocolate cookie dough that's made with cake flour, cocoa, a minimal amount of butter, and plenty of semisweet chocolate, these Savannah Chocolate Drops probably had the greatest influence of all. I tweaked all three formulas into a cookie dough by overwhelming it with good bittersweet chocolate (to create the taste-and-texture experience of eating truffle candies), minimizing the amount of sugar (because the bittersweet chocolate provided just the right amount of sweetness), adding an abundance of nuts, and using

MOCHA COOKIE DOUGH

2½ teaspoons instant (not granular) espresso powder

2¾ teaspoons pure vanilla extract

⅓ cup unsifted bleached all-purpose flour

3 tablespoons plus 2 teaspoons unsifted bleached cake flour

3 tablespoons unsweetened, alkalized cocoa

¼ teaspoon baking powder

¼ teaspoon baking soda

⅛ teaspoon cream of tartar

¼ teaspoon salt

13 ounces bittersweet chocolate, melted and cooled to tepid

3 ounces (3 squares) unsweetened chocolate, melted and cooled to tepid

5 tablespoons unsalted butter, melted and cooled to tepid

3 large eggs

3 large egg yolks

1⅓ cups plus 2 tablespoons superfine sugar

BITTERSWEET CHOCOLATE AND PECAN STIR-IN

15 ounces bittersweet chocolate, chopped into small chunks

2½ cups pecan halves and pieces (or 2 cups very coarsely chopped pecans)

several cookie sheets

a small quantity—just enough to bind the ingredients—of bleached all-purpose and bleached cake flour. I also incorporated cocoa powder to raise the overall chocolate intensity of the dough.

PREHEAT THE OVEN AND PREPARE THE COOKIE SHEETS Preheat the oven to 325° F. Line the cookie sheets with lengths of cooking parchment paper; set aside.

MIX THE MOCHA COOKIE DOUGH In a small ramekin, combine the espresso powder and vanilla extract; set aside.

Sift the all-purpose flour, cake flour, cocoa, baking powder, baking soda, cream of tartar, and salt onto a sheet of waxed paper.

Beat the melted bittersweet chocolate, melted unsweetened chocolate, and melted butter in the large bowl of a freestanding electric mixer on moderate speed for 30 seconds to 1 minute, or until just combined. Blend in the whole eggs and egg yolks, and mix until just combined. Blend in the superfine sugar and vanilla extract-espresso blend. Mix on moderately low speed for 1 to 2 minutes, or until well combined. *Beating observation* Do not beat until aerated and lightened in texture or it will spoil the tender fudge texture of the baked cookies. On low speed, add the sifted mixture and mix just until the particles of flour are absorbed. Scrape down the sides of the mixing bowl two or three times with a rubber spatula to keep the cookie dough even-textured.

INCORPORATE THE BITTERSWEET CHOCOLATE AND PECAN STIR-IN AND ADD TO THE COOKIE DOUGH Add the bittersweet chocolate chunks and pecans to the batter, and with a wooden spoon (or sturdy rubber spatula), stir the additions into the chocolate mixture. *Dough texture observation* The dough will be creamy-thick and chunky with chocolate and nuts. Let dough stand for 4 to 5 minutes. It will firm up slightly as it stands.

SPOON THE DOUGH ONTO THE PREPARED COOKIE SHEETS Spoon generous 2-tablespoon-size mounds of dough onto the lined cookie sheets, spacing the mounds about 3 inches apart. Place nine mounds of dough on each sheet.

BEST BAKING ADVICE
Allowing the cookies to cool completely on sheets of parchment paper keeps them moist and creamy-textured.

BAKE AND COOL THE COOKIES Bake the cookies in the preheated oven for 15 to 16 minutes, or until just set (the interiors should be softly set). The tops of the baked cookies will have small hairline cracks here and there—this is traditional. Let the cookies stand on the sheets for 10 minutes, then remove them to clean sheets of parchment paper, using an offset metal spatula.

❋ *For an aromatic topnote of flavor,* use intensified vanilla extract (see page 52) in place of plain vanilla extract in the cookie dough.

FRESHLY BAKED, THE COOKIES KEEP FOR 2 DAYS.

Variations: For mocha truffle cookies with Dutch-process black cocoa, substitute 1 tablespoon Dutch-process black cocoa for the unsweetened, alkalized cocoa. Use 2 tablespoons unsweetened, alkalized cocoa.

For bittersweet chocolate cookies, an all-chocolate version of this cookie without the undertone of coffee, omit the vanilla extract-espresso blend. Instead, add 2½ teaspoons pure vanilla extract after the superfine sugar has been incorporated.

ESPRESSO CHOCOLATE CHIP SHORTBREAD
One 9½-inch shortbread, creating 12 triangular pieces

THERE ARE TWO KEY ELEMENTS in flavoring the dough: to build the taste of the cookie, the instant espresso powder is dissolved in the flavoring extract, rather than hot water; and the dough is sweetened exclusively with brown sugar to frame the taste of the coffee. You can dress up triangles of this chocolate-laced, coffee-flavored shortbread with the Caramel Nut Topping on page 232. Decked out in a cover of drizzly caramel, this sweet becomes a sublime holiday cookie.

PREHEAT THE OVEN AND PREPARE THE TART PAN Preheat the oven to 350° F. Have the tart pan at hand.

MAKE THE COFFEE-CHOCOLATE CHIP SHORTBREAD DOUGH Place the espresso powder in a ramekin, stir in the vanilla extract, and mix well; set aside.

Sift the all-purpose flour, cake flour, rice flour, baking powder, and salt onto a sheet of waxed paper.

2 teaspoons instant (not granular)
    espresso powder

2 teaspoons pure vanilla extract

1 cup unsifted bleached all-purpose
    flour

¼ cup unsifted bleached cake flour

¼ cup rice flour

¼ teaspoon baking powder

⅛ teaspoon salt

12 tablespoons (1½ sticks) unsalted
    butter, softened

⅓ cup firmly packed light brown
    sugar, sieved if lumpy

1 teaspoon pure vanilla extract

1 cup semisweet chocolate chips

About 2 tablespoons granulated sugar,
    for sprinkling on top of the baked
    shortbread

BAKEWARE

fluted 9½-inch round tart pan (with a
    removable bottom)

Cream the butter in the large bowl of a freestanding electric mixer for 3 minutes on low speed. Add the light brown sugar and vanilla extract, and continue creaming for 2 minutes longer. Add the flour mixture and combine slowly to form a soft, smooth dough. Scrape down the sides of the mixing bowl once or twice to keep the dough even-textured. Blend in the chocolate chips.

PRESS THE DOUGH INTO THE PAN Place the dough in the pan and press it into an even layer, using your fingertips to push the dough out to the sides and gently pat down the top.

With the tines of a fork, prick the dough lightly in 12 to 15 random places.

BAKE, COOL, AND CUT THE SHORTBREAD Bake the shortbread in the preheated oven for 30 to 35 minutes, or until set and firm.

Let the shortbread stand in the pan on a cooling rack for 10 minutes, Carefully unmold the shortbread, removing the outer ring. Leave the shortbread on its round base and cool for 10 to 15 minutes. With a sharp chef's knife, cut the cookie into wedges. Cool completely.

※ *For an aromatic topnote of flavor,* use intensified vanilla extract (see page 52) in place of plain vanilla extract in the shortbread dough.

※ *For a textural contrast,* blend ⅓ cup chopped walnuts or pecans into the shortbread dough along with the chocolate chips.

FRESHLY BAKED, THE COOKIE KEEPS FOR 1 WEEK.

BEST BAKING ADVICE
The combination of all-purpose flour, cake flour, and rice flour produces a beautifully tender, pleasingly sandy cookie. Rice flour is essential to its texture, but you can use 1¼ cups bleached all-purpose flour and omit the cake flour.

MOCHA CHIP POUND CAKE

One 10-inch cake, creating about 20 slices

WITH ITS SUPERB KEEPING QUALITIES and soft chocolate taste, this big, chip-spotted butter cake has a tempered mocha flavor and moist crumb.

Shortening and bleached all-purpose flour, for preparing the cake pan

MOCHA-CHOCOLATE CHIP-SOUR CREAM CAKE BATTER

2½ teaspoons instant (not granular) espresso powder

2 teaspoons pure vanilla extract

¼ teaspoon hot water

2¾ cups unsifted bleached all-purpose flour

¼ cup unsifted bleached cake flour

⅓ cup plus 1 tablespoon unsweetened, alkalized cocoa

⅛ teaspoon baking powder

⅛ teaspoon baking soda

1 teaspoon salt

2 cups miniature semisweet chocolate chips

½ pound (16 tablespoons or 2 sticks) unsalted butter, softened

2 cups granulated sugar

¾ cup firmly packed light brown sugar, sieved if lumpy

5 large eggs

1 cup thick, cultured sour cream

2 tablespoons heavy cream

Coffee Syrup (see page 57), for brushing on the warm, baked cake

PREHEAT THE OVEN AND PREPARE THE CAKE PAN Preheat the oven to 325° F. Grease the inside of the tube pan with shortening. Line the bottom of the pan with a circle of waxed paper cut to fit, and grease the paper. Dust the inside of the pan with all-purpose flour. Tap out any excess flour; set aside.

MIX THE MOCHA-CHOCOLATE CHIP-SOUR CREAM CAKE BATTER Combine the espresso powder, vanilla extract, and hot water in a small ramekin.

Sift the all-purpose flour, cake flour, cocoa, baking powder, baking soda, and salt onto a sheet of waxed paper. In a medium-size mixing bowl, toss the chocolate chips with 1 tablespoon of the sifted mixture.

Cream the butter in the large bowl of a freestanding electric mixer on moderate speed for 2 minutes. Add the granulated sugar in three additions, beating for about 1 minute after each portion is added. Add the light brown sugar and beat for a minute longer. Blend in the eggs, one at a time, beating for 45 seconds after each addition. Scrape down the sides of the mixing bowl frequently with a rubber spatula to keep the batter even-textured. Blend in the coffee-vanilla extract mixture.

On low speed, add the sifted ingredients in three additions with the sour cream in two additions, beginning and ending with the sifted mixture. Blend in the heavy cream. Scrape down the sides of the mixing bowl frequently with a rubber spatula to keep the batter even-textured. Stir in the chocolate chips.

Spoon the batter into the prepared pan. Smooth the top lightly, using a rubber spatula.

Vanilla Whipped Cream (see page 530), to accompany the cake (optional)

BAKEWARE

plain 10-inch tube pan

BAKE THE CAKE Bake the cake for 1 hour and 20 minutes to 1 hour and 25 minutes, or until risen, set, and a wooden pick inserted in the cake withdraws clean. The baked cake will pull away slightly from the sides of the baking pan.

COOL AND APPLY THE FINISH TO THE WARM CAKE Cool the cake in the pan on a rack for 5 to 10 minutes. Carefully invert the cake onto another cooling rack, peel off the waxed paper circle, then invert again to cool right side up.

Using a soft, 1-inch-wide pastry brush, paint the coffee wash on the top and sides of the cake. Cool completely before slicing and serving. *Slicing observation* Use a serrated knife to cut the cake neatly and cleanly.

❋ *For an aromatic topnote of flavor,* use intensified vanilla extract (see page 52) in place of plain vanilla extract in the cake batter.

❋ *For a textural contrast,* stir ½ cup chopped walnuts into the cake batter along with the chocolate chips.

FRESHLY BAKED, THE CAKE KEEPS FOR 5 DAYS.

Variations: For mocha double chip pound cake, use 1 cup cappuccino-flavored chips and 1 cup miniature semisweet chocolate chips.

For mocha chip pound cake with Dutch-process black cocoa, use 2 tablespoons plus 1 teaspoon Dutch-process black cocoa and ¼ cup unsweetened, alkalized cocoa in the cake batter.

BEST BAKING ADVICE
To keep the baked crumb of the cake velvety, use softened (but not oily) butter, and mix the batter carefully with each addition of the sifted ingredients. The particles of flour should be integrated and absorbed, but take care not to overbeat the batter, which would create a less than tender texture.

COFFEE AND MILK CHOCOLATE CHIP CAKE

One 10-inch fluted tube cake, creating 16 slices

CREAMY MORSELS OF MILK CHOCOLATE drift through a brown sugar and coffee-endowed batter in this simple, homestyle coffee cake. The way in which the coffee flavor unfolds in the cake is simple—powdered espresso is dissolved in the vanilla extract, then combined with buttermilk. The vanilla extract, in addition to the hint of cinnamon and nutmeg, boosts the coffee taste.

Nonstick cookware spray, for preparing the cake pan

COFFEE-BROWN SUGAR-CHOCOLATE CHIP BUTTER CAKE BATTER

2¾ teaspoons instant (not granular) espresso powder

2 teaspoons pure vanilla extract

1 cup buttermilk

3 cups unsifted bleached all-purpose flour

2¼ teaspoons baking powder

½ teaspoon baking soda

1 teaspoon salt

¼ teaspoon ground cinnamon

¼ teaspoon freshly grated nutmeg

2 cups milk chocolate chips

12 tablespoons (1½ sticks) unsalted butter, softened

¼ cup shortening

1 cup firmly packed light brown sugar, sieved if lumpy

¾ cup plus 1 tablespoon granulated sugar

4 large eggs

PREHEAT THE OVEN AND PREPARE THE CAKE PAN Preheat the oven to 350° F. Film the inside of the Bundt pan with nonstick cooking spray, and set aside.

MIX THE COFFEE-BROWN SUGAR-CHOCOLATE CHIP BUT-TER CAKE BATTER Combine the espresso powder and vanilla extract in a mixing bowl, and mix well to dissolve the coffee. Whisk in the buttermilk. Set aside.

Sift the flour, baking powder, baking soda, salt, cinnamon, and nutmeg onto a sheet of waxed paper. In a medium-size mixing bowl, toss the milk chocolate chips with 1 tablespoon of the sifted mixture.

Cream the butter and shortening in the large bowl of a free-standing electric mixer on moderately low speed for 3 minutes. Add the light brown sugar and beat for 1 minute; add the granulated sugar and beat for 1 to 2 minutes longer. Beat in the eggs, one at a time, blending well after each addition.

On low speed, alternately add the sifted ingredients in three additions with the buttermilk-espresso mixture in two additions, beginning and ending with the dry ingredients. Scrape down the sides of the mixing bowl frequently with a rubber spatula to keep the batter even-textured. *Batter texture observation* The batter will be moderately thick and creamy. Stir in the milk chocolate chips.

Coffee-Sugar Wash (see page 60), for applying to the baked cake

BAKEWARE
10-inch Bundt pan

BEST BAKING ADVICE
Use softened, not oily, butter. Thoroughly stir the floured milk chocolate chips into the batter.

Spoon the batter into the prepared Bundt pan. Smooth over the top with a rubber spatula.

BAKE AND COOL THE CAKE Bake the cake in the preheated oven for 50 to 55 minutes, or until risen, set, and a wooden pick inserted in the cake withdraws clean. The baked cake will pull away slightly from the sides of the baking pan. Let the cake stand in the pan on a cooling rack for 5 to 8 minutes. Invert the cake onto another cooling rack. Place a sheet of waxed paper under the cooling rack to catch any drips of glaze or topping.

APPLY THE WASH TO THE BAKED CAKE Using a soft, 1-inch-wide pastry brush, paint the coffee-sugar wash over the top and sides of the cake. Cool completely before slicing and serving. *Slicing observation* Use a serrated knife to cut the cake neatly and cleanly.

❀ *For an aromatic topnote of flavor,* use intensified vanilla extract (see page 52) in place of plain vanilla extract in the cake batter.

FRESHLY BAKED, THE CAKE KEEPS FOR 2 TO 3 DAYS.

Variation: For coffee and cappuccino chip cake, substitute 2 cups cappuccino-flavored chips for the milk chocolate chips.

MOCHA PECAN WAFFLES

5 deep, Belgian-style 2-sided waffles,
each waffle section measuring 4½ by 4½ inches

Cocoa powder and coffee-scented milk are the dominant flavoring agents in this playful dessert waffle batter reinforced with chopped pecans and milk chocolate. As the batter cooks, the bits of milk chocolate become small pools that turn into sweet pockets of flavor.

MOCHA PECAN WAFFLE BATTER

1¼ cups milk

1 tablespoon plus 2 teaspoons instant (not granular) espresso powder

1¼ cups unsifted bleached all-purpose flour

¼ cup unsifted bleached cake flour

⅔ cup plus 2 tablespoons unsweetened, alkalized cocoa

1¼ teaspoons baking powder

½ teaspoon baking soda

¼ teaspoon salt

1 cup superfine sugar

3 large eggs

2 teaspoons pure vanilla extract

¼ pound (8 tablespoons or 1 stick) unsalted butter, melted and cooled to tepid

3 (1.55 ounces each) milk chocolate candy bars (Hershey's Milk Chocolate), chopped into small chunks

¾ cup chopped pecans

Confectioners' sugar, for sprinkling over the waffles

MAKE THE MOCHA PECAN WAFFLE BATTER Heat ¼ cup milk in a small saucepan until very warm, stir in the espresso powder, and remove from the heat. Pour into a medium-size heatproof bowl. Cool for 10 minutes, then stir in the remaining milk and cool completely.

Sift the all-purpose flour, cake flour, cocoa, baking powder, baking soda, salt, and superfine sugar into a large mixing bowl.

In a medium-size mixing bowl, whisk together the eggs, vanilla extract, melted butter, and cooled coffee-milk.

Pour the liquid ingredients over the sifted mixture, add the chopped milk chocolate and pecans, and stir to form a batter. Mix until all the particles of flour are absorbed, using a wooden spoon or flat wooden paddle. Scrape down the sides of the mixing bowl with a rubber spatula and mix briefly.

MAKE THE WAFFLES Preheat a deep-dish waffle iron. Spoon a generous ⅓ cup of batter onto the center of each square (this allows the batter to flow out toward all sides as the waffle iron is closed). Cook the waffles until set, 1 minute to 1 minute and 15 seconds, and serve.

Variations: For mocha pecan waffles with Dutch-process black cocoa, use 2 tablespoons Dutch-process black cocoa and ⅔ cup unsweetened, alkalized cocoa in the waffle batter.

For mocha pecan waffles with cappuccino chips, add ½ cup cappuccino-flavored chips to the batter along with the chopped milk chocolate and pecans.

ICED COFFEE CHOCOLATE LAYER CAKE

One two-layer, 9-inch cake, creating about 12 slices

Y EARS AGO, my mother made a chocolate layer cake with brewed coffee, and she assembled the cake with a creamy chocolate filling, then enveloped the whole cake in frosting—a delicious idea. The addition of ice-cold coffee to a creamed batter creates a chocolate layer cake with a divine texture. This is my version of her cake batter, which I've intensified with a fanciful coffee pastry cream filling, a direct and delicious contrast to the frosting.

Shortening and bleached all-purpose flour, for preparing the layer cake pans

ICED COFFEE-CHOCOLATE LAYER CAKE BATTER

1¾ cups unsifted bleached all-purpose flour

½ cup unsifted bleached cake flour

1¼ teaspoons baking powder

¼ teaspoon baking soda

¼ teaspoon salt

10 tablespoons (1 stick plus 2 tablespoons) unsalted butter, softened

1⅓ cups plus 3 tablespoons granulated sugar

3 large eggs

2 teaspoons pure vanilla extract

3 ounces (3 squares) unsweetened chocolate, melted and cooled

¾ cup strong brewed coffee, cold

2 tablespoons milk

Coffee Cream Filling (see page 373), for spreading between the cake layers

Buttery Chocolate Frosting (see page 285), for spreading on the baked cake layers

BAKEWARE

two 9-inch round layer cake pans

PREHEAT THE OVEN AND PREPARE THE LAYER CAKE PANS
Preheat the oven to 350° F. Lightly grease the inside of the cake pans with shortening. Line the bottom of each pan with a circle of waxed paper, grease the paper, and dust the inside with all-purpose flour. Tap out any excess flour; set aside.

MIX THE ICED COFFEE-CHOCOLATE LAYER CAKE BATTER
Sift the all-purpose flour, cake flour, baking powder, baking soda, and salt onto a sheet of waxed paper.

Cream the butter in the large bowl of a freestanding electric mixer on moderately low speed for 2 to 3 minutes. Add half of the granulated sugar and beat for 1 to 2 minutes; add the balance of the sugar, and continue beating for 1 minute longer. Blend in the eggs, one at a time, beating for 30 to 45 seconds after each addition. Blend in the vanilla extract and melted unsweetened chocolate.

On low speed, alternately add the sifted mixture in three additions with the cold coffee in two additions, beginning and ending with the sifted mixture. Scrape down the sides of the mixing bowl frequently with a rubber spatula to keep the batter even-textured. Blend in the milk. *Batter texture observation* The batter will be billowy, thick and creamy.

Spoon the batter into the prepared cake pans, dividing it evenly between them. Level the batter with a rubber spatula.

BAKE AND COOL THE CAKE LAYERS Bake the layers for 30 minutes, or until set and a wooden pick inserted 1 inch from the center of each cake layer withdraws clean. The baked layers will pull away slightly from the sides of the baking pans. Let the cake layers stand in the pans on cooling racks for 5 minutes.

Invert each layer onto another cooling rack, peel off the waxed paper round, then invert again to cool right side up. Cool completely.

ASSEMBLE AND FROST THE CAKE Tear off four 3-inch-wide strips of waxed paper. Place the strips in the shape of a square around the outer 3 inches of a cake plate. Center one cake layer on the plate; the layer will partially cover the waxed paper square; the strips should extend by at least 1 inch.

With a flexible palette knife, spread all of the coffee cream filling to ¼ inch of the edge of the cake layer, smoothing it over as you go.

Carefully place the second layer on top, then ice the entire cake in sweeps of frosting, using a flexible palette knife. When the frosting has set (usually about 45 minutes in a cool kitchen), gently slide out and discard the waxed paper strips.

Cut the cake into slices for serving. The cream-filled cake is delicate and must be refrigerated within 2 hours of assembly. Serve the cake on the day it is baked, filled, and frosted.

❉ *For an aromatic topnote of flavor,* use intensified vanilla extract (see page 52) in place of plain vanilla extract in the cake batter.

COFFEE CREAM FILLING

About 1 cup

*T*HE FLAVOR OF THIS PASTRY CREAM, rich and coffee-scented, is especially marvelous sandwiched between layers of cake.

COFFEE CREAM FILLING

1 cup light (table) cream

2 tablespoons heavy cream

½ teaspoon instant (not granular) espresso powder

1 tablespoon cornstarch

⅓ cup plus 1 tablespoon superfine sugar

pinch of salt

3 large egg yolks

½ teaspoon pure vanilla extract

2 teaspoons unsalted butter, softened

MAKE THE COFFEE CREAM FILLING Place the table cream, heavy cream, and espresso powder in a small saucepan; set over moderately low heat to dissolve the coffee and warm the liquid. Whisk once or twice as the mixture is heating. When the cream mixture is warm and the coffee has dissolved completely, remove the saucepan from the heat. Cool to tepid.

Sift the cornstarch, superfine sugar, and salt into a small (5-cup), heavy saucepan (preferably enameled cast iron). Whisk the sugar-cornstarch mixture well to combine. Whisk in the egg yolks. Place a small fine-meshed sieve over the saucepan and add 1 tablespoon of the tepid cream-milk mixture, and immediately stir it in. Add 3 more tablespoons of the liquid in this way to temper the egg yolks. Add the remaining liquid in three additions, mixing well. *Straining observation* Straining the liquid into the yolk mixture through a sieve keeps back any fragments of film that may have formed on top of the liquid.

Bring the filling mixture to a boil over gentle heat, stirring slowly all the while with a wooden spoon. As soon as the thickened cream comes to a low boil, regulate the heat so that it bubbles gently for about 1 minute to 1 minute and 30 seconds. *Cream filling texture observation* The cream filling will be smooth if you watch over the cooking carefully and bring the mixture to a boil slowly; otherwise it will form small lumps. If small lumps appear, the cream filling will smooth out when strained in the next step.

STRAIN AND FLAVOR THE CREAM Press the cream through a fine-meshed sieve into a heatproof bowl. Slowly stir in the vanilla extract and butter. Quickly press a sheet of plastic wrap directly over the surface of the cream to prevent a skin from forming. Cool. Refrigerate the cream in an airtight container for at least 6 hours before using. The cream can be made a day in advance and stored in the refrigerator.

MEGA MOCHA PECAN CHIP MUFFINS

11 jumbo muffins

THESE ARE LIVELY, TEXTURAL MUFFINS, what with the pecans, chocolate chips, substantial crumble mixture, and mocha batter creating a compelling combination. Enjoy them freshly baked, when all the full, rounded flavors come forward.

Nonstick cooking spray, for preparing the muffin pans

PECAN CHIP STREUSEL

⅔ cup plus 3 tablespoons unsifted bleached all-purpose flour

pinch of salt

⅔ cup firmly packed light brown sugar, sieved if lumpy

7 tablespoons (1 stick less 1 tablespoon) unsalted butter, cool, cut into chunks

½ teaspoon pure vanilla extract

½ cup chopped pecans

½ cup miniature semisweet chocolate chips

MOCHA CHIP MUFFIN BATTER

1 tablespoon plus 2 teaspoons instant (not granular) espresso powder

2 teaspoons pure vanilla extract

3⅓ cups plus 3 tablespoons unsifted bleached all-purpose flour

3 tablespoons unsweetened, alkalized cocoa

3½ teaspoons baking powder

½ teaspoon baking soda

¾ teaspoon salt

¼ teaspoon freshly grated nutmeg

1⅓ cups miniature semisweet chocolate chips

PREHEAT THE OVEN AND PREPARE THE MUFFIN PANS Preheat the oven to 375° F. Film the inside of the crown muffin cups with nonstick cooking spray; set aside.

MAKE THE PECAN CHIP STREUSEL Thoroughly combine the flour, salt, and light brown sugar in a medium-size mixing bowl. Toss over the chunks of butter and, using a pastry blender, cut in the fat until reduced to small nuggets, about the size of small dried lima beans. Add the vanilla extract. Spoon in the pecans and chocolate chips. Firmly knead-and-crumble the mixture together with your fingers until reduced to moist, cohesive lumps.

MAKE THE MOCHA CHIP MUFFIN BATTER Combine the espresso powder and vanilla extract in a small ramekin; set aside.

Sift the flour, cocoa, baking powder, baking soda, salt, and nutmeg into a large mixing bowl. In a small mixing bowl, toss the chocolate chips and pecans with 1 tablespoon of the sifted mixture.

In a medium-size mixing bowl, whisk the melted butter, melted shortening, light brown sugar, granulated sugar, eggs, and vanilla extract-espresso mixture. Thoroughly blend in the milk-cream mixture. Pour the liquid ingredients over the dry ingredients, add the chocolate chips and pecans, and stir with a wooden spoon or flat wooden paddle to form a batter. Make sure that all particles of flour are absorbed into the batter.

FILL THE MUFFIN CUPS AND TOP THE UNBAKED MUFFINS WITH THE CRUMBLE MIXTURE Spoon the batter into the prepared muffin cups (each cup will be a generous three-fourths full),

¾ cup chopped pecans

6 tablespoons (¾ stick) unsalted butter, melted and cooled

3 tablespoons shortening, melted and cooled

1 cup firmly packed light brown sugar, sieved if lumpy

3 tablespoons granulated sugar

4 large eggs

1 cup milk blended with ⅓ cup plus 3 tablespoons light (table) cream

BAKEWARE

11 jumbo, crown top muffin cups (two pans, each holding six individual muffin cups), each cup measuring about 3¼ inches in diameter and 2 inches deep, with a capacity of scant cup

dividing it evenly among them. Scatter and lightly pat down 2 to 3 rounded tablespoons of the crumble mixture onto the top of each muffin.

BAKE AND COOL THE MUFFINS Bake the muffins for 25 minutes, or until risen, set, and a wooden pick inserted in the center of a baked muffin will withdraw clean, or with a few moist crumbs adhering to it. Place the muffin pans on cooling racks. Let the muffins stand for 20 minutes, then carefully remove them to another cooling rack. Serve warm the muffins warm or at room temperature.

❋ *For an aromatic topnote of flavor,* use intensified vanilla extract (see page 52) in place of plain vanilla extract in the streusel mixture and muffin batter.

FRESHLY BAKED, THE MUFFINS KEEP FOR 2 TO 3 DAYS.

Variation: For mega mocha pecan chip muffins with Dutch-process black cocoa, use 1 tablespoon Dutch-process black cocoa and 2 tablespoons unsweetened, alkalized cocoa in the muffin batter.

*t*he potency of ginger, in the form of ground ginger, grated fresh gingerroot, chopped crystallized ginger, or ginger preserved in syrup, comes through directly—and pungently—in a batter or dough. For the heat of the spice to be appealing, it needs to be balanced by a sweetener (primarily granulated sugar, brown sugar, honey, or molasses, alone or in combination), modified by the presence of butter, milk, sour cream, or buttermilk, and pointed up with a spoonful of vanilla extract.

Although zesty in its own right, the flavor of ginger is emphasized when used along with other spices, such as cinnamon, nutmeg, allspice, cloves, and cardamom, which broaden its taste and complexity. In baked goods, ginger also requires a certain amount of butter for enrichment and balance.

Powdered China #1 Ginger (see "Selected Sources") has a bold character and direct flavor, and is wonderful to use in my Spicy Gingerbread Cookies, Ginger Butter Balls, Gingerbread Waffles, and Spicy Molasses Gingerbread.

16

GINGER

PUMPKIN GINGER CAKE

One 9 by 9-inch cake, creating 12 squares

PUMPKIN PUREE, ADDED TO A BATTER, makes it particularly moist, soft-textured, and slightly dense. The taste of the pumpkin is enhanced by the molasses and brown sugar, and the spices scent the batter in a fragrant way. This plain (but delicious) cake is modeled after my Spicy Molasses Gingerbread on page 391, and my mother's buttermilk pumpkin spice cake. It can be graced with nuts, seeds, or dried fruit: vary the look and taste by adding ½ cup chopped walnuts, ⅓ cup lightly toasted pumpkin seeds, ½ cup golden or dark raisins, or ¾ cup diced dried apricots to the batter just before it's turned into the baking pan. Any additions should be dusted in a light coating of the sifted flour mixture (about 1 teaspoon for the nuts and 2 teaspoons for the fruit) before incorporation into the batter. Warm squares of the cake would be a lavish addition to the Thanksgiving bread basket.

Softened unsalted butter and bleached all-purpose flour, for preparing the baking pan

PUMPKIN GINGERBREAD BATTER

2⅓ cups plus 2 tablespoons unsifted all-purpose flour

¾ teaspoon baking soda

¼ teaspoon baking powder

¼ teaspoon salt

2½ teaspoons ground ginger

¾ teaspoon ground cinnamon

½ teaspoon freshly grated nutmeg

¼ teaspoon ground cloves

6 tablespoons (¾ stick) unsalted butter, softened

2 tablespoons shortening

¼ cup granulated sugar

¼ cup firmly packed light brown sugar, sieved if lumpy

2 large eggs

2 teaspoons pure vanilla extract

⅔ cup plain pumpkin puree

⅓ cup plus 2 tablespoons mild, unsulphured molasses

⅔ cup plus 1 tablespoon buttermilk

BAKEWARE

9 by 9 by 2-inch baking pan

PREHEAT THE OVEN AND PREPARE THE BAKING PAN Preheat the oven to 350° F. Lightly butter and flour the baking pan. Tap out any excess flour; set aside.

MIX THE PUMPKIN GINGER CAKE BATTER Sift the flour, baking soda, baking powder, salt, ginger, cinnamon, nutmeg, and cloves onto a sheet of waxed paper.

Cream the butter and shortening in the large bowl of a free-standing electric mixer on moderately low speed for 2 to 3 minutes. Add the granulated sugar and beat for 1 minute; add the light brown sugar and beat for a minute longer. Blend in the eggs. Blend in the vanilla extract and the pumpkin puree. Add the molasses and beat on low speed for 1 to 2 minutes, or until thoroughly combined. *Batter appearance observation* The batter will look curdled at this point.

On low speed, add the sifted flour mixture in three additions with the buttermilk in two additions, mixing just until the particles of flour are absorbed. Scrape down the sides of the mixing bowl frequently with a rubber spatula to keep the batter even-textured. *Batter texture observation* The batter will be moderately thick and creamy.

Spoon the batter into the prepared baking pan. Smooth over the top with a rubber spatula.

BAKE AND COOL THE GINGER CAKE Bake the cake for 35 minutes, or until risen, set, and a wooden pick inserted in the cake withdraws clean. Let the cake stand in the pan on a cooling rack. Serve the cake warm or at room temperature, cut into squares directly from the pan.

❋ *For an extra surge of flavor,* toss ¼ cup finely chopped crystallized ginger with ½ teaspoon of the sifted mixture and stir into the batter after the last portion of flour has been added.

❋ *For an aromatic topnote of flavor,* use intensified vanilla extract (see page 52) in place of plain vanilla extract in the cake batter.

FRESHLY BAKED, THE CAKE KEEPS FOR 4 DAYS.

CHOCOLATE-GINGER SOUFFLÉ CAKE

One 9-inch cake, creating 8 to 10 slices

THE ZIP OF CRYSTALLIZED GINGER, paired with the intensity of bittersweet chocolate, makes this cake sing.

Softened unsalted butter and unsweetened, alkalized cocoa, for preparing the cake pan

CHOCOLATE-GINGER CAKE BATTER

5 eggs, separated

2 teaspoons pure vanilla extract

⅛ teaspoon salt

½ cup superfine sugar sifted with 2 tablespoons unsweetened, alkalized cocoa and ¼ teaspoon ground ginger

¼ pound (8 tablespoons or 1 stick) unsalted butter, melted and cooled to tepid

12 ounces bittersweet chocolate, melted and cooled to tepid

½ cup minced crystallized ginger

¼ teaspoon cream of tartar

Vanilla Whipped Cream (see page 530), to accompany the cake (optional)

BAKEWARE

9-inch springform pan (2¾ inches deep)

PREHEAT THE OVEN AND PREPARE THE CAKE PAN Preheat the oven to 350° F. Lightly butter the inside of the springform pan. Dust the inside of the pan with unsweetened, alkalized cocoa. Tap out any excess cocoa; set aside.

MIX THE CHOCOLATE-GINGER CAKE BATTER Place the egg yolks and vanilla in a large mixing bowl and whisk for 30 to 45 seconds. Add the salt and resift the superfine sugar-cocoa-ground ginger mixture over the egg yolks; whisk for 1 minute, or until just combined.

In a small mixing bowl, thoroughly combine the melted butter and melted bittersweet chocolate with a rubber spatula or wooden spoon. *Mixture texture observation* The melted butter-chocolate mixture will be shiny and moderately thick.

Blend the butter-chocolate mixture into the egg yolk mixture, making sure that it's a uniform color. Stir in the crystallized ginger. *Mixture texture observation* The mixture will be thick.

Using an electric hand mixer, beat the egg whites in a clean, dry mixing bowl until just beginning to mound. Add the cream of tartar and continue beating until firm (not stiff) peaks are formed. Stir two large spoonfuls of the beaten whites into the chocolate batter, then fold in the remaining whites. *Folding texture observation* As you fold in the whites, the chocolate mixture will thicken and turn slightly ropy. Continue to mix the two components until the whites are integrated into the chocolate mixture. Carefully scrape the batter into the prepared springform pan. Smooth over the top lightly with a rubber spatula.

BAKE AND COOL THE CAKE Bake the cake for 30 to 35 minutes, or until risen and set. The center of the cake should be softly set and not at all wobbly. Cool the cake completely in the pan on a rack. As the cake cools, it will fall, leaving the surface somewhat uneven. Release the sides of the springform pan and cut the cake into wedges for serving. Serve the cake with dollops of whipped cream, if you wish.

FRESHLY BAKED, THE CAKE KEEPS FOR 1 DAY.

Variation: For chocolate-ginger soufflé with Dutch-process black cocoa, use 1 tablespoon Dutch-process black cocoa and 1 tablespoon unsweetened, alkalized cocoa in the sifted sugar-cocoa-ground ginger mixture for the cake batter.

SPICY GINGERBREAD COOKIES
About 3 dozen cookies using a 3-inch cutter

DEEPLY GINGERY, with brazen blasts of ground ginger, cinnamon, nutmeg, all-spice, and cloves, this batch of gingerbread cookies is spicy and full of savor. I love to stamp out the dough into traditional or fanciful shapes and decorate the baked cut-outs. I use gingerbread men and women from my collection of antique cutters, as well as some contemporary shapes, such as a big cactus, an old-fashioned tea pot, a slender chili pepper, a sensual(!) reclining woman, and a ballerina in mid-air. For the best results, this recipe guides you in working with well-chilled dough that is quick-frozen just before cutting; the absence of an overload of flour (which would ulti-mately toughen the dough) yields tender-textured cookies that look good and taste delicious.

GINGERBREAD COOKIE DOUGH

5¾ cups unsifted bleached all-purpose
    flour
1 teaspoon baking powder
1 teaspoon baking soda
1 teaspoon salt

MIX THE GINGERBREAD COOKIE DOUGH Whisk the flour, baking powder, baking soda, salt, ginger, cinnamon, nutmeg, all-spice, and cloves in a medium-size mixing bowl.

Cream the butter in the large bowl of a freestanding electric mixer on moderate speed for 2 to 3 minutes. Beat in the dark brown sugar and superfine sugar. Blend in the vanilla extract and

2 tablespoons ground ginger

1 tablespoon ground cinnamon

2 teaspoons freshly grated nutmeg

¾ teaspoon ground allspice

¾ teaspoon ground cloves

½ pound (16 tablespoons or 2 sticks) unsalted butter, softened

⅔ cup plus 1 tablespoon firmly packed dark brown sugar, sieved if lumpy

3 tablespoons superfine sugar

1 tablespoon pure vanilla extract

2 large eggs

¾ cup plus 2 tablespoons mild, unsulphured molasses

2 tablespoons honey

Granulated sugar or turbinado sugar, for sprinkling; or Royal Icing Made with Meringue Powder (see page 384)

BAKEWARE

several cookie sheets

eggs. Beat in the molasses and honey. Mix well. On low speed, add the whisked, spiced flour mixture, a third at a time, to the creamed mixture, beating just until the particles of flour have been absorbed. As the flour mixture is added, scrape down the sides of the mixing bowl frequently with a rubber spatula to keep the cookie dough even-textured.

ROLL THE DOUGH Divide the dough into four portions and roll each between two sheets of waxed paper to a thickness of a generous ¼ inch. Stack the sheets of dough on a cookie sheet. Refrigerate the dough overnight. Place the dough in the freezer 1 to 2 hours before cutting out and baking the cookies. *Dough freezing observation* Freezing the sheets of dough allows you to cut the cookies neatly.

PREHEAT THE OVEN AND PREPARE THE COOKIE SHEETS Preheat the oven to 350° F. Line several cookie sheets with lengths of cooking parchment paper; set aside.

CUT OUT THE COOKIES Working with one sheet of dough at a time from the freezer, peel off both sheets of waxed paper and place the dough on a lightly floured work surface. Stamp out cookies with a floured 3-inch cookie cutter and place them, 2½ inches apart, on the lined cookie sheets. If you are decorating the cookies with sprinklings of sugar, do so now. If you are making traditional gingerbread boys or girls, and are using raisins or currants for buttons or eyes, press them on at this point, too.

BAKE AND COOL THE COOKIES Bake the cookies for 10 to 12 minutes, or until set. Let the cookies rest on the sheet for 1 minute, then remove them to a cooling rack using a wide metal offset spatula. Cool completely before storing or decorating with icing.

Working with royal icing

COAT THE SURFACE OF THE COOKIE WITH ROYAL ICING You can cover the entire surface of each cookie with a smooth veneer of royal icing. Prepare the icing to a coating consistency: it should be as fluid as all-purpose Elmer's glue. You can adjust the density with water.

To ice the surface of a cookie with a coating of royal icing, use a firm, ½-inch-wide pastry brush, dip it into the icing, and smooth the icing on in light, large dabs, coaxing it to the edge. Actually painting on the icing leaves brush marks and uneven streaks. This takes a little practice, but goes along quickly once you understand how the icing behaves. Let the cookies stand until the icing is completely firm, 2 to 4 hours, before decorating further with additional royal icing piped through a pastry bag. This drying time is necessary so that any additional applications of colored icing do not meld into (or tint) the surface below.

At this point, you can apply very small candies to the cookies as soon as the icing begins to reach the point of setting (2 to 4 minutes, depending upon the ambient temperature of your kitchen and humidity in the air). Anything applied to the top of the cookies must be edible. Use a pair of clean tweezers to set the candies in place.

DECORATE THE COOKIES WITH ROYAL ICING To decorate with royal icing, use 10-inch pastry bags. Outfit the bag with the coupler and selected tip, twist and tuck about 1 inch of the bag into the tip, and bend a collar on the bag. Holding the bag by the inside of the collar, fill halfway full with the icing, undo the bottom twist, and flip up the collar. Carefully smooth the icing down toward the tip with your fingers, lightly twist the top to close, and squeeze (from the top) to decorate the cookie.

Working with many colors of royal icing observation When decorating the cookies with more than one overlapping color, you must let each color dry before applying the next one. If the colors are not dry, they will bleed together.

STORING COOKIES DECORATED WITH ROYAL ICING Let the decorated cookies stand until both the base coat icing and all decorative icing work applied with a pastry bag are completely firm and dry, at least 5 to 6 hours (and longer if the day is humid). To preserve your handiwork, store the cookies in a single layer in an airtight container.

❉ *For an aromatic topnote of flavor,* use intensified vanilla extract (see page 52) in place of plain vanilla extract in the cookie dough.

FRESHLY BAKED, THE COOKIES KEEP FOR 1 WEEK.

Royal Icing Made with Meringue Powder

About 2⅔ cups

Royal icing dries firm and polished. As an undercoating for another layer of decorative piping, it creates a smooth surface for designs that give the cookies depth and complexity. To use the icing for coating the tops of baked cookies, thin it out a little at a time with ¼-teaspoon amounts of water; to use the icing for piping, stiffen it by beating in extra confectioners' sugar, a tablespoon at a time. Royal icing can be tinted with paste food colors, creating a vivid range of hues. Always make a little more colored icing than you think you'll need, because it's difficult to duplicate the exact hue of coloring in subsequent batches.

Meringue powder is the all-important icing ingredient. Wilton Enterprises (see page 546) makes an excellent meringue powder. Royal icing made with meringue powder maintains just the right firmness on baked cookies.

ROYAL ICING

4 tablespoons plus 2½ teaspoons meringue powder

6 cups unsifted confectioners' sugar

½ cup water

2 teaspoons strained, freshly squeezed lemon juice

2½ teaspoons pure vanilla extract

Paste food colors, for coloring the icing (optional)

MIX THE ICING Place the meringue powder, confectioners' sugar, water, lemon juice, and vanilla extract in the large bowl of a freestanding electric mixer. Beat on low speed for 1 minute, or until the ingredients are combined. Scrape down the sides of the mixing bowl with a rubber spatula and beat for 30 seconds longer, or until the icing is smooth and glossy (but not fluffy).

CURE THE ICING Scrape the icing into a clean, dry glass bowl, cover tightly with plastic wrap, and refrigerate for 2 hours. *Storage equipment observation* Glass can be cleaned free of an oily or buttery residue, and doesn't readily absorb food odors.

COLOR THE ICING WITH PASTE FOOD COLOR To color the icing with paste food color, place the icing in a glass bowl. Dip the end of a wooden pick in a trace of color and mix well. Cover the bowl with plastic wrap. Let the icing "bloom" for 10 minutes. Add extra specks of color to achieve the desired intensity.

CRYSTALLIZED GINGER GINGERBREAD

One 9 by 9-inch gingerbread, creating 16 squares

PATTERNED AFTER THE SPICY MOLASSES GINGERBREAD on page 391, this version of the time-honored American bakery delight is somewhat darker, has fewer spices, and is peppered with chopped crystallized ginger. It has a little more depth and ginger intensity than the Spicy Molasses Gingerbread. Cut into squares and dusted with confectioners' sugar, it's the perfect sweet to serve with poached fruit, particularly pears.

Softened unsalted butter and bleached all-purpose flour, for preparing the baking pan

CRYSTALLIZED GINGER GINGERBREAD BATTER

2½ cups unsifted bleached all-purpose flour

1¼ teaspoons baking soda

½ teaspoon salt

2½ teaspoons ground ginger

1 teaspoon ground cinnamon

¼ teaspoon ground allspice

⅓ cup finely chopped crystallized ginger

6 tablespoons (¾ stick) unsalted butter, softened

2 tablespoons solid shortening

½ cup firmly packed dark brown sugar, sieved if lumpy

1 large egg

1½ teaspoons pure vanilla extract

1 cup mild, unsulphured molasses

1 cup boiling water

Confectioners' sugar, for sprinkling on the squares (optional)

BAKEWARE

9 by 9 by 2-inch baking pan

PREHEAT THE OVEN AND PREPARE THE BAKING PAN Preheat the oven to 350° F. Lightly butter and flour the inside of the baking pan. Tap out any excess flour; set aside.

MIX THE GINGERBREAD BATTER Sift the flour, baking soda, salt, ginger, cinnamon, and allspice onto a sheet of waxed paper. Toss the chopped crystallized ginger with 1 teaspoon of the sifted mixture.

Cream the butter and shortening in the large bowl of a freestanding electric mixer on moderately low speed for 2 minutes. Add the dark brown sugar and beat for 1 minute. Blend in the egg and vanilla extract. Add the molasses and beat for 1 minute.

On low speed, add the sifted flour mixture, blending until smooth. Add the boiling water and beat until smooth, scraping down the sides of the mixing bowl with a rubber spatula to keep the batter even-textured. *Batter texture observation* The batter will be moderately thin. Stir in the crystallized ginger. Immediately pour the batter into the prepared baking pan.

BAKE AND COOL THE GINGERBREAD Bake the gingerbread for 35 minutes, or until risen, set, and a wooden pick inserted withdraws clean. Serve the gingerbread warm or at room temperature, cut into squares. Sprinkle squares with confectioners' sugar, if you wish.

FRESHLY BAKED, THE GINGERBREAD KEEPS FOR 4 DAYS.

SOUR CREAM GINGER KEEPING CAKE

One 10-inch cake, creating about 20 slices

M OIST, WITH A SOFT BUT COMPACT CRUMB, this is a wonderful cake to have on hand for serving with coffee or tea, a dried fruit compote, or fresh fruit salad. Or simply slice and toast the cake, and serve with strokes of softened sweet butter.

Shortening and bleached all-purpose
   flour, for preparing the cake pan

SOUR CREAM GINGER
CAKE BATTER

2⅔ cups unsifted bleached all-purpose
   flour

⅓ cup unsifted bleached cake flour

¼ teaspoon baking soda

¾ teaspoon salt

2½ teaspoons ground ginger

½ teaspoon freshly grated nutmeg

¼ teaspoon ground allspice

½ cup finely chopped crystallized
   ginger

½ pound (16 tablespoons or 2 sticks)
   unsalted butter, softened

2¾ cups superfine sugar

6 large eggs

1 tablespoon plus 1 teaspoon finely
   grated fresh gingerroot

2 teaspoons pure vanilla extract

1 cup thick, cultured sour cream

Confectioners' sugar, for sifting over
   the top of the baked cake (optional)

BAKEWARE

plain 10-inch tube pan

PREHEAT THE OVEN AND PREPARE THE CAKE PAN Preheat the oven to 325° F. Grease the inside of the tube pan with shortening. Line the bottom of the pan with a circle of waxed paper cut to fit, and grease the paper. Dust the inside of the pan with all-purpose flour. Tap out any excess flour; set aside. *Baking pan observation* The batter for this cake is ample, and it rises impressively in the pan. Don't substitute a 10-inch Bundt pan for the larger, plain 10-inch tube pan, because it isn't roomy enough and the batter will bake unevenly in it.

MIX THE SOUR CREAM GINGER CAKE BATTER Sift the all-purpose flour, cake flour, baking soda, salt, ginger, nutmeg, and allspice onto a sheet of waxed paper. In a small bowl, toss the crystallized ginger with ½ teaspoon of the sifted mixture.

Cream the butter in the large bowl of a freestanding electric mixer on moderately low speed for 3 to 4 minutes. Add the superfine sugar in three additions, beating for 1 minute on moderate speed after each portion is added. Beat in the eggs, one at a time, blending for 45 seconds after each addition. Blend in the grated gingerroot and vanilla extract.

On low speed, alternately add the sifted mixture in three additions with the sour cream in two additions, beginning and ending with the sifted ingredients. Scrape down the sides of the mixing bowl frequently with a rubber spatula to keep the batter even-textured. Stir in the crystallized ginger.

Spoon the batter into the prepared tube pan. Smooth over the top with a rubber spatula.

BAKE AND COOL THE CAKE Bake the cake in the preheated oven for 1 hour and 20 minutes to 1 hour and 25 minutes, or until risen, set, and a wooden pick inserted in the cake withdraws clean. The top of the cake will have formed a crackly top crust in large patches; the cake must be baked through, or the top will be gummy once it is cooled. The baked cake will pull away slightly from the sides of the baking pan.

Cool the cake in the pan on a rack for 10 minutes. Carefully invert the cake onto another cooling rack, peel off the waxed paper circle, then invert again to cool right side up. Cool completely. Sift confectioners' sugar on top of the cake, just before slicing and serving, if you wish. *Slicing observation* Use a serrated knife to cut the cake neatly and cleanly.

❋ *For an aromatic topnote of flavor,* use intensified vanilla extract (see page 52) in place of plain vanilla extract in the cake batter.

❋ *For a textural contrast,* stir ⅔ cup chopped walnuts into the cake batter along with the crystallized ginger.

FRESHLY BAKED, THE CAKE KEEPS FOR 1 WEEK.

GINGER AND MACADAMIA NUT SHORTBREAD

One 9½-inch shortbread, creating 12 triangular pieces

A ROUGH, CRUNCHY SURFACE OF MACADAMIA NUTS paves this tender, but crumbly, shortbread. The nut topping, a fast and fashionable way to glamorize short-bread, is softly sweetened and lightly redolent of ginger.

Nonstick cooking spray, for preparing the tart pan

GINGER SHORTBREAD DOUGH

1¼ cups unsifted bleached all-purpose flour

¼ cup rice flour

¼ teaspoon baking powder

⅛ teaspoon salt

1 teaspoon ground ginger

¼ teaspoon freshly grated nutmeg

12 tablespoons (1½ sticks) unsalted butter, softened

½ cup unsifted confectioners' sugar

1¼ teaspoons pure vanilla extract

½ cup coarsely chopped crystallized ginger

GINGER-MACADAMIA NUT TOPPING

¾ cup coarsely chopped unsalted macadamia nuts

2 teaspoons unsalted butter, melted and cooled

2 tablespoons granulated sugar blended with ⅛ teaspoon ground ginger

BAKEWARE

fluted 9½-inch round tart pan (with a removable bottom)

PREHEAT THE OVEN AND PREPARE THE TART PAN Preheat the oven to 350° F. Film the inside of the tart pan with nonstick cooking spray; set aside.

MIX THE GINGER SHORTBREAD DOUGH Sift the all-purpose flour, rice flour, baking powder, salt, ginger, and nutmeg onto a sheet of waxed paper.

Cream the butter in the large bowl of a freestanding electric mixer on low speed for 3 minutes. Blend in the confectioners' sugar and vanilla extract. Beat in the crystallized ginger. Blend in the sifted flour mixture in two additions, mixing slowly until the particles of flour are absorbed and the dough is creamy-textured and smooth.

PAT THE DOUGH INTO THE PREPARED PAN Transfer the dough to the tart pan, and lightly press it into an even layer. Prick the shortbread with the tines of a fork in 10 to 15 random places.

MAKE THE MACADAMIA NUT TOPPING AND TOP THE SHORTBREAD In a small bowl, toss the macadamia nuts with the melted butter, then toss again with the sugar-ginger blend.

Scatter the nut mixture over the top of the dough and, using your fingertips, press it lightly onto the surface. *Dough texture observation* Pressing the nuts too firmly on the dough will compact it and prevent the shortbread from baking into a delicate, tender cookie.

Sprinkle sugar-ginger mixture over and about the nuts and surface of the cookie dough.

BAKE AND COOL THE SHORTBREAD Bake the shortbread in the preheated oven for 30 minutes, or until set and a medium golden color on top. Place the pan of shortbread on a cooling rack and cool for 15 minutes.

UNMOLD AND CUT THE SHORTBREAD Carefully unmold the shortbread, removing the tart pan's outer ring. Leave the shortbread on its round base and cool for 10 to 15 minutes. With a sharp chef's knife, cut the cookie into wedges. Cool completely.

FRESHLY BAKED, THE SHORTBREAD KEEPS FOR 1 WEEK.

GINGER BUTTER BALLS

About 30 cookies

BOTH THE FORWARD, tingly flavor of crystallized ginger and the secondary, mellower flavor of ground ginger build the flavor in this delicate butter cookie. Crystallized ginger is spicy and forthcoming in a butter cookie dough—it adds a nice jolt of seasoning.

GINGER BUTTER COOKIE DOUGH

2¼ cups unsifted bleached all-purpose flour

¾ teaspoon baking powder

⅛ teaspoon salt

¾ teaspoon ground ginger

¼ teaspoon freshly grated nutmeg

½ pound (16 tablespoons or 2 sticks) unsalted butter, melted and cooled

⅓ cup very finely chopped walnuts

3 tablespoons very finely chopped crystallized ginger

⅓ cup unsifted confectioners' sugar

PREHEAT THE OVEN AND PREPARE THE COOKIE SHEETS Preheat the oven to 350° F. Line the cookie sheets with lengths of cooking parchment paper.

MIX THE GINGER BUTTER COOKIE DOUGH Sift the all-purpose flour, baking powder, salt, ground ginger, and nutmeg onto a sheet of waxed paper.

In a large mixing bowl, whisk the melted butter, walnuts, crystallized ginger, confectioners' sugar, and vanilla extract. At this point, the sugar will form small clumps; it will mix in and blend well with the other ingredients in the next step. Using a rubber spatula, stir in the flour mixture in three additions, mixing to form a dough. Let the dough stand for 5 minutes.

1 teaspoon pure vanilla extract

Confectioners' sugar, for rolling the baked cookies

BAKEWARE

several cookie sheets

FORM THE COOKIE BALLS Spoon out scant tablespoon-size quantities of dough and roll into plump, round balls. Place the balls, 2 inches apart, on the lined cookie sheets. Arrange 12 to 16 cookies to a sheet (depending on the size of the cookie sheets).

BAKE AND COOL THE COOKIES Bake the cookies for 13 to 15 minutes, or until set, with light golden bottoms.

Let the cookies stand on the sheets for 5 minutes, then remove them to cooling racks, using an offset metal spatula. Cool for 5 to 10 minutes. Line a work surface with waxed paper.

COAT THE COOKIES WITH CONFECTIONERS' SUGAR Place about 3 cups of confectioners' sugar (or more as needed) in a shallow bowl. Gently, dredge the warm (not hot) cookies in the confectioners' sugar, and place them on the waxed paper as they are coated. Let the cookies stand for about 10 minutes, then redredge them a second time in confectioners' sugar. Cool the cookies completely.

FRESHLY BAKED, THE COOKIES KEEP FOR **4** TO **5** DAYS.

BEST BAKING ADVICE

Use thoroughly cooled melted butter. Letting the dough stand for 5 minutes before rolling into balls allows the dough to absorb the flour properly. This improves the baked texture of the cookies.

SPICY MOLASSES GINGERBREAD

One 9 by 9-inch gingerbread, creating 16 squares

To CHANNEL THE GINGER FLAVOR INTO GINGERBREAD, use mild unsulphured molasses, ground ginger (along with cinnamon, nutmeg, allspice, cloves, and cardamom), and vanilla extract in the batter. The interplay of the various spices unites the flavor of the ginger and molasses. This plain gingerbread has a classic flavor and beautifully moist and feathery crumb.

Softened unsalted butter and bleached all-purpose flour, for preparing the baking pan

MOLASSES GINGERBREAD BATTER

2½ cups unsifted bleached all-purpose flour

1¼ teaspoons baking soda

½ teaspoon salt

2½ teaspoons ground ginger

1 teaspoon ground cinnamon

¾ teaspoon freshly grated nutmeg

¼ teaspoon ground allspice

¼ teaspoon ground cloves

⅛ teaspoon ground cardamom

¼ pound (8 tablespoons or 1 stick) unsalted butter, softened

⅓ cup plus 3 tablespoons granulated sugar

1 large egg

2 teaspoons pure vanilla extract

2 teaspoons finely grated fresh gingerroot

1 cup mild, unsulphured molasses

1 cup boiling water

BAKEWARE

9 by 9 by 2-inch baking pan

PREHEAT THE OVEN AND PREPARE THE BAKING PAN Preheat the oven to 350° F. Lightly butter and flour the inside of the baking pan. Tap out any excess flour; set aside.

MIX THE MOLASSES GINGERBREAD BATTER Sift the flour, baking soda, salt, ginger, cinnamon, nutmeg, allspice, cloves, and cardamom onto a sheet of waxed paper.

Cream the butter in the large bowl of a freestanding electric mixer on moderately low speed for 2 minutes. Add the granulated sugar and beat for 1 minute. Blend in the egg, vanilla extract, and grated ginger. Add the molasses and beat for 1 minute.

On low speed, add the sifted flour mixture, blending until smooth. Add the boiling water and beat until the mixture is smooth, scraping down the sides of the mixing bowl with a rubber spatula to keep the batter even-textured. *Batter texture observation* The batter will be moderately thin and smooth. Pour the batter into the prepared baking pan.

BAKE AND COOL THE GINGERBREAD Bake the gingerbread for 35 minutes, or until risen, set, and a wooden pick inserted withdraws clean. Let the gingerbread stand in the pan on a cooling rack. Serve the gingerbread warm or at room temperature, cut into squares directly from the pan.

FRESHLY BAKED, THE GINGERBREAD KEEPS FOR 4 DAYS.

GINGER CRACKS

About 3 dozen cookies

$\mathcal{T}$HE INTENSE AND RADIANT FLAVOR of crystallized ginger brightens these spicy, chewy-crisp cookies. About the dough: The shortening creates a well-developed cookie with a crunchy shear to it, while the butter adds flavor; the four spices offset the dusky taste of the molasses, and the vanilla extract balances both the ground and the crystallized ginger.

GINGER COOKIE DOUGH

2 cups plus 1 tablespoon unsifted bleached all-purpose flour

1¾ teaspoons baking soda

¼ teaspoon baking powder

½ teaspoon salt

2¼ teaspoons ground ginger

1 teaspoon ground cinnamon

¾ teaspoon freshly grated nutmeg

¼ teaspoon ground allspice

½ cup shortening

4 tablespoons (½ stick) unsalted butter, softened

¾ cup plus 2 tablespoons granulated sugar

1 large egg

¼ cup plus 1 tablespoon mild, unsulphured molasses

1 teaspoon pure vanilla extract

⅔ cup chopped crystallized ginger

About 1 cup granulated sugar, for rolling the unbaked balls of cookie dough

BAKEWARE

heavy cookie sheets

MIX THE GINGER COOKIE DOUGH Sift the flour, baking soda, baking powder, salt, ginger, cinnamon, nutmeg, and allspice onto a sheet of waxed paper.

Cream the shortening and butter in the large bowl of a freestanding electric mixer on low speed for 2 to 3 minutes. Add the granulated sugar and beat on moderate speed for 1 minute. Blend in the egg, molasses, and vanilla extract. Scrape down the sides of the mixing bowl frequently with a rubber spatula to keep the mixture even-textured. On low speed, add the sifted ingredients in two additions, beating just until the particles of flour are absorbed. Blend in the crystallized ginger. *Dough texture observation* At this point, the dough will be soft and somewhat sticky.

FREEZE (OR REFRIGERATE) THE DOUGH Scrape the dough onto a large sheet of plastic wrap, and flatten it into a shallow cake, using a rubber spatula. Wrap up the dough, place it in a baking pan, and freeze for 30 minutes, or until firm enough to roll into balls; or, refrigerate the dough for 2 to 3 hours so that it's manageable. (The dough can be stored in the refrigerator for up to 2 days in advance of baking.)

PREHEAT THE OVEN AND PREPARE THE COOKIE SHEETS Preheat the oven to 375° F. Line the cookie sheets with cooking parchment paper. The baking sheets need to be heavy if the cookies are to bake evenly without scorching. Double-pan the sheets, if necessary.

Placing a maximum nine balls of dough on a large cookie sheet gives them enough room to bake without merging into each other. In a hot kitchen or on a very humid day, refrigerate the dough balls on the cookie sheets for about 15 minutes before baking; if they have been refrigerated, bake the cookies for an additional minute.

FORM THE COOKIES Place the granulated sugar in a shallow bowl and have at hand. Spoon up rounded tablespoon quantities of dough and roll into balls. Roll the balls in granulated sugar and place them, 3 inches apart, on the lined cookie sheets. Arrange nine balls of dough on each sheet. The dough balls will spread and flatten as they bake.

BAKE AND COOL THE COOKIES Bake the cookies for 12 to 13 minutes, or until set. As the cookies bake, they will puff up, then flatten out; the surfaces of the baked cookies will appear crackly and crinkly. Let the cookies stand on the sheets for 1 minute, then remove them to cooling racks, using a wide, offset metal spatula. Cool completely.

❄ *For an extra surge of flavor,* blend ½ teaspoon ground ginger into the 1 cup granulated sugar used for rolling the unbaked cookie dough balls.

FRESHLY BAKED, THE COOKIES KEEP FOR 3 TO 4 DAYS.

GINGER SCONES

6 scones

AROMATIC, WITH BURSTS OF CHOPPED CRYSTALLIZED GINGER, the scones balance a variety of spices and a hint of molasses. These are substantial and moist.

GINGER SCONE DOUGH

2 cups plus 3 tablespoons unsifted bleached all-purpose flour

2½ teaspoons baking powder

¼ teaspoon baking soda

¼ teaspoon salt

2½ teaspoons ground ginger

1 teaspoon ground cinnamon

⅛ teaspoon ground allspice

PREHEAT THE OVEN AND PREPARE THE BAKING SHEET Preheat the oven to 425° F. Line the cookie sheet or sheet pan with a length of cooking parchment paper; set aside. *Bakeware observation* The baking sheets must be heavy, or the ginger dough will scorch on the bottom as the scones bake. Double-pan the sheets, if necessary.

MIX THE GINGER SCONE DOUGH In a large mixing bowl, whisk together the flour, baking powder, baking soda, salt, ginger,

⅛ teaspoon ground cloves

½ cup unsifted confectioners' sugar

6 tablespoons (¾ stick) unsalted butter, cold, cut into tablespoon pieces

5 tablespoons heavy cream

3 tablespoons mild, unsulphured molasses

2 large eggs

2 teaspoons pure vanilla extract

½ cup chopped crystallized ginger

About 2 tablespoons turbinado sugar, for sprinkling on top of the unbaked scones (or substitute granulated sugar)

BAKEWARE

large, heavy cookie sheet or rimmed sheet pan

cinnamon, allspice, cloves, and confectioners' sugar. Drop over the cold chunks of butter and, using a pastry blender, cut the fat into the flour until it is reduced to small pieces the size of dried lima beans. Dip into the mixture with your fingertips and crumble it lightly for about 1 minute, reducing the butter to smaller flakes.

Whisk the heavy cream, molasses, eggs, and vanilla extract in a medium-size mixing bowl. Pour the whisked liquid mixture over the dry ingredients, add the crystallized ginger, and stir to form the beginning of a firm, but moist, dough. With lightly floured hands, gather up the dough and knead it in the bowl for 10 to 15 seconds, until it comes together.

FORM THE DOUGH INTO SCONES Turn dough onto a lightly floured work surface and pat into a round cake 7½ to 8 inches in diameter. Cut the cake into six wedges, using a sharp chef's knife. Using an offset metal spatula, transfer the wedges to the lined baking sheet, placing them 2½ to 3 inches apart. Sprinkle the tops of the scones with the turbinado sugar.

BAKE AND COOL THE SCONES Bake the scones in the preheated oven for 16 to 18 minutes, or until set. Let the scones stand on the baking sheet for 1 minute, then remove them to a cooling rack, using a wide, metal offset spatula. Serve the scones warm or at room temperature.

❊ For an aromatic topnote of flavor, use intensified vanilla extract (see page 52) in place of plain vanilla extract in the scone dough.

FRESHLY BAKED, THE SCONES KEEP FOR 2 DAYS.

Variations: For chocolate chip-ginger scones, add ⅔ cup semisweet chocolate chips to the scone ingredients along with the chopped crystallized ginger.

For bittersweet chocolate chunk-ginger scones, add 6 ounces bittersweet chocolate, cut into chunks, to the scone ingredients along with the chopped crystallized ginger.

BEST BAKING ADVICE

If you are making the scones in a hot kitchen or on a very humid day, refrigerate the cake of dough for 30 minutes, then cut, top with sugar, and bake.

For ginger-walnut scones, add ⅔ cup chopped walnuts (lightly toasted and cooled completely) to the scone ingredients along with the chopped crystallized ginger.

GINGERBREAD WAFFLES

About 4 deep, Belgian-style 2-sided waffles,
each waffle section measuring 4½ by 4½ inches

With all the haunting flavors of gingerbread, this waffle batter packs in the spices and is reinforced with a little whole wheat flour. The batter, which is lightly sweetened, tenderized by buttermilk, and enriched with melted butter, bakes into the perfect cushion for toppings such as butter-sautéed apples, oven-roasted pears, or dollops of apple butter.

GINGERBREAD WAFFLE BATTER

1¾ cups unsifted bleached all-purpose flour

¼ cup unsifted whole wheat flour

2 teaspoons baking powder

½ teaspoon baking soda

¼ teaspoon salt

2¾ teaspoons ground ginger

¾ teaspoon ground cinnamon

½ teaspoon freshly grated nutmeg

¼ teaspoon ground allspice

¼ teaspoon ground cloves

⅓ cup plus 1 tablespoon granulated sugar

3 large eggs

5 tablespoons unsalted butter, melted and cooled to tepid

2 teaspoons pure vanilla extract

2 tablespoons mild, unsulphured molasses

1¾ cups buttermilk, plus 1 to 2 tablespoons extra, as needed

Confectioners' sugar, for sprinkling on the waffles

MAKE THE GINGERBREAD WAFFLE BATTER Sift the all-purpose flour, whole wheat flour, baking powder, baking soda, salt, ginger, cinnamon, nutmeg, allspice, cloves, and granulated sugar into a large mixing bowl.

In a medium-size mixing bowl, whisk the eggs, melted butter, vanilla extract, molasses, and buttermilk. Pour the liquid ingredients over the dry ingredients and stir to form a batter, using a rubber spatula or wooden spoon, mixing until the particles of flour are absorbed. *Batter consistency observation* The batter will be moderately thick, but creamy-textured. (If the batter is too thick, stir in a little more buttermilk, a tablespoon at a time.)

MAKE THE WAFFLES Preheat the deep-dish waffle iron. Spoon a generous ⅓ cup of batter onto the center of each square of the iron. Cook the waffles until golden, about 1 minute and 30 seconds. Serve the waffles piping hot, sprinkled with confectioners' sugar if you wish, and apple butter, ginger preserves, or pure maple syrup.

❋ *For an extra surge of flavor,* stir 3 tablespoons chopped ginger preserved in syrup (well drained) into the prepared waffle batter.

❋ *For a textural contrast,* scatter ½ cup golden raisins over the liquid ingredients as soon as the whisked mixture is poured on the dry ingredients, then stir to form a batter.

GINGER MOLASSES SWEET POTATO PIE

One 9-inch pie, creating about 8 slices

GINGER PRESERVED IN SYRUP, along with a flavor-charge of molasses and vanilla extract, sharpens a sweet potato pie filling in the most glorious of ways.

Vanilla Pie Crust (see page 520)

GINGER MOLASSES SWEET
POTATO PIE FILLING

2 cups freshly cooked and pureed
   sweet potatoes

½ cup granulated sugar blended with
   1¼ teaspoons ground ginger,
   ½ teaspoon freshly grated nutmeg,
   ½ teaspoon ground cinnamon,
   ¼ teaspoon ground cloves, and
   ¼ teaspoon salt

¼ cup firmly packed light brown
   sugar, sieved if lumpy

3 tablespoons mild, unsulphured
   molasses

2 teaspoons finely grated fresh
   gingerroot

1½ teaspoons pure vanilla extract

3 large eggs, lightly beaten

3 tablespoons unsalted butter, melted
   and cooled

1¼ cups heavy cream

3 tablespoons finely chopped ginger
   preserved in syrup, patted dry on
   paper towels

BAKEWARE

9-inch pie pan

PREPARE THE VANILLA PIE CRUST Make the pie dough, line the pie pan, and prebake the crust as directed in the recipe on page 520.

PREHEAT THE OVEN Preheat the oven to 400° F.

MIX THE GINGER MOLASSES SWEET POTATO PIE FILLING Place the sweet potatoes, granulated sugar-spice blend, light brown sugar, molasses, and grated gingerroot in a large mixing bowl. Stir well to combine, using a wooden spoon or rubber spatula. Blend in the vanilla extract and eggs. Mix in the melted butter. Slowly blend in the heavy cream. Stir in the chopped preserved ginger.

Scrape the filling into the prebaked pie crust. Smooth over the top, using a rubber spatula.

BAKE AND COOL THE PIE Bake the pie in the preheated oven for 10 minutes. Reduce the oven temperature to 325° F. and continue baking for 30 to 35 minutes longer, or until just set. Cool the pie on a rack. Slice and serve with spoonfuls of Vanilla Whipped Cream (see page 530), if you wish. The pie is best served freshly baked. Refrigerate any leftover pie in an airtight container.

❋ *For an aromatic topnote of flavor,* use intensified vanilla extract (see page 530) in place of plain vanilla extract in the pie filling.

BEST BAKING ADVICE
Mix the filling ingredients slowly but thoroughly to keep the filling smooth and dense, rather than airy or fluffy.

GINGER BROWNIES

16 brownies

L ITTLE BURSTS OF PRESERVED GINGER, set against the creaminess of chocolate and butter, make up this luscious brownie batter. A dash of ground cardamom deepens the ginger flavor. Ginger undeniably thrives in the company of
chocolate, for its sweet heat is at once tempered and amplified in its presence.

Nonstick cooking spray, for preparing
the baking pan

GINGER AND CHOCOLATE
BROWNIE BATTER

1 cup unsifted bleached all-purpose
flour

2 tablespoons unsweetened, alkalized
cocoa

¼ teaspoon baking powder

¼ teaspoon ground ginger

¼ teaspoon salt

¾ cup miniature semisweet chocolate
chips

½ pound (16 tablespoons or 2 sticks)
unsalted butter, melted and cooled
to tepid

4 ounces (4 squares) unsweetened
chocolate, melted and cooled
to tepid

4 large eggs

1¾ cups plus 2 tablespoons granulated
sugar

2 teaspoons pure vanilla extract

⅓ cup chopped ginger preserved in
syrup, well drained and patted dry
on paper towels

Confectioners' sugar, for sifting over
the top of the brownies (optional)

BAKEWARE

9 by 9 by 2-inch baking pan

PREHEAT THE OVEN AND PREPARE THE BAKING PAN Preheat
the oven to 325° F. Film the inside of the baking pan with nonstick cooking spray; set aside.

MIX THE GINGER AND CHOCOLATE BROWNIE BATTER Sift
the flour, cocoa, baking powder, ginger, and salt onto a sheet of
waxed paper. In a bowl, toss the chocolate chips with 1¼ teaspoons of the sifted mixture.

Whisk the melted butter and melted unsweetened chocolate
in a medium-size mixing bowl until thoroughly combined.

In a large mixing bowl, whisk the eggs to blend well, about 45
seconds. Add the granulated sugar, and whisk until just combined,
about 1 minute. Blend in the melted chocolate-butter mixture and
vanilla extract. Sift over the sifted ingredients and whisk until the
particles of flour are completely absorbed. Stir in the chocolate chips
and preserved ginger, using a wooden spoon or flat wooden paddle.

Scrape the batter into the prepared baking pan. Smooth over
the top with a rubber spatula.

BAKE AND COOL THE BROWNIES Bake the brownies for 35 to
38 minutes, or until set. Let the brownies stand in the pan on a
cooling rack for 3 hours, then refrigerate for 30 minutes, or until
firm enough to cut. (In hot or humid weather, or in a warm
kitchen, freeze the pan of brownies for 20 minutes before cutting,
or until firm enough to cut.) Cut the entire cake of brownies into

four quarters, then cut each quarter into four squares, using a small, sharp knife. Remove the brownies from the pan, using a small, offset metal spatula. Sprinkle the top of the brownies with confectioners' sugar, just before serving, if you wish.

FRESHLY BAKED, THE BROWNIES KEEP FOR 4 DAYS.

Variation: For ginger brownies with Dutch-process black cocoa, use 1 tablespoon Dutch-process black cocoa and 1 tablespoon unsweetened, alkalized cocoa in the brownie batter.

GINGERY PUMPKIN MUFFINS WITH GINGER–SUGAR SPRINKLE

1 dozen muffins

CHOPPED CRYSTALLIZED GINGER and a simple topping made by combining granulated sugar and ground ginger add great flavor to these tender little quick breads. The aromatic batter, which is made by hand without too much fuss, turns out soft-textured muffins that are moist and plump.

Nonstick cooking spray, for preparing the muffin pan

GINGER-SUGAR SPRINKLE
5 tablespoons granulated sugar
½ teaspoon ground ginger
pinch of freshly grated nutmeg

SPICED PUMPKIN
MUFFIN BATTER
1½ cup unsifted bleached all-purpose flour
¼ cup unsifted bleached cake flour

PREHEAT THE OVEN AND PREPARE THE MUFFIN PANS Preheat the oven to 400° F. Film the inside of the muffin cups with nonstick cooking spray; set aside.

MAKE THE GINGER SUGAR–SPRINKLE Sift the granulated sugar, ground ginger, and nutmeg into a small mixing bowl. Whisk the sugar to distribute the spice evenly. Set aside.

MIX THE SPICED PUMPKIN MUFFIN BATTER Sift the all-purpose flour, cake flour, whole wheat flour, baking powder, salt, ginger, cinnamon, nutmeg, cloves, and granulated sugar into a large mixing bowl.

¼ cup unsifted whole wheat flour

2 teaspoons baking powder

½ teaspoon salt

1¼ teaspoons ground ginger

½ teaspoon ground cinnamon

½ teaspoon freshly grated nutmeg

¼ teaspoon ground cloves

⅔ cup granulated sugar

6 tablespoons (¾ stick) unsalted butter, melted and cooled

2 tablespoons shortening, melted and cooled

2 large eggs

2 teaspoons pure vanilla extract

¾ cup plain canned pumpkin puree (not pumpkin pie filling)

¾ cup milk

½ cup chopped crystallized ginger

BAKEWARE

standard (12-cup) muffin pan (each cup measuring about 2¾ inches in diameter and 1⅜ inches deep, with a capacity of ½ cup)

Whisk the melted butter, melted shortening, eggs, vanilla, pumpkin puree, and milk. Pour the whisked pumpkin mixture over the sifted mixture, and add the crystallized ginger. Stir to form a batter.

Spoon the batter into the prepared muffin cups, dividing it evenly among them. As you fill the cups with the batter, mound it softly in the center. Sprinkle a little of the ginger-sugar sprinkle over the top of each muffin.

BAKE AND COOL THE MUFFINS Bake the muffins in the preheated oven for 17 to 19 minutes, or until risen, set, and a wooden pick inserted in a muffin withdraws clean. The baked muffins will pull away slightly from the sides of the cups. Place the muffin pan on a cooling rack and let stand for 6 to 8 minutes. Carefully remove the muffins to another cooling rack. Serve the muffins warm.

❋ For an aromatic topnote of flavor, use intensified vanilla extract (see page 52) in place of plain vanilla extract in the muffin batter.

❋ For a textural contrast, stir ½ cup chopped walnuts into the muffin batter along with the crystallized ginger.

FRESHLY BAKED, THE MUFFINS KEEP FOR 2 DAYS.

BEST BAKING ADVICE

Ginger preserved in syrup—chopped, well drained on paper towels, air-dried for 20 minutes, and lightly tossed in 2 teaspoons of the sifted flour mixture—can be substituted for the crystallized variety.

*t*he dynamic flavor of lemon can be as rich, gratifying, and potent as chocolate or almond, but in a sweet and sharp way. What distinguishes the taste of lemon from other prominent flavors is the welcoming presence of acid, which, when paired with butter, sugar, and eggs, turns an aggressively sour component into one that is tingly, tangy, and pleasingly astringent.

The passageway to expanding the flavor of lemon in batters and doughs can be direct or indirect: freshly grated lemon rind, lemon juice, and lemon extract, in various combinations, can charge up a cake batter directly and immediately. These would be classified as dominant flavoring agents. On a more subtle, layered level are lemon-scented granulated sugar, candied lemon peel "threads," lemon glaze, or lemon icing, as accessory flavoring agents.

When buying lemons at the market, look for firm-surfaced, bright-skinned fruit that are heavy in the hand, indicating that they're full of juice. Avoid lemons with any soft, slightly dimpled areas. When a recipe calls for grated lemon peel, use cold lemons, for the chilled peel is easiest to grate and produces the fluffiest rind. Fluffy-textured rind—rather than dense, tough rind—produces the best flavor in a batter because it's easily absorbed. To generate the most juice from lemons, squeeze at room temperature after you've rolled them firmly on the countertop with the palm of your hand.

17

LEMON

ULTRA-LEMON CAKE

One 10-inch fluted tube cake, creating 16 slices

*T*HIS FINE-GRAINED, softly textured cake is finished with two toppings—a sheer syrup and a spoonable confectioners' sugar icing. It's an energetic and intense way to develop the essence of lemon in a cake. Here you have an excellent cake to serve at brunch, or to offer as dessert, along with a spoonful of summer's ripest berries.

Nonstick cooking spray, for preparing the cake pan

LEMON RIND SOAK

1 tablespoon plus 1 teaspoon freshly grated lemon rind

1½ teaspoons pure lemon extract

1 tablespoon freshly squeezed and strained lemon juice

LEMON BUTTER CAKE BATTER

3 cups unsifted bleached all-purpose flour

½ teaspoon baking soda

¾ teaspoon salt

14 tablespoons (1¾ sticks) unsalted butter, softened

2 tablespoons shortening

2 cups lemon-scented granulated sugar (see page 55)

4 large eggs, separated

1 cup buttermilk

⅛ teaspoon cream of tartar

3 tablespoons lemon-scented granulated sugar (see page 55)

Lemon "Soaking" Glaze (see page 404), for spooning onto the baked cake

MAKE THE LEMON RIND SOAK Combine the lemon rind, lemon extract, and lemon juice in a small nonreactive bowl. Set aside for 15 minutes.

PREHEAT THE OVEN AND PREPARE THE CAKE PAN Preheat the oven to 350° F. Film the inside of the Bundt pan with nonstick cooking spray; set aside.

MIX THE LEMON BUTTER CAKE BATTER Sift the flour, baking soda, and salt onto a sheet of waxed paper.

Cream the butter and shortening in the large bowl of a free-standing electric mixer on moderate speed for 3 to 4 minutes. Beat in 2 cups of the lemon-scented granulated sugar in three additions, mixing on moderately high speed for 1 minute after each portion is added. Beat in the egg yolks, then the lemon rind mixture.

On low speed, alternately add the sifted ingredients in three additions with the buttermilk in two additions, beginning and ending with the sifted mixture. Scrape down the sides of the mixing bowl frequently with a rubber spatula to keep the batter even-textured. The batter will be thick.

Using an electric hand mixer, beat the egg whites in a clean, dry bowl until frothy, add the cream of tartar, and continue beating until soft peaks are formed. Sprinkle over 3 tablespoons lemon-scented granulated sugar and continue beating until firm (but not stiff) peaks are formed.

Lemon "Pouring" Topping (see page 405), for spooning onto the baked cake

BAKEWARE

10-inch Bundt pan

Stir one-quarter of the beaten egg whites into the batter, then fold in the remaining whites. *Batter observation* All large clumps of egg white (about the size of a whole walnut) and even slender wisps should be incorporated into the batter, but be careful not to deflate the batter by overfolding the mixture.

Scrape the batter into the prepared Bundt pan. Gently shake the pan (once or twice) from side to side to level the top.

BAKE AND COOL THE CAKE Bake the cake for 55 minutes, or until risen, set, and a wooden pick inserted in the cake withdraws clean, or with a few moist crumbs adhering to it. The baked cake will pull away slightly from the sides and central tube of the baking pan.

Let the cake stand in the pan on a cooling rack for 10 minutes. Invert the cake onto another cooling rack. Place a sheet of waxed paper under the cooling rack to catch any drips of glaze or topping.

GLAZE AND TOP THE CAKE Spoon the "soaking" glaze over the surface of the cake, taking care to moisten the sides of the cake as well as the top. After 15 minutes (or when the top of the cake is no longer very moist to the touch), spoon or pour over the "pouring" topping, letting it cascade from the top of the cake down the sides. *Technique observation* It's important to wait until the glaze has permeated the cake before pouring the topping; otherwise the topping may not set up properly. Cool completely before slicing and serving. *Slicing observation* Use a serrated knife to cut the cake neatly and cleanly.

FRESHLY BAKED, THE CAKE KEEPS FOR 2 DAYS.

LEMON "SOAKING" GLAZE

Makes about ⅔ cup

A LIGHT SYRUP, BREEZY, sweet and tart, for dousing lemon cakes, cupcakes, or tea breads.

LEMON GLAZE

½ cup freshly squeezed and strained lemon juice

⅓ cup plus 2 teaspoons granulated sugar

¼ teaspoon pure lemon extract

MAKE THE LEMON GLAZE Combine the lemon juice and granulated sugar in a small nonreactive saucepan (preferably enameled cast iron). Cover and set over moderately low heat to dissolve the sugar completely, about 5 minutes. Uncover and simmer for 1 minute. Pour into a bowl. Stir in the lemon extract.

You can use the warm or hot glaze over a warm or cool cake (or batch of muffins or cupcakes). Or, use the cool glaze over a warm or hot cake. *Avoid using the cool glaze on a cool cake.* (If the glaze is made in advance and stored in the refrigerator, bring to room temperature before using over a warm or hot cake.)

❊ *For an extra surge of flavor,* use lemon-scented granulated sugar (see page 55) in place of the plain granulated sugar.

Lemon "Pouring" Topping

Makes about 1¼ cups

Spreading a sparkling lemon icing on baked loaf and Bundt cakes, sweet yeast breads, tea biscuits, or muffins is a bright and tangy finish, and a pretty way to spruce up a plain bakery sweet.

LEMON TOPPING

2 cups plus 3½ tablespoons unsifted confectioners' sugar

5 tablespoons plus ¼ teaspoon freshly squeezed and strained lemon juice

2 tablespoons unsalted butter, melted and cooled

MAKE THE LEMON TOPPING Place the confectioners' sugar, lemon juice, and melted butter in a medium-size mixing bowl. With an electric hand mixer, blend the ingredients on low speed for 30 seconds, or until just combined. Scrape down the sides of the mixing bowl once or twice with a rubber spatula to keep the topping smooth-textured. Do not overbeat. *Topping consistency observation* The topping should be slightly thick, but still pourable. You can adjust the density of the mixture by adding up to a tablespoon (a teaspoon at a time) of confectioners' sugar or lemon juice to the topping, if necessary.

Use the topping immediately, before it begins to firm up.

Baby Lemon Muffins

About 23 teacake-size muffins

Lemon-accented muffins as adorable as these belong in the brunch bread basket, for they are light and tangy enough to accompany any kind of morning food. The sheer finishing glaze, made up of fresh lemon juice and sugar, adds to the lemon flavor impact and keeps these little gems moist.

Nonstick cooking spray, for preparing the muffin pan

PREHEAT THE OVEN AND PREPARE THE MUFFIN PAN Preheat the oven to 400° F. Film the inside of the muffin cups with nonstick cookware spray; set aside.

2½ teaspoons freshly grated lemon rind

1 teaspoon pure lemon extract

2 cups unsifted bleached all-purpose flour

1 teaspoon baking powder

¾ teaspoon baking soda

½ teaspoon salt

1 cup lemon-scented granulated sugar (see page 55)

6 tablespoons (¾ stick) unsalted butter, melted and cooled

2 tablespoons shortening, melted and cooled

¾ cup plus 1 tablespoon thick, cultured sour cream

½ cup milk

1 large egg

Lemon "Soaking" Glaze (see page 404), for brushing on the warm, baked muffins

BAKEWARE

23 teacake-size miniature muffin cups (each large pan contains 24 muffin cups, each cup measuring 2 inches in diameter by 1³⁄₁₆ inches deep, with a capacity of 3 tablespoons)

MIX THE LEMON MUFFIN BATTER **Combine** the grated lemon rind and lemon extract in a small ramekin; set aside.

Sift the flour, baking powder, baking soda, salt, and lemon-scented granulated sugar into a large mixing bowl. In a medium-size bowl, whisk together the melted butter, melted shortening, sour cream, milk, egg, and lemon rind-lemon extract mixture. Pour the liquid ingredients over the dry ingredients and stir to form a batter.

Divide the batter among the 23 miniature muffin cups, filling each cup a scant three-quarters full to allow room for rising.

BAKE THE MUFFINS Bake the muffins for 15 minutes, or until risen, plump, set, and a wooden pick inserted in a muffin withdraws clean. Place the muffin pan on a cooling rack. Let the muffins cool for 5 minutes, then gently (they're really tender at this point) remove them to another cooling rack.

GLAZE AND COOL THE MUFFINS Using a soft pastry brush (or small teaspoon), moisten the top of each warm muffin with some of the spooning glaze. Serve the muffins very fresh, warm or at room temperature.

FRESHLY BAKED, THE MUFFINS KEEP FOR 1 DAY.

BEST BAKING ADVICE

Carefully remove the baked muffins from the pan to cooling racks. Let the completed muffins stand for at least 30 minutes to allow for a thorough absorption of the glaze.

LEMON RICOTTA PANCAKES

About 27 pancakes

THE WHOLE-MILK RICOTTA CHEESE and buttermilk make these pancakes a combination of creamy and tangy. I love them hot off the griddle, sprinkled with lots of confectioners' sugar and served with a spoonful of raspberry preserves and a scattering of fresh raspberries.

LEMON RICOTTA
PANCAKE BATTER

1 cup unsifted bleached all-purpose flour

1 teaspoon baking powder

pinch of salt

¾ cup whole-milk ricotta cheese

3 tablespoons granulated sugar

1 teaspoon freshly grated lemon rind

2 large eggs

¾ cup milk

4 tablespoons (½ stick) unsalted butter, melted and cooled to tepid

½ teaspoon pure lemon extract

Clarified butter (see page 66), for the griddle

Confectioners' sugar, for sprinkling on the griddled pancakes

MAKE THE LEMON RICOTTA PANCAKE BATTER Sift the flour, baking powder, and salt into a medium-size mixing bowl.

Thoroughly blend the ricotta cheese, granulated sugar, lemon rind, and eggs in a small mixing bowl, using a wooden spoon or flat wooden paddle. Blend in the milk, melted butter, and lemon extract.

Blend the whisked ricotta cheese mixture into the sifted ingredients, and stir to form an evenly textured batter, using a wooden spoon or flat wooden paddle. *Batter consistency observation* The batter will be moderately thick.

GRIDDLE THE PANCAKES Place 2-tablespoon amounts of batter onto a hot griddle greased with a film of clarified butter. Cook the pancakes for about 1 minute, until the undersides are golden and bubbles appear here and there on the surface. Flip over with a wide, offset metal spatula and continue cooking until golden on the bottom, completely set, and cooked through, about 1 minute longer.

Serve the pancakes piping hot, sprinkled with confectioners' sugar, if you wish.

✳ *For an extra surge of flavor,* use lemon-scented granulated sugar (see page 55) in place of the plain granulated sugar in the pancake batter.

✳ *For a textural contrast,* blend ½ cup chopped walnuts into the whisked ricotta mixture just before combining with the sifted dry ingredients to create the pancake batter.

LEMON TEA LOAF

One 9 by 5-inch loaf cake, creating about 12 slices

TEA CAKE SORCERY: a plain, old-fashioned loaf cake batter turns contemporary with flashes of lemon in the batter and in a sheer sugar topping.

Shortening and all-purpose flour, for preparing the loaf pan

LEMON RIND-LEMON EXTRACT SOAK

2½ teaspoons freshly grated lemon rind

1½ teaspoons pure lemon extract

LEMON BUTTER CAKE BATTER

2 cups unsifted all-purpose flour

1¼ teaspoons baking powder

½ teaspoon salt

¼ pound (8 tablespoons or 1 stick) unsalted butter, softened

1 cup lemon-scented granulated sugar (see page 55)

2 large eggs

¾ cup half-and-half

Lemon-Sugar Wash (see page 59), for brushing on the warm, baked tea loaf

BAKEWARE

9 by 5 by 3-inch loaf pan

MAKE THE LEMON RIND-LEMON EXTRACT SOAK Combine the grated lemon rind and lemon extract in a small nonreactive ramekin. Set aside for 10 minutes.

PREHEAT THE OVEN AND PREPARE THE LOAF PAN Preheat the oven to 350° F. Lightly grease the inside of the loaf pan with shortening. Dust the inside of the pan with all-purpose flour. Tap out any excess flour; set aside.

MAKE THE LEMON BUTTER CAKE BATTER Sift the flour, baking powder, and salt onto a sheet of waxed paper.

Cream the butter in the large bowl of a freestanding electric mixer on moderate speed for 3 minutes. Add half of the lemon-scented granulated sugar and beat for 1 minute; add the balance of the sugar and continue beating for a minute longer. Beat in the eggs, one at a time, mixing for about 45 seconds after each is added. Beat in the lemon rind-lemon extract soak.

On low speed, alternately add the sifted mixture in three additions with the half-and-half in two additions, beginning and ending with the sifted mixture. Scrape down the sides of the mixing bowl frequently with a rubber spatula to keep the batter even-textured.

Spoon the batter into the prepared loaf pan, mounding it slightly in the center.

BAKE AND COOL THE TEA LOAF Bake the loaf for 50 to 55 minutes, or until risen, set, and a wooden pick inserted in the cake withdraws clean. When fully baked, the tea cake will crown beautifully in the center and pull away slightly from the sides of the baking pan.

*Half-and-half makes a creamy-textured,
slightly firm crumb that holds up to the
lemon-sugar wash brushed over the
surface of the baked loaf. The half-and-
half gives the loaf a poundcake-like
texture.*

Let the tea loaf stand in the pan on a cooling rack for 5 minutes, then carefully tip out onto another cooling rack. Stand the
loaf right side up. Place a sheet of waxed paper under the cooling
rack to catch any dribbles of the topping.

FINISH THE TEA LOAF WITH THE LEMON-SUGAR WASH
Immediately apply the lemon-sugar wash over the top and sides of
the warm loaf cake, using a soft, 1-inch-wide pastry brush. Cool
completely before slicing and serving. *Slicing observation* Use a serrated knife to cut the
cake neatly and cleanly.

FRESHLY BAKED, THE TEA LOAF KEEPS FOR 2 DAYS.

LEMON-LIME CAKE WITH
GLAZED CITRUS THREADS

One 10-inch fluted tube cake, creating 16 slices

*F*INE, LONG SHREDS OF GLAZED LEMON AND LIME peel, glistening and bright, weave through this citrus-spiked butter cake batter. For a keen flavor impact, the baked cake is finished with fresh sweet-sharp glaze (it's actually uncooked), which you brush over the cake when it's released from the baking pan. This cake is sweet and tart, and delicious served with a raspberry or blueberry compote.

Nonstick cooking spray, for preparing
   the cake pan

GLAZED LEMON AND
LIME THREADS

3 lemons, washed well and dried

1 lime, washed well and dried

⅓ cup plus 1 tablespoon granulated
   sugar

¼ cup water

LEMON-LIME BUTTER
CAKE BATTER

2¾ cups unsifted bleached all-purpose
   flour

⅓ cup unsifted bleached cake flour

½ teaspoon baking powder

½ teaspoon baking soda

¾ teaspoon salt

½ pound (16 tablespoons or 2 sticks)
   unsalted butter, softened

2 cups superfine sugar

1 tablespoon freshly grated lemon rind

2 teaspoons pure lemon extract

4 large eggs

⅞ cup (1 cup less 2 tablespoons)
   buttermilk, whisked well

2 tablespoons freshly squeezed lime
   juice

MAKE THE GLAZED LEMON AND LIME THREADS Remove the outer peel from each lemon and the lime in thin shreds with a zester, producing fine julienne threads. Place the shreds in a medium-size nonreactive saucepan, cover with 2 inches of cold water, and bring to a boil. Boil for 30 seconds, then pour into a small stainless steel strainer.

Place the granulated sugar and ¼ cup water in a small nonreactive saucepan (preferably enameled cast iron), cover, and cook over low heat until the sugar has dissolved completely. Uncover, add the citrus threads, and simmer for 5 to 8 minutes, or until the threads look glossy and there is a scant 1 tablespoon of syrup left in the saucepan.

Drain the citrus threads of any syrup, except what clings lightly to them, turn into a small ramekin, and cool completely.

PREHEAT THE OVEN AND PREPARE THE CAKE PAN Preheat the oven to 350° F. Film the inside of the Bundt pan with nonstick cooking spray; set aside.

MIX THE LEMON-LIME BUTTER CAKE BATTER Sift the all-purpose flour, cake flour, baking powder, baking soda, and salt onto a sheet of waxed paper.

¼ cup freshly squeezed and strained
lemon juice

¼ cup freshly squeezed and strained
lime juice

½ cup superfine sugar

BAKEWARE

10-inch Bundt pan

Cream the butter in the large bowl of a freestanding electric mixer on moderate speed for 3 minutes. Add the superfine sugar in three additions, beating on moderate speed for 1 minute after each portion is added. Beat in the grated lemon rind and lemon extract. Add the eggs, one at a time, beating for 30 seconds after each addition.

On low speed, alternately add the sifted ingredients in three additions with the buttermilk in two additions, beginning and ending with the sifted mixture. Scrape down the sides of the mixing bowl frequently to keep the batter even-textured. Blend in the lime juice and cooled, glazed citrus threads.

Scrape the batter into the prepared Bundt pan. Gently shake the pan (once or twice) from side to side to level the top.

BAKE AND COOL THE CAKE Bake the cake for 55 minutes to 1 hour, or until risen, set, and a wooden pick inserted in the cake withdraws clean. The baked cake will pull away slightly from the sides and central tube of the baking pan.

Let the cake stand in the pan on a cooling rack for 5 to 8 minutes. Invert the cake onto another cooling rack. Place a sheet of waxed paper under the cooling rack to catch any drips of glaze.

MIX THE LEMON-LIME BRUSHING GLAZE Make the brushing glaze while the cake is cooling in the pan. Combine the lemon juice, lime juice, and sugar in a small non-reactive bowl.

BEST BAKING ADVICE

The glazed citrus threads can be made up to 2 days in advance. Refrigerate the simmered citrus threads in the remaining syrup in a tightly covered, nonreactive storage container, but use them at room temperature.

GLAZE THE HOT CAKE Using a soft, 1-inch pastry brush, paint the citrus glaze over the surface of the hot cake, taking care to dampen the sides of the cake as well as the top. Cool completely before slicing and serving. *Slicing observation* Use a serrated knife to cut the cake neatly and cleanly.

FRESHLY BAKED, THE CAKE KEEPS FOR 3 DAYS.

LEMON POUND CAKE

One 10-inch cake, creating about 20 slices

A THOROUGHLY PAMPERED LEMON BATTER—with a blushing number of eggs—makes a bountiful cake: This version might actually reshape your idea of how pound cake should taste. The flavor scale is tipped by using a citrus rind-juice-extract mixture and lemony topping, but for the lemon intensity to come through, sour cream must be present. It typically adds moisture to a batter, but also allows a lemon-flavored cake to develop that mellow citric edge.

Shortening and bleached all-purpose flour, for preparing the cake pan

Lemon Peel Infusion (see page 60), for adding to the batter

SOUR CREAM LEMON CAKE BATTER

3 cups unsifted all-purpose flour

¼ teaspoon baking soda

1 teaspoon salt

½ pound (16 tablespoons or 2 sticks) unsalted butter, softened

3 cups superfine sugar

6 large eggs

1 cup thick, cultured sour cream

Lemon-Sugar Wash (see page 59), for brushing on the warm, baked cake

BAKEWARE

plain 10-inch tube pan

PREHEAT THE OVEN AND PREPARE THE CAKE PAN Preheat the oven to 325° F. Grease the inside of the tube pan with shortening. Line the bottom of the pan with a circle of waxed paper cut to fit and grease the paper. Dust the inside of the pan with all-purpose flour. Tap out any excess flour; set aside.

MAKE THE LEMON INFUSION Make the lemon rind-lemon juice-lemon extract mixture and set aside for 15 minutes.

MIX THE SOUR CREAM LEMON CAKE BATTER Sift the flour, baking soda, and salt onto a sheet of waxed paper.

Cream the butter in the large bowl of a freestanding electric mixer on moderately low speed for 4 minutes. Add the superfine sugar in three additions, beating for 1 minute on moderate speed after each portion is added. Beat in the eggs, one at a time, blending for 45 seconds after each addition.

On low speed, alternately add the sifted mixture in three additions with the sour cream in two additions, beginning and ending with the sifted ingredients. Scrape down the sides of the mixing bowl frequently with a rubber spatula to keep the batter even-textured. Blend in the prepared lemon infusion.

Spoon the batter into the prepared tube pan. Smooth over the top with a rubber spatula.

BAKE THE CAKE Bake the cake in the preheated oven for 1 hour and 15 minutes to 1 hour and 20 minutes, or until risen, set, and a wooden pick inserted in the cake withdraws clean. The baked cake will pull away slightly from the sides of the baking pan.

COOL AND APPLY THE FINISH TO THE CAKE Cool the cake in the pan on a rack for 10 minutes. Carefully invert the cake onto another cooling rack, peel off the waxed paper circle, then invert again onto another rack to cool right side up. Place a sheet of waxed paper under the cooling rack to catch any drips of the topping.

Using a soft, 1-inch-wide pastry brush, brush the lemon-sugar wash on the surface of the warm cake. Cool completely before slicing and serving. *Slicing observation* Use a serrated knife to cut the cake neatly and cleanly.

FRESHLY BAKED, THE POUND CAKE KEEPS FOR 5 DAYS.

LEMON LAYER CAKE

One three-layer, 8-inch cake, creating about 10 slices

THE JOY OF LEMON: a sweet-and-tangy stovetop-cooked custard joins together three light layers of lemon cake, and the stacked layers are covered in a buttery, lemon-stroked confectioners' sugar frosting.

Shortening and all-purpose flour, for preparing the layer cake pans

LEMON BUTTER CAKE BATTER

3 cups sifted bleached cake flour

2½ teaspoons baking powder

½ teaspoon salt

½ pound (16 tablespoons or 2 sticks) unsalted butter, softened

2 cups lemon-scented granulated sugar (see page 55)

2 teaspoons pure lemon extract

2 tablespoons freshly grated lemon rind

1 cup milk, cold

PREHEAT THE OVEN AND PREPARE THE LAYER CAKE PANS Preheat the oven to 350° F. Lightly grease the inside of the cake pans with shortening. Line the bottom of each pan with a circle of waxed paper, grease the paper, and dust the inside with all-purpose flour. Tap out any excess flour; set aside.

MIX THE LEMON LAYER CAKE BATTER Sift the flour, baking powder, and salt onto a sheet of waxed paper.

Cream the butter in the large bowl of a freestanding electric mixer on moderate speed for 2 minutes. Add 1¾ cups of the lemon-scented granulated sugar in three additions (reserving ¼ cup to use with the egg whites below), beating for 1 minute on moderate speed after each portion is added. Blend in the lemon extract and lemon rind.

3 tablespoons water, cold

5 large egg whites

⅛ teaspoon cream of tartar

Lemon Custard Filling (see page 415), for spreading on the baked cake layers

Lemon Frosting (see page 416), for spreading on the top and sides of the baked cake layers

BAKEWARE

three 8-inch round layer cake pans

On low speed, add the sifted ingredients in three additions with the cold milk in two additions, beginning and ending with the sifted mixture. Blend in the cold water. Scrape down the sides of the mixing bowl frequently with a rubber spatula to keep the batter even-textured.

Using an electric hand mixer, beat the egg whites in a clean, dry bowl until foamy, add the cream of tartar, and continue beating until soft peaks are formed. Sprinkle over the remaining ¼ cup lemon-scented granulated sugar and continue beating until firm (but not stiff) peaks are formed.

Stir 3 large spoonfuls of the beaten whites into the lemon butter cake batter, then fold in the remaining whites, combining the two mixtures lightly but thoroughly until the whites are completely incorporated.

Spoon the batter into the cake pans, dividing it evenly among them. Smooth over the batter with a rubber spatula or flexible palette knife.

BAKE AND COOL THE CAKE LAYERS Bake the layers for 30 minutes, or until nicely risen, set, golden on top, and a wooden pick withdraws clean 1 inch from the center of each layer. Each baked layer will pull away slightly from the sides of the cake pan. Cool the cake layers in the pans on racks for 6 to 8 minutes. Invert each layer onto another rack, peel off the waxed-paper round, then invert again to cool right side up. Cool completely.

ASSEMBLE AND FROST THE CAKE Have the custard filling and frosting at hand.

Tear off four 3-inch-wide strips of waxed paper. Place the strips in the shape of a square around the outer 3 inches of a cake plate. Center one cake layer on the plate (partially covering the waxed paper square; at least 1 inch of the strip should be visible). Spread half of the filling on the cake layer evenly, using a flexible palette knife. Carefully place the second layer on top, and cover that layer with the remaining filling. Carefully place the third layer on top. Frost the sides and top of the cake. When the frosting has set, in about 45 minutes, gently slide out and discard the waxed paper strips.

BEST BAKING ADVICE

Cold milk and cold water, in addition to the beaten egg whites, lighten the texture of the baked cake layers.

Cut the cake into slices for serving. Serve the cake very fresh, within 4 hours of filling and frosting. The custard-filled cake is fragile and must be refrigerated after 1 hour. Refrigerate any leftover cake in an airtight cake keeper.

LEMON CUSTARD FILLING

Makes about 1¼ cups

*T*HIS TANGY LEMON FILLING is delicious spread on layers of white or yellow cake. It can be made a day in advance.

LEMON CUSTARD FILLING

1 cup lemon-scented granulated sugar (see page 55)

2 tablespoons cornstarch

pinch of salt

½ cup water

½ cup plus 3 tablespoons freshly squeezed lemon juice

4 large egg yolks, lightly beaten to mix in a small bowl

2 teaspoons freshly grated lemon rind

2 tablespoons unsalted butter, softened

BEST BAKING ADVICE

Adding the remaining tablespoon lemon juice at the end (with the lemon rind and butter) brightens the taste of the filling.

MAKE THE LEMON FILLING Sift the lemon-scented granulated sugar, cornstarch, and salt into a heavy, nonreactive 2-quart saucepan (preferably enameled cast iron). Whisk the cornstarch-sugar mixture thoroughly to blend. Stir in the water and blend well. Stir in ½ cup plus 2 tablespoons lemon juice, reserving 1 tablespoon lemon juice.

Set the saucepan over moderately high heat and bring to the boil, stirring slowly with a wooden spoon. Do not use a whisk. Do not stir rapidly. *Stirring observation* Stirring too quickly or using a whisk would break down the bonds of cornstarch built up at the filling mixture heats and thickens.

Bring the mixture to the boil, stirring, and cook at a low boil for 1 minute. Stir 3 tablespoons of the hot lemon mixture into the eggs yolks. Remove the saucepan from the heat, slowly and carefully stir in the tempered egg yolks, return to the heat, and let the mixture cook at a low to moderate boil for 1 minute longer, or until thickened.

STRAIN, FINISH, AND COOL THE LEMON FILLING Place a fine-meshed stainless steel sieve over a medium-size nonreactive bowl. Scrape the hot filling into the sieve and press it through, using a rubber spatula. Using a wooden spoon or flat wooden paddle, gently stir in the lemon rind, butter, and the remaining 1 tablespoon lemon juice. Transfer the filling to a storage container, press a piece of food-safe plastic wrap directly on the surface, and cool for 20 minutes. Cover the container with the lid and refrigerate for 6 hours (or up to 24 hours) before using.

LEMON FROSTING

Makes about 3⅔ cups

THIS CONFECTIONERS' SUGAR FROSTING is uplifted with lemon juice, lemon rind, and pure lemon extract, and its creaminess is an excellent counterpoint to satiny layers of cake.

LEMON FROSTING

6 cups confectioners' sugar

large pinch of salt

5 tablespoons freshly squeezed and strained lemon juice

3 tablespoons heavy cream

1¼ teaspoons pure lemon extract

8 tablespoons (1 stick) unsalted butter, cut into tablespoon chunks, softened

2 tablespoons plus 1 teaspoon freshly grated lemon rind

MAKE THE LEMON FROSTING Place the confectioners' sugar in a large mixing bowl. Add the salt, lemon juice, heavy cream, and lemon extract. Scatter over the chunks of butter. Beat the ingredients together with an electric hand mixer on moderate speed for 2 minutes, or until smooth. Scrape down the sides of the mixing bowl once or twice with a rubber spatula to keep the frosting even-textured. Add the grated lemon rind, raise the speed to moderately high, and beat for 3 minutes longer, or until the frosting is somewhat lightened in texture.

Use the frosting immediately on thoroughly cooked layers of cake.

LEMON-POPPYSEED CAKE

One 10-inch tube cake, creating about 20 slices

I N T H E A M E R I C A N P A N O R A M A O F B U T T E R C A K E S, the combination of lemon and poppyseed is an enduring and treasured one. In all its many forms and variations, this type of cake is adored for its clean citrus flavor and subtle crunch of seeds.

Shortening and bleached all-purpose flour, for preparing the cake pan

Lemon Peel Infusion (see page 60), for adding to the batter

LEMON-POPPYSEED SOUR CREAM CAKE BATTER

3 cups unsifted bleached all-purpose flour

½ teaspoon baking soda

1 teaspoon salt

½ pound (16 tablespoons or 2 sticks) unsalted butter, softened

2¾ cups lemon-scented granulated sugar (see page 55)

6 large eggs

1 cup thick, cultured sour cream

3 tablespoons milk

⅓ cup poppyseeds

Lemon-Sugar Wash (see page 59), for brushing on the warm, baked cake

BAKEWARE

plain 10-inch tube pan

MIX THE LEMON INFUSION Mix the ingredients for the Lemon Peel Infusion as described on page 60; set aside for 15 minutes.

PREHEAT THE OVEN AND PREPARE THE CAKE PAN Preheat the oven to 350° F. Grease the inside of the tube pan with shortening. Line the bottom of the pan with waxed paper cut to fit, and grease the paper. Dust the inside of the pan with all-purpose flour. Tap out any excess flour; set aside.

MIX THE LEMON-POPPYSEED SOUR CREAM CAKE BATTER Sift the flour, baking soda, and salt two times onto a sheet of waxed paper.

Cream the butter in the large bowl of a freestanding electric mixer on moderate speed for 4 minutes. Add the lemon-scented granulated sugar in three additions, beating for 1 minute after each portion is added. Add the eggs, one at a time, mixing for 45 seconds after each addition. Blend in the lemon infusion.

On low speed, alternately add the sifted ingredients in three additions with the sour cream in two additions, beginning and ending with the sifted mixture. Scrape down the sides of the mixing bowl frequently with a rubber spatula to keep the batter even-textured. *Batter texture observation* The batter will be creamy and moderately thick. Blend in the milk. Stir in the poppyseeds.

Spoon the batter into the prepared tube pan. Shake the pan gently from side to side, once or twice, to level the top.

BAKE AND COOL THE CAKE Bake the cake in the preheated oven for 1 hour and 20 minutes to 1 hour and 25 minutes, or until risen, set, and a wooden pick inserted in the cake withdraws clean. The baked cake will pull away slightly from the sides of the

Use softened (but not oily) butter. The sour cream in the batter and the final brush-on of a lemon-sugar wash are two elements that make this cake ultra-moist.

baking pan. Let the cake stand in the pan on a cooling rack for 10 minutes. Invert the cake, peel off the waxed paper circle, then invert again to stand right side up. Place a sheet of waxed paper under the cooling rack to catch any drips of sugar wash.

FINISH THE CAKE WITH THE LEMON-SUGAR WASH Using a soft, 1-inch pastry brush, apply the wash over the top and sides of the cake. Cool completely before slicing and serving. *Slicing observation* Use a serrated knife to cut the cake neatly and cleanly. Store in an airtight cake keeper.

FRESHLY BAKED, THE CAKE KEEPS FOR 5 DAYS.

LEMON-WALNUT BREAD

One 9 by 5-inch loaf, creating about 12 slices

Bᴜᴛᴛᴇʀʏ ᴇɴᴏᴜɢʜ ᴛᴏ ʙʀɪɴɢ ᴏᴜᴛ the soft citrus fragrance, this is a loaf that is welcome at breakfast, brunch, or tea time.

Shortening and bleached all-purpose flour, for preparing the loaf pan

LEMON-WALNUT BATTER

1¾ cups unsifted bleached all-purpose flour

1¼ teaspoons baking powder

¼ teaspoon salt

¼ pound (8 tablespoons or 1 stick) unsalted butter, softened

1 cup lemon-scented granulated sugar (see page 55)

2 large eggs

2 tablespoons ground walnuts

1½ teaspoons pure lemon extract

1 tablespoon freshly grated lemon rind

½ cup plus 2 tablespoons heavy cream

½ cup chopped walnuts, lightly toasted and cooled

Lemon "Soaking" Glaze (see page 404), for brushing on the warm, baked bread

BAKEWARE

9 by 5 by 3-inch loaf pan

Pʀᴇʜᴇᴀᴛ ᴛʜᴇ ᴏᴠᴇɴ ᴀɴᴅ ᴘʀᴇᴘᴀʀᴇ ᴛʜᴇ ʟᴏᴀꜰ ᴘᴀɴ Preheat the oven to 350° F. Lightly grease the inside of the loaf pan with shortening. Dust the inside of the pan with all-purpose flour. Tap out any excess flour; set aside.

Mᴀᴋᴇ ᴛʜᴇ ʟᴇᴍᴏɴ-ᴡᴀʟɴᴜᴛ ʙᴀᴛᴛᴇʀ Sift the flour, baking powder, and salt onto a sheet of waxed paper.

Cream the butter in the large bowl of a freestanding electric mixer on moderate speed for 3 minutes. Add the lemon-scented granulated sugar in three additions, beating for about 45 seconds after each portion is added. Beat in the eggs, one at a time, mixing for about 45 seconds after each is added. Blend in the ground walnuts, lemon extract, and grated lemon rind.

On low speed, add half of the sifted mixture, the cream, then the balance of the sifted mixture. Scrape down the sides of the mixing bowl frequently with a rubber spatula to keep the batter even-textured. *Batter texture observation* The batter will be smooth and moderately thick. Blend in the chopped walnuts. Spoon the batter into the prepared loaf pan.

Bᴀᴋᴇ ᴀɴᴅ ᴄᴏᴏʟ ᴛʜᴇ ʟᴏᴀꜰ Bake the loaf for 50 minutes, or until risen, set, and a wooden pick inserted in the cake withdraws clean. When baked, the bread will pull away slightly from the sides of the baking pan.

Let the cake stand in the pan on a cooling rack for 5 minutes, then carefully remove it to another cooling rack. Stand the bread right side up. Place a sheet of waxed paper under the cooling rack to catch any drips of the wash.

The ground walnuts add a reinforcing and subtle texture to the baked loaf, and the nut flavor is repeated by adding chopped, lightly toasted walnuts.

FINISH THE LOAF WITH THE LEMON GLAZE Immediately coat the top and sides of the loaf with the lemon-sugar glaze, using a soft, 1-inch-wide pastry brush. Cool completely before slicing and serving. *Slicing observation* Use a serrated knife to cut the cake neatly and cleanly.

FRESHLY BAKED, THE TEA BREAD KEEPS FOR 2 TO 3 DAYS.

Suzanne's Lemon Tart

RADIANT, LEMONY, AND RAVISHING—and it's all in the filling. A perfect, easy-to-make filling mixture that's sweet-sharp and lemon-intense is contained in a cookie dough crust, and the merger of the two shapes is a tart that you're not likely to forget.

This lemon tart is named for Suzanne Reifers, who owned a wine bar and bistro in the Dupont Circle section of Washington, D.C. This exceptionally popular dessert was available in the restaurant and in the prepared food carry-out section, too. To this day, people remember the tart. The tart was composed of a cookie dough crust, sweet-tart lemon filling, apricot glaze, and thin slices of lemon carefully placed on top of the warm glaze. Years ago, Suzanne was kind enough to share with me the recipe for the filling, the procedure for baking the tart, and the garnish. I devised my own cookie dough crust and apricot glaze to go with it.

Butter Cookie Tart Dough, prepared and prebaked (see page 423)

SUZANNE'S LEMON TART FILLING

5 large eggs

1⅛ cups granulated sugar

4 tablespoons (½ stick) unsalted butter, melted and cooled

¾ cup freshly squeezed and strained lemon juice

1 tablespoon freshly grated lemon rind

APRICOT GLAZE FOR FINISHING THE TART

1 cup apricot preserves

1 teaspoon freshly squeezed lemon juice

1 teaspoon water

Paper-thin slices of lemon, for garnishing the tart (optional)

BAKEWARE

fluted 9½-inch round tart pan (with a removable bottom)

cookie sheet or rimmed sheet pan

PREPARE THE TART DOUGH AND PREBAKE THE TART SHELL Make the dough, line the tart pan, and prebake the crust as directed in the recipe for Butter Cookie Tart Dough on page 423.

PREHEAT THE OVEN Preheat the oven to 325° F. Have a cookie sheet or sheet pan at hand.

MIX THE LEMON TART FILLING In a medium-size mixing bowl, whisk the eggs lightly to combine them, add the granulated sugar, and whisk until well blended. Blend in the melted butter, lemon juice, and grated lemon rind, mixing thoroughly and slowly to create as little surface foam as possible. *Mixing observation* The filling must be mixed well; otherwise the melted butter won't fully disperse in the filling mixture and will puddle on top of the tart as it bakes.

Blend together the ingredients for the
filling thoroughly and, as quickly as
possible, get it into the tart shell and onto
the oven rack.

FILL THE TART SHELL WITH THE LEMON MIXTURE Place the tart shell on the cookie sheet. Since the filling is liquidy, filling and baking the tart on the cookie sheet makes it easier to navigate it in and out of the oven. Pour the filling into the tart shell.

BAKE AND COOL THE TART Carefully transfer the filled tart-cookie sheet assembly to the oven rack. Bake the tart in the preheated oven for 20 minutes, or until just set. Transfer the tart (on the cookie sheet) to a cooling rack and let stand for 5 minutes. Carefully move the tart (in its pan) from the cookie sheet to a cooling rack. Cool for 30 minutes.

MAKE THE APRICOT GLAZE While the tart is baking, make the glaze: Combine the apricot preserves, lemon juice, and water in a small, heavy nonreactive saucepan (preferably enameled cast iron). Set over moderately high heat and bring to a rapid simmer, stirring occasionally. Strain the preserves through a medium-size fine-meshed sieve into a heatproof bowl. Rinse and dry the saucepan. Scrape the glaze back into the saucepan.

GLAZE THE TART Just before you are about to finish the tart, bring the glaze to a simmer. Let it bubble for 30 seconds. Dip a 1-inch-wide pastry brush into the hot glaze. Lightly dab the glaze on top of the tart, letting it flow down from the pastry brush onto the surface of the tart, and smooth it on lightly. *Glazing observation* Dabbing, rather than actually painting, the glaze on the top preserves the fragile surface of the tart.

If you are finishing the tart with the lemon slices, immediately set them randomly (or in a pattern) on top of the freshly glazed tart. Cool completely. Carefully release the tart from the pan's outer ring, leaving it on its base. Serve the tart at room temperature, or lightly chilled. Cut the tart into wedges for serving.

FRESHLY BAKED, THE TART KEEPS FOR 2 DAYS.

BUTTER COOKIE TART DOUGH

One 9½-inch tart crust

*T*HE CLEAR, SWEET TASTE OF BUTTER comes through in this egg yolk-fortified tart crust. This cookie dough, which I've perfected over the years, has enough sugar to tenderize, egg yolks to color and enrich, and butter to flavor.

BUTTER COOKIE DOUGH

1¼ cups unsifted bleached all-purpose flour

⅛ teaspoon salt

6 tablespoons (¾ stick) unsalted butter, cool but still firm, cut into teaspoon-size pieces

¼ cup plus 1 tablespoon superfine sugar

3 large egg yolks, lightly beaten

½ teaspoon pure vanilla extract

BAKEWARE

fluted 9½-inch round tart pan (with a removable bottom)

cookie sheet or rimmed baking pan

MAKE THE BUTTER COOKIE TART DOUGH BY HAND **Combine** the flour and salt in a medium-size mixing bowl. Drop in the chunks of butter and, using a pastry blender, cut the fat into the flour until reduced to bits about the size of dried navy beans. Sprinkle the superfine sugar over the mixture and thoroughly mix it in, using a rubber spatula.

In a small ramekin, whisk the egg yolks and vanilla extract. Pour the egg yolk mixture over the tart dough mixture, and mix with a rubber spatula to incorporate the egg yolks into the flour-butter mixture.

With your fingertips, work the mixture until it forms a solid dough by lightly rubbing the mixture together. *Dough observation* The little clusters of dough should be a uniform color, with the pieces of butter worked in; if a few big pieces of butter are visible, work them into the dough.

MAKE THE BUTTER COOKIE TART DOUGH IN A FOOD PROCESSOR **Place the flour** and salt in the container of a food processor fitted with the steel knife. Cover and process, using two quick on-off pulses, to combine the flour and salt. Add the butter pieces, cover, and process, using about eight on-off pulses, to reduce the butter into small bits. Sprinkle over the sugar, cover, and process to combine, using two quick on-off pulses. Whisk the egg yolks and vanilla extract in a small mixing bowl, pour over the flour-butter-sugar combination, and process, using eight to ten on-off pulses, until the dough mixture forms very small pellets. Avoid processing the dough until it bonds together into a mass. *Dough texture observation* The dough should be a uniform golden color, free of streaks and in small, moist-looking beads. At this point, the dough mixture will appear more granular than that of a handmade dough.

CREATE A CAKE OF DOUGH, ROLL IT INTO A ROUND, AND REFRIGERATE Turn the fragments of handmade dough or loose-textured food processor-created dough onto a work surface. Gather and press the dough into a cake. (Don't worry about overworking it at this point.) Gently knead the dough with the heel of your hand to allow the elements to coalesce. Roll the dough to a 10½-inch round between two sheets of waxed paper. Transfer the dough round to a cookie sheet and refrigerate for 15 minutes.

LINE THE TART PAN WITH THE DOUGH Have the tart pan at hand.

Remove the sheet of dough from the refrigerator, peel away the top sheet of waxed paper, and let the dough stand for about 2 minutes.

Invert the dough onto the tart pan and peel off the top sheet of waxed paper. Set the dough in place by pressing it first onto the bottom of the tart pan (using the pads of your fingertips). Press the dough up and onto the fluted sides of the tart pan. With your thumb, press back a ¼-inch ridge of dough (using the dough that extends past the rim) all around the edges of the pan. Roll over the top of the dough with a rolling pin to cut away the overhang of tart dough; there should be a small amount to cut off. Now, press up on the tucked-in ¼ inch of dough—all around the perimeter of the pan—to create a reinforcing edge that extends about ⅛ inch above the rim. This heightened rim is necessary in order to contain all of the tart filling.

Prick the bottom of the crust lightly with the tines of a fork (in about 10 random places).

REFRIGERATE THE DOUGH–LINED TART PAN Refrigerate the crust for 2 hours. The tart shell can be made in advance and stored in the refrigerator overnight. To do so, after 1 hour and once the dough is firm, slide the lined tart pan into a large, self-sealing plastic bag and refrigerate.

PREBAKE THE TART SHELL On baking day, preheat the oven to 375° F. Place the cookie sheet or baking pan on the oven rack about 10 minutes before you are ready to bake the tart shell.

Line the dough-lined tart pan with a sheet of aluminum foil, very lightly pressing the foil against the bottom and sides of the dough. *Technique observation* Firmly pressing the foil against the tart crust would actually bond a thin layer of the crust to the foil, and when you remove the foil insert, some of the crust might stick to it and peel away from the inner part of the crust.

Fill the lined tart pan with raw rice. (The container of rice should be stored exclusively for this purpose.) Place on the cookie sheet and bake for 15 minutes. Carefully spoon out about one-third of the rice, then lift away the foil with its contents and return the remaining rice to the container.

Reduce the heat to 350° F., return the tart shell to the oven, and continue baking for 15 minutes longer, or until light golden and set. *Dough color observation* The bottom (base) of the tart dough will be a pale tan (biscuit) color, and the edges a golden color.

Transfer the tart shell (still on the cookie sheet) to a cooling rack and let stand for 5 minutes. The tart shell is now ready to be filled.

LEMON ROLL

One 9½-inch roll, creating 8 slices

THE LIGHT CAKE BATTER, softly seasoned with lemon extract and lemon rind, bakes into a sheet that forms a tender and delicate cushion for whipped cream-lightened lemon curd. Serve slices of the roll, cut on the diagonal, with a compote of fresh berries.

Shortening, softened unsalted butter, and bleached all-purpose flour, for preparing the jellyroll pan

LEMON ROLL CAKE BATTER

¾ cup plus 3 tablespoons unsifted bleached cake flour

½ teaspoon baking powder

⅛ teaspoon salt

4 large eggs

1 cup superfine sugar

1¼ teaspoons pure lemon extract

2 teaspoons freshly grated lemon rind

¼ cup milk

LEMON FILLING FOR SPREADING ON THE BAKED JELLYROLL CAKE LAYER

Silky Lemon Cream (see page 428), well chilled, without the final stir-in of ¼ cup heavy cream

½ cup heavy cream, cold

Confectioners' sugar, for sprinkling on the finished roll

BAKEWARE

10½ by 15½ by 1¾-inch jelly roll pan

PREHEAT THE OVEN AND PREPARE THE JELLYROLL PAN
Preheat the oven to 375° F. Dab a little shortening on the surface at the four bottom corners and in the middle of the jellyroll pan. Line the inside of the pan with waxed paper, allowing the paper to extend about 3 inches above the short sides. Butter the bottom and sides of the waxed paper and dust with a haze of all-purpose flour. Carefully tap out any excess flour; set aside.

MIX THE LEMON ROLL CAKE BATTER Sift the flour two times with the baking powder and salt onto a sheet of waxed paper.

With the whisk attachment in place, beat the eggs in the large bowl of a heavy-duty freestanding electric mixer on moderately high speed for 2 minutes (#6 speed on a KitchenAid mixer). Add the superfine sugar and beat for 4 minutes longer on moderately high speed. Blend in the lemon extract and grated lemon rind. Add the milk and beat for 30 seconds on low speed (#1 on a KitchenAid mixer). Remove the mixing bowl from the stand.

Sift half of the dry ingredients over the eggs-sugar-milk mixture. By hand, whisk the two together lightly until the particles of flour have disappeared. Sift over the remaining flour and whisk to combine. Avoid overwhisking the batter. *Batter texture observation* The batter will be very light and billowy.

Pour and scrape the batter into the prepared jellyroll pan. Smooth over the batter with a rubber spatula, making sure that it flows into the corners of the pan evenly.

Bake and cool the cake roll Bake the cake roll for 12 to 13 minutes, or until light golden on top and set. Let the roll stand on a cooling rack for 2 minutes.

Trim the cake roll Sprinkle a haze of confectioners' sugar on top of the roll. Place a large sheet of parchment paper on top and invert onto a cooling rack. Remove the baking pan. Carefully peel away the waxed paper. Trim off the firmer edges with a serrated knife. Starting at one of the short ends, roll up the sheet of cake, rolling the parchment paper along with the cake as you go. Cool completely. This will take about 1 hour.

Finish the cake roll filling Whip the cream until moderately soft peaks are formed in a small, chilled mixing bowl. Stir a spoonful of the whipped cream into the curd. Fold in the remaining cream until thoroughly combined.

Fill the roll Carefully unroll the sheet of cake. Spread the filling on the surface of cake to within about ¾ inch of the four sides. Roll up the cake beginning at one of the short ends, using the end of the sheet of parchment to help you push along the roll (but don't enclose the parchment this time!). Chill for 1 hour.

Sift confectioners' sugar generously over the top and sides of the cake and serve very fresh, cut into slices on the diagonal, using a serrated knife.

SILKY LEMON CREAM

About 2⅔ cups

THIS IS JUST ABOUT as fine a lemon filling as you could imagine—sharp, sweet, tangy, and lightly creamy. The silky quality of the filling is cultivated by employing three tricks: the lemon base is cooked slowly to silkiness, "quick-chilled" in an ice water bath as soon as it is cooked, and embellished with heavy cream after it has been refrigerated. Quick-chilling the base after it has been cooked on the stove top virtually guarantees a lithe and gracefully soft texture.

LEMON CREAM

6 large egg yolks

1 cup plus 2 tablespoons superfine sugar

⅔ cup freshly squeezed and strained lemon juice

7 tablespoons (1 stick less 1 tablespoon) unsalted butter, softened, cool (but not soft), cut into small cubes

1 tablespoon freshly grated lemon rind

pinch of salt

¼ cup heavy cream

Years ago, with the memory of my mother's and grandmother's lemon custard sauce firmly secured in my consciousness, I worked out a formula for a lemon cream dessert sauce (it's actually a softer, flowing version of this filling thickened a bit with arrowroot); it contains half as many yolks as this filling, a little less than half the amount of butter and sugar and a splash of light cream. I decided to modify the formula to make a rich lemon filling, one that would stand up to the addition of heavy cream, whipped or unwhipped. Unlike many lemon fillings, this one uses egg yolks alone and less butter than some versions of lemon cream.

The lemon cream is as good hidden within the fold of a crêpe, as it is spooned to the side of a crispy waffle, a mound of fresh berries, or a thick slice of buttery pound cake.

MAKE THE LEMON BASE Combine the egg yolks, granulated sugar, and salt in a large (7½- to 8-cup), heavy nonreactive saucepan (preferably enameled cast iron), using a wooden spoon or flat wooden paddle. *Mixture texture observation* At first the mixture will be heavy, wet, and sandy textured, but after a minute or so of mixing, will become a little more stirable. Whisk for 1 to 2 minutes.

Stir in the lemon juice and cold cubes of butter. Set the saucepan over moderate heat and cook, stirring continuously, for 10 to 11 minutes, or until lightly thickened. Do not allow the mixture to simmer merrily along, or the lemon base will have a gummy texture when chilled. Using a heavy pan for this step is important because it diffuses and moderates the heat. *Thickness observation* At this point, the lemon base should lightly coat a wooden spoon or paddle and will be ultra-smooth. Using cool butter initially helps to keep the lemon mixture creamy-textured, rather than dense or oily. (If it is overcooked in the saucepan to very thick, the lemon mixture will have gluey, slightly adhesive quality.)

Turn off the heat and let the lemon base stand in the pan for 2 to 3 minutes, stirring continuously. The residual heat will finish the thickening process. Stir in the lemon rind and salt. Scrape the lemon base in to a nonreactive medium-size mixing bowl.

QUICK-CHILL THE LEMON BASE Set the bowl containing the lemon base in a large mixing bowl one-third filled with cold water and two or three handfuls of ice cubes. Let the lemon mixture cool down for 20 minutes, stirring frequently with a rubber spatula. *Thickness observation* After 20 minutes, the lemon base will be as thick as soft pudding, and thickly coat a wooden spoon, spatula, or flat wooden paddle. Remove the bowl containing the lemon base from the water bath and thoroughly dry the outside.

REFRIGERATE THE LEMON BASE Scrape the lemon mixture into a nonreactive storage container, cover, and refrigerate overnight. It will firm up a little more after an overnight refrigeration. The lemon base can be stored in the refrigerator for 2 days.

FINISH THE LEMON FILLING WITH THE CREAM ADDITION Just before using it, scrape the lemon base into a medium-size bowl. Gently stir in the heavy cream. Use immediately.

LEMON CRÊPES WITH SILKY LEMON CREAM

About 3 cups crêpe batter, creating 22 to 24 five-inch crêpes

Wɪᴛʜ ᴀ sᴛᴏᴠᴇ ᴛᴏᴘ-ᴄᴏᴏᴋᴇᴅ lemon custard mixture on hand, and a quick-blending of ingredients for a crêpe batter just minutes in the making, this most ethereal and intensely lemon of desserts will grace your dessert plates in fine style. The two components can be made ahead, but thin, freshly made pancakes should be used right out of the pan, and the heavy cream should be stirred into the thickened lemon mixture just before the crêpes are assembled.

Dᴇʟɪᴄᴀᴛᴇ ʟᴇᴍᴏɴ ᴄʀᴇ̂ᴘᴇ ʙᴀᴛᴛᴇʀ

2 large eggs

2 large egg yolks

7 tablespoons (1 stick less 1 tablespoon) unsalted butter, melted and cooled

3 tablespoons superfine sugar

½ teaspoon pure lemon extract

⅛ teaspoon salt

1⅓ cups plus 2 tablespoons milk

1 cup plus 1½ tablespoons unsifted bleached all-purpose flour

⅓ cup plus 2 tablespoons unsifted bleached cake flour

1 teaspoon fresh, finely grated lemon rind

Clarified butter (see page 66), for cooking the crêpes

Silky Lemon Cream (see page 428), for filling the crêpes

Confectioners' sugar, for sprinkling on top of the filled and folded crêpes

Mᴀᴋᴇ ᴛʜᴇ ʟᴇᴍᴏɴ ᴄʀᴇ̂ᴘᴇ ʙᴀᴛᴛᴇʀ Place the whole eggs, egg yolks, melted butter, superfine sugar, lemon extract, salt, and milk in the container of a 40-ounce-capacity blender. Cover securely and blend on low speed for 30 seconds. Uncover the blender. Add the all-purpose flour and cake flour. Cover tightly and blend on high speed to form a batter. Uncover, then scrape down the sides of the blender with a rubber spatula to distribute the flour evenly and to break up any lingering clumps of flour. Cover the blender and blend for 30 seconds on high speed. *Consistency observation* The batter should resemble medium-thick cream. After chilling, stir in up to 2 to 3 tablespoons additional milk to restore the consistency, if necessary.

Strain the batter through a large fine-meshed sieve into a bowl. Stir in the grated lemon rind. Cover and refrigerate the batter for at least 3 hours before using. The batter must mellow in the refrigerator so that the flour is dispelled throughout the dairy mixture. The batter can be stored in the refrigerator overnight, but must be used on the following day. Remove the batter from the refrigerator about 5 minutes before cooking the crêpes. Whisk well.

Mᴀᴋᴇ ᴛʜᴇ ᴄʀᴇ̂ᴘᴇs Heat a 6-inch-diameter crêpe pan over moderately high heat. (The base of the pan will turn out a 5-inch crêpe.) Dip a double thickness of folded-over paper towels in a little softened clarified butter.

The combination of all-purpose flour and cake flour makes the tenderest crêpes. Superfine sugar is used to sweeten the batter because of its superb dissolving ability. Clarified butter is used to gloss over the crêpe pan as the cooking medium because it can tolerate high heat without burning.

Wearing a heatproof oven glove to protect your hand, and lifting the pan off the heat at a slight tilt, quickly and carefully coat the bottom of the pan with the butter. Return the pan to the heat and let it sit on the burner for 30 seconds.

Again, using a padded glove to hold the handle, lift it away from the heat, add 2 tablespoons of the batter to the hot pan, and quickly circulate it around to coat the bottom evenly. *Procedure observation* The trick is to cover the entire bottom of the pan with the batter quickly before it has the chance to set in one area.

Return the pan to the heat and cook for about 45 seconds, or until the crepe is a lacy medium-golden color underneath. Using a slender wooden crêpe spatula or other thin wooden spatula, lift the crêpe away from the edges of the pan and carefully turn it over. Cook the crêpe on the second side (this side will turn a mottled brown), for 15 to 20 seconds longer. Continue to make crêpes in this way, buttering the pan as necessary and overlapping the crêpes slightly on a cookie sheet lined with plastic wrap.

FILL THE CRÊPES For each serving, place a scant-tablespoon of the lemon cream on the spotty brown side of each warm crêpe, and fold in half and in half again. Sprinkle the tops lightly with the confectioners' sugar just before serving.

*r*oasted peanuts and peanut butter add a distinctive edge to bar and drop cookie doughs, cake batters, and the dough for hand-formed scones. The slick, creamy density of peanut butter gives a buttery edge to bakery sweets in a way that other nut butters cannot, as the peanut variety has a faintly sweet and mellow undertone coupled with a rich consistency. Peanut butter labeled all-natural, which often appears to have separated in the container, produces inadequate results in doughs; supermarket brands such as Skippy, Jif, Reese's, or Peter Pan are preferable. In addition to peanut butter, whole or chopped peanuts and peanut butter-flavored chips add crunch and texture while creating dashes and dabs of flavor.

Spices that highlight the peanut taste are cinnamon, allspice, nutmeg, cloves, and cardamom; light or dark brown sugar builds the rounded, earthy flavor of the nut; and vanilla extract mellows its intensity.

18

PEANUT AND PEANUT BUTTER

COCOA-DOUBLE PEANUT SCONES

12 scones

PEANUT BUTTER CHIPS AND PEANUTS, along with roasted peanuts, are enveloped in a tender, cocoa-tinted scone dough: I adore the textural drama and contrast of the chips, nuts, and chocolate-flavored dough.

PEANUT BUTTER CHIP
SCONE DOUGH

4 cups unsifted bleached all-purpose flour

5 tablespoons unsweetened, alkalized cocoa, sifted

4¼ teaspoons baking powder

1 teaspoon salt

½ cup plus 2 tablespoons superfine sugar

12 tablespoons (1½ sticks) unsalted butter, cold, cut into tablespoon-size chunks

4 large eggs

2 tablespoons creamy (smooth) peanut butter

1 cup heavy cream

1 tablespoon pure vanilla extract

1½ cups peanut butter-flavored chips

¾ cup whole, roasted unsalted peanuts

BAKEWARE

2 large, heavy cookie sheets or rimmed sheet pans

PREHEAT THE OVEN AND PREPARE THE COOKIE SHEETS
Preheat the oven to 400° F. Line the cookie sheets or sheet pans with cooking parchment paper; set aside. *Bakeware observation* The baking sheets must be heavy, or the dough will scorch on the bottom as the scones bake. Double-pan the sheets, if necessary.

MIX THE PEANUT BUTTER CHIP SCONE DOUGH Whisk the flour, sifted cocoa, baking powder, salt, and superfine sugar in a large mixing bowl.

Drop in the chunks of butter and, using a pastry blender, reduce the fat to pieces about the size of dried navy beans.

Whisk the eggs and peanut butter in a medium-size mixing bowl. *Whisked mixture observation* The peanut butter will appear in small flecks and speckle the egg mixture, but will blend into the dough later on. Add the heavy cream and vanilla extract, and whisk until completely blended.

Pour the heavy cream-egg mixture over the flour-cocoa mixture, add the peanut butter chips and roasted peanuts, and combine to form a dough, using a wooden spoon or flat wooden paddle. *Dough texture observation* The dough will be somewhat stiff but moist, and because it's dense, will take 1 or 2 minutes to come together. Lightly knead the dough in the bowl, giving it about 6 turns and pushes.

FORM THE DOUGH INTO TWO CAKES AND CUT INTO SCONES On a lightly floured work surface, divide the dough in half. Form each half into a cake measuring about 7 inches in diameter. Using a sharp chef's knife, cut the cake into six wedges. Transfer the scones to the lined cookie sheets, spacing them 3 inches apart, and six to a sheet,

The small quantity of peanut butter adds a surprisingly well-developed flavor to the scone dough without making it gummy.

using a offset metal spatula. *Nuts or chips observation* Press back in any nuts or chips that may be peeking out of the dough after you've cut the scones. If the scones seem soft after cutting, refrigerate them on the cookie sheets for 20 minutes.

BAKE AND COOL THE SCONES Bake the scones for 17 minutes, or until set. Let the scones stand on the baking pans for 2 minutes, then remove them to cooling racks, using an offset metal spatula. Serve the scones warm or at room temperature.

FRESHLY BAKED, THE SCONES KEEP FOR 2 DAYS.

Variation: For cocoa-double peanut scones with Dutch-process black cocoa, use 2 tablespoons Dutch-process black cocoa and 3 tablespoons unsweetened, alkalized cocoa in the scone dough.

Retro Peanut Butter Cookies

About 4 dozen cookies

Cherished by many as, perhaps, one of the favorite souvenirs of old-fashioned baking, peanut butter cookies are an undisputed delight. Both the brown sugar and cluster of spices are present to emphasize the rich peanut butter flavor.

PEANUT BUTTER COOKIE DOUGH

2¼ cups unsifted bleached all-purpose flour

¾ teaspoon baking soda

¼ teaspoon baking powder

¾ teaspoon salt

¾ teaspoon freshly grated nutmeg

½ teaspoon ground cinnamon

¼ teaspoon ground allspice

⅛ teaspoon ground cloves

9 tablespoons (1 stick plus 1 tablespoon) unsalted butter, softened

3 tablespoons shortening

1 cup firmly packed light brown sugar, sieved if lumpy

½ cup vanilla-scented granulated sugar (see page 53)

⅔ cup creamy (smooth) peanut butter

2 large eggs

2 teaspoons pure vanilla extract

1 cup coarsely chopped roasted unsalted peanuts

BAKEWARE

several cookie sheets, preferably the insulated type

PREPARE THE COOKIE SHEETS Line the cookie sheets with lengths of cooking parchment paper; set aside.

MIX THE PEANUT BUTTER COOKIE DOUGH Sift the flour, baking soda, baking powder, salt, nutmeg, cinnamon, allspice, and cloves onto a sheet of waxed paper.

Cream the butter and shortening in the large bowl of a free-standing electric mixer on low speed for 3 minutes. Add the light brown sugar and beat on moderate speed for 1 minute; add the vanilla-scented granulated sugar and continue beating for a minute longer. Blend in the peanut butter, eggs, and vanilla extract. Scrape down the sides of the mixing bowl frequently with a rubber spatula to keep the batter even-textured.

On low speed, add the sifted mixture in two additions, beating just until the particles of flour are absorbed. Mix in the chopped peanuts.

QUICK-FREEZE THE DOUGH Turn the dough onto a large sheet of plastic wrap, press into a flat cake, enclose in the wrap, and place in a small baking pan. Freeze the dough for 20 minutes. Alternately, refrigerate the dough for 4 hours, or until firm enough to handle. (The dough may be made in advance and stored in the refrigerator for up to 2 days.)

PREHEAT THE OVEN AND FORM THE COOKIES Preheat the oven to 375° F. in advance of baking the cookies. Have a shallow plate of all-purpose flour at your work surface.

Remove the cake of dough from the freezer. Spoon out the dough by heaping tablespoons and roll into balls. Place the balls of dough, 3 inches apart, on the lined cookie sheets, arranging them nine to a sheet. Flatten the balls slightly with the lightly floured bottom of a juice glass, a smooth stainless steel meat pounder, or the palm of your hand. Lightly dip the tines of a fork into flour and crisscross the cookies twice (from top to bottom and from side to side), pressing down lightly into the dough rounds to level them a bit.

BAKE AND COOL THE COOKIES Bake the cookies in the preheated oven for 10 to 12 minutes, or until just set. Remove the cookies to cooling racks, using a wide, offset metal spatula. Cool completely.

❋ *For an aromatic topnote of flavor,* use intensified vanilla extract (see page 52) in place of plain vanilla extract in the cookie dough.

FRESHLY BAKED, THE COOKIES KEEP FOR 3 DAYS.

TISH'S CHOCOLATE–PEANUT BUTTER CLOUD PIE

One 9-inch pie, creating about 8 slices

TISH BOYLE, Food Editor of *Chocolatier* and *Pastry Art & Design* magazines, created this outstanding pie, and gave the recipe to me to share with all lovers of peanut butter (and chocolate). Tish describes the pie as a "chewy, intensely peanutty cookie crust" that "provides the foundation for a filling of half chocolate-tinged peanut butter pudding and half peanut butter mousse." The filling is a dramatic alliance of chocolate and peanut butter, and the crust, which encloses it, is a delicious cookie dough. Whipped cream tops it all off.

PEANUT BUTTER COOKIE CRUST

⅔ cup unsifted bleached all-purpose flour

½ teaspoon baking powder

⅛ teaspoon baking soda

pinch of salt

4 tablespoons (½ stick) unsalted butter, softened

⅓ cup creamy (smooth) peanut butter

¼ cup granulated sugar

¼ cup firmly packed dark brown sugar

1 large egg yolk

½ teaspoon pure vanilla extract

MIX THE PEANUT BUTTER COOKIE CRUST In a small bowl, whisk together the flour, baking powder, baking soda, and salt.

Cream the butter and peanut butter in the large bowl of a freestanding electric mixer on medium speed until smooth, about

2 ounces bittersweet chocolate, finely
chopped

2 tablespoons cornstarch

½ cup granulated sugar

pinch of salt

1¾ cups milk

2 large egg yolks

½ cup creamy (smooth) peanut butter

½ teaspoon pure vanilla extract

1 cup heavy cream, chilled

WHIPPED CREAM FOR TOPPING
THE PIE

1 cup heavy cream, chilled

1 tablespoon superfine sugar

½ teaspoon pure vanilla extract

About 3 tablespoons chopped roasted
unsalted peanuts, for sprinkling
around the edge of the whipped
cream-topped pie

BAKEWARE

9-inch pie pan

2 minutes. Add the granulated sugar and beat for 1 minute; add the dark brown sugar and beat for a minute longer. Blend in the egg yolk and vanilla extract. On low speed, add the whisked sifted mixture in two additions, beating just until the particles of flour are absorbed. Scrape down the sides of the mixing bowl with a rubber spatula once or twice to keep the dough even-textured.

Turn the dough onto a sheet of plastic wrap and shape into a disk about ½ inch thick. Wrap it up and refrigerate for 45 minutes to 1 hour, or until slightly firm and lightly chilled.

LINE THE PIE PAN WITH THE COOKIE CRUST AND REFRIGERATE Place the disk of dough in the bottom of the pie pan. With your fingertips, press the dough evenly on the bottom and up the sides of the pan. Refrigerate the cookie crust for 45 minutes.

BAKE AND COOL THE PIE CRUST Preheat the oven to 375° F. in advance of baking. Bake the crust for 13 to 15 minutes, or until it is golden brown around the edges. *Baked crust observation* The crust will be soft and puffed when you take it out of the oven, but will firm up and flatten as it cools. Place the crust-lined pan on a cooling rack. Cool completely.

MIX THE CHOCOLATE-PEANUT BUTTER MOUSSE FILLING Place the chopped chocolate in a medium-size mixing bowl.

Sift the cornstarch, sugar, and salt into a medium-size heavy saucepan, preferably enameled cast iron, then whisk to combine thoroughly. Slowly blend in the milk. Bring the mixture to a low boil over moderately high heat, stirring slowly (this will take 5 to 7 minutes) as it thickens. In a small, heat-proof bowl, whisk the egg yolks. Stir 3 to 4 spoonfuls of the hot cream into the yolks to temper them. Off the heat, stir the tempered egg yolk mixture back into the cream, then let it bubble slowly until thickened, 2 to 3 minutes longer. Remove the pan from the heat and, lightly but thoroughly, stir in the peanut butter and vanilla extract. *Technique observation* The quickest and easiest way to incorporate the peanut butter is to drop tablespoons of it on the surface of the hot pudding, add the vanilla extract, and stir carefully but thoroughly.

COMBINE PART OF THE FILLING WITH THE BITTERSWEET CHOCOLATE, FILL THE COOLED PIE CRUST, AND REFRIGERATE Slowly but thoroughly, stir 1 cup of the hot peanut butter mixture into the chopped bittersweet chocolate. Combine the mixture until the chocolate is completely melted down and incorporated into the filling.

Scrape the chocolate mixture into the prepared crust. Smooth over the top with a flexible palette knife. Refrigerate for 1 hour to 1 hour and 30 minutes, or until completely set.

COOL DOWN THE REMAINING PEANUT BUTTER FILLING Transfer the remaining peanut butter filling to a medium-size bowl, press a sheet of plastic wrap directly over the surface, and chill for 45 minutes, or until cool but not set.

LIGHTEN THE REMAINING FILLING MIXTURE WITH WHIPPED CREAM Place the chilled heavy cream in a medium-size bowl and beat on moderately high speed until soft peaks are formed. Stir 2 or 3 large spoonfuls of the whipped cream into the cooled filling mixture, then fold in the remaining cream.

ASSEMBLE THE SECOND LAYER OF THE PIE Spoon and scrape the whipped cream-enriched filling over the chocolate-peanut butter layer. Smooth over the top with a flexible palette knife. Chill until set, 4 to 6 hours.

MAKE THE WHIPPED CREAM FOR TOPPING THE PIE Place the chilled heavy cream in a medium-size bowl and beat on moderately high speed until just beginning to mound. Add the superfine sugar and vanilla extract and continue beating until softly firm peaks are formed. Top the pie with the whipped cream and refrigerate for 1 hour. Just before serving, sprinkle the edges of the whipped cream with the chopped peanuts.

PEANUT MADNESS CHUNKS

About 27 cookies

T HESE ARE VOLUPTUOUS COOKIES, with generous hunks of candy and roasted peanuts snared in a brown-sugar and vanilla-scented dough. A batch of cookie dough can be made up and refrigerated for up to 3 days (or frozen for a month) before baking, so you can have the cookies freshly baked, when the peanut flavor is at its peak.

PEANUT BUTTER CANDY COOKIE DOUGH

Eighteen (.6 ounce each) snack-size milk chocolate peanut butter cups (Reese's Milk Chocolate Peanut Butter Cups), each cup cut into ½-inch chunks

1½ cups unsifted all-purpose flour

⅛ teaspoon cream of tartar

¼ teaspoon salt

9 tablespoons (1 stick plus 1 tablespoon) unsalted butter, softened

2 tablespoons shortening

¾ cup granulated sugar

¼ cup firmly packed light brown sugar, sieved if lumpy

1 tablespoon creamy (smooth) peanut butter

1 large egg

1½ teaspoons pure vanilla extract

1 cup whole roasted unsalted peanuts

BAKEWARE

several cookie sheets

CHILL THE PEANUT BUTTER CANDY CHUNKS Place the cut-up candy in a bowl and refrigerate for 20 minutes. *Candy chilling observation* Refrigerating the chunks of candy will help to keep them intact as they are worked into the cookie dough.

MIX THE PEANUT BUTTER CANDY COOKIE DOUGH Whisk the flour, cream of tartar, and salt in a small mixing bowl.

Cream the butter and shortening in the large bowl of a freestanding electric mixer on low speed for 2 minutes. Add the granulated sugar and beat for 1 minute on moderate speed. Add the light brown sugar and beat for a minute longer. Beat in the peanut butter and egg. Blend in the vanilla extract. Scrape down the sides of the mixing bowl frequently with a rubber spatula to keep the dough even-textured. On low speed, add the sifted mixture in two additions, beating just until the particles of flour are absorbed. Work in the candy chunks and peanuts, using a wooden spoon or flat wooden paddle. *Dough texture observation* The cookie dough will be stiff and chunky with candy and nuts.

CHILL THE COOKIE DOUGH Cover the bowl with a sheet of plastic wrap and refrigerate for 15 to 20 minutes.

PREHEAT THE OVEN AND PREPARE THE COOKIE SHEETS Preheat the oven to 325° F. in advance of baking. Line the cookie sheets with lengths of cooking parchment paper.

SPOON THE DOUGH ONTO THE PREPARED COOKIE SHEETS Place rounded, lightly domed 2-tablespoon mounds of dough, 3 inches apart, onto the lined cookie sheets, about nine mounds to a sheet. For the best shaped cookies, push any chunks of candy that jut out back into the cookie dough mound.

BAKE AND COOL THE COOKIES Bake the cookies in the preheated oven for 15 to 17 minutes, or until just set, with pale golden edges. Let the cookies stand on the sheets for 1 minute, then remove them to cooling racks, using a wide, offset metal spatula. Cool completely.

❊ *For an aromatic topnote of flavor,* use intensified vanilla extract (see page 52) in place of plain vanilla extract in the cookie dough.

FRESHLY BAKED, THE COOKIES KEEP FOR 2 TO 3 DAYS.

RICH AND CHEWY PEANUT BUTTER SQUARES

16 squares

PEANUT BUTTER, WHOLE ROASTED PEANUTS, peanut butter candy, and peanut butter-flavored chips all help to develop the rich, nutty flavor in these sumptuous cut-from-the-pan bar cookies. The combination of butter in the melted, tepid state and moist brown sugar softens the texture and contributes to the chewy quality of the squares.

Nonstick cooking spray, for preparing the baking pan

PEANUT BUTTER–PEANUT BUTTER CANDY BATTER

1 cup unsifted bleached all-purpose flour

¼ cup unsifted bleached cake flour

¾ teaspoon baking powder

⅛ teaspoon salt

½ teaspoon freshly grated nutmeg

⅓ cup creamy (smooth) peanut butter

PREHEAT THE OVEN AND PREPARE THE BAKING PAN Preheat the oven to 350° F. Film the inside of the baking pan with nonstick cooking spray; set aside.

MIX THE PEANUT BUTTER–PEANUT BUTTER CANDY BATTER Sift the all-purpose flour, cake flour, baking powder, salt, and nutmeg onto a sheet of waxed paper.

¼ pound (8 tablespoons or 1 stick)
   unsalted butter, melted and cooled
   to tepid

1 cup firmly packed light brown sugar,
   sieved if lumpy

1 large egg

1 large egg yolk

¾ teaspoon intensified vanilla extract
   (see page 52)

3 packages (1.6 oz each) milk
   chocolate peanut butter cups
   (Reese's Milk Chocolate Peanut
   Butter Cups), cut into chunks

½ cup peanut butter-flavored chips

⅓ cup whole roasted salted peanuts

BAKEWARE

8 by 8 by 2-inch baking pan

In a medium-size mixing bowl, whisk the peanut butter and melted butter. Whisk in the light brown sugar, egg, egg yolk, and vanilla extract. With a wooden spoon or flat wooden paddle, stir in the sifted mixture along with the peanut butter candy chunks, peanut butter chips, and peanuts, mixing until the particles of flour are absorbed. *Batter texture observation* The batter will be very thick and chunky.

Scrape the batter into the prepared baking pan. Spread the batter evenly, using a flexible palette knife or rubber spatula.

BAKE, COOL, AND CUT THE SQUARES Bake the sweet for 25 to 30 minutes, or until set. Transfer the pan to a cooling rack. Cool completely. With a small, sharp knife, cut the entire cake into four quarters, then cut each quarter into four squares. Remove the squares from the baking pan with a small, offset metal spatula.

FRESHLY BAKED, THE SQUARES KEEP FOR 3 DAYS.

BEST BAKING ADVICE

In very humid weather, or in a humid kitchen, refrigerate the peanut butter cup chunks for 15 to 20 minutes before adding to the batter so they stay relatively distinct and don't muddy it.

DOUBLE PEANUT BARS

2 dozen bar cookies

*P*EANUT BUTTER CHIPS AND ROASTED PEANUTS add a playful—but rich—contrast of flavor to this fudgy bar cookie batter.

Nonstick cooking spray, for preparing the baking pan

PEANUT-CHOCOLATE
BAR COOKIE BATTER

1 cup unsifted bleached all-purpose flour

2 tablespoons unsweetened, alkalized cocoa

¼ teaspoon baking powder

¼ teaspoon salt

1 cup peanut butter-flavored chips

¾ cup whole roasted unsalted peanuts

½ pound (16 tablespoons or 2 sticks) unsalted butter, melted and cooled to tepid

4 ounces (4 squares) unsweetened chocolate, melted and cooled to tepid

4 large eggs

1¾ cups plus 2 tablespoons superfine sugar

2 teaspoons pure vanilla extract

Confectioners' sugar, for sifting over the top of the bars (optional)

BAKEWARE
9 by 9 by 2-inch baking pan

PREHEAT THE OVEN AND PREPARE THE BAKING PAN Preheat the oven to 325° F. Film the inside of the baking pan with non-stick cooking spray; set aside.

MIX THE PEANUT-CHOCOLATE BAR COOKIE BATTER Sift the flour, cocoa, baking powder, and salt onto a sheet of waxed paper. In a bowl, toss the peanut butter-flavored chips and peanuts with 2½ teaspoons of the sifted mixture.

Whisk the melted butter and melted unsweetened chocolate in a medium-size mixing bowl until thoroughly combined.

In a large mixing bowl, whisk the eggs to blend, add the superfine sugar, and whisk until just combined, about 1 minute. Blend in the melted chocolate-butter mixture and vanilla extract. Sift over the sifted mixture and whisk until the particles of flour are completely absorbed and a thick batter is formed. Stir in the peanut butter chips and peanuts, using a wooden spoon or flat wooden paddle.

Scrape the batter into the prepared baking pan. Smooth over the top with a rubber spatula.

BAKE, COOL, AND CUT THE BARS Bake the sweet for 33 to 38 minutes, or until set. Let the sweet stand in the pan on a cooling rack for 3 hours, then refrigerate for 45 minutes, or until firm enough to cut. Cut the sweet into four quarters, then cut each quarter into six bars, using a small, sharp knife. Remove the bars from the baking pan, using a small, offset metal spatula. Sprinkle the top of the bars with confectioners' sugar just before serving, if you wish.

FRESHLY BAKED, THE BARS KEEP FOR 4 DAYS.

Variation: For double peanut bars with Dutch-process black cocoa, use 1 tablespoon Dutch-process black cocoa and 1 tablespoon unsweetened, alkalized cocoa.

PEANUT BUTTER CHIP COFFEE CAKE

One 9 by 9-inch cake, creating 16 squares

A CAKE THAT INCLUDES ALL THE GOODIES: the batter for this whimsical coffee-time sweet is accented with peanut butter-flavored chips and chopped peanuts, and topped with more peanuts tossed in a mixture of sugar, melted butter, and vanilla extract. The brown sugar present in the topping and batter heightens the peanut butter taste.

Nonstick cooking spray, for preparing the baking pan

BROWN SUGAR-PEANUT TOPPING

½ cup firmly packed light brown sugar, sieved if lumpy

3 tablespoons granulated sugar

½ cup chopped roasted unsalted peanuts

2 tablespoons unsalted butter, melted and cooled

½ teaspoon pure vanilla extract

PEANUT BUTTER CHIP COFFEE CAKE BATTER

2 cups unsifted bleached all-purpose flour

1½ teaspoons baking powder

½ teaspoon baking soda

¼ teaspoon salt

½ teaspoon freshly grated nutmeg

¼ teaspoon ground allspice

¾ cup peanut butter-flavored chips

⅓ cup chopped, roasted unsalted peanuts

¼ pound (8 tablespoons or 1 stick) unsalted butter, softened

¾ cup granulated sugar

¼ cup firmly packed light brown sugar, sieved if lumpy

2 large eggs

PREHEAT THE OVEN AND PREPARE THE BAKING PAN Preheat the oven to 375° F. Film the inside of the baking pan with nonstick cooking spray; set aside.

MAKE THE BROWN SUGAR-PEANUT TOPPING In a small mixing bowl, combine the light brown sugar, granulated sugar, and peanuts. Drizzle over the melted butter and vanilla extract; mix well to lightly moisten the sugar-peanut mixture. Set aside.

MIX THE PEANUT BUTTER CHIP COFFEE CAKE BATTER Sift the flour, baking powder, baking soda, salt, nutmeg, and allspice onto a sheet of waxed paper. In a medium-size mixing bowl, toss the peanut butter chips and chopped peanuts with 1½ teaspoons of the sifted mixture.

Cream the butter in the large bowl of a freestanding electric mixer on moderate speed for 2 minutes. Add the granulated sugar and beat for 1 minute; add the light brown sugar and beat for a minute longer. Beat in the eggs, one at a time, mixing well after each addition. Blend in the vanilla extract.

On low speed, alternately add the sifted ingredients in three additions with the sour cream-milk blend in two additions, beginning and ending with the sifted mixture. Scrape down the sides of the mixing bowl frequently with a rubber spatula to keep the batter even-textured. Stir in the peanut butter chips and chopped peanuts.

1¾ teaspoons pure vanilla extract

½ cup thick, cultured sour cream blended with ½ cup milk

BAKEWARE

9 by 9 by 2-inch baking pan

ASSEMBLE THE COFFEE CAKE Scrape the batter into the prepared baking pan. Smooth over the top with a flexible palette knife or rubber spatula. Sprinkle the peanut topping evenly over the surface of the batter.

BAKE AND COOL THE COFFEE CAKE Bake the cake in the preheated oven for 35 minutes, or until risen, set, and a wooden pick inserted in the cake withdraws clean, or with a few moist crumbs attached to it. Cool the cake in the pan on a rack. Serve the cake cut into squares directly from the pan.

FRESHLY BAKED, THE CAKE KEEPS FOR 2 DAYS.

BEST BAKING ADVICE

The combination of sour cream and milk gives the cake batter a creamy, lightened texture.

CHOCOLATE, PEANUT, AND PEANUT BUTTER CANDY FUDGE CAKE

One 9-inch cake, creating about 10 slices

Wᴛʜ ʟᴏᴛs ᴏꜰ ᴄʜᴏᴘᴘᴇᴅ ᴘᴇᴀɴᴜᴛ ʙᴜᴛᴛᴇʀ ᴄᴀɴᴅʏ, roasted peanuts, peanut butter, and a full quarter-pound of chocolate in the batter, it's an enjoyable challenge to decide whether this sweet is actually a cake or a confection. I say that its fudgy excess puts it instantly in the category of confection, and a dense and extravagant one at that. Peanutty, indeed.

Softened, unsalted butter, for preparing the cake pan

CHOCOLATE AND PEANUT BUTTER CANDY FUDGE CAKE BATTER

1½ cups unsifted bleached all-purpose flour

1 tablespoon unsweetened, alkalized cocoa

¼ teaspoon baking powder

¼ teaspoon salt

5 packages (1.6 ounces each) milk chocolate peanut butter cups (Reese's Milk Chocolate Peanut Butter Cups), each cup cut into 6 chunks

¾ cup whole roasted unsalted peanuts

½ pound (16 tablespoons or 2 sticks) unsalted butter, melted and cooled to tepid

4 ounces (4 squares) unsweetened chocolate, melted and cooled to tepid

2 tablespoons creamy (smooth) peanut butter

4 large eggs

1¾ cups plus 2 tablespoons superfine sugar

2 teaspoons pure vanilla extract

Pʀᴇʜᴇᴀᴛ ᴛʜᴇ ᴏᴠᴇɴ ᴀɴᴅ ᴘʀᴇᴘᴀʀᴇ ᴛʜᴇ ᴄᴀᴋᴇ ᴘᴀɴ Preheat the oven to 325° F. Butter the inside of the springform pan; set aside. Have the sheet pan at hand.

Mɪx ᴛʜᴇ ᴄʜᴏᴄᴏʟᴀᴛᴇ ᴀɴᴅ ᴘᴇᴀɴᴜᴛ ʙᴜᴛᴛᴇʀ ᴄᴀɴᴅʏ ꜰᴜᴅɢᴇ ᴄᴀᴋᴇ ʙᴀᴛᴛᴇʀ Sift the flour, cocoa, baking powder, and salt onto a sheet of waxed paper. In a medium-size mixing bowl, toss the peanut butter candy chunks and peanuts with 2 teaspoons of the flour mixture.

Whisk the melted butter, melted unsweetened chocolate, and peanut butter in a medium-size mixing bowl until very smooth. Whisk in the eggs in a large mixing bowl for 1 minute. Add the superfine sugar and whisk for 1 minute, or until just combined. Blend in the vanilla extract. Sift over the sifted mixture and whisk until the particles of flour are absorbed. Stir in the peanut butter candy chunks and peanuts, using a wooden spoon or flat wooden paddle. *Batter texture observation* The batter will be thick.

Scrape the batter into the prepared cake pan. Smooth over the top with a rubber spatula.

Bᴀᴋᴇ ᴀɴᴅ ᴄᴏᴏʟ ᴛʜᴇ ᴄᴀᴋᴇ Place the springform pan on the rimmed sheet pan and bake the cake in the preheated oven for 45 minutes, or until set. Cool the cake in the pan on a rack. Open the

Confectioners' sugar, for sprinkling on top of the baked cake (optional)

BAKEWARE

9-inch springform pan (2¾ inches deep)
rimmed sheet pan

hinge on the side of the springform pan and carefully lift the outer ring away from the cake, allowing the cake to stand on the base. Dredge the top of the cake with sifted confectioners' sugar, if you wish, just before slicing into wedges and serving. *Slicing observation* Use a serrated knife or long chef's knife to cut the cake neatly and cleanly. Refrigerate any cake that is left over in an airtight cake keeper.

FRESHLY BAKED, THE CAKE KEEPS FOR 3 DAYS.

BABY PEANUT BUTTER CAKES

14 small Bundt (Bundt-lette) cakes

THE BATTER FOR THESE CURVY AND PLUMP peanut-flavored cakes is baked in small fluted tube pans. The peanut taste is spotlighted—and expanded—by using a combination of peanut butter-flavored chips, peanut butter, and roasted peanuts, in addition to dark brown sugar and several "sweet" spices that add depth and intensity to the batter.

Nonstick cooking spray, for preparing the cake pans

BUTTERY PEANUT BUTTER CAKE BATTER

3 cups unsifted bleached all-purpose flour
½ cup unsifted bleached cake flour
3 teaspoons baking powder
1 teaspoon baking soda
1 teaspoon salt
1 teaspoon freshly grated nutmeg
¼ teaspoon ground allspice
¼ teaspoon ground cardamom
¼ teaspoon ground cloves
2 cups peanut butter-flavored chips

PREHEAT THE OVEN AND PREPARE THE CAKE PANS Preheat the oven to 350° F. Film the inside of the Bundt-lette cups with nonstick cooking spray; set aside.

MIX THE BUTTERY PEANUT BUTTER CAKE BATTER Sift the all-purpose flour, cake flour, baking powder, baking soda, salt, nutmeg, allspice, cardamom, and cloves onto a sheet of waxed paper. In a small mixing bowl, toss the peanut butter chips with 1 heaping tablespoon of the sifted mixture.

Beat the melted butter, dark brown sugar, granulated sugar, peanut butter, eggs, egg yolk, and vanilla extract in the large bowl of a freestanding electric mixer on moderately low speed until very

- ½ pound (2 sticks or 16 tablespoons) unsalted butter, melted and cooled
- ⅔ cup firmly packed dark brown sugar, sieved if lumpy
- ½ cup plus 2 tablespoons granulated sugar
- 1¼ cups plus 1 tablespoon creamy (smooth) peanut butter
- 2 large eggs
- 1 large egg yolk
- 1 tablespoon pure vanilla extract
- 1 cup milk
- ½ cup heavy cream
- 1⅓ cups whole, roasted salted peanuts

- Confectioners' sugar, for sifting over the baked tea cakes (optional)

BAKEWARE

14 Bundt-lette (small Bundt) cake cups (3 pans, each pan containing 6 cake cups and each cup measuring 4 inches in diameter and a scant 2 inches deep, with a capacity of 1 cup)

BEST BAKING ADVICE

The heavy cream rounds out the peanut butter flavor and moistens the crumb of the baked cakes.

smooth, about 2 minutes. Blend in the milk and heavy cream. On low speed, add the sifted mixture in two additions, blending to form a batter. Scrape down the sides of the mixing bowl several times with a rubber spatula to keep the mixture even-textured. Stir in the peanut butter chips and peanuts.

Spoon the batter into the prepared Bundt-lette cake cups, dividing it evenly among them.

BAKE AND COOL THE CAKES Bake the cakes in the preheated oven for 22 to 25 minutes, or until risen, plump, and a wooden pick inserted in a cake withdraws clean. The baked cakes will pull away slightly from the sides of the baking pan.

Cool the cakes in the pans on racks for 5 to 8 minutes, then invert them, one tray at a time, onto other cooling racks. Cool completely. Sift confectioners' sugar over the top, just before serving, if you wish.

FRESHLY BAKED, THE CAKES KEEP FOR 2 DAYS.

LAYERED CHOCOLATE AND PEANUT CARAMEL SQUARES

16 squares

Nonstick cooking spray, for preparing the baking pan

CHOCOLATE COOKIE CRUMB LAYER

¼ pound (8 tablespoons or 1 stick) unsalted butter, melted and cooled

¼ teaspoon pure vanilla extract

1½ cups chocolate wafer cookie crumbs

COCONUT, PEANUT, AND CHOCOLATE AND PEANUT BUTTER CHIP LAYER

1⅓ cups lightly packed sweetened flaked coconut

¾ cup semisweet chocolate chips

¾ cup peanut butter-flavored chips

1¼ cups whole roasted unsalted peanuts

One 14-ounce can sweetened condensed milk

Caramel Nut Topping (see page 232), using whole, roasted unsalted peanuts, for applying to the baked squares

BAKEWARE

10 by 10 by 2-inch baking pan

WITH ALL THE INGREDIENTS TUCKED AWAY on a pantry shelf, these peanut gems are crunchy-chewy, rich, and easily made. Chocolate and caramel support—and deliciously exploit—the peanut taste. And if you love the contrast of salty and sweet, use lightly salted peanuts in the coconut, peanut, and chocolate and peanut butter chip layer.

PREHEAT THE OVEN AND PREPARE THE BAKING PAN Preheat the oven to 350° F. Film the inside of the baking pan with nonstick cooking spray; set aside.

PUT TOGETHER THE CHOCOLATE COOKIE CRUMB LAYER In a small bowl, whisk the melted butter and vanilla extract. Pour the butter mixture into the prepared baking pan. Sprinkle the cookie crumbs evenly over the butter. Using a small, offset metal spatula, lightly press down the cookie crumbs to form a solid layer.

COVER THE COOKIE BASE WITH THE TOPPING Sprinkle the coconut over the chocolate cookie base. Top with the chocolate chips, peanut butter chips, and peanuts. Pour the sweetened condensed milk evenly over all, making sure to drizzle it along the edges of the baking pan.

BAKE THE BAR COOKIES Bake the bar cookies in the preheated oven for 30 minutes, or until just set.

COOL, TOP, AND CUT THE BAR COOKIES Let the entire cake of bar cookies stand in the pan on a cooling rack for 15 minutes. Drizzle the warm caramel topping on top of the bar cookies. Sprinkle the peanuts on top of the caramel. Cool completely. With a small, sharp knife, cut the cake into quarters, then cut each quarter into four squares. Remove the squares from the baking pan with a small, offset metal spatula.

FRESHLY BAKED, THE SQUARES KEEP FOR 3 DAYS.

a layering of flavors develops the full flavor-impact of rum: for the taste of rum to come forward in a cake, as an example, add dark rum to a batter sweetened with vanilla-scented sugar, spiced with nutmeg, cinnamon, and allspice, and seasoned with vanilla extract. Finally, brush a glaze, made of butter, sugar, rum, and vanilla extract, over the warm, baked cake. This cake (actually the Butter Rum Cake on page 452) is suffused with the taste of rum in a tempered, not harsh, way. The prominence of the rum flavor and the direction that it takes is generally accomplished by orchestrating a series of ingredients, and this cake is a good model of that process.

The ingredients that support the taste of rum in a cake, waffle, or pancake batter; sweet sauce; confectioners' sugar icing; and yeast and biscuit dough emphasize it gently, in a rounded way. These ingredients are spices (cinnamon, freshly grated nutmeg, allspice, and cloves), pure vanilla extract, unsalted butter and heavy cream, dark brown sugar, and sweetened flaked coconut.

19

Rum

BUTTER RUM CAKE

One 10-inch fluted tube cake, creating 16 slices

BUTTER AND RUM are an exceptional match in baking, for the richness of the butter makes the deep flavor of rum flourish. Count on the rum taste to shine in this cake—it appears in the butter-imbued batter and again in the glaze, uplifted by a small amount of vanilla extract.

Shortening and bleached all-purpose flour, for preparing the cake pan

BUTTER RUM CAKE BATTER

3 cups unsifted bleached all-purpose flour

¼ teaspoon baking soda

1 teaspoon salt

¾ teaspoon freshly grated nutmeg

½ pound (16 tablespoons or 2 sticks) unsalted butter, softened

2¼ cups superfine sugar, preferably vanilla-scented (see page 54)

4 large eggs

2 teaspoons pure vanilla extract

¾ cup plus 1 tablespoon buttermilk

3 tablespoons dark rum

BUTTER RUM GLAZE FOR BRUSHING ON THE WARM, BAKED CAKE

5 tablespoons unsalted butter, cut into chunks

½ cup granulated sugar

⅓ cup dark rum

½ teaspoon pure vanilla extract

PREHEAT THE OVEN AND PREPARE THE CAKE PAN Preheat the oven to 350° F. Grease the inside of the Bundt pan with shortening and dust with all-purpose flour. Tap out any excess flour; set aside.

MIX THE BUTTER RUM CAKE BATTER Sift the flour, baking soda, salt, and nutmeg onto a sheet of waxed paper.

Cream the butter in the large bowl of a freestanding electric mixer on moderate speed for 3 to 4 minutes. Add the superfine sugar in three additions, beating for 1 minute after each portion is added. Add the eggs, one at a time, beating for 45 seconds after each is added. Blend in the vanilla extract.

On low speed, alternately add the sifted mixture in three additions with the buttermilk in two additions, beginning and ending with the sifted mixture. Scrape down the sides of the mixing bowl frequently with a rubber spatula to keep the batter even-textured. Add the rum and beat for 30 seconds. *Batter texture observation* The batter will be medium-thick and very creamy.

Spoon the batter into the prepared Bundt pan. Lightly smooth over the top with a flexible rubber spatula.

BAKE THE CAKE Bake the cake in the preheated oven for 55 minutes, or until risen, set, and a wooden pick inserted in the cake withdraws clean. The baked cake will pull away slightly from the sides of the Bundt pan. Let the cake stand in the pan on a cooling rack for 5 to 8 minutes.

Rum Custard Sauce (see page 454), for serving with the cake (optional)

BAKEWARE
10-inch Bundt pan

BEST BAKING ADVICE

Buttermilk and superfine sugar create a cake with a fine crumb that readily absorbs the finishing glaze. Use the butter rum glaze while warm so that it permeates the surface of the freshly baked cake.

MAKE THE BUTTER RUM GLAZE While the cake is cooling in the pan, place the butter, granulated sugar, and rum in a small, heavy nonreactive saucepan (preferably enameled cast iron). Set over low heat and cook the mixture until the sugar dissolves completely. Bring to the boil. Simmer for 2 minutes. Off the heat, stir in the vanilla extract.

UNMOLD, GLAZE, AND COOL THE CAKE Invert the cake onto another cooling rack. Place a sheet of waxed paper under the cooling rack to catch any drips of glaze. Using a 1-inch-wide pastry brush, apply the warm glaze to the top and sides of the cake. Cool completely before slicing and serving. *Slicing observation* Use a serrated knife to cut the cake neatly and cleanly. Serve the cake with a spoonful or two of the custard sauce, if you wish.

❋ *For an aromatic topnote of flavor,* use intensified vanilla extract (see page 52) in place of plain vanilla extract in both the cake batter and the glaze.

FRESHLY BAKED, THE CAKE KEEPS FOR 4 DAYS.

Variation: For spiced butter rum cake, add ¾ teaspoon ground cinnamon, ¼ teaspoon ground allspice, and ¼ teaspoon ground cardamom to the ingredients to be sifted along with the nutmeg.

RUM CUSTARD SAUCE

About 1¾ cups

*F*OR A RUM-TINGED CUSTARD SAUCE to be suffused with flavor, it must include a splash of vanilla extract and dash of nutmeg. The seasoning extract and spice cultivate the taste of the rum, and give it complexity.

CUSTARD SAUCE

1 cup heavy cream

¾ cup milk

pinch of salt

5 large egg yolks

⅓ cup plus 1 tablespoon superfine sugar

½ teaspoon pure vanilla extract

big pinch freshly grated nutmeg

1 tablespoon plus 1 teaspoon dark rum

MAKE THE CUSTARD SAUCE Warm the cream, milk, and salt in a small saucepan (to about 110° to 115° F.). Cool to tepid. In a medium-size mixing bowl, whisk the egg yolks and superfine sugar for 2 to 3 minutes or until lightly thickened. Place a small fine-meshed sieve over the saucepan and add 1 tablespoon of the tepid cream-milk mixture, and immediately stir it in. Slowly add 3 tablespoons of the liquid through the sieve, and stir it in. Add the remaining liquid a little at a time, in this way, mixing thoroughly. *Technique observation* It's essential to stir in the tepid liquid gradually to avoid curdling the egg yolks.

Pour the egg yolk-cream-sugar mixture into a heavy, medium-size saucepan (preferably enameled cast iron). Cook over low heat until thickened, about 10 minutes, stirring constantly with a wooden spoon.

STRAIN, FLAVOR, AND COOL THE SAUCE Strain the sauce through a medium-size fine-meshed sieve into a medium-size storage container, pressing the sauce through with a rubber spatula. Stir in the vanilla extract, nutmeg, and rum. Place a sheet of plastic wrap directly over the surface. Cool. Cover the container tightly and refrigerate.

The sauce may be stored in the refrigerator for up to 2 days. It will thicken somewhat after 24 hours. After that time, add an additional 1 to 2 tablespoons of milk to restore the consistency.

RUM BUNS

1 dozen jumbo buns

*T*ALL AND HANDSOME, these bountiful sweet rolls are filled simply with butter, spiced sugar, and raisins; once baked, they are glossed over generously with rum icing. The rum flavor comes through in the marinated raisins and icing it emboldens, and that taste is offset nicely by the pillowy, downy, and buttery texture of the dough.

Softened unsalted butter, for preparing the baking pan

RUM-MARINATED RAISINS

1 cup dark, seedless raisins

2 tablespoons light rum

SPICED YEAST DOUGH

1 tablespoon active dry yeast

¾ teaspoon granulated sugar

¼ cup warm (110° to 115° F.) water

1 cup milk

¼ pound (8 tablespoons or 1 stick) unsalted butter, cut into chunks

¼ cup granulated sugar

2 teaspoons pure vanilla extract

1 teaspoon freshly grated lemon rind

3 large eggs, lightly beaten

4¾ cups unsifted unbleached all-purpose flour, plus more as needed

1 teaspoon salt

¾ teaspoon ground cinnamon

¾ teaspoon freshly grated nutmeg

½ teaspoon ground cloves

¼ teaspoon ground allspice

MAKE THE RUM-MARINATED RAISINS Place the raisins in a small nonreactive bowl and toss with the rum; set aside, uncovered.

MAKE THE SPICED YEAST DOUGH Combine the yeast and ¾ teaspoon granulated sugar in a bowl. Stir in the warm water and let stand until the yeast has dissolved into a swollen mass, 7 to 8 minutes. In the meantime, place the milk, butter, and ¼ cup granulated sugar in a small, heavy saucepan and scald. Remove from the heat, stir well, and blend in the vanilla extract and lemon rind. Pour the milk mixture into a medium-size heatproof bowl. When the liquid has reached 110° to 115° F., blend in the beaten eggs.

Combine 3 cups of flour with the salt, cinnamon, nutmeg, cloves, and allspice. Stir the yeast mixture into the cooled egg-milk mixture and pour it over the spiced flour. Stir well.

Add the remaining 1¾ cups of flour, ½ cup at a time, mixing well. Add an additional ¼ cup flour, a few tablespoons at a time, as needed, to create a moistly soft (but not too sticky) dough. Turn out the dough onto a floured work surface and knead until smooth and resilient, about 8 minutes.

SET THE DOUGH TO RISE Place the dough in a lightly buttered bowl, turn to coat all sides in the butter, and cut a large cross in the top with a pair of kitchen scissors (this will help the dough to rise). Cover the bowl tightly with a sheet of plastic wrap and let stand until doubled in bulk, about 1½ hours.

2 tablespoons unsalted butter, melted,
cooled and blended with ¼
teaspoon pure vanilla extract

SPICED SUGAR AND RUM-
MARINATED RAISIN FILLING

5 tablespoons unsalted butter, softened

⅔ cup granulated sugar blended with
1¼ teaspoon ground cinnamon and
¼ teaspoon freshly grated nutmeg

Rum Icing (see page 457), for
spreading over the warm,
baked buns

BAKEWARE

12 by 8 by 3-inch baking pan

PREPARE THE BAKING PAN Lightly butter the baking pan;
set aside.

ROLL, FILL, AND CUT THE BUNS Gently deflate the dough by
compressing the top with the palms of your hands. Roll the dough
into a sheet measuring about 16 by 16 inches. Brush the butter
and vanilla wash on the surface of the dough, and let stand for
10 minutes.

Spread the 5 tablespoons softened butter over the surface of
the dough. Sprinkle over the sugar-spice blend. Scatter over the
rum-marinated raisins and press them down lightly with your fingertips. Roll up the dough into a long coil, just as you would a jellyroll, tucking in the edges as you go. Pinch closed the end of the
long seam.

With a sharp chef's knife, cut the coil into 12 even-sized
slices. Place the buns in the prepared pan, cut side up to reveal the
spiral of filling. Bun placement observation For now, there will be
gaps between the buns, but as they rise, the gaps will vanish.

SET THE BUNS TO RISE Cover the pan loosely with a sheet of plastic wrap. Let the
buns rise until doubled in bulk, 1 hour and 15 minutes to 1 hour and 25 minutes.

PREHEAT THE OVEN AND BAKE THE BUNS Preheat the oven to 375° F. in advance of
baking. Remove the sheet of plastic wrap covering the baking pan. Bake the buns for 30
to 35 minutes, or until set, plump, and golden on top. Cool the buns in the pan on a
rack for 10 minutes, invert them onto another cooling rack, and carefully reinvert to
right side up. Let stand for 5 minutes. Have the prepared rum icing at hand.

SPREAD THE ICING ON THE BUNS Smooth the icing thickly over the tops of the
warm buns, using a flexible palette knife; it will puddle in places where the natural (and
irregular) surface of the block of buns forms dips and peaks. The icing will melt slightly
and flow easily over the tops of the warm buns. Let the buns stand
until the icing has set up, about 1 hour. Serve the buns freshly
baked and iced.

BEST BAKING ADVICE

*Applying the icing to the warm buns is the
most efficient way of coating them. The
icing will melt over and about the buns,
and firm up as the buns cool.*

❋ For an aromatic topnote of flavor, use intensified vanilla
extract (see page 52) in place of plain vanilla extract in the
yeast dough.

RUM ICING

About 1⅓ cups

SMOOTH AND CREAMY, this is the icing to use on warm biscuits, scones, and sweet rolls that contain spices, dried fruit, chocolate, or coconut. The small amount of vanilla extract in the icing acts as a sensual, flavor-expanding counterpoint to the rum.

RUM ICING

1½ cups unsifted confectioners' sugar

⅛ teaspoon freshly grated nutmeg

1½ tablespoons unsalted butter, softened

1 tablespoon light rum

1 tablespoon plus ½ teaspoon milk

½ teaspoon pure vanilla extract

BEST BAKING ADVICE
Mix the icing slowly on low speed until very smooth.

MIX THE RUM ICING Place the confectioners' sugar, nutmeg, butter, rum, milk, and vanilla extract in a medium-size mixing bowl. Using an electric hand mixer, beat the ingredients on low speed for 1 minute or until just combined and smooth, scraping down the sides of the mixing bowl two or three times with a rubber spatula to keep the icing even-textured. Press a sheet of plastic wrap directly on the surface of the icing until you are ready to use it. Use the icing freshly made, within 1 hour of mixing.

ICED RUM-RAISIN TEA BISCUITS

16 biscuits

SOULFUL AND ALTOGETHER TENDER-RICH, these biscuits are spiced just right and adorned with an audacious slick of rum-scented icing. The sweetness of the icing balances the creaminess of the biscuits' baked crumb. They are divine with good coffee.

Long ago, this recipe began with the dough that I routinely made into scones. They were delicious, but plain. Many batches later, I transformed it into a dough that would contain lots of raisins marinated in rum and a sleek coat of icing. Seasoned fruit is a good way to flavor a substantial quick bread dough, and this one is as fine with raisins as it would be with currants, chopped dried figs, apricots, or dried cherries.

RUM-MARINATED RAISINS

1¼ cups dark raisins

1½ tablespoons dark rum

1 teaspoon pure vanilla extract

LIGHTLY SPICED CREAM BISCUIT DOUGH

4¼ cups unsifted bleached all-purpose flour

4¾ teaspoons baking powder

1 teaspoon salt

1¼ teaspoons freshly grated nutmeg

½ teaspoon ground cinnamon

½ teaspoon ground allspice

¼ teaspoon ground cloves

½ cup plus 2 tablespoons unsifted confectioners' sugar

10 tablespoons (1 stick plus 2 tablespoons) unsalted butter, cold, cut into tablespoon chunks

2 tablespoons shortening, cold

MARINATE THE RAISINS Place the raisins in a small nonreactive mixing bowl and toss with the rum and vanilla extract. Set aside, uncovered, to marinate for 30 minutes.

PREHEAT THE OVEN AND PREPARE THE BAKING SHEETS Preheat the oven to 400° F. Line the cookie sheets or sheet pans with cooking parchment paper; set aside. *Bakeware observation* The baking sheets must be heavy, or the dough will scorch on the bottom as the biscuits bake. Double-pan the sheets, if necessary.

MIX THE LIGHTLY SPICED CREAM BISCUIT DOUGH Whisk the flour, baking powder, salt, nutmeg, cinnamon, allspice, cloves, and confectioners' sugar in a large mixing bowl. Add the chunks of butter and shortening and, using a pastry blender, cut the butter into small pieces about the size of dried lima beans. Lightly and quickly, crumble the mixture between your fingertips until the butter is reduced to small, lentil-size bits.

In a medium-size mixing bowl, whisk the eggs, heavy cream, and vanilla extract. Pour the egg-cream mixture over the dry ingredients, add the marinated raisins, and stir to form a batter. The

4 large eggs

1 cup heavy cream

1 teaspoon pure vanilla extract

Rum Icing (see page 457), for
spreading over the warm biscuits

2 large, heavy cookie sheets or rimmed
sheet pans

BEST BAKING ADVICE

*Marinating the raisins for 30 minutes
allows the fruit to draw in a good amount
of rum flavor, and, in turn, convey it to
the batter.*

dough will be moist and slightly sticky, but workable. With
floured hands, lightly knead the dough in the bowl about 10
times. If the dough seems very sticky, sprinkle over 1 to 2 tablespoons of all-purpose flour to keep the dough manageable, and
continue kneading gently and quickly.

FORM THE DOUGH INTO BISCUITS On a floured work surface,
divide the dough in half and form each half into an 8-inch disk.
With a sharp chef's knife, cut each disk into eight wedges. Using a
wide, offset metal spatula, transfer the biscuits to the lined cookie sheets, arranging them
about 3 inches apart, eight to a sheet.

BAKE THE BISCUITS Bake the biscuits in the preheated oven for 15 to 18 minutes, or
until set.

COOL AND ICE THE BISCUITS Remove the biscuits to cooling racks, using a wide,
offset metal spatula, and let them stand for 3 to 4 minutes. Place a sheet of waxed paper
under each cooling rack to catch any drips of icing.

With a flexible palette knife, spread the rum icing lavishly on
each biscuit, letting it flow over the surface. Let the biscuits stand for
at least 30 minutes to firm up the icing. Serve the biscuits fresh.

❋ *For an extra surge of flavor and texture,* shower the tops
of the biscuits with the Golden Oatmeal Sprinkle (see page
65). The glaze should still be somewhat moist so that the sprinkle sticks to it.

PECAN, RUM, AND BROWN SUGAR KEEPING CAKE

One 10-inch cake, creating about 20 slices

Unsalted butter and sour cream, pure and fresh tasting, form the backdrop for the flavors of brown sugar and rum to expand in the batter. A few supporting spices—nutmeg, cinnamon, and allspice—balance the potency of the rum. The crumb of the cake is moderately fine-grained and dense, and superbly moist.

Shortening and bleached all-purpose flour, for preparing the cake pan

BROWN SUGAR, PECAN, AND RUM BUTTER CAKE BATTER

3 cups unsifted bleached all-purpose flour

¾ teaspoon baking powder

¼ teaspoon baking soda

1 teaspoon salt

1 teaspoon freshly grated nutmeg

½ teaspoon ground cinnamon

¼ teaspoon ground allspice

¼ teaspoon ground cloves

½ pound (16 tablespoons or 2 sticks) unsalted butter, softened

2 cups firmly packed dark brown sugar, sieved if lumpy

¼ cup granulated sugar

5 large eggs

2 teaspoons pure vanilla extract

1 cup thick, cultured sour cream

3 tablespoons dark rum

1 cup finely chopped pecans

PREHEAT THE OVEN AND PREPARE THE CAKE PAN Preheat the oven to 325° F. Grease the inside of the tube pan with shortening, line the bottom of the pan with a circle of waxed paper cut to fit, and grease the paper. Dust the inside of the pan with all-purpose flour. Tap out any excess flour; set aside.

MIX THE BROWN SUGAR, PECAN, AND RUM BUTTER CAKE BATTER Sift the flour, baking powder, baking soda, salt, nutmeg, cinnamon, allspice, and cloves onto a sheet of waxed paper.

Cream the butter in the large bowl of a freestanding electric mixer on moderately low speed for 3 minutes. Add the dark brown sugar in two additions, beating for 1 minute after each portion is added. Add the granulated sugar and continue beating for 1 to 2 minutes longer. Add the eggs, one at a time, beating for 1 minute after each addition. Blend in the vanilla extract.

On low speed, add the sifted mixture in three additions alternately with the sour cream in two additions, beginning and ending with the sifted ingredients. Scrape down the sides of the mixing bowl frequently with a rubber spatula to keep the batter even-textured. Blend in the rum. *Batter texture observation* The batter will be soft and gently thickened, and very creamy. Stir in the pecans. Spoon the batter into the prepared tube pan. Smooth over the top with a rubber spatula.

Rum Syrup (see page 56), for brushing over the warm, baked cake

Rum Custard Sauce (see page 454), for serving with the cake (optional)

BAKEWARE

plain 10-inch tube pan

BAKE AND COOL THE CAKE Bake the cake for 1 hour and 15 minutes to 1 hour and 20 minutes, or until risen, set, and a wooden pick inserted in the cake withdraws clean. Cool the cake in the pan on a rack for 10 minutes. Invert the cake onto another cooling rack, peel off the waxed paper circle, then invert again to stand right side up.

APPLY THE RUM SYRUP TO THE HOT CAKE Using a soft 1-inch-wide pastry brush, apply the syrup to the top and sides of the cake. Cool completely before slicing and serving. *Slicing observation* Use a serrated knife to cut the cake neatly and cleanly. Accompany slices of cake with spoonfuls of the custard sauce, if you wish.

❋ *For an aromatic topnote of flavor,* use intensified vanilla extract (see page 52) in place of plain vanilla extract in the cake batter.

FRESHLY BAKED, THE CAKE KEEPS FOR **5** TO **7** DAYS.

BEST BAKING ADVICE
Apply the rum syrup to the warm cake in several coatings so that it's evenly saturated and absorbs all of the syrup you have made.

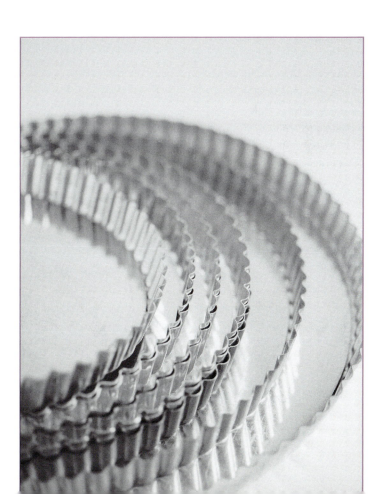

Rum Pound Cake

One 10-inch cake, creating about 20 slices

Many of the ingredients that maintain and promote the flavor of rum are present in this cake—flaked coconut, heavy cream, freshly grated nutmeg, ground allspice, and vanilla extract among them. The texture of the cake is creamy and moist, established by the use of basic dairy staples fundamental to good baking.

Shortening and bleached all-purpose flour, for preparing the cake pan

RUM BUTTER CAKE BATTER

3 cups unsifted bleached all-purpose flour

¼ teaspoon baking powder

1 teaspoon salt

1 teaspoon freshly grated nutmeg

¼ teaspoon ground cinnamon

⅛ teaspoon ground allspice

⅛ teaspoon cloves

½ pound (16 tablespoons or 2 sticks) unsalted butter, softened

4 tablespoons shortening

2¾ cups plus 2 tablespoons superfine sugar

6 large eggs

2½ teaspoons pure vanilla extract

½ teaspoon pure almond extract

¾ cup heavy cream

¼ cup dark rum

1 cup lightly packed sweetened flaked coconut

PREHEAT THE OVEN AND PREPARE THE CAKE PAN Preheat the oven to 325° F. Grease the inside of the tube pan with shortening, line the bottom of the pan with a circle of waxed paper cut to fit, and grease the paper. Dust the inside of the pan with all-purpose flour. Tap out any excess flour; set aside.

MIX THE RUM BUTTER CAKE BATTER Sift the flour, baking powder, salt, nutmeg, cinnamon, allspice, and cloves onto a sheet of waxed paper.

Cream the butter and shortening in the large bowl of a free-standing electric mixer on moderate speed for 3 to 4 minutes. Add the superfine sugar in three additions, beating for 1 minute after each portion is added. Blend in the eggs, one at a time, beating for 30 to 45 seconds after each is added. Blend in the vanilla and almond extracts.

On low speed, alternately add the sifted mixture in three additions with the heavy cream in two additions, beginning and ending with the sifted ingredients. Scrape down the sides of the mixing bowl frequently with a rubber spatula to keep the batter even-textured. Blend in the rum. *Batter texture observation* The batter will be creamy. Stir in the coconut.

Spoon the batter into the prepared tube pan. Lightly smooth over the top with a flexible rubber spatula.

BAKE AND COOL THE CAKE Bake the cake for 1 hour and 20 minutes to 1 hour and 25 minutes, or until risen, set, and a wooden pick inserted in the cake withdraws clean. Cool the cake in the pan on a rack for 10 minutes. Invert the cake onto another cooling

¼ cup dark rum

3 tablespoons granulated sugar

¼ teaspoon pure vanilla extract

BAKEWARE

plain 10-inch tube pan

rack, peel off the waxed paper circle, then invert again to stand right side up. Place a sheet of waxed paper underneath the cooling rack to catch any drips of the sugar-rum glaze.

MAKE THE SUGAR-RUM GLAZE AND BRUSH IT ON THE CAKE Combine the rum, sugar, and vanilla extract in a small mixing bowl. The sugar does not need to dissolve. Using a soft, 1-inch-wide pastry brush, paint the glaze over the top and sides of the cake.

Cool the cake completely before cutting into slices for serving.

❋ *For an extra surge of flavor,* serve the pound cake with spoonfuls of Rum Custard Sauce (see page 454).

FRESHLY BAKED, THE CAKE KEEPS FOR 5 DAYS.

BEST BAKING ADVICE

Use softened (but not oily) butter. When applying the glaze on the cake, take care to dip into the sugar (which usually settles at the bottom of the sugar-rum glaze) with the pastry brush.

FEATHERY RUM PANCAKES

About 3 dozen pancakes

*T*HIS LIGHT, RUM-CHARGED PANCAKE BATTER is delicate and tender—the buttermilk and beaten egg whites make it so. To elevate the rum flavor, serve these ethereal pancakes with little splashes of the Creamy Brown Sugar and Rum Sauce (see page 466).

RUM-MARINATED RAISINS

½ cup dark raisins

1 tablespoon dark rum

RUM PANCAKE BATTER

1¼ cups unsifted bleached all-purpose flour

¼ cup unsifted bleached cake flour

1 teaspoon baking powder

¾ teaspoon baking soda

⅛ teaspoon salt

¼ teaspoon freshly grated nutmeg

⅛ teaspoon ground cinnamon

¼ cup granulated sugar

3 large eggs, separated

1¼ cups buttermilk

4 tablespoons (½ stick) unsalted butter, melted and cooled to tepid

1 tablespoon dark rum

1½ teaspoons pure vanilla extract

⅛ teaspoon cream of tartar

Clarified butter (see page 66), for the griddle

MAKE THE RUM-MARINATED RAISINS Place the raisins in a small, nonreactive mixing bowl, spoon over the rum, toss, and let stand for 15 minutes.

MAKE THE RUM PANCAKE BATTER Sift the all-purpose flour, cake flour, baking powder, baking soda, salt, nutmeg, cinnamon, and granulated sugar into a large mixing bowl.

Whisk the egg yolks, buttermilk, melted butter, rum, and vanilla extract in a medium-size mixing bowl.

Using a rotary egg beater (or an electric hand mixer), beat the egg whites in a clean, dry mixing bowl until soft peaks are formed, add the cream of tartar, and continue beating until firm (not stiff) peaks are formed.

Pour the egg yolk–buttermilk mixture over the dry ingredients and stir to form a batter, using a rubber spatula. Stir in the rum-raisin mixture. Let the batter stand for 1 minute. Mix a large spoonful of the beaten egg whites into the batter to lighten it, then blend in the remaining whites, mixing to incorporate all of the beaten whites into the batter. *Batter texture observation* Fully integrate the beaten egg whites into the batter without leaving behind any streaks or "cotton ball" fluffs of egg white.

GRIDDLE THE PANCAKES Place a griddle over moderate high heat and film the surface with a little clarified butter, using a wad of paper toweling to spread it in a translucent layer. Place 2-tablespoon-size puddles of batter on the preheated

Confectioners' sugar, for sprinkling on the griddled pancakes (optional)

Creamy Brown Sugar and Rum Sauce (see page 466), for serving with the pancakes

griddle and cook the pancakes for about 1 minute, until the edges are set and the undersides are golden. Flip the pancakes with a wide, offset metal spatula and continue cooking until they are a spotty golden color on the bottoms and completely set, 45 seconds to 1 minute.

Serve the pancakes hot off the griddle, sprinkled with confectioners' sugar, if you wish, and with a generous spoonful of the creamy rum sauce.

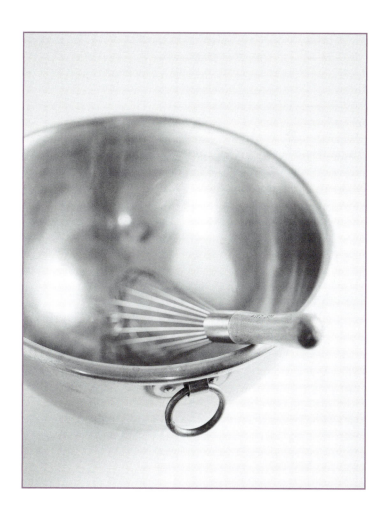

CREAMY BROWN SUGAR AND RUM SAUCE

1⅓ cups, without the optional addition of chopped nuts

FOLDING LIGHTLY TOASTED CHOPPED WALNUTS or pecans through this sauce just before serving expands the flavor and adds a definite textural relief to its buttery-creamy character. Dark rum, an excellent flavoring agent for a brown sugar–based sauce, is added at the beginning and at the end. This strategy is what gives the sauce its rounded taste.

CREAMY RUM SAUCE

½ cup firmly packed light brown sugar, sieved if lumpy

3 tablespoons granulated sugar

⅓ cup plus 2 tablespoons heavy cream

6 tablespoons (¾ stick) unsalted butter, cut into chunks

pinch of salt

2½ tablespoons dark rum

1 teaspoon pure vanilla extract

⅓ cup chopped pecans or walnuts, lightly toasted and cooled completely (optional)

MAKE THE CREAMY RUM SAUCE Place the light brown sugar, granulated sugar, heavy cream, butter, salt, and 1½ tablespoons rum in a heavy, medium-size (2-quart) saucepan, preferably enameled cast iron. Set over moderately low heat and cook slowly until the sugar melts down completely, about 3 minutes, stirring with a wooden spoon or flat wooden paddle. Raise the heat to high, bring to the boil (the sauce will begin to bubble around the perimeter of the pan at first), then reduce the heat and cook at a low boil for 3 to 4 minutes, or until lightly thickened.

Remove the saucepan from the heat. Stir in the vanilla extract and remaining 1 tablespoon rum. Stir in the optional nuts. Use the sauce while it's warm and fluid.

To use the refrigerated sauce, heat the sauce in a heavy saucepan until smooth and liquefied, bring to the simmer, and simmer steadily for 2 to 3 minutes before using. Stir in the nuts, if you are using them, and serve.

THE SAUCE—WITHOUT THE ADDITION OF THE CHOPPED NUTS—MAY BE STORED IN AN AIRTIGHT CONTAINER AND REFRIGERATED FOR UP TO 2 DAYS AHEAD OF SERVING.

RUM AND MILK CHOCOLATE WAFFLES

6 deep, Belgian-style 2-sided waffles,
each waffle section measuring 4½ by 4½ inches

A GOOD SPLASH OF RUM, a big handful of milk chocolate chips to beautify the batter (in a way only chocolate can), and a pouring of cream mingle with basic baking ingredients to form regal waffles. The milk chocolate morsels add a sweetness all their own to the batter, and act as a chocolaty counterpoint to the flavor of the dark rum, butter, and vanilla extract. Finely chopped milk chocolate, hand-cut from top-quality candy bars, may be substituted for the chips.

RUM AND MILK CHOCOLATE CHIP WAFFLE BATTER

2 cups unsifted bleached all-purpose flour

2½ teaspoons baking powder

¼ teaspoon salt

¼ teaspoon ground allspice

⅓ cup plus 1 tablespoon superfine sugar

3 large eggs

6 tablespoons (¾ stick) unsalted butter, melted and cooled to tepid

2 teaspoons pure vanilla extract

½ teaspoon pure almond extract

¼ cup dark rum

1 cup milk

½ cup light (table) cream

1 cup milk chocolate chips

Confectioners' sugar, for sprinkling on the waffles (optional)

Creamy Brown Sugar and Rum Sauce (see page 466), to serve with the waffles

BEST BAKING ADVICE

Let the waffle batter stand for a full 5 minutes so that the flour is absorbed and the batter doesn't overrun the waffle iron when spooned onto the grids.

MAKE THE RUM AND MILK CHOCOLATE CHIP WAFFLE BATTER Sift the flour, baking powder, salt, allspice, and superfine sugar into a large mixing bowl.

In a medium-size mixing bowl, whisk together the eggs, melted butter, vanilla extract, almond extract, rum, milk, and cream. Pour the liquid ingredients over the sifted mixture, add the milk chocolate chips, and stir to form a batter, using a rubber spatula, mixing until the sifted ingredients are completely incorporated. Let the batter stand for 5 minutes. *Batter texture observation* The batter should be lightly thickened.

MAKE THE WAFFLES Preheat a deep-dish waffle iron. Spoon ⅓ cup of batter onto the center of each square of the preheated iron. Cook the waffles until golden, 1 minute to 1 minute and 15 seconds. Dust the tops of the waffles with confectioners' sugar, if you wish, and serve with the rum sauce.

a blend of spices—among them cinnamon, allspice, nutmeg, cloves, ginger, and cardamom—characterizes the composite flavor called spice, and in an aromatic way, colors a batter or dough. Usually, three dominant spices—such as cinnamon, nutmeg, and cloves, or cinnamon, ginger, and allspice—are enough to carry the spice flavor in a batter, as each spice plays on the intensity of the others.

A spice-enhanced batter or dough becomes pronounced with the use of dairy products such as heavy cream, buttermilk, whole milk, half-and-half, and sour cream, in addition to enough eggs and butter and a judicious amount of vanilla extract. Spices used in baking should be fresh and pungent if they are to convey maximum flavor, and must be measured in level, not rounded, amounts—just as you would baking powder or baking soda. Jars of ground spices should be stored tightly closed and kept on a cool and dark pantry shelf.

20

SPICE

SWEET OATMEAL-RAISIN SPICE BUNS

1 dozen buns

W**HEN THIS BUTTERY OATMEAL YEAST DOUGH IS ROLLED**, filled, formed into buns, and baked, its craggy, rustic quality disappears into a completely gorgeous batch of sweet rolls. The spices wind their way through the yeast dough, the spiral of sugar and raisins, and the icing in the most alluring of ways. This recipe evolved in my kitchen as the oatmeal variation of the dough for the Cinnamon Butter Rosebuds on page 304 (with many twists and turns along the way), and the formula you have here combines the best buttery qualities of a yeast dough with the superb taste of an oatmeal-raisin cookie dough. The sweet rolls (which I've been baking for more than 15 years) are an inviting sight at Sunday brunch.

The yeast dough can be made up and baked into buns on the same day, or, if it is more convenient, refrigerated overnight, and rolled, filled, and formed the next day.

Nonstick cooking spray and softened, unsalted butter, for preparing the baking pan

SPICED OATMEAL YEAST DOUGH

2¾ teaspoons active dry yeast

½ teaspoon granulated sugar

¼ cup warm (110° to 115° F.) water

¼ cup granulated sugar

1 cup milk

6 tablespoons (¾ stick) unsalted butter, cut into chunks

2 teaspoons pure vanilla extract

⅔ cup quick-cooking (not instant) rolled oats

2 large eggs and 1 large egg yolk, lightly beaten

1 cup unsifted bleached all-purpose flour

2¾ cups plus 2 tablespoons unsifted unbleached all-purpose flour, plus more as needed for kneading and the work surface

1 teaspoon salt

2½ teaspoons ground cinnamon

1½ teaspoons freshly grated nutmeg

¾ teaspoon ground allspice

¾ teaspoon ground cardamom

½ teaspoon ground cloves

MAKE THE OATMEAL YEAST DOUGH Combine the yeast and ½ teaspoon granulated sugar in a bowl. Stir in the warm water and let stand until the yeast has dissolved, 7 to 8 minutes. Place the ¼ cup granulated sugar, the milk, and butter in a small saucepan and scald. Remove from the heat, stir well, and blend in the vanilla extract. Place the rolled oats in a medium-size heatproof bowl and pour over the milk mixture. Cool the oatmeal mixture to 115° F.; blend in the beaten eggs and egg yolk.

Combine 1 cup of the bleached flour and 2 cups of unbleached flour with the salt, cinnamon, nutmeg, allspice, cardamom, and cloves in a large mixing bowl. Stir the yeast mixture into the cooled egg-milk-oatmeal mixture, and add it to the spiced flour. Stir well, using a wooden spoon or flat wooden paddle.

6 tablespoons (¾ stick) unsalted
butter, softened

½ cup granulated sugar blended
with 2 teaspoons ground cinnamon,
1 teaspoon freshly grated nutmeg,
⅛ teaspoon ground allspice, and
⅛ teaspoon ground cardamom

1 cup dark raisins

SPICE ICING FOR SPREADING
OVER THE WARM, BAKED BUNS

1 cup unsifted confectioners' sugar

¼ teaspoon ground cinnamon

¼ teaspoon freshly grated nutmeg

pinch of ground allspice

pinch of ground cardamom

pinch of salt

1 tablespoon unsalted butter, softened

2 tablespoons light (table) cream

½ teaspoon pure vanilla extract

BAKEWARE

12 by 8 by 3-inch baking pan

Add the remaining ¾ cup plus 2 tablespoons unbleached flour, a little at a time, mixing well, to form a soft, malleable dough. Knead the dough on a well-floured work surface until supple and smooth, 8 to 9 minutes.

SET THE DOUGH TO RISE Place the dough in a lightly buttered bowl and turn to coat all sides in the butter. Cover the bowl tightly with a sheet of plastic wrap and let stand until doubled in bulk, about 1 hour and 15 minutes.

At this point, the once-risen dough can be used immediately, or refrigerated overnight, if it is more convenient to bake the rolls the next day. *To refrigerate the once-risen dough,* place the dough in a gallon-size, food-safe self-locking plastic bag and seal. Refrigerate the dough overnight.

PREPARE THE BAKING PAN Film the baking pan with nonstick cooking spray. Thickly butter the inside of the pan; set aside.

ASSEMBLE THE SPICED BUTTER AND RAISIN FILLING In a small mixing bowl, cream the butter with the spiced sugar. Have the raisins at hand.

ROLL, FILL, AND CUT THE DOUGH Gently compress the risen dough to deflate, or remove the dough from the refrigerator if it has rested there overnight.

Generously flour your work surface and rolling pin. Roll the dough into a sheet measuring about 15 by 16 inches. Spread the spiced butter on the surface of the dough and sprinkle over the raisins. Press down on the raisins so that they stick to the seasoned butter.

Roll up the dough tightly into a long coil, jellyroll-style, tucking in and crimping the edges with your fingertips as you roll. Brush excess flour off the dough as you roll it, using a soft pastry brush. *Rolling technique observation* Rolling the dough tightly will keep the spiral intact. Pinch the long seam end to close it. Gently roll the coil to extend it to about 19 inches in length.

With a sharp chef's knife, cut the coil into 12 even-sized slices. Place the buns, cut side down, in the prepared pan, in four rows of three. *Bun placement observation* At this point, there will be spaces between the buns, but they will disappear as the buns rise.

SET THE BUNS TO RISE Cover the pan loosely with a sheet of plastic wrap. Let the buns rise until doubled in bulk, about 1 hour and 10 minutes if you are using the room temperature-risen dough, or 2 hours to 2 hours and 20 minutes if you are working with refrigerated dough. The rolls should rise to about ½ inch of the top of the pan.

PREHEAT THE OVEN AND BAKE THE BUNS Preheat the oven to 375° F. in advance of baking. Remove and discard the sheet of plastic wrap covering the baking pan. Bake the buns for 25 to 30 minutes, or until plump, golden, and set. Cool the buns in the pan on a rack for 10 minutes, then invert them onto another cooling rack; invert again to cool right side up.

MIX THE SPICE ICING While the buns are cooling (and just before releasing them from the pan), make the icing. Sift the confectioners' sugar, cinnamon, nutmeg, allspice, cardamom, and salt into a medium-size mixing bowl. Add the butter, cream, and vanilla extract. Using an electric hand mixer, beat the ingredients on low speed for 1 minute or until just combined and smooth, scraping down the sides with a rubber spatula once or twice to keep the frosting even-textured.

SPREAD THE ICING ON THE WARM BUNS Spread the icing over the top of the warm buns, using a flexible palette knife. As you spread the icing over the surface of the warm buns, it will follow the surface pattern and melt down slightly, then firm up. Let the buns stand until the icing has set, about 1 hour. Serve the buns fresh.

❀ *For an aromatic topnote of flavor,* use intensified vanilla extract (see page 52) in place of plain vanilla extract in the yeast dough.

SPICED APPLE WAFFLES

7 deep, Belgian-style 2-sided waffles,
each waffle section measuring 4½ by 4½ inches

THE COMBINATION OF CINNAMON, nutmeg, ginger, and allspice absolutely blooms in a buttermilk and sour cream–based waffle batter. This batter catches shreds of freshly grated apple, which add a fruity topnote of flavor and gentle tang. Moist dried currants (½ cup), finely chopped crystallized ginger (¼ cup), or chopped walnuts (½ cup) can be added to the batter as you're stirring in the apples, for that extra bit of savor or crunch.

SPICED APPLE WAFFLE BATTER

2 cups unsifted bleached all-purpose flour

2¼ teaspoons baking powder

½ teaspoon baking soda

¼ teaspoon salt

2½ teaspoons ground cinnamon

1 teaspoon freshly grated nutmeg

½ teaspoon ground ginger

½ teaspoon ground allspice

⅛ teaspoon ground cloves

⅓ cup plus 2 tablespoons superfine sugar

½ cup thick, cultured sour cream

3 large eggs

7 tablespoons (1 stick less 1 tablespoon) unsalted butter, melted and cooled to tepid

1 cup buttermilk, plus extra as needed

2½ teaspoons pure vanilla extract

1 cup peeled and shredded apples

Confectioners' sugar, for sprinkling over the waffles (optional)

BEST BAKING ADVICE

When reducing the apples to shreds, use the large holes of a four-sided box grater to create shreds that stay suspended in the waffle batter.

MAKE THE SPICED APPLE WAFFLE BATTER Sift the flour, baking powder, baking soda, salt, cinnamon, nutmeg, ginger, allspice, cloves, and superfine sugar into a large mixing bowl.

Whisk the sour cream, eggs, and melted butter in a medium-size mixing bowl; slowly whisk in the buttermilk. Blend in the vanilla extract. Pour the liquid ingredients over the dry ingredients, add the shredded apples, and stir to form a batter, using a wooden spoon, flat wooden paddle, or rubber spatula. *Batter observation* The batter will be moderately thick. If the batter gets too thick as it stands, stir in additional buttermilk, a tablespoon or two at a time.

MAKE THE WAFFLES Preheat the waffle iron. Spoon a generous ⅓ cup of batter onto the center of each square of the preheated iron. Cook the waffles until golden, 1 minute to 1 minute and 15 seconds. Serve the waffles hot out the iron, sprinkled with confectioners' sugar, and topped, if you wish, with apple butter or maple-walnut syrup or honey-butter.

SUGAR AND SPICE BREAKFAST CAKE

One 9-inch cake, creating 12 slices

WHEN A BUTTER-AND-SPICE CRUMBLE MIXTURE is sprinkled on top of a sour cream cake batter, the crumble sticks to the top of the batter and turns into a buttery layer of sweet and lightly crunchy "gravel." To drive up the flavor, I spread half of the batter in the prepared baking pan and sift a mixture of cinnamon and nutmeg over the layer of filling just before adding the remaining batter. This tactic manages to give the cake that extra boost of flavor that I love.

The recipe for the sour cream batter used in this cake comes from my paternal grandmother, Lilly, and my mother, Irene; both baked a thoroughly cinnamon version of this cake in a springform cake pan. For the sake of nostalgia, and to keep the memory of their creative handiwork alive, I use the same style pan.

Nonstick cooking spray, for preparing the cake pan

SPICE CRUMBLE TOPPING

½ cup plus 2 tablespoons unsifted bleached all-purpose flour

½ cup firmly packed dark brown sugar, sieved if lumpy

½ cup firmly packed light brown sugar, sieved if lumpy

¼ cup granulated sugar

½ teaspoon ground cinnamon

½ teaspoon freshly grated nutmeg

¼ teaspoon ground cardamom

pinch of salt

6 tablespoons (¾ stick) unsalted butter, cold, cut into small chunks

⅔ cup chopped pecans or walnuts

SOUR CREAM SPICE
CAKE BATTER

2 cups unsifted bleached all-purpose flour

¼ cup unsifted bleached cake flour

1 teaspoon baking powder

½ teaspoon baking soda

¼ teaspoon salt

1½ teaspoons ground cinnamon

¾ teaspoon freshly grated nutmeg

¼ teaspoon ground allspice

¼ teaspoon ground cardamom

PREHEAT THE OVEN AND PREPARE THE CAKE PAN Preheat the oven to 350° F. Film the inside of the springform pan with nonstick cooking spray; set aside.

MAKE THE SPICE CRUMBLE TOPPING Thoroughly combine the flour, dark brown sugar, light brown sugar, granulated sugar, cinnamon, nutmeg, cardamom, and salt in a medium-size mixing bowl. Drop in the chunks of butter and, using a pastry blender, cut the fat into the flour until reduced to small clumps about the size of dried lima beans. Blend in the nuts. With your fingertips, rub-and-crumble the mixture until it comes together into large and small moist lumps. Set aside.

MIX THE SOUR CREAM SPICE CAKE BATTER Sift the all-purpose flour, cake flour, baking powder, baking soda, salt, cinnamon, nutmeg, allspice, and cardamom onto a sheet of waxed paper.

¼ pound (8 tablespoons or 1 stick) unsalted butter, softened

1 cup plus 2 tablespoons granulated sugar

2 large eggs

2 teaspoons intensified vanilla extract (see page 52)

1¼ cups thick, cultured sour cream

1 tablespoon ground cinnamon blended with ½ teaspoon freshly grated nutmeg and pinch of ground allspice

BAKEWARE

9-inch springform pan (2¾ inches deep)

Cream the butter in the large bowl of a freestanding electric mixer on moderate speed for 2 minutes. Add the granulated sugar in three additions; beat for 1 minute longer. Blend in the eggs, one at a time, mixing for 1 minute after each addition. Blend in the vanilla extract.

On low speed, alternately add the sifted mixture in three additions with the sour cream in two additions, beginning and ending with the sifted mixture. Scrape down the sides of the mixing bowl frequently with a rubber spatula to keep the batter even-textured. *Batter texture observation* The batter will be thick.

ASSEMBLE THE CAKE BATTER WITH THE TOPPING AND SPICE MIXTURE Spoon half of the batter into the prepared cake pan. Sift the cinnamon-nutmeg-allspice blend evenly over the top. Spoon on the remaining cake batter; as you spread the batter, it will lift away, but keep spreading. It will cling and settle down. Lightly swirl together the two layers of batter, using a small, flexible palette knife. Sprinkle the topping mixture on the top of the cake.

BAKE AND COOL THE CAKE Bake the cake in the preheated oven for 1 hour to 1 hour and 10 minutes, or until set and a wooden pick inserted in the center of the cake withdraws clean or with a few moist crumbs attached to it. The baked cake will pull away slightly from the sides of the baking pan.

Cool the cake in the pan on a rack. When it is completely cool, release the sides, and cut the cake into wedges.

FRESHLY BAKED, THE CAKE KEEPS FOR 3 DAYS.

SPICE RIPPLE KEEPING CAKE

One 10-inch tube cake, creating about 20 slices

*I*N THIS RECIPE, the spices are put in the context of a buttery, creamy batter. The dairy ingredients allow the spices to unfold and enlarge, and produce an aromatic cake that's delicious served with brewed tea or strong coffee.

Shortening and bleached all-purpose flour, for preparing the cake pan

SWEET SPICE RIPPLE

2 teaspoons ground cinnamon

½ teaspoon freshly grated nutmeg

½ teaspoon ground ginger

¼ teaspoon ground allspice

¼ teaspoon ground cardamom

¼ cup granulated sugar

SPICED BUTTER AND SOUR CREAM CAKE BATTER

3 cups unsifted bleached all-purpose flour

¼ teaspoon baking powder

1 teaspoon salt

1 tablespoon ground cinnamon

1 teaspoon freshly grated nutmeg

1 teaspoon ground ginger

½ teaspoon ground allspice

¼ teaspoon ground cloves

¼ teaspoon ground cardamom

¾ pound (3 sticks) unsalted butter, softened

2½ cups superfine sugar

5 large eggs

2 teaspoons pure vanilla extract

1 cup heavy cream

PREHEAT THE OVEN AND PREPARE THE CAKE PAN Preheat the oven to 325° F. Grease the inside of the tube pan with shortening. Line the bottom of the pan with a circle of waxed paper cut to fit, and grease the paper. Dust the inside of the pan with all-purpose flour. Tap out any excess flour; set aside.

MAKE THE SWEET SPICE RIPPLE Whisk together the cinnamon, nutmeg, ginger, allspice, cardamom, and granulated sugar in a small mixing bowl; set aside.

MIX THE SPICED BUTTER AND SOUR CREAM CAKE BATTER Sift the all-purpose flour, baking powder, salt, cinnamon, nutmeg, ginger, allspice, cloves, and cardamom onto a sheet of waxed paper.

Cream the butter in the large bowl of a freestanding electric mixer on moderate speed for 3 minutes. Add the superfine sugar in four additions, beating for 1 minute after each portion is added. Add the eggs, one at a time, beating for 45 seconds after each addition. Blend in the vanilla extract.

On low speed, alternately add the sifted mixture in three additions with the heavy cream in two additions, beginning and ending with the sifted mixture. Scrape down the sides of the mixing bowl frequently with a rubber spatula to keep the batter even-textured. *Batter texture observation* The batter will be moderately thick and very creamy.

ASSEMBLE THE BATTER WITH THE SPICE RIPPLE Spoon a little more than half of the batter into the prepared cake pan. Sprinkle over the spice mixture. Spoon over the remaining batter.

Confectioners' sugar, for sifting over top of the cooled cake (optional)

plain 10-inch tube pan

Lightly swirl the two levels of batter together with a flexible palette knife.

Gently shake the pan (once or twice) from side to side to level the top.

BAKE AND COOL THE CAKE Bake the cake in the preheated oven for 1 hour and 20 minutes to 1 hour and 25 minutes, or until risen, set, and a wooden pick inserted in the cake withdraws clean. The baked cake will pull away slightly from the sides of the baking pan.

Cool the cake in the pan on a rack for 7 to 10 minutes. Invert the cake onto another cooling rack. Cool completely. Sift confectioners' sugar over the top of the cake before slicing and serving, if you wish. *Slicing observation* Use a serrated knife to cut the cake neatly and cleanly.

❊ *For an aromatic topnote of flavor,* use intensified vanilla extract (see page 52) in place of plain vanilla extract in the cake batter.

FRESHLY BAKED, THE CAKE KEEPS FOR 5 TO 7 DAYS.

BEST BAKING ADVICE
So that the filling swirls into the cake batter evenly, make sure that the ingredients for the sweet spice ripple are thoroughly combined to incorporate the spices and the sugar.

SPICED AND GLAZED CHOCOLATE CHIP CAKE

One 10-inch fluted tube cake, creating 16 slices

Butter and spices go together handily, and are equal partners in taste in this chocolate chip–freckled pound cake. The chips add another layer of flavor to the cake and meld agreeably with the "sweet" ground spices. For a diversion in texture, chopped walnuts or pecans can be added to the batter, along with the chips, for crunch.

The neighborhood bakery of my childhood sold a special chocolate spice cake on the weekends only, and it is the memory of that cake that inspired this recipe.

Nonstick cooking spray, for preparing the cake pan

SPICED CHOCOLATE CHIP BUTTER CAKE BATTER

2½ cups unsifted bleached all-purpose flour

½ cup unsifted bleached cake flour

1¾ teaspoons baking powder

1 teaspoon salt

1½ teaspoons ground cinnamon

1 teaspoon freshly grated nutmeg

¾ teaspoon ground ginger

¼ teaspoon ground allspice

¼ teaspoon ground cloves

2 cups miniature semisweet chocolate chips

½ pound (16 tablespoons or 2 sticks) unsalted butter, softened

2 cups vanilla-scented granulated sugar (see page 53)

4 large eggs

2¾ teaspoons intensified vanilla extract (see page 52)

1 cup milk

Chocolate Glaze (see page 479), for spooning over the baked cake

BAKEWARE

10-inch Bundt pan

PREHEAT THE OVEN AND PREPARE THE CAKE PAN Preheat the oven to 350° F. Film the inside of the Bundt pan with nonstick cooking spray; set aside.

MIX THE SPICED CHOCOLATE CHIP BUTTER CAKE BATTER Sift the all-purpose flour, cake flour, baking powder, salt, cinnamon, nutmeg, ginger, allspice, and cloves onto a sheet of waxed paper. In a medium-size mixing bowl, toss the chocolate chips with 1 tablespoon of the sifted mixture.

Cream the butter in the large bowl of a freestanding electric mixer on moderate speed for 3 minutes. Add the vanilla-scented granulated sugar in three additions, beating on moderate speed for 30 seconds after each portion is added. Beat for a minute longer. Beat in the eggs, one at a time, mixing for 30 seconds after each addition. Blend in the vanilla extract. Scrape down the sides of the mixing bowl frequently with a rubber spatula to keep the batter even-textured.

On low speed, alternately add the sifted mixture in three additions with milk in two additions, beginning and ending with the sifted mixture. Stir in the chocolate chips.

Scrape the batter into the prepared Bundt pan. Lightly smooth over the top with a flexible spatula.

BAKE THE CAKE Bake the cake in the preheated oven for 55 minutes to 1 hour, or until risen, set, and a wooden pick inserted in the cake withdraws clean.

COOL THE CAKE Cool the cake in the pan on a rack for 5 to 10 minutes. Invert the cake onto another cooling rack and cool completely. Place a sheet of waxed paper under the cooling rack to catch any drips of glaze.

GLAZE THE CAKE Spoon the glaze over the cooled cake, letting it flow down the sides and central tube. Let the glaze firm up for at least 2 hours before slicing and serving. *Slicing observation* Use a serrated knife to cut the cake neatly and cleanly.

FRESHLY BAKED, THE CAKE KEEPS FOR 2 DAYS.

CHOCOLATE GLAZE

About 1¼ cups

SET AGAINST A BUTTERY BACKDROP, this glaze has a full jolt of chocolate and balanced vanilla undertone. It's a superb counterpoint to the spicy chocolate chip Bundt cake on page 478, as well as a noble finish to any buttery chocolate, buttercrunch, or vanilla cake baked in a plain or fluted tube pan.

CHOCOLATE GLAZE

3 ounces (3 squares) unsweetened chocolate, coarsely chopped

6 tablespoons (¾ stick) unsalted butter, cut into tablespoon chunks

⅓ cup plus 2½ tablespoons superfine sugar

1 tablespoon cornstarch

pinch of salt

½ cup milk

1¼ teaspoons pure vanilla extract

¼ teaspoon light corn syrup

MAKE THE CHOCOLATE GLAZE Place the chopped unsweetened chocolate and butter in a heavy, medium-size saucepan, preferably enameled cast iron. Set over low heat and cook slowly until the chocolate and butter are melted. Remove from the heat and whisk well to combine.

Sift the superfine sugar, cornstarch, and salt into a small mixing bowl. Slowly whisk in the milk in a steady stream, blending well. Stir the cornstarch-sugar-milk mixture into the melted butter-chocolate. Place over moderate to moderately high heat and bring to the boil, stirring slowly and thoroughly all the while. Do not beat the mixture rapidly. Do not use a whisk for stirring the mixture. When the glaze reaches a low boil, let it bubble for 1 to 2 minutes, or until lightly thickened. The glaze will be shiny.

STRAIN THE GLAZE Remove the saucepan from the heat. Pour the glaze into a large fine-meshed sieve set over a heatproof bowl. Press the glaze through the sieve, using a rubber spatula. Stir in the vanilla extract and corn syrup.

COOL THE GLAZE Let the glaze cool for 2 minutes, stirring continuously to keep it smooth and homogenous, before spooning it over a thoroughly cooled bundt or pound cake. *Glaze temperature observation* The glaze must be used when freshly made and very warm, before it has the chance to set up. Reheating the glaze would ruin its finished texture.

SPICE CAKE

One 13 by 9-inch cake, creating 20 pieces

THE BACKDROP OF BUTTER, brown sugar, and buttermilk clearly strengthens the taste of the spices, and makes the cake sparkle. The buttery confectioners' sugar frosting is a typical, and classic, way to top the sheet cake.

Nonstick cooking spray, for preparing the baking pan

BUTTERMILK SPICE
CAKE BATTER

2 cups unsifted bleached all-purpose flour

½ cup unsifted bleached cake flour

1 teaspoon baking soda

¼ teaspoon baking powder

1 teaspoon salt

2½ teaspoons ground cinnamon

PREHEAT THE OVEN AND PREPARE THE BAKING PAN Preheat the oven to 350° F. Film the inside of the baking pan with nonstick cooking spray; set aside.

MIX THE BUTTERMILK SPICE CAKE BATTER Sift the all-purpose flour, cake flour, baking soda, baking powder, salt, cinnamon, nutmeg, ginger, allspice, and cloves onto a sheet of waxed paper.

Cream the butter and shortening in the large bowl of a freestanding electric mixer on moderate speed for 3 minutes. Add the dark brown sugar and beat for 1 minute; add the granulated sugar and beat for a minute longer. Blend in the eggs, one at a

1 teaspoon freshly grated nutmeg

1 teaspoon ground ginger

¾ teaspoon ground allspice

½ teaspoon ground cloves

¼ pound (8 tablespoons or 1 stick) unsalted butter, softened

3 tablespoons shortening

1 cup firmly packed dark brown sugar, sieved if lumpy

¾ cup granulated sugar

3 large eggs

2 teaspoons intensified vanilla extract (see page 52)

¾ cup buttermilk, whisked well

Spice Cake Frosting (see page 482), for spreading on the baked cake layer

BAKEWARE

13 by 9 by 2-inch baking pan

time, beating for 45 seconds after each addition. Beat in the vanilla extract.

On low speed, alternately add the sifted ingredients in three additions with the buttermilk in two additions, beginning and ending with the sifted mixture. Scrape down the sides of the mixing bowl frequently with a rubber spatula to keep the batter even-textured.

Spoon the batter into the prepared baking pan. Smooth over the top with a rubber spatula.

BAKE AND COOL THE CAKE Bake the cake for 35 minutes, or until risen, set, and a wooden pick inserted in the center of the cake withdraws clean. Cool the cake in the pan on a rack.

FROST THE CAKE Place large spoonfuls of the frosting over the surface of the cake. With a flexible palette knife, spread and swirl the frosting over the top of the cake, taking care to cover the corners and edges. Let the cake stand for 2 hours (to set the frosting) before cutting into squares for serving.

❊ *For an extra surge of flavor and texture,* sprinkle some Golden Oatmeal Sprinkle (see page 65) on top of the freshly frosted cake just before cutting and serving. The oatmeal crumble mixture is a crunchy, buttery counterpoint to the softness of the cake and creaminess of the frosting.

FRESHLY BAKED, THE CAKE KEEPS FOR 2 DAYS.

SPICE CAKE FROSTING

About 2⅔ cups

A BUTTER AND CREAM-BASED FROSTING is a traditional complement to a soft, fine-grained spice cake. This frosting is laced with nutmeg and vanilla extract, two flavoring components that cultivate the taste of the butter.

SPICE CAKE FROSTING

7 tablespoons (1 stick less 1 tablespoon) unsalted butter, softened, cut into tablespoon pieces

4¼ cups unsifted confectioners' sugar

big pinch of salt

2¼ teaspoons pure vanilla extract

¼ cup plus 2 tablespoons half-and-half

MAKE THE FROSTING Place the butter, confectioners' sugar, salt, vanilla extract, and half-and-half in a large mixing bowl. Using an electric hand mixer, beat the ingredients together on moderately low speed until smooth, scraping down the sides of the mixing bowl frequently with a rubber spatula. Beat the frosting on moderately high speed for 1 minute, or until creamy. *Frosting consistency observation* The frosting should be smooth, creamy, and spreadable. If the frosting is too soft, add additional confectioners' sugar, a tablespoon at a time.

Use the frosting immediately on a thoroughly cooled cake.

SPICE SCONES

1 dozen scones

T HE GLOW OF GROUND CINNAMON, nutmeg, allspice, ginger, and cloves tints and infuses this buttery, golden raisin-flecked scone dough. Dredging the unbaked wedges with cinnamon-sugar is a simple way to add a tasty and decorative finish.

SPICED SCONE DOUGH

4¼ cups unsifted bleached all-purpose flour

5 teaspoons baking powder

PREHEAT THE OVEN AND PREPARE THE BAKING SHEETS Preheat the oven to 400° F. Line the cookie sheets or sheet pans with cooking parchment paper; set aside. *Bakeware observation* The baking sheets must be heavy, or the spice dough will scorch

1 teaspoon salt

1 tablespoon ground cinnamon

1¼ teaspoons freshly grated nutmeg

1 teaspoon ground ginger

¼ teaspoon ground allspice

⅛ teaspoon ground cloves

⅔ cup granulated sugar

12 tablespoons (1½ sticks) unsalted butter, cold, cut into tablespoon chunks

4 large eggs

1 cup heavy cream

2½ teaspoons pure vanilla extract

1 cup golden raisins

CINNAMON-SUGAR MIXTURE FOR SPRINKLING OVER THE UNBAKED SCONES

¼ cup granulated sugar blended with 1 teaspoon ground cinnamon

BAKEWARE

2 large, heavy cookie sheets or rimmed sheet pans

on the bottom as the scones bake. Double-pan the sheets, if necessary.

MIX THE SPICED SCONE DOUGH Whisk the flour, baking powder, salt, cinnamon, nutmeg, ginger, allspice, cloves, and granulated sugar in a large mixing bowl. Add the chunks of butter, and using a pastry blender, cut the butter into small pea-sized bits. Lightly and quickly, crumble the mixture between your fingertips until the butter is reduced to smaller flakes.

In a medium-size mixing bowl, whisk the eggs, heavy cream, and vanilla extract. Pour the egg-cream mixture over the dry ingredients, scatter over the raisins, and stir to form the beginnings of a dough. With lightly floured hands, knead the mixture until it comes together in to a firm, manageable (but moist) dough. Knead the dough in the bowl, using 10 to 12 light pushes.

FORM THE DOUGH INTO SCONES On a floured work surface, divide the dough in half and form each half into an 8-inch disk. Cut each disk into six wedges. With a wide, offset metal spatula, transfer the scones to the lined cookie sheets, placing them about 3 inches apart, six to a sheet. Sprinkle a little of the cinnamon-sugar on top of each scone.

BAKE AND COOL THE SCONES Bake the scones in the preheated oven for 17 to 20 minutes, or until set. Remove the scones to cooling racks, using a wide metal spatula. Serve the scones warm or at room temperature.

FRESHLY BAKED, THE SCONES KEEP FOR 2 DAYS.

BEST BAKING ADVICE

Be sure to knead the dough in the bowl before forming and shaping to develop its texture and height as the scones bake.

SPICED PUMPKIN AND
CHOCOLATE CHIP TEA LOAF

Two 9 by 5 by 3-inch loaves, each loaf creating 10 slices

Pumpkin puree, as a both a vegetable and a flavoring agent, is an excellent vehicle for carrying and expanding the taste of many spices, and is also a terrific complement to chocolate. The batter for these moist, soft-textured, chocolate chip-decorated loaves actually radiates spice—it's built on the mingling of cinnamon, nutmeg, ginger, allspice, and cardamom, which taken together are deep, mellow, and rich. Although the chocolate chip version is delicious, 1¼ cups of chopped nuts (walnuts, pecans, or Brazil nuts), or 1 cup of diced dates, golden or dark raisins, or chopped dried (or glazed) apricots can replace the chocolate chips.

Shortening and bleached all-purpose flour, for preparing the loaf pans

SPICED PUMPKIN-CHOCOLATE CHIP LOAF CAKE BATTER

3 cups unsifted bleached all-purpose flour

2¼ teaspoons baking powder

1 teaspoon salt

2 teaspoons ground cinnamon

¾ teaspoon freshly grated nutmeg

¾ teaspoon ground ginger

½ teaspoon ground allspice

¼ teaspoon ground cardamom

2 cups miniature semisweet chocolate chips

2 large eggs

2 large egg yolks

2¾ cups granulated sugar

½ cup plain vegetable oil, such as soybean

¼ pound (8 tablespoons or 1 stick) unsalted butter, melted and cooled

1 tablespoon pure vanilla extract

One 1-pound can plain pumpkin puree (not pumpkin pie filling)

BAKEWARE

two 9 by 5 by 3-inch loaf pans

PREHEAT THE OVEN AND PREPARE THE LOAF PANS Preheat the oven to 350° F. Lightly grease the loaf pans with shortening. Dust the inside of each pan with all-purpose flour. Tap out any excess flour; set aside. *Equipment observation* For the best-looking loaves, be sure to use pans with sloping sides.

MAKE THE SPICED PUMPKIN-CHOCOLATE CHIP LOAF CAKE BATTER Sift the flour, baking powder, salt, cinnamon, nutmeg, ginger, allspice, and cardamom onto a sheet of waxed paper. In a medium-size mixing bowl, toss the chocolate chips with 1 tablespoon of the sifted mixture.

Beat the eggs and egg yolks in the large bowl of a freestanding electric mixer on moderately low speed for 1 minute. Add the granulated sugar and beat for 1 to 2 minutes on moderately low speed. Blend in the oil and butter, mixing for 1 minute longer. Blend in the vanilla extract and pumpkin puree.

On low speed, add the sifted flour mixture in three additions, mixing just until the particles of flour are absorbed before adding the next batch. Scrape down the sides of the mixing bowl frequently with a rubber spatula to keep the batter even-textured. *Batter texture observation* The batter will be smooth and moderately thick. Stir in the chocolate chips. Spoon the batter into the prepared loaf pans, dividing it evenly between them.

BAKE AND COOL THE LOAVES Bake the loaves for 1 hour and 5 minutes to 1 hour and 10 minutes, or until risen, set, and a wooden pick inserted in the cake withdraws clean. The baked loaves will pull away slightly from the sides of the pans. Let the loaves stand in the pans on cooling racks for 5 minutes, carefully invert onto other cooling racks, then stand them right side up. Cool completely before slicing and serving. *Slicing observation* Use a serrated knife to cut the loaf neatly and cleanly.

FRESHLY BAKED, THE TEA LOAVES KEEP FOR **2** TO **3** DAYS.

*C*ream cheese is dense and smooth, and amenable to flavoring, and produces rich and indulgent bakery sweets. Cream cheese can be transformed into a glimmery filling or turned into a cheesecake-like topping for swirling into a bar cookie or torte batter, or to dollop onto the top of unbaked muffins or cupcakes. It can also spotlight itself in a cake or torte by adding a distinctly creamy, vaguely (and pleasantly) acidic richness. The moistness intrinsic to cream cheese makes it an ideal addition to sweet yeast roll fillings. Cream cheese creates heavenly textured batters that can be fine-grained and close-textured, or light and delicate.

21

SWEET CHEESE

CREAM CHEESE POUND CAKE

One 10-inch tube cake, creating about 20 slices

THE FRESHLY GRATED NUTMEG and the interplay of three flavoring extracts (vanilla, lemon, and almond) softly accent this fine-grained pound cake. Not only do these ingredients impact the overall flavor of the cake, but they also serve to bring out the tanginess of the cream cheese. And since the cake is rich in butter, cream cheese, and eggs, the batter doesn't require any liquid in the form of milk, heavy cream, or sour cream to establish its volume or texture.

Shortening and bleached all-purpose flour, for preparing the cake pan

BUTTER AND CREAM CHEESE CAKE BATTER

2¾ cups unsifted bleached all-purpose flour

¼ cup unsifted bleached cake flour

¼ teaspoon baking soda

1 teaspoon salt

¾ teaspoon freshly grated nutmeg

½ pound (16 tablespoons or 2 sticks) unsalted butter, softened

One 8-ounce package cream cheese, softened

3 tablespoons shortening

3 cups vanilla-scented superfine sugar (see page 54)

2½ teaspoons pure vanilla extract

1 teaspoon pure lemon extract

1 teaspoon pure almond extract

6 large eggs

Vanilla-scented confectioners' sugar (see page 54), for sifting over the top of the cooled cake (optional)

BAKEWARE

plain 10-inch tube pan

PREHEAT THE OVEN AND PREPARE THE CAKE PAN Preheat the oven to 325° F. Lightly grease the bottom of the tube pan with shortening; cut a circle of waxed paper to fit the bottom of the pan and smooth it onto the bottom. Grease the waxed paper-lined bottom and sides of the pan with a film of shortening, then dust the pan with all-purpose flour. Tap out any excess flour; set aside.

PREPARE THE BUTTER AND CREAM CHEESE CAKE BATTER Sift the all-purpose flour, cake flour, baking soda, salt, and nutmeg onto a sheet of waxed paper.

Cream the butter, cream cheese, and shortening in the large bowl of a freestanding electric mixer on moderate speed for 4 minutes, or until quite smooth. Add the vanilla-scented superfine sugar in three additions, beating on moderate speed for about 1 minute after each portion is added. Blend in the vanilla, lemon, and almond extracts. Beat in the eggs, one at a time, mixing on moderate speed for 30 seconds after each addition. Scrape down the sides of the mixing bowl frequently with a rubber spatula to keep the batter even-textured.

On low speed, add the sifted ingredients in three additions, blending just until the particles of flour have been absorbed. Scrape down the sides of the bowl with a rubber spatula after each addition of flour has been added to the batter.

Spoon the batter into the prepared tube pan, lightly smoothing over the top with a flexible palette knife or rubber spatula.

BAKE THE CAKE Bake the cake in the preheated oven for 1 hour and 20 minutes to 1 hour and 25 minutes, or until risen, set, and a wooden pick inserted in the cake withdraws clean. The baked cake will pull away slightly from the sides of the baking pan.

COOL THE CAKE Cool the cake in the pan on a rack for 10 minutes, then carefully invert onto another cooling rack. Peel off the waxed paper circle, then invert to cool right side up. Cool completely before slicing and serving. *Slicing observation* Use a serrated knife to cut the cake neatly and cleanly. For serving, sift confectioners' sugar generously over the top of the cake, if you wish.

FRESHLY BAKED, THE CAKE KEEPS FOR 5 DAYS.

SWEET CHEESE BUNS

18 buns

*T*HESE SWEET ROLLS, made of a fluffy brioche-style dough, a glamorous cream cheese and raisin filling, and a spiced crumble topping, are lush and flavorful. Two spices—nutmeg and cinnamon—that are present in all three components unify this sweet and serve as an appropriate background of flavor to the cream cheese.

Softened unsalted butter, for preparing the baking pans

LIGHTLY SWEETENED
BRIOCHE-STYLE YEAST DOUGH

4½ teaspoons active dry yeast

¾ teaspoon granulated sugar

3 tablespoons warm (110° to 115° F.) water

MAKE THE BRIOCHE-STYLE YEAST DOUGH Combine the yeast and ¾ teaspoon granulated sugar in a small heatproof bowl. Stir in the warm water and let stand until the yeast dissolves and the mixture is lightened and swollen, 7 to 8 minutes.

Whisk the eggs in a large mixing bowl. Mix in the ⅓ cup plus 2 tablespoons granulated sugar, nutmeg, cinnamon, and vanilla extract. Blend in the frothy and expanded yeast mixture. Combine the bleached and unbleached all-purpose flour with the salt in a

6 large eggs

⅓ cup plus 2 tablespoons granulated
   sugar

1 teaspoon freshly grated nutmeg

1 teaspoon ground cinnamon

1 tablespoon pure vanilla extract

2 cups unsifted bleached all-purpose
   flour

2 cups unsifted unbleached all-purpose
   flour

1 teaspoon salt

½ pound plus 2 tablespoons
   (18 tablespoons or 2 sticks plus
   2 tablespoons) unsalted butter,
   lightly softened but cool

SCENTED CREAM CHEESE,
WALNUT, AND RAISIN FILLING

One 8-ounce package cream cheese,
   softened

2 tablespoons unsalted butter, softened

5 tablespoons granulated sugar
   blended with ½ teaspoon ground
   cinnamon and ½ teaspoon freshly
   grated nutmeg

2 teaspoons pure vanilla extract

1 large egg

⅓ cup ground walnuts

1 cup moist golden raisins

Buttery Spiced Streusel (see page 61)
   or Nut Streusel (see page 63), using
   walnuts, for scattering over the
   fully risen buns

BAKEWARE

two 9 by 9 by 3-inch baking pans

medium-size bowl. Using a sturdy wooden spoon or flat wooden paddle, add the flour combination a cup at a time, mixing well. *Dough texture observation* As you add the last cup of flour, the dough will appear slightly shaggy and somewhat roughhewn, but will smooth out in a few minutes.

Transfer the dough to the bowl of a heavy-duty, freestanding electric mixer fitted with the flat paddle. Beat the dough for 4 minutes on moderate to moderately low speed, or until somewhat smooth.

Place the butter on a flat plate and smear it out slightly with a flexible palette knife or rubber spatula. The butter should be cool but malleable, and not oily. Add the softened, cool butter to the dough, about a tablespoon at a time, beating until it has assimilated into the dough before adding the next piece. Beat for 1 to 2 minutes longer. During the beating process, the dough should make a slapping noise against the sides of the mixing bowl. *Dough texture observation* Allowing the dough to absorb the butter a little at a time will create a silky dough with a good pull and satiny sheen. Rushing the process (by adding too much butter at once) will underdevelop—and then spoil—the composition of the yeast dough.

SET THE DOUGH TO RISE Lightly place the dough in a buttered bowl. Cover the top with a sheet of plastic wrap. Let the dough rise until doubled in bulk, 2 hours to 2 hours and 30 minutes.

PREPARE THE DOUGH FOR REFRIGERATION With your cupped hands, place the dough on a lightly floured work surface. Gently press the dough into a 10 by 10-inch square. Fold the dough in half and press down lightly. Place the dough in a self-sealing plastic bag and refrigerate. After 3 hours, lightly compress the dough with your fingertips. Over the next 3 hours, pat down the dough two or three times more. Refrigerate the dough overnight.

MIX THE SCENTED CREAM CHEESE, WALNUT, AND RAISIN FILLING Using an electric hand mixer, beat the cream cheese and butter on moderately low speed for 3 minutes, or until smooth. Blend in the granulated sugar-spice mixture and beat for 1 minute. Blend in the vanilla extract and egg, and beat until smooth, scraping down the sides of the mixing bowl with a rubber spatula, about a minute longer. Blend in the ground walnuts. Have the raisins at hand in a small bowl.

PREPARE THE BAKING PANS Lightly butter the inside of the baking pans; set aside.

ROLL, FILL, AND CUT THE BUNS Remove the dough from the refrigerator and place on a floured work surface. Flour a rolling pin. *Dough texture observation* The dough, although well chilled, will still be somewhat sticky. It's important to keep the rolling pin and work surface well floured.

Roll out the dough into a sheet measuring about 15 by 16 inches. Spread the filling on the surface of the dough to within about 1 inch of all four sides. Scatter over the raisins. With the help of a pastry scraper to lift the dough, roll it into a long jellyroll. With a soft pastry brush, dust off the flour on the underside of the roll. *Ooze of filling observation* As you are rolling, the filling will be soft and might ooze here and there, but any imperfections will be concealed when the buns are arranged in the pan and covered with the topping. Pinch the long seam and two ends closed. Carefully lengthen the coil until it measures about 23 inches by stretching and pulling it a section at a time.

With a sharp chef's knife, cut the coil into 18 slices. The filling will seep a bit as the buns are cut. Place nine buns (in rows of three), cut side up, in each buttered pan.

SET THE BUNS TO RISE Cover each pan loosely with a sheet of plastic wrap. Let the buns rise until doubled in bulk at cool room temperature, 2 hours and 30 minutes to 3 hours. *Dough rising observation* A long, tempered rise, not accelerated by heat, will create the best-textured buns. Both the density of the buttery dough and the filling are what account for the long rising time.

PREHEAT THE OVEN, AND TOP AND BAKE THE BUNS Preheat the oven to 375° F. Remove and discard the sheets of plastic wrap covering both pans of buns. Just before baking, scatter the streusel mixture in large and small clumps over the buns, dividing the mixture evenly between the two pans. Bake the buns for 30 minutes, or until well risen and set, and the streusel is firm and amber-colored.

COOL THE BUNS Let the buns stand in the pans on cooling racks for 20 minutes. Remove them, individually or in blocks of three, using a wide metal spatula, cutting them as they split naturally as they have connected while rising. Serve the buns slightly warm, or at room temperature. Refrigerate any buns not eaten within 3 hours of cooling, in an airtight container.

✻ *For an aromatic topnote of flavor,* use intensified vanilla extract (see page 52) in place of plain vanilla extract in the yeast dough.

FRESHLY BAKED, THE BUNS KEEP FOR 3 DAYS.

CREAM CHEESE–SWIRLED BROWNIES

16 brownies

*T*HICK RIPPLES OF A LIGHTLY SWEETENED, chocolate chip–dotted cream cheese mixture meander through this vividly chocolate batter, and the combination bakes into a distinguished bar cookie.

Nonstick cooking spray, for preparing the baking pan

CHOCOLATE CHIP–CREAM CHEESE SWIRL

Two 3-ounce packages cream cheese, softened

⅓ cup vanilla-scented granulated sugar (see page 53)

2 large egg yolks

pinch of salt

1¼ teaspoons pure vanilla extract

⅓ cup miniature semisweet chocolate chips

COCOA-CHIP BROWNIE BATTER

⅔ cup plus 2 tablespoons unsifted bleached all-purpose flour

1 tablespoon unsweetened, alkalized cocoa

¼ teaspoon baking powder

¼ teaspoon salt

½ cup miniature semisweet chocolate chips

6 tablespoons (¾ stick) unsalted butter, melted and cooled

3 ounces (3 squares) unsweetened chocolate, melted and cooled

2 large eggs

1 cup vanilla-scented granulated sugar (see page 53)

PREHEAT THE OVEN AND PREPARE THE BAKING PAN Preheat the oven to 325° F. Film the inside of the baking pan with nonstick cooking spray; set aside.

MIX THE CHOCOLATE CHIP–CREAM CHEESE SWIRL Using an electric hand mixer, beat the cream cheese and vanilla-scented granulated sugar in a small bowl on moderate speed for 2 minutes. Add the egg yolks, salt, and vanilla extract and blend slowly until thoroughly combined. *Batter texture observation* The batter will be moderately thick, but creamy. Scrape down the sides of the mixing bowl two or three times with a rubber spatula to keep the mixture smooth. Stir in the chocolate chips. Set aside.

MIX THE COCOA-CHIP BROWNIE BATTER Sift the flour, cocoa, baking powder, and salt onto a sheet of waxed paper. In a small bowl, toss the chocolate chips with 1½ teaspoons of the sifted mixture.

Whisk the melted butter and melted unsweetened chocolate in a small mixing bowl. In a medium-size mixing bowl, whisk the eggs for 1 minute. Add the vanilla-scented granulated sugar and whisk for 45 seconds, or until just combined; whisk in the melted butter-chocolate mixture. Blend in the vanilla extract. Sift over the sifted ingredients and whisk to form a batter, mixing until the particles of flour are completely absorbed. Blend in the heavy cream. *Batter texture observation* The batter will be somewhat thick. Stir in the chocolate chips, using a wooden spoon or flat wooden paddle.

ASSEMBLE THE BROWNIE BATTER AND CREAM CHEESE SWIRL Scrape the brownie batter into the prepared baking pan.

1½ teaspoons pure vanilla extract

2 tablespoons heavy cream

BAKEWARE

8 by 8 by 2-inch baking pan

Smooth over the top with a flexible palette knife (or rubber spatula). Spoon the cream cheese mixture on top of the brownie batter in nine large dollops. Using a flexible palette knife, swirl the two mixtures together, using an up and over motion. *Swirling technique observation* The batters are thick, so make wide, looping swirls by dipping into the chocolate batter, folding it up and over the cheesecake batter, then dipping down again to finish the swirl. Shake the pan vigorously from side to side two or three times to level the top. *Leveling the top of the brownies observation* Smoothing over the top of the batter with a rubber spatula would create a muddy-looking surface.

BAKE, COOL, AND CUT THE BROWNIES Bake the brownies in the preheated oven for 40 minutes, or until set. Let the brownies stand in the pan on a cooling rack for at least 2 hours. With a small, sharp knife, cut the brownie cake into four equal quarters, cut each section into four squares, and remove from the pan, using a small, offset metal spatula. Refrigerate any brownies not eaten within 2 hours after cooling, in an airtight container.

❋ *For an aromatic topnote of flavor,* use intensified vanilla extract (see page 52) in place of plain vanilla extract in the brownie batter.

FRESHLY BAKED, THE BROWNIES KEEP FOR 4 DAYS.

VANILLA AND CARAMEL NOUGAT CHEESECAKE TORTE

One 9-inch cake, creating 10 slices

A LAYER OF NOUGAT AND CARAMEL CANDY BAR CHUNKS flavors this rich-in-cream-cheese torte batter. The cheesecake batter itself, which sits on a chocolate cookie crumb base, is flavored only with vanilla extract, which balances the intensity of the candy. For this cookie crumb crust, I use Nabisco Oreo Chocolate Sandwich Cookies.

Nonstick cooking spray, for preparing the cake pan

CHOCOLATE, CARAMEL, AND NOUGAT COOKIE CRUMB CRUST

1⅔ cups chocolate sandwich cookie crumbs

3 tablespoons plus 2 teaspoons unsalted butter, melted, cooled, and blended with ¼ teaspoon pure vanilla extract

Five bars (1.76 ounces each) dark chocolate-covered caramel and vanilla nougat candy (Milky Way Dark), cut into small chunks

SOUR CREAM CHEESECAKE BATTER

Four 8-ounce packages cream cheese, softened

1 cup vanilla-scented granulated sugar blended with 2 teaspoons cornstarch

⅛ teaspoon salt

4 large eggs

2 teaspoons intensified vanilla extract (see page 52)

⅓ cup thick, cultured sour cream

Buttery Caramel Sauce (see page 237), for serving with the torte (optional)

BAKEWARE

9-inch springform pan

PREHEAT THE OVEN AND PREPARE THE CAKE PAN Preheat the oven to 325° F. Film the inside of the springform pan with nonstick cooking spray and have a cookie sheet (or sheet pan) at hand.

ASSEMBLE AND BAKE THE CHOCOLATE, CARAMEL, AND NOUGAT COOKIE CRUMB CRUST Thoroughly combine the cookie crumbs and melted butter–vanilla blend in a medium-size mixing bowl. Press the crumb crust mixture evenly over the bottom of the prepared cake pan.

Bake the crust for 7 minutes. Transfer the cookie crust–lined cake pan to a cooling rack. Cool for 10 minutes. Scatter the chunks of candy on the bottom of the cookie crust; set aside.

MIX THE SOUR CREAM CHEESECAKE BATTER Beat the cream cheese in the large bowl of a freestanding electric mixer on moderate speed for 2 minutes. Add the vanilla-scented granulated sugar–cornstarch blend and salt; beat for 2 minutes. On low speed, mix in the eggs, one at a time, blending just until mixed, about 20 seconds after each addition. *Batter texture observation* Adding the eggs on low speed and mixing until just combined creates a smooth and creamy-textured cheesecake. Scrape down the sides of the mixing bowl frequently with a rubber spatula to keep the batter even-textured. Lightly blend in the vanilla extract and sour cream.

ASSEMBLE THE TORTE WITH THE CREAM CHEESE BATTER Pour the vanilla cheesecake batter on top of the candy bar-covered crust.

Place the springform pan on the cookie sheet (or sheet pan). Bake the torte in the preheated oven for 1 hour to 1 hour and 5 minutes, or until set. The baked cheesecake will be pale golden on top, with a golden edge. Turn off the oven, partially open the oven door, and let the torte stand for 20 minutes.

Cool the torte completely in the pan on a rack. Release the sides of the pan and refrigerate the torte for at least 8 hours, or until well chilled, before slicing and serving. *Slicing observation* Use a long chef's knife to cut the torte neatly and cleanly. Store the cake in an airtight cake keeper in the refrigerator.

FRESHLY BAKED, THE TORTE KEEPS FOR **2** TO **3** DAYS.

CREAM CHEESE SCHNECKEN

3 dozen pastries

*C*OILS OF SOUR CREAM YEAST DOUGH enveloping a lightly sweetened cream cheese filling, set on a buttery brown sugar and vanilla mixture, bake into exceptional sweet rolls. Variations of this dough abound and are based on how much butter and sour cream is worked into the dough. The vanilla-based dough that follows differs from the one for the Apricot Schnecken on page 146; this dough uses butter in the melted state, more sour cream, whole eggs (rather than egg yolks), and a good dose of vanilla extract. It's rich. The cream cheese filling keeps the inside folds of the dough moist as the pastries bake, and the honey-butter-brown sugar spread gives the bottoms a flavorful sheen.

VANILLA, BUTTER, AND SOUR CREAM YEAST DOUGH

3 teaspoons active dry yeast

½ teaspoon granulated sugar

⅓ cup warm (110° to 115° F.) water

1½ cups thick, cultured sour cream

12 tablespoons (1½ sticks) unsalted butter, melted and cooled

2 large eggs

1 tablespoon pure vanilla extract

½ cup superfine sugar

5⅓ cups unsifted unbleached all-purpose flour, plus more as needed

1 teaspoon salt

1 teaspoon freshly grated nutmeg

MAKE THE VANILLA, BUTTER, AND SOUR CREAM YEAST DOUGH Combine the yeast and ½ teaspoon granulated sugar in a small heatproof bowl. Stir in the warm water and let stand until the yeast dissolves and the mixture is puffy, 7 to 8 minutes.

CREAM CHEESE, WALNUT, AND RAISIN FILLING

Two 8-ounce packages cream cheese, softened

⅓ cup plus 2 tablespoons granulated sugar

2 large egg yolks

¼ cup plus 1 tablespoon ground walnuts

¾ teaspoon ground cinnamon

½ teaspoon freshly grated nutmeg

2 teaspoons pure vanilla extract

1 cup dark raisins

BROWN SUGAR AND BUTTER SPREAD

12 tablespoons (1½ sticks) unsalted butter, softened

1½ cups firmly packed dark brown sugar, sieved if lumpy

¼ cup mild honey, such as clover

1 teaspoon pure vanilla extract

1 cup walnut halves or pieces, for assembling the schnecken

BAKEWARE

3 standard (12-cup) muffin pans (each cup measuring about 2¾ inches in diameter and 1⅜ inches deep, with a capacity of ½ cup)

Whisk the sour cream, melted butter, eggs, vanilla extract, and ½ cup superfine sugar in a medium-size mixing bowl. Stir in the swollen yeast mixture.

Combine 4 cups flour, salt, and nutmeg in a large mixing bowl. Add the sour cream–butter-egg-yeast mixture and stir well, using a sturdy wooden spoon or flat wooden paddle. *Dough texture observation* At this point, the dough will be a thick, heavy batter-like mixture.

Add the remaining 1⅓ cups of flour in four portions (⅓ cup at a time) to make a soft, smooth dough. With well-floured hands, knead the dough lightly in the bowl for 3 minutes. It will be soft and sticky. If it is too sticky, add up to an additional ½ cup of flour.

SET THE DOUGH TO RISE IN THE REFRIGERATOR Place the dough in a food-safe, self-sealing 1-gallon plastic bag. Refrigerate the dough for 8 hours or, preferably, overnight. Do not compress the dough during this time. Both the cream cheese filling and the brown sugar and butter spread should be made on baking day and refrigerated.

MAKE THE CREAM CHEESE FILLING Using an electric hand mixer, beat the cream cheese and granulated sugar in a medium-size mixing bowl. Blend in the egg yolks, walnuts, cinnamon, nutmeg, and vanilla extract. Refrigerate the filling in a covered bowl for 1 hour, or until needed. Have the raisins at hand in a small bowl.

MAKE THE BROWN SUGAR AND BUTTER SPREAD Beat the butter, dark brown sugar, honey, and vanilla extract in a medium-size mixing bowl until well combined and creamy, using a wooden spoon or flat wooden paddle. Set aside. Have the walnut pieces at hand in a small bowl.

PREPARE THE MUFFIN PANS AND SMEAR THE BROWN SUGAR AND BUTTER SPREAD ON THE BOTTOM OF THE PANS Film the cups of the muffin pans with non-stick cooking spray. Place dollops of the buttery brown sugar spread on the bottom of each muffin cup, dividing it evenly among them. Push several walnut pieces onto the spread in each cup, dividing the nuts evenly among the muffin cups. Set aside.

ROLL THE DOUGH, FILL, AND CUT THE SCHNECKEN Remove the dough from the refrigerator and place it on a well-floured work surface. Flour a rolling pin. Roll out the dough into a sheet measuring about 18 by 21 inches. Place the cream cheese filling on the dough in large dollops; spread it evenly over the surface of the dough, using a

Use thoroughly softened cream cheese in the filling for the creamiest texture. Roll the cream cheese–spread dough into as tight and plump a jellyroll as possible.

medium-size flexible palette knife (or rubber spatula). Sprinkle over the raisins. With your fingertips, lightly press the raisins into the cream cheese filling.

Roll the dough into a long, tight jellyroll, tucking in the ends and pinching them closed as you go. With a soft pastry brush, carefully sweep away any flour clinging to the outside of the dough as it is rolled. *Dough rolling observation* The filled dough must be tightly (and carefully) rolled if the filling is to bake evenly in the schnecken, or the dough will collapse as it bakes. Pinch the long seam and two ends closed. Extend the roll, by rolling it lightly with the palms of your hands, to a coil measuring about 28 inches long.

Cut the coil into 36 slices, using a sharp chef's knife. Place each slice, spiral side down, in a prepared muffin cup, pressing down lightly.

SET THE SCHNECKEN TO RISE Cover each pan loosely with a sheet of plastic wrap. Let the pastries rise until swollen and risen nearly to a scant ¼ inch of the top of the cups, about 2 hours (if you are working with dough refrigerated for 8 hours) or 2 hours and 45 minutes to 3 hours (if you are working with dough refrigerated overnight).

PREHEAT THE OVEN AND BAKE THE SCHNECKEN Preheat the oven to 375° F. Remove and discard the sheets of plastic wrap covering the pans of pastries. Place each muffin pan on a rimmed baking sheet to catch any drips of the brown sugar and butter spread as it bubbles around the rims of the muffin cups. Bake the pastries for 25 to 30 minutes, or until set and golden on top. This dough has good oven spring—the initial boost of yeast dough during the first 5 minutes of baking.

To bake the pastries in shifts (depending upon oven space), hold one pan of risen schnecken in the refrigerator while the first two pans bake.

COOL THE SCHNECKEN Let the schnecken stand in the pans on cooling racks for 5 minutes. Using a small, flexible metal palette knife, carefully remove the pastries (they are tender at this stage), bottom side up, to cooling racks. Protect your hands when handling the schnecken, for the caramel-like brown sugar glaze is very hot. Spoon the brown sugar and butter mixture (and walnuts, if not clinging to the pastries) sitting on the bottom of the baking sheet over the warm pastries. Cool completely. Refrigerate all schnecken not eaten within 2 hours of cooling in airtight containers.

❋ *For an aromatic topnote of flavor,* use intensified vanilla extract (see page 52) in place of plain vanilla extract in the yeast dough, filling, and spread.

FRESHLY BAKED, THE SCHNECKEN KEEPS FOR 3 DAYS.

CAPPUCCINO CREAM CHEESE FUDGE CAKE

One 9-inch cake, creating about 12 slices

CREAMY. CHOCOLATY. SOFTLY COFFEE-SEASONED. A rippled fudge cake, flaunting two batters, is easy to build, baking-wise: the brownie-like fudge cake batter is poured into a springform pan and topped with contrasting cream cheese-based chocolate chip topping. The two batters are marbleized for a blend of flavors, and a swirly appearance.

Nonstick cooking spray, for preparing the cake pan

CREAMY CHOCOLATE CHIP TOPPING

2 packages (3 ounces each) cream cheese, softened

⅓ cup granulated sugar blended with 2 teaspoons unsifted bleached cake flour

1 large egg

1 tablespoon thick, cultured sour cream

1½ teaspoons pure vanilla extract

pinch of salt

⅓ cup semisweet chocolate chips

FUDGE CAKE BATTER

1 cup unsifted bleached cake flour

1 tablespoon unsweetened, alkalized cocoa

¼ teaspoon baking powder

½ teaspoon salt

¼ teaspoon ground cinnamon

12 tablespoons (1½ sticks) unsalted butter, melted and cooled to tepid

4 ounces (4 squares) unsweetened chocolate, melted and cooled to tepid

4 large eggs

1⅔ cups vanilla-scented superfine sugar (see page 54)

PREHEAT THE OVEN AND PREPARE THE CAKE PAN Preheat the oven to 350° F. Film the inside of the springform pan with nonstick cooking spray; set aside.

MAKE THE CREAMY CHOCOLATE CHIP TOPPING For the topping, place the cream cheese and granulated sugar-cake flour blend in a medium-size mixing bowl, and using an electric hand mixer, beat on moderate speed for 2 minutes. Reduce the speed to low and blend in the egg, sour cream, vanilla extract, and salt. Scrape down the sides of the mixing bowl with a rubber spatula to keep the batter even-textured. Stir in the chocolate chips. Set aside.

MAKE THE FUDGE CAKE BATTER Sift the flour, cocoa, baking powder, salt, and cinnamon onto a sheet of waxed paper.

In a medium-size mixing bowl, whisk together the melted butter and melted unsweetened chocolate. Whisk the eggs in a large mixing bowl for 1 minute. Add the vanilla-scented granulated sugar, vanilla extract, and dissolved coffee mixture; whisk for 1 minute, or until just combined. Sift over the sifted flour mixture, and whisk lightly until all particles of flour are absorbed.

ASSEMBLE THE FUDGE CAKE BATTER AND CHOCOLATE CHIP TOPPING Spoon the fudge cake batter into the prepared cake pan. Scrape the topping over the chocolate batter and, using a flexible palette knife, gently swirl together the two mixtures. Shake the pan lightly from side to side two or three times to level the top.

1½ teaspoons pure vanilla extract

2 teaspoons instant (not granular) espresso powder dissolved in 1 teaspoon hot water and cooled completely

9-inch springform pan (2¾ inches deep)

BAKE AND COOL THE CAKE Bake the cake in the preheated oven for 40 to 45 minutes, or until set. The cake will rise and puff slightly, and the center will be set but soft, with the surrounding edges a bit firmer. Cool the cake in the pan on a rack. When it is completely cool, release the sides, slice the cake, and serve. On slicing, the center of the torte will be a bit creamier than the sides. *Slicing observation* Use a long chef's knife to cut the cake neatly and cleanly. Refrigerate any cake not eaten within 2 hours of cooling in an airtight cake keeper.

❊ *For an extra surge of flavor,* toss ½ cup cappuccino-flavored chips with 1 teaspoon of the sifted flour mixture from the fudge cake batter. Stir the chips into the batter after the flour mixture has been whisked in.

❊ *For an aromatic topnote of flavor,* use intensified vanilla extract (see page 52) in place of plain vanilla extract in the cake batter.

FRESHLY BAKED, THE CAKE KEEPS FOR 3 DAYS.

CREAM CHEESE AND ALMOND TEA RING

2 petal-shaped rings, each creating 10 to 12 slices

THE DOUGH FOR THESE COFFEE CAKES IS LIGHT, buttery, and a pleasure to form into pretty petal-shaped tea rings. Each ring, made from a coil of dough filled with a cream cheese and almond mixture, is cut into spiral sections, and each section is folded out to form slightly overlapping petals. The sweet rings are fabulous to serve at brunch, when guests are sure to be charmed by this baking "arts-and-crafts" project.

SWEET YEAST DOUGH

1 tablespoon plus 1 teaspoon active dry yeast

1 teaspoon granulated sugar

MAKE THE SWEET YEAST DOUGH Combine the yeast and 1 teaspoon granulated sugar in a small heatproof bowl. Stir in the warm water and let stand until the yeast dissolves and the mixture is expanded and puffy, about 8 minutes.

⅓ cup warm (110° to 115° F.) water

6 tablespoons (¾ stick) unsalted butter, cut into chunks

⅓ cup granulated sugar

1 cup milk

2 teaspoons intensified vanilla extract (see page 52)

2 teaspoons pure almond extract

2 large eggs

About 4½ cups unsifted unbleached all-purpose flour, plus more as needed

1 teaspoon salt

1 teaspoon freshly grated nutmeg

½ teaspoon ground cardamom

CREAM CHEESE AND
ALMOND FILLING

One 8-ounce can almond paste

4 tablespoons (½ stick) unsalted butter, softened

Two 3-ounce packages cream cheese, cut into chunks, softened

⅓ cup granulated sugar

1½ teaspoons pure almond extract

1 tablespoon unsifted bleached all-purpose flour

1 large egg

1 large egg yolk

¼ teaspoon freshly grated nutmeg

GLAZE FOR BRUSHING OVER
THE UNBAKED RINGS

1 large egg

2 teaspoons milk

ALMOND ICING FOR SPREADING
OVER THE TOP OF THE WARM,
BAKED RINGS

1¼ cups unsifted confectioners' sugar

1 tablespoon plus 1½ teaspoons unsalted butter, softened

pinch of salt

Place the butter, ⅓ cup granulated sugar, and the milk in a small saucepan, set over low heat, and cook until the sugar has melted down, stirring occasionally with a wooden spoon. Remove from the heat and pour into a medium-size heatproof bowl. Stir in the vanilla and almond extracts, and cool to 110° to 115° F. Blend in the eggs and swollen yeast mixture.

Combine 3 cups flour, salt, nutmeg, and cardamom in a large mixing bowl. Stir in the yeast mixture, using a sturdy wooden spoon or flat wooden paddle. *Dough texture observation* At this stage, the dough will resemble a sticky batter. Work in 1 cup of flour, about ⅓ cup at a time; the dough will be moist.

KNEAD THE DOUGH Place the remaining ½ cup flour on a work surface. Turn the dough onto the surface and knead for 8 to 9 minutes, adding additional sprinkles of flour to prevent the dough from adhering to the surface. Add only enough flour to keep the dough workable; the dough should remain supple and bouncy.

SET THE DOUGH TO RISE Place the dough in a buttered bowl, turn to coat all sides in the butter, and cover tightly with a sheet of plastic wrap. Let rise in a cozy, sheltered spot until doubled in bulk, about 1 hour.

MIX THE CREAM CHEESE AND ALMOND FILLING Crumble the almond paste in the work bowl of a food processor fitted with the steel knife. Add the butter, cream cheese, and granulated sugar. Cover and process, using short on-off bursts, until thoroughly combined and smooth, stopping two or three times to scrape down the sides of the container with a rubber spatula. Add the almond extract, flour, whole egg, egg yolk, and nutmeg; cover and process until smooth, scraping down the sides of the mixing bowl once or twice more. Scrape the filling into a small mixing bowl, cover, and refrigerate. *Texture observation* Remove the filling from the refrigerator to soften its texture (about 20 to 30 minutes) before spreading it on the yeast dough.

ASSEMBLE THE COOKIE SHEETS AND OVENPROOF RAMEKINS Line the cookie sheets with lengths of cooking parchment paper. Lightly butter the exterior sides of two ovenproof ramekins measuring 3 inches in diameter.

½ teaspoon pure almond extract

¼ teaspoon pure vanilla extract

1 tablespoon almond liqueur, such as Amaretto

1 tablespoon plus 2 teaspoons milk

Whole blanched almonds, lightly toasted and cooled, and whole dried cherries, for decorating the iced rings

BAKEWARE

2 large cookie sheets

ROLL OUT THE DOUGH, FILL, AND FORM THE PETAL-SHAPED RINGS Have the cookie sheets and buttered ramekins at hand.

Gently deflate the dough by compressing it with the palms of your hands. Divide the dough in half. Work with one piece of dough at a time, and keep the remaining portion covered with a sheet of plastic wrap.

For each tea ring, roll each piece of dough into a sheet measuring 12 by 16 inches. Spread half of the cream cheese and almond filling over the surface of the dough. Roll up the dough as you would a jellyroll, tucking in and pinching closed the sides as you go. Pinch closed the long seam end. Roll the coil on the work surface, using the palms of your hands, to elongate it to 26 to 27 inches.

Carefully transfer the coil to one of the lined cookie sheets. Connect the ends of the coil by pressing them together to form a circle. Shift the circle of dough into the center of the cookie sheet. With a sharp, medium-size knife, make 12 cuts every 2 inches at the outer edge of the dough up to about ½ inch of the inner edge. (Do not cut all the way through to the center end of the ring.) With your fingers, turn out one spiral of dough toward the outside of the ring; turn out the next spiral toward the inside of the ring. Put the buttered ramekin in the center of the ring, carefully placing the dough around it. The ramekin will keep the center of the spirals from closing together as the ring bakes. Make another ring with the remaining piece of dough and filling.

SET THE FORMED RINGS TO RISE Cover each ring loosely with a sheet of plastic wrap. Let the rings rise (with each ramekin intact) until just doubled in bulk, about 50 minutes. *Rising observation* If the rings rise too much, the texture of the baked coffee cake will be cobweb-like, rather than fine-grained and moist, and the shape of each will be distorted.

MIX THE GLAZE FOR BRUSHING OVER THE UNBAKED RINGS In a small bowl, whisk the egg and milk until well combined.

BAKE AND COOL THE RINGS Preheat the oven to 375° F. in advance of baking. Remove and discard the plastic wrap covering the rings.

Using a soft, 1-inch-wide pastry brush, apply the egg-and-milk glaze lightly on the surface of each ring.

Bake the rings (still with the ovenproof ramekins intact) in the preheated oven for about 25 minutes, or until golden and set. Let the rings stand on the cookie sheets for 10 minutes to firm up (they are tender at this point), carefully remove each ramekin, then slide each ring (still on the parchment paper) onto a cooling rack. Cool for 10 minutes. Place a sheet of waxed paper under the cooling rack of each ring to catch any drips of icing. Make the glaze while the rings are cooling.

PREPARE THE ALMOND ICING AND APPLY TO THE WARM, BAKED RINGS Place the confectioners' sugar, butter, salt, almond and vanilla extracts, almond liqueur, and milk in a small mixing bowl. Using an electric hand mixer, mix the ingredients on low speed for about 45 seconds, or until just combined and smooth. Scrape down the sides of the mixing bowl two or three times with a rubber spatula to keep the icing even-textured. Do not overbeat.

Carefully remove the length of parchment paper from the bottom of each ring by slipping a long, offset metal spatula between the bottom of the ring and the paper, and gently pulling away the paper. Leave the rings on the cooling racks.

While the rings are still warm, apply the icing over the top and sides of each, using a flexible palette knife to smooth over large dabs of icing. Since the coffee cakes are warm, the icing will melt randomly over them. While the icing is still wet, place whole almonds and cherries decoratively on top. Let the icing set before cutting the rings into slices for serving (at least 45 minutes to 1 hour). Serve the rings fresh.

MARBLED COCONUT, CHOCOLATE, AND CREAM CHEESE CAKE

One 9-inch cake, creating 10 slices

A SWEET CHEESE AND WALNUT MIXTURE, marbled around and about a buttery dark chocolate, coconut-spattered batter makes a creamy, dreamy, chocolaty cake.

Nonstick cooking spray, for preparing the cake pan

CHOCOLATE CAKE BATTER

1 cup unsifted bleached all-purpose flour

½ teaspoon baking powder

¼ teaspoon salt

PREHEAT THE OVEN AND PREPARE THE CAKE PAN Preheat the oven to 325° F. Film the inside of the springform pan with nonstick cooking spray; set aside.

MIX THE CHOCOLATE CAKE BATTER Sift the flour, baking powder, and salt onto a sheet of waxed paper.

Whisk the melted butter, melted bittersweet chocolate, and vanilla extract in a medium-size mixing bowl. Whisk in the eggs

¼ pound (8 tablespoons or 1 stick) unsalted butter, melted and cooled to tepid

3 ounces bittersweet chocolate, melted and cooled to tepid

2 teaspoons pure vanilla extract

4 large eggs

1⅓ cups plus 2 tablespoons granulated sugar

1 cup lightly packed sweetened flaked coconut

VANILLA-CREAM CHEESE MIXTURE

Two 3-ounce packages cream cheese, softened

5 tablespoons unsalted butter, softened

⅓ cup plus 3 tablespoons granulated sugar

1¼ teaspoons pure vanilla extract

2 tablespoons unsifted bleached cake flour

2 large eggs

¼ cup chopped walnuts

BAKEWARE

9-inch springform pan (2¾ inches deep)

and granulated sugar, mixing until just combined. Add the sifted mixture and whisk, making sure that all particles of flour are absorbed into the batter. Stir in the coconut. *Batter texture observation* The batter will be moderately thick. Set aside.

MIX THE CREAM CHEESE BATTER Place the cream cheese, butter, and granulated sugar in a small mixing bowl and beat until smooth, using an electric hand mixer. Beat in the vanilla extract, cake flour, and eggs. Scrape down the sides of the mixing bowl (once or twice) with a rubber spatula to keep the batter even-textured. *Batter texture observation* The batter will be creamy. Stir in the walnuts.

ASSEMBLE THE CAKE BY MARBLEIZING THE CHOCOLATE BATTER AND THE CREAM CHEESE BATTER Scrape the chocolate batter into the prepared cake pan. Place big spoonfuls of the cream cheese batter over the chocolate batter.

With a small, flexible palette knife (or small, narrow rubber spatula), swirl the batter by lightly dragging the knife (or spatula) through the batter in slightly exaggerated S-shaped waves, bringing chocolate batter up and over the cream cheese batter, and so creating distinct patches of dark and light batter.

BAKE, COOL, AND REFRIGERATE THE CAKE Bake the cake for 50 to 55 minutes, or until completely set. The lighter-colored cream cheese batter will be golden and the baked cake will pull away slightly from the sides of the baking pan. Let the cake stand in the pan on a rack until completely cooled. Release the sides of the pan, leaving the cake on its flat metal base. Refrigerate the cake for 3 hours, or until lightly chilled, then slice and serve. *Slicing observation* Use a serrated knife or long chef's knife to cut the cake neatly and cleanly. Store the cake in an airtight container in the refrigerator.

FRESHLY BAKED, CAKE KEEPS FOR 2 TO 3 DAYS.

BEST BAKING ADVICE

Use thoroughly softened cream cheese and butter for the cream cheese mixture. The baked cake should stand in the pan, with the wrap-around ring intact, until completely cooled.

Chocolate and Cream Cheese–Chocolate Chip Muffins

3 dozen muffins

*T*HESE SIMPLE-TO-MAKE, CHOCOLATE-BOTTOMED MUFFINS (also known as black bottom cupcakes) have a baked-in cheesecakelike filling dotted with semi-sweet chocolate chips. This version of my mother's recipe (which is more than 25 years old) includes melted chocolate and melted butter in the batter.

CREAM CHEESE–MINIATURE CHOCOLATE CHIP TOPPING

Four 3-ounce packages cream cheese, softened

½ cup plus 2 tablespoons superfine sugar

2 large eggs

2 teaspoons intensified vanilla extract (see page 52)

⅛ teaspoon salt

1 cup miniature semisweet chocolate chips tossed with 1 teaspoon unsifted bleached all-purpose flour

DARK CHOCOLATE MUFFIN BATTER

3 cups unsifted bleached all-purpose flour

2 cups superfine sugar

⅓ cup plus 3 tablespoons unsweetened, alkalized cocoa

2 teaspoons baking powder

½ teaspoon salt

6 tablespoons plain vegetable oil (such as canola)

5 tablespoons unsalted butter, melted and cooled

PREHEAT THE OVEN AND PREPARE THE MUFFIN PANS Preheat the oven to 350° F. Line the muffin cups with ovenproof cupcake paper liner cups; set aside.

MIX THE CREAM CHEESE–MINIATURE CHOCOLATE CHIP TOPPING Place the cream cheese in a medium-size mixing bowl and beat with an electric hand mixer on moderately low speed for 1 minute. Add the superfine sugar and beat for 1 minute longer. Blend in the eggs, one at a time, beating well after each addition. Scrape down the sides of the mixing bowl with a rubber spatula to keep the batter even-textured. Mix in the vanilla and salt. Stir in the chocolate chips. Set aside.

MIX THE DARK CHOCOLATE MUFFIN BATTER Sift the flour, superfine sugar, cocoa, baking powder, and salt into the large bowl of a freestanding electric mixer. In a medium-size bowl, whisk the oil, melted butter, melted unsweetened chocolate, water, vinegar, and vanilla extract. Pour the liquid ingredients over the dry ingredients. Beat the ingredients on moderate speed until combined and smooth, about 2 minute, scraping down the sides of the mixing bowl once or twice to keep the batter even-textured.

ASSEMBLE THE MUFFINS WITH THE CREAM CHEESE–CHOCOLATE CHIP TOPPING AND THE MUFFIN BATTER Pour the muffin batter into a pitcher. Fill the cups a little more than

1 ounce (1 square) unsweetened chocolate, melted and cooled

1¾ cups plus 2 tablespoons water

1 tablespoon white vinegar

1 tablespoon intensified vanilla extract (see page 52)

BAKEWARE

3 standard (12-cup) muffin pans (each cup measuring about 2¾ inches in diameter and 1⅜ inches deep, with a capacity of ½ cup)

three-quarters full with batter. Spoon generous tablespoons of the topping into the center of each cup.

BAKE AND COOL THE MUFFINS Bake the muffins for 25 minutes, or until set. Let the muffins stand for 5 minutes, then remove them to cooling racks. Cool completely. Refrigerate any muffins not eaten within 2 hours of cooling.

FRESHLY BAKED, THE MUFFINS KEEP FOR 2 DAYS.

Variation: For chocolate and cream cheese-chocolate chip muffins with Dutch-process black cocoa, use 3 tablespoons Dutch-process black cocoa and ⅓ cup unsweetened, alkalized cocoa in the muffin batter.

BEST BAKING ADVICE

For the topping, use thoroughly softened cream cheese. In the muffin batter, use plain distilled white vinegar (not a flavored or wine vinegar), which has an effectively neutral taste, and the just the right acidity (5%).

*p*lain vanilla is very much like that little black cocktail dress—always welcome, simply chic, so quietly dramatic. As a flavor, vanilla reigns supreme in cookie doughs, butter cake batters, and yeast-risen sweet rolls. Who would turn down a vanilla sugar cookie, a slice of vanilla-imbued pound cake, or a vanilla cream crumb bun?

The vanilla bean is a pod that contains many tiny, moist seeds, the fruit of a vine that is a member of the orchid family. Vanilla extract is the liquid that results when the beans are immersed in alcohol and water. Tahiti, Mexico, and Madagascar all produce vanilla beans that are exceptionally flexible and succulent, with a forward fragrance. Tahitian beans are especially aromatic (and expensive); their bold, flowery bouquet and concentrated flavor make them especially prized for baking. When purchasing vanilla beans, look for plump, moist pods. Lilly Joss Reich, author of *The Viennese Pastry Cookbook* (New York: Collier Books, 1970), suggests storing a vanilla bean in a container along with some raisins to keep it supple.

Unsalted butter is the single most important accompanying ingredient in vanilla-based bakery sweets. Without butter, the full impact of vanilla could not be achieved, resulting in a less intense flavor. Conversely, when vanilla is not added to a butter-based sweet batter or dough, the end result usually tastes greasy. Butter unleashes the flavor of vanilla, and vanilla tempers and rounds out the taste of all the warm spices (such as cinnamon, nutmeg, and ginger), eggs (whole eggs or yolks alone), sweetened flaked coconut, almond, chocolate, butterscotch, rum, and buttercrunch.

22

VANILLA

VANILLA BEAN CREAM CAKE

One 10-inch tube cake, creating about 20 slices

A DASH OF ALMOND EXTRACT acts as an indirect—but amplifying—backdrop of flavor in this predominantly vanilla-flavored butter-and-cream cake. The cake is finished with a light, shimmery glaze (touched with 2 teaspoons of rum) that flavors the soft, fine-textured cake once it's baked and unmolded from the pan.

Shortening and bleached all-purpose flour, for preparing the cake pan

VANILLA BUTTER AND CREAM CAKE BATTER

2½ cups unsifted bleached all-purpose flour

1 cup unsifted bleached cake flour

½ teaspoon baking powder

1 teaspoon salt

¾ teaspoon freshly grated nutmeg

½ pound (16 tablespoons or 2 sticks) unsalted butter, softened

½ cup shortening

seed scrapings from a plump vanilla bean, reserving vanilla bean for glaze

2¾ cups plus 1 tablespoon vanilla-scented superfine sugar (see page 54)

2¾ teaspoons intensified vanilla extract (see page 52)

½ teaspoon pure almond extract

5 large eggs

1 cup light (table) cream

PREHEAT THE OVEN AND PREPARE THE CAKE PAN Preheat the oven to 325° F. Grease the inside of the tube pan with shortening. Line the bottom of the pan with a circle of waxed paper cut to fit, and grease the paper. Dust the inside of the pan with all-purpose flour. Tap out any excess flour; set aside.

MIX THE VANILLA BUTTER AND CREAM CAKE BATTER Sift the all-purpose flour, cake flour, baking powder, salt, and nutmeg onto a sheet of waxed paper.

Cream the butter and shortening in the large bowl of a free-standing electric mixer on moderate speed for 4 minutes. Blend in the seed scrapings from the vanilla bean. Add the vanilla-scented superfine sugar in three additions, beating for 1 minute after each portion is added. Blend in the vanilla and almond extracts. Beat in the eggs, one at a time, beating for 20 seconds after each egg is added.

On low speed, add the sifted mixture in three additions with the cream in two additions, beginning and ending with the sifted mixture. Scrape down the sides of the mixing bowl with a rubber spatula to keep the batter even-textured. *Batter texture observation* The batter will be smooth and creamy-textured.

Pour and scrape the batter into the prepared tube pan. Gently shake the pan from side to side (once or twice) to level the top.

BAKE THE CAKE Bake the cake for 1 hour and 20 minutes to 1 hour and 25 minutes, or until the cake is risen, set, and a wooden pick inserted in the cake withdraws clean. The baked cake will pull away slightly from the sides and central tube of the baking pan.

⅓ cup granulated sugar

⅓ cup water

the reserved vanilla bean, cut into
  2-inch lengths

2 teaspoons dark rum

1½ teaspoons pure intensified vanilla
  extract (see page 52)

¼ teaspoon pure almond extract

BAKEWARE

plain 10-inch tube pan

MAKE THE VANILLA-RUM GLAZE Place the granulated sugar, water, and reserved vanilla bean pieces in a small, heavy nonreactive saucepan, preferably enameled cast iron. Cover the saucepan and set over low heat. When the sugar has dissolved, raise the heat, bring the contents of the saucepan to a boil, and reduce the heat so that the mixture simmers actively. Simmer for 3 to 4 minutes, or until lightly condensed. *Glaze consistency observation* The syrup should be spoonable and slightly dense, neither watery nor too viscous. Add the rum and simmer for 30 seconds longer.

Take the syrup off the heat, and remove and discard the vanilla pieces. Stir in the vanilla and almond extracts. Pour the syrup into a small bowl and let stand until you are ready to use it.

COOL THE CAKE Let the cake stand in the pan on a cooling rack for 5 to 10 minutes. Invert the cake onto another cooling rack. Place a sheet of waxed paper under the cooling rack to catch any drips of glaze.

GLAZE THE WARM CAKE With a soft, 1-inch-wide pastry brush, paint the glaze over the top and sides of the warm cake. Cool the cake completely before cutting into slices for serving. *Slicing observation* Use a serrated knife to cut the cake neatly and cleanly.

FRESHLY BAKED, THE CAKE KEEPS FOR 2 TO 3 DAYS.

GLAZED VANILLA POUND CAKE

One 10-inch tube cake, creating about 20 slices

To DEVISE A POUND CAKE that brims with vanilla, you'll need to use vanilla in as many forms as possible: in a flavored sugar, as a heightened extract, and in an icing, in addition to incorporating the seed scrapings from a vanilla bean. For vanilla-lovers, this cake is a charmer.

Shortening and bleached all-purpose flour, for preparing the cake pan

VANILLA POUND CAKE BATTER

3 cups unsifted bleached all-purpose flour

¼ cup unsifted bleached cake flour

½ teaspoon baking soda

1 teaspoon salt

1 teaspoon freshly grated nutmeg

½ pound (16 tablespoons or 2 sticks) unsalted butter, softened

¼ cup shortening

seed scrapings from the inside of a plump vanilla bean

3 cups vanilla-scented granulated sugar (see page 53)

6 large eggs

1 tablespoon intensified vanilla extract (see page 52)

1 cup thick, cultured sour cream

CREAMY VANILLA "SPREADING" ICING FOR APPLYING TO THE WARM, BAKED CAKE

1½ cups unsifted confectioners' sugar

2 tablespoons unsalted butter

2 tablespoons plus 1 teaspoon heavy cream

PREHEAT THE OVEN AND PREPARE THE CAKE PAN Preheat the oven to 325° F. Grease the inside of the tube pan with shortening. Line the bottom of the pan with waxed paper cut to fit, and grease the surface of the paper. Dust the inside of the pan with all-purpose flour. Tap out any excess flour; set aside.

MIX THE VANILLA POUND CAKE BATTER Sift the all-purpose flour, cake flour, baking soda, salt, and nutmeg onto a sheet of waxed paper twice.

Cream the butter and shortening in the large bowl of a free-standing electric mixer on moderate speed for 4 minutes. Blend in the vanilla bean seed scrapings. Add the vanilla-scented granulated sugar in three additions, beating for 1 minute after each portion is added. Beat in the eggs, one at a time, beating for 30 seconds after each egg is added. Blend in the vanilla extract.

On low speed, add the sifted mixture in three additions with the sour cream in two additions, beginning and ending with the sifted mixture. Scrape down the sides of the mixing bowl frequently with a rubber spatula to keep the batter even-textured. *Batter texture observation* The batter will be creamy-smooth and moderately thick.

Scrape the batter into the prepared tube pan. Gently shake the pan from side to side (once or twice) to level the top.

BAKE THE CAKE Bake the cake for 1 hour and 20 minutes, or until the cake is risen, set, and a wooden pick inserted in the cake

1 teaspoon intensified vanilla extract
  (see page 52)

pinch of freshly grated nutmeg

plain 10-inch tube pan

withdraws clean. The bake cake will pull away slightly from the sides of the baking pan.

PREPARE THE CREAMY VANILLA "SPREADING" ICING Place the confectioners' sugar, butter, heavy cream, vanilla extract, and nutmeg in a medium-size mixing bowl. Using an electric hand mixer, beat the ingredients together for 1 minute on moderate speed, or until just combined and smooth. Scrape down the sides of the mixing bowl once or twice with a rubber spatula. There will be about ¾ cup of icing. *Icing consistency observation* The icing will be moderately thick, but will soften as it's spread on a hot or warm cake.

Press a sheet of plastic wrap directly on the surface of the icing; set aside.

COOL THE CAKE Let the cake stand in the pan on a cooling rack for 5 to 10 minutes. Invert the cake onto another cooling rack, peel off the waxed paper circle, then place another cooling rack on top and reinvert the cake to stand right side up. Place a sheet of waxed paper under the cooling rack to catch any drips of icing. Cool for 5 minutes.

APPLY THE ICING TO THE WARM CAKE Coat the top of the cake with the icing, using a small metal spatula to smooth it over; the icing will melt down nicely as you are applying it to the warm cake.

Cool the cake completely before cutting into slices for serving. *Slicing observation* Use a serrated knife to cut the cake neatly and cleanly.

BEST BAKING ADVICE

Sifting the flour mixture twice aerates it thoroughly enough to establish a smooth, creamy-textured batter.

FRESHLY BAKED, THE CAKE KEEPS FOR 3 TO 4 DAYS.

VANILLA CRUMB BUNS

16 buns

COAXING AN ALLURING VANILLA FLAVOR into sweet yeast rolls is simple, once you recognize the elements involved in devising such a sublime breakfast treat. This large pan of delectable crumb buns is something of a project, but for those of us who love to bake it's an activity that can be accomplished in two sessions—one to make the dough, prepare the filling, and combine the crumb topping, and another to assemble and bake the buns.

These are just the sort of sweet buns to have on hand for weekend guests (they'll store magnificently in the freezer and reheat nicely) and, of course, yourself.

Nonstick cookware spray and softened, unsalted butter, for preparing the baking pan

RICH VANILLA YEAST DOUGH

4½ teaspoons active dry yeast

¾ teaspoon granulated sugar

⅓ cup warm (110° to 115° F.) water

¼ cup half-and-half

⅓ cup vanilla-scented granulated sugar (see page 53)

1 tablespoon intensified vanilla extract (see page 52)

seed scrapings from a plump vanilla bean

5 large eggs

2 large egg yolks

2 cups unsifted unbleached all-purpose flour

2¾ cups plus 1 tablespoon unsifted bleached all-purpose flour

1¼ teaspoons freshly grated nutmeg

1 teaspoon salt

½ pound plus 4 tablespoons (20 tablespoons or 2½ sticks) unsalted butter, softened but cool

VANILLA-NUTMEG FILLING

1½ cups half-and-half

1 tablespoon plus 1½ teaspoons cornstarch

½ cup vanilla-scented superfine sugar (see page 54)

MAKE THE RICH VANILLA YEAST DOUGH Combine the yeast and ¾ teaspoon granulated sugar in a small heatproof bowl. Stir in the warm water and let stand until the yeast is dissolved and the mixture is swollen, 7 to 8 minutes. In the meantime, place the half-and-half and ⅓ cup vanilla-scented granulated sugar in a small saucepan and set over low heat to dissolve the sugar. Remove from the heat and pour into a medium-size heatproof bowl; cool to 115° F. Blend in the vanilla extract and vanilla bean seed scrapings; beat in the whole eggs and egg yolks. Stir in the yeast mixture.

In a large mixing bowl, combine the unbleached flour, 2 cups of the bleached flour, nutmeg, and salt. Stir in the milk-yeast-egg mixture with a sturdy wooden spoon or flat wooden paddle. *Dough texture observation* The dough will come together in a sticky, slightly shaggy mass. Two tablespoons at a time, smear half of the butter into the dough by working it into the dough with a flat wooden paddle or your fingertips. Use a slightly exaggerated slapping motion to integrate the butter into the dough. Work in ¼ cup of the bleached flour; add the remaining softened butter, kneading it in 2 tablespoons at a time.

large pinch of salt

4 large egg yolks

1 tablespoon unsalted butter, cut into bits, softened

2 teaspoons intensified vanilla extract (see page 52)

¼ teaspoon freshly grated nutmeg

1 tablespoon half-and-half

2 teaspoons intensified vanilla extract (see page 52)

Vanilla Streusel (see page 62), for sprinkling on the unbaked buns

BAKEWARE

13 by 18 by 1-inch rimmed sheet pan

Transfer the dough to the bowl of a heavy-duty freestanding electric mixer fitted with the dough hook. Beat the dough for 1 minute on moderate speed. Add ¼ cup bleached flour and beat for 2 minutes. Add another ¼ cup bleached flour and beat for 5 minutes on moderate speed. *Dough texture observation* The dough will be smooth and elastic.

Remove the bowl from the mixing stand. Sprinkle over the remaining 1 tablespoon bleached flour; knead the dough in the bowl for 1 minute. *Dough texture observation* The completed dough will be soft, with a tender, pliant pull. Lightly press the dough into a rough, squarish cake and fold into thirds.

SET THE DOUGH TO RISE AND REFRIGERATE Transfer the dough to a gallon-size, food-safe self-locking plastic bag, and seal. Let the dough rise at cool room temperature for 1 hour. Refrigerate the dough overnight, gently compressing the dough with the cupped palms of your hands once after 1 hour, and again after 2 more hours.

MAKE THE VANILLA-NUTMEG FILLING Warm the half-and-half in a small, heavy saucepan to 115° F. Cool to tepid. Sift the cornstarch, vanilla-scented superfine sugar, and salt into a heavy, medium-size saucepan (preferably enameled cast iron), then whisk thoroughly to combine. Whisk in the egg yolks. Strain the tepid half-and-half over the beaten yolk-sugar mixture: Set a medium-size fine-meshed sieve over the yolk mixture and add the liquid, a few tablespoons at a time, mixing well with a wooden spoon to gradually introduce the warm liquid. Slowly add the remaining liquid, mixing thoroughly. Set the pan over moderate heat and bring to the boil, stirring slowly with a wooden spoon. When the mixture thickens considerably and comes to a bubbly boil, reduce the heat and simmer for 2 minutes. *Filling density observation* The filling will be medium-dense, and will thicken further as it cools and chills.

Strain the filling through a medium-size fine-meshed sieve into a heatproof bowl. Lightly smooth the filling through the strainer with a rubber spatula. Slowly stir in the softened butter, vanilla extract, and nutmeg. Immediately place a sheet of plastic wrap directly on top of the filling to prevent a surface skin from forming. Cool the filling, cover tightly, and refrigerate for at least 8 hours. (The cream filling can be prepared and refrigerated up to 2 days in advance.)

PREPARE THE BAKING PAN Film the inside of the rimmed sheet pan with nonstick cookware spray. Butter the bottom and sides of the pan; set aside.

REST THE REFRIGERATED DOUGH AT COOL ROOM TEMPERATURE Remove the dough from the refrigerator and let stand in the bag at cool room temperature for 30 minutes.

MAKE THE VANILLA WASH Combine the half-and-half and vanilla extract in a small ramekin; set aside.

ROLL, FILL, AND CUT THE BUNS Place the dough on a well-floured work surface. Flour a rolling pin. Roll out the dough to a sheet measuring about 17 by 18 inches, lightly flouring the surface as necessary as you go along; the dough will be slightly sticky. Using a pastry brush, dust off any surface flour and paint the dough with the vanilla wash. Let stand for 15 minutes.

Spread the filling evenly over the surface of the dough, to about ¾ inch of the four sides. Roll up the dough into a coil as snugly as possible, pressing over the sides as you go to enclose the filling. *Rolling observation* The filling is moist and will soften the dough a bit. Carefully elongate the coil until it measures about 23 inches in length.

With a sharp chef's knife, cut the coil in half, and cut each half into eight even-sized slices, forming 16 slices in total. The filling will ooze from the sides as the rolls are cut, and the rolls will be moist, a bit slippery, and relatively flaccid at this point. Pat the slices into neat ovals and place them in the prepared pan, arranging them in four rows of four. Lightly flatten the buns with your fingertips.

SET THE BUNS TO RISE Cover the pan loosely with a sheet of plastic wrap. Let the buns rise at cool room temperature for 1 hour to 1 hour and 15 minutes, or until puffy (a little less than doubled in bulk). The edges of the buns will have converged. *Bun rising observation* The buns should be swollen and look light. Be watchful: if the buns have risen too much (or in a very warm kitchen), the spiral of dough will disconnect from the filling and collapse on baking.

PREHEAT THE OVEN, COVER WITH THE VANILLA CRUMB TOPPING, AND BAKE THE BANS Preheat the oven to 375° F. in advance of baking the buns. Have the vanilla crumb topping at hand. Remove and discard the plastic wrap covering the pan. Scatter the streusel mixture in large and small lumps evenly on top of the buns; use all of it. Do not press it down.

Bake the buns for 25 to 30 minutes, or until set and the topping is a light-golden brown; the buns at the edge of the pan will be golden brown. The buns will rise nicely and pull away ever-so-slightly from the sides of the baking pan.

COOL THE BUNS Let the buns stand in the pan on a large cooling rack for 30 minutes. Cut the buns within their natural edges with a small, sharp knife and remove them individually, using a wide, offset metal spatula. Serve the buns warm or at room temperature. Refrigerate any buns not eaten within 2 hours of cooling in an airtight container.

FRESHLY BAKED, THE BUNS KEEP FOR 2 DAYS.

Variation: To add a subtle, nut-flavored dimension to these crumb buns, substitute Nut Streusel (see page 63) for the Vanilla Streusel above.

Vanilla Cream Waffles

6 deep, Belgian-style 2-sided waffles,
each waffle section measuring 4½ by 4½ inches

WITH THE PRESENCE OF GOOD DAIRY INGREDIENTS front and center, these waffles are completely lush. Serve them with berries, lightly sweetened berry syrup, whipped cream, and sprinkles of confectioners' sugar.

VANILLA CREAM WAFFLE BATTER

1 cup unsifted bleached all-purpose flour

1 cup unsifted bleached cake flour

1¾ teaspoons baking powder

¼ teaspoon salt

½ teaspoon freshly grated nutmeg

¼ cup vanilla-scented granulated sugar (see page 53)

7 tablespoons unsalted butter, melted and cooled to tepid

5 large eggs

1 tablespoon intensified vanilla extract (see page 52)

seed scrapings from ½ vanilla bean

1¼ cups heavy cream

pinch of cream of tartar

Confectioners' sugar, for sprinkling on the waffles

MAKE THE VANILLA CREAM WAFFLE BATTER Sift the all-purpose flour, cake flour, baking powder, salt, nutmeg, and vanilla-scented granulated sugar into a large mixing bowl.

In a medium-size mixing bowl, whisk together the melted butter, 3 whole eggs, 2 egg yolks (reserving the 2 egg whites in a clean, dry bowl), vanilla extract, vanilla bean seed scrapings, and heavy cream. Using an electric hand mixer, beat the 2 egg whites in a clean, dry bowl until frothy, add the cream of tartar, and continue beating until firm (not stiff) peaks are formed.

Whisk the liquid ingredients once again to blend, pour them over the sifted mixture, and stir to form a batter, using a rubber spatula, mixing until the particles of flour are absorbed. Be sure to swipe the bottom and sides of the mixing bowl to dispel any lingering pockets of flour. *Batter consistency observation* At this point, the batter will be thick, with many small lumps; it isn't necessary to beat or whisk out the lumps. Stir one-quarter of the beaten whites into the batter, then fold in the remaining whites until all streaks and small patches are incorporated.

MAKE THE WAFFLES Preheat the deep-dish waffle iron. Spoon about ½ cup of batter onto each square of the preheated iron. Cook the waffles until golden, 1 minute and 30 seconds to 2 minutes. Serve the waffles piping hot, sprinkled with confectioners' sugar if you wish, and fruit preserves, fruit syrup, and fresh berries, or pure maple syrup.

Vanilla Crêpes with Soft Vanilla "Spooning" Cream

3 cups crêpe batter, creating 22 to 24 five-inch crêpes

A PLATE OF SMALL, "HANDKERCHIEF"-SIZE CRÊPES, filled with a little vanilla pastry cream, folded over, glazed, and served with fresh berries is my notion of a wonderful late-day breakfast. The vanilla "spooning" cream is a less compact, slightly creamier version of a pastry cream—it will remind you of soft vanilla pudding.

The crêpe batter, which I've refined over the years, is easy to make in the blender and can be stored overnight in the refrigerator. I've made batches of batter with a smaller amount of butter, but it seems that the vanilla flavor is less voluptuous with the smaller quantities. And, of course, the compatibility of butter and vanilla is a classic one.

Without the "spooning" cream, warm-from-the-pan crêpes are also very good simply spread with apricot or blueberry preserves and sprinkled with confectioners' sugar. With the batter at hand, a sweet crêpe becomes a tasty wrapper for sliced, lightly sweetened fresh fruit or berries, too.

VANILLA CRÊPE BATTER

3 large eggs

6 tablespoons (¾ stick) unsalted butter, melted and cooled to tepid

2½ teaspoons intensified vanilla extract (see page 52)

2 tablespoons plus 2 teaspoons vanilla-scented granulated sugar (see page 53)

⅛ teaspoon salt

1⅓ cups plus 1 tablespoon milk

1 cup unsifted bleached all-purpose flour

¼ cup plus 1 tablespoon unsifted bleached cake flour

⅛ teaspoon freshly grated nutmeg

VANILLA "SPOONING" CREAM, FOR FILLING THE CRÊPES

2½ teaspoons cornstarch

¼ cup vanilla-scented granulated sugar (see page 53)

large pinch of salt

1¼ cups half-and-half

3 large egg yolks

1 tablespoon unsalted butter, softened

1 teaspoon intensified vanilla extract (see page 52)

MAKE THE VANILLA CRÊPE BATTER Place the eggs, melted butter, vanilla extract, vanilla-scented granulated sugar, salt, and milk in the container of a 40-ounce capacity blender. Cover securely and blend on low speed for 30 seconds. Uncover the blender and add the all-purpose flour and cake flour. Cover tightly and blend on low speed to form a batter. Uncover and scrape down the sides of the blender with a rubber spatula to distribute the flour evenly and to break up any pockets of flour. Cover the

Clarified butter (see page 66), for cooking the crêpes

Vanilla-scented superfine sugar (see page 54), for sprinkling on the tops of filled and folded crêpes before glazing

Firm, fresh raspberries or blueberries, picked over, or halved ripe figs, to accompany the filled and glazed crêpes

blender, and blend for 30 seconds on high speed. *Consistency observation* The batter should resemble unwhipped heavy cream.

Strain the batter through a large fine-meshed sieve into a bowl. Stir in the nutmeg, cover, and refrigerate for at least 3 hours before using. The batter must mellow in the refrigerator to allow the flour to be fully absorbed into the liquid ingredients, but do not store it any longer than overnight for use the next day.

MAKE THE VANILLA "SPOONING" CREAM Sift the cornstarch, vanilla-scented granulated sugar, and salt into a small, heavy saucepan, preferably enameled cast iron, then whisk to combine thoroughly. Slowly blend in the half-and-half. Bring the mixture to a low boil, stirring slowly, then let it bubble for 1 minute.

In a small heatproof bowl, whisk the egg yolks. Stir a few spoonfuls of the hot cream into the yolks to temper them. With the pan off the heat, stir the tempered egg yolk mixture back into the cream, then simmer for 1 to 2 minutes, or until thickened.

Strain the cream through a large fine-meshed sieve into a bowl, smoothing it through with a rubber spatula. Stir in the butter and vanilla extract. Press a sheet of plastic wrap directly on top to prevent a skin from forming. Cool, cover the cream with a tight-fitting lid, and refrigerate. (The cream can be stored in the refrigerator for up to 2 days. *Storage observation* The cream must be stored with a tight-fitting lid; otherwise it will surely absorb any strong smells lurking in the refrigerator.)

Note that you'll be using 2 teaspoons of filling for each crêpe; for a fuller, slightly bulkier (and much richer) filling, you can prepare a double amount of "spooning" cream.

MAKE THE CRÊPES Remove the batter from the refrigerator about 5 minutes before cooking the crêpes. Whisk the batter.

Heat a 6-inch-diameter crêpe pan over moderately high heat. Wearing heatproof oven gloves to protect your hands, and lifting the pan off the heat at an angle, quickly and carefully swipe the bottom of the pan with the clarified butter. Return it to the heat and let it sit on the burner for 30 seconds.

Again, using a padded glove (or a comfortable potholder) to hold the handle, lift it away from the heat, add 2 tablespoons of the batter to the hot pan, and quickly swirl it around to coat the bottom evenly. *Procedure observation* The trick is to coat the bottom of the pan completely before the batter has the chance to set up.

Return the pan to the heat and cook for about 45 seconds, or until the crêpe is a lacy golden brown underneath. Using a slender wooden crêpe spatula (specifically designed for this purpose), or other thin wooden spatula, lift the crêpe away from the edges of the pan and carefully turn it over. Cook the crêpe on the second side (this side will be a spotty brown), for 15 to 20 seconds longer. Continue to make crêpes in this fashion, overlapping them slightly on a cookie sheet lined with plastic wrap.

FILL AND GLAZE THE CRÊPES For each serving, place 2 teaspoons of the vanilla "spooning" cream on the spotty brown side of each crêpe, and fold in half. Slightly overlap three crêpes on a ovenproof plate. Sprinkle the tops lightly with the sugar. Place the plate under a hot, preheated broiler briefly to glaze the top a medium golden. (Alternatively, overlap the crêpes in a 14-inch gratin dish that has been lightly buttered on the bottom, sprinkle with sugar, and glaze.) Serve the crêpes immediately, with fresh berries or sliced figs scattered over each helping.

VANILLA PECAN PIE

One 9-inch pie, creating about 8 slices

THE COMPLEXITY OF SPICES, a splash of bourbon, light brown sugar, dark corn syrup, vanilla bean scrapings and extract, and butter combine with plenty of chopped pecans to form a rich-tasting pie filling. The bourbon balances the sweetness of the filling, making the spices sparkle and intensifying the presence of the vanilla.

SINGLE-CRUST PIE DOUGH

Vanilla Pie Crust, prepared and prebaked (see page 520)

VANILLA PECAN PIE FILLING

⅓ cup vanilla-scented granulated sugar (see page 53)

3 tablespoons firmly packed light brown sugar, sieved if lumpy

½ teaspoon ground cinnamon

¼ teaspoon freshly grated nutmeg

¼ teaspoon ground cloves

¼ teaspoon ground allspice

PREPARE THE VANILLA PIE CRUST Make the pie dough, line the pie pan, and prebake the crust as directed in the recipe for Vanilla Pie Crust on page 520.

PREHEAT THE OVEN Preheat the oven to 300° F.

MAKE THE VANILLA PECAN PIE FILLING In a heavy, 2-quart saucepan (preferably enameled cast iron), thoroughly combine the vanilla-scented granulated sugar, light brown sugar, cinnamon, nutmeg, cloves, and allspice, making sure that the spices are dispersed in the sugar. Whisk in the corn syrup, bourbon, and salt. Add the butter. Place the saucepan over moderately low heat and

1 cup dark corn syrup

1 tablespoon bourbon

⅛ teaspoon salt

5 tablespoons unsalted butter, cut into chunks

3 large eggs

2 teaspoons intensified vanilla extract (see page 52)

seed scrapings from ½ vanilla bean

2 cup coarsely chopped pecans

Vanilla Custard Sauce (see page 531) *or* Vanilla Whipped Cream (see page 530), for serving with the pie

BAKEWARE

9-inch pie pan

cook, stirring with a wooden spoon or flat wooden paddle, until the sugar and butter have melted down. Raise the heat to moderately high, bring the mixture just to the boil, then simmer for 3 minutes. Pour the syrup mixture into a large (4-cup capacity) heat-proof measuring cup. Cool to warm.

In a large mixing bowl, whisk the eggs, vanilla extract, and vanilla bean seed scrapings to combine. Slowly whisk about ½ cup of the warm syrup mixture into the egg mixture to temper it, then quickly stir in the remaining syrup, adding it in a thin stream. Blend in the pecans.

Turn the filling into the prebaked pie crust.

BAKE AND COOL THE PIE Bake the pie in the preheated oven for 40 to 45 minutes, or until just set. The filling will have thickened to a soft set, meaning that its consistency is rather like lightly thickened fruit preserves, but not at all liquid. Cool the pie on a rack. Slice and serve with a spoonful of custard sauce or whipped cream. Refrigerate any leftover pie in an airtight container.

FRESHLY BAKED, THE PIE KEEPS FOR 2 DAYS.

BEST BAKING ADVICE

A cooked syrup mixture serves as a lightly thickened, flavorful foundation to use as the base for the addition of eggs, vanilla, and pecans.

VANILLA PIE CRUST

One 9-inch pie crust

Vanilla extract and vanilla-scented sugar give this butter pie dough a certain vitality.

VANILLA-SCENTED PIE DOUGH

1½ cups unsifted bleached all-purpose flour

⅛ teaspoon salt

1 tablespoon shortening, frozen

7 tablespoons unsalted butter, cold, cut into tablespoon chunks

2½ teaspoons vanilla-scented granulated sugar (see page 53)

1 large egg yolk, cold

1 teaspoon intensified vanilla extract (see page 52)

1 tablespoon ice-cold milk

1 tablespoon ice-cold water

BAKEWARE

9-inch pie pan

TO MAKE THE VANILLA-SCENTED PIE DOUGH BY HAND Whisk the flour and salt in a medium-size mixing bowl. Drop in the shortening and chunks of butter, and using a pastry blender, cut the fat into the flour until reduced to pieces the size of dried navy beans.

Mix in the vanilla-scented granulated sugar. Dip into the flour-butter mixture and crumble it lightly between your fingertips for about 1 minute. This will disperse the butter into slightly smaller fragments. In a small bowl or cup, whisk the egg yolk, vanilla extract, milk, and water. Pour the egg yolk mixture over the flour and, using your fingertips, quickly mix to form a dough. *Dough texture observation* The dough should come together as a moderately firm, but not dry, mass. Add extra ice-cold water, ½ teaspoon at a time, if the dough seems very dry. Pat the dough into a 4- to 5-inch round cake on a sheet of waxed paper, wrap it up, and refrigerate for 10 minutes.

TO MAKE THE VANILLA-SCENTED PIE DOUGH IN A FOOD PROCESSOR Place the flour and salt in the container of a food processor fitted with the steel knife. Cover and process, using two quick on-off pulses, to combine the flour and salt. Add the shortening and chunks of butter, cover, and process, using 7 to 8 on-off pulses, to reduce the butter into small morsels. Sprinkle over the vanilla-scented sugar, cover, and process to combine, using one or two quick on-off pulses. Whisk the egg yolk, vanilla extract, milk, and water in a small mixing bowl, pour the liquid over the flour-butter-sugar combination, and process, using 10 to 12 quick on-off bursts, until the dough mixture gathers together into small clumps.

Turn the fragments of dough onto a sheet of waxed paper and gather into a 4- to 5-inch flat cake, wrap it up, and refrigerate for 10 minutes.

ROLL THE DOUGH AND LINE THE PIE PAN Have the pie pan at hand. Roll the dough between two large sheets of waxed paper to a round, about 13 inches in diameter. Refrigerate the dough on a cookie sheet for 15 minutes.

Remove the top layer of waxed paper from the sheet of dough. In order to build up the edge of the crust so that you can flute it, cut ½-inch strips of dough from the outside of the sheet of pie crust, keeping the circle intact. Press these strips on the rim of the pan.

Quickly invert the dough over a 9-inch pie pan. Press the dough onto the bottom of the pie pan first, then press it up the sides and onto the dough-lined rim. With a small, sharp knife, cut away any excess dough that overhangs the edge of the rim. Using a round-edged table knife, make tiny horizontal scoring marks against the cut edge of the dough to give it texture. Flute or crimp the edges decoratively. Prick the bottom of the pie lightly with tines of table fork.

WRAP AND REFRIGERATE THE PIE CRUST Wrap the dough loosely in plastic wrap and carefully slip into a large self-sealing plastic bag. Refrigerate the pie crust for at least 5 hours, or overnight.

PREBAKE THE PIE CRUST On baking day, preheat the oven to 425° F. About 10 minutes before prebaking the crust, place a cookie sheet on the oven rack.

Line the pie crust with a sheet of aluminum foil, allowing the foil to extend up the sides. Fill with raw rice (kept exclusively for this purpose) up to ¼ inch of the rim. Place the pie shell on the cookie sheet in the preheated oven and bake for 10 minutes. Carefully remove the aluminum foil and rice. (Cool the rice completely before storing.) Reduce the oven temperature to 375° F. and continue baking for about 15 minutes longer, or until a golden amber color. Transfer the pie crust to a cooling rack. *Procedural observation* To preserve its texture, fill the pie crust when it's freshly baked and still warm, so plan on preparing the filling while the crust is prebaking.

VANILLA CRESCENTS

2½ to 3 dozen cookies

Like most fragile-textured cookies, these crescents rely on the forthright, pure flavor of butter to carry the vanilla flavor and tenderize the dough. Structurally, what sets this dough apart from others of its kind is the presence of baking powder. The leavening actually opens up the crumb of the dough and prevents it from turning dense and pastelike. And the chopped nuts—make sure the walnuts are finely chopped—add volume and a second plane of flavor to the dough.

VANILLA COOKIE DOUGH

2¼ cups unsifted bleached all-purpose flour

¾ teaspoon baking powder

⅛ teaspoon salt

¼ teaspoon freshly grated nutmeg

½ pound (16 tablespoons or 2 sticks) unsalted butter, melted and cooled

seed scrapings from ½ vanilla bean

⅓ cup plus 2 tablespoons unsifted vanilla-scented confectioners' sugar (see page 54)

⅓ cup finely chopped walnuts

1¼ teaspoons intensified vanilla extract (see page 52)

About 3 cups vanilla-scented confectioners' sugar (see page 54), for rolling the baked cookies

BAKEWARE

several cookie sheets, preferably the insulated kind

PREHEAT THE OVEN AND PREPARE THE COOKIE SHEETS Preheat the oven to 350° F. Line the cookie sheets with lengths of cooking parchment paper; set aside.

MIX THE VANILLA COOKIE DOUGH Sift the all-purpose flour, baking powder, salt, and nutmeg onto a sheet of waxed paper.

Whisk the melted butter and vanilla bean seeds in a large mixing bowl. Blend in the vanilla-scented confectioners' sugar, walnuts, and vanilla extract. Using a flexible rubber spatula, stir in the flour mixture in three additions, mixing to form a dough. *Dough texture observation* The dough will be soft but not sticky and easy to shape.

SHAPE THE DOUGH INTO CRESCENTS Spoon out scant tablespoon-size quantities of dough and form into 2¼- to 2½-inch logs. Arrange the logs on the lined cookie sheets, about 2 inches apart, then bend and curve each into a crescent shape, tapering the ends slightly. Place 12 to 16 crescents on each cookie sheet, depending on the size of the sheet.

BAKE AND COOL THE CRESCENTS Bake the cookies in the preheated oven for 13 to 15 minutes, or until set, with light golden bottoms. The baked cookies may have small, fine cracks here and there.

Let the cookies stand on the sheets for 1 minute, then remove them to cooling racks, using a wide, offset metal spatula. *Cooling observation* Delicately shaped cookies such as these formed into half-moons need to firm up longer on the cookie sheets after baking than those formed into buttons, pillows, or balls.

COAT THE CRESCENTS Line a work surface with waxed paper. Place the confectioners' sugar in a shallow bowl. While the cookies are warm, carefully nestle and dredge them, a few at a time, in the sugar to coat, and place them on the waxed paper. After 30 minutes, coat the cookies again.

FRESHLY BAKED, THE CRESCENTS KEEP FOR 4 DAYS.

VANILLA LAYER CAKE

One two-layer, 9-inch cake, creating about 12 slices

 A SWEEP OF CHOCOLATE FROSTING, in between layers and around the cake, is a good contrast to the light, vanilla-flavored layers. The cake batter is rich in butter and eggs, which shape the vanilla taste.

Shortening and bleached all-purpose flour, for preparing the layer cake pans

VANILLA AND BUTTER LAYER CAKE BATTER

1¾ cups unsifted bleached all-purpose flour

½ cup unsifted bleached cake flour

1¾ teaspoons baking powder

¼ teaspoon salt

10 tablespoons (1 stick plus 2 tablespoons) unsalted butter, softened

1½ cups vanilla-scented superfine sugar (see page 54)

seed scrapings from ½ vanilla bean

2 teaspoons intensified vanilla extract (see page 52)

3 large eggs

¾ cup milk blended with ¼ cup plus 2 tablespoons heavy cream

Buttery Chocolate Frosting (see page 285) *or* Chocolate Cream Frosting (see page 272), for spreading on the baked cake layers

BAKEWARE

two 9-inch round layer cake pans (1½ inches deep)

PREHEAT THE OVEN AND PREPARE THE LAYER CAKE PANS Preheat the oven to 350° F. Lightly grease the inside of the cake pans with shortening. Line the bottom of each pan with a circle of waxed paper, grease the paper, then dust the inside with all-purpose flour. Tap out any excess flour; set aside.

MAKE THE VANILLA AND BUTTER LAYER CAKE BATTER Sift the all-purpose flour, cake flour, baking powder, and salt onto a sheet of waxed paper.

Cream the butter in the large bowl of a freestanding electric mixer on moderate speed for 3 minutes. Add the vanilla-scented superfine sugar in three batches, beating for 1 minute after each portion is incorporated. Blend in the vanilla bean seed scrapings and vanilla extract; beat for a minute longer. Beat in the eggs, one at a time, blending well after each addition.

On low speed, alternately add the sifted mixture in three additions with the milk-heavy cream blend in two additions, beginning and ending with the sifted mixture. Scrape down the sides of the mixing bowl frequently with a rubber spatula to keep the batter even-textured. *Batter texture observation* The batter will be moderately thick and creamy.

Spoon the batter into the prepared cake pans, dividing it evenly between them. Shake each pan gently from side to side, once or twice, to level the batter, or smooth it with a flexible rubber spatula.

BAKE AND COOL THE CAKE LAYERS Bake the layers for 25 to 30 minutes, or until set and a wooden pick inserted 1 inch from the center of each cake layer withdraws clean.

BEST BAKING ADVICE

Beating the superfine sugar into the butter for a full minute after each portion is added gives the baked cake layers a gossamer texture.

Cool the layers in the pans on racks for 5 minutes. Invert each layer onto another cooling rack, peel off the waxed paper round, then invert again to cool right side up. Cool completely.

ASSEMBLE AND FROST THE CAKE Tear off four 3-inch-wide strips of waxed paper. Place the strips in the shape of a square at the rim of a 10-inch cake plate. Position one cake layer on the plate; about 1 inch of waxed paper should extend past the circle of cake on all four sides, and the waxed paper should protect the cake plate as you are applying the frosting. Using a flexible palette knife, spread the top with frosting, set on the second layer, and frost the top and sides of the cake. When the frosting has firmed up, gently pull away the waxed paper strips and discard them.

Cut the cake into slices for serving.

FRESHLY BAKED, THE CAKE KEEPS FOR 2 TO 3 DAYS.

Vanilla Sugar Cookies

2½ to 3 dozen cookies

THE FLAVORS OF VANILLA AND BUTTER are spotlighted in this rolled cookie dough, and the two tastes are so compatible that they need little more than the basic baking staples to compose a dough. That little extra is freshly grated nutmeg, which helps to cultivate the vanilla taste.

VANILLA BUTTER COOKIE DOUGH

3 cups unsifted bleached all-purpose flour

½ teaspoon baking powder

¼ teaspoon salt

½ teaspoon freshly grated nutmeg

½ pound (16 tablespoons or 2 sticks) unsalted butter, softened

1½ cups vanilla-scented granulated sugar (see page 53)

2 large eggs

2 teaspoons intensified vanilla extract (see page 52)

2 tablespoons milk

Granulated sugar, for sprinkling on top of the unbaked cookies

BAKEWARE

several cookie sheets

MIX THE VANILLA BUTTER COOKIE DOUGH Whisk the flour, baking powder, salt, and nutmeg in a medium-size mixing bowl.

Cream the butter in the large bowl of a freestanding electric mixer on moderate speed for 2 minutes. Add the vanilla-scented granulated sugar; beat for 2 minutes. Blend in the eggs, vanilla extract, and milk.

On low speed, add the whisked flour mixture in three additions, beating just until the particles of flour are absorbed.

ROLL THE DOUGH Divide the dough into three portions and roll each between two sheets of waxed paper to a thickness of a scant ¼ inch. Stack the sheets of dough on a cookie sheet and refrigerate overnight. Transfer the sheets of dough to the freezer 30 minutes before cutting into cookies.

PREHEAT THE OVEN AND PREPARE THE COOKIE SHEETS Preheat the oven to 375° F. Line several cookie sheets with lengths of cooking parchment paper; set aside.

STAMP OUT THE COOKIES Working with one sheet of dough at a time, peel off the waxed paper, and place on a lightly floured work surface. Stamp out cookies with a floured 3-inch cookie cutter, and place them 2 inches apart on the cookie sheets. Dredge the tops with granulated sugar.

BEST BAKING ADVICE

Refrigerating the dough overnight sets the texture, and freezing the sheets of dough for 30 minutes before cutting gives the cut cookies a nice, clean edge.

BAKE AND COOL THE COOKIES Bake the cookies in the preheated oven for 10 to 12 minutes, or until golden and set. Remove the cookies to cooling racks, using a wide, offset metal spatula. Cool completely.

FRESHLY BAKED, THE COOKIES KEEP FOR 5 DAYS.

Vanilla Bean Shortbread

One 9½-inch shortbread, creating 12 triangular pieces

THE HEADY FRAGRANCE OF VANILLA is baked into this simple, lightly sweetened shortbread. The butter illuminates the vanilla taste, and the rice flour imparts a tender-crisp texture to the cookie.

VANILLA BEAN SHORTBREAD DOUGH

1 cup unsifted bleached all-purpose flour

¼ cup unsifted bleached cake flour

¼ cup rice flour

¼ teaspoon baking powder

⅛ teaspoon salt

¼ teaspoon freshly grated nutmeg

12 tablespoons (1½ sticks) unsalted butter, softened

seed scrapings from ½ vanilla bean

¼ cup plus 2 tablespoons vanilla-scented superfine sugar (see page 54)

2 teaspoons intensified vanilla extract (see page 52)

About 2 tablespoons vanilla-scented superfine sugar (see page 54), for sprinkling on top of the baked shortbread

BAKEWARE

fluted 9½-inch round tart pan (with a removable bottom)

BEST BAKING ADVICE

Beating both the butter and superfine sugar on low speed, and mixing in the sifted flour mixture only until absorbed, makes tender-textured shortbread.

PREHEAT THE OVEN AND PREPARE THE TART PAN Preheat the oven to 350° F. Have the tart pan at hand.

MIX THE VANILLA BEAN SHORTBREAD DOUGH Sift the all-purpose flour, cake flour, rice flour, baking powder, salt, and nutmeg onto a sheet of waxed paper.

Cream the butter in the large bowl of a freestanding electric mixer on low speed for 2 minutes. Beat in the vanilla bean seed scrapings. Blend in the vanilla-scented superfine sugar and vanilla extract. Beat on low speed for 2 minutes. Add the flour mixture in two additions, beating slowly until the particles of flour are absorbed and a smooth, soft dough forms. Scrape down the sides of the mixing bowl once or twice to keep the dough even-textured.

PRESS THE DOUGH INTO THE PREPARED PAN Turn the dough into the tart pan. Press it into an even layer, using your fingertips. Prick the dough in 15 random places, with the tines of a fork.

BAKE AND COOL THE SHORTBREAD Bake the shortbread in the preheated oven for 30 minutes or until it turns an all-over medium tan color and is set. Immediately dust the top with the superfine sugar. Cool the shortbread in the pan on a rack for 10 minutes.

UNMOLD AND CUT THE SHORTBREAD Carefully unmold the shortbread, leaving it on its round base. After 10 to 15 minutes, cut into wedges and cool completely. Store in an airtight tin.

FRESHLY BAKED, THE SHORTBREAD KEEPS FOR I WEEK.

Vanilla Madeleines

19 small cakes

THE VANILLA VERSION of these little cakes has a plain buttery taste and a delicate texture. My batter uses a combination of all-purpose flour and cake flour, which tenderizes the internal grain of the little baked cakes, and just enough baking powder to lighten its composition.

Melted clarified butter (see page 66) and bleached all-purpose flour, for preparing the madeleine molds

VANILLA MADELEINE BATTER

½ cup plus 2 tablespoons unsifted bleached all-purpose flour

¼ cup unsifted bleached cake flour

¼ teaspoon baking powder

⅛ teaspoon salt

⅛ teaspoon freshly grated nutmeg

6 tablespoons (¾ stick) unsalted butter, softened

⅓ cup plus 3 tablespoons vanilla-scented superfine sugar (see page 54)

seed scrapings from ¼ vanilla bean

2 large eggs

1 teaspoon intensified vanilla extract (see page 52)

2 teaspoons heavy cream

Confectioners' sugar, for sprinkling on top of the baked madeleines (optional)

BAKEWARE

3 *plaques à coques* (stylized madeleine molds, eight 2½-inch shells to each plaque)

PREHEAT THE OVEN AND PREPARE THE BAKING MOLDS
Preheat the oven to 375° F. Film the inside of the *plaques à coques* with clarified butter, using a soft pastry brush. Let stand for 5 minutes, or until completely set, then dust the inside of each shell with all-purpose flour. Tap out any excess flour; there should be a very thin coating. Set aside.

MIX THE VANILLA MADELEINE BATTER Sift the all-purpose flour, cake flour, baking powder, salt, and nutmeg onto a sheet of waxed paper twice.

Using an electric hand mixer, cream the butter in a medium-size mixing bowl on moderate speed for 2 minutes. Add the vanilla-scented superfine sugar and vanilla bean seed scrapings, and beat for 1 minute longer. Beat in the eggs, one at a time, mixing for 30 to 45 seconds after each addition. Scrape down the sides of the mixing bowl frequently with a rubber spatula to keep the batter even-textured. Blend in the vanilla extract. Add the sifted ingredients and mix on low speed until the particles of flour are absorbed. Scrape down the sides of the mixing bowl frequently to keep the batter even-textured. Blend in the heavy cream. *Batter texture observation* The batter will be thick but creamy-textured.

FILL THE MADELEINE MOLDS Fill the prepared molds with the batter, dividing it evenly among them. Uniformly mound the batter evenly in the center of each shell. *Batter position observation* Placing the batter in a rounded mound creates evenly plump baked cakes.

BAKE AND COOL THE MADELEINES Bake the cakes in the preheated oven for 10 to 12 minutes, or until plump, set, and a wooden pick inserted in the middle of a madeleine withdraws clean. The edges of the fully baked cakes will be light golden.

Cool the madeleines in the pans on racks for 1 minute, then lift them out of the pan at one side, using the rounded tip of a flexible palette knife. Place the madeleines, rounded (shell) side up, on cooling racks. Just before serving, sift confectioners' sugar over the tops of the madeleines, if you wish. Serve the madeleines warm, or within 2 to 3 hours of baking.

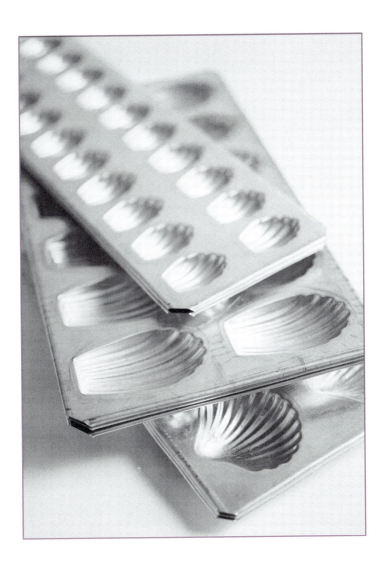

VANILLA WHIPPED CREAM

About 1½ cups

USING THE FLAVOR-HEIGHTENED VANILLA EXTRACT on page 52 deepens the taste of this simple whipped cream accompaniment. Superfine sugar, rather than confectioners' sugar, sweetens the cream perfectly without adding a chalky edge. Soft and delicate, drifts of cream are so good alongside a slice of cake or pie or spooned over dessert waffles or crêpes.

Whipped cream with the silkiest texture is made by using a whisk (rather than an electric hand mixer or a manual rotary egg beater) as the beating device. Whisking the cream by hand requires a bit of patience and premium-quality heavy cream with a high butterfat content. You can approximate the fine quality of hand-whipped cream by using electric (or rotary) beaters to thicken the cream sufficiently before the sugar is added. Then, add the sugar and complete the beating of the cream with a whisk.

VANILLA-SCENTED
WHIPPED CREAM

1 cup heavy cream, cold

1 tablespoon superfine sugar

1 teaspoon intensified vanilla extract
(see page 52)

CHILL THE WHISK (OR BEATERS) AND MIXING BOWL At least 1½ hours before making the flavored cream, place the whisk (or beaters of choice) and a medium-size stainless steel mixing bowl in the refrigerator for 30 to 45 minutes.

WHIP, SWEETEN, AND FLAVOR THE CREAM Pour the heavy cream into the mixing bowl and beat rapidly until the cream begins to thicken and swell. When the cream is very lightly thickened and just beginning to mound, sprinkle over the superfine sugar and beat until soft, billowy peaks are formed. Blend in the vanilla extract.

Use the whipped cream immediately.

Vanilla Custard Sauce

About 2 cups

A POURING OF CUSTARD SAUCE—lightly thickened and vanilla charged—is so appealing served alongside a slice of cake or pie. As an accompaniment, it adds a creamy topnote of flavor and satiny, contrasting texture.

VANILLA CUSTARD SAUCE

1¼ cups heavy cream

½ cup milk

pinch of salt

½ vanilla bean, split to expose the tiny seeds

5 large egg yolks

⅓ cup plus 2 tablespoons vanilla-scented superfine sugar (see page 54)

1 teaspoon intensified vanilla extract (see page 52)

MAKE THE VANILLA CUSTARD SAUCE Warm the heavy cream, milk, salt, and vanilla bean in a small saucepan (to 110° to 115° F.). Carefully remove the vanilla bean from the saucepan and scrape the seeds into the milk. Set the cream-milk mixture aside; cool to tepid. Remove and discard the vanilla bean.

Whisk the egg yolks in a medium-size mixing bowl. Add the vanilla-scented superfine sugar and whisk for 1 minute. Blend in 3 tablespoons of the warm liquid, adding it through a fine-meshed sieve. Add the remaining liquid, a few tablespoons at a time through the sieve, blending each batch in.

Pour the custard mixture into a heavy, medium-size saucepan, preferably enameled cast iron. Place the saucepan over low heat and cook the sauce, stirring with a wooden spoon until it's lightly thickened and heavily coats the back of the spoon, 10 to 12 minutes. Don't rush the process by raising the heat. *Sauce consistency observation* The thickened custard sauce will look shiny and silky-smooth.

STRAIN, COOL, AND FLAVOR THE SAUCE Strain the custard sauce through a fine-meshed sieve into a heatproof storage container. Smooth the mixture through the strainer with a rubber spatula. Stir in the vanilla extract. Press a sheet of plastic wrap on the surface of the sauce to prevent a skin from forming. Cool, cover, and refrigerate. *Storage observation* On chilling, the sauce will thicken somewhat, and can be restored by stirring in an extra tablespoon (or two) of milk. The custard can be refrigerated for 1 day.

BEST BAKING ADVICE

Straining the finished custard sauce through a fine-meshed sieve virtually guarantees that it will be extra-velvety.

Variation: For almond custard sauce, replace the vanilla-scented superfine sugar with plain superfine sugar, reduce the pure vanilla extract to ¼ teaspoon, and stir it in along with ½ teaspoon pure almond extract and 1 tablespoon almond liqueur (Amaretto).

*P*reserving the life of baked goods essentially comes down to maintaining quality: while you *could* freeze anything, you can compromise the sparkle and vitality—and the absolute lusciousness—of some of what you bake. However, many items can be frozen quite well and revived by a short reheat in a moderate oven, or by slicing and toasting.

The following chart shows which recipes in this book take well to freezer storage. Many recipes call for freezing the item once it is baked; others recommend simply freezing the dough in its unbaked form. Some of the baked goods must be reheated in the oven or toasted, and some are delicious when thawed gently in the refrigerator (like a fudge brownie).

Any material that comes in contact with food, either baked or as a dough, must be food-safe. For freezer storage, first enclose the freshly baked item in clinging plastic wrap, then in a square of aluminum foil; muffins or rolls can be wrapped individually, while bar cookies can be packaged in clusters. Bundle the baked goods in self-sealing plastic bags. Date and label the contents of the packages. Depending on the amount, a recipe of cookie dough should be divided in half or into thirds, carefully pressed into flat cakes on sheets of plastic wrap, and slipped into a plastic bag. Cookie doughs, and all baked goods, should be initially *thawed in their wrappings* before proceeding. A temperature-controlled thawing in the refrigerator, although more time-consuming, is the best way to ease the sweet out of its frozen firmness.

To reheat muffins, scones, and sweet rolls or streusel buns, bundle them in aluminum foil, leaving some open air space at the top. The gap will keep the baked goods from steaming.

ABOUT FREEZING
BAKED GOODS

Freezing and Reheating

BAKING CATEGORY AND SPECIFIC BAKERY ITEM	OPTIMUM FREEZER STORAGE TIME	REHEATING RECOMMENDATIONS: OVEN OR TOASTER PREHEATED OVEN/ REHEATING TIME
BISCUITS AND SCONES		
Sweet Almond and Chocolate Chip Drop Biscuits	2 months	350° F. oven 10 to 12 minutes
Apricot Oatmeal Breakfast Scones	unglazed, 2 months	350° F. oven 10 to 12 minutes, then glaze
Sweet Banana and Chocolate Chip Scones	2 months	350° F. oven 10 to 12 minutes
Sweet Blueberry Breakfast Biscuits	6 weeks	350° F. oven 10 to 12 minutes
Butter Biscuits	4 to 6 weeks	350° F. oven 10 to 12 minutes
Buttercrunch Tea Biscuits	6 weeks	350° F. oven 10 minutes
Double Chocolate Scones	2 months	325° F. oven 10 to 12 minutes
Cinnamon Chip Scones with Cinnamon-Pecan Streusel	2 months	325° F. oven 12 to 15 minutes
Toasted Coconut and Macadamia Nut Scones	2 months	350° F. oven 10 to 12 minutes
Ginger Scones	2 months	350° F. oven 10 to 12 minutes
Cocoa-Double Peanut Scones	2 months	325° F. oven 12 minutes
Iced Rum-Raisin Tea Biscuits	uniced, 2 months	350° F. oven 10 to 12 minutes, then apply icing
Spice Scones	2 months	350° F. oven 10 to 12 minutes

(continued)

Freezing and Reheating

BAKING CATEGORY AND SPECIFIC BAKERY ITEM	OPTIMUM FREEZER STORAGE TIME	REHEATING RECOMMENDATIONS: OVEN OR TOASTER PREHEATED OVEN/ REHEATING TIME
CAKES AND TORTES		
Pumpkin-Almond Keeping Cake	6 weeks	slice and lightly toast
Almond Butter Cake	2 months	slice and toast
Buttery Glazed Almond Ring	unglazed, 1 month	350° F. oven 15 minutes, then finish with almond-butter glaze
Blueberry Coffee Cake	3 weeks	350° F. oven 10 to 12 minutes
Blueberries and Cream Breakfast Cake	3 weeks	350° F. oven 10 to 12 minutes
Grandma Lilly's Butter Pound Cake	1 month	slice and lightly toast
Buttermilk Butter Pound Cake	1 month	slice and lightly toast
Golden Butter Cake	2 months	slice and lightly toast
Caramel and Butterscotch Chip Pound Cake	6 weeks	350° F. oven 15 minutes, then apply caramel basting sauce
Butterscotch Sour Cream Coffee Cake	2 months	350° F. oven 15 minutes
Lavish Cinnamon Brunch Cake	2 months	350° F. oven 12 to 15 minutes
Cinnamon Chip Cinnamon Cake	2 months	slice and lightly toast
Ultra-Cinnamon Pound Cake with Macadamia-Spice Ribbon	2 months	slice and lightly toast
Cinnamon Sour Cream Coffee Cake	2 months	slice and lightly toast
Sour Cream Ginger Keeping Cake	2 months	slice and lightly toast

(continued)

FREEZING AND REHEATING

BAKING CATEGORY AND SPECIFIC BAKERY ITEM	OPTIMUM FREEZER STORAGE TIME	REHEATING RECOMMENDATIONS: OVEN OR TOASTER PREHEATED OVEN/ REHEATING TIME
CAKES AND TORTES (CONT'D)		
Butter Rum Cake	unglazed, 2 months	325° F. 15 to 20 minutes, then apply butter rum glaze
Pecan, Rum, and Brown Sugar Keeping Cake	without rum syrup, 1 month	325° F. 15 to 20 minutes, then apply rum syrup
Rum Pound Cake	unglazed, 6 weeks	325° F. 15 to 20 minutes, then apply sugar rum glaze
Sugar and Spice Breakfast Cake	1 month	350° F. 12 minutes
Spice Ripple Keeping Cake	1 month	slice and lightly toast
Cream Cheese Pound Cake	1 month	slice and lightly toast
COOKIES (baked or frozen unbaked dough)		
Bittersweet Almond Chunk Brownies (baked)	4 to 6 weeks	—
Apricot Sandwich Cookies (unbaked dough)	6 weeks (freeze in rolled-out sheets)	—
Apricot Thumbprint Cookies (unbaked dough)	6 weeks (freeze in flat cakes)	—
Butter Crescents (unbaked dough)	6 weeks (freeze in flat cakes)	—
Butter Cookie Cut-Outs (unbaked dough)	6 weeks (freeze in rolled-out sheets)	—
Buttercrunch Melt-a-Ways (unbaked dough)	6 weeks (freeze in flat cakes)	—

(continued)

FREEZING AND REHEATING

BAKING CATEGORY AND SPECIFIC BAKERY ITEM	OPTIMUM FREEZER STORAGE TIME	REHEATING RECOMMENDATIONS: OVEN OR TOASTER PREHEATED OVEN/ REHEATING TIME
COOKIES (CONT'D)		
Buttercrunch Flats (unbaked dough)	2 months (freeze in flat cakes)	—
Almond Fudge Buttercrunch Brownies (baked)	4 to 6 weeks	—
Butterscotch Oatmeal Cookies (unbaked dough)	2 months (freeze in flat cakes)	—
Chocolate-covered Caramel and Peanut Candy Bar Brownies (baked)	4 to 6 weeks	—
Truffled Chocolate-Walnut Brownies (baked)	6 weeks	—
Cocoa-Chocolate Chip Pillows (unbaked dough)	6 weeks (freeze in flat cakes)	—
Bittersweet Chocolate Brownies with Pecans (baked)	4 to 6 weeks	—
Simply Intense Chocolate Brownies (baked)	4 weeks	—
Coconut-Chocolate Chip Cookies (unbaked dough)	6 weeks (freeze in flat cakes)	—
Coconut Washboards (unbaked dough)	4 to 6 weeks (freeze in flat cakes)	—
Coconut Jumbles (unbaked dough)	6 weeks (freeze in rolled-out sheets)	—
Soft Coconut Oatmeal Cookies with Dried Fruit (unbaked dough)	2 months (freeze in flat cakes)	—
Coconut and Almond Fudge Squares (baked)	4 to 6 weeks	—

(continued)

BAKING CATEGORY AND SPECIFIC BAKERY ITEM	OPTIMUM FREEZER STORAGE TIME	REHEATING RECOMMENDATIONS: OVEN OR TOASTER PREHEATED OVEN/ REHEATING TIME
COOKIES (CONT'D)		
Double Chocolate-Coconut Brownies (baked)	4 to 6 weeks	—
Mocha Bars (baked)	4 to 6 weeks	—
Mocha Truffle Cookies (unbaked dough)	1 month (freeze in flat cakes)	—
Spicy Gingerbread Cookies (unbaked dough)	6 weeks (freeze in rolled-out sheets)	—
Ginger Butter Balls (unbaked dough)	6 weeks (freeze in flat cakes)	—
Ginger Cracks (unbaked dough)	6 weeks (freeze in flat cakes)	—
Ginger Brownies (baked)	1 month	—
Retro Peanut Butter Cookies (unbaked dough)	6 weeks (freeze in flat cakes)	—
Peanut Madness Chunks (unbaked dough)	4 to 6 weeks	—
Cream Cheese-Swirled Brownies (baked)	6 weeks	—
Vanilla Crescents (unbaked dough)	6 weeks (freeze in flat cakes)	—
Vanilla Sugar Cookies (unbaked dough)	6 weeks (freeze in rolled-out sheets)	—

(continued)

FREEZING AND REHEATING

BAKING CATEGORY AND SPECIFIC BAKERY ITEM	OPTIMUM FREEZER STORAGE TIME	REHEATING RECOMMENDATIONS: OVEN OR TOASTER PREHEATED OVEN/ REHEATING TIME
MUFFINS		
Texas-Size Banana Muffins	2 months	350° F. 10 to 12 minutes
Tender, Cakelike Blueberry Muffins	6 weeks	350° F. 10 to 12 minutes
Baby Blueberry Corn Muffins	1 month	350° F. 10 minutes
Sour Cream Blueberry Muffins	2 months	350° F. 10 to 12 minutes
Texas-Size Buttercrunch-Pecan-Chip Muffins	6 weeks	350° F. 10 minutes
Big Chocolate-Chocolate Chip Muffins	2 months	350° F. 10 to 12 minutes
Cinnamon-Walnut Muffins with Spiced Sugar-Butter Dunk	without sugar-butter dunk, 2 months	350° F. 10 to 12 minutes, then finish with sugar-butter dunk
Mega Mocha Pecan Chip Muffins	2 months	325° F. 12 to 15 minutes
Gingery Pumpkin Muffins with Ginger-Sugar Sprinkle	1 month	350° F. 10 minutes

(continued)

FREEZING AND REHEATING

BAKING CATEGORY AND SPECIFIC BAKERY ITEM	OPTIMUM FREEZER STORAGE TIME	REHEATING RECOMMENDATIONS: OVEN OR TOASTER PREHEATED OVEN/ REHEATING TIME
SWEET LOAVES AND TEA BREADS		
Spiced Banana Breakfast Loaf	2 months	350° F. about 15 minutes, or slice and lightly toast
Banana and Dried Cranberry Tea Cake	2 months	350° F. 15 minutes
Cocoa Banana Loaf	2 months	325° F. 15 minutes
Blueberry Loaf	6 weeks	325° F. 15 minutes
Blueberry-Banana Tea Loaf	6 weeks	325° F. 15 minutes
Crystallized Ginger Gingerbread	4 to 6 weeks	325° F. 15 minutes
Spicy Molasses Gingerbread	4 to 6 weeks	325° F. 15 minutes
Spiced Pumpkin and Chocolate Chip Tea Loaf	2 months	325° F. 15 minutes
SWEET YEAST ROLLS, COFFEE CAKES AND BUNS		
Almond Pull-Aparts	3 months	350° F. 10 to 12 minutes
Apricot Babka	unglazed, 2 months	350° F. about 15 minutes, then apply apricot glaze
Apricot Schnecken	3 months	350° F. 10 to 12 minutes
Buttercrunch Butter Buns	3 months	350° F. 10 to 12 minutes

(continued)

FREEZING AND REHEATING

BAKING CATEGORY AND SPECIFIC BAKERY ITEM	OPTIMUM FREEZER STORAGE TIME	REHEATING RECOMMENDATIONS: OVEN OR TOASTER PREHEATED OVEN/ REHEATING TIME
SWEET YEAST ROLLS, COFFEE CAKES AND BUNS (CONT'D)		
Bittersweet Chocolate Stollen	1 month	325° F. 15 minutes
Cinnamon Sticky Buns	1 month	325° F. about 15 minutes
Cinnamon Butter Rosebuds	2 months	350° F. 12 to 15 minutes
Cinnamon Ripple Rolls	uniced, 2 months	350° F. 12 to 15 minutes, then top with icing
Coconut Cream Coffee Cake Buns	3 months	350° F. 12 minutes
Iced Mocha Sweet Rolls	uniced, 3 months	350° F. 10 to 12 minutes, then apply coffee icing
Rum Buns	uniced, 3 months	350° F. 12 minutes, then apply rum icing
Sweet Oatmeal-Raisin Spice Buns	uniced, 3 months	350° F. 10 to 15 minutes, then apply spice icing
Sweet Cheese Buns	2 months	325° F. 12 to 15 minutes
Cream Cheese Schnecken	2 months	325° F. 12 to 15 minutes
Cream Cheese and Almond Tea Ring	uniced, 2 months	325° F. 15 to 20 minutes, then apply almond icing
Vanilla Crumb Buns	3 months	325° F. 12 to 15 minutes

SELECTED SOURCES FOR EQUIPMENT AND SUPPLIES

THE FOLLOWING RESOURCES offer baking materials—food and equipment—for stocking your pantry and outfitting your kitchen. Verify prices and confirm current stock before placing an order.

AMERICAN SPOON FOODS

P.O. Box 566
Petoskey, Michigan 49770-0566
616-347-9030
Toll Free 888-735-6700 or 231-347-9030
Fax 800-647-2512 or 231-347-2512
Customer Service 800-222-5886

American Spoon Foods carries a wonderful range of preserves, jellies, and jams; fruit butters; and excellent dried fruit such as dried red tart cherries, dried Michigan blueberries, dried wild blueberries, and dried cranberries, in addition to other assorted treats.

THE BAKER'S CATALOGUE

King Arthur Flour
Box 876
Norwich, Vermont 05055-0876
800-827-6836 Monday through Friday 8:30 A.M.–8:00 P.M., 9:00 A.M.–5:00 P.M. Saturday, 11:00 A.M.–4:00 P.M. Sunday (Sunday hours through April 5)
Fax 800-343-3002
Baker's Hotline 802-649-3717, Monday through Friday, 9:00 A.M.–5:00 P.M.

The Baker's Catalogue is a resource for measuring equipment; baking pans; cooling racks; pastry brushes; cookie cutters; all kinds of flour, including specialty flours and grains, individual and blended; Dutch-process black cocoa (see page 68) and the dark micro-chips (see page 68); distinctive bread-baking ingredients; flavorings; dried fruits; sugars, including the Snow White Non-Melting Sugar (see page 73); hard-to-find flavored baking chips, such as cinnamon, cappuccino, and caramel—all this in addition to cookbooks, baking advice, and so much more.

BRIDGE KITCHENWARE CORPORATION

214 East 52 Street
New York, New York 10022
For catalog orders only: 800-BRIDGE K
(800-274-3435), Ext. 3
In New York: 212-838-1901, Extension 3
For all other information and customer service:
212-838-6746, Extension 5
Fax: 212-758-5387

Bridge Kitchenware is a source for high-quality baking tools that include sifters and dredgers; measuring equipment; bench knives; pastry blenders; cake pans; muffin pans; tart pans; pastry cutter sets; baking sheets; spoons and spatulas; rolling pins; pastry brushes; pastry bags and tips; cooling racks, and other fine supplies.

A COOK'S WARES

211 37 Street
Beaver Falls, Pennsylvania 15010-2103
Orders, toll free, any time, any day: 800-915-9788
Fax 800-916-2886
Information and inquiries, 724-846-9490
Monday–Friday 8:00 A.M.–5:00 P.M.,
Saturday 9:00 A.M.–1:00 P.M. EST

A Cook's Wares sells several sizes of heat-resistant spatulas and spoons; muffin pans; springform pans; parchment paper; bakeware gear such as pastry blenders, cooling racks, sugar sprinklers, and rolling pins; cookie cutters; tart pans; whisks; measuring equipment; knives and offset spatulas, and more.

FRAN'S CAKE & CANDY SUPPLIES

10396 Willard Way
Fairfax, Virginia 22030
Telephone 703-352-1471
Monday through Saturday 10:00 A.M. to 6:00 P.M.

Fran Wheat's shop is headquarters for those who love to bake and decorate cakes and cookies, and make all kinds of candy as well. She stocks a large selection of cookie cutters; cake pans of all types and styles; decorative molds; paper goods used in packaging and presenting baked cookies and candies; sanding sugars and sprinkles in a wide range of colors; plus pastry bags, a comprehensive assortment of pastry tips, paste food colors of all hues, and other ingredients required in decorative work. Fran's presence in the store and her extensive knowledge of cake decorating and styling make this largess comprehensible.

KITCHEN ETC.

Catalog services
Department DM 999
32 Industrial Drive
Exeter, New Hampshire 03833-4557
To place order 800-232-4070
Outside the U.S. 603-773-0020
Customer service hours: Monday 9:00 A.M.–9:00 P.M. EST
Tuesday–Friday 9:00 A.M.–5:00 P.M.
Saturday 10:00 A.M.–5:00 P.M.
Fax credit card order 603-778-0777

In addition to china, crystal, and flatware, Kitchen etc. stocks a range of cookware and knives, including cookie sheets; enameled cast iron saucepans; spoons and spatulas; jellyroll and cake pans; peelers; and various types of serrated, chopping, and utility knives.

KITCHEN GLAMOR

Corporate Offices Warehouse
39049 Webb Court
Westland, Michigan 48185-7606
Quick delivery 800-641-1252
Telephone 734-641-1244
Fax 734-641-1240 (24-hour)
Toll Free Order 800-641-1252
Customer Service 800-641-1252

Kitchen Glamor stocks tools for the baker, including mixers, cake pans, tart pans, muffin pans, and cookie sheets.

KITCHEN KRAFTS

The Foodcrafter's Supply Catalog
P.O. Box 442-ORD
Waukon, Iowa 52172-0442
Toll-free telephone orders 8:00 A.M.–5:00 P.M. CST, 800-776-0575
319-535-8000
Fax toll-free 24 hours a day/365 days a year
800-850-3093
Fax 319-535-8001

Kitchen Krafts carries equipment and supplies that include electric mixers, cooling racks, sifters, dough scrapers, spatulas, measuring equipment, and cake pans.

LA CUISINE

323 Cameron Street
Alexandria, Virginia 22314
Telephone 703-836-4435
Fax 703-836-8925
USA and Canada 800-521-1176

La Cuisine is an excellent source for classic bakeware, including an impressive selection of madeleine *plaques*; tart, muffin, and cake pans; heat-resistant spatulas; boxwood spoons and paddles; stainless steel strainers; rolling pins and pastry scrapers; whisks and icing spatulas; citrus zesters and nutmeg graters; glorious cookie cutters; pastry bags and tips; knives; crêpe pans in many sizes, in addition to a range of top-quality chocolate, extracts, and nut flours. La Cuisine also stocks a selection of copper.

MARTHA BY MAIL

P.O. Box 60060
Tampa, Florida 33660-0060
800-950-7130, 24 hours a day, 7 days a week

In Martha By Mail, Martha Stewart offers bakers cookie cutters, cake and cookie-decorating kits, petit-fours kits, cake molds, sanding sugars for cookie decorating, mixing bowls, copper trays, and unusual seasonal goods for the home.

Department 6600, 1950 Waldorf NW
Grand Rapids, Michigan 49550-6600
Telephone 800-832-9993
Fax 309-689-3893

Mauna Loa® is the source for coconut candy-glazed macadamia nuts.

New York Cake & Baking Distributor
56 West 22 Street
New York, New York 10010
Telephone 212-675-CAKE; 800-94-CAKE-9,
10:00 A.M.–5:00 P.M. EST
Fax 212-675-7099

New York Cake & Baking Distributor is a source for baking and decorating supplies. The extensive bakeware available includes cake pans in all shapes, sizes, and depths (including 3-inch-deep square and rectangular pans); pie and tart pans; muffin pans; cake rings; cookie cutters; cooling racks; rolling pins (including the nylon variety); molds; sifters, strainers, and measuring equipment (including nonstick measuring spoons); ramekins; whisks; all kinds of spatulas; pastry (decorating) bags, tips, and paste colors; flavorings; and chocolate. This is only a partial listing of the equipment and tools for the dedicated baker.

Penzeys Spices
Catalog of seasonings
Post Office Box 933
Muskego, Wisconsin 53150
Telephone 800-741-7787
Fax 262-679-7878
8:00 A.M.–5:00 P.M. Monday through Friday;
9:00 A.M.–3:00 P.M. Saturdays (Central Time)

Penzeys Spices carries a complete stock of whole and ground spices. The China cassia cinnamon, with its bold flavor, is wonderful for baking, as is the more modulated Korintje cassia cinnamon; the Whole Grenadian West Indian nutmeg has a beautifully intense flavor and grates into an aromatic powder; and the Whole Root China #1 ginger, grated, intensifies gingerbread cookie dough and gingerbread batter in a wonderful way. Penzeys also stocks Madagascar, Indonesian, and Mexican vanilla beans, and pure single and double-strength vanilla extracts (35% alcohol each), both made from Madagascar vanilla beans.

Prévin Incorporated
2044 Rittenhouse Square
Philadelphia, Pennsylvania 19103
Telephone 215-985-1996
Fax 215-985-0323

Prévin stocks a superb collection of ovenproof porcelain (including ramekins), spoons, tongs, pastry spatulas, pastry cutters, dough scrapers, decorating bags and tips, rolling pins, baking sheets, molds and Bundt pans, springform pans and cake pans, in addition to other baking accessories and supplies.

J.B. Prince Company, Inc.
36 East 31 Street
11th Floor
New York, New York 10016
Telephone 212-683-3553; 800-473-0577; phone orders
9:00 A.M.–5:00 P.M. Eastern time
Fax 212-683-4488
Telephone order 9:00 A.M.–5:00 P.M., Eastern time,
Monday through Friday

J.B. Prince is a good place to shop for cutlery, cookware, and bakeware, including pastry bags and tips; pastry brushes; cutters; cooling racks; spoons and spatulas; serrated knives; fluted tart pans; madeleine pans; plain and fluted cake pans; extra deep, plain-sided tube pans; sheet pans; whisks; strainers; tongs; and a fine selection of special preparation tools, such as zesters, stripers, melon ball cutters, peelers, and scoops.

Catalog Division
1765 Sixth Avenue South
Seattle, Washington 98134-1608
Telephone 800-243-0852 (24 hours a day)
Fax 206-682-1026
Customer Service 800-243-0852

Sur La Table carries electric mixers, cake molds, knives, cookie cutters, and other tools for the baker.

Sweet Celebrations Inc.

General catalog
P.O. Box 39426
Edina, Minnesota 55439-0426
To order: 800-328-6722
Fax 612-943-1688
Twin City Metro 612-943-1508

Sweet Celebrations (Maid of Scandinavia division of Sweet Celebrations, Inc.) offers, in the general catalog, a range of baking tools, including cutters, cake decorating equipment and baking pans, chocolate, and flavorings.

Williams-Sonoma, Inc.

Mail Order Department
P.O. Box 7456
San Francisco, California 94120-7456
Order by telephone: 800-541-2233
Fax 702-363-2541
Customer Service 800-541-1262

Williams-Sonoma is a source for equipment, tools, and baking supplies that include electric mixers, blenders, measuring equipment, mixing bowls, strainers, knives, baking pans, tart pans, muffin pans, cake pans, spatulas, vanilla extract, vanilla bean paste, vanilla beans, and more.

Wilton Enterprises

Caller Service No. 1604
2440 W. 75 Street
Woodridge, Illinois 60517-0750
Telephone 630-963-1818
Fax 888-824-9520

The Wilton Enterprises Cake Decorating Yearbook (produced annually) is a classic handbook, resource, and reference guide for decorating supplies and ideas. The "Decorating Tips Guide," an indispensable section of the yearbook, sets out pastry tips available by shape, appearance, and number; a squirt of colored icing accompanies each tip so that you can see the design it creates. The company is an excellent source for icing ingredients, decorating (pastry) bags, a full range of decorating tips, spatulas, couplers, and cleaning brushes for pastry tips.

BIBLIOGRAPHY: A SELECTION OF BOOKS FOR REFERENCE AND REFERRAL

THE FOLLOWING REFERENCE LIST—composed mostly of books on baking and desserts—will sharpen your skills and provide many hours of delicious reading.

Adams, Marcia. *Cooking from Quilt Country*. New York: Clarkson Potter, 1989.

Allison, Sonia. *The English Biscuit and Cookie Cookbook*. New York: St. Martin's Press, 1983.

Appel, Jennifer, and Allysa Torey. *The Magnolia Bakery Cookbook*. New York: Simon & Schuster, 1999.

Baggett, Nancy. *The International Chocolate Cookbook*. New York: Stewart, Tabori & Chang, 1991.

———. *The International Cookie Cookbook*. New York: Stewart, Tabori & Chang, 1993.

Boyle, Tish. *Diner Desserts*. San Francisco: Chronicle Books, 2000.

———, and Timothy Moriarty. *Chocolatepassion*. New York: John Wiley & Sons, 2000.

———, and Timothy Moriarty. *Grand Finales: A Neoclassic View of Plated Desserts*. New York: John Wiley & Sons, 2000.

Beard, James. *Beard on Bread*. New York: Alfred A. Knopf, 1973.

———. *James Beard's American Cookery*. Boston: Little, Brown and Company, 1972.

Beranbaum, Rose Levy. *The Cake Bible*. New York: William Morrow and Company, 1988.

———. *The Pie and Pastry Bible*. New York: Scribners, 1998.

Bergin, Mary, and Judy Gethers. *Spago Desserts*. New York: Random House, 1994.

———. *Spago Chocolate*. New York: Random House, 1999.

Berl, Christine. *The Classic Art of Viennese Pastry*. New York: John Wiley & Sons, 1998.

Bodger, Lorraine. *Chocolate Cookies*. New York: St. Martin's Griffin, 1998.

Bradshaw, Lindsay John. *The Ultimate Book of Royal Icing*. London: Merehurst, 1992.

Brachman, Wayne Harley. *Cakes and Cowpokes*. New York: William Morrow and Company, 1995.

Braker, Flo. *Sweet Miniatures*. New York: William Morrow and Company, 1991.

———. *The Simple Art of Perfect Baking*, Updated and Revised. Shelburne: Chapters Publishing Ltd., 1992, 1985.

Butts, Diana Collingwood, and Carol V. Wright. *Sugarbakers' Cookie Cutter Cookbook*. New York: Simon & Schuster, 1997.

Byrn, Anne. *The Cake Mix Doctor*. New York: Workman Publishing Company, 1999.

Child, Julia, Louisette Bertholle, and Simone Beck. *Mastering the Art of French Cooking*, Volume One. New York: Alfred A. Knopf, 1961.

———, and Simone Beck. *Mastering the Art of French Cooking*, Volume Two. New York: Alfred A. Knopf, 1970.

———. *The French Chef Cookbook*. New York: Alfred A. Knopf, 1968.

Claiborne, Craig. *The New York Times Cookbook*. New York: Harper & Row Publishers, 1961.

Clayton, Bernard, Jr. *Bernard Clayton's New Complete Book of Breads*. New York: Simon and Schuster, 1973, 1987.

———. *The Complete Book of Pastry Sweet and Savory*. New York: Simon & Schuster, 1981, First Fireside Edition, 1984.

Corriher, Shirley O. *CookWise*. New York: William Morrow and Company, 1997.

Cunningham, Marion. *The Fanny Farmer Baking Book*. New York: Alfred A. Knopf, 1984.

Dannenberg, Linda. *French Tarts*. New York: Artisan, 1997.

Desaulniers, Marcel. *Death by Chocolate*. New York: Rizzoli International Publications, 1992.

———, recipes with Jon Pierre Peavey. *Desserts to Die For*. New York: Simon & Schuster, 1995.

Dodge, Jim, with Elaine Ratner. *The American Baker*. New York: Simon & Schuster, 1987.

———. *Baking with Jim Dodge*. New York: Simon & Schuster, 1991.

Elbert, Virginie & George. *Dolci*. New York: Simon & Schuster, 1987.

Flatt, Letty Halloran. *Chocolate Snowball and other Fabulous Pastries from Deer Valley*. Helena: Falcon Publishing, 1999.

Fobel, Jim. *Jim Fobel's Old-Fashioned Baking Book*. New York: Ballantine Books, 1987.

Friberg, Bo. *The Professional Pastry Chef*, Third Edition. New York: John Wiley & Sons, 1996.

Fussell, Betty. *I Hear America Cooking*. New York: Viking, 1986.

Galli, Franco. *The Il Fornaio Baking Book*. San Francisco: Chronicle Books, 1993.

Good Cooking School, James Beard, Alexis Bespaloff, Philip Brown, John Clancy, Edward Giobbi, George Lang, Leon Llanides, Helen McCully, Maurice Moore-Betty, Jacques Pépin and Felipe Rojas-Lombardi. *The Great Cooks Cookbook*. New York: Ferguson/Doubleday The Good Cooking School, 1974.

Gorman, Judy. *Judy Gorman's Breads of New England*. Camden: Yankee Books, 1988.

Gourley, Robbin. *Cakewalk*. New York: Doubleday, 1994.

Gourmet, Editors of. *Gourmet's Best Desserts*. New York: Condé Nast Books, 1987.

Greenspan, Dorie. *Baking with Julia*. New York: William Morrow and Company, 1996.

———. *Sweet Times*. New York: William Morrow and Company, 1991.

Greenstein, George. *Secrets of a Jewish Baker*. Freedom: Crossing Press, 1993.

Hadda, Ceri. *Coffee Cakes*. New York: Simon & Schuster, 1992.

———. *Cupcakes*. New York: Simon & Schuster, 1995.

Halberstadt. Piet. *The Illustrated Cookie*. New York: Macmillan, 1994.

Hazelton, Nika. *American Home Cooking*. New York: Viking Press, 1980.

Healy, Bruce, with Paul Bugat. *The French Cookie Cookbook*. New York: William Morrow and Company, 1994.

———. *Mastering the Art of French Pastry*. New York: Barrons, 1984.

———. *The Art of the Cake*. New York: William Morrow and Company, 1999.

Heatter, Maida. *Maida Heatter's Book of Great American Desserts*. New York: Alfred A. Knopf, 1983.

———. *Maida Heatter's Book of Great Desserts*. New York: Alfred A. Knopf, 1974.

Hensperger, Beth. *Beth's Basic Bread Book*. San Francisco: Chronicle Books, 1999.

———. *The Art of Quick Breads*. San Francisco: Chronicle Books, 1994.

Hermé, Pierre, and Dorie Greenspan. *Desserts by Pierre Hermé*. Boston: Little, Brown and Company, 1998.

Hewitt, Mary-Jo. *The Biscuit Basket Lady*. New York: Hearst Books, 1995.

Hilburn, Prudence. *A Treasury of Southern Baking*. New York: HarperPerennial, 1993.

Johnson, Jann. *The Art of the Cookie*. San Francisco: Chronicle Books, 1994.

Jones, Judith and Evan. *The Book of Bread*. New York: Harper & Row Publishers, 1982.

Kamman, Madeleine. *The New Making of a Cook*. New York: William Morrow and Company, 1997.

Kennedy, Teresa. *American Pie*. New York: Workman Publishing Company, 1984.

Klivans, Elinor. *Bake and Freeze Desserts*. New York: William Morrow and Company, 1994.

Kosoff, Susan. *Good Old-Fashioned Cakes*. New York: St. Martin's Press, 1989.

Knipe, Judy, and Barbara Marks. *The Christmas Cookie Book*. New York: Ballantine Books, 1990.

Laver, Norma. *The Art of Sugarcraft Piping*. London: Merehurst Press, 1986.

Lawhon, Charla. *Heartland Baking*. New York: Dell Publishing, 1991.

Lenôtre, Gaston, revised and adapted by Philip and Mary Hyman. *Lenôtre's Desserts and Pastries*. Woodbury: Barrons, 1977.

Levy, Faye. *Dessert Sensations Fresh From France*. New York: Dutton, 1990.

———. *Sensational Chocolate*. Los Angeles: HPBooks, a division of Price Stern Sloan, 1986, 1992 HPBooks revised addition.

Lebovitz, David. *Room for Dessert*. New York: HarperCollins, 1999.

Luchetti, Emily. *Stars Desserts*. New York: HarperCollins, 1991.

MacLauchlan, Andrew. *New Classic Desserts*. New York: John Wiley & Sons, 1995.

Maher, Barbara. *Classic Cakes and Cookies*. New York: Pantheon Books, 1986.

Malgieri, Nick. *Chocolate*. New York: HarperCollins, 1998.

———. *Great Italian Desserts*. Boston: Little Brown and Company, 1990.

———. *How to Bake*. New York: HarperCollins, 1995.

———. *Nick Malgieri's Perfect Pastry*. New York: Macmillan Publishing Company, 1989.

Margittai, Tom, and Paul Kovi. *The Four Seasons*. New York: Simon & Schuster, 1980.

McGee, Harold. *On Food and Cooking*. New York: Scribner's, 1984.

McNair, James. *James McNair's Cakes*. San Franscisco: Chronicle Books, 1999.

Medrich, Alice. *Cocolat*. New Work: Warner Books, 1990.

Miller, Mark, and Andrew MacLauchlan, with Jon Harrisson. *Flavored Breads*. Berkeley: Ten Speed Press, 1996.

Moore, Marilyn, M. *The Wooden Spoon Bread Book*. New York: Atlantic Monthly Press, 1987.

Nathan, Joan. *The Jewish Holiday Baker*. New York: Schocken Books, 1997.

Ojakangas, Beatrice. *The Great Scandinavian Baking Book*. Boston: Little, Brown & Company, 1988.

Olivier, Raymond. *La Cuisine*. New York: Leon Amiel, 1969.

Olney, Judith. *Judith Olney on Bread*. New York: Crown Publishers, 1985.

Ortiz, Gayle and Joe, with Louisa Beers. *The Village Baker's Wife*. Berkeley: Ten Speed Press, 1997.

———, Joe. *The Village Baker*. Berkeley: Ten Speed Press, 1993.

Payard, François, with Tim Moriarty and Tish Boyle. *Simply Sensational Desserts*. New York: Broadway Books, 1999.

Peck, Paula. *The Art of Fine Baking*. New York: Simon & Schuster, 1961.

Peery, Susan Mahnke. *The Wellesley Cookie Exchange Cookbook*. New York: Simon & Schuster, 1986.

Pépin, Jacques. *La Methode*. New York: Times Books, 1979.

———. *La Technique*. New York: Pocket Books, 1976.

Purdy, Susan G. *A Piece of Cake*. New York: Atheneum, 1989.

Reich, Lilly Joss. *The Viennese Pastry Cookbook*. New York: Collier Books, A Division of Macmillan Publishing Co., 1970.

Reinhart, Peter. *Crust and Crumb*. Berkeley: Ten Speed Press, 1998.

Robbins, Maria Polushkin, Editor. *Blue Ribbon Cookies*. New York: St. Martin's Press, 1988.

Rodgers, Rick. *Best-Ever Chocolate Desserts*. Chicago: Contemporary Books, 1992.

Rosenberg, Judy, with Nan Levinson. *Rosie's Bakery All-Butter, Fresh Cream, Sugar-Packed, No-Holds-Barred Baking Book*. New York: Workman Publishing Company, 1991.

———. *Rosie's Bakery Chocolate-Packed, Jam-Filled, Butter-Rich, No-Holds-Barred Cookie Book*. New York: Workman Publishing Company, 1996.

Roux, Michel and Albert. *The Roux Brothers on Patisserie*. New York: Prentice-Hall, 1986.

Rubin, Maury. *Book of Tarts*. New York: William Morrow and Company, 1995.

Rushing, Lilith, and Ruth Voss. *The Cake Cook Book*. Philadelphia: Chilton Books, 1965.

Sax, Richard. *Classic Home Desserts*. Shelburne: Chapters Publishing, Ltd., 1994.

———. *The Cookie Lover's Cookbook*. New York: Harper & Row, 1986.

Schinz, Marina. *The Book of Sweets*. New York: Harry N. Abrams, 1994.

Schulz, Philip Stephen. *As American as Apple Pie*. New York: Simon & Schuster, 1990.

Scherber, Amy, and Toy Kim Dupree. *Amy's Bread*. William Morrow and Company, 1996.

Scicolone, Michele. *La Dolce Vita*. New York: William Morrow and Company, 1993.

Shere, Lindsey Remolif. *Chez Panisse Desserts*. New York: Random House, 1985.

Silverton, Nancy, in collaboration with Heidi Yorkshire. *Desserts by Nancy Silverton*. New York: Harper & Row, 1986.

———, in collaboration with Laurie Ochoa. *Nancy Silverton's Breads from the La Brea Bakery*. New York: Villard Books, 1996.

Simmons, Marie. *A to Z Bar Cookies*. Shelburne: Chapters Publishing, 1994.

Standard, Stella. *Our Daily Bread*. New York: Funk and Wagnalls, 1970.

Stewart, Martha. *Martha Stewart's Pies and Tarts*. New York: Clarkson Potter, 1985.

Thompson, Sylvia. *The Birthday Cake Book*. San Francisco: Chronicle Books, 1993.

Truax, Carol, Editor. *Ladies' Home Journal Dessert Cookbook*. Garden City: Nelson Doubleday & Company, 1964.

Van Cleave, Jill. *Icing the Cake*. Chicago: Contemporary Books, 1990.

Walter, Carole. *Great Cakes*. New York: Ballantine Books, 1991.

Warren, Ann, with Joan Lilly. *The Cupcake Café Cookbook*. New York: Doubleday, 1998.

Welch, Adrienne. *Sweet Seduction*. New York: Harper & Row, 1984.

Weinstock, Sylvia, with Kate Manchester. *Sweet Celebrations*. New York: Simon & Schuster, 1999.

Wilkerson, Arnold, Patricia Henly, and Michael Deraney, with Evie Righter. *The Little Pie Company of the Big Apple Pies and Other Dessert Favorites*. New York: HarperPerennial, 1993.

Willan, Anne. *Anne Willan's Look and Cook Chocolate Desserts*. New York: Dorling Kindersley, 1992.

Witty, Helen. *Mrs. Witty's Monster Cookies*. New York: Workman Publishing Company, 1983.

Yockelson, Lisa. *Baking for Gift-Giving*. New York: HarperCollins, 1993.

———. *Brownies and Blondies*. New York: HarperCollins, 1992.

———. *A Country Baking Treasury*. New York: HarperCollins, 1995.

———. *Layer Cakes and Sheet Cakes*. New York: HarperCollins, 1996.

INDEX